PARADE'S END

Ford Madox Ford

PARADE'S END

With an introduction by
ROBIE MACAULEY

PENGUIN MODERN CLASSICS

Penguin Books Ltd, Harmondsworth, Middlesex, England
Penguin Books, 625 Madison Avenue, New York, New York 10022, U.S.A.
Penguin Books, Australia Ltd, Ringwood, Victoria, Australia
Penguin Books Canada Ltd, 2801 John Street, Markham, Ontario, Canada L3R 1B4
Penguin Books (N.Z.) Ltd, 182-190 Wairau Road, Auckland 10, New Zealand

"Some Do Not..." first published by Duckworth 1924
Copyright © Janice Biala, 1924
"No More Parades" first published by Duckworth 1925
Copyright © Janice Biala, 1925
"A Man Could Stand Up—" first published by Duckworth 1926
Copyright © Janice Biala, 1926
"The Last Post" first published by Duckworth 1928
Copyright © Janice Biala, 1928

This edition published in Penguin Books 1982

Made and printed in the United States of America by R. J. Carroll/Banta Inc.

Introduction

THE YEAR BEFORE HE DIED Ford Madox Ford used to walk around the campus at Olivet College like a pensioned veteran of forgotten wars. We took him for a kind of vast, benevolent and harmless Uncle Toby, leaning on his stick in class or sitting in his dark little basement office and wheezing out his stories of Henry James as Toby might have spoken of Marlborough. His books seemed like medals achieved, perhaps, in the Crimea; and we read Auden, Kafka, Evelyn Waugh.

We were no different from the rest of the world. We knew vaguely that his Tietjens books were about the first World War and we suspected that they might be a good enough account of a soldier's disillusioning experiences — but we had read all that before. If any of us went far enough to look at the introductory letter to A Man Could Stand Up —, the third in the series, he would find Ford confirming it:

"This is what the late war was like: this is how modern fighting of the organized, scientific type affects the mind. If, for reasons of gain, or, as is still more likely out of dislike for collective types other than your own, you choose to permit your rulers to embark on another war, this — or something very accentuated along similar lines — is what you will have to put up with! I hope, in fact, that this series of books, for what it is worth, may make war seem undesirable."

A little afterward some of us went to war ourselves and later, coming back, took Ford's novels down from the shelf to see if his easy prediction had come true. It seemed impossible that we could have been so wrong.

For some peculiar reason of his own he had hoaxed us; he was

neither benevolent nor harmless and his books were by no means a
simple warning as to what modern warfare is like. To read the
Tietjens story for that would be like going through Henry James
to improve one's manners or through Conrad to learn how to navi-
gate a ship.

Nevertheless, this is the way the novels were taken when they were
first published. They were thought to be books of "experiences" and
they sold well. The reaction came when Ford's readers discovered
that what he had actually given them was not another *Under Fire* or
What Price Glory? but something complex and baffling. There was
a love story with no passionate scenes; there were trenches but no
battles; there was a tragedy without a denouement. Ford was quickly
and easily forgotten.

We are a little older now and perhaps a little less superficial. We
have been living a little longer with the great, enveloping tragedy
Ford set out to describe. Perhaps in this edition we can take a second
look at the Tietjens story and discover that it is less about the incident of a single war than about a whole era, more about our own
world than his.

II

"The two young men — they were of the English public official
class — sat in the perfectly appointed railway carriage." So begins
the Tietjens story. Everything is excellent, comfortable, predictable:
the leather window straps are of virgin newness, the mirrors immaculate, as if they had reflected very little, the upholstery a luxuriant scarlet and yellow design, the air smelling faintly of varnish.
The train runs as smoothly as (Tietjens thinks) British gilt-edged
securities. Moreover, the two young men are of the class that ad-
ministers the world. "If they saw a policeman misbehave, railway
porters lack civility, an insufficiency of street lamps, defects in public
services or in foreign countries, they saw to it either with nonchalant
Balliol voices or with letters to the *Times*, asking with regretful indignation, 'Has the British This or That come to *this?*' " Under their
care are manners, the arts, diplomacy, inter-imperial trade and the
personal reputations of prominent men. They do not realize that
their train has got on the wrong line.

Actually it is not running from London to Rye as they think, but from the past into the future, and ahead of them on their one-way journey is a chaotic country of ripped battlefields and disordered towns. Their fellow-passengers will grow hysterical and unpredictable, station masters will put up the wrong signals, troops will come aboard and get off again, the good furnishings of the train will get worn and broken, the schedule will go to pieces. And, experiencing all this, Christopher Tietjens will learn to expect that somewhere, beyond some bridge or tunnel, the tracks themselves will finally disappear into the dry sands of the wasteland.

But to begin where Ford did we must return to take a look at the unsuspecting passenger as he sits in his comfortable seat at the start of the journey. The beginning of the Tietjens story took form in Ford's mind just after the war. He had returned to France and was spending the summer in Harold Monro's villa on the deserted Riviera, a discharged officer, a cast-off writer immersed in a sense of disaster. As he walked in the garden of the Villa des Moulins, his ideas, cloudy at first but growing more precise, began to gather around the memory of an old friend, now dead.

Arthur Marwood had been enough of a paradox in himself to suggest greater ones. He was the son of a good Yorkshire country family, a mathematician of brilliance in the government office of statistics and Ford's associate in publishing *The English Review*. His mind was "acute and scornful" Ford says. "He possessed the clear Eighteenth-century English mind which has disappeared from the earth, leaving the earth very much the poorer." However, "he was, beneath the surface, extraordinarily passionate — with the abiding passion for the sort of truth that makes for intellectual accuracy . . ." In spite of his brilliance, Marwood had no career.

It was tuberculosis, actually, that forced him into a retired and inactive life, yet Ford, going beyond that, saw a tragedy of disinheritance. His kind of intelligence and what it represented passed through the metamorphosis of the author's imagination and became Christopher Tietjens. "I seemed," Ford says, "to see him stand in some high place in France during the period of hostilities taking in not only what was visible but all the causes and all the motive powers of infinitely distant places. And I seemed to hear his infinitely scornful comment on those places. It was as if he lived again."

So Marwood furnished the outline and the intellect, but there had to be more to Tietjens than that alone. Through the course of the four books the development of his personality is one of the most elaborate and singular accomplishments of modern writing.

His character is synonymous with the character of an ordered, bounded, and harmonious past. Socially, this means the England of gentry and farms before the middle classes built it into an empire. Morally, it means a code of honor and self-respect in contrast to business honesty and puritan habits. It means that Tietjens is humane in his relationships, feudal in his outlook, Christian in his beliefs, a classicist by education, a Tory in politics. He is, in fact, "the last English Tory." Mirrored in this "clear Eighteenth-century mind," the world is an equable and logical mechanism in which God, Man, and Nature have a balanced relationship. It is not specifically an English view; it has belonged to every Western nation.

In one place in *No More Parades* Tietjens concocts a kind of fable for himself. He sees:

"The Almighty as, on a colossal scale, a great English landowner, a benevolently awful duke who never left his study and was thus invisible, but knowing all about the estate down to the last hind at the home farm and the last oak; Christ an almost too-benevolent land-steward, son of the Owner, knowing all about the estate down to the last child at the porter's lodge, apt to be got around by the more detrimental tenants; the Third Person of the Trinity, the spirit of the estate, the Game as it were, as distinct from the players of the game; the atmosphere of the estate, that of Winchester cathedral just after a Handel anthem has been played."

Tietjens means it as a semi-humorous comment on himself, but beyond that it is serious. Heaven is a Platonic reflection of earth, a place of feudal order and harmony and there are laws of science, morality, or theology to cover every event.

But Tietjens is out of his time in a world where the laws have lost their reality, the system has collapsed and the synthesis of knowledge and belief has lost its validity; under his feet he feels the great landslip. England (his specific example) once had a defined and integrated culture, but during the Nineteenth century it had become a kind of pseudo-civilization marked for export. Like cheap trading-goods, imitations, her morals, manners, and religion were shipped to every part of the world. It was a process of weakening, dilution, and overextension in more than a physical sense. Earning great paper profits, she had actually been spending her capital.

Ford saw the war as simply a dramatic heightening of the inevitable processes of ruin. England's victory was only an irony, a catalytic occurrence and she emerged from it into a social and intellectual chaos. The telling thing, Ford thought, was not that the world had changed physically to any great extent, but that the lines of communication had broken down. There was no longer a recognized continuity between past or present or present and future. The traditional modes of relationship among people had disappeared and there were no new ones to take the place.

We are likely to judge history as the blind men took the elephant; it is too big for us and too misleading in its various parts. The historian may offer a splendid, documented, analytical narrative; and yet we feel the lack of a plot. The novelist of history offers us a kind of mystery-play in which the great mass of ideas and events are concentrated into a sharp and comprehensible drama. Shakespeare's historical cycle and *War and Peace* are such mystery-plays. Though I do not wish to suggest a qualitative comparison — those two works are almost the grandest of their kind — Ford's Tietjens novel at least belongs in the same category. But with a difference. Ford was trying to define dramatically a thing that was only a direction or indication in his own time and his story includes the future. Looking at England today we can see more plainly what he meant. Tolstoy left the future out or, rather, he saw it as a twin-brother to the past and the cycle of his novel goes through the sequence of revolt and disorder back to order again. Chekhov, seeing differently, implied the future and we know now that the ring of the axe on the cherry tree outside the Ranevskys' windows was a more prophetic sound than the laughter in the Behuzovs' drawing-room at the end of *War and Peace*.

Therefore, Ford took as the scheme for his allegory the life of one man, Christopher Tietjens, a member of an extinct species, which, as he says, "died out sometime in the Eighteenth century." Representing in himself the order and stability of another age, he must experience the disruptive present.

III

I have been trying to give a bare idea of the abstract concepts which govern the development of the Tietjens novel, "the game," Ford says, "as distinct from the players of the game." One of Flau-

bert's important insistences was that the writer deal directly and exclusively with the explicit, leaving value judgments to implication.
For a novelist whose abstract meaning is readily available this is not
hard. The younger Flaubert, for instance, demonstrates just the right
evidence to make the case of *Madame Bovary* clear. But it is a relatively simple case. The older Flaubert, dealing with the greater and
more complicated issues of *L'Education sentimentale*, produces a
story whose surface is difficult, contrasting, and perplexed. Ford went
along the same path; the lucidity and perfect form of *The Good
Soldier* was followed ten years later by the slippery indirections of
the Tietjens story. (The comparison is even more exact if we remember that Ford's early enthusiasm was for *Madame Bovary* but
that in later life, he said, he read *L'Education sentimentale* fourteen
times.)

There is perhaps one central question arising from the events and
circumstances of the Tietjens story that seems almost unexplainable
in terms of the plot alone. It is one of the chief ambiguities that
must exasperate and rebuff the unwary reader and yet it seems to lie
in wait for him in almost every phase of the entire story. A workable
answer to it should supply a great deal.

Why is Christopher Tietjens so endlessly persecuted? Nearly everyone else in the novel, consciously or unconsciously, tries to discredit,
injure, attack, or betray him. He seems to be the object of a kind of
compulsive hatred, yet in himself he is honorable, amiable, apparently a danger to nobody. In various ways this enmity appears in his
friends, his acquaintances, fellow-officers, superiors, but most particularly and significantly in his wife. It is the last, his relationship
with Sylvia, that offers the decisive clue to the seemingly purposeless affliction that he finds on every side.

At the beginning of *Some Do Not* . . . the domestic situation of
the two is outlined. Sylvia has had a child whose paternity is doubtful
and more recently she has run away to the Continent with another
man. Then she has changed her mind and asked Tietjens to have
her back again, a proposal to which he assents by cable. Sylvia, in
Germany, is shown in a scene with a Socratic Irish priest, Father
Consett, who draws from her the admission that what she hates most
about her husband and what she can't live with is his essential and
imperturbable goodness. In the meantime Tietjens has met a young
woman named Valentine Wannop at Rye and taken a long ride in
the fog with her. The first part is chiefly an establishment of charac-

ter and the lines are drawn between Sylvia, an arrogant, reckless, and morally chaotic woman and Christopher, the wise and enduring man.

The antagonism gets dramatic exposition in the second part of *Some Do Not . . .* through a long scene which is built up by one of Ford's favorite devices, the *progression d'effet*. It is a psychological melodrama which gradually produces an intolerable pressure.

Tietjens, in the interval between the two parts, has been in the early battles of the war. A portion of his mind has been numbed by amnesia and he is wondering if this may be the first terrible sign. At the same time Sylvia is attacking his mental security in her own way. "I'll torment him," she has promised herself and she proceeds by accusation, sarcasm, lies, and open hatred. She has slandered him to his friends, whispered that he is keeping a mistress, that he has had a child by another woman; she has involved him in financial trouble. She is trying by all desperate means to reduce him to her own state of emotional anarchy — one sign of anger or weakness is all that she needs. "If," Sylvia went on with her denunciation, "you had once in your life said to me: 'You whore, you bitch . . . May you rot in hell . . .' you might have done something to bring us together."

But Tietjens grows stronger under the assault. Bit by bit his memory is returning and with it the emotional and intellectual equilibrium that belongs to him. He treats her violence with his odd courtesy, dispassion, and forgiveness.

"There is only one man from whom a woman could take '*Neither I condemn thee*' and not hate him more than she hates the fiend!" Sylvia says, and finally gives her last furious thrust: Tietjens' father, she says, was driven to commit suicide by hearing the report that Christopher had got the daughter of his oldest friend with child.

Tietjens answers. "Oh! Ah! Yes! I suspected that. I knew it really. I suppose the poor dear knows better now. Or perhaps he doesn't . . . It doesn't matter." Instead of the expected explosion there has been a deflation and Sylvia has lost again.

Later on in *No More Parades* Tietjens's relationship with Sylvia is developed in another crucial scene. It is in France during wartime and Tietjens, now in command of a base camp, is suffering from enormous nervous stresses. Sylvia has managed to get there by unofficial means and they meet at a hotel during an engagement party. She is unable to explain to herself exactly why she has come; she confronts herself with the apparently insoluble paradox that Christopher, whom she detests so much, is actually the only man in the world

she can love. But once there, she gives herself up to the luxury of torturing and trying to ruin him. Though she cannot quite see what it
means, her memory furnishes her with an exquisite sadistic example of
her motives in the anecdote of a white purebred bulldog (looking
something like Tietjens) that she had once whipped raw and left out
in the weather to freeze.

Sylvia has no difficulty raising all kinds of troubles, official, domestic, and personal, around Tietjens's head. She seems to arouse
the hidden or latent antagonism of everyone else towards him.
("Christopher . . . A Socialist!" gasps General Campion when Sylvia tells him an absurd lie. "By God, I *will* have him drummed out
of the service . . .") It ends in a strange muddle in her hotel room
and as a result Tietjens is transferred to the front lines.

The portrayal of Sylvia is as remarkable as that of Christopher.
The unusual thing that Ford manages to transmit is not only Sylvia's
insecurity and self-doubt, but her real terror at the idea of her husband. The intolerable fact to her is that he is sane.

And some of this terror at Tietjens is shared by everyone around.
They are fragmentary people, uncertain, confused, without values.
They sense that Tietjens belongs to a moral frame of reference that
both makes the world intelligible and wards off its shocks. To their
jumbled and neurotic lives he stands as a reproach, and they must
destroy him if possible.

IV

The two middle books of the novel, No More Parades and A Man
Could Stand Up — might be described as concurrent with the war
rather than about it. The scene is France during the hostilities and
Ford manages to show a great deal of Tietjens's life, first as an administrative officer in charge of organizing drafts of replacements
and later as commander of a front-line unit. It is often vivid, always
well-observed and convincing; yet the mere fact of the war has a
curiously secondary importance.

Fiction about war has always been, essentially, a kind of adventure fiction. With the older novelists it was an adventure of sides
or armies seen from a high hill. How will the English (or the Scotch
or the French) win this battle? was the question we were supposed

to hang on. Victor Hugo's Waterloo is the most elaborate example. Then came Stendhal, the innovator, and wrote the adventure story of a single man lost in the tremendous confusion. How will Fabrizio escape? he asks. It seemed to be a much more interesting question.

Tolstoy and Crane followed his line and so did nearly all of Ford's contemporaries who wrote about the first World War. To it they added their own generation's contempt for illusion and made the point that such an adventure must turn out badly. War was a savage, hideous thing and had to be shown as such. Nevertheless, it was a kind of entity in itself, an unexplained adventure that had little to do with the normal course of the world.

Ford saw the war as a concentrated specimen of the whole history of his time, a bloody dumb-show imitating the bigger drama. If there is any adventure in Ford's war it is a cerebral adventure and if there is any danger it is psychological danger. Tietjens's question: "Am I going mad?" becomes a universal one and while protagonists of other war novels see villages wrecked, Tietjens sees a civilization going to ruin.

Ford always felt somewhat embarrassed in trying to explain his own work; the great artistic immodesty of James's prefaces was something he could not understand. Consequently, his prefatory remarks to these books might have been written by a mild, slightly deprecating friend who had little idea of their subject. In a typical understatement to be found in the dedicatory letter to *No More Parades* he says that the book is about Worry:

"That immense army was . . . depressed by the idea that those who controlled it overseas would — I will not use the word 'betray' since that implies volition — but 'let us down.' We were oppressed, ordered, counter-ordered, commanded, countermanded, harassed, strafed, denounced — and, above all, dreadfully worried. The never-ending sense of worry, in fact, far surpassed any of the 'exigencies of troops actually in contact with the enemy forces,' and that applied not merely to the bases, but to the whole field of military operations. Unceasing worry!"

This statement hints at something, but by no means expresses it. The more valuable idea that Ford's war is seen as something like a violent intensification of all the troubles of a foundering society comes out a little more clearly in his remarks concerning his "war books" in the autobiographical volume, *It Was the Nightingale*:

"A man at this point is subject to exactly the same disasters and perplexities as his temperament prepares him for in time of peace. If he is the sort of man to have put up with the treachery of others, his interest at home will suffer from treasons; if he is the man to incur burdens of debts, debts will unaccountably mass themselves; if he is a man destined to be betrayed by women, his women will betray him exaggeratedly and without shame. For all these vicissitudes will be enlarged by the strident note that in time of war gets into both speeches and events . . . And he is indeed then *homo duplex*: a poor fellow whose body is tied in one place but whose mind and personality brood over another distant locality."

In *No More Parades* the "disasters and perplexities" that haunt Tietjens have actually taken possession of those around him. Lt. McKechnie is the lunatic remnant of a brave officer, a classical scholar. His troubles with his wife are a wildly exaggerated version of Tietjens's relations with Sylvia and he has got to the point where he hears a kind of shelling within his brain. "The memory seemed to burst inside him like one of those enormous tin-pot crashes." For Tietjens he is like a horrible premonition.

There is the Welsh private, O Nine Morgan. His wife has gone off with a prize-fighter and when he applied for leave to go home Tietjens refused it in order to save him from being killed by the fighter. Morgan is a dispatch-runner; he is hit by a shell-burst in the street just outside the door of Tietjens's office and he falls inside to die in Tietjens's arms. "So he was better dead," Tietjens thinks. "Or perhaps not."

"Is death better than discovering that your wife is a whore and being done in by her cully? *Gwell angau na gwillth*, their own regimental badge bore the words. 'Death is better than dishonor.' . . . No, not death, *angau* means pain. Anguish! Anguish is better than dishonor. The devil it is! . . . He was born to be a blooming casualty. Either by shellfire or by the fist of the prize-fighter."

O Nine Morgan, the semi-anonymous man, is an example or a parable. He is truly *homo duplex*, born to be a casualty wherever he might go — either from fists at home or splinters of iron abroad, both of which, in the final view, are aspects of the same thing.

The war experiences, in a way, represent Tietjens's dark night. *No More Parades* piles injustice on injustice, but one of the things that helps Tietjens remain firm is the increasing realization that he is experiencing no simple personal nemesis but the total breakup. "We were fitted neither for victory nor defeat," he thinks; "we

could be true neither to friend nor foe. Not even to ourselves." He
sees the clearest irony in his story of a visit to the War Office in 1914
where he had seen an official preparing the one ceremony of the
war for which (Tietjens thinks) England was prepared — the disbanding of troops. It would close with the band's playing *Land of
Hope and Glory*. The adjutant would then say, *"There will be no
more parades."* And, Tietjens adds, "Don't you see how symbolical
it was? . . . For there won't. There damn well won't. No more
Hope, no more Glory, no more parades for you and me any more.
Not for the country . . . Not for the world, I daresay."

A *Man Could Stand Up* — begins with a telephone message to
Valentine Wannop in England, informing her that Tietjens has
come home but that he seems to have lost his mind. With this
ominous suggestion about him, the novel takes a step backward in
time to show the history of one day in the trenches. The major part
of it takes place in Tietjens's mind, an interior monologue that
mingles a thousand fragments of the past with a thousand details
of the present. Tietjens is second-in-command of a thinned-out battalion awaiting a German attack. As he goes about the routine business of the day Tietjens makes an effort of memory and imagination
to hold off the gathering insanity he feels all about him. He must
quiet the frenzied McKechnie and deal with his colonel who, losing
control, has taken to drink. He tries to keep up the morale of his men.

Most important of all, he must keep his own balance. One night
Tietjens had awakened to hear a voice coming from a mine almost
beneath his feet, *"Bringt dem Hauptmann eine Kerze,"* it said.
"Bring a candle to the captain." Was it real? he wonders. Or is his
mind becoming a tangle of fantasy like all the others'?

But Tietjens has an amulet to carry him through. It is the recurring thought of George Herbert on a hill above Bemerton parsonage
composing the line, *"Sweet day so cool, so calm, so bright, the bridal
of the earth and sky . . ."* It is a vision of serenity and sanity. It
serves to remind Tietjens that he belongs to a consistent system of
belief, that there is or has been once a regular, logical, beautiful
order to nature of which he is part. As long as that idea remains, as
long as he can distinguish the song of the larks from the noise of the
barrage, he will be safe.

The battlefield of A *Man Could Stand Up* —, thus, is more mental
than physical and only one actual shell falls on it. It comes as a climax to the scene, burying Tietjens, a lance-corporal, and a lieutenant

under a pile of earth. Tietjens crawls out, uncovers the others and carries the lieutenant away under fire. Immediately he is ordered to report to General Campion who, spic and span, is visiting the trenches on a tour of inspection. He is enraged that Tietjens has not reported before, that his uniform is dirty and that he has a hand in one pocket. The general relieves him of his command and with this unexpected little irony the war is over for Tietjens.

The third part of the book begins where the first left off, bringing Tietjens and Valentine together in his empty house in London. He is not mad, but just saved from madness. At last they are ready to admit they love each other, but as the horns and bells of Armistice Night sound, the crazy spectres from the trenches drift in one by one. Now that the ordeal is over, they seem simply harmless scarecrows and Tietjens and Valentine give them something to drink to celebrate the war's end.

Before looking at the final book of the Tietjens story, I should mention the matter of style. It is quite possible that Ford knew as many of the trade-secrets of writing as did any author of his time and a real discussion of his technique would be more extensive than an introduction allows. A few important methods and intentions, however, can be noted.

The language of the Tietjens story is one of simplicity and understatement. It is neither commonplace nor rhetorical and it manages to reveal exciting events without any surface theatricality of its own.

The chief strategems of narrative or dramatic style are somewhat more difficult to describe; they are the *progression d'effet*, the time-shift and the interior monologue. I have noted a good example of the first in the breakfast scene between Tietjens and Sylvia in *Some Do Not . . .* , in which all the nerves are slowly drawn to the snapping point.

In the Tietjens novel the time-shift and interior monologue are employed simultaneously. Ford often translates the scene of his story into the mind of one character or another and then uses all the tenses of memory as if they formed a keyboard. A scene from the far past is juxtaposed significantly with a present incident; the happening of a year ago has some bearing on yesterday. The "stream-of-consciousness" techniques (Woolf, Joyce, Proust, Richardson) bear both similarities and differences, though Ford at this time had not read the work of his contemporary experimenters.

In all, Ford cannot be called a great stylistic innovator. Rather he tried to use the best techniques of others with great care and imagination. He himself called his style "impressionistic." If a term is needed, that word seems both sufficiently general and sufficiently descriptive.

V

The Last Post is the strangely inconclusive conclusion of the Tietjens story. In form it is the most oblique of any of the books, the most extreme example of what might be called Ford's "tangential relevance." Christopher Tietjens is present physically for only one moment at the end of the book and yet he is the most central being in it. The system of the book might be thought of as a temporarily eclipsed sun with a number of visible satellite consciousnesses surrounding and defining its position. There are nine relative and interconnected interior monologues representing several people in the general vicinity of the cottage to which Christopher and Valentine and Mark and his long-time French mistress (now his wife) have gone after the war.

Each one of these monologues is a digressive collection of commentary, gloss, footnote, addenda, and paraphrase of the whole Tietjens story. The mind of Marie (Mark's wife) is described as being like a cupboard, "stuffed, packed with the most incongruous materials, tools, vessels and debris. Once you opened the door you never knew what would tumble out or be followed by what." Nearly all of the incongruous material that tumbles out of each mind, however, is pertinent somehow to the life of Tietjens.

Each one of these minds floats in the atmosphere of time, crossing and recrossing the orbits of the others, yet there must be a binding device to connect each one with the here-and-now of the book and to remind the reader of real people in a real place. Ford introduces a certain amount of present incident into the story to effect this (a woman entering the garden, Marie making cider) and each present incident is viewed from a different perspective by several different characters. The whole book is like an immense juggling act of time and point of view.

In the fantastic trench-world, Tietjens had wished for peace: "to stand up on a hill." The post-war world seems to be an image of his hope — placid and rural. But when the minds are opened we realize

that nothing has actually changed and that the chaos, disorder and
combat are still there. It is a non-sequitur world just as the memories
of its inhabitants are non-sequitur.

Christopher's elder brother Mark becomes the Tietjens symbol.
He has been paralyzed by a stroke (the Tietjenses can no longer be
an effective force actually, physically), but his mind is as active and
perceptive as ever (the intellectual dominance remains). He lies on
a cot under a thatch roof, staring out at a landscape. He knows that
he will soon die. His consciousness is thus purified of all physical
dross and from him we can expect some definition, a statement removed into the realm of the absolute and final by death itself.

To the other six mental discussions of the Tietjens story, which
are ambiguous, unreliable, partial views, Mark's three sequences of
thought stand as a kind of framework. He appears at the beginning,
middle, and end. (The actual succession follows this order: Mark;
Marie-Leonie, his wife; Cramp, a farmer; an American woman, a
stranger; Mark again; Marie; Sylvia Tietjens; Valentine Wannop;
finally, Mark.)

In Mark's thoughts the various puzzles of the Tietjens history are
solved at last. He knows now that his father's "suicide" was really
an accident, that Christopher's son is truly Christopher's son. Now
that the ancient tree of Groby is to be cut down and the family
estate passed into the hands of a Catholic, he knows that the traditional curse will be off the Tietjens — in effect, the dire but honorable curse of simply being what they are. Last night he had heard
a rushing sound and had been "sensible of the presence of the Almighty walking upon the firmament." He is ready for death and sure
of heaven.

He hears the people in the garden as voices from the past. "Damn
it all could they all be ghosts drifting before the wind?" Christopher
stands in front of his eyes for a moment with a chunk of the fallen
Groby great tree in his hands and then Mark is dead; and the time of
the Tietjenses is dead with him.

Mark's final statement is beyond emotion; the "curse" has always
implied a future and it is now lifted. He presents both a summation
of the Tietjens's case and a reconciliation with its destruction. Both
their strength and their failure lie in the fact that they have been
true to something in a world where no one is true to anything. They
are an anachronism and, as an anachronism, must disappear. It is
inevitable that one theory of Truth, one systematic idea of how man

may lead a "good" life, will be swallowed up in a world of Untruth, but that is according to history's law — not its equity.

VI

In his crotchety book on the English novel, Ford found much to complain of. He could see in its history no progressive intellectual maturation, no regular development of a tradition and no continuing attempt to uphold the artist's responsibility of "rendering" the life he saw. There were, however, a few writers here and there who understood that responsibility and lived up to it.

The difference between the general library of English novels and these few isolated achievements is partly a matter of method and partly of artistic integrity. Fielding, Smollett, Dickens, Thackeray — and most of the others we are inclined to call the major English novelists — failed, Ford thought, in the peculiar duty of an artist to his work. It resulted in, "mere relating of a more or less arbitrary tale so turned as to insure a complacent view of life." "Complacent" is the important word. It recalls, as a near-perfect example, the ending of *Tom Jones* when Tom, outcast and disinherited because of his honesty and courage, is welcomed back again simply because Fielding has performed the magician's trick of discovering his gentle birth. This complacency, this annihilating compromise with banality Ford thought to be a result of the English writer's continual urge to be considered "respectable" in a country where the artist had no honor and no social place.

The working toward ultimate conformity produced another commitment, which was one of method and viewpoint. The novelist presupposes a whole social scheme; within that circumference he arranges the smaller scheme of his plot and within the plot he assigns his characters various appropriate roles. When Fielding or Thackeray suddenly surprise us by showing their faces over the tops of their puppet theatres, we realize exactly what the novelist should keep us from realizing: that these are not self-directing people involved in a situation that seems to generate its own drama, but contrivances of cloth and wood assigned to their roles of good or evil.

According to Ford's view, the other kind of novel — in distinction it might be called the "intensive" novel — was produced intermittently during the eighteenth and nineteenth centuries by, first, Richardson, later Austen and Trollope, finally Conrad and James. (His own name belongs next.) In France it became a tradition; in England it remained a series of singular performances.

This kind of novelist pursues an intense inquiry into the behavior of a certain group of characters both as unique beings and as part of an interweaving, interacting system of relationship. Finally he reasons, or suggests that we reason, from the particular to the general. All society, he declares, is simply a sum total of how human beings behave towards each other and if he is fortunate enough or gifted enough to select for his study circumstances of relationship that have a widespread application, he will have achieved, into his contemporary world, the most penetrating act of inquiry possible. In this kind of novel we surprise the individual situation in the very act of turning into the general circumstance.

We can imagine Mansfield Park as the geographical center of an early nineteenth-century culture and its concerns — love, money, manners, personal virtue — being pivotal to that culture. Visibly, things changed so little during the next seven decades that these could still remain preoccupations for that great pedant of the sensibilities, Henry James.

But geological shifts had been taking place in the culture and those values, by the end of the nineteenth century, no longer represented the same importance. Conrad had to deal with an expanding world and Ford an exploding one. In the Tietjens novel Ford had not only to consider a greater multiplicity of values (all of them changing, becoming ambiguous) but the greater question of value itself. If the quiet but intricate life of Mansfield Park is the proper symbol of one period, the wartime life of the Tietjens book is a symbol of our own destructive, inchoate time.

In this way Ford expanded the dimensions of the "intensive" novel to fulfill a more complicated assignment, yet he retained the central principle of precise moral-emotional-psychological investigation. The general argument or "meaning" of his book is not, of course, unique. In different ways and under different disguises it is one of the common motives of most important twentieth-century writers; Mann, Joyce, Gide, Eliot, Proust have all shared it and projected it in their various ways.

Each one of these writers has produced his response — Ford has not. It may be that the Tietjens novel demands a greater effort of self-recognition from the world, but if this effort can be made we shall not only have added a major novel to our literature but shall have performed a major act of understanding about ourselves and our era.

VII

I have been referring to the Tietjens story as one novel divided into four different books and I think it can be comprehended in no other way. There is a misleading note in Ford's dedicatory letter to *The Last Post* which seems to indicate that he added this book as a kind of sequel to show "how things turned out." Addressing it to Isabel Paterson, he says:

"For, but for you, this book would only nebularly have existed — in space, in my brain, where you will so it be not on paper or between boards. But, that is to say, for your stern, contemptuous and almost virulent insistence on knowing 'what became of Tietjens' I never should have conducted this chronicle to the stage it has now reached."

Most likely, this should be taken more as a compliment to a literary friend than as exact truth. Without *The Last Post*, the novel would have been sadly truncated and though it could never "turn out" as an ordinary novel must turn out, the recapitulation and final statement of *The Last Post* is indispensable. In his book on Conrad, Ford explains that it was necessary for him to have a whole design in mind (contrary to Conrad's procedure) before he could begin.

The entire novel was written over a period of five years, *Some Do Not . . .* appearing in 1924, *No More Parades* in 1925, *A Man Could Stand Up —* in 1926, and *The Last Post* in 1928. It was begun at St. Jean Cap Ferrat, continued during Ford's wanderings from there to Paris, from Paris to Guermantes, to Toulon, Paris again, Avignon, and was finally finished in New York on November 2nd, 1927.

Previous to this edition it has not been published in its proper form, as a unit. *Parade's End*, the present title, was Ford's own choice as a designation for the whole.

It seems the most appropriate of any. With an immense sense of tragedy, Ford saw the long and splendid procession of the Western

nations coming to an end and Tietjens is the ghostly voice of the
adjutant at the final disbanding. He says, "There will be no more
Hope, no more Glory. Not for the nation. Not for the world, I daresay. *There will be no more parades.*"

ROBIE MACAULEY

Contents

Some Do Not...

Part One

T HE TWO YOUNG MEN — they were of the English public official class — sat in the perfectly appointed railway carriage. The leather straps to the windows were of virgin newness; the mirrors beneath the new luggage racks immaculate as if they had reflected very little; the bulging upholstery in its luxuriant, regulated curves was scarlet and yellow in an intricate, minute dragon pattern, the design of a geometrician in Cologne. The compartment smelt faintly, hygienically of admirable varnish; the train ran as smoothly — Tietjens remembered thinking — as British gilt-edged securities. It travelled fast; yet had it swayed or jolted over the rail joints, except at the curve before Tonbridge or over the points at Ashford where these eccentricities are expected and allowed for, Macmaster, Tietjens felt certain, would have written to the company. Perhaps he would even have written to the *Times*.

Their class administered the world, not merely the newly created Imperial Department of Statistics under Sir Reginald Ingleby. If they saw policemen misbehave, railway porters lack civility, an insufficiency of street lamps, defects in public services or in foreign countries, they saw to it, either with nonchalant Balliol voices, or with letters to the *Times*, asking in regretful indignation: "Has the British This or That come to *this!*" Or they wrote, in the serious reviews of which so many still survived, articles taking under their care, manners, the Arts, diplomacy, inter-Imperial trade, or the personal reputations of deceased statesmen and men of letters.

Macmaster, that is to say, would do all that: of himself Tietjens was not so certain. There sat Macmaster; smallish; Whig; with a

3

trimmed, pointed black beard, such as a smallish man might wear to enhance his already germinated distinction; black hair of a stubborn fibre, drilled down with hard metal brushes; a sharp nose; strong, level teeth; a white, butterfly collar of the smoothness of porcelain; a tie confined by a gold ring, steel-blue speckled with black — to match his eyes, as Tietjens knew.

Tietjens, on the other hand, could not remember what coloured tie he had on. He had taken a cab from the office to their rooms, had got himself into a loose, tailored coat and trousers, and a soft shirt, had packed quickly, but still methodically, a great number of things in an immense two-handled kit-bag, which you could throw into a guard's van if need be. He disliked letting that "man" touch his things; he had disliked letting his wife's maid pack for him. He even disliked letting porters carry his kit-bag. He was a Tory — and as he disliked changing his clothes, there he sat, on the journey, already in large, brown, hugely welted and nailed golf boots, leaning forward on the edge of the cushion, his legs apart, on each knee an immense white hand — and thinking vaguely.

Macmaster, on the other hand, was leaning back, reading some small, unbound printed sheets, rather stiff, frowning a little. Tietjens knew that this was, for Macmaster, an impressive moment. He was correcting the proofs of his first book.

To this affair, as Tietjens knew, there attached themselves many fine shades. If, for instance, you had asked Macmaster whether he were a writer, he would have replied with the merest suggestion of a deprecatory shrug.

"No, dear lady!" for of course no man would ask the question of anyone so obviously a man of the world. And he would continue with a smile: "Nothing so fine! A mere trifler at odd moments. A critic, perhaps. Yes! A little of a critic."

Nevertheless Macmaster moved in drawing-rooms that, with long curtains, blue china plates, large-patterned wallpapers and large, quiet mirrors, sheltered the long-haired of the Arts. And, as near as possible to the dear ladies who gave the At Homes, Macmaster could keep up the talk — a little magisterially. He liked to be listened to with respect when he spoke of Botticelli, Rossetti, and those early Italian artists whom he called "The Primitives." Tietjens had seen him there. And he didn't disapprove.

For, if they weren't, these gatherings, Society, they formed a stage on the long and careful road to a career in a first-class Government office. And, utterly careless as Tietjens imagined himself of careers or offices, he was, if sardonically, quite sympathetic towards his friend's ambitiousnesses. It was an odd friendship, but the oddnesses of friendships are a frequent guarantee of their lasting texture.

The youngest son of a Yorkshire country gentleman, Tietjens himself was entitled to the best — the best that first-class public offices and first-class people could afford. He was without ambition, but these things would come to him as they do in England. So he could afford to be negligent of his attire, of the company he kept, of the opinions he uttered. He had a little private income under his mother's settlement; a little income from the Imperial Department of Statistics; he had married a woman of means, and he was, in the Tory manner, sufficiently a master of flouts and jeers to be listened to when he spoke. He was twenty-six; but, very big, in a fair, untidy, Yorkshire way, he carried more weight than his age warranted. His chief, Sir Reginald Ingleby, when Tietjens chose to talk of public tendencies which influenced statistics, would listen with attention. Sometimes Sir Reginald would say: "You're a perfect encyclopædia of exact material knowledge, Tietjens," and Tietjens thought that that was his due, and he would accept the tribute in silence.

At a word from Sir Reginald, Macmaster, on the other hand, would murmur: "You're very good, Sir Reginald!" and Tietjens thought that perfectly proper.

Macmaster was a little the senior in the service as he was probably a little the senior in age. For, as to his room-mate's years, or as to his exact origins, there was a certain blank in Tietjens' knowledge. Macmaster was obviously Scotch by birth, and you accepted him as what was called a son of the manse. No doubt he was really the son of a grocer in Cupar or a railway porter in Edinburgh. It does not matter with the Scotch, and as he was very properly reticent as to his ancestry, having accepted him, you didn't, even mentally, make any enquiries.

Tietjens always had accepted Macmaster — at Clifton, at Cambridge, in Chancery Lane and in their rooms at Gray's Inn. So for Macmaster he had a very deep affection — even a gratitude. And Macmaster might be considered as returning these feelings. Certainly he had always done his best to be of service to Tietjens. Already at the Treasury and attached as private secretary to Sir Reginald Ingleby, whilst Tietjens was still at Cambridge, Macmaster had brought to the notice of Sir Reginald Tietjens' many great natural gifts, and

Sir Reginald, being on the look-out for young men for his ewe lamb, his newly-found department, had very readily accepted Tietjens as his third in command. On the other hand, it had been Tietjens' father who had recommended Macmaster to the notice of Sir Thomas Block at the Treasury itself. And indeed, the Tietjens family had provided a little money — that was Tietjens' mother really — to get Macmaster through Cambridge and install him in Town. He had repaid the small sum — paying it partly by finding room in his chambers for Tietjens when in turn he came to Town.

With a Scots young man such a position had been perfectly possible. Tietjens had been able to go to his fair, ample, saintly mother in her morning-room and say:

"Look here, mother, that fellow Macmaster! He'll need a little money to get through the University," and his mother would answer:

"Yes, my dear. How much?"

With an English young man of the lower orders that would have left a sense of class obligation. With Macmaster it just didn't.

During Tietjens' late trouble — for four months before Tietjens' wife had left him to go abroad with another man — Macmaster had filled a place that no other man could have filled. For the basis of Christopher Tietjens' emotional existence was a complete taciturnity — at any rate as to his emotions. As Tietjens saw the world, you didn't "talk." Perhaps you didn't even think about how you felt.

And, indeed, his wife's flight had left him almost completely without emotions that he could realise, and he had not spoken more than twenty words at most about the event. Those had been mostly to his father, who, very tall, very largely built, silver-haired and erect, had drifted, as it were, into Macmaster's drawing-room in Gray's Inn, and after five minutes of silence had said:

"You will divorce?"

Christopher had answered:

"No! No one but a blackguard would ever submit a woman to the ordeal of divorce."

Mr. Tietjens had suggested that, and after an interval had asked:

"You will permit her to divorce you?"

He had answered:

"If she wishes it. There's the child to be considered."

Mr. Tietjens said:

"You will get her settlement transferred to the child?"

Christopher answered:

"If it can be done without friction."

Mr. Tietjens had commented only:

"Ah!" Some minutes later he had said:

"Your mother's very well." Then: "That motor-plough *didn't* answer," and then: "I shall be dining at the club."

Christopher said:

"May I bring Macmaster in, sir? You said you would put him up."

Mr. Tietjens answered:

"Yes, do. Old General ffolliott will be there. He'll second him. He'd better make his acquaintance." He had gone away.

Tietjens considered that his relationship with his father was an almost perfect one. They were like two men in the club — the *only* club; thinking so alike that there was no need to talk. His father had spent a great deal of time abroad before succeeding to the estate. When, over the moors, he went into the industrial town that he owned, he drove always in a coach-and-four. Tobacco smoke had never been known inside Groby Hall: Mr. Tietjens had twelve pipes filled every morning by his head gardener and placed in rose bushes down the drive. These he smoked during the day. He farmed a good deal of his own land; had sat for Holdernesse from 1876 to 1881, but had not presented himself for election after the redistribution of seats; he was patron of eleven livings; rode to hounds every now and then, and shot fairly regularly. He had three other sons and two daughters, and was now sixty-one.

To his sister Effie, on the day after his wife's elopement, Christopher had said over the telephone:

"Will you take Tommie for an indefinite period? Marchant will come with him. She offers to take charge of your two youngest as well, so you'll save a maid, and I'll pay their board and a bit over."

The voice of his sister — from Yorkshire — had answered:

"Certainly, Christopher." She was the wife of a vicar, near Groby, and she had several children.

To Macmaster Tietjens had said:

"Sylvia has left me with that fellow Perowne."

Macmaster had answered only: "Ah!"

Tietjens had continued:

"I'm letting the house and warehousing the furniture. Tommie is going to my sister Effie. Marchant is going with him."

Macmaster had said:

"Then you'll be wanting your old rooms." Macmaster occupied a very large storey of the Gray's Inn buildings. After Tietjens had left him on his marriage he had continued to enjoy solitude, except that his man had moved down from the attic to the bedroom formerly occupied by Tietjens.

Tietjens said:

"I'll come in to-morrow night if I may. That will give Ferens time to get back into his attic."

That morning, at breakfast, four months having passed, Tietjens had received a letter from his wife. She asked, without any contrition at all, to be taken back. She was fed up with Perowne and Brittany.

Tietjens looked up at Macmaster. Macmaster was already half out of his chair, looking at him with enlarged, steel-blue eyes, his beard quivering. By the time Tietjens spoke Macmaster had his hand on the neck of the cut-glass brandy decanter in the brown wood tantalus.

Tietjens said:

"Sylvia asks me to take her back."

Macmaster said:

"Have a little of this!"

Tietjens was about to say: "No," automatically. He changed that to:

"Yes. Perhaps. A liqueur glass."

He noticed that the lip of the decanter agitated, tinkling on the glass. Macmaster must be trembling.

Macmaster, with his back still turned, said:

"Shall you take her back?"

Tietjens answered:

"I imagine so." The brandy warmed his chest in its descent. Macmaster said:

"Better have another."

Tietjens answered:

"Yes. Thanks."

Macmaster went on with his breakfast and his letters. So did Tietjens. Ferens came in, removed the bacon plates and set on the table a silver water-heated dish that contained poached eggs and haddock. A long time afterwards Tietjens said:

"Yes, in principle I'm determined to. But I shall take three days to think out the details."

He seemed to have no feelings about the matter. Certain insolent phrases in Sylvia's letter hung in his mind. He preferred a letter like that. The brandy made no difference to his mentality, but it seemed to keep him from shivering.

Macmaster said:

"Suppose we go down to Rye by the 11.40. We could get a round after tea now the days are long. I want to call on a parson near there. He has helped me with my book."

Tietjens said:

"Did your poet know parsons? But of course he did. Duchemin is the name, isn't it?"

Macmaster said:

"We could call about two-thirty. That will be all right in the country. We stay till four with a cab outside. We can be on the first tee at five. If we like the course we'll stay next day: then Tuesday at Hythe and Wednesday at Sandwich. Or we could stay at Rye all your three days."

"It will probably suit me better to keep moving," Tietjens said. "There are those British Columbia figures of yours. If we took a cab now I could finish them for you in an hour and twelve minutes. Then British North America can go to the printers. It's only 8.30 now."

Macmaster said, with some concern:

"Oh, but you *couldn't*. I can make our going all right with Sir Reginald."

Tietjens said:

"Oh, yes I can. Ingleby will be pleased if you tell him they're finished. I'll have them ready for you to give him when he comes at ten."

Macmaster said:

"What an extraordinary fellow you are, Chrissie. Almost a genius!"

"Oh," Tietjens answered. "I was looking at your papers yesterday after you'd left and I've got most of the totals in my head. I was thinking about them before I went to sleep. I think you make a mistake in overestimating the pull of Klondyke this year on the population. The passes are open, but relatively no one is going through. I'll add a note to that effect."

In the cab he said:

"I'm sorry to bother you with my beastly affairs. But how will it affect you and the office?"

"The office," Macmaster said, "not at all. It is supposed that Sylvia is nursing Mrs. Satterthwaite abroad. As for me, I wish . . ." — he closed his small, strong teeth — "I wish you would drag the woman through the mud. By God I do! Why should she mangle you for the rest of your life? She's done enough!"

Tietjens gazed out over the flap of the cab.

That explained a question. Some days before, a young man, a friend of his wife's rather than of his own, had approached him in the club and had said that he hoped Mrs. Satterthwaite — his wife's mother — was better. He said now:

"I see. Mrs. Satterthwaite has probably gone abroad to cover up Sylvia's retreat. She's a sensible woman, if a bitch."

The hansom ran through nearly empty streets, it being very early for the public official quarters. The hoofs of the horse clattered precipitately. Tietjens preferred a hansom, horses being made for gentle-folk. He had known nothing of how his fellows had viewed his affairs. It was breaking up a great, numb inertia to enquire.

During the last few months he had employed himself in tabulating from memory the errors in the *Encyclopædia Britannica*, of which a new edition had lately appeared. He had even written an article for a dull monthly on the subject. It had been so caustic as to miss its mark, rather. He despised people who used works of reference; but the point of view had been so unfamiliar that his article had galled no one's withers, except possibly Macmaster's. Actually it had pleased Sir Reginald Ingleby, who had been glad to think that he had under him a young man with a memory so tenacious, and so encyclopædic a knowledge. . . .

That had been a congenial occupation, like a long drowse. Now he had to make enquiries. He said:

"And my breaking up the establishment at twenty-nine? How's that viewed? I'm not going to have a house again."

"It's considered," Macmaster answered, "that Lowndes Street did not agree with Mrs. Satterthwaite. That accounted for her illness. Drains wrong. I may say that Sir Reginald entirely — expressly — approves. He does not think that young married men in Government offices should keep up expensive establishments in the S.W. district."

Tietjens said:

"Damn him." He added: "He's probably right, though." He then said: "Thanks. That's all I want to know. A certain discredit has always attached to cuckolds. Very properly. A man ought to be able to keep his wife."

Macmaster exclaimed anxiously:

"No! No! Chrissie."

Tietjens continued:

"And a first-class public office is very like a public school. It might very well object to having a man whose wife had bolted amongst its members. I remember Clifton hated it when the Governors decided to admit the first Jew and the first nigger."

Macmaster said:

"I wish you wouldn't go on."

"There was a fellow," Tietjens continued, "whose land was next to ours. Conder his name was. His wife was habitually unfaithful to him. She used to retire with some fellow for three months out of every year. Conder never moved a finger. But we felt Groby and the neighbourhood were unsafe. It was awkward introducing him — not to mention her — in your drawing-room. All sorts of awkwardnesses. Everyone knew the younger children weren't Conder's. A fellow married the youngest daughter and took over the hounds. And not a soul called on her. It wasn't rational or just. But that's why society distrusts the cuckold, really. It never knows when it mayn't be driven into something irrational and unjust."

"But you *aren't*," Macmaster said with real anguish, "going to let Sylvia behave like that."

"I don't know," Tietjens said. "How am I to stop it? Mind you, I think Conder was quite right. Such calamities are the will of God. A gentleman accepts them. If the woman won't divorce, he *must* accept them, and it gets talked about. You seem to have made it all right this time. You and, I suppose, Mrs. Satterthwaite between you. But you won't be always there. Or I might come across another woman."

Macmaster said:

"Ah!" and after a moment:

"What then?"

Tietjens said:

"God knows . . . There's that poor little beggar to be considered. Marchant says he's beginning to talk broad Yorkshire already."

Macmaster said:

"If it wasn't for that. . . . That would be a solution."

Tietjens said: "Ah!"

When he paid the cabman, in front of a grey cement portal with a gabled arch, reaching up, he said:

"You've been giving the mare less licorice in her mash. I told you she'd go better."

The cabman, with a scarlet, varnished face, a shiny hat, a drab box-cloth coat and a gardenia in his buttonhole, said:

"Ah! Trust you to remember, sir."

In the train, from beneath his pile of polished dressing and despatch cases — Tietjens had thrown his immense kit-bag with his own hands into the guard's van — Macmaster looked across at his friend. It was, for him, a great day. Across his face were the proof-sheets of his first, small, delicate-looking volume. . . . A small page, the type black and still odorous! He had the agreeable smell of the printer's ink in his nostrils; the fresh paper was still a little damp. In his white, rather spatulate, always slightly cold fingers, was the pressure of the small, flat, gold pencil he had purchased especially for these corrections. He had found none to make.

He had expected a wallowing of pleasure — almost the only sensuous pleasure he had allowed himself for many months. Keeping up the appearances of an English gentleman on an exiguous income was no mean task. But to wallow in your own phrases, to be rejoiced by the savour of your own shrewd pawkinesses, to feel your rhythm balanced and yet sober — that is a pleasure beyond most, and an inexpensive one at that. He had had it from mere "articles" — on the philosophies and domestic lives of such great figures as Carlyle and Mill, or on the expansion of inter-colonial trade. This was a book.

He relied upon it to consolidate his position. In the office they were mostly "born," and not vastly sympathetic. There was a sprinkling, too — it was beginning to be a large one — of young men who had obtained their entry by merit or by sheer industry. These watched promotions jealously, discerning nepotic increases of increment and clamouring amongst themselves at favouritisms.

To these he had been able to turn a cold shoulder. His intimacy with Tietjens permitted him to be rather on the "born" side of the institution, his agreeableness — he knew he was agreeable and useful! — to Sir Reginald Ingleby, protecting him in the main from unpleasantness. His "articles" had given him a certain right to an austerity of demeanour; his book he trusted to let him adopt an almost judicial attitude. He would then be *the* Mr. Macmaster, the critic, the authority. And the first-class departments are not adverse to having distinguished men as ornaments to their company; at any rate the promotion of the distinguished are not objected to. So Macmaster saw — almost physically — Sir Reginald Ingleby perceiving the empressement with which his valued subordinate was treated in the drawing-rooms of Mrs. Leamington, Mrs. Cressy, the Hon. Mrs. de Limoux; Sir Reginald would perceive that, for he was not a reader himself of much else than Government publications, and he would feel fairly safe in making easy the path of his critically gifted and austere young helper. The son of a very poor shipping clerk in an obscure Scotch harbour town, Macmaster had very early decided on the career that he would make. As between the heroes of Mr. Smiles, an author enormously popular in Macmaster's boyhood, and the more distinctly intellectual achievements open to the very poor Scot, Macmaster had had no difficulty in choosing. A pit lad *may* rise to be a mine owner; a hard, gifted, unsleeping Scots youth, pursuing unobtrusively and unobjectionably a course of study and of public usefulness, *will* certainly achieve distinction, security and the quiet admiration of those around him. It was the difference between the *may* and the *will*, and Macmaster had had no difficulty in making his choice. He saw himself by now almost certain of a career that should give him at fifty a knighthood, and long before that a competence, a drawing-room of his own, and a lady who should contribute to his unobtrusive fame, she moving about, in that room, amongst the best of the intellects of the day, gracious, devoted, a tribute at once to his discernment and his achievements. Without some disaster he was sure of himself. Disasters come to men through drink, bankruptcy, and women. Against the first two he knew himself immune, though his expenses had a tendency to outrun his income, and he was always a little in debt to Tietjens. Tietjens fortunately had means. As to the third, he was not so certain. His life had necessarily been starved of women, and, arrived at a stage when the female element might, even with due respect to caution, be considered as a legitimate feature of his life, he had to fear a rashness of choice due to that very starvation. The type of woman he needed he knew to exactitude: tall, graceful, dark, loose-gowned, passionate yet circumspect, oval-featured, deliberative, gracious to everyone around her. He could almost hear the very rustle of her garments.

And yet . . . He had had passages when a sort of blind unreason had attracted him almost to speechlessness towards girls of the most giggling, behind-the-counter order, big-bosomed, scarlet-cheeked. It was only Tietjens who had saved him from the most questionable entanglements.

"Hang it," Tietjens would say, "don't get messing round that trollop. All you could do with her would be to set her up in a tobacco shop, and she would be tearing your beard out inside the quarter. Let alone, you can't afford it."

And Macmaster, who would have sentimentalised the plump girl to the tune of *Highland Mary*, would for a day damn Tietjens up and down for a coarse brute. But at the moment he thanked God for Tietjens. There he sat, near to thirty, without an entanglement, a blemish on his health, or a worry with regard to any woman.

With deep affection and concern he looked across at his brilliant junior, who hadn't saved himself. Tietjens had fallen into the most barefaced snare, into the cruellest snare, of the worst woman that could be imagined.

And Macmaster suddenly realised that he wasn't wallowing, as he had imagined that he would, in the sensuous current of his prose. He had begun spiritedly with the first neat square of a paragraph. . . . Certainly his publishers had done well by him in the matter of print:

> "Whether we consider him as the imaginer of mysterious, sensuous and exact plastic beauty; as the manipulator of sonorous, rolling and full-mouthed lines; of words as full of colour as were his canvases; or whether we regard him as the deep philosopher, elucidating and drawing his illumination from the arcana of a mystic hardly greater than himself, to Gabriel Charles Dante Rossetti, the subject of this little monograph, must be accorded the name of one who has profoundly influenced the outward aspects, the human contacts, and all those things that go to make up the life of our higher civilisation as we live it to-day. . . ."

Macmaster realised that he had only got thus far with his prose, and had got thus far without any of the relish that he had expected, and that then he had turned to the middle paragraph of page three — after the end of his exordium. His eyes wandered desultorily along the line:

> "The subject of these pages was born in the western central district of the metropolis in the year . . ."

The words conveyed nothing to him at all. He understood that that was because he hadn't got over that morning. He had looked up from his coffee-cup — over the rim — and had taken in a blue-grey sheet of notepaper in Tietjens' fingers, shaking, inscribed in the large, broad-nibbed writing of that detestable harridan. And Tietjens had been staring — staring with the intentness of a maddened horse — at his, Macmaster's, face! And grey! Shapeless! The nose like a pallid triangle on a bladder of lard! That was Tietjens' face. . . .

He could still feel the blow, physical, in the pit of his stomach! He had thought Tietjens was going mad: that he *was* mad. It had passed. Tietjens had assumed the mask of his indolent, insolent self. At the office, but later, he had delivered an extraordinarily forceful — and quite rude — lecture to Sir Reginald on his reasons for differing from the official figures of population movements in the western territories. Sir Reginald had been much impressed. The figures were wanted for a speech of the Colonial Minister — or an answer to a question — and Sir Reginald had promised to put Tietjens' views before the great man. That was the sort of thing to do a young fellow good — because it got kudos for the office. They had to work on figures provided by the Colonial Governments, and if they could correct those fellows by sheer brain work — that scored.

But there sat Tietjens, in his grey tweeds, his legs apart, lumpish, clumsy, his tallowy, intelligent-looking hands drooping inert between his legs, his eyes gazing at a coloured photograph of the port of Boulogne beside the mirror beneath the luggage rack. Blond, high-coloured, vacant apparently, you couldn't tell what in the world he was thinking of. The mathematical theory of waves, very likely, or slips in someone's article on Arminianism. For, absurd as it seemed, Macmaster knew that he knew next to nothing of his friend's feelings. As to them, practically no confidences had passed between them. Just two: On the night before his starting for his wedding in Paris Tietjens had said to him:

"Vinny, old fellow, it's a back door way out of it. She's bitched *me*."

And once, rather lately, he had said:

"Damn it! I don't even know if the child's my own!"

This last confidence had shocked Macmaster so irremediably — the child had been a seven months' child, rather ailing, and Tietjens' clumsy tenderness towards it had been so marked that, even without this nightmare, Macmaster had been affected by the sight of them together — that confidence then had pained Macmaster so frightfully, it was so appalling, that Macmaster had regarded it almost as an insult. It was the sort of confidence a man didn't make to his equal, but only to solicitors, doctors, or the clergy who are not quite men. Or, at any rate, such confidences are not made between men without appeals for sympathy, and Tietjens had made no appeal for sympathy. He had just added sardonically:

"She gives me the benefit of the agreeable doubt. And she's as good as said as much to Marchant" — Marchant had been Tietjens' old nurse.

Suddenly — and as if in a sort of unconscious losing of his head — Macmaster remarked:

"You can't say the man wasn't a poet!"

The remark had been, as it were, torn from him, because he had observed, in the strong light of the compartment, that half of Tietjens' forelock and a roundish patch behind it was silvery white. That might have been going on for weeks: you live beside a man and notice his changes very little. Yorkshire men of fresh colour, and blondish, often go speckled with white very young; Tietjens had had a white hair or two at the age of fourteen, very noticeable in the sunlight when he had taken his cap off to bowl.

But Macmaster's mind, taking appalled change, had felt assured that Tietjens had gone white with the shock of his wife's letter — in four hours! That meant that terrible things must be going on within him; his thoughts, at all costs, must be distracted. The mental process in Macmaster had been quite subconscious. He would not, advisedly, have introduced the painter-poet as a topic.

Tietjens said:

"I haven't said anything at all that I can remember."

The obstinacy of his hard race awakened in Macmaster:

"Since," he quoted, "when we stand side by side

> Only hands may meet,
> Better half this weary world
> Lay between us, sweet!
> Better far tho' hearts may break
> Bid farewell for aye!
> Lest thy sad eyes, meeting mine,
> Tempt my soul away!"

"You can't," he continued, "say that that isn't poetry! Great poetry."

"I can't say," Tietjens answered contemptuously. "I don't read poetry except Byron. But it's a filthy picture. . . ."

Macmaster said uncertainly:

"I don't know that I know the picture. Is it in Chicago?"

"It isn't painted!" Tietjens said. "But it's there!"

He continued with sudden fury:

"Damn it. What's the sense of all these attempts to justify fornication? England's mad about it. Well, you've got your John Stuart Mill's and your George Eliot's for the high-class thing. Leave the furniture out! Or leave me out, at least I tell you it revolts me to think of that obese, oily man who never took a bath, in a grease-spotted dressing-gown and the underclothes he's slept in, standing beside a five-shilling model with crimped hair, or some Mrs. W. Three Stars, gazing into a mirror that reflects their fetid selves and gilt sunfish and drop chandeliers and plates sickening with cold bacon fat and gurgling about passion."

Macmaster had gone chalk white, his short beard bristling:

"You daren't . . . you daren't talk like that," he stuttered.

"I *dare*!" Tietjens answered; "but I oughtn't to . . . to you! I admit that. But you oughtn't, almost as much, to talk about that stuff to me, either. It's an insult to my intelligence."

"Certainly," Macmaster said stiffly, "the moment was not opportune."

"I don't understand what you mean," Tietjens answered. "The moment can never be opportune. Let's agree that making a career is a dirty business — for me as for you! But decent augurs grin behind their masks. They never preach to each other."

"You're getting esoteric," Macmaster said faintly.

"I'll underline," Tietjens went on. "I quite understand that the favour of Mrs. Cressy and Mrs. de Limoux is essential to you! They have the ear of that old don Ingleby."

Macmaster said:

"Damn!"

"I quite agree," Tietjens continued, "I quite approve. It's the game as it has always been played. It's the tradition, so it's right. It's been sanctioned since the days of the *Précieuses Ridicules*."

"You've a way of putting things," Macmaster said.

"I haven't," Tietjens answered. "It's just because I haven't that what I *do* say sticks out in the minds of fellows like you who are always fiddling about after literary expression. But what I do say is this: I stand for monogamy."

Macmaster uttered a "*You!*" of amazement.

Tietjens answered with a negligent "*I!*" He continued·

"I stand for monogamy and chastity. And for no talking about it. Of course if a man who's a man wants to have a woman he has her. And again, no talking about it. He'd no doubt be in the end better, and better off, if he didn't. Just as it would probably be better for him if he didn't have the second glass of whisky and soda. . . ."

"You call that monogamy and chastity!" Macmaster interjected.

"I do," Tietjens answered. "And it probably is, at any rate it's clean. What is loathesome is all your fumbling in placket-holes and polysyllabic Justification by Love. You stand for lachrymose polygamy. That's all right if you can get your club to change its rules."

"You're out of my depth," Macmaster said. "And being very disagreeable. You appear to be justifying promiscuity. I don't like it."

"I'm probably being disagreeable," Tietjens said. "Jeremiahs usually are. But there ought to be a twenty years' close time for discussions of sham sexual morality. Your Paolo and Francesca — and Dante's — went, very properly, to Hell, and no bones about it. You don't get Dante justifying them. But your fellow whines about creeping into Heaven."

"He *doesn't*," Macmaster exclaimed. Tietjens continued with equanimity:

"Now your novelist who writes a book to justify his every tenth or fifth seduction of a commonplace young woman in the name of the rights of shop boys. . . ."

"I'll admit," Macmaster coincided, "that Briggs is going too far. I told him only last Thursday at Mrs. Limoux's . . ."

"I'm not talking of anyone in particular," Tietjens said. "I don't read novels. I'm supposing a case. And it's a cleaner case than that of your pre-Raphaelite horrors! No! I don't read novels, but I follow tendencies. And if a fellow chooses to justify his seductions of uninteresting and viewy young females along the lines of freedom and the rights of man, it's relatively respectable. It would be better just to boast about his conquests in a straightforward and exultant way. But . . ."

"You carry joking too far sometimes," Macmaster said. "I've warned you about it."

"I'm as solemn as an owl!" Tietjens rejoined. "The lower classes are becoming vocal. Why shouldn't they? They're the only people in this country who are sound in wind and limb. They'll save the country if the country's to be saved."

"And you call yourself a Tory!" Macmaster said.

"The lower classes," Tietjens continued equably, "such of them as get through the secondary schools, want irregular and very transitory unions. During holidays they go together on personally conducted tours to Switzerland and such places. Wet afternoons they pass in their tiled bathrooms, slapping each other hilariously on the backs and splashing white enamel paint about."

"You say you don't read novels," Macmaster said, "but I recognise the quotation."

"I don't *read* novels," Tietjens answered. "I know what's in 'em. There has been nothing worth *reading* written in England since the eighteenth century except by a woman. . . . But it's natural for your enamel splashers to want to see themselves in a bright and variegated literature. Why shouldn't they? It's a healthy, human desire, and now that printing and paper are cheap they get it satisfied. It's healthy, I tell you. Infinitely healthier than . . ." He paused.

"Than what?" Macmaster asked.

"I'm thinking," Tietjens said, "thinking how not to be too rude."

"You want to be rude," Macmaster said bitterly, "to people who lead the contemplative . . . the circumspect life."

"It's precisely that," Tietjens said. He quoted:

> She walks, the lady of my delight,
> A shepherdess of sheep;
> She is so circumspect and right:
> She has her thoughts to keep.

Macmaster said:
"Confound you, Chrissie. You know everything."

"Well, yes," Tietjens said musingly, "I think I should want to be rude to her. I don't say I should be. Certainly I shouldn't if she were good looking. Or if she were your soul's affinity. You can rely on that."

Macmaster had a sudden vision of Tietjens' large and clumsy form walking beside the lady of his, Macmaster's, delight, when ultimately she was found — walking along the top of a cliff amongst tall grass and poppies and making himself extremely agreeable with talk of Tasso and Cimabue. All the same, Macmaster imagined, the lady wouldn't like Tietjens. Women didn't as a rule. His looks and his silences alarmed them. Or they hated him. . . . Or they like him very much indeed. And Macmaster said conciliatorily:

"Yes, I think I could rely on that!" He added: "All the same I don't wonder that . . ."

He had been about to say:

"I don't wonder that Sylvia calls you immoral." For Tietjens' wife alleged that Tietjens was detestable. He bored her, she said, by his silences; when he did speak she hated him for the immorality of his views. . . . But he did not finish his sentence, and Tietjens went on:

"All the same when the war comes it will be these little snobs who will save England, because they've the courage to know what they want and to say so."

Macmaster said loftily:

"You're extraordinarily old-fashioned at times, Chrissie. You ought to know as well as I do that a war is impossible — at any rate with this country in it. Simply because . . ." He hesitated and then emboldened himself: "*We* — the circumspect — yes, the circumspect classes, will pilot the nation through the tight places."

"War, my good fellow," Tietjens said — the train was slowing down preparatorily to running into Ashford — "is inevitable, and with this country plumb centre in the middle of it. Simply because you fellows are such damn hypocrites. There's not a country in the world that trusts us. We're always, as it were, committing adultery — like your fellow! — with the name of Heaven on our lips." He was jibing again at the subject of Macmaster's monograph.

"He never!" Macmaster said in almost a stutter. "He never whined about Heaven."

"He did," Tietjens said: "The beastly poem you quoted ends:

> Better far though hearts may break,
>   Since we dare not love,
> Part till we once more may meet
>   In a Heaven above."

And Macmaster, who had been dreading that shot — for he never knew how much or how little of any given poem his friend would have by heart — Macmaster collapsed, as it were, into fussily getting down his dressing-cases and clubs from the rack, a task he usually left to a porter. Tietjens who, however much a train might be running into a station he was bound for, sat like a rock until it was dead-still, said:

"Yes, a war is inevitable. Firstly, there's you fellows who can't be trusted. And then there's the multitude who mean to have bathrooms and white enamel. Millions of them; all over the world. Not merely here. And there aren't enough bathrooms and white enamel in the world to go round. It's like you polygamists with women. There aren't enough women in the world to go round to satisfy your insatiable appetites. And there aren't enough men in the world to give each woman one. And most women want several. So you have divorce cases. I suppose you won't say that because you're so circumspect and right there shall be no more divorce? Well, war is as inevitable as divorce. . . ."

Macmaster had his head out of the carriage window and was calling for a porter.

On the platform a number of women in lovely sable cloaks, with purple or red jewel cases, with diaphanous silky scarves flying from motor hoods, were drifting towards the branch train for Rye, under the shepherding of erect, burdened footmen. Two of them nodded to Tietjens.

Macmaster considered that he was perfectly right to be tidy in his dress; you never knew whom you mightn't meet on a railway journey. This confirmed him as against Tietjens, who preferred to look like a navvy.

A tall, white-haired, white-moustached, red-cheeked fellow limped after Tietjens, who was getting his immense bag out of the guard's van. He clapped the young man on the shoulder and said:

"Hullo! How's your mother-in-law? Lady Claude wants to know. She says come up and pick a bone tonight if you're going to Rye." He had extraordinarily blue, innocent eyes.

Tietjens said:

"Hullo, General," and added: "I believe she's much better. Quite restored. This is Macmaster. I think I shall be going over to bring my wife back in a day or two. They're both at Lobscheid . . . a German spa."

The general said:

"Quite right. It isn't good for a young man to be alone. Kiss Sylvia's finger-tips for me. She's the real thing, you lucky beggar." He added, a little anxiously: "What about a foursome to-morrow? Paul Sandbach is down. He's as crooked as me. We can't do a full round at singles."

"It's your own fault," Tietjens said. "You ought to have gone to my bone-setter. Settle it with Macmaster, will you?" He jumped into the twilight of the guard's van.

The general looked at Macmaster, a quick, penetrating scrutiny:
"You're *the* Macmaster," he said. "You would be if you're with
Chrissie."

A high voice called:
"General! General!"

"I want a word with you," the general said, "about the figures in
that article you wrote about Pondoland. Figures are all right. But
we shall lose the beastly country if . . . But we'll talk about it after
dinner to-night. You'll come up to Lady Claudine's. . . ."

Macmaster congratulated himself again on his appearance. It was
all very well for Tietjens to look like a sweep; he was of these people.
He, Macmaster, wasn't. He had, if anything, to be an authority, and
authorities wear gold tie-rings and broadcloth. General Lord Edward
Campion had a son, a permanent head of the Treasury department
that regulated increases of salaries and promotions in all the public
offices. Tietjens only caught the Rye train by running alongside it,
pitching his enormous kit-bag through the carriage window and
swinging on the foot-board. Macmaster reflected that if he had done
that half the station would have been yelling, "Stand away there."

As it was Tietjens, a stationmaster was galloping after him to open
the carriage door and grinningly to part:
"Well caught, sir!" for it was a cricketing county.

"Truly," Macmaster quoted to himself.

> The gods to each ascribe a differing lot:
> Some enter at the portal. Some do not!

II

MRS. SATTERTHWAITE with her French maid, her priest, and her
disreputable young man, Mr. Bayliss, were at Lobscheid, an unknown and little-frequented air resort amongst the pinewoods of the
Taunus. Mrs. Satterthwaite was ultra-fashionable and consummately
indifferent — she only really lost her temper if at her table and under
her nose you consumed her famous Black Hamburg grapes without
taking their skin and all. Father Consett was out to have an up-
roarious good time during his three weeks' holiday from the slums of
Liverpool; Mr. Bayliss, thin like a skeleton in tight blue serge, golden-

haired and pink, was so nearly dead of tuberculosis, was so dead penniless, and of tastes so costly that he was ready to keep stone quiet, drink six pints of milk a day and behave himself. On the face of it he was there to write the letters of Mrs. Satterthwaite, but the lady never let him enter her private rooms for fear of infection. He had to content himself with nursing a growing adoration for Father Consett. This priest, with an enormous mouth, high cheek-bones, untidy black hair, a broad face that never looked too clean and waving hands that always looked too dirty, never kept still for a moment, and had a brogue such as is seldom heard outside old-fashioned English novels of Irish life. He had a perpetual laugh, like the noise made by a steam roundabout. He was, in short, a saint, and Mr. Bayliss knew it, though he didn't know how. Ultimately, and with the financial assistance of Mrs. Satterthwaite, Mr. Bayliss became almoner to Father Consett, adopted the rule of St. Vincent de Paul and wrote some very admirable, if decorative, devotional verse.

They proved thus a very happy, innocent party. For Mrs. Satterthwaite interested herself — it was the only interest she had — in handsome, thin, and horribly disreputable young men. She would wait for them, or send her car to wait for them, at the gaol gates. She would bring their usually admirable wardrobes up to date and give them enough money to have a good time. When contrary to all expectations — but it happened more often than not! — they turned out well, she was lazily pleased. Sometimes she sent them away to a gay spot with a priest who needed a holiday; sometimes she had them down to her place in the west of England.

So they were a pleasant company and all very happy. Lobscheid contained one empty hotel with large verandahs and several square farmhouses, white with grey beams, painted in the gables with bouquets of blue and yellow flowers or with scarlet huntsmen shooting at purple stags. They were like gay cardboard boxes set down in fields of long grass; then the pinewoods commenced and ran, solemn, brown and geometric for miles up and down hill. The peasant girls wore black velvet waistcoats, white bodices, innumerable petticoats and absurd parti-coloured headdresses of the shape and size of halfpenny buns. They walked about in rows of four to six abreast, with a slow step, protruding white-stockinged feet in dancing pumps, their headdresses nodding solemnly; young men in blue blouses, kneebreeches and, on Sundays, in three-cornered hats, followed behind singing part-songs.

The French maid — whom Mrs. Satterthwaite had borrowed from
the Duchesse de Carbon Châteaulherault in exchange for her own
maid — was at first inclined to find the place *maussade*. But getting
up a tremendous love affair with a fine, tall, blond young fellow,
who included a gun, a gold-mounted hunting knife as long as his
arm, a light, grey-green uniform, with gilt badges and buttons, she
was reconciled to her lot. When the young Förster tried to shoot her
— *"et pour cause,"* as she said — she was ravished and Mrs. Satterthwaite lazily amused.

They were sitting playing bridge in the large, shadowy dining-hall
of the hotel: Mrs. Satterthwaite, Father Consett, Mr. Bayliss. A
young blond sub-lieutenant of great obsequiousness who was there
as a last chance for his right lung and his career, and the bearded
Kur-doctor cut in. Father Consett, breathing heavily and looking
frequently at his watch, played very fast, exclaiming: "Hurry up now;
it's nearly twelve. Hurry up wid ye." Mr. Bayliss being dummy, the
Father exclaimed: "Three, no trumps; I've to make. Get me a whisky
and soda quick, and don't drown it as ye did the last." He played his
hand with extreme rapidity, threw down his last three cards, exclaimed: "Ach! Botheranouns an' all; I'm two down and I've revoked
on the top av it," swallowed down his whisky and soda, looked at his
watch and exclaimed: "Done it to the minute! Here, doctor, take my
hand and finish the rubber." He was to take the mass next day for
the local priest, and mass must be said fasting from midnight, and
without cards played. Bridge was his only passion; a fortnight every
year was what, in his worn-out life, he got of it. On his holiday he
rose at ten. At eleven it was: "A four for the Father." From two to
four they walked in the forest. At five it was: "A four for the Father."
At nine it was: "Father, aren't you coming to your bridge?" And
Father Consett grinned all over his face and said: "It's good ye are
to a poor ould soggart. It will be paid back to you in Heaven."

The other four played on solemnly. The Father sat himself down
behind Mrs. Satterthwaite, his chin in the nape of her neck. At excruciating moments he gripped her shoulders, exclaimed: "Play the
queen, woman!" and breathed hard down her back. Mrs. Satterthwaite would play the two of diamonds, and the Father, throwing
himself back, would groan. She said over her shoulder:

"I want to talk to you to-night, Father," took the last trick of the
rubber, collected 17 marks 50 from the doctor and 8 marks from
the unter-leutnant. The doctor exclaimed:

"You gan't dake that immense sum from us and then ko off. Now we shall be ropped py Herr Payliss at gutt-throat!"

She drifted, all shadowy black silk, across the shadows of the dining-hall, dropping her winnings into her black satin vanity bag and attended by the priest. Outside the door, beneath the antlers of a royal stag, in an atmosphere of paraffin lamps and varnished pitch-pine, she said:

"Come up to my sitting-room. The prodigal's returned. Sylvia's here."

The Father said:

"I thought I saw her out of the corner of my eye in the 'bus after dinner. She'll be going back to her husband. It's a poor world."

"She's a wicked devil!" Mrs. Satterthwaite said.

"I've known her myself since she was nine," Father Consett said, "and it's little I've seen in her to hold up to the commendation of my flock." He added: "But maybe I'm made unjust by the shock of it."

They climbed the stairs slowly.

Mrs. Satterthwaite sat herself on the edge of a cane chair. She said: "Well!"

She wore a black hat like a cart-wheel and her dresses appeared always to consist of a great many squares of silk that might have been thrown on to her. Since she considered that her complexion, which was mat white, had gone slightly violet from twenty years of make up, when she was not made up — as she never was at Lobscheid — she wore bits of puce-coloured satin ribbon stuck here and there, partly to counteract the violet of her complexion, partly to show she was not in mourning. She was very tall and extremely emaciated; her dark eyes that had beneath them dark brown thumb-marks were very tired or very indifferent by turns.

Father Consett walked backwards and forwards, his hands behind his back, his head bent, over the not too well polished floor. There were two candles, lit but dim, in imitation pewter *nouvel art* candle-sticks, rather dingy; a sofa of cheap mahogany with red plush cushions and rests, a table covered with a cheap carpet and an American roll-top desk that had thrown into it a great many papers in scrolls or flat. Mrs. Satterthwaite was extremely indifferent to her surroundings, but she insisted on having a piece of furniture for her papers. She liked also to have a profusion of hot-house, not garden, flowers, but as there were none of these at Lobscheid she did without them. She insisted also, as a rule, on a comfortable chaise longue which she rarely, if ever, used; but the German Empire of those days did not contain a comfortable chair, so she did without it, lying down on her bed when she was really tired. The walls of the large room were completely covered with pictures of animals in death agonies: capercailzies giving up the ghost with gouts of scarlet blood on the snow; deer dying with their heads back and eyes glazing, gouts of red blood on their necks; foxes dying with scarlet blood on green grass. These pictures were frame to frame, representing sport, the hotel having been a former Grand Ducal hunting-box, freshened to suit the taste of the day with varnished pitch-pine, bath-rooms, verandahs, and excessively modern but noisy lavatory arrangements which had been put in for the delight of possible English guests.

Mrs. Satterthwaite sat on the edge of her chair; she had always the air of being just about to go out somewhere or of having just come in and being on the point of going to take her things off. She said:

"There's been a telegram waiting for her all the afternoon. I knew she was coming."

Father Consett said:

"I saw it in the rack myself. I misdoubted it." He added: "Oh dear, oh dear! After all we've talked about it; now it's come."

Mrs. Satterthwaite said:

"I've been a wicked woman myself as these things are measured; but . . ."

Father Consett said:

"Ye have! It's no doubt from you she gets it, for your husband was a good man. But one wicked woman is enough for my contemplation at a time. I'm no St. Anthony. . . . The young man says he will take her back?"

"On conditions," Miss Satterthwaite said. "He is coming here to have an interview."

The priest said:

"Heaven knows, Mrs. Satterthwaite, there are times when to a poor priest the rule of the Church as regards marriage seems bitter hard and he almost doubts her inscrutable wisdom. He doesn't mind you. But at times I wish that that young man would take what advantage — it's all there is! — that he can of being a Protestant and divorce Sylvia. For I tell you, there are bitter things to see amongst my flock over there. . . ." He made a vague gesture towards the infinite. "And bitter things I've seen, for the heart of man is a wicked place. But never a bitterer than this young man's lot."

"As you say," Mrs. Satterthwaite said, "my husband was a good man. I hated him, but that was as much my fault as his. More! And the only reason I don't wish Christopher to divorce Sylvia is that it would bring disgrace on my husband's name. At the same time, Father . . ."

The priest said:

"I've heard near enough."

"There's this to be said for Sylvia," Mrs. Satterthwaite went on. "There are times when a woman hates a man — as Sylvia hates her husband. . . . I tell you I've walked behind a man's back and nearly screamed because of the desire to put my nails into the veins of his neck. It was a fascination. And it's worse with Sylvia. It's a natural antipathy."

"Woman!" Father Consett fulminated, "I've no patience wid ye! If the woman, as the Church directs, would have children by her husband and live decent, she would have no such feelings. It's unnatural living and unnatural practises that cause these complexes. Don't think I'm an ignoramus, priest if I am."

Mrs. Satterthwaite said:

"But Sylvia's had a child."

Father Consett swung round like a man that has been shot at.

"Whose?" he asked, and he pointed a dirty finger at his interlocutress. "It was that blackguard Drake's, wasn't it? I've long suspected that."

"It was probably Drake's," Mrs. Satterthwaite said.

"Then," the priest said, "in the face of the pains of the hereafter, how could you let that decent lad in the hotness of his sin . . . ?"

"Indeed," Mrs. Satterthwaite said, "I shiver sometimes when I think of it. Don't believe that I had anything to do with trepanning him. But I couldn't hinder it. Sylvia's my daughter, and dog doesn't eat dog."

"There are times when it should," Father Consett said contemptuously.

"You don't seriously," Mrs. Satterthwaite said, "say that I, a mother, if an indifferent one, with my daughter appearing in trouble, as the kitchenmaids say, by a married man — that I should step in and stop a marriage that was a Godsend. . . ."

"Don't," the priest said, "introduce the sacred name into an affair of Piccadilly bad girls. . . ." He stopped. "Heaven help me," he said again, "don't ask me to answer the question of what you should or shouldn't have done. You know I loved your husband like a brother, and you know I've loved you and Sylvia ever since she was a tiny. And I thank God that I am not your spiritual adviser, but only your friend in God. For if I had to answer your question I could answer it only in one way." He broke off to ask: "Where is that woman?"

Mrs. Satterthwaite called:

"Sylvia! Sylvia! Come here!"

A door in the shadows opened and light shone from another room behind a tall figure leaning one hand on the handle of the door. A very deep voice said:

"I can't understand, mother, why you live in rooms like a sergeants' mess." And Sylvia Tietjens wavered into the room. She added: "I suppose it doesn't matter. I'm bored."

Father Consett groaned:

"Heaven help us, she's like a picture of Our Lady by Fra Angelico."

Immensely tall, slight, and slow in her movements, Sylvia Tietjens wore her reddish, very fair hair in great bandeaux right down over her ears. Her very oval, regular face had an expression of virginal lack of interest such as used to be worn by fashionable Paris courtesans a decade before that time. Sylvia Tietjens considered that, being privileged to go everywhere where one went and to have all men at her feet, she had no need to change her expression or to infuse into it the greater animation that marked the more common beauties of the early twentieth century. She moved slowly from the door and sat languidly on the sofa against the wall.

"There you are, Father," she said. "I'll not ask you to shake hands with me. You probably wouldn't."

"As I am a priest," Father Consett answered, "I could not refuse. But I'd rather not."

"This," Sylvia repeated, "appears to be a boring place."

"You won't say so to-morrow," the priest said. "There's two young fellows. . . . And a sort of policeman to trepan away from your mother's maid!"

"That," Sylvia answered, "is meant to be bitter. But it doesn't hurt. I am done with men." She added suddenly: "Mother, didn't you one day, while you were still young, say that you had done with men? Firmly! And mean it?"

Mrs. Satterthwaite said:

"I did."

"And did you keep to it?" Sylvia asked.

Mrs. Satterthwaite said:

"I did."

"And shall I, do you imagine?"

Mrs. Satterthwaite said:

"I imagine you will."

Sylvia said:

"Oh dear!"

The priest said:

"I'd be willing to see your husband's telegram. It makes a difference to see the words on paper."

Sylvia rose effortlessly.

"I don't see why you shouldn't," she said. "It will give you no pleasure." She drifted towards the door.

"If it would give me pleasure," the priest said, "you would not show it me."

"I would not," she said.

A silhouette in the doorway, she halted, drooping, and looked over her shoulder.

"Both you and mother," she said, "sit there scheming to make life bearable for the Ox. I call my husband the Ox. He's repulsive: like a swollen animal. Well . . . you can't do it." The lighted doorway was vacant. Father Consett sighed.

"I told you this was an evil place," he said. "In the deep forests. She'd not have such evil thoughts in another place."

Mrs. Satterthwaite said:

"I'd rather you didn't say that, Father. Sylvia would have evil thoughts in any place."

"Sometimes," the priest said, "at night I think I hear the claws of evil things scratching on the shutters. This was the last place in Europe to be christianised. Perhaps it wasn't ever even christianised and they're here yet."

Mrs. Satterthwaite said:

"It's all very well to talk like that in the day-time. It makes the place seem romantic. But it must be near one at night. And things are bad enough as it is."

"They are," Father Consett said. "The devil's at work."

Sylvia drifted back into the room with a telegram of several sheets.

Father Consett held it close to one of the candles to read, for he was short-sighted.

"All men are repulsive," Sylvia said; "don't you think so, mother?"

Mrs. Satterthwaite said:

"I do not. Only a heartless woman would say so."

"Mrs. Vanderdecken," Sylvia went on, "says all men are repulsive and it's woman's disgusting task to live beside them."

"You've been seeing that foul creature?" Mrs. Satterthwaite said. "She's a Russian agent. And worse!"

"She was at Gosingeux all the time we were," Sylvia said. "You needn't groan. She won't split on us. She's the soul of honour."

"It wasn't because of that I groaned, if I did," Mrs. Satterthwaite answered.

The priest, from over his telegram, exclaimed:

"Mrs. Vanderdecken! God forbid."

Sylvia's face, as she sat on the sofa, expressed languid and incredulous amusement.

"What do you know of her?" she asked the Father.

"I know what you know," he answered, "and that's enough."

"Father Consett," Sylvia said to her mother, "has been renewing his social circle."

"It's not," Father Consett said, "amongst the dregs of the people that you must live if you don't want to hear of the dregs of society."

Sylvia stood up. She said:

"You'll keep your tongue off my best friends if you want me to stop and be lectured. But for Mrs. Vanderdecken I should not be here, returned to the fold!"

Father Consett exclaimed:

"Don't say it, child. I'd rather, heaven help me, you had gone on living in open sin."

Sylvia sat down again, her hands listlessly in her lap.

"Have it your own way," she said, and the Father returned to the fourth sheet of the telegram.

"What does this mean?" he asked. He had returned to the first sheet. "This here: '*Accept resumption yoke*'?" he read, breathlessly.

"Sylvia," Mrs. Satterthwaite said, "go and light the spirit lamp for some tea. We shall want it."

"You'd think I was a district messenger boy," Sylvia said as she rose. "Why don't you keep your maid up? . . . It's a way we had of referring to our . . . union," she explained to the Father.

"There was sympathy enough between you and him then," he said, "to have bywords for things. It was that I wanted to know. I understood the words."

"They were pretty bitter bywords, as you call them," Sylvia said. "More like curses than kisses."

"It was you that used them then," Mrs. Satterthwaite said. "Christopher never said a bitter thing to you."

An expression like a grin came slowly over Sylvia's face as she turned back to the priest.

"That's mother's tragedy," she said. "My husband's one of her best boys. She adores him. And he can't bear *her*." She drifted behind the wall of the next room and they heard her tinkling the tea-things as the Father read on again beside the candle. His immense shadow began at the centre and ran along the pitchpine ceiling, down the wall and across the floor to join his splay feet in their clumsy boots.

"It's bad," he muttered. He made a sound like "Umbleumbleumble. . . . Worse than I feared . . . umbleumble. . . . '*accept resumption yoke but on rigid conditions.*' What's this: *esoecially*; it ought to be a 'p,' '*especially regards child reduce establishment ridiculous our position remake settlements in child's sole interests flat not house entertaining minimum am prepared resign office settle Yorkshire but imagine this not suit you child remain sister Effie open visits both wire if this rough outline provisionally acceptable in that case will express draft general position Monday for you and mother reflect upon follow self Tuesday arrive Thursday Lobscheid go Wiesbaden fortnight on social task discussion Thursday limited solely comma emphasised comma to affairs.*' "

"That means," Mrs. Satterthwaite said, "that he doesn't mean to reproach her. *Emphasised* applies to the word *solely*. . . ."

"Why d'you take it . . ." Father Consett asked, "did he spend an immense lot of money on this telegram? Did he imagine you were in such trepidation. . . ." He broke off. Walking slowly, her long arms extended to carry the tea-tray, over which her wonderfully moving face had a rapt expression of indescribable mystery, Sylvia was coming through the door.

"Oh, child," the Father exclaimed, "whether it's St. Martha or that Mary that made the bitter choice, not one of them ever looked more virtuous than you. Why aren't ye born to be a good man's helpmeet?"

A little tinkle sounded from the tea-tray and three pieces of sugar fell on to the floor. Mrs. Tietjens hissed with vexation.

"I *knew* that damned thing would slide off the tea-cups," she said. She dropped the tray from an inch or so of height on to the carpeted table. "I'd made it a matter of luck between myself and myself," she said. Then she faced the priest.

"I'll tell you," she said, "why he sent the telegram. It's because of that dull display of the English gentleman that I detested. He gives himself the solemn airs of the Foreign Minister, but he's only a youngest son at the best. That is why I loathe him."

Mrs. Satterthwaite said:

"That isn't the reason why he sent the telegram."

Her daughter had a gesture of amused, lazy tolerance.

"Of course it isn't," she said. "He sent it out of consideration: the lordly, full dress consideration that drives me distracted. As he would say: He'd imagine I'd find it convenient to have ample time for reflection. It's like being addressed as if one were a monument and by a herald according to protocol. And partly because he's the soul of truth like a stiff Dutch doll. He wouldn't write a letter because he couldn't without beginning it 'Dear Sylvia' and ending it 'Yours sincerely' or 'truly' or 'affectionately.' He's that sort of precise imbecile. I tell you he's so formal he can't do without all the conventions there are and so truthful he can't use half of them."

"Then," Father Consett said, "if ye know him so well, Sylvia Satterthwaite, how is it ye can't get on with him better? They say: *Tout savoir c'est tout pardonner*."

"It isn't," Sylvia said. "To know everything about a person is to be bored . . . bored . . . bored!"

"And how are ye going to answer this telegram of his?" the Father asked. "Or have ye answered it already?"

"I shall wait until Monday night to keep him as bothered as I can to know whether he's to start on Tuesday. He fusses like a hen over his packings and the exact hours of his movements. On Monday I shall telegraph: 'Righto' and nothing else."

"And why," the Father asked, "will ye telegraph him a vulgar word that you never use, for your language is the one thing about you that isn't vulgar?"

Sylvia said:

"Thanks!" She curled her legs up under her on the sofa and laid her head back against the wall so that her Gothic arch of a chinbone pointed at the ceiling. She admired her own neck, which was very long and white.

"I know!" Father Consett said. "You're a beautiful woman. Some men would say it was a lucky fellow that lived with you. I don't ignore the fact in my cogitation. He'd imagine all sorts of delights to lurk in the shadow of your beautiful hair. And they wouldn't."

Sylvia brought her gaze down from the ceiling and fixed her brown eyes for a moment on the priest, speculatively.

"It's a great handicap we suffer from," he said.

"I don't know why I selected that word," Sylvia said, "it's one word, so it costs only fifty pfennigs. I couldn't hope really to give a jerk to his pompous self-sufficiency."

"It's great handicaps we priests suffer from," the Father repeated. "However much a priest may be a man of the world — and he has to be to fight the world. . . ."

Mrs. Satterthwaite said:

"Have a cup of tea, Father, while it's just right. I believe Sylvia is the only person in Germany who knows how to make tea."

"There's always behind him the Roman collar and the silk bib, and you don't believe in him," Father Consett went on, "yet he knows ten — a thousand times! — more of human nature than ever you can."

"I don't see," Sylvia said placably, "how you can learn in your slums anything about the nature of Eunice Vanderdecken, or Elizabeth B., or Queenie James, or any of my set." She was on her feet pouring cream into the Father's tea. "I'll admit for the moment that you aren't giving me pi-jaw."

"I'm glad," the priest said, "that ye remember enough of yer school-days to use the old term."

Sylvia wavered backwards to her sofa and sank down again.

"There you are," she said, "you can't really get away from preachments. Me for the pyore young girl is always at the back of it."

"It isn't," the Father said. "I'm not one to cry for the moon."

"You don't want me to be a pure young girl," Sylvia asked with lazy incredulity.

"I do not!" the Father said, "but I'd wish that at times ye'd remember you once were."

"I don't believe I ever was," Sylvia said, "if the nuns had known I'd have been expelled from the Holy Child."

"You would not," the Father said. "Do stop your boasting. The nuns have too much sense. . . . Anyhow, it isn't a pure young girl

I'd have you or behaving like a Protestant deaconess for the craven fear of hell. I'd have ye be a physically healthy, decently honest-with-yourself young devil of a married woman. It's them that are the plague and the salvation of the world."

"You admire mother?" Mrs. Tietjens asked suddenly. She added in parenthesis: "You see you can't get away from salvation."

"I mean keeping bread and butter in their husband's stomachs," the priest said. "Of course I admire your mother."

Mrs. Satterthwaite moved a hand slightly.

"You're at any rate in league with her against me," Sylvia said. She asked with more interest: "Then would you have me model myself on her and do good works to escape hell fire? She wears a hair shirt in Lent."

Mrs. Satterthwaite started from her doze on the edge of her chair. She had been trusting the Father's wit to give her daughter's insolence a run for its money, and she imagined that if the priest hit hard enough he might, at least, make Sylvia think a little about some of her ways.

"Hang it, no, Sylvia," she exclaimed more suddenly. "I may not be much, but I'm a sportsman. I'm afraid of hell fire; horribly, I'll admit. But I don't bargain with the Almighty. I hope He'll let me through; but I'd go on trying to pick men out of the dirt — I suppose that's what you and Father Consett mean — if I were as certain of going to hell as I am of going to bed to-night. So that's that!"

" 'And lo! Ben Adhem's name led all the rest!' " Sylvia jeered softly. "All the same I bet you wouldn't bother to reclaim men if you could not find the young, good-looking, interestingly vicious sort."

"I wouldn't," Mrs. Satterthwaite said. "If they didn't interest me, why should I?"

Sylvia looked at Father Consett.

"If you're going to trounce me any more," she said, "get a move on. It's late, I've been travelling for thirty-six hours."

"I will," Father Consett said. "It's a good maxim that if you swat flies enough some of them stick to the wall. I'm only trying to make a little mark on your common sense. Don't you see what you're going to?"

"What?" Sylvia said indifferently. "Hell?"

"No," the Father said, "I'm talking of this life. Your confessor must talk to you about the next. But I'll not tell you what you're going to. I've changed my mind. I'll tell your mother after you're gone."

"Tell me," Sylvia said.

"I'll not," Father Consett answered. "Go to the fortune-tellers at the Earl's Court exhibition; they'll tell ye all about the fair woman you're to beware of."

"There's some of them said to be rather good," Sylvia said. "Di Wilson's told me about one. She said she was going to have a baby. . . . You don't mean that, Father? For I swear I never will. . . ."

"I daresay not," the priest said. "But let's talk about men."

"There's nothing you can tell me I don't know," Sylvia said.

"I daresay not," the priest answered. "But let's rehearse what you do know. Now suppose you could elope with a new man every week and no questions asked? Or how often would you want to?"

Sylvia said:

"Just a moment, Father," and she addressed Mrs. Satterthwaite: "I suppose I shall have to put myself to bed."

"You will," Mrs. Satterthwaite said. "I'll not have any maid kept up after ten in a holiday resort. What's she to do in a place like this? Except listen for the bogies it's full of?"

"Always considerate!" Mrs. Tietjens gibed. "And perhaps it's just as well. I'd probably beat that Marie of your's arms to pieces with a hair-brush if she came near me." She added: "You were talking about men, Father. . . ." And then began with sudden animation to her mother:

"I've changed my mind about that telegram. The first thing to-morrow I shall wire: '*Agreed entirely but arrange bring Hullo Central with you.*'"

She addressed the priest again:

"I call my maid Hullo Central because she's got a tinny voice like a telephone. I say: 'Hullo Central' — when she answers 'Yes, modd'm,' you'd swear it was the Exchange speaking. . . . But you were telling me about men."

"I was reminding you!" the Father said. "But I needn't go on. You've caught the drift of my remarks. That is why you are pretending not to listen."

"I assure you, no," Mrs. Tietjens said. "It is simply that if a thing comes into my head I have to say it. You were saying that if one went away with a different man for every week-end. . . ."

"You've shortened the period already," the priest said. "I gave a full week to every man."

"But, of course, one would have to have a home," Sylvia said, "an address. One would have to fill one's mid-week engagements. Really it comes to it that one has to have a husband and a place to store one's maid in. Hullo Central's been on board-wages all the time. But I don't believe she likes it. . . . Let's agree that if I had a different man every week I'd be bored with the arrangement. That's what you're getting at, isn't it?"

"You'd find," the priest said, "that it whittled down until the only divvy moment was when you stood waiting in the booking-office for the young man to take the tickets. And then gradually that wouldn't be divvy any more. . . . And you'd yawn and long to go back to your husband."

"Look here," Mrs. Tietjens said, "you're abusing the secrets of the confessional. That's exactly what Tottie Charles said. She tried it for three months while Freddie Charles was in Madeira. It's *exactly* what she said down to the yawn and the booking-office. *And* the 'divvy.' It's only Tottie Charles who uses it every two words. Most of us prefer ripping! It *is* more sensible."

"Of course I haven't been abusing the secrets of the confessional," Father Consett said mildly.

"Of course you haven't," Sylvia said with affection. "You're a good old stick and no end of a mimic, and you know us all to the bottom of our hearts."

"Not all that much," the priest said, "there's probably a good deal of good at the bottom of your hearts."

Sylvia said: .

"Thanks." She asked suddenly: "Look here. *Was* it what you saw of us — the future mothers of England, you know, and all — at Miss Lampeter's — that made you take to the slums? Out of disgust and despair?"

"Oh, let's not make melodrama out of it," the priest answered. "Let's say I wanted a change. I couldn't see that I was doing any good."

"You did us all the good there was done," Sylvia said. "What with Miss Lampeter always drugged to the world, and all the French mistresses as wicked as hell."

"I've heard you say all this before," Mrs. Satterthwaite said. "But it was supposed to be the best finishing school in England. I know it cost enough!"

"Well, say it was we who were a rotten lot," Sylvia concluded; and then to the Father: "We *were* a lot of rotters. weren't we?"

The priest answered:

"I don't know. I don't suppose you were — or are — any worse than your mother or grandmother, or the patricianesses of Rome or the worshippers of Ashtaroth. It seems we have to have a governing class and governing classes are subject to special temptations."

"Who's Ashtaroth?" Sylvia asked. "Astarte?" and then: "Now, Father, after your experiences would you say the factory girls of Liverpool, or any other slum, are any better women than us that you used to look after?"

"Astarte Syriaca," the Father said, "was a very powerful devil. There's some that hold she's not dead yet. I don't know that I do myself."

"Well, I've done with her," Sylvia said.

The Father nodded:

"You've had dealings with Mrs. Profumo?" he asked. "And that loathsome fellow. . . . What's his name?"

"Does it shock you?" Sylvia asked. "I'll admit it was a bit thick. . . . But I've done with it. I prefer to pin my faith to Mrs. Vanderdecken. And, of course, Freud."

The priest nodded his head and said:

"Of course! Of course. . . ."

But Mrs. Satterthwaite exclaimed, with sudden energy:

"Sylvia Tietjens, I don't care what you do or what you read, but if you ever speak another word to that woman, you never do to me!"

Sylvia stretched herself on her sofa. She opened her brown eyes wide and let the lids slowly drop again.

"I've said once," she said, "that I don't like to hear my friends miscalled. Eunice Vanderdecken is a bitterly misjudged woman. She's a real good pal."

"She's a Russian spy," Mrs. Satterthwaite said.

"Russian grandmother," Sylvia answered. "And if she is, who cares? She's welcome for me. . . . Listen now, you two. I said to myself when I came in: 'I daresay I've given them both a rotten time.' I know you're both more nuts on me than I deserve. And I said I'd sit and listen to all the pi-jaw you wanted to give me if I sat till dawn. And I will. As a return. But I'd rather you let my friends alone."

Both the elder people were silent. There came from the shuttered windows of the dark room a low, scratching rustle.

"You hear!" the priest said to Mrs. Satterthwaite.

"It's the branches," Mrs. Satterthwaite answered.

The Father answered: "There's no tree within ten yards! Try bats as an explanation."

"I've said I wish you wouldn't, once," Mrs. Satterthwaite shivered. Sylvia said:

"I don't know what you two are talking about. It sounds like superstition. Mother's rotten with it."

"I don't say that it's devils trying to get in," the Father said. "But it's just as well to remember that devils *are* always trying to get in. And there are especial spots. These deep forests are noted among others." He suddenly turned his back and pointed at the shadowy wall. "Who," he asked, "but a savage possessed by a devil could have conceived of *that* as a decoration?" He was pointing at a life-sized, coarsely daubed picture of a wild boar dying, its throat cut, and gouts of scarlet blood. Other agonies of animals went away into all the shadows.

"*Sport!*" he hissed. "It's devilry!"

"That's perhaps true," Sylvia said. Mrs. Satterthwaite was crossing herself with great rapidity. The silence remained.

Sylvia said:

"Then if you're both done talking I'll say what I have to say. To begin with . . ." She stopped and sat rather erect, listening to the rustling from the shutters.

"To begin with," she began again with impetus, "you spared me the catalogue of the defects of age; I know them. One grows skinny — my sort — the complexion fades, the teeth stick out. And then there is the boredom. I know it; one is bored . . . bored . . . bored! You can't tell me anything I don't know about that. I'm thirty. I know what to expect. You'd like to have told me, Father, only you were afraid of taking away from your famous man of the world effect — you'd like to have told me that one can insure against the boredom and the long, skinny teeth by love of husband and child. The home stunt! I believe it! I do quite believe it. Only I hate my husband . . . and I hate . . . I hate my child."

She paused, waiting for exclamations of dismay or disapprobation from the priest. These did not come.

"Think," she said, "of all the ruin that child has meant for me; the pain in bearing him and the fear of death."

"Of course," the priest said, "child-bearing is for women a very terrible thing."

"I can't say," Mrs. Tietjens went on, "that this has been a very decent conversation. You get a girl . . . fresh from open sin, and make her talk about it. Of course you're a priest and mother's mother; we're *en famille*. But Sister Mary of the Cross at the convent had a maxim: 'Wear velvet gloves in family life.' We seem to be going at it with the gloves off."

Father Consett still didn't say anything.

"You're trying, of course, to draw me," Sylvia said. "I can see that with half an eye. . . . Very well then, you shall."

She drew a breath.

"You want to know why I hate my husband. I'll tell you; it's because of his simple, sheer immorality. I don't mean his actions; his views! Every speech he utters about everything makes me — I swear it makes me — in spite of myself, want to stick a knife into him, and I can't prove he's wrong, not ever, about the simplest thing. But I can pain him. And I will. . . . He sits about in chairs that fit his back, clumsy, like a rock, not moving for hours. . . . And I can make him wince. Oh, without showing it. . . . He's what you call . . . oh, loyal. There's an absurd little chit of a fellow . . . oh, Macmaster . . . and his mother whom he persists in a silly, mystical way in calling a saint . . . a Protestant saint! And his old nurse, who looks after the child . . . and the child itself. . . . I tell you I've only got to raise an eyelid . . . yes, cock an eyelid up a little when any one of them is mentioned, and it hurts him dreadfully. His eyes roll in a sort of mute anguish. . . . Of course he doesn't say anything. He's an English country gentleman."

Father Consett said:

"This immorality you talk about in your husband. . . I've never noticed it. I saw a good deal of him when I stayed with you for the week before your child was born. I talked with him a great deal. Except in matters of the two communions — and even in these I don't know that we differed so much — I found him perfectly sound."

"Sound!" Mrs. Satterthwaite said with sudden emphasis; "of course he's sound. It isn't even the word. He's the best ever. There was your father, for a good man . . . and him. That's an end of it."

"Ah," Sylvia said, "you don't know. Look here. Try and be just. Suppose I'm looking at the *Times* at breakfast and say, not having spoken to him for a week: 'It's wonderful what the doctors are doing. Have you seen the latest?' And at once he'll be on his high-horse — he knows everything! — and he'll prove, *prove* that all unhealthy children must be lethal-chambered or the world will go to pieces.

And it's like being hypnotised; you can't think of what to answer him. Or he'll reduce you to speechless rage by proving that murderers ought not to be executed. And then I'll ask, casually, if children ought to be lethal-chambered for being constipated. Because Marchant — that's the nurse — is always whining that the child's bowels aren't regular and the dreadful diseases that leads to. Of course *that* hurts him. For he's perfectly soppy about that child, though he half knows it isn't his own. . . . But that's what I mean by immorality. He'll profess that murderers ought to be preserved in order to breed from because they're bold fellows, and innocent little children executed because they're sick. And he'll almost make you believe it, though you're on the point of retching at the ideas."

"You wouldn't now," Father Consett began, and almost coaxingly, "think of going into retreat for a month or two."

"I wouldn't," Sylvia said. "How could I?"

"There's a convent of female Premonstratensians near Birkenhead, many ladies go there," the Father went on. "They cook very well, and you can have your own furniture and your own maid if ye don't like nuns to wait on you."

"It can't be done," Sylvia said, "you can see for yourself. It would make people smell a rat at once. Christopher wouldn't hear of it. . . ."

"No, I'm afraid it can't be done, Father," Mrs. Satterthwaite interrupted finally. "I've hidden here for four months to cover Sylvia's tracks. I've got Wateman's to look after. My new land steward's coming in next week."

"Still," the Father urged, with a sort of tremulous eagerness, "if only for a month. . . . If only for a fortnight. . . . So many Catholic ladies do it. . . . Ye might think of it."

"I see what you're aiming at," Sylvia said with sudden anger; "you're revolted at the idea of my going straight from one man's arms to another."

"I'd be better pleased if there could be an interval," the Father said. "It's what's called bad form."

Sylvia became electrically rigid on her sofa.

"Bad form!" she exclaimed. "You accuse me of bad form."

The Father slightly bowed his head like a man facing a wind.

"I do," he said. "It's disgraceful. It's unnatural. I'd travel a bit at least."

She placed her hand on her long throat.

"I know what you mean," she said, "you want to spare Christopher . . . the humiliation. The . . . the nausea. No doubt he'll feel nauseated. I've reckoned on that. It will give me a little of my own back."

The Father said:

"That's enough, woman. I'll hear no more."

Sylvia said:

"You will then. Listen here. . . . I've always got this to look forward to: I'll settle down by that man's side. I'll be as virtuous as any woman. I've made up my mind to it and I'll be it. And I'll be bored stiff for the rest of my life. Except for one thing. I can torment that man. And I'll do it. Do you understand how I'll do it? There are many ways. But if the worst comes to the worst, I can always drive him silly . . . by corrupting the child!" She was panting a little, and round her brown eyes the whites showed. "I'll get even with him. I can. I know how, you see. And with you, through him, for tormenting me. I've come all the way from Brittany without stopping. I haven't slept. . . . But I can . . ."

Father Consett put his hand beneath the tail of his coat.

"Sylvia Tietjens," he said, "in my pistol pocket I've a little bottle of holy water which I carry for such occasions. What if I was to throw two drops of it over you and cry: *Exorciso te Ashtaroth in nomine*? . . ."

She erected her body above her skirts on the sofa, stiffened like a snake's neck above its coils. Her face was quite pallid, her eyes staring out.

"You . . . you *daren't*," she said. "To me . . . an outrage!" Her feet slid slowly to the floor; she measured the distance to the doorway with her eyes. "You *daren't*," she said again; "I'd denounce you to the Bishop. . . ."

"It's little the Bishop would help you with them burning into your skin," the priest said. "Go away, I bid you, and say a Hail Mary or two. Ye need them. Ye'll not talk of corrupting a little child before me again."

"I won't," Sylvia said. "I shouldn't have . . ."

Her black figure showed in silhouette against the open doorway.

When the door was closed upon them, Mrs. Satterthwaite said:

"Was it necessary to threaten her with that? You know best, of course. It seems rather strong to me."

"It's a hair from the dog that's bit her," the priest said. "She's a silly girl. She's been playing at black masses. along with that Mrs. Profumo and the fellow whose name I can't remember. You could tell that. They cut the throat of a white kid and splash its blood about. That was at the back of her mind. . . . It's not very serious. A parcel of silly, idle girls. It's not much more than palmistry or fortune-telling to them if one has to weigh it, for all its ugliness, as a sin. As far as their volition goes, and it's volition that's the essence of prayer, black or white. . . . But it was at the back of her mind, and she won't forget to-night."

"Of course, that's your affair, Father," Mrs. Satterthwaite said lazily. "You hit her pretty hard. I don't suppose she's ever been hit so hard. What was it you wouldn't tell her?"

"Only," the priest said, "I wouldn't tell her because the thought's best not put in her head. . . . But her hell on earth will come when her husband goes running, blind, head down, mad after another woman."

Mrs. Satterwaite looked at nothing; then she nodded.

"Yes," she said; "I hadn't thought of it. . . . But will he? He *is* a very sound fellow, isn't he?"

"What's to stop it?" the priest asked. "*What* in the world but the grace of our blessed Lord, which he hasn't got and doesn't ask for? And then . . . he's a young man, full-blooded, and they won't be living . . . *maritalement.* Not if I know him. And then. . . . *Then* she'll tear the house down. The world will echo with her wrongs."

"Do you mean to say," Mrs. Satterthwaite said, "that Sylvia would do anything vulgar?"

"Doesn't every woman who's had a man to torture for years when she loses him?" the priest asked. "The more she's made an occupation of torturing him the less right she thinks she has to lose him."

Mrs. Satterthwaite looked gloomily into the dusk."

"That poor devil . . ." she said. "Will he get any peace anywhere? . . . What's the matter, Father?"

The Father said:.

"I've just remembered she gave me tea and cream and I drank it. Now I can't take mass for Father Reinhardt. I'll have to go and knock up his curate, who lives away in the forest."

At the door, holding the candle, he said:

"I'd have you not get up to-day nor yet to-morrow, if ye can stand it. Have a headache and let Sylvia nurse you. . . . You'll have to tell how she nursed you when you get back to London. And I'd rather ye

didn't lie more out and out than ye need, if it's to please me. . . .
Besides, if ye watch Sylvia nursing you, you might hit on a characteristic touch to make it seem more truthful. . . . How her sleeves
brushed the medicine bottles and irritated you, maybe . . . or —
you'll know! If we can save scandal to the congregation, we may as
well."

He ran downstairs.

III

AT the slight creaking made by Macmaster in pushing open his door,
Tietjens started violently. He was sitting in a smoking-jacket, playing patience engrossedly in a sort of garret bedroom. It had a sloping
roof outlined by black oak beams, which cut into squares the cream-
coloured patent distemper of the walls. The room contained also a
four-post bedstead, a corner cupboard in black oak, and many rush
mats on a polished oak floor of very irregular planking. Tietjens, who
hated these disinterred and waxed relics of the past, sat in the centre
of the room at a flimsy card-table beneath a white-shaded electric
light of a brillance that, in those surroundings, appeared unreasonable. This was one of those restored old groups of cottages that it
was at that date the fashion to convert into hostelries. To it Macmaster, who was in search of the inspiration of the past, had preferred to come. Tietjens, not desiring to interfere with his friend's
culture, had accepted the quarters, though he would have preferred
to go to a comfortable modern hotel as being less affected and
cheaper. Accustomed to what he called the grown oldnesses of a
morose, rambling Yorkshire manor house, he disliked being among
collected and rather pitiful bits which, he said, made him feel ridiculous, as if he were trying to behave seriously at a fancy-dress ball.
Macmaster, on the other hand, with gratification and a serious air,
would run his finger tips along the bevellings of a darkened piece of
furniture, and would declare it genuine "Chippendale" or "Jacobean
oak," as the case might be. And he seemed to gain an added seriousness and weight of manner with each piece of ancient furniture that
down the years he thus touched. But Tietjens would declare that
you could tell the beastly thing was a fake by just cocking an eye at
it and, if the matter happened to fall under the test of professional
dealers in old furniture, Tietjens was the more often in the right of

it, and Macmaster, sighing slightly, would prepare to proceed still
further along the difficult road to connoisseurship. Eventually, by
conscientious study, he got so far as at times to be called in by Somer-
set House to value great properties for probate — an occupation at
once distinguished and highly profitable.

Tietjens swore with the extreme vehemence of a man who has
been made, but who much dislikes being seen, to start.

Macmaster — in evening dress he looked extremely miniature! —
said:

"I'm sorry, old man, I know how much you dislike being interrupted. But the General is in a terrible temper."

Tietjens rose stiffly, lurched over to an eighteenth-century rose-
wood folding washstand, took from its top a glass of flat whisky
and soda, and gulped down a large quantity. He looked about
uncertainly, perceived a notebook on a "Chippendale" bureau,
made a short calculation in pencil and looked at his friend momentarily.

Macmaster said again:

"I'm sorry old man. I must have interrupted one of your immense
calculations."

Tietjens said:

"You haven't. I was only thinking. I'm just as glad you've come.
What did you say?"

Macmaster repeated:

"I said the General is in a terrible temper. It's just as well you
didn't come up to dinner."

Tietjens said:

"He isn't . . . He isn't in a temper. He's as pleased as punch at
not having to have these women up before him."

Macmaster said:

"He says he's got the police scouring the whole county for them,
and that you'd better leave by the first train to-morrow."

Tietjens said:

"I won't. I can't. I've got to wait here for a wire from Sylvia."

Macmaster groaned:

"Oh dear! Oh dear!" Then he said hopefully: "But we could have
it forwarded to Hythe."

Tietjens said with some vehemence:

"I tell you I won't leave here. I tell you I've settled it with the police and that swine of a Cabinet Minister. I've mended the leg of the canary of the wife of the police-constable. Sit down and be reasonable. The police don't touch people like us."

Macmaster said:

"I don't believe you realise the public feeling there is . . ."

"Of course I do, amongst people like Sandbach," Tietjens said. "Sit down I tell you. . . . Have some whisky. . . ." He filled himself out another long tumbler and, holding it, dropped into a too low-seated, reddish wicker armchair that had cretonne fixings. Beneath his weight the chair sagged a good deal and his dress-shirt front bulged up to his chin.

Macmaster said:

"What's the matter with you?" Tietjens' eyes were bloodshot.

"I tell you," Tietjens said, "I'm waiting for a wire from Sylvia."

Macmaster said:

"Oh!" And then: "It can't come to-night, it's getting on for one."

"It can," Tietjens said, "I've fixed it up with the postmaster — all the way up to Town! It probably won't come because Sylvia won't send it until the last moment, to bother me. None the less I'm waiting for a wire from Sylvia, and this is what I look like."

Macmaster said:

"That woman's the cruellest beast. . . ."

"You might," Tietjens interrupted, "remember that you're talking about my wife."

"I don't see," Macmaster said, "how one can talk about Sylvia without . . ."

"The line is a perfectly simple one to draw," Tietjens said. "You can relate a lady's actions if you know them and are asked to. You mustn't comment. In this case you don't know the lady's actions even, so you may as well hold your tongue." He sat looking straight in front of him.

Macmaster sighed from deep in his chest. He asked himself if this was what sixteen hours' waiting had done for his friend, what were all the remaining hours going to do?

Tietjens said:

"I shall be fit to talk about Sylvia after two more whiskies. Let's settle your other perturbations first. . . . The fair girl is called Wannop: Valentine Wannop."

"That's the Professor's name," Macmaster said.

"She's the late Professor Wannop's daughter," Tietjens said. "She's also the daughter of the novelist."

Macmaster interjected:

"But . . ."

"She supported herself for a year after the Professor's death as a domestic servant," Tietjens said. "Now she's housemaid for her mother, the novelist, in an inexpensive cottage. I should imagine the two experiences would make her desire to better the lot of her sex."

Macmaster again interjected a "But . . ."

"I got that information from the policeman whilst I was putting his wife's canary's leg in splints."

Macmaster said:

"The policeman you knocked down?" His eyes expressed unreasoning surprise. He added: "He knew Miss . . . eh . . . Wannop then!"

"You would not expect much intelligence from the police of Sussex," Tietjens said. "But you would be wrong. P.C. Finn is clever enough to recognise the young lady who for several years past has managed the constabulary's wives' and children's annual tea and sports. He says Miss Wannop holds the quarter-mile, half-mile, high jump, long jump and putting the weight records for East Sussex. That explains how she went over that dyke in such tidy style. . . . And precious glad the good, simple man was when I told him he was to leave the girl alone. He didn't know, he said, how he'd ever a had the face to serve the warrant on Miss Wannop. The other girl — the one that squeaked — is a stranger, a Londoner probably."

Macmaster said:

"You told the policeman . . ."

"I gave him," Tietjens said, "the Rt. Hon. Stephen Fenick Waterhouse's compliments, and he'd be much obliged if the P.C. would hand in a 'No Can Do' report in the matter of those ladies every morning to his inspector. I gave him also a brand new fi' pun note — from the Cabinet Minister — and a couple of quid and the price of a new pair of trousers from myself. So he's the happiest constable in Sussex. A very decent fellow; he told me how to know a dog otter's spoor from a gravid bitch's. . . . But that wouldn't interest you."

He began again:

"Don't look so inexpressibly foolish. I told you I'd been dining with that swine. . . . No, I oughtn't to call him a swine after eating his dinner. Besides, he's a very decent fellow. . . ."

"You didn't tell me you'd been dining with Mr. Waterhouse," Macmaster said. "I hope you remembered that, as he's amongst other things the President of the Funded Debt Commission, he's the power of life and death over the department and us."

"You didn't think," Tietjens answered, "that you are the only one to dine with the great ones of the earth! I wanted to talk to that fellow . . . about those figures their cursed crowd made me fake. I meant to give him a bit of my mind."

"You *didn't!*" Macmaster said with an expression of panic. "Besides, they didn't ask you to fake the calculation. They only asked you to work it out on the basis of given figures."

"Anyhow," Tietjens said, "I gave him a bit of my mind. I told him that, at threepence, it must run the country — and certainly himself as a politician! — to absolute ruin."

Macmaster uttered a deep "Good Lord!" and then: "But won't you ever remember you're a Government servant. He could . . ."

"Mr. Waterhouse," Tietjens said, "asked me if I wouldn't consent to be transferred to his secretary's department. And when I said: 'Go to hell!' he walked the streets with me for two hours arguing. . . . I was working out the chances on a 4½d. basis for him when you interrupted me. I've promised to let him have the figures when he goes by up the 1.30 on Monday."

Macmaster said:

"You haven't. . . . But by Jove you're the only man in England that could do it."

"That was what Mr. Waterhouse said," Tietjens commented. "He said old Ingleby had told him so."

"I do hope," Macmaster said, "that you answered him politely!"

"I told him," Tietjens answered, "that there were a dozen men who could do it as well as I, and I mentioned your name in particular."

"But I *couldn't,*" Macmaster answered. "Of course I could convert a 3d. rate into 4½d. But these are the actuarial variations; they're infinite. I couldn't touch them."

Tietjens said negligently: "I don't want my name mixed up in the unspeakable affair. When I give him the papers on Monday I shall tell him you did most of the work."

Again Macmaster groaned.

Nor was this distress mere altruism. Immensely ambitious for his brilliant friend, Macmaster's ambition was one ingredient of his strong desire for security. At Cambridge he had been perfectly content with a moderate, quite respectable place on the list of mathematical postulants. He knew that that made him safe, and he had still more satisfaction in the thought that it would warrant him in never being brilliant in after life. But when Tietjens, two years after, had come out as a mere Second Wrangler, Macmaster had been bitterly and loudly disappointed. He knew perfectly well that Tietjens simply hadn't taken trouble; and, ten chances to one, it was on purpose that Tietjens hadn't taken trouble. For the matter of that, for Tietjens it wouldn't have been trouble.

And, indeed, to Macmaster's upbraidings, which Macmaster hadn't spared him, Tietjens had answered that he hadn't been able to think of going through the rest of his life with a beastly placard like Senior Wrangler hung round his neck.

But Macmaster had early made up his mind that life for him would be safest if he could go about, not very much observed but still an authority, in the midst of a body of men all labelled. He wanted to walk down Pall Mall on the arm, precisely, of a largely-lettered Senior Wrangler; to return eastward on the arm of the youngest Lord Chancellor England had ever seen; to stroll down Whitehall in familiar converse with a world-famous novelist, saluting on the way a majority of My Lords Commissioners of the Treasury. And, after tea, for an hour at the club all these, in a little group, should treat him with the courtesy of men who respected him for his soundness. Then he would be safe.

And he had no doubt that Tietjens was the most brilliant man in England of that day, so that nothing caused him more anguish than the thought that Tietjens might not make a brilliant and rapid career towards some illustrious position in the public services. He would very willingly — he desired, indeed, nothing better! — have seen Tietjens pass over his own head! It did not seem to him a condemnation of the public services that this appeared to be unlikely.

Yet Macmaster was still not without hope. He was quite aware that there are other techniques of careers than that which he had prescribed for himself. He could not imagine himself, even in the most deferential way, correcting a superior; yet he could see that, though Tietjens treated almost every hierarch as if he were a born fool, no one very much resented it. Of course Tietjens was a Tietjens of Groby; but was that going to be enough to live on for ever? Times were changing, and Macmaster imagined this to be a democratic age.

But Tietjens went on, with both hands as it were, throwing away opportunity and committing outrage. . . .

That day Macmaster could only consider to be one of disaster. He got up from his chair and filled himself another drink; he felt himself to be distressed and to need it. Slouching amongst his cretonnes, Tietjens was gazing in front of him. He said:

"Here!" without looking at Macmaster, and held out his long glass. Into it Macmaster poured whisky with a hesitating hand. Tietjens said: "Go on!"

Macmaster said:

"It's late; we're breakfasting at the Duchemin's at ten."

Tietjens answered:

"Don't worry, sonny. We'll be there for your pretty lady." He added: "Wait another quarter of an hour. I want to talk to you."

Macmaster sat down again and deliberately began to review the day. It had begun with disaster, and in disaster it had continued.

And, with something like a bitter irony, Macmaster remembered and brought up now for digestion the parting words of General Campion to himself. The General had limped with him to the hall door up at Mountsby and, standing patting him on the shoulder, tall, slightly bent and very friendly, had said:

"Look here. Christopher Tietjens is a splendid fellow. But he needs a good woman to look after him. Get him back to Sylvia as quick as you can. Had a little tiff, haven't they? Nothing serious? Chrissie hasn't been running after the skirts? No? I daresay a little. No? Well then . . ."

Macmaster had stood like a gate-post, so appalled. He had stuttered:

"No! No."

"We've known them both so long," the General went on. "Lady Claudine in particular. And, believe me, Sylvia is a splendid girl. Straight as a die; the soul of loyalty to her friends. And fearless. She'd face the devil in his rage. You should have seen her out with the Belvoir! Of course you know her. . . . Well then!"

Macmaster had just managed to say that he knew Sylvia, of course.

"Well then," the General had continued, "you'll agree with me that if there *is* anything wrong between them he's to blame. And it will be resented. Very bitterly. He wouldn't set foot in this house again. But he says he's going out to her and Mrs. Satterthwaite. . . ."

"I believe . . ." Macmaster had begun, "I believe he is . . ."

"Well then!" the General had said: "It's all right. . . . But Christopher Tietjens needs a good woman's backing. He's a splendid fellow. There are few young fellows for whom I have more . . . I could almost say respect. . . . But he needs that. To ballast him."

In the car, running down the hill from Mountby, Macmaster had exhausted himself in the effort to restrain his execrations of the General. He wanted to shout that he was a pig-headed old fool: a meddlesome ass. But he was in the car with the two secretaries of the Cabinet Minister: the Rt. Hon. Edward Fenwick Waterhouse, who, being himself an advanced Liberal down for a week-end of golf, preferred not to dine at the house of the Conservative member. At that date there was, in politics, a phase of bitter social feud between the parties: a condition that had not till lately been characteristic of English political life. The prohibition had not extended itself to the two younger men.

Macmaster was not unpleasurably aware that these two fellows treated him with a certain deference. They had seen Macmaster being talked to familiarly by General Lord Edward Campion. Indeed, they and the car had been kept waiting whilst the General patted their fellow guest on the shoulder; held his upper arm and spoke in a low voice into his ear.

But that was the only pleasure that Macmaster got out of it.

Yes, the day had begun disastrously with Sylvia's letter; it ended — if it was ended! — almost more disastrously with the General's eulogy of that woman. During the day he had nerved himself to having an immensely disagreeable scene with Tietjens. Tietjens _must_ divorce the woman; it was necessary for the peace of mind of himself, of his friends, of his family; for the sake of his career; in the very name of decency!

In the meantime Tietjens had rather forced his hand. It had been a most disagreeable affair. They had arrived at Rye in time for lunch — at which Tietjens had consumed the best part of a bottle of Burgundy. During lunch Tietjens had given Macmaster Sylvia's letter to read, saying that, as he should later consult his friend, his friend had better be made acquainted with the document.

The letter had appeared extraordinary in its effrontery, for it said nothing. Beyond the bare statement, "I am now ready to return to you," it occupied itself simply with the fact that Mrs. Tietjens wanted — could no longer get on without — the services of her maid, whom she called Hullo Central. If Tietjens wanted her, Mrs. Tietjens, to return to him he was to see that Hullo Central was waiting on the doorstep for her, and so on. She added the detail that there was *no one* else, underlined, she could bear round her while she was retiring for the night. On reflection Macmaster could see that this was the best letter the woman could have written if she wanted to be taken back; for, had she extended herself into either excuses or explanations, it was ten chances to one Tietjens would have taken the line that he couldn't go on living with a woman capable of such a lapse in taste. But Macmaster had never thought of Sylvia as wanting in *savoir faire*.

It had none the less hardened him in his determination to urge his friend to divorce. He had intended to begin this campaign in the fly, driving to pay his call on the Rev. Mr. Duchemin, who, in early life, had been a personal disciple of Mr. Ruskin and a patron and acquaintance of the poet-painter, the subject of Macmaster's monograph. On this drive Tietjens preferred not to come. He said that he would loaf about the town and meet Macmaster at the golf club towards four-thirty. He was not in the mood for making new acquaintances. Macmaster, who knew the pressure under which his friend must be suffering, thought this reasonable enough, and drove off up Iden Hill by himself.

Few women had ever made so much impression on Macmaster as Mrs. Duchemin. He knew himself to be in a mood to be impressed by almost any woman, but he considered that that was not enough to account for the very strong influence she at once exercised over him. There had been two young girls in the drawing-room when he had been ushered in, but they had disappeared almost simultaneously, and although he had noticed them immediately afterwards riding past the window on bicycles, he was aware that he would not have recognised them again. From her first words on rising to greet him: "Not *the* Mr. Macmaster!" he had had eyes for no one else.

It was obvious that the Rev. Mr. Duchemin must be one of those clergymen of considerable wealth and cultured taste who not infrequently adorn the Church of England. The rectory itself, a great, warm-looking manor house of very old red brick, was abutted on to by one of the largest tithe barns that Macmaster had ever seen; the church itself, with a primitive roof of oak shingles, nestled in the corner formed by the ends of rectory and tithe barn, and was by so much the smallest of the three and so undecorated that but for its little belfry it might have been a good cow-byre. All three buildings stood on the very edge of the little row of hills that looks down on the Romney Marsh; they were sheltered from the north wind by a great symmetrical fan of elms and from the south-west by a very tall hedge and shrubbery, all of remarkable yews. It was, in short, an ideal cure of souls for a wealthy clergyman of cultured tastes, for there was not so much as a peasant's cottage within a mile of it.

To Macmaster, in short, this was the ideal English home. Of Mrs. Duchemin's drawing-room itself, contrary to his habit, for he was sensitive and observant in such things, he could afterwards remember little except that it was perfectly sympathetic. Three long windows gave on to a perfect lawn, on which, isolated and grouped, stood standard rose trees, symmetrical half globes of green foliage picked out with flowers like bits of carved pink marble. Beyond the lawn was a low stone wall; beyond that the quiet expanse of the marsh shimmered in the sunlight.

The furniture of the room was, as to its woodwork, brown, old, with the rich softnesses of much polishing with beeswax. What pictures there were Macmaster recognised at once as being by Simeon Solomon, one of the weaker and more frail æsthetes — aureoled, palish heads of ladies carrying lilies that were not very like lilies. They were in the tradition — but not the best of the tradition. Macmaster understood — and later Mrs. Duchemin confirmed him in the idea — that Mr. Duchemin kept his more precious specimens of work in a sanctum, leaving to the relatively public room, good-humouredly and with slight contempt, these weaker specimens. That seemed to stamp Mr. Duchemin at once as being of the elect.

Mr. Duchemin in person was, however, not present; and there seemed to be a good deal of difficulty in arranging a meeting between the two men. Mr. Duchemin, his wife said, was much occupied at the week-ends. She added, with a faint and rather absent smile, the word, "Naturally." Macmaster at once saw that it was natural for a clergyman to be much occupied during the week-ends. With a little hesitation Mrs. Duchemin suggested that Mr. Macmaster and his friend might come to lunch on the next day — Saturday. But Macmaster had made an engagement to play the foursome with General Campion — half the round from twelve till one-thirty: half the round from three to half-past four. And, as their then present arrangements stood, Macmaster and Tietjens were to take the 6.30 train to Hythe; that ruled out either tea or dinner next day.

With sufficient, but not too extravagant regret, Mrs. Duchemin raised her voice to say:

"Oh dear! Oh dear! But you must see my husband and the pictures after you have come so far."

A rather considerable volume of harsh sound was coming through the end wall of the room — the barking of dogs, apparently the hurried removal of pieces of furniture or perhaps of packing cases, guttural ejaculations. Mrs. Duchemin said, with her far away air and deep voice:

"They are making a good deal of noise. Let us go into the garden and look at my husband's roses, if you've a moment more to give us."

Macmaster quoted to himself:

" 'I looked and saw your eyes in the shadow of your hair. . . .' "

There was no doubt that Mrs. Duchemin's eyes, which were of a dark, pebble blue, were actually in the shadow of her blue-black, very regularly waved hair. The hair came down on the square, low forehead. It was a phenomenon that Macmaster had never before really seen, and, he congratulated himself, this was one more confirmation — if confirmation were needed! — of the powers of observation of the subject of his monograph!

Mrs. Duchemin bore the sunlight! Her dark complexion was clear; there was, over the cheekbones, a delicate suffusion of light carmine. Her jawbone was singularly clear-cut, to the pointed chin — like an alabaster, mediæval saint's.

She said:

"Of course you're Scotch. I'm from Auld Reekie myself."

Macmaster would have known it. He said he was from the Port of Leith. He could not imagine hiding anything from Mrs. Duchemin. Mrs. Duchemin said with renewed insistence:

"Oh, but of *course* you must see my husband and the pictures. Let me see. . . . We must think. . . . Would breakfast now? . . ."

Macmaster said that he and his friend were Government servants and up to rising early. He had a great desire to breakfast in that house. She said:

"At a quarter to ten, then, our car will be at the bottom of your street. It's a matter of ten minutes only, so you won't go hungry long!"

She said, gradually gaining animation, that of course Macmaster would bring his friend. He could tell Tietjens that he should meet a very charming girl. She stopped and added suddenly: "Probably, at any rate." She said the name which Macmaster caught as "Wanstead." And possibly another girl. And Mr. Horsted, or something like it, her husband's junior curate. She said reflectively:

"Yes, we might try quite a party . . ." and added, "quite noisy and gay. I hope your friend's talkative!"

Macmaster said something about trouble.

"Oh, it can't be too much trouble," she said. "Besides it might do my husband good." She went on: "Mr. Duchemin is apt to brood. It's perhaps too lonely here." And added the rather astonishing words: "After all."

And, driving back in the fly, Macmaster said to himself that you couldn't call Mrs. Duchemin ordinary, at least. Yet meeting her was like going into a room that you had long left and never ceased to love. It felt good. It was perhaps partly her Edinburgh-ness. Macmaster allowed himself to coin that word. There was in Edinburgh a society — he himself had never been privileged to move in it, but its annals are part of the literature of Scotland! — where the ladies are all great ladies in tall drawing-rooms; circumspect yet shrewd; still yet with a sense of the comic; frugal yet warmly hospitable. It was perhaps just Edinburgh-ness that was wanting in the drawing-rooms of his friends in London. Mrs. Cressy, the Hon. Mrs. Limoux and Mrs. Delawnay were all almost perfection in manner, in speech, in composure. But, then, they were not young, they weren't Edinburgh — and they weren't strikingly elegant!

Mrs. Duchemin was all three! Her assured, tranquil manner she would retain to any age: it betokened the enigmatic soul of her sex, but, physically, she couldn't be more than thirty. That was unimportant, for she would never want to do anything in which physical youth counted. She would never, for instance, have occasion to run; she would always just "move" — floatingly! He tried to remember the details of her dress.

It had certainly been dark blue — and certainly of silk: that rather coarsely-woven, exquisite material that has on its folds as of a silvery shimmer with minute knots. But very dark blue. And it contrived to be at once artistic — absolutely in the tradition! And yet well cut! Very large sleeves, of course, but still with a certain fit. She had worn

an immense necklace of yellow polished amber: on the dark blue!
And Mrs. Duchemin had said, over her husband's roses, that the
blossoms always reminded her of little mouldings of pink cloud come
down for the cooling of the earth. . . . A charming thought!

Suddenly he said to himself:

"What a mate for Tietjens!" And his mind added: "Why should
she not become an Influence!"

A vista opened before him, in time! He imagined Tietjens, in some
way proprietarily responsible for Mrs. Duchemin: quite *pour le bon*,
tranquilly passionate and accepted, *motif*; and "immensely improved"
by the association. And himself, in a year or two, bringing the at last
found Lady of his Delight to sit at the feet of Mrs. Duchemin — the
Lady of his Delight whilst circumspect would be also young and im-
pressionable! — to learn the mysterious assuredness of manner, the
gift of dressing, the knack of wearing amber and bending over standard roses — and the Edinburgh-ness!

Macmaster was thus not a little excited, and finding Tietjens at
tea amid the green-stained furnishings and illustrated papers of the
large, corrugated iron golf-house, he could not help exclaiming:

"I've accepted the invitation to breakfast with the Duchemins to-
morrow for us both. I hope you won't mind," although Tietjens was
sitting at a little table with General Campion and his brother-in-law,
the Hon. Paul Sandbach, Conservative member for the division and
husband of Lady Claudine. The General said pleasantly to Tietjens:.

"Breakfast! With Duchemin! You go, my boy! You'll get the best
breakfast you ever had in your life."

He added to his brother-in-law: "Not the eternal mock kedgeree
Claudine gives us every morning."

Sandbach grunted:

"It's not for want of trying to steal their cook. Claudine has a shy
at it every time we come down here."

The General said pleasantly to Macmaster — he spoke always
pleasantly, with a half smile and a slight sibilance:

"My brother-in-law isn't serious, you understand. My sister
wouldn't think of stealing a cook. Let alone from Duchemin. She'd
be frightened to."

Sandbach grunted:

"Who wouldn't?"

Both these gentlemen were very lame: Mr. Sandbach from birth
and the General as the result of a slight but neglected motor acci-

dent. He had practically only one vanity, the belief that he was qualified to act as his own chauffeur, and since he was both inexpert and
very careless, he met with frequent accidents. Mr. Sandbach had a
dark, round, bull-dog face and a violent manner. He had twice been
suspended from his Parliamentary duties for applying to the then
Chancellor of the Exchequer the epithet "lying attorney," and he was
at that moment still suspended.

Macmaster then became unpleasantly perturbed. With his sensi-
tiveness he was perfectly aware of an unpleasant chill in the air.
There was also a stiffness about Tietjens' eyes. He was looking
straight before him; there was a silence too. Behind Tietjens' back
were two men with bright green coats, red knitted waistcoats and
florid faces. One was bald and blond, the other had black hair, remarkably oiled and shiny; both were forty-fiveish. They were regarding the occupants of the Tietjens' table with both their mouths
slightly open. They were undisguisedly listening. In front of each were
three empty sloe-gin glasses and one half-filled tumbler of brandy and
soda. Macmaster understood why the General had explained that
his sister had not tried to steal Mrs. Duchemin's cook.

Tietjens said:

"Drink up your tea quickly and let's get started." He was drawing
from his pocket a number of telegraph forms which he began arranging. The General said:

"Don't burn your mouth. We can't start off before all . . . all
these other gentlemen. We're too slow."

"No; we're beastly well stuck," Sandbach said.

Tietjens handed the telegraph forms over to Macmaster.

"You'd better take a look at these," he said. "I mayn't see you
again to-day after the match. You're dining up at Mountby. The
General will run you up. Lady Claude will excuse me. I've got work
to do."

This was already matter for dismay for Macmaster. He was aware
that Tietjens would have disliked dining up at Mountby with the
Sandbachs, who would have a crowd, extremely smart, but more than
usually unintelligent. Tietjens called this crowd, indeed, the plague-
spot of the party — meaning of Toryism. But Macmaster couldn't
help thinking that a disagreeable dinner would be better for his
friend than brooding in solitude in the black shadows of the huddled
town. Then Tietjens said:

"I'm going to have a word with that swine!" He pointed his square

chin rather rigidly before him, and looking past the two brandy
drinkers, Macmaster saw one of those faces that frequent caricature
made familiar and yet strange. Macmaster couldn't, at the moment,
put a name to it. It must be a politician, probably a Minister. But
which? His mind was already in a dreadful state. In the glimpse he
had caught of the telegraph form now in his hand he had perceived
that it was addressed to Sylvia Tietjens and began with the word
"agreed." He said swiftly:

"Has that been sent or is it only a draft?"

Tietjens said:

"That fellow is the Rt. Hon. Stephen Fenwick Waterhouse. He's
chairman of the Funded Debt Commission. He's the swine who made
us fake that return in the office."

That moment was the worst Macmaster had ever known. A worse
came. Tietjens said:

"I'm going to have a word with him. That's why I'm not dining
at Mountby. It's a duty to the country."

Macmaster's mind simply stopped. He was in a space, all windows.
There was sunlight outside. And clouds. Pink and white. Woolly!
Some ships. And two men: one dark and oily, the other rather blotchy
on a blond baldness. They were talking, but their words made no
impression on Macmaster. The dark, oily man said that he was not
going to take Gertie to Budapest. Not half! He winked like a nightmare. Beyond were two young men and a preposterous face. . . .
It was all so like a nightmare that the Cabinet Minister's features
were distorted for Macmaster. Like an enormous mask of pantomime:
shiny, with an immense nose and elongated, Chinese eyes.

Yet not unpleasant! Macmaster was a Whig by conviction, by nation, by temperament. He thought that public servants should abstain
from political activity. Nevertheless, he couldn't be expected to think
a Liberal Cabinet Minister ugly. On the contrary, Mr. Waterhouse
appeared to have a frank, humorous, kindly expression. He listened
deferentially to one of his secretaries, resting his hand on the young
man's shoulder, smiling a little, rather sleepily. No doubt he was
overworked. And then, letting himself go in a side-shaking laugh.
Putting on flesh!

What a pity! What a *pity!* Macmaster was reading a string of incomprehensible words in Tietjens' heavily scored writing. *Not entertain . . . flat not house . . . child remain at sister.* . . . His eyes
went backwards and forwards over the phrases. He could not connect

the words without stops. The man with the oily hair said in a sickly
voice that Gertie was hot stuff, but not the one for Budapest with
all the Gitana girls you were telling me of! Why, he'd kept Gertie
for five years now. More like the real thing! His friend's voice was like
a result of indigestion. Tietjens, Sandbach, and the General were
stiff, like pokers.

What a pity! Macmaster thought.

He ought to have been sitting. . . . It would have been pleasant
and right to be sitting with the pleasant Minister. In the ordinary
course he, Macmaster, would have been. The best golfer in the place
was usually set to play with distinguished visitors, and there was
next to no one in the south of England who ordinarily could beat
him. He had begun at four, playing with a minature cleek and a
found shilling ball over the municipal links. Going to the poor school
every morning and back to dinner; and back to school and back to
bed! Over the cold, rushy, sandy links, beside the grey sea. Both
shoes full of sand. The found shilling ball had lasted him three
years. . . .

Macmaster exclaimed: "Good God!" He had just gathered from
the telegram that Tietjens meant to go to Germany on Tuesday. As
if at Macmaster's ejaculation Tietjens said:

"Yes. It *is* unbearable. If you don't stop those swine, General, I
shall."

The General sibilated low, between his teeth:

"Wait a minute. . . . Wait a minute. . . . Perhaps that other
fellow will."

The man with the black oily hair said:

"If Budapest's the place for the girls you say it is, old pal, with the
Turkish baths and all, we'll paint the old town red all right, next
month," and he winked at Tietjens. His friend, with his head down,
seemed to make internal rumblings, looking apprehensively beneath
his blotched forehead at the General.

"Not," the other continued argumentatively, "that I don't love
my old woman. She's all right. And then there's Gertie. 'Ot stuff, but
the real thing. But I say a man wants . . ." He ejaculated, "Oh!"

The General, his hands in his pockets, very tall, thin, red-cheeked,
his white hair combed forward in a fringe, sauntered towards the
other table. It was not two yards, but it seemed a long saunter. He
stood right over them, they looking up, open-eyed, like schoolboys at
a balloon. He said:

"I'm glad you're enjoying our links, gentlemen."

The bald man said: "We are! We are! First-class. A treat!"

"But," the General said, "it isn't wise to discuss one's . . . eh . . . domestic circumstances . . . at . . . at mess, you know, or in a golf house. People might hear."

The gentleman with the oily hair half rose and exclaimed:

"Oo, the . . ." The other man mumbled: "Shut up, Briggs."

The General said:

"I'm the president of the club, you know. It's my duty to see that the *majority* of the club and its visitors are pleased. I hope you don't mind."

The General came back to his seat. He was trembling with vexation.

"It makes one as beastly a bounder as themselves," he said. "But what the devil else was one to do?" The two city men had ambled hastily into the dressing-rooms; the dire silence fell. Macmaster realised that, for these Tories at least, this was really the end of the world. The last of England! He returned, with panic in his heart, to Tietjens' telegram. . . . Tietjens was going to Germany on Tuesday. He offered to throw over the department. These were unthinkable things. You couldn't imagine them!

He began to read the telegram all over again. A shadow fell upon the flimsy sheets. The Rt. Hon. Mr. Waterhouse was between the head of the table and the windows. He said:

"We're much obliged, General. It was impossible to hear ourselves speak for those obscene fellows' smut. It's fellows like that that make our friends the suffragettes! That warrants them. . . ." He added: "Hullo! Sandbach! Enjoying your rest?"

The General said:

"I was hoping you'd take on the job of telling these fellows off."

Mr. Sandbach, his bull-dog jaw sticking out, the short black hair on his scalp appearing to rise, barked:

"Hullo, Waterslop. Enjoying your plunder?"

Mr. Waterhouse, tall, slouching and untidy-haired, lifted the flaps of his coat. It was so ragged that it appeared as if straws stuck out of the elbows.

"All that the suffragettes have left of me," he said, laughingly. "Isn't one of you fellows a genius called Tietjens?" He was looking at Macmaster. The General said:

"Tietjens . . . Macmaster . . ." The Minister went on very friendly:

"Oh, it's you? . . . I just wanted to take the opportunity of thanking you."

Tietjens said:

"Good God! What for?"

"*You* know!" the Minister said. "We couldn't have got the Bill before the House till next session without your figures. . . ." He said slyly: "Could we, Sandbach?" and added to Tietjens: "Ingleby told me. . . ."

Tietjens was chalk-white and stiffened. He stuttered:

"I can't take any credit. . . . I consider . . ."

Macmaster exclaimed:

"Tietjens . . . you . . ." he didn't know what he was going to say.

"Oh, you're too modest," Mr. Waterhouse overwhelmed Tietjens. "We know whom we've to thank. . . ." His eyes drifted to Sandbach a little absently. Then his face lit up.

"Oh! Look here, Sandbach," he said. "Come here, will you?" He walked a pace or two away, calling to one of his young men: "Oh, Sanderson, give the bobbie a drink. A good stiff one." Sandbach jerked himself awkwardly out of his chair and limped to the Minister.

Tietjens burst out:

"Me too modest! *Me!* . . . The swine. . . . The unspeakable swine!"

The General said:

"What's it all about, Chrissie? You probably are too modest."

Tietjens said:

"Damn it. It's a serious matter. It's driving me out of the unspeakable office I'm in."

Macmaster said:

"No! No! You're wrong. It's a wrong view you take." And with a good deal of real passion he began to explain to the General. It was an affair that had already given him a great deal of pain. The Government had asked the statistical department for figures illuminating a number of schedules that they desired to use in presenting their new Bill to the Commons. Mr. Waterhouse was to present it.

Mr. Waterhouse at the moment was slapping Mr. Sandbach on the back, tossing the hair out of his eyes and laughing like a hysterical schoolgirl. He looked suddenly tired. A police constable, his buttons shining, appeared, drinking from a pewter-pot outside the glazed door. The two city men ran across the angle from the dressing-room to the same door, buttoning their clothes. The Minister said loudly:

"Make it guineas!"

It seemed to Macmaster painfully wrong that Tietjens should call anyone so genial and unaffected an unspeakable swine. It was unjust. He went on with his explanation to the General.

The Government had wanted a set of figures based on a calculation called B 7. Tietjens, who had been working on one called H 19 — for his own instruction — had persuaded himself that H 19 was the lowest figure that was actuarially sound.

The General said pleasantly: "All this is Greek to me."

"Oh, no, it needn't be," Macmaster heard himself say. "It amounts to this. Chrissie was asked by the Government — by Sir Reginald Ingleby — to work out what 3 × 3 comes to: it was that sort of thing in principle. He said that the only figure that would not ruin the country was nine times nine. . . ."

"The Government wanted to shovel money into the working man's pockets, in fact," the General said. "Money for nothing — or votes, I suppose."

"But that isn't the point, sir," Macmaster ventured to say. "All that Chrissie was asked to do was to say what 3 × 3 was."

"Well, he appears to have done it and earned no end of kudos," the General said. "That's all right. We've all, always, believed in Chrissie's ability. But he's a strong-tempered beggar."

"He was extraordinarily rude to Sir Reginald over it," Macmaster went on.

The General said:

"Oh dear! Oh dear!" He shook his head at Tietjens and assumed with care the blank, slightly disappointing air of the regular officer. "I don't like to hear of rudeness to a superior. In *any* service."

"I don't think," Tietjens said with extreme mildness, "that Macmaster is quite fair to me. Of course he's a right to his opinion as to what the discipline of a service demands. I certainly told Ingleby that I'd rather resign than do that beastly job. . . ."

"You shouldn't have," the General said. "What would become of the services if everyone did as you did?"

Sandbach came back laughing and dropped painfully into his low arm-chair.

"That fellow . . ." he began.

The General slightly raised his hand.

"A minute!" he said. "I was about to tell Chrissie, here, that if I am offered the job — of course it's an order really — of suppressing the Ulster Volunteers . . . I'd rather cut my throat than do it. . . ."

Sandbach said:

"Of course you would, old chap. They're our brothers. You'd see the beastly, lying Government damned first."

"I was going to say that I should accept," the General said, "I shouldn't resign my commission."

Sandbach said:

"Good God!"

Tietjens said:

"Well, I didn't."

Sandbach exclaimed:

"General! You! After all Claudine and I have said. . . ."

Tietjens interrupted:

"Excuse me, Sandbach. I'm receiving this reprimand for the moment. I wasn't, then, rude to Ingleby. If I'd expressed contempt for what he said or for himself, that would have been rude. I didn't. He wasn't in the least offended. He looked like a cockatoo, but he wasn't offended. And I let him overpersuade me. He was right, really. He pointed out that, if I didn't do the job, those swine would put on one of our little competition wallah head clerks and get all the schedules faked, as well as starting off with false premises!"

"That's the view I take," the General said, "if I don't take the Ulster job the Government will put on a fellow who'll burn all the farmhouses and rape all the women in the three counties. They've got him up their sleeve. He only asks for the Connaught Rangers to go through the north with. And you know what *that* means. All the same . . ." he looked at Tietjens: "one should not be rude to one's superiors."

"I tell you I wasn't rude," Tietjens exclaimed. "Damn your nice, paternal old eyes. Get that into your mind!"

The General shook his head:

"You brilliant fellows!" he said. "The country, or the army, or anything, could not be run by you. It takes stupid fools like me and Sandbach, along with sound, moderate heads like our friend here." He indicated Macmaster and, rising, went on: "Come along. You're playing me, Macmaster. They say you're hot stuff. Chrissie's no good. He can take Sandbach on."

He walked off with Macmaster towards the dressing-room.

Sandbach, wriggling awkwardly out of his chair, shouted:

"Save the country. . . . Damn it. . . ." He stood on his feet. "I and Campion . . . look at what the country's come to. What with swine like these two in our club houses! And policemen to go round the links with Ministers to protect them from the wild women. . . . By God! I'd like to have the flaying of the skin off some of their backs. I would. By God I would."

He added:

"That fellow Waterslops is a bit of a sportsman. I haven't been able to tell you about our bet, you've been making such a noise. . . . Is your friend really plus one at North Berwick? What are you like?"

"Macmaster is a good plus two anywhere when he's in practice." Sandbach said:

"Good Lord. . . . A stout fellow. . . ."

"As for me," Tietjens said, "I loathe the beastly game."

"So do I," Sandbach answered. "We'll just lollop along behind them."

IV

THEY came out into the bright open where all the distances under the tall sky showed with distinct prismatic outlines. They made a little group of seven — for Tietjens would not have a caddy — waiting on the flat, first teeing ground. Macmaster walked up to Tietjens and said under his voice:

"You've really *sent* that wire?"

Tietjens said:

"It'll be in Germany by now!"

Mr. Sandbach hobbled from one to the other explaining the terms of his wager with Mr. Waterhouse. Mr. Waterhouse had backed one of the young men playing with him to drive into and hit twice in the eighteen holes the two city men who would be playing ahead of them. As the Minister had taken rather short odds, Mr. Sandbach considered him a good sport.

A long way down the first hole Mr. Waterhouse and his two companions were approaching the first green. They had high sandhills to the right and, to their left, a road that was fringed with rushes and a narrow dyke. Ahead of the Cabinet Minister the two city men and their two caddies stood on the edge of the dyke or poked downwards into the rushes. Two girls appeared and disappeared on the tops of the sandhills. The policeman was strolling along the road, level with Mr. Waterhouse. The General said:

"I think we could go now."

Sandbach said:

"Waterslops will get a hit at them from the next tee. They're in the dyke."

The General drove a straight, goodish ball. Just as Macmaster was in his swing Sandbach shouted:

"By God! He nearly did it. See that fellow jump!"

Macmaster looked round over his shoulder and hissed with vexation between his teeth:

"Don't you know that you don't shout while a man is driving? Or haven't you played golf?" He hurried fussily after his ball.

Sandbach said to Tietjens:

"Golly! That chap's got a temper!"

Tietjens said:

"Only over this game. You deserved what you got."

Sandbach said:

"I did. . . . But I didn't spoil his shot. He's outdriven the General twenty yards."

Tietjens said:

"It would have been sixty but for you."

They loitered about on the tee waiting for the others to get their distance. Sandbach said:

"By Jove, your friend is on with his second . . . You wouldn't believe it of such a *little* beggar!" He added: "He's not much class, is he?"

Tietjens looked down his nose.

"Oh, about *our* class!" he said. "He wouldn't take a bet about driving into the couple ahead."

Sandbach hated Tietjens for being a Tietjens of Groby: Tietjens was enraged by the existence of Sandbach, who was the son of an ennobled mayor of Middlebrough, seven miles or so from Groby. The feuds between the Cleveland landowners and the Cleveland plutocrats are very bitter. Sandbach said:

"Ah, I suppose he gets you out of scrapes with girls and the Treasury, and you take him about in return. It's a practical combination."

"Like Pottle Mills and Stanton," Tietjens said. The financial operations connected with the amalgamating of these two steelworks had earned Sandbach's father a good deal of odium in the Cleveland district. . . . Sandbach said:

"Look here, Tietjens. . . ." But he changed his mind and said:

"We'd better go now." He drove off with an awkward action but not without skill. He certainly outplayed Tietjens.

Playing very slowly, for both were desultory and Sandbach very lame, they lost sight of the others behind some coastguard cottages and dunes before they had left the third tee. Because of his game leg, Sandbach sliced a good deal. On this occasion he sliced right into the gardens of the cottages and went with his boy to look for his ball among potato-haulms, beyond a low wall. Tietjens patted his own ball lazily up the fairway and, dragging his bag behind him by the strap, he sauntered on.

Although Tietjens hated golf as he hated any occupation that was of a competitive nature, he could engross himself in the mathematics of trajectories when he accompanied Macmaster in one of his expeditions for practice. He accompanied Macmaster because he liked there to be one pursuit at which his friend undisputably excelled himself, for it was a bore always browbeating the fellow. But he stipulated that they should visit three different and, if possible, unknown courses every week-end when they golfed. He interested himself then in the way the courses were laid out, acquiring thus an extraordinary connoisseurship in golf architecture, and he made abstruse calculations as to the flight of balls off sloped club-faces, as to the foot-poundals of energy exercised by one muscle or the other, and as to theories of spin. As often as not he palmed Macmaster off as a fair, average player on some other unfortunate fair, average stranger. Then he passed the afternoon in the club-house studying the pedigrees and forms of racehorses, for every club-house contained a copy of Ruff's guide. In the spring he would hunt for and examine the nests of soft-billed birds, for he was interested in the domestic affairs of the cuckoo, though he hated natural history and field botany.

On this occasion he had just examined some notes of other mashie shots, had put the notebook back in his pocket, and had addressed his ball with a niblick that had an unusually roughened face and a head like a hatchet. Meticulously, when he had taken his grip he removed his little and third fingers from the leather of the shaft. He was thanking heaven that Sandbach seemed to be accounted for for ten minutes at least, for Sandbach was miserly over lost balls and, very slowly, he was raising his mashie to half cock for a sighting shot.

He was aware that someone, breathing a little heavily from small lungs, was standing close to him and watching him: he could indeed, beneath his cap-rim, perceive the tips of a pair of boy's white sand-shoes. It in no way perturbed him to be watched since he was avid of no personal glory when making his shots. A voice said:

"I say . . ." He continued to look at his ball.

"Sorry to spoil your shot," the voice said. "But . . ."

Tietjens dropped his club altogether and straightened his back. A fair young woman with a fixed scowl was looking at him intently. She had a short skirt and was panting a little.

"I say," she said, "go and see they don't hurt Gertie. I've lost her . . ." She pointed back to the sandhills. "There looked to be some beasts among them."

She seemed a perfectly negligible girl except for the frown: her eyes blue, her hair no doubt fair under a white canvas hat. She had a striped cotton blouse, but her fawn tweed skirt was well hung.

Tietjens said:

"You've been demonstrating."

She said:

"Of course we have, and of course you object on principle. But you won't let a girl be man-handled. Don't wait to tell me I know it. . . ."

Noises existed. Sandbach, from beyond the low garden wall fifty yards away, was yelping, just like a dog: "Hi! Hi! Hi! Hi!" and gesticulating. His little caddy, entangled in his golf-bag, was trying to scramble over the wall. On top of a high sandhill stood the policeman: he waved his arms like a windmill and shouted. Beside him and behind, slowly rising, were the heads of the General, Macmaster and their two boys. Further along, in completion were appearing the figures of Mr. Waterhouse, his two companions and *their* three boys. The Minister was waving his driver and shouting. They all shouted.

"A regular rat-hunt," the girl said; she was counting. "Eleven and two more caddies!" She exhibited satisfaction. "I headed them all off except two beasts. They couldn't run. But neither can Gertie. . . ."

She said urgently:

"Come along! You aren't going to leave Gertie to those beasts! They're drunk."

Tietjens said:

"Cut away then. I'll look after Gertie." He picked up his bag.

"No, I'll come with you," the girl said.

Tietjens answered: "Oh, you don't want to go to gaol. Clear out!" She said:

"Nonsense. I've put up with worse than that. Nine months as a slavey. . . . Come *along!*"

Tietjens started to run — rather like a rhinoceros seeing purple. He had been violently spurred, for he had been pierced by a shrill, faint scream. The girl ran beside him.

"You . . . can . . . run!" she panted, "put on a spurt."

Screams protesting against physical violence were at that date rare things in England. Tietjens had never heard the like. It upset him frightfully, though he was aware only of an expanse of open country. The policeman, whose buttons made him noteworthy, was descending his conical sandhill, diagonally, with caution. There is something grotesque about a town policeman, silvered helmet and all, in the open country. It was so clear and still in the air; Tietjens felt as if he were in a light museum looking at specimens.

A little young woman, engrossed, like a hunted rat, came round the corner of a green mound. "This is an assaulted female!" the mind of Tietjens said to him. She had a black skirt covered with sand, for she had just rolled down the sandhill; she had a striped grey and black silk blouse, one shoulder torn completely off, so that a white camisole showed. Over the shoulder of the sandhill came the two city men, flushed with triumph and panting; their red knitted waistcoats moved like bellows. The black-haired one, his eyes lurid and obscene, brandished aloft a fragment of black and grey stuff. He shouted hilariously:

"Strip the bitch naked! . . . Ugh . . . Strip the bitch stark naked!" and jumped down the little hill. He cannoned into Tietjens, who roared at the top of his voice:

"You infernal swine. I'll knock your head off if you move!"

Behind Tietjens' back the girl said:

"Come along, Gertie. . . . It's only to there . . ."

A voice panted in answer:

"I . . . can't. . . . My heart . . ."

Tietjens kept his eye upon the city man. His jaw had fallen down, his eyes stared! It was as if the bottom of his assured world, where all men desire in their hearts to bash women, had fallen out. He panted:

"Ergle! Ergle!"

Another scream, a little further than the last voices from behind his back, caused in Tietjens a feeling of intense weariness. What did beastly women want to scream for? He swung round, bag and all. The policeman, his face scarlet like a lobster just boiled, was lumbering unenthusiastically towards the two girls who were trotting towards the dyke. One of his hands, scarlet also, was extended. He was not a yard from Tietjens.

Tietjens was exhausted, beyond thinking or shouting. He slipped his clubs off his shoulder and, as if he were pitching his kit-bag into a luggage van, threw the whole lot between the policeman's running legs. The man, who had no impetus to speak of, pitched forward on to his hands and knees. His helmet over his eyes, he seemed to reflect for a moment; then he removed his helmet and with great delibera-tion rolled round and sat on the turf. His face was completely with-out emotion, long, sandy-moustached and rather shrewd. He mopped his brow with a carmine handkerchief that had white spots.

Tietjens walked up to him.

"Clumsy of me!" he said. "I hope you're not hurt." He drew from his breast pocket a curved silver flask. The policeman said nothing. His world, too, contained uncertainties and he was profoundly glad to be able to sit still without discredit. He muttered:

"Shaken. A bit! Anybody would be!"

That let him out and he fell to examining with attention the bayo-net catch of the flask top. Tietjens opened it for him. The two girls, advancing at a fatigued trot, were near the dyke side. The fair girl, as they trotted, was trying to adjust her companion's hat; attached by pins to the back of her hair, it flapped on her shoulder.

All the rest of the posse were advancing at a very slow walk, in a converging semi-circle. Two little caddies were running, but Tietjens saw them check, hesitate and stop. And there floated to Tietjens' ears the words:

"Stop, you little devils. She'll knock your heads off."

Rt. Hon. Mr. Waterhouse must have found an admirable voice trainer somewhere. The drab girl was balancing tremulously over a plank on the dyke; the other took it at a jump: up in the air — down on her feet; perfectly business-like. And, as soon as the other girl was off the plank, she was down on her knees before it, pulling it towards her, the other girl trotting away over the vast marsh field.

The girl dropped the plank on the grass. Then she looked up and

faced the men and boys who stood in a row on the road. She called
in a shrill, high voice, like a young cockerel's:

"Seventeen to two! The usual male odds! You'll *have* to go round
by Camber railway bridge, and we'll be in Folkestone by then. We've
got bicycles!" She was half going when she checked and, searching out
Tietjens to address, exclaimed: "I'm sorry I said that. Because some
of you didn't want to catch us. But some of you *did*. And you *were*
seventeen to two." She addressed Mr. Waterhouse:

"Why *don't* you give women the vote?" she said. "You'll find it will
interfere a good deal with your indispensable golf if you don't. Then
what becomes of the nation's health?"

Mr. Waterhouse said:

"If you'll come and discuss it quietly . . ."

She said:

"Oh, tell that to the marines," and turned away, the men in a row
watching her figure disappear into the distance of the flat land. Not
one of them was inclined to risk that jump: there was nine foot of
mud in the bottom of the dyke. It was quite true that, the plank
being removed, to go after the women they would have had to go
several miles round. It had been a well-thought-out raid. Mr. Waterhouse said that girl was a ripping girl: the others found her just
ordinary. Mr. Sandbach, who had only lately ceased to shout: "Hi!"
wanted to know what they were going to do about catching the
women, but Mr. Waterhouse said: "Oh, chuck it, Sandy," and
went off.

Mr. Sandbach refused to continue his match with Tietjens. He
said that Tietjens was the sort of fellow who was the ruin of England. He said he had a good mind to issue a warrant for the arrest of
Tietjens — for obstructing the course of justice. Tietjens pointed out
that Sandbach wasn't a borough magistrate and so couldn't. And
Sandbach went off, dot and carry one, and began a furious row with
the two city men who had retreated to a distance. He said they were
the sort of men who were the ruin of England. They bleated like
rams. . . .

Tietjens wandered slowly up the course, found his ball, made his
shot with care and found that the ball deviated several feet less to
the right of a straight line than he had expected. He tried the shot
again, obtained the same result and tabulated his observations in his
notebook. He sauntered slowly back towards the club-house. He was
content.

He felt himself to be content for the first time in four months. His pulse beat calmly; the heat of the sun all over him appeared to be a beneficent flood. On the flanks of the older and larger sandhills he observed the minute herbage, mixed with little purple aromatic plants. To these the constant nibbling of sheep had imparted a protective tininess. He wandered, content, round the sandhills to the small, silted harbour mouth. After reflecting for some time on the wave-curves in the sloping mud of the water sides he had a long conversation, mostly in signs, with a Finn who hung over the side of a tarred, stump-masted, battered vessel that had a gaping, splintered hole where the anchor should have hung. She came from Archangel; was of several hundred tons burthen, was knocked together anyhow, of soft wood, for about ninety pounds, and launched, sink or swim, in the timber trade. Beside her, taut, glistening with brasswork, was a new fishing boat, just built there for the Lowestoft fleet. Ascertaining her price from a man who was finishing her painting, Tietjens reckoned that you could have built three of the Archangel timber ships for the cost of that boat, and that the Archangel vessel would earn about twice as much per hour per ton.

It was in that way his mind worked when he was fit: it picked up little pieces of definite, workmanlike information. When it had enough it classified them: not for any purpose, but because to know things was agreeable and gave a feeling of strength, of having in reserve something that the other fellow would not suspect. . . . He passed a long, quiet, abstracted afternoon.

In the dressing-room he found the General, among lockers, old coats, and stoneware, washing basins set in scrubbed wood. The General leaned back against a row of these things.

"You are the ruddy *limit*!" he exclaimed.

Tietjens said:

"Where's Macmaster?"

The General said he had sent Macmaster off with Sandbach in the two-seater. Macmaster had to dress before going up to Mountby. He added: "The *ruddy* limit!" again.

"Because I knocked the bobbie over?" Tietjens asked. "He liked it."

The General said:

"Knocked the bobbie over . . . I didn't see that."

"He didn't want to catch the girls," Tietjens said, "you could see him — oh, yearning not to."

"I don't want to know anything about that," the General said. "I shall hear enough about it from Paul Sandbach. Give the bobbie a quid and let's hear no more of it. I'm a magistrate."

"Then what have I done?" Tietjens said. "I helped those girls to get off. You didn't want to catch them; Waterhouse didn't, the policeman didn't. No one did except the swine. Then what's the matter?"

"Damn it all!" the General said, "don't you remember that you're a young married man?"

With the respect for the General's superior age and achievements, Tietjens stopped himself laughing.

"If you're really serious, sir," he said, "I always remember it very carefully. I don't suppose you're suggesting that I've ever shown want of respect for Sylvia."

The General shook his head.

"I don't know," he said. "And damn it all I'm worried. I'm . . . hang it, I'm your father's oldest friend." The General looked indeed worn and saddened in the light of the sand-drifted, ground glass, windows. He said: "Was that skirt a . . . a friend of yours? Had you arranged it with her?"

Tietjens said:

"Wouldn't it be better, sir, if you said what you had on your mind? . . ."

The old General blushed a little.

"I don't like to," he said straightforwardly. "You brilliant fellows.. . . . I only want, my dear boy, to hint that . . ."

Tietjens said, a little more stiffly:

"I'd prefer you to get it out, sir. . . . I acknowledge your right as my father's oldest friend."

"Then," the General burst out, "who was the skirt you were lolloping up Pall Mall with? On the last day they trooped the colours? . . . I didn't see her myself. Was it this same one? Paul said she looked like a cook maid."

Tietjens made himself a little more rigid.

"She was, as a matter of fact, a bookmaker's secretary," Tietjens said. "I imagine I have the right to walk where I like, with whom I like. And no one has the right to question it. . . . I don't mean you, sir. But no one else."

The General said puzzledly:

"It's you *brilliant* fellows. . . . They all say you're brilliant. . . ."

Tietjens said:

"You might let your rooted distrust of intelligence . . . .. It's natural of course; but you might let it allow you to be just to me. I assure you there was nothing discreditable."

The General interrupted:

"If you were a stupid young subaltern and told me you were show-ing your mother's new cook the way to the Piccadilly tube I'd believe you. . . . But, then, no young subaltern would do such a damn, blasted, tomfool thing! Paul said you walked beside her like the king in his glory! Through the crush outside the Haymarket, of all places in the world!"

"I'm obliged to Sandbach for his commendation. . . ." Tietjens said. He thought a moment. Then he said:

"I was trying to get that young woman. . . . I was taking her out to lunch from her office at the bottom of the Haymarket. . . . To get her off a friend's back. That is, of course, between ourselves."

He said this with great reluctance because he didn't want to cast reflection on Macmaster's taste, for the young lady had been by no means one to be seen walking with a really circumspect public official. But he had said nothing to indicate Macmaster, and he had other friends.

The General choked.

"Upon my soul," he said, "what do you take me for?" He repeated the words as if he were amazed. "If," he said, "my G.S.O. II. — who's the stupidest ass I know — told me such a damn-fool lie as that I'd have him broke to-morrow." He went on expostulatorily: "Damn it all, it's the first duty of a soldier — it's the first duty of all Englishmen — to be able to tell a good lie in answer to a charge. But a lie like that . . ."

He broke off breathless, then he began again:

"Hang it all, I told that lie to my grandmother and my grandfather told it to *his* grandfather. And they call you brilliant! . . ." He paused and then asked reproachfully: "Or do you think I'm in a state of senile decay?"

Tietjens said:

"I know you, sir, to be the smartest general of division in the Brit-ish Army. I leave you to draw your own conclusions as to why I said what I did. . . ." He had told the exact truth, but he was not sorry to be disbelieved.

The General said:

"Then I'll take it that you tell me a lie meaning me to know that it's a lie. That's quite proper. I take it you mean to keep the woman officially out of it. But look here, Chrissie" — his tone took a deeper seriousness — "if the woman that's come between you and Sylvia — that's broken up your home, damn it, for that's what it is! — is little Miss Wannop . . ."

"Her name was Julia Mandelstein," Tietjens said.

The General said:

"Yes! Yes! Of course! . . . But if it *is* the little Wannop girl and it's not gone too far . . . put her back . . . put her back, as you used to be a good boy! It would be too hard on the mother. . . ."

Tietjens said:

"General! I give you my word . . ."

The General said:

"I'm not asking any questions, my boy; I'm talking now. You've told me the story you want told and it's the story I'll tell for you! But that little piece is . . . she use to be! . . . as straight as a die. I daresay you know better than I. Of course when they get among the wild women there's no knowing what happens to them. They say they're all whores. . . . I beg your pardon, if you like the girl . . ."

"Is Miss Wannop," Tietjens asked, "the girl who demonstrates?"

"Sandbach said," the General went on, "that he couldn't see from where he was whether that girl was the same as the one in the Haymarket. But he thought it was. . . . He was pretty certain."

"As he's married your sister," Tietjens said, "one can't impugn his taste in women."

"I say again, I'm not asking," the General said. "But I do say again too: put her back. Her father was a great friend of your father's: or your father was a great admirer of his. They say he was the most brilliant brain of the party."

"Of course I know who Professor Wannop was," Tietjens said. "There's nothing you could tell me about him."

"I daresay not," the General said drily. "Then you know that he didn't leave a farthing when he died and the rotten Liberal Government wouldn't put his wife and children on the Civil List because he'd sometimes written for a Tory paper. And you know that the mother has had a deuced hard row to hoe and has only just turned the corner. If she can be said to have turned it. I know Claudine takes them all the peaches she can cadge out of Paul's gardener."

Tietjens was about to say that Mrs. Wannop, the mother, had written the only novel worth reading since the eighteenth century. . . . But the General went on:

"Listen to me, my boy. . . . If you can't get on without women
. . . I should have thought Sylvia was good enough. But I know what
we men are. . . . I don't set up to be a saint. I heard a woman in the
promenade of the Empire say once that it was the likes of them that
saved the lives and figures of all the virtuous women of the country.
And I daresay it's true. But choose a girl that you can set up in a
tobacco shop and do your courting in the back parlour. Not in the
Haymarket. . . . Heaven knows if you can afford it. That's your
affair. You appear to have been sold up. And from what Sylvia's let
drop to Claudine . . ."

"I don't believe," Tietjens said, "that Sylvia's said anything to Lady
Claudine . . . She's too straight."

"I didn't say 'said,'" the General exclaimed, "I particularly said
'let drop.' And perhaps I oughtn't to have said as much as that, but
you know what devils for ferreting out women are. And Claudine's
worse than any woman I ever knew."

"And, of course, she's had Sandbach to help," Tietjens said.

"Oh, that fellow's worse than any woman," the General exclaimed.

"Then what does the whole indictment amount to?" Tietjens
asked.

"Oh, hang it," the General brought out, "I'm not a beastly detective, I only want a plausible story to tell Claudine. Or not even plausible. An obvious lie as long as it shows you're not flying in the face
of society — as walking up the Haymarket with the little Wannop
when your wife's left you because of her would be."

"What does it amount to?" Tietjens said patiently: "What Sylvia
'let drop'?"

"Only," the General answered, "that you are — that your views are
— immoral. Of course they often puzzle me. And, of course, if you
have views that aren't the same as other people's, and don't keep
them to yourself, other people will suspect you of immorality. That's
what put Paul Sandbach on your track! . . . and that you're extravagant. . . . Oh, hang it. . . . Eternal hansoms, and taxis and tele-
grams. . . . You know, my boy, times aren't what they were when
your father and I married. We used to say you could do it on five
hundred a year as a younger son. . . . And then this girl too. . . ."
His voice took on a more agitated note of shyness — pain. "It probably hadn't occurred to you. . . . But, of course, Sylvia has an income of her own. . . . And, don't you see . . . if you outrun the
constable and . . . In short, you're spending Sylvia's money on the

other girl, and that's what people can't stand." He added quickly:
"I'm bound to say that Mrs. Satterthwaite backs you through thick
and thin. Thick and thin! Claudine wrote to her. But you know what
women are with a handsome son-in-law that's always polite to them.
But I may tell you that but for your mother-in-law, Claudine would
have cut you out of her visiting list months ago. And you'd have been
cut out of some others too. . . ."

Tietjens said:

"Thanks. I think that's enough to go on with. Give me a couple of
minutes to reflect on what you've said . . ."

"I'll wash my hands and change my coat," the General said with
intense relief.

At the end of two minutes Tietjens said:

"No; I don't see that there is anything I want to say."

The General exclaimed with enthusiasm:

"That's my good lad! Open confession is next to reform. . . .
And . . . and try to be more respectful to your superiors. . . .
Damn it; they say you're brilliant. But I thank heaven I haven't got
you in my command. . . . Though I believe you're a good lad. But
you're the sort of fellow to set a whole division by the ears. . . . A
regular . . . what's 'is name? A regular Dreyfus!"

"Did you think Dreyfus was guilty?" Tietjens asked.

"Hang it," the General said, "he was worse than guilty — the sort
of fellow you couldn't believe in and yet couldn't prove anything
against. The curse of the world. . . ."

Tietjens said:

"Ah "

"Well, they are," the General said: "fellows like that *unsettle*
society. You don't know where you are. You can't judge. They
make you uncomfortable. . . . A brilliant fellow too! I believe he's
a brigadier-general by now. . . ." He put his arm round Tietjen's
shoulders.

"There, there, my dear boy," he said, "come and have a sloe gin.
That's the real answer to all beastly problems."

It was some time before Tietjens could get to think of his own
problems. The fly that took them back went with the slow pomp of
a procession over the winding marsh road in front of the absurdly
picturesque red pyramid of the very old town. Tietjens had to listen
to the General suggesting that it would be better if he didn't come
to the golf-club till Monday. He would get Macmaster some good

games. A good, sound fellow that Macmaster, now. It was a pity Tiet-jens hadn't some of his soundness!

The two city men had approached the General on the course and had used some violent invectives against Tietjens: they had objected to being called ruddy swine to their faces; they were going to the po-lice. The General said that he had told them himself, slowly and dis-tinctly, that they *were* ruddy swine and that they would never get another ticket at that club after Monday. But till Monday, appar-ently, they had the right to be there and the club wouldn't want scenes. Sandbach, too, was infuriated about Tietjens.

Tietjens said that the fault lay with the times that permitted the introduction into gentlemen's company of such social swipes as Sand-bach. One acted perfectly correctly and then a dirty little beggar like that put dirty little constructions on it and ran about and bleated. He added that he knew Sandbach was the General's brother-in-law, but he couldn't help it. That was the truth. . . . The General said: "I know, my boy: I know. . . ." But one had to take society as one found it. Claudine had to be provided for and Sandbach made a very good husband, careful, sober, and on the right side in politics. A bit. of a rip; but they couldn't ask for everything! And Claudine was using all the influence she had with the other side — which was not a little, women were so wonderful! — to get him a diplomatic job in Turkey, so as to get him out of the way of Mrs. Crundall! Mrs. Crundall was the leading Anti-Suffragette of the little town. That was what made Sandbach so bitter against Tietjens. He told Tietjens so that Tiet-jens might understand.

Tietjens had hitherto flattered himself that he could examine a subject swiftly and put it away in his mind. To the General he hardly listened. The allegations against himself were beastly; but he could usually ignore allegations against himself and he imagined that if he said no more about them he would himself hear no more. If there were, in clubs and places where men talk, unpleasant rumours as to himself he preferred it to be thought that he was the rip, not his wife the strumpet. That was normal, male vanity; the preference of the English gentleman! Had it been a matter of Sylvia spotless and him-self as spotless as he was — for in all these things he knew himself to be spotless! — he would certainly have defended himself, at least, to the General. But he had acted practically in not defending himself more vigorously. For he imagined that, had he really tried, he could have made the General believe him. But he had behaved rightly! It was not mere vanity. There was the child up at his sister Effie's. It was better for a boy to have a rip of a father than a whore for mother!

The General was expatiating on the solidity of a squat castle, like a pile of draughts, away to the left, in the sun, on the flatness. He was saying that we didn't build like that nowadays.

Tietjens said:

"You're perfectly wrong, General. All the castles that Henry VIII built in 1543 along this coast are mere monuments of jerry-building. . . . 'In 1543 *jactat castra Delis, Sandgatto, Reia, Hastingas Henricus Rex*' . . . That means he chucked them down. . . ."

The General laughed:

"You are an incorrigible fellow. . . . If ever there's any known, certain fact . . ."

"But go and *look* at the beastly things," Tietjens said. "You'll see they've got just a facing of Caen stone that they tide-floated here, and the fillings-up are just rubble, any rubbish. Look here! It's a known certain fact, isn't it, that your eighteen-pounders are better than the French seventy-fives. They tell us so in the House, on the hustings, in the papers; the public believes it. . . . But would you put one of your tin-pot things firing — what is it? — four shells a minute? — with the little bent pins in their tails to stop the recoil — against their seventy-fives with the compressed-air cylinders. . . ."

The General sat stiffly upon his cushions:

"That's different," he said. "How the devil do you get to know these things?"

"It isn't different," Tietjens said, "it's the same muddle-headed frame of mind that sees good building in Henry VIII as lets us into wars with hopelessly antiquated field guns and rottenly inferior ammunition. You'd fire any fellow on your staff who said we could stand up for a minute against the French."

"Well, anyhow," the General said, "I thank heaven you're not on my staff for you'd talk my hind leg off in a week. It's perfectly true that the public . . ."

But Tietjens was not listening. He was considering that it was natural for an unborn fellow like Sandbach to betray the solidarity that should exist between men. And it was natural for a childless woman like Lady Claudine Sandbach with a notoriously, a flagrantly unfaithful husband to believe in the unfaithfulness of the husbands of other women!

The General was saying:

"Who did you hear that stuff from about the French field gun?"
Tietjens said:
"From you. Three weeks ago!"
And all the other society women with unfaithful husbands. . . .
They must do their best to down and out a man. They would cut
him off their visiting lists! Let them. The barren harlots mated to
faithless eunuchs! . . . Suddenly he thought that he didn't know
for certain that he was the father of his child, and he groaned.

"Well, what have I said wrong now?" the General asked. "Surely
you don't maintain that pheasants do eat mangolds. . . ."
Tietjens proved his reputation for sanity with:
"No! I was just groaning at the thought of the Chancellor! That's
sound enough for you, isn't it?" But it gave him a nasty turn. He
hadn't been able to pigeon-hole and padlock his disagreeable reflections. He had been as good as talking to himself.

In the bow-window of another hostelry than his own he caught the
eye of Mr. Waterhouse, who was looking at the view over the
marshes. The great man beckoned to him and he went in. Mr. Waterhouse was anxious that Tietjens — whom he assumed to be a man of
sense — should get any pursuit of the two girls stopped off. He
couldn't move in the matter himself, but a five pound note and possibly a police promotion or so might be handed round if no advertisement were given to the mad women on account of their raid of that
afternoon.

It was not a very difficult matter: for where the great man was to
be found in the club lounge, there, in the bar, the mayor, the town
clerk, the local head of the police, the doctors and solicitors would
be found drinking together. And after it was arranged the great man
himself came into the bar, had a drink and pleased them all immensely by his affability. . . .

Tietjens himself, dining alone with the Minister to whom he
wanted to talk about his Labour Finance Act, didn't find him a disagreeable fellow: not really foolish, not sly except in his humour,
tired obviously, but livening up after a couple of whiskies, and certainly not as yet plutocratic; with tastes for apple-pie and cream of a
fourteen-year-old boy. And, even as regards his famous Act, which
was then shaking the country to its political foundations, once you
accepted its fundamental unsuitedness to the temperament and needs
of the English working-class, you could see that Mr. Waterhouse
didn't want to be dishonest. He accepted with gratitude several of

Tietjens' emendations in the actuarial schedules. .... And over their
port they agreed on two fundamental legislative ideals: every working
man to have a minimum of four hundred a year and every beastly
manufacturer who wanted to pay less to be hung. That, it appeared,
was the High Toryism of Tietjens as it was the extreme Radicalism
of the extreme Left of the Left.

And Tietjens, who hated no man, in face of this simple-minded
and agreeable schoolboy type of fellow, fell to wondering why it was
that humanity that was next to always agreeable in its units was, as
a mass, a phenomenon so hideous. You look at a dozen men, each of
them not by any means detestable and not uninteresting, for each
of them would have technical details of their affairs to impart; you
formed them into a Government or a club and at once, with oppressions, inaccuracies, gossip, backbiting, lying, corruptions and vileness,
you had the combination of wolf, tiger, weasel and louse-covered ape
that was human society. And he remembered the words of some
Russian: "Cats and monkeys. Monkeys and cats. All humanity is
there."

Tietjens and Mr. Waterhouse spent the rest of the evening together.

Whilst Tietjens was interviewing the policeman, the Minister sat
on the front steps of the cottage and smoked cheap cigarettes, and
when Tietjens went to bed Mr. Waterhouse insisted on sending by
him kindly messages to Miss Wannop, asking her to come and discuss female suffrage any afternoon she liked in his private room at
the House of Commons. Mr. Waterhouse flatly refused to believe
that Tietjens hadn't arranged the raid with Miss Wannop. He said
it had been too neatly planned for any woman, and he said Tietjens
was a lucky fellow, for she was a ripping girl.

Back in his room under the rafters, Tietjens fell, nevertheless, at
once a prey to real agitation. For a long time he pounded from wall
to wall and, since he could not shake off the train of thought, he got
out at last his patience cards, and devoted himself seriously to thinking out the conditions of his life with Sylvia. He wanted to stop
scandal if he could; he wanted them to live within his income, he
wanted to subtract that child from the influence of its mother. These
were all definite but difficult things. . . . Then one half of his mind
lost itself in the rearrangement of schedules, and on his brilliant table
his hands set queens on kings and checked their recurrences.

In that way the sudden entrance of Macmaster gave him a really terrible physical shock. He nearly vomited; his brain reeled and the room fell about. He drank a great quantity of whisky in front of Mac-master's goggling eyes; but even at that he couldn't talk, and he dropped into his bed faintly aware of his friend's efforts to loosen his clothes. He had, he knew, carried the suppression of thought in his conscious mind so far that his unconscious self had taken command and had, for the time, paralysed both his body and his mind.

V

"It doesn't seem quite fair, Valentine," Mrs. Duchemin said. She was rearranging in a glass bowl some minute flowers that floated on water. They made there, on the breakfast-table, a patch, as it were, of mosaic amongst silver chafing dishes, silver épergnes piled with peaches in pyramids, and great silver rose-bowls filled with roses, that drooped to the damask cloth. A congeries of silver largenesses made as if a fortification for the head of the table; two huge silver urns, a great silver kettle on a tripod and a couple of silver vases filled with the extremely tall blue spikes of delphiniums that, spreading out, made as if a fan. The eighteenth-century room was very tall and long; panelled in darkish wood. In the centre of each of four of the panels, facing the light, hung pictures, a mellowed orange in tone, representing mists and the cordage of ships in mists at sunrise. On the bottom of each large gold frame was a tablet bearing the ascrip-tion: "J. M. W. Turner." The chairs, arranged along the long table that was set for eight people had the delicate, spidery, mahogany backs of Chippendale; on the golden mahogany sideboard that had behind it green silk curtains on a brass-rail were displayed an im-mense, crumbed ham, more peaches on an épergne, a large meat-pie with a varnished crust, another épergne that supported the large pale globes of grape-fruit, a galantine, a cube of inlaid meats, encased in thick jelly.

"Oh, women have to back each other up in these days," Valentine Wannop said. "I couldn't let you go through this alone after break-fasting with you every Saturday since I don't know when."

"I do feel," Mrs. Duchemin said, "immensely grateful to you for your moral support. I ought not, perhaps, to have risked this morning. But I've told Parry to keep him out till 10.15."

"It's, at any rate, tremendously sporting of you," the girl said. "I think it was worth trying."

Mrs. Duchemin, wavering round the table, slightly changed the position of the delphiniums.

"I think they make a good screen," Mrs. Duchemin said.

"Oh, nobody will be able to see him," the girl answered reassuringly. She added with a sudden resolution, "Look here, Edie. Stop worrying about my mind. If you think that anything I hear at your table after nine months as an ash-cat at Ealing, with three men in the house, an invalid wife and a drunken cook, can corrupt my mind, you're simply mistaken. You can let your conscience be at rest, and let's say no more about it."

Mrs. Duchemin said, "Oh, Valentine! How could your mother let you?"

"She didn't know," the girl said. "She was out of her mind for grief. She sat for most of the whole nine months with her hands folded before her in a board and lodging house at twenty-five shillings a week, and it took the five shillings a week that I earned to make up the money." She added, "Gilbert had to be kept at school of course. And in the holidays, too."

"I don't understand!" Mrs. Duchemin said. "I simply don't understand."

"Of course you wouldn't," the girl answered. "You're like the kindly people who subscribed at the sale to buy my father's library back and present it to my mother. That cost us five shillings a week for warehousing, and at Ealing they were always nagging at me for the state of my print dresses. . . ."

She broke off and said:

"Let's not talk about it any more if you don't mind. You have me in your house, so I suppose you've a right to references, as the mistresses call them. But you've been very good to me and never asked. Still, its come up; do you know I told a man on the links yesterday that I'd been a slavey for nine months. I was trying to explain why I was a suffragette; and, as I was asking him a favour, I suppose I felt I needed to give *him* references too."

Mrs. Duchemin, beginning to advance towards the girl impulsively, exclaimed:

"You darling!"

Miss Wannop said:

"Wait a minute. I haven't finished. I want to say this: I never talk

about that stage of my career because I'm ashamed of it. I'm ashamed
of it because I think I did the wrong thing, not for any other reason.
I did it on impulse and I stuck to it out of obstinacy. I mean it would
probably have been more sensible to go round with the hat to benevolent people, for the keep of mother and to complete my education.
But if we've inherited the Wannop ill-luck, we've inherited the Wannop pride. And I *couldn't* do it. Besides I was only seventeen, and I
gave out we were going into the country after the sale. I'm not educated at all, as you know, or only half, because father, being a brilliant man, had ideas. And one of them was that I was to be an athletic, not a classical don at Cambridge, or I might have been, I believe. I don't know why he had that tic. . . . But I'd like you to
understand two things. One I've said already: what I hear in this
house won't ever shock or corrupt me; that it's said in Latin is neither
here nor there. I understand Latin almost as well as English because
father used to talk it to me and Gilbert as soon as we talked at all.
. . . And, oh yes: I'm a suffragette because I've been a slavey. But
I'd like you to understand that, though I was a slavey and am a
suffragette — you're an old-fashioned woman and queer things are
thought about these two things — then I'd like you to understand
that in spite of it all I'm pure! Chaste, you know. . . . Perfectly
virtuous."

Mrs. Duchemin said:

"Oh, Valentine! Did you wear a cap and apron? You! In a cap and
apron."

Miss Wannop replied:

"Yes! I wore a cap and apron and sniffled, 'M'm!' to the mistress;
and slept under the stairs too. Because I would not sleep with the
beast of a cook."

Mrs. Duchemin now ran forward and catching Miss Wannop by
both hands kissed her first on the left and then on the right cheek.

"Oh, Valentine," she said, "you're a heroine. And you only twenty-
two! . . . Isn't that the motor coming?"

But it wasn't the motor coming and Miss Wannop said:

"Oh, no! I'm not a heroine. When I tried to speak to that Minister
yesterday, I just couldn't. It was Gertie who went for him. As for me,
I just hopped from one leg to the other and stuttered: 'V . . .
V . . . Votes for W . . . W . . . W . . . omen!' . . . If I'd been
decently brave I shouldn't have been too shy to speak to a strange
man. . . . For that was what it really came to."

"But that surely," Mrs. Duchemin said — she continued to hold both the girl's hands — "makes you all the braver. . . . It's the person who does the thing he's afraid of who's the real hero, isn't it?"

"Oh, we used to argue that old thing over with father when we were ten. You can't tell. You've got to define the term brave. I was just abject. . . . I could harangue the whole crowd when I got them together. But speak to one man in cold blood I couldn't. . . . Of course I *did* speak to a fat golfing idiot with bulging eyes, to get him to save Gertie. But that was different."

Mrs. Duchemin moved both the girl's hands up and down in her own.

"As you know, Valentine," she said, "I'm an old-fashioned woman. I believe that woman's true place is at her husband's side. At the same time . . ."

Miss Wannop moved away.

"Now, don't, Edie, don't!" she said. "If you believe that, you're an anti. Don't run with the hare and hunt with the hounds. It's your defect really. . . . I tell you I'm *not* a heroine. I *dread* a prison: I *hate* rows. I'm thankful to goodness that it's my duty to stop and housemaid-typewrite for mother, so that I can't really *do things*. . . . Look at that miserable, adenoidy little Gertie, hiding upstairs in our garret. She was crying all last night — but that's just nerves. Yet she's been in prison five times, stomach-pumped and all. Not a moment of funk about her! . . . But as for me, a girl as hard as a rock that prison wouldn't touch. . . . Why, I'm all of a jump now. That's why I'm talking nonsense like a pert schoolgirl. I just dread that every sound may be the police coming for me."

Mrs. Duchemin stroked the girl's fair hair and tucked a loose strand behind her ear.

"I wish you'd let me show you how to do your hair," she said. "The right man might come along at any moment."

"Oh, the right man!" Miss Wannop said. "Thanks for tactfully changing the subject. The right man for me, when he comes along, will be a married man. That's the Wannop luck!"

Mrs. Duchemin said, with deep concern:

"Don't talk like that. . . . Why should you regard yourself as being less lucky than other people? Surely your mother's done well. She has a position; she makes money. . . ."

"Ah, but mother isn't a Wannop," the girl said, "only by marriage. The real Wannops . . . they've been executed, and attain-dered, and falsely accused and killed in carriage accidents and married adventurers or died penniless like father. Ever since the dawn of history. And then, mother's got her mascot . . ."

"Oh, what's that?" Mrs. Duchemin asked, almost with animation, "a relic . . ."

"Don't you know mother's mascot?" the girl asked. "She tells everybody. . . . Don't you know the story of the man with the champagne? How mother was sitting contemplating suicide in her bed-sitting room and there came in a man with a name like Tea-tray; she always calls him the mascot and asks us to remember him as such in our prayers. . . . He was a man who'd been at a German university with father years before and loved him very dearly, but not kept touch with him. And he'd been out of England for nine months when father died and found about it. And he said: 'Now Mrs. Wannop, what's this?' And she told him. And he said, 'What you want is champagne!' And he sent the slavey out with a sovereign for a bottle of Veuve Cliquot. And he broke the neck of the bottle off against the mantelpiece because they were slow in bringing an opener. And he stood over her while she drank half the bottle out of her tooth-glass. And he took her out to lunch . . . oh . . . oh . . . oh, it's cold! . . . And lectured her . . . And got her a job to write leaders on a paper he had shares in . . ."

Mrs. Duchemin said:

"You're shivering!"

"I know I am," the girl said. She went on very fast. "And of course, mother always *wrote* father's articles for him. He found the ideas, but couldn't write, and she's a splendid style. . . . And, since then, he — the mascot — Tea-tray — has always turned up when she's been in tight places. When the paper blew her up and threatened to dismiss her for inaccuracies! She's frightfully inaccurate. And he wrote her out a table of things every leader writer must know, such as that 'A. Ebor' is the Archbishop of York, and that the Government is Liberal. And one day he turned up and said: 'Why don't you write a novel on that story you told me?' And he lent her the money to buy the cottage we're in now to be quiet and write in . . . Oh, I can't go on!"

Miss Wannop burst into tears.

"It's thinking of those beastly days," she said. "And that beastly, *beastly* yesterday!" She ran the knuckles of both her hands fiercely into her eyes, and determinedly eluded Mrs. Duchemin's handkerchief and embraces. She said almost contemptuously:

"A nice, considerate person I am. And you with this ordeal hanging over you! Do you suppose I don't appreciate all your silent heroism of the home, while we're marching about with flags and shouting? But it's just to stop women like you being tortured, body and soul, week in, week out, that we . . ."

Mrs. Duchemin had sat down on a chair near one of the windows; she had her handkerchief hiding her face.

"Why women in your position don't take lovers . . ." the girl said, hotly. "Or that women in your position *do* take lovers . . ."

Mrs. Duchemin looked up; in spite of its tears her white face had an air of serious dignity:

"Oh, *no*, Valentine," she said, using her deeper tones. "There's something beautiful, there's something *thrilling* about chastity. I'm not narrow-minded. Censorius! I don't *condemn*! But to preserve in word, thought and action a lifelong fidelity. . . . It's no mean achievement. . . ."

"You mean like an egg and spoon race," Miss Wannop said.

"It isn't," Mrs. Duchemin replied gently, "the way I should have put it. Isn't the real symbol Atalanta, running fast and not turning aside for the golden apple? That always seemed to me the real truth hidden in the beautiful old legend. . . ."

"I don't know," Miss Wannop said, "when I read what Ruskin says about it in the *Crown of Wild Olive*. Or no! It's the *Queen of the Air*. That's his Greek rubbish, isn't it? I always think it seems like an egg-race in which the young woman didn't keep her eyes in the boat. But I suppose it comes to the same thing."

Mrs. Duchemin said:

"My *dear*! Not a word against John Ruskin in *this* house."

Miss Wannop screamed.

An immense voice had shouted:

"This way! This way! . . . The ladies will be here!"

Of Mr. Duchemin's curates — he had three of them, for he had three marshland parishes almost without stipend, so that no one but a very rich clergyman could have held them — it was observed that they were all very large men with the physiques rather of prize-fighters than of clergy. So that when by any chance at dusk, Mr.

Duchemin, who himself was of exceptional stature, and his three assistants went together along a road the hearts of any malefactors whom in the mist they chanced to encounter went pit-a-pat.

Mr. Horsley — the number two — had in addition an enormous voice. He shouted four or five words, interjected "tee-hee," shouted four or five words more and again interjected "tee-hee." He had enormous wrist-bones that protruded from his clerical cuffs, an enormous Adam's apple, a large, thin, close-cropped, colourless face like a skull, with very sunken eyes, and when he was once started speaking it was impossible to stop him, because his own voice in his ears drowned every possible form of interruption.

This morning, as an inmate of the house, introducing to the break-fast-room Messrs. Tietjens and Macmaster, who had driven up to the steps just as he was mounting them, he had a story to tell. The introduction was, therefore, not, as such, a success. . . .

"A STATE OF SIEGE, LADIES! Tee-hee!" he alternately roared and giggled. "We're living in a regular state of siege. . . . What with . . ." It appeared that the night before, after dinner, Mr. Sandbach and rather more than half-a-dozen of the young bloods who had ʼined at Mountby, had gone scouring the country lanes, mounted on motor bicycles and armed with loaded canes . . . for Suffragettes! Every woman they had come across in the darkness they had stopped, abused, threatened with their loaded canes and subjected to cross-examination. The countryside was up in arms.

As a story this took, with the appropriate reflections and repetitions, a long time in telling, and afforded Tietjens and Miss Wannop the opportunity of gazing at each other. Miss Wannop was frankly afraid that this large, clumsy, unusual-looking man, now that he had found her again, might hand her over to the police whom she imagined to be searching for herself and her friend Gertie, Miss Wilson, at that moment in bed, under the care, as she also imagined, of Mrs. Wannop. On the links he had seemed to her natural and in place; here, with his loosely hung clothes and immense hands, the white patch on the side of his rather cropped head and his masked, rather shapeless features, he affected her queerly as being both in and out of place. He seemed to go with the ham, the meat-pie, the galantine and even at a pinch with the roses; but the Turner pictures, the æsthetic curtain and Mrs. Duchemin's flowing robes, amber and rose in the hair did not go with him at all. Even the Chippendale chairs hardly did. And she felt herself thinking oddly, be-

neath her perturbations of a criminal and the voice of the Rev.
Horsley that *his* Harris tweeds went all right with her skirt, and she
was glad that she had on a clean, cream-coloured silk blouse, not a
striped pink cotton.

She was right as to that.

In every man there are two minds that work side by side, the one
checking the other; thus emotion stands against reason, intellect
corrects passion and first impressions act a little, but very little, before
quick reflection. Yet first impressions have always a bias in their favour, and even quiet reflection has often a job to efface them.

The night before, Tietjens had given several thoughts to this young
woman. General Campion had assigned her to him as *maîtresse en
titre.* He was said to have ruined himself, broken up his home and
spent his wife's money on her. Those were lies. On the other hand
they were not inherent impossibilities. Upon occasion and given the
right woman, quite sound men have done such things. He might,
heaven knows, himself be so caught. But that he should have ruined
himself over an unnoticeable young female who had announced herself as having been a domestic servant, and wore a pink cotton blouse
. . . that had seemed to go beyond the bounds of even the unreason
of club gossip!

That was the strong, first impression! It was all very well for his
surface mind to say that the girl was not by birth a tweeny maid; she
was the daughter of Professor Wannop and she could jump! For
Tietjens held very strongly the theory that what finally separated the
classes was that the upper could lift its feet from the ground whilst
common people couldn't. . . . But the strong impression remained.
Miss Wannop was a tweeny maid. Say a lady's help, by nature. She
was of good family, for the Wannops were first heard of at Birdlip
in Gloucestershire in the year 1417 — no doubt enriched after Agin-
court. But even brilliant men of good family will now and then throw
daughters who are lady helps by nature. That was one of the queernesses of heredity. . . . And, though Tietjens had even got as far as
to realise that Miss Wannop must be a heroine who had sacrificed
her young years to her mother's gifts, and no doubt to a brother at
school — for he had guessed as far as that — even then Tietjens
couldn't make her out as more than a lady help. Heroines are all very
well, admirable, they may even be saints; but if they let themselves
get careworn in face and go shabby. . . . Well, they must wait for
the gold that shall be amply stored for them in heaven. On this

earth you could hardly accept them as wives for men of your own
set. Certainly you wouldn't spend your own wife's money on them.
That was what it really came to.

But, brightened up as he now suddenly saw her, with silk for the
pink cotton, shining coiled hair for the white canvas hat, a charming
young neck, good shoes beneath neat ankles, a healthy flush taking
the place of yesterday's pallor of fear for her comrade; an obvious
equal in the surroundings of quite good people; small, but well-
shaped and healthy; immense blue eyes fixed without embarrassment
on his own. . . .

"By Jove . . ." he said to himself: "It's true! What a jolly little
mistress she'd make!"

He blamed Campion, Sandbach, and the club gossips for the form
the thought had taken. For the cruel, bitter and stupid pressure of
the world has yet about it something selective; if it couples male and
female in its inexorable rings of talk it will be because there is something harmonious in the union. And there exists then the pressure of
suggestion!

He took a look at Mrs. Duchemin and considered her infinitely
commonplace and probably a bore. He disliked her large-shouldered,
many-yarded style of blue dress and considered that no woman should
wear clouded amber, for which the proper function was the provision
of cigarette holders for bounders. He looked back at Miss Wannop,
and considered that she would make a good wife for Macmaster;
Macmaster liked bouncing girls and this girl was quite lady enough.

He heard Miss Wannop shout against the gale to Mrs. Duchemin:
"Do I sit beside the head of the table and pour out?"

Mrs. Duchemin answered:

"No! I've asked Miss Fox to pour out. She's nearly stone deaf."
Miss Fox was the penniless sister of a curate deceased. "You're to
amuse Mr. Tietjens."

Tietjens noticed that Mrs. Duchemin had an agreeable throat-
voice; it penetrated the noises of Mr. Horsley as the missel-thrush's
note penetrates a gale. It was rather agreeable. He noticed that Miss
Wannop made a little grimace.

Mr. Horsley, like a megaphone addressing a crowd, was turning
from side to side, addressing his hearers by rotation. At the moment
he was bawling at Macmaster; it would be Tietjens' turn again in a
moment to hear a description of the heart attacks of old Mrs. Haglen
at Nobeys. But Tietjens' turn did not come. . . .

A high-complexioned, round-cheeked, forty-fiveish lady, with agreeable eyes, dressed rather well in the black of the not-very-lately widowed, entered the room with precipitation. She patted Mr. Horsley on his declamatory right arm and, since he went on talking, she caught him by the hand and shook it. She exclaimed in high, commanding tones:

"Which is Mr. Macmaster, the critic?" and then, in the dead lull to Tietjens: "Are you Mr. Macmaster, the critic? No! . . . Then *you* must be."

Her turning to Macmaster and the extinction of her interest in himself had been one of the rudest things Tietjens had ever experienced, but it was an affair so strictly businesslike that he took it without any offence. She was remarking to Macmaster:

"Oh, Mr. Macmaster, my new book will be out on Thursday week," and she had begun to lead him towards a window at the other end of the room.

Miss Wannop said:

"What have you done with Gertie?"

"Gertie!" Mrs. Wannop exclaimed with the surprise of one coming out of a dream. "Oh yes! She's fast asleep. She'll sleep till four. I told Hannah to give a look at her now and then."

Miss Wannop's hands fell open at her side.

"Oh, *mother!*" forced itself from her.

"Oh, yes," Mrs. Wannop said, "we'd agreed to tell old Hannah we didn't want her to-day. So we had!" She said to Macmaster: "Old Hannah is our charwoman," wavered a little and then went on brightly: "Of course it will be of use to you to hear about my new book. To you journalists a little bit of previous explanation . . ." and she dragged off Macmaster. . . .

That had come about because just as she had got into the dog-cart to be driven to the rectory — for she herself could not drive a horse — Miss Wannop had told her mother that there would be two men at breakfast, one whose name she didn't know; the other, a Mr. Macmaster, a celebrated critic. Mrs. Wannop had called up to her:

"A critic? Of what?" her whole sleepy being electrified.

"I don't know," her daughter had answered. "Books, I daresay."

A second or so after, when the horse, a large black animal that wouldn't stand, had made twenty yards at several bounds, the handy man who drove had said:

"Yer mother's 'owlin' after yer." But Miss Wannop had answered

that it didn't matter. She was confident that she had arranged for
everything. She was to be back to get lunch; her mother was to give
an occasional look at Gertie Wilson in the garret; Hannah, the daily
help, was to be told she could go for the day. It was of the highest importance that Hannah should not know that a completely strange
young woman was asleep in the garret at eleven in the morning. If
she did, the news would be all over the neighbourhood at once, and
the police instantly down on them.

But Mrs. Wannop was a woman of business. If she heard of a re-
viewer within driving distance she called on him with eggs as a
present. The moment the daily help had arrived, she had set out and
walked to the rectory. No consideration of danger from the police
would have stopped her; besides, she had forgotten all about the
police.

Her arrival worried Mrs. Duchemin a good deal, because she
wished all her guests to be seated and the breakfast well begun before
the entrance of her husband. And this was not easy. Mrs. Wannop,
who was uninvited, refused to be separated from Mr. Macmaster.
Mr. Macmaster had told her that he never wrote reviews in the daily
papers, only articles for the heavy quarterlies, and it had occurred to
Mrs. Wannop that an article on her new book in one of the quarterlies was just what was needed. She was, therefore, engaged in telling Mr. Macmaster how to write about herself, and twice after Mrs.
Duchemin had succeeded in shepherding Mr. Macmaster nearly to
his seat, Mrs. Wannop had conducted him back to the embrasure
of the window. It was only by sitting herself firmly in her chair next
to Macmaster that Mrs. Duchemin was able to retain for herself this
all-essential, strategic position. And it was only by calling out:

"Mr. Horsley, *do* take Mrs. Wannop to the seat beside you and
feed her," that Mrs. Duchemin got Mrs. Wannop out of Mr. Duchemin's own seat at the head of the table, for Mrs. Wannop, having
perceived this seat to be vacant and next to Mr. Macmaster,
had pulled out the Chippendale armchair and had prepared to sit
down in it. This could only have spelt disaster, for it would have
meant turning Mrs. Duchemin's husband loose amongst the other
guests.

Mr. Horsley, however, accomplished his duty of leading away this
lady with such firmness that Mrs. Wannop conceived of him as a very
disagreeable and awkward person. Mr. Horsley's seat was next to Miss
Fox, a grey spinster, who sat, as it were, within the fortification of

silver urns and deftly occupied herself with the ivory taps of these machines. This seat, too, Mrs. Wannop tried to occupy, imagining that, by moving the silver vases that upheld the tall delphiniums, she would be able to get a diagonal view of Macmaster and so to shout to him. She found, however, that she couldn't, and so resigned herself to taking the chair that had been reserved for Miss Gertie Wilson, who was to have been the eighth guest. Once there she sat in distracted gloom, occasionally saying to her daughter:

" I think it's very bad management. I think this party's very badly arranged." Mr. Horsley she hardly thanked for the sole that he placed before her; Tietjens she did not even look at.

Sitting beside Macmaster, her eyes fixed on a small door in the corner of a panelled wall, Mrs. Duchemin became a prey to a sudden and overwhelming fit of apprehension. It forced her to say to her guest, though she had resolved to chance it and say nothing:

"It wasn't perhaps fair to ask you to come all this way. You may get nothing out of my husband. He's apt . . . especially on Saturdays. . . ."

She trailed off into indecision. It was possible that nothing might occur. On two Saturdays out of seven nothing *did* occur. Then an admission would be wasted; this sympathetic being would go out of her life with a knowledge that he needn't have had — to be a slur on her memory in his mind. . . . But then, overwhelmingly, there came over her the feeling that, if he knew of her sufferings, he might feel impelled to remain and comfort her. She cast about for words with which to finish her sentence. But Macmaster said:

"Oh, dear lady!" (And it seemed to her to be charming to be addressed thus!) "One understands . . . one is surely trained and adapted to understand . . . that these great scholars, these abstracted cognoscenti . . ."

Mrs. Duchemin breathed a great "Ah!" of relief. Macmaster had used the exactly right words.

"And," Macmaster was going on, "merely to spend a short hour; a shallow flight . . . 'As when the swallow gliding from lofty portal to lofty portal' . . . You know the lines . . . in these, your perfect surroundings. . . ."

Blissful waves seemed to pass from him to her. It was in this way that men should speak; in that way — steel-blue tie, true-looking gold ring, steel-blue eyes beneath black brows! — that men should look. She was half-conscious of warmth; this suggested the bliss of falling asleep, truly, in perfect surroundings. The roses on the table were lovely; their scent came to her.

A voice came to her:

"You *do* do the thing in style, I must say."

The large, clumsy, but otherwise unnoticeable being that this fascinating man had brought in his train was setting up pretensions to her notice. He had just placed before her a small blue china plate that contained a little black caviare and a round of lemon; a small Sevres, pinkish, delicate plate that held the pinkest peach in the room. She had said to him: "Oh . . . a little caviare! A peach!" a long time before, with the vague under-feeling that the names of such comestibles must convey to her person a charm in the eyes of Caliban.

She buckled about her her armour of charm; Tietjens was gazing with large, fishish eyes at the caviare before her.

"How do you get *that*, for instance?" he asked.

"Oh!" she answered: "If it wasn't my husband's doing it would look like ostentation. I'd find it ostentatious for myself." She found a smile, radiant, yet muted. "He's trained Simpkins of New Bond Street. For a telephone message overnight special messengers go to Billingsgate at dawn for salmon, and red mullet, this, in ice, and great blocks of ice too. It's such pretty stuff . . . and then by seven the car goes to Ashford Junction. . . . All the same, it's difficult to give a breakfast before ten."

She didn't want to waste her careful sentences on this grey fellow; she couldn't, however, turn back, as she yearned to do, to the kindredly running phrases — as if out of books she had read! — of the smaller man.

"Ah, but it isn't," Tietjens said, "ostentation. It's the great Tradition. You mustn't ever forget that your husband's Breakfast Duchemin of Magdalen."

He seemed to be gazing, inscrutably, deep into her eyes. But no doubt he meant to be agreeable.

"Sometimes I wish I could," she said. "He doesn't get anything out of it himself. He's ascetic to unreasonableness. On Fridays he eats nothing at all. It makes me quite anxious . . . for Saturdays."

Tietjens said:

"I know."

She exclaimed — and almost with sharpness:

"You *know*!"

He continued to gaze straight into her eyes:

"Oh, of course one knows all about Breakfast Duchemin!" he said.
"He was one of Ruskin's road-builders. He was said to be the most
Ruskin-like of them all!"

Mrs. Duchemin cried out: "Oh!" Fragments of the worst stories
that in his worst moods her husband had told her of his old preceptor
went through her mind. She imagined that the shameful parts of
her intimate life must be known to this nebulous monster. For
Tietjens, turned sideways and facing her, had seemed to grow monstrous, with undefined outlines. He was the male, threatening,
clumsily odious and external! She felt herself say to herself: "I will
do you an injury, if ever . . ." For already she had felt herself swaying the preferences, the thoughts and the future of the man on
her other side. He was the male, tender, in-fitting; the complement
of the harmony, the meat for consumption, like the sweet pulp of
figs. . . . It was inevitable; it was essential to the nature of her relationship with her husband that Mrs. Duchemin should have these
feelings. . . .

She heard, almost without emotion, so great was her disturbance,
from behind her back the dreaded, high, rasping tones:

"*Post coitum tristis!* Ha! Ha! That's what it is?" The voice repeated the words and added sardonically: "You know what *that*
means?" But the problem of her husband had become secondary;
the real problem was: "What was this monstrous and hateful man
going to say of her to his friend, when, for long hours, they were
away?"

He was still gazing into her eyes. He said nonchalantly, rather low:

"I wouldn't look round if I were you. Vincent Macmaster is quite
up to dealing with the situation."

His voice had the familiarity of an elder brother's. And at once
Mrs. Duchemin knew — that *he* knew that already close ties were
developing between herself and Macmaster. He was speaking as a
man speaks in emergencies to the mistress of his dearest friend. He
was then one of those formidable and to be feared males who possess
the gift of right intuitions. . . .

Tietjens said: "You heard!"

To the gloating, cruel tones that had asked:

"You know what that means?" Macmaster had answered clearly,
but with the snappy intonation of a reproving Don:

"Of course I know what it means. It's no discovery!" That was exactly the right note. Tietjens — and Mrs. Duchemin too — could hear Mr. Duchemin, invisible behind his rampart of blue spikes and silver, give the answering snuffle of a reproved schoolboy. A hard-faced, small man, in grey tweed that buttoned, collar-like, tight round his throat, standing behind the invisible chair, gazed straight forward into infinity.

Tietjens said to himself:

"By God! Parry! the Bermondsey light middle-weight! He's there to carry Duchemin off if he becomes violent!"

During the quick look that Tietjens took round the table Mrs. Duchemin gave, sinking lower in her chair, a short gasp of utter relief. Whatever Macmaster was going to think of her, he thought now. He knew the worst! It was settled, for good or ill. In a minute she would look round at him.

Tietjens said:

"It's all right, Macmaster will be splendid. We had a friend up at Cambridge with your husband's tendencies, and Macmaster could get him through *any* social occasion. . . . Besides, we're all gentle-folk here!"

He had seen the Rev. Horsley and Mrs. Wannop both interested in their plates. Of Miss Wannop he was not so certain. He had caught, bent obviously on himself, from large, blue eyes, an appealing glance. He said to himself: "She must be in the secret. She's appealing to me not to show emotion and upset the apple-cart! It is a shame that she should be here: a girl!" and into his answering glance he threw the message: "It's all right as far as this end of the table is concerned."

But Mrs. Duchemin had felt come into herself a little stiffening of morale. Macmaster by now knew the worst; Duchemin was quoting snuffingly to him the hot licentiousness of the *Trimalchion* of Petronius; snuffling into Macmaster's ear. She caught the phrase: *Festinans, puer calide.* . . . Duchemin, holding her wrist with the painful force of the maniac, had translated it to her over and over again. . . . No doubt, that too, this hateful man beside her would have guessed!

She said: "Of course we should be all gentlefolk here. One naturally arranges that. . . ."

Tietjens began to say:

"Ah! But it isn't so easy to arrange nowadays. All sorts of bounders get into all sorts of holies of holies!"

Mrs. Duchemin turned her back on him right in the middle of his sentence. She devoured Macmaster's face with her eyes, in an infinite sense of calm.

Macmaster four minutes before had been the only one to see the entrance, from a small panelled door that had behind it another of green baize, of the Rev. Mr. Duchemin, and following him a man whom Macmaster, too, recognised at once as Parry, the ex-prize-fighter. It flashed through his mind at once that this was an extraordinary conjunction. It flashed through his mind, too, that it was extraordinary that anyone so ecstatically handsome as Mrs. Duchemin's husband should not have earned high preferment in a church always hungry for male beauty. Mr. Duchemin was extremely tall, with a slight stoop of the proper clerical type. His face was of alabaster; his grey hair, parted in the middle, fell brilliantly on his high brows; his glance was quick, penetrating, austere; his nose very hooked and chiselled. He was the exact man to adorn a lofty and gorgeous fane, as Mrs. Duchemin was the exact woman to consecrate an episcopal drawing-room. With his great wealth, scholarship and tradition. . . . "Why then?" went through Macmaster's mind in a swift pinprick of suspicion, "isn't he at least a dean?"

Mr. Duchemin had walked swiftly to his chair which Parry, as swiftly walking behind him, drew out. His master slipped into it with a graceful, sideways motion. He shook his head at grey Miss Fox who had moved a hand towards an ivory urn-tap. There was a glass of water beside his plate, and round it his long, very white fingers closed. He stole a quick glance at Macmaster, and then looked at him steadily with glittering eyes. He said: "Good-morning, doctor," and then, drowning Macmaster's quiet protest: "Yes! Yes! The stethoscope meticulously packed into the top-hat and the shining hat left in the hall."

The prize-fighter, in tight box-cloth leggings, tight whipcord breeches, and a short tight jacket that buttoned up at the collar to his chin — the exact stud-groom of a man of property, gave a quick glance of recognition to Macmaster and then to Mr. Duchemin's back another quick look, raising his eyebrows. Macmaster, who knew him very well because he had given Tietjens boxing lessons at Cambridge, could almost hear him say: "A queer change this, sir! Keep your eyes on him a second!" and, with the quick, light, tip-toe of the pugilist he slipped away to the sideboard. Macmaster stole a quick glance on his own account at Mrs. Duchemin. She had her back to him, being deep in conversation with Tietjens. His heart jumped a little when, looking back again, he saw Mr. Duchemin half raised to his feet, peering round the fortifications of silver. But he sank down again in his chair, and surveying Macmaster with an expression of cunning singular on his ascetic features, exclaimed:

"And your friend? Another medical man! All with stethoscope complete. It takes, of course, two medical men to certify . . ."

He stopped and with an expression of sudden, distorted rage, pushed aside the arm of Parry, who was sliding a plate of sole-fillets on to the table beneath his nose.

"Take away," he was beginning to exclaim thunderously, "these conducements to the filthy lusts of . . ." But with another cunning and apprehensive look at Macmaster, he said: "Yes! yes! Parry! That's right. Yes! Sole! A touch of kidney to follow. Another! Yes! Grape-fruit! With sherry!" He had adopted an old Oxford voice, spread his napkin over his knees and hastily placed in his mouth a morsel of fish.

Macmaster with a patient and distinct intonation said that he must be permitted to introduce himself. He was Macmaster, Mr. Duchemin's correspondent on the subject of his little monograph. Mr. Duchemin looked at him, hard, with an awakened attention that gradually lost suspicion and became gloatingly joyful:

"Ah, yes, Macmaster" he said. "Macmaster. A budding critic. A little of a hedonist perhaps? And yes . . . you wired that you were coming. Two friends! Not medical men! Friends!" He moved his face closer to Macmaster and said:

"How tired you look! Worn! Worn!"

Macmaster was about to say that he was rather hard-worked when, in a harsh, high cackle close to his face there came the Latin words. Mrs. Duchemin — and Tietjens! — had heard. Macmaster knew then what he was up against. He took another look at the prize-fighter; moved his head to one side to catch a momentary view of the gigantic Mr. Horsley, whose size took on a new meaning. Then he settled down in his chair and ate a kidney. The physical force present was no doubt enough to suppress Mr. Duchemin should he become violent. And trained! It was one of the curious, minor coincidences of life that, at Cambridge, he had once thought of hiring this very Parry to follow round his dear friend Sim. Sim, the most brilliant of sardonic ironists, sane, decent and ordinarily a little prudish on the surface, had been subject to just such temporary lapses as Mr. Duche-min. On society occasions he would stand up and shout or sit down and whisper the most unthinkable indecencies. Macmaster, who had loved him very much, had run round with Sim as often as he could, and had thus gained skill in dealing with these manifestations. . . . He felt suddenly a certain pleasure! He thought he might gain prestige in the eyes of Mrs. Duchemin if he dealt quietly and effi-ciently with this situation. It might even lead to an intimacy. He asked nothing better!

He knew that Mrs. Duchemin had turned towards him: he could feel her listening and observing him; it was as if her glance was warm on his cheek. But he did not look round; he had to keep his eyes on the gloating face of her husband. Mr. Duchemin was quoting Pe-tronius, leaning towards his guest. Macmaster consumed kidneys stiffly.

He said:

"That isn't the amended version of the iambics. Willamovitz Möllendorf that we used . . ."

To interrupt him Mr. Duchemin put his thin hand courteously on Macmaster's arm. It had a great cornelian seal set in red gold on the third finger. He went on, reciting in ecstasy, his head a little on one side as if he were listening to invisible choristers. Macmaster really disliked the Oxford intonation of Latin. He looked for a short mo-ment at Mrs. Duchemin; her eyes were upon him; large, shadowy, full of gratitude. He saw, too, that they were welling over with wet-ness.

He looked quickly back at Duchemin. And suddenly it came to him; she was suffering! She was probably suffering intensely. It had not occurred to him that she would suffer — partly because he was without nerves himself, partly because he had conceived of Mrs. Duchemin as firstly feeling admiration for himself. Now it seemed to him abominable that she should suffer.

Mrs. Duchemin was in an agony. Macmaster had looked at her intently and looked away! She read into his glance contempt for her situation, and anger that he should have been placed in such a posi-tion. In her pain she stretched out her hand and touched his arm.

Macmaster was aware of her touch; his mind seemed filled with sweetness. But he kept his head obstinately averted. For her sake he did not dare to look away from the maniacal face. A crisis was com-ing. Mr. Duchemin had arrived at the English translation. He placed his hands on the table-cloth in preparation for rising; he was going to stand on his feet and shout obscenities wildly to the other guests. It was the exact moment.

Macmaster made his voice dry and penetrating to say:

" 'Youth of tepid loves' is a lamentable rendering of *puer calide*! It's lamentably antiquated . . ."

Duchemin choked and said:

"What? What? What's that?"

"It's just like Oxford to use an eighteenth-century crib. I suppose that's Whiston and Ditton? Something like that . . ." He observed Duchemin, brought out of his impulse, to be wavering — as if he were coming awake in a strange place! He added:

"Anyhow it's wretched schoolboy smut. Fifth form. Or not even that. Have some galantine. I'm going to. Your sole's cold."

Mr. Duchemin looked down at his plate.

"Yes! Yes!" he muttered. "Yes! With sugar and vinegar sauce!" The prize-fighter slipped away to the sideboard, an admirable quiet fellow; as unobtrusive as a burying beetle. Macmaster said:

"You were about to tell me something for my little monograph. What became of Maggie . . . Maggie Simpson. The Scots girl who was Rossetti's model for *Alla Finestra del Cielo*?"

Mr. Duchemin looked at Macmaster with sane, muddled, rather exhausted eyes:

"*Alla Finestra!*" he exclaimed: "Oh yes! I've got the water-colour. I saw her sitting for it and bought it on the spot. . . ." He looked again at his plate, started at sight of the galantine and began to eat ravenously: "A beautiful girl!" he said: "Very long-necked . . . She wasn't of course . .•. eh . . . respectable! She's living yet, I think. Very old. I saw her two years ago. She had a lot of pictures. Relics of course! . . . In the Whitechapel Road she lived. She was naturally of that class. . . ." He went muttering on, his head above his plate. Macmaster considered that the fit was over. He was irresistibly impelled to turn to Mrs. Duchemin; her face was rigid, stiff. He said swiftly:

"If he'll eat a little: get his stomach filled . . . It calls the blood down from the head. . . ."

She said:

"Oh, forgive! It's dreadful for you! Myself I will never forgive!"

He said:

"No! No! . . . Why; it's what I'm *for*!"

A deep emotion brought her whole white face to life:

"Oh, you *good* man!" she said in her profound tones, and they remained gazing at each other.

Suddenly, from behind Macmaster's back Mr. Duchemin shouted:

"I say he made a settlement on her, *dum casta et sola,* of course. Whilst she remained chaste and alone!"

Mr. Duchemin, suddenly feeling the absence of the powerful will that had seemed to overweigh his own like a great force in the darkness, was on his feet, panting and delighted:

"Chaste!" He shouted. "Chaste, you observe! What a world of suggestion in the word . . ." He surveyed the opulent broadness of his tablecloth; it spread out before his eyes as if it had been a great expanse of meadow in which he could gallop, relaxing his limbs after long captivity. He shouted three obscene words and went on in his Oxford Movement voice: "But chastity . . ."

Mrs. Wannop suddenly said:

"Oh!" and looked at her daughter, whose face grew slowly crimson as she continued to peel a peach. Mrs. Wannop turned to Mr. Horsley beside her and said:

"You write, too, I believe, Mr. Horsley. No doubt something more learned than my poor readers would care for . . ." Mr. Horsley had been preparing, according to his instructions from Mrs. Duchemin, to shout a description of an article he had been writing about the *Mosella* of Ausonius, but as he was slow in starting the lady got in first. She talked on serenely about the tastes of the large public. Tietjens leaned across to Miss Wannop and, holding in his right hand a half-peeled fig, said to her as loudly as he could:

"I've got a message for you from Mr. Waterhouse. He says if you'll . . ."

The completely deaf Miss Fox — who had had her training by writing — remarked diagonally to Mrs. Duchemin:

"I think we shall have thunder to-day. Have you remarked the number of minute insects. . . ."

"When my revered preceptor," Mr. Duchemin thundered on, "drove away in the carriage on his wedding day he said to his bride: 'We will live like the blessed angels!' How sublime! I, too, after my nuptials . . ."

Mrs. Duchemin suddenly screamed:

"Oh . . . *no!*"

As if checked for a moment in their stride all the others paused —

for a breath. Then they continued talking with polite animation and listening with minute attention. To Tietjens that seemed the highest achievement and justification of English manners!

Parry, the prize-fighter, had twice caught his master by the arm and shouted that breakfast was getting cold. He said now to Macmaster that he and the Rev. Horsley could get Mr. Duchemin away, but there'd be a hell of a fight. Macmaster whispered: "Wait!" and, turning to Mrs. Duchemin he said: "I can stop him. Shall I?" She said:

"Yes! Yes! Anything!" He observed tears; isolated upon her cheeks, a thing he had never seen. With caution and with hot rage he whispered into the prize-fighter's hairy ear that was held down to him:

"Punch him in the kidney. With your thumb. As *hard* as you can without breaking your thumb . . ."

Mr. Duchemin had just declaimed:

"I, too, after my nuptials . . ." He began to wave his arms, pausing and looking from unlistening face to unlistening face. Mrs. Duchemin had just screamed.

Mr. Duchemin thought that the arrow of God struck him. He imagined himself an unworthy messenger. In such pain as he had never conceived of he fell into his chair and sat huddled up, a darkness covering his eyes.

"He won't get up again." Macmaster whispered to the appreciative pugilist. "He'll want to. But he'll be afraid."

He said to Mrs. Duchemin:

"Dearest lady! It's all over. I assure you of that. It's a scientific nerve counter-irritant."

Mrs. Duchemin said:

"Forgive!" with one deep sob: "You can never respect . . ." She felt her eyes explore his face as the wretch in a cell explores the face of his executioner for a sign of pardon. Her heart stayed still: her breath suspended itself. . . .

Then complete heaven began. Upon her left palm she felt cool fingers beneath the cloth. This man knew always the exact right action! Upon the fingers, cool, like spikenard and ambrosia, her fingers closed themselves.

In complete bliss, in a quiet room, his voice went on talking. At first with great neatness of phrase, but with what refinement! He explained that certain excesses being merely nervous cravings, can be combatted if not, indeed, cured altogether, by the fear of, by the determination not to ensue, sharp physical pain — which of course is a nervous matter, too! . . .

Parry, at a given moment, had said into his master's ear:

"It's time you prepared your sermon for to-morrow, sir," and Mr. Duchemin had gone as quietly as he had arrived, gliding over the thick carpet to the small door.

Then Macmaster said to her:

"You come from Edinburgh? You'll know the Fifeshire coast then."

"Do I not?" she said. His hand remained in hers. He began to talk of the whins on the links and the sanderlings along the flats, with such a Scots voice and in phrases so vivid that she saw her childhood again, and had in her eyes a wetness of a happier order. She released his cool hand after a long gentle pressure. But when it was gone it was as if much of her life went. She said: "You'll be knowing Kingussie House, just outside your town. It was there I spent my holidays as a child."

He answered:

"Maybe I played round it a barefoot lad and you in your grandeur within."

She said:

"Oh, no! Hardly! There would be the difference of our ages! And . . . And indeed there are other things I will tell you."

She addressed herself to Tietjens, with all her heroic armour of charm buckled on again:

"Only think! I find Mr. Macmaster and I almost played together in our youths."

He looked at her, she knew, with a commiseration that she hated:

"Then you're an older friend than I," he asked, "though I've known him since I was fourteen, and I don't believe you could be a better. He's a good fellow. . . ."

She hated him for his condescension towards a better man and for his warning — she *knew* it was a warning — to her to spare his friend.

Mrs. Wannop gave a distinct, but not an alarming scream. Mr. Horsley had been talking to her about an unusual fish that used to inhabit the Moselle in Roman times. The *Mosella* of Ausonius; the subject of the essay he was writing is mostly about fish. . . .

"No," he shouted, "it's been said to be the roach. But there are no roach in the river now. V*annulis viridis, oculisque*. No. It's the other way round: *Red* fins . . ."

Mrs. Wannop's scream and her wide gesture: her hand, indeed, was nearly over his mouth and her trailing sleeve across his plate! — were enough to interrupt him.

"*Tietjens!*" she again screamed. "Is it possible? . . ."

She pushed her daughter out of her seat and, moving round beside the young man, she overwhelmed him with vociferous love. As Tietjens had turned to speak to Mrs. Duchemin she had recognized his aquiline half-profile as exactly that of his father at her own wedding-breakfast. To the table that knew it by heart — though Tietjens himself didn't! — she recited the story of how his father had saved her life, and was her mascot. And she offered the son — for to the father she had never been allowed to make any return — her house, her purse, her heart, her time, her all. She was so completely sincere that, as the party broke up, she just nodded to Macmaster and, catching Tietjens forcibly by the arm, said perfunctorily to the critic:

"Sorry I can't help you any more with the article. But my dear Chrissie must have the books he wants. At once! This very minute!"

She moved off, Tietjens grappled to her, her daughter following as a young swan follows its parents. In her gracious manner Mrs. Duchemin had received the thanks of her guests for her wonderful breakfast, and had hoped that now that they had found their ways there. . . .

The echoes of the dispersed festival seemed to whisper in the room. Macmaster and Mrs. Duchemin faced each other, their eyes wary — and longing.

He said:

"It's dreadful to have to go now. But I have an engagement."

She said:

"Yes! I know! With your great friends."

He answered:

"Oh, only with Mr. Waterhouse and General Campion . . . and Mr. Sandbach, of course. . . ."

She had a moment of fierce pleasure at the thought that Tietjens was not to be of the company: *her* man would be outsoaring the vulgarian of his youth, of his past that she didn't know. . . . Almost harshly she exclaimed:

"I don't want you to be mistaken about Kingussie House. It was just a holiday school. Not a grand place."

"It was very costly," he said, and she seemed to waver on her feet.

"Yes! yes!" she said, nearly in a whisper. "But you're so grand now! I was only the child of very poor bodies. Johnstons of Midlothian. But very poor bodies. . . . I . . . He bought me, you might say. You know. . . . Put me to very rich schools: when I was fourteen . . . my people were glad. . . . But I think if my mother had known when I married . . ." She writhed her whole body. "Oh, dreadful! dreadful!" she exclaimed. "I want you to know . . ."

His hands were shaking as if he had been in a jolting cart. . . .

Their lips met in a passion of pity and tears. He removed his mouth to say: "I must see you this evening. . . . I shall be mad with anxiety about you." She whispered: "Yes! yes! . . . In the yew walk." Her eyes were closed, she pressed her body fiercely into his. "You are the . . . first . . . man . . ." she breathed.

"I will be the only one for ever," he said.

He began to see himself: in the tall room, with the long curtains: a round, eagle mirror reflected them gleaming: like a bejewelled picture with great depths: the entwined figures.

They drew apart to gaze at each other, holding hands. . . . The voice of Tietjens said:

"Macmaster! You're to dine at Mrs. Wannop's to-night. Don't dress; I shan't." He was looking at them without any expression, as if he had interrupted a game of cards; large, grey, fresh-featured, the white patch glistening on the side of his grizzling hair.

Macmaster said:

"All right. It's near here, isn't it? . . . I've got an engagement just after . . ." Tietjens said that that would be all right: he would be working himself. All night probably. For Waterhouse . . .

Mrs. Duchemin said with swift jealousy:

"You let him order you about . . ." Tietjens was gone.

Macmaster said absently:

"Who? Chrissie? Yes! Sometimes I him, sometimes he me. . . . We make engagements. My best friend. The most brilliant man in England, of the best stock too. Tietjens of Groby. . . ." Feeling that she didn't appreciate his friend he was abstractly piling on commendations: "He's making calculations now. For the Government that no other man in England could make. But he's going . . ."

An extreme languor had settled on him, he felt weakened but yet triumphant with the cessation of her grasp. It occurred to him

numbly that he would be seeing less of Tietjens. A grief. He heard
himself quote:

" 'Since when we stand side by side!' " His voice trembled.

"Ah yes!" came in her deep tones: "The beautiful lines . . .
They're true. We must part. In this world . . ." They seemed to her
lovely and mournful words to say; heavenly to have them to say, vi-
bratingly, arousing all sorts of images. Macmaster, mournfully too,
said:

"We must wait." He added fiercely: "But to-night, at dusk!" He
imagined the dusk, under the yew hedge. A shining motor drew up
in the sunlight under the window.

"Yes! yes!" she said. "There's a little white gate from the lane."
She imagined their interview of passion and mournfulness amongst
dim objects half seen. So much of glamour she could allow herself.

Afterwards he must come to the house to ask after her health and
they would walk side by side on the lawn, publicly, in the warm light,
talking of indifferent but beautiful poetries, a little wearily, but with
what currents electrifying and passing between their flesh. . . . And
then: long, circumspect years. . . .

Macmaster went down the tall steps to the car that gleamed in the
summer sun. The roses shone over the supremely levelled turf. His
heel met the stones with the hard tread of a conqueror. He could
have shouted aloud!

VI

TIETJENS lit a pipe beside the stile, having first meticulously cleaned
out the bowl and the stem with a surgical needle, in his experience
the best of all pipe-cleaners, since, made of German silver, it is flex-
ible, won't corrode and is indestructible. He wiped off methodically
with a great dock-leaf, the glutinous brown products of burnt tobacco, the young woman, as he was aware, watching him from behind his back. As soon as he had restored the surgical needle to the
notebook in which it lived, and had put the notebook into its bulky
pocket, Miss Wannop moved off down the path: it was only suited
for Indian file, and had on the left hand a ten-foot, untrimmed
quicken hedge, the hawthorn blossoms just beginning to blacken at

the edges and small green haws to show. On the right the grass was above knee high and bowed to those that passed. The sun was exactly vertical; the chaffinchs said: "Pink! pink!" The young woman had an agreeable back.

This, Tietjens thought, is England! A man and a maid walk through Kentish grass fields: the grass ripe for the scythe. The man honourable, clean, upright; the maid virtuous, clean, vigorous; he of good birth; she of birth quite as good; each filled with a too good breakfast that each could yet capably digest. Each come just from an admirably appointed establishment: a table surrounded by the best people, their promenade sanctioned, as it were, by the Church — two clergy — the State, two Government officials; by mothers, friends, old maids.

Each knew the names of birds that piped and grasses that bowed: chaffinch, greenfinch, yellow-ammer (*not*, my dear, hammer! *ammer* from the Middle High German for "finch"), garden warbler, Dartford warbler, pied-wagtail, known as "dishwasher." (These *charming* local dialect names.) Marguerites over the grass, stretching in an infinite white blaze; grasses purple in a haze to the far distant hedgerow; coltsfoot, wild white clover, sainfoin, Italian rye grass (all technical names that the best people must know: the best grass mixture for permanent pasture on the Wealden loam). In the hedge: Our Lady's bedstraw, dead-nettle, bachelor's button (but in *Sussex* they call it ragged robin, my dear), so interesting! Cowslip (paigle, you know, from old French *pasque*, meaning Easter); burr, burdock (farmer that thy wife may thrive, but not burr and burdock wive!); violet leaves, the flowers, of course, over; black briony; wild clematis: later it's old man's beard; purple loose-strife. (That our young maids long purples call and literal shepherds give a grosser name. *So* racy of the soil!) . . . Walk, then, through the field, gallant youth and fair maid, minds cluttered up with all these useless anodynes for thought, quotation, imbecile epithets! Dead silent, unable to talk, from too good breakfast to probably extremely bad lunch. The young woman, so the young man is duly warned, to prepare it: pink india-rubber half-cooked cold beef, no doubt; tepid potatoes, water in the bottom of willow-pattern dish. (*No! Not* genuine willow-pattern, of *course*, Mr. Tietjens.) Overgrown lettuce with wood-vinegar to make the mouth scream with pain; pickles, also preserved in wood-vinegar; two bottles of public-house beer that, on opening, squirts to the wall. A glass of invalid port . . . for the *gentleman*! . . . and the jaws hardly able to open after the too enormous breakfast at 10.15. Midday now!

"God's England!" Tietjens exclaimed to himself in high good humour. "'Land of Hope and Glory!' — F natural descending to tonic, C major: chord of 6–4, suspension over dominant seventh to common chord of C major. . . . All absolutely correct! Double basses, 'cellos, all violins, all woodwind, all brass. Full grand organ, all stops, special *vox humana* and key-bugle effect. . . . Across the counties came the sound of bugles that his father knew. . . . Pipe exactly right. It must be: pipe of Englishman of good birth; ditto tobacco. Attractive young woman's back. English midday midsummer. Best climate in the world! No day on which man may not go abroad!" Tietjens paused and aimed with his hazel stick an immense blow at a tall spike of yellow mullein with its undecided, furry, glaucous leaves and its undecided, buttony, unripe lemon-coloured flower. The structure collapsed, gracefully, like a woman killed among crinolines!

"Now I'm a bloody murderer!" Tietjens said. "Not gory! Green stained with vital fluid of innocent plant . . . And by God! Not a woman in the country who won't let you rape her after an hour's acquaintance!" He slew two more mulleins and a sow-thistle! A shadow, but not from the sun, a gloom, lay across the sixty acres of purple grass bloom and marguerites, white: like petticoats of lace over the grass!

"By God," he said, "Church! State! Army! H.M. Ministry: H.M. Opposition: H.M. City Man. . . . All the governing class! All rotten! Thank God we've got a navy! . . . But perhaps that's rotten too! Who knows! Britannia needs no bulwarks . . . Then thank God for the upright young man and the virtuous maiden in the summer fields: he Tory of the Tories as he should be: she suffragette of the militants: militant here in earth . . . as she should be! As she should be! In the early decades of the twentieth century however else can a woman keep clean and wholesome! Ranting from platforms, splendid for the lungs, bashing in policemen's helmets. . . . No! It's I do that: my part, I think, miss! . . . Carrying heavy banners in twenty-mile processions through streets of Sodom. All splendid! I bet she's virtuous. But you don't have to bet. It isn't done on certainties. You can tell it in the eye. Nice eyes! Attractive back. Virginal cockiness. . . . Yes, better occupation for mothers of empire than attending on lewd husbands year in year out till you're as hysterical as a female cat

in heat. . . . You could see it in her, that woman, you can see it in
most of 'em! Thank God then for the Tory, upright young married
man and the Suffragette kid . . . Backbone of England! . . ."

He killed another flower.

"But by God! we're both under a cloud! Both! . . . That kid and
I! And General Lord Edward Campion, Lady Claudine Sandbach,
and the Hon. Paul, M.P. (suspended) to spread the tale. . . . And
forty toothless fogies in the club to spread it; and no end visiting
books yawning to have your names cut out of them, my boy! . . .
My dear boy: I so regret: your father's oldest friend. . . . By jove,
the pistachio nut of that galantine! Repeating! Breakfast gone wrong;
gloomy reflections! Thought I could stand anything; digestion of an
ostrich. . . . But no! Gloomy reflections! I'm hysterical like that
large-eyed whore! For same reason! Wrong diet and wrong life: diet
meant for partridge shooters over the turnips consumed by the sedentary. England the land of pills . . . *Das Pillen-Land*, the Germans
call us. Very properly . . . And, damn it, outdoor diet: boiled mutton, turnips, sedentary life . . . and forced up against the filthiness
of the world; your nose in it all day long! Why, hang it, I'm as badly
off as she. Sylvia's as bad as Duchemin! . . . I'd never have thought
that . . . No wonder meat's turned to uric acid . . . prime cause of
neurasthenia. . . . What a beastly muddle! Poor Macmaster! He's
finished. Poor devil: he'd better have ogled this kid. He could have
sung: 'Highland Mary' a better tune than 'This is the end of every
man's desire' . . . You can cut it on his tombstone, you can write it
on his card that a young man tacked on to a paulo-post pre-Raphaelite
prostitute. . . ."

He stopped suddenly in his walk. It had occurred to him that he
ought not to be walking with this girl!

"But damn it all," he said to himself, "she makes a good screen for
Sylvia . . . who cares! She must chance it. She's probably struck off
all their beastly visiting lists already . . . as a suffragette!"

Miss Wannop, a cricket pitch or so ahead of him, hopped over a
stile; felt foot on the step, right on the top bar, a touch of the left
on the other steps, and down on the white, drifted dust of a road
they no doubt had to cross. She stood waiting, her back still to him.
. . . Her nimble foot-work, her attractive back, seemed to him, now,
infinitely pathetic. To let scandal attach to her was like cutting the
wings of a goldfinch: the bright creature, yellow, white, golden and

delicate that in the sunlight makes a haze with its wings beside thistle-tops. No; damn it! it was worse; it was worse than putting out, as the bird-fancier does, the eyes of a chaffinch. . . . Infinitely pathetic!

Above the stile, in an elm, a chaffinch said: "Pink! pink!"

The imbecile sound filled him with rage; he said to the bird: "Damn your eyes! *Have* them put out, then!" The beastly bird that made the odious noise, when it had its eyes put out, at least squealed like any other skylark or tom-tit. Damn all birds, field naturalists, botanists! In the same way he addressed the back of Miss Wannop: "Damn your eyes! *Have* your chastity impugned them? What do you speak to strange men in public for! You know you can't do it in this country. If it were a decent, straight land like Ireland where people cut each other's throats for clean issues: Papist versus Prot . . . well, you could! You could walk through Ireland from east to west and speak to every man you met. . . . 'Rich and rare were the gems she wore . . .' To every man you met as long as he wasn't an Englishman of good birth; *that* would deflower you!" He was scrambling clumsily over the stile. "Well! *be* deflowered then: *lose* your infantile reputation. You've spoken to strange pitch: you're defined . . . with the benefit of Clergy, Army, Cabinet, Administration, Opposition, mothers and old maids of England. . . . They'd all tell you you can't talk to a strange man, in the sunlight, on the links, without becoming a screen for some Sylvia or other. . . . Then *be* a screen for Sylvia: *get* struck off the visiting books! The deeper you're implicated, the more bloody villain I am! I'd like the whole lot to see us here; that would settle it. . . ."

Nevertheless, when at the roadside he stood level with Miss Wannop who did not look at him, and saw the white road running to right and left with no stile opposite, he said gruffly to her:

"Where's the next stile? I hate walking on roads!" She pointed with her chin along the opposite hedgerow. "Fifty yards!" she said.

"Come along!" he exclaimed, and set off at a trot almost. It had come into his head that it would be just the beastly sort of thing that would happen if a car with General Campion and Lady Claudine and Paul Sandbach all aboard should come along that blinding stretch of road, or one alone — perhaps the General driving the dog-car he affected. He said to himself:

"By God! If they cut this girl I'd break their backs over my knee!" and he hastened. "Just the beastly thing that *would* happen." The road probably led straight in at the front door of Mountby!

Miss Wannop trotted along a little in his rear. She thought him the most extraordinary man: as mad as he was odious. Sane people, if they're going to hurry — but *why* hurry! — do it in the shade of field hedgerows, not in the white blaze of county council roads. Well, he could go ahead. In the next field she was going to have it out with him: she didn't intend to be hot with running; let him be, his hateful, but certainly noticeable eyes, protruding at her like a lobster's; but she cool and denunciatory in her pretty blouse. . . .

There was a dog-cart coming behind them!

Suddenly it came into her head: that fool had been lying when he had said that the police meant to let them alone: lying over the breakfast-table. . . . The dog-cart contained the police: after them! She didn't waste time looking round: she wasn't a fool like Atalanta in the egg race. She picked up her heels and sprinted. She beat him by a yard and a half to the kissing-gate, white in the hedge: panicked, breathing hard. He panted into it, after her: the fool hadn't the sense to let her through first. They were jammed in together: face to face, panting! An occasion on which sweethearts kiss in Kent: the gate being made in three, the inner flange of the V moving on hinges. It stops cattle getting through, but this great lout of a Yorkshireman didn't know, trying to push through like a mad bullock! Now they were caught. Three weeks in Wandsworth gaol. . . . Oh hang. . . .

The voice of Mrs. Wannop — of course it was only mother! Twenty feet on high or so behind the kicking mare, with a good, round face like a peony — said:

"Ah, you can jam my Val in a gate and hold her . . . but she gave you seven yards in twenty and beat you to the gate. That was her father's ambition!" She thought of them as children running races. She beamed down, round-faced and simple, on Tietjens from beside the driver, who had a black, slouch hat and the grey beard of St. Peter.

"My dear boy!" she said, "my dear boy; it's such a satisfaction to have you under my roof!"

The black horse reared on end, the patriarch sawing at its mouth. Mrs. Wannop said unconcernedly: "Stephen Joel! I haven't done talking."

Tietjens was gazing enragedly at the lower part of the horse's sweat-smeared stomach.

"You soon will have," he said, "with the girth in that state. Your neck will be broken."

"Oh, I don't think so," Mrs. Wannop said. "Joel only bought the turn-out yesterday."

Tietjens addressed the driver with some ferocity:

"Here; get down, you," he said. He held, himself, the head of the horse whose nostrils were wide with emotion; it rubbed its forehead almost immediately against his chest. He said: "Yes! yes! There! there!" Its limbs lost their tautness. The aged driver scrambled down from the high seat, trying to come down at first forward and then backwards. Tietjens fired indignant orders at him:

"Lead the horse into the shade of that tree. Don't touch his bit: his mouth's sore. Where did you get this job lot? Ashford market, thirty pounds; it's worth more. . . . But, blast you, don't you see you've got a thirteen hands pony's harness for a sixteen and a half hands horse. Let the bit out three holes: it's cutting the animal's tongue in half. . . . This animal's a rig. Do you know what a rig is? If you give it corn for a fortnight it will kick you and the cart and the stable to pieces in five minutes one day." He led the conveyance, Mrs. Wannop triumphantly complacent and all, into a patch of shade beneath elms.

"Loosen that bit, confound you," he said to the driver. "Ah! you're afraid."

He loosened the bit himself, covering his fingers with greasy harness polish which he hated. Then he said:

"Can you hold his head or are you afraid of that too? You *deserve* to have him bite your hands off." He addressed Miss Wannop: "Can *you?*" She said: "No! I'm afraid of horses. I can drive any sort of car, but I'm afraid of horses." He said: "Very proper!" He stood back and looked at the horse: it had dropped its head and lifted its near hind foot, resting the toe on the ground: an attitude of relaxation.

"He'll stand now!" he said. He undid the girth, bending down uncomfortably, perspiring and greasy; the girth-strap parted in his hand.

"It's true," Mrs. Wannop said. "I'd have been dead in three minutes if you hadn't seen that. The cart would have gone over backwards . . ."

Tietjens took out a large, complicated, horn-handled knife like a schoolboy's. He selected a punch and pulled it open. He said to the driver:

"Have you got any cobbler's thread? Any string? Any copper wire? A rabbit wire, now? Come, you've got a rabbit wire or you're not a handy-man."

The driver moved his slouch hat circularly in negation. This seemed to be Quality who summons you for poaching if you own to possessing rabbit wires.

Tietjens laid the girth along the shaft and punched into it with his punch.

"Woman's work!" he said to Mrs. Wannop, "but it'll take you home and last you six months as well . . . But I'll sell this whole lot for you to-morrow."

Mrs. Wannop sighed:

"I suppose it'll fetch a ten pound note . . ." She said: "I ought to have gone to market myself."

"No!" Tietjens answered: "I'll get you fifty for it or I'm no Yorkshireman. This fellow hasn't been swindling you. He's got you deuced good value for money, but he doesn't know what's suited for ladies; a white pony and a basket-work chaise is what you want."

"Oh, I like a bit of spirit," Mrs. Wannop said.

"Of course you do," Tietjens answered: "but this turn-out's too much."

He sighed a little and took out his surgical needle.

"I'm going to hold this band together with this," he said. "It's so pliant it will make two stitches and hold for ever. . . ."

But the handy-man was beside him, holding out the contents of his pockets: a greasy leather pouch, a ball of beeswax, a knife, a pipe, a bit of cheese and a pale rabbit wire. He had made up his mind that *this* Quality was benevolent and he made offering of all his possessions.

Tietjens said: "Ah," and then, while he unknotted the wire:

"Well! Listen . . . you bought this turn-out of a higgler at the back door of the Leg of Mutton Inn."

"Saracen's 'Ed!" the driver muttered.

"You got it for thirty pounds because the higgler wanted money bad. *I* know. And dirt cheap. . . . But a rig isn't everybody's driving. All right for a vet or a horse-coper. Like the cart that's too tall! . . . But you did damn well. Only you're not what you were, are you, at thirty? And the horse looked to be a devil and the cart so high you couldn't get out once you were in. And you kept it in the sun for two hours waiting for your mistress."

"There wer' a bit o' lewth 'longside stable wall," the driver muttered.

"Well! He didn't like waiting," Tietjens said placably. "You can be thankful your old neck's not broken. Do this band up, one hole less for the bit I've taken in."

He prepared to climb into the driver's seat, but Mrs. Wannop was there before him, at an improbable altitude on the sloping watch-box with strapped cushions.

"Oh, no, you don't," she said, "no one drives me and my horse but me or my coachman when I'm about. Not even you, dear boy."

"I'll come with you then," Tietjens said.

"Oh, no, you don't," she answered. "No one's neck's to be broken in this conveyance but mine and Joel's," she added: "perhaps to-night if I'm satisfied the horse is fit to drive."

Miss Wannop suddenly exclaimed:

"Oh, *no*, mother." But the handy-man having climbed in, Mrs. Wannop flirted her whip and started the horse. She pulled up at once and leaned over to Tietjens:

"*What* a life for that poor woman," she said. "We must *all* do all we can for her. She could have her husband put in a lunatic asylum to-morrow. It's sheer self-sacrifice that she doesn't."

The horse went off at a gentle, regular trot.

Tietjens addressed Miss Wannop:

"What hands your mother's got," he said, "it isn't often one sees a woman with hands like that on a horse's mouth. Did you see how she pulled up? . . ."

He was aware that, all this while, from the road-side, the girl had been watching him with shining eyes, intently, even with fascination.

"I suppose you think that a mighty fine performance," she said.

"I didn't make a very good job of the girth," he said. "Let's get off this road."

"Setting poor, weak women in their places," Miss Wannop continued. "Soothing the horse like a man with a charm. I suppose you soothe women like that too. I pity your wife. . . . The English country male! And making a devoted vassal at sight of the handy-man. The feudal system all complete. . . ."

Tietjens said:

"Well, you know, it'll make him all the better servant to you if he thinks you've friends in the know. The lower classes are like that. Let's get off this road."

She said: '

"You're in a mighty hurry to get behind the hedge. Are the police after us or aren't they? Perhaps you were lying at breakfast: to calm the hysterical nerves of a weak woman."

"I wasn't lying," he said, "but I hate roads when there are field-paths . . ."

"That's a phobia, like any woman's," she exclaimed.

She almost ran through the kissing-gate and stood awaiting him:

"I suppose," she said, "if you've stopped off the police with your high and mighty male ways you think you've destroyed my romantic young dream. You haven't. I don't *want* the police after me. I believe I'd *die* if they put me in Wandsworth. I'm a coward."

"Oh, no, you aren't," he said, but he was following his own train of thought, just as she wasn't in the least listening to him. "I daresay you're a heroine all right. *Not* because you persevere in actions the consequences of which you fear. But I daresay you can touch pitch and not be defiled."

Being too well brought up to interrupt she waited till he had said all he wanted to say, then she exclaimed:

"Let's settle the preliminaries. It's obvious mother means us to see a great deal of you. *You're* going to be a mascot too, like your father. I suppose you think you are: you saved me from the police yesterday, you appear to have saved mother's neck to-day. You appear, too, to be going to make twenty pounds profit on a horse deal. You say you will and you seem to be that sort of a person . . . Twenty pounds is no end in a family like ours . . . Well, then, you appear to be going to be the regular *bel ami* of the Wannop family . . ."

Tietjens said:

"I hope not."

"Oh, I don't mean," she said, "that you're going to rise to fame by making love to all the women of the Wannop family. Besides, there's only me. But mother will press you into all sorts of odd jobs; and there will always be a plate for you at the table. Don't shudder! I'm a regular good cook — *cuisine bourgeoise* of course. I learned under a real professed cook, though a drunkard. That meant I used to do half the cooking and the family was particular. Ealing people are: county councillors, half of them, and the like. So I know what men are . . ."

She stopped and said good-naturedly: "But do, for goodness' sake, get it over. I'm sorry I was rude to you. But it *is* irritating to have to stand like a stuffed rabbit while a man is acting like a regular Admirable Crichton, and cool and collected, with the English country gentleman air and all."

Tietjens winced. The young woman had come a little too near the knuckle of his wife's frequent denunciations of himself. And she exclaimed:

"No! That's not fair! I'm an ungrateful pig! You didn't show a bit more side really than a capable workman must who's doing his job in the midst of a crowd of incapable duffers. But just get it out, will you? Say once and for all that — you know the proper, pompous manner: you are not without sympathy with our aims, but you disapprove — oh, immensely, strongly — of our methods."

It struck Tietjens that the young woman was a good deal more interested in the cause — of votes for women — than he had given her credit for. He wasn't much in the mood for talking to young women, but it was with considerably more than the surface of his mind that he answered:

"I don't. I approve entirely of your methods: but your aims are idiotic."

She said:

"You don't know, I suppose, that Gertie Wilson, who's in bed at our house, is wanted by the police: not only for yesterday, but for putting explosives in a whole series of letter-boxes?"

He said:

"I didn't . . . but it was a perfectly proper thing to do. She hasn't burned any of my letters or I might be annoyed, but it wouldn't interfere with my approval."

"You don't think," she asked earnestly, "that we . . . mother and I . . . are likely to get heavy sentences for shielding her. It would be beastly bad luck on mother. Because she's an anti . . ."

"I don't know about the sentence," Tietjens said, "but we'd better get the girl off your premises as soon as we can. . . ."

She said:

"Oh, you'll *help*?"

He answered:

"Of course, your mother can't be incommoded. She's written the only novel that's been fit to read since the eighteenth century."

She stopped and said earnestly:

"Look here. *Don't* be one of those ignoble triflers who say the vote won't do women any good. Women have a rotten time. They do, really. If you'd seen what I've seen, I'm not talking through my hat." Her voice became quite deep: she had tears in her eyes: "*Poor* women *do!*" she said, "little insignificant creatures. We've *got* to change the divorce laws. We've *got* to get better conditions. *You* couldn't stand it if you knew what I know."

Her emotion vexed him, for it seemed to establish a sort of fraternal intimacy that he didn't at the moment want. Women do not show emotion except before their familiars. He said drily:

"I daresay I shouldn't. But I don't know, so I can!"

She said with deep disappointment:

"Oh, you *are* a beast! And I shall never beg your pardon for saying that. I don't believe you mean what you say, but merely to say it is heartless."

This was another of the counts of Sylvia's indictment and Tietjens winced again. She explained:

"You don't know the case of the Pimlico army clothing factory workers or you wouldn't say the vote would be no use to women."

"I know the case perfectly well," Tietjens said: "It came under my official notice, and I remember thinking that there never was a more signal instance of the uselessness of the vote to anyone."

"We can't be thinking of the same case," she said.

"We are," he answered. "The Pimlico army clothing factory is in the constituency of Westminster; the Under-Secretary for War is member for Westminster; his majority at the last election was six hundred. The clothing factory employed seven hundred men at 1s. 6d. an hour, all these men having votes in Westminster. The seven hundred men wrote to the Under-Secretary to say that if their screw wasn't raised to two bob they'd vote solid against him at the next election. . . ."

Miss Wannop said: "Well then!"

"So," Tietjens said: "The Under-Secretary had the seven hundred men at eighteenpence fired and took on seven hundred women at tenpence. What good did the vote do the seven hundred men? What good did a vote ever do anyone?"

Miss Wannop checked at that and Tietjens prevented her exposure of his fallacy by saying quickly:

"Now, if the seven hundred women, backed by all the other ill-used, sweated women of the country, had threatened the Under-Secretary, burned the pillar-boxes, and cut up all the golf greens round his country-house, they'd have had their wages raised to half-a-crown next week. That's the only straight method. It's the feudal system at work."

"Oh, but we couldn't cut up *golf* greens," Miss Wannop said. "At

least the W.S.P.U. debated it the other day, and decided that anything so unsporting would make us *too* unpopular. I was for it personally."

Tietjens groaned:

"It's maddening," he said, "to find women, as soon as they get in
Council, as muddleheaded and as afraid to face straight issues as
men! . . ."

"You won't, by-the-by," the girl interrupted, "be able to sell our
horse to-morrow. You've forgotten that it will be Sunday."

"I shall have to on Monday, then," Tietjens said. "The point about
the feudal system . . ."

Just after lunch — and it was an admirable lunch of the cold lamb,
new potatoes and mint-sauce variety, the mint-sauce made with white
wine vinegar and as soft as kisses, the claret perfectly drinkable and
the port much more than that, Mrs. Wannop having gone back to
the late professor's wine merchants — Miss Wannop herself went
to answer the telephone.

The cottage had no doubt been a cheap one, for it was old, roomy
and comfortable; but effort had no doubt, too, been lavished on its
low rooms. The dining-room had windows on each side and a beam
across; the dining silver had been picked up at sales, the tumblers
were old cut glass; on each side of the ingle was a grandfather's chair.
The garden had red brick paths, sunflowers, hollyhocks and scarlet
gladioli. There was nothing to it all, but the garden-gate was well
hung.

To Tietjens all this meant effort. Here was a woman who, a few
years ago, was penniless, in the most miserable of circumstances, supporting life with the most exiguous of all implements. What effort
hadn't it meant! and what effort didn't it mean? There was a boy at
Eton . . . a senseless, but a gallant effort.

Mrs. Wannop sat opposite him in the other grandfather's chair;
an admirable hostess, an admirable lady. Full of spirit in dashes, but
tired. As an old horse is tired that, taking three men to harness it in
the stable yard, starts out like a stallion, but soon drops to a jog-trot.
The face tired, really; scarlet-cheeked with the good air, but seamed
downward. She could sit there at ease, the plump hands covered with
a black lace shawl, and descending on each side of her lap, as much
at ease as any other Victorian great lady. But at lunch she had let
drop that she had written for eight hours every day for the last four

years — till that day — without missing a day. To-day being Saturday, she had no leader to write:

"And, my darling boy," she had said to him. "I'm giving it to you. I'd give it to no other soul but your father's son. Not even to —— " And she had named the name that she most respected. "And that's the truth," she had added. Nevertheless, even over lunch, she had fallen into abstractions, heavily and deeply, and made fantastic mis-statements, mostly about public affairs. It all meant a tremendous record.

And there he sat, his coffee and port on a little table beside him; the house belonging to him.

She said:

"My dearest boy . . . you've so much to do. Do you think you ought really to drive the girls to Plimsoll to-night? They're young and inconsiderate; work comes first."

Tietjens said:

"It isn't the distance . . ."

"You'll find that it is," she answered humorously. "It's twenty miles beyond Tenterden. If you don't start till ten when the moon sets, you won't be back till five, even if you've no accidents. . . . The horse is all right, though . . ."

Tietjens said:

"Mrs. Wannop, I ought to tell you that your daughter and I are being talked about. Uglily!"

She turned her head to him, rather stiffly. But she was only coming out of an abstraction.

"Eh?" she said, and then: "Oh! About the golf-links episode. . . . It must have looked suspicious. I daresay you made a fuss, too, with the police, to head them off her." She remained pondering for a moment, heavily, like an old pope:

"Oh, you'll live it down," she said.

"I ought to tell you," he persisted, "that it's more serious than you think. I fancy I ought not to be here."

"Not here!" she exclaimed. "Why, where else in the world should you be? You don't get on with your wife; I know. She's a regu-lar wrong 'un. Who else could look after you as well as Valentine and I."

In the acuteness of that pang, for, after all, Tietjens cared more for his wife's reputation than for any other factor in a complicated world,

Tietjens asked rather sharply why Mrs. Wannop had called Sylvia a
wrong 'un. She said in rather a protesting, sleepy way:

"My dear boy, nothing! I've guessed that there are differences between you; give me credit for some perception. Then, as you're perfectly obviously a right 'un, she must be a wrong 'un. That's all, I
assure you."

In his relief Tietjens' obstinacy revived. He liked this house; he
liked this atmosphere; he liked the frugality, the choice of furniture,
the way the light fell from window to window; the weariness after
hard work; the affection of mother and daughter; the affection, indeed, that they both had for himself, and he was determined, if he
could help it, not to damage the reputation of the daughter of the
house.

Decent men, he held, don't do such things, and he recounted with
some care the heads of the conversation he had had with General
Campion in the dressing-room. He seemed to see the cracked wash-
bowls in their scrubbed oak settings. Mrs. Wannop's face seemed to
grow greyer, more aquiline; a little resentful! She nodded from time
to time; either to denote attention or else in sheer drowsiness.

"My dear boy," she said at last, "it's pretty damnable to have such
things said about you. I can see that. But I seem to have lived in a
bath of scandal all my life. Every woman who has reached my age has
that feeling . . . Now it doesn't seem to matter." She really nodded
nearly off: then she started. "I don't see . . . I really don't see how I
can help you as to your reputation. I'd do it if I could, believe me.
. . . But I've other things to think of. . . . I've this house to keep
going and the children to keep fed and at school. I can't give all the
thought I ought to to other people's troubles. . . ."

She started into wakefulness and right out of her chair.

"But what a beast I am!" she said, with a sudden intonation that
was exactly that of her daughter; and, drifting with a Victorian
majesty of shawl and long skirt behind Tietjens' high-backed chair,
she leaned over it and stroked the hair on his right temple:

"My dear boy," she said. "Life's a bitter thing. I'm an old novelist
and know it. There you are working yourself to death to save the
nation with a wilderness of cats and monkeys howling and squalling
your personal reputation away. . . . It was Dizzy himself said these
words to me at one of our receptions. 'Here I am, Mrs. Wannop,' he
said . . . And . . ." she drifted for a moment. But she made another
effort: "My dear boy," she whispered, bending down her head to get

it near his ear, "my dear boy; it doesn't matter; it doesn't really matter. You'll live it down. The only thing that matters is to do good work. Believe an old woman that has lived very hard; 'Hard lying money' as they call it in the navy. It sounds like cant, but it's the only real truth. . . . You'll find consolation in that. And you'll live it all down. Or perhaps you won't; that's for God in His mercy to settle. But it won't matter; believe me, as thy day so shall thy strength be." She drifted into other thoughts; she was much perturbed over the plot of a new novel and much wanted to get back to the consideration of it. She stood gazing at the photograph, very faded, of her husband in side-whiskers and an immense shirt-front, but she continued to stroke Tietjens' temple with a subliminal tenderness.

This kept Tietjens sitting there. He was quite aware that he had tears in his eyes; this was almost too much tenderness to bear, and, at bottom his was a perfectly direct, simple, and sentimental soul. He always had bedewed eyes at the theatre, after tender love scenes, and so avoided the theatre. He asked himself twice whether he should or shouldn't make another effort, though it was almost beyond him. He wanted to sit still.

The stroking stopped; he scrambled on to his feet:

"Mrs. Wannop," he said, facing her, "it's perfectly true. I oughtn't to care what these swine say about me, but I do. I'll reflect about what you say till I get it into my system . . ."

She said:

"Yes, yes! My dear," and continued to gaze at the photograph.

"But," Tietjens said; he took her mittened hand and led her back to her chair: "what I'm concerned for at the moment is not my reputation, but your daughter Valentine's."

She sank down into the high chair, balloon-like and came to rest.

"Val's reputation!" she said, "Oh! you mean they'll be striking *her* off their visiting lists. It hadn't struck me. So they will!" She remained lost in reflection for a long time.

Valentine was in the room, laughing a little. She had been giving the handy-man his dinner, and was still amused at his commendations of Tietjens.

"You've got one admirer," she said to Tietjens. " 'Punched that rotten strap,' he goes on saying, 'like a gret ol' yaffle punchin' a 'ollow log!' He's had a pint of beer and said it between each gasp." She continued to narrate the quaintnesses of Joel which appealed to her;

informed Tietjens that "yaffle" was Kentish for great green wood-
pecker, and then said:

"You haven't got any friends in Germany, have you?" She was beginning to clear the table.

Tietjens said:

"Yes, my wife's in Germany; at a place called Lobscheid."

She placed a pile of plates on a black japanned tray.

"I'm so sorry," she said, without an expression of any deep regret.
"It's the ingenious clever stupidities of the telephone. I've got a tele-
graph message for you then. I thought it was the subject for mother's
leader. It always comes through with the initials of the paper which
are not unlike Tietjens, and the girl who always sends it is called
Hopside. It seemed rather inscrutable, but I took it to have to do with
German politics and I thought mother would understand it. . . .
You're not both asleep, are you?"

Tietjens opened his eyes; the girl was standing over him, having
approached from the table. She was holding out a slip of paper on
which she had transcribed the message. She appeared all out of drawing and the letters of the message ran together. The message was:

"Righto. But arrange for certain Hullo Central travels with you.
Sylvia Hopside Germany."

Tietjens leaned back for a long time looking at the words; they
seemed meaningless. The girl placed the paper on his knee, and went
back to the table. He imagined the girl wrestling with these incomprehensibilities on the telephone.

"Of course if I'd had any sense," the girl said, "I should have known
it couldn't have been mother's leader note; she never gets one on a
Saturday."

Tietjens heard himself announce clearly, loudly and with between
each word a pause:

"It means I go to my wife on Tuesday and take her maid with me."

"Lucky you!" the girl said, "I wish I was you. I've never been in
the Fatherland of Goethe and Rosa Luxemburg." She went off with
her great tray load, the table-cloth over her forearm. He was dimly
aware that she had before then removed the crumbs with a crumb-
brush. It was extraordinary with what swiftness she worked, talking
all the time. That was what domestic service had done for her; an
ordinary young lady would have taken twice the time, and would
certainly have dropped half her words if she had tried to talk. Efficiency! He had only just realised that he was going back to Sylvia,

and of course to Hell! Certainly it was Hell. If a malignant and skilful devil . . . though the devil of course is stupid and uses toys like
fireworks and sulphur; it is probably only God who can, very properly,
devise the long ailings of mental oppressions . . . if God then desired (and one couldn't object but one hoped He would not!) to
devise for him, Christopher Tietjens, a cavernous eternity of weary
hopelessness. . . . But He had done it; no doubt as retribution. What
for? Who knows what sins of his own are heavily punishable in the
eyes of God, for God is just? . . . Perhaps God then, after all, visits
thus heavily sexual offences.

There came back into his mind, burnt in, the image of their breakfast-room, with all the brass, electrical fixings, poachers, toasters,
grillers, kettle-heaters, that he detested for their imbecile inefficiency;
with gross piles of hothouse flowers — that he detested for their exotic
waxennesses! — with white enamelled panels that he disliked and
framed, weak prints — quite genuine of course, my dear, guaranteed
so by Sotheby — pinkish women in sham Gainsborough hats, selling
mackerel or brooms. A wedding present that he despised. And Mrs.
Satterthwaite, in negligé, but with an immense hat, reading the *Times*
with an eternal rustle of leaves because she never could settle down
to any one page; and Sylvia walking up and down because she could
not sit still, with a piece of toast in her fingers or her hands behind
her back. Very tall, fair, as graceful, as full of blood and as cruel
as the usual degenerate Derby winner. In-bred for generations for one
purpose: to madden men of one type. . . . Pacing backwards and
forwards, exclaiming: "I'm bored! Bored!" Sometimes even breaking
the breakfast plates. . . . And talking! For ever talking: usually,
cleverly, with imbecility; with maddening inaccuracy, with wicked
penetration, and clamouring to be contradicted; a gentleman has to
answer his wife's questions. . . . And in his forehead the continual
pressure; the determination to sit putt; the *décor* of the room seeming to burn into his mind. It was there, shadowy before him now. And
the pressure upon his forehead. . . .

Mrs. Wannop was talking to him now; he did not know what she
said; he never knew afterwards what he had answered.

"God!" he said within himself, "if it's sexual sins God punishes,
He indeed is just and inscrutable!" Because he had had physical contact with this woman before he married her; in a railway carriage,
coming down from the Dukeries. An extravagantly beautiful girl!

Where was the physical attraction of her gone to now? Irresistible;

reclining back as the shires rushed past. . . . His mind said that she
had lured him on. His intellect put the idea from him. No gentleman
thinks such things of his wife.

No gentleman thinks. . . . By God; she must have been with child
by another man. . . . He had been fighting the conviction down all
the last four months. He knew now that he had been fighting the conviction all the last four months whilst, anæsthetised, he had bathed
in figures and wave-theories. Her last words had been, her very last
words, late, all in white she had gone up to her dressing-room, and
he had never seen her again; her last words had been about the child.
. . . "Supposing," she had begun . . . He didn't remember the rest.
But he remembered her eyes. And her gesture as she peeled off her
long white gloves. . . .

He was looking at Mrs. Wannop's ingle; he thought it a mistake
in taste, really, to leave logs in an ingle during the summer. But
then what are you to do with an ingle in summer. In Yorkshire
cottages they shut the ingles up with painted doors. But that is
stuffy, too!

He said to himself:

"By God! I've had a stroke!" and he got out of his chair to test his
legs. . . . But he hadn't had a stroke. It must then, he thought, be
that the pain of his last consideration must be too great for his mind
to register, as certain great physical pains go unperceived. Nerves,
like weighing machines, can't register more than a certain amount,
then they go out of action. A tramp who had had his leg cut off by
a train had told him that he had tried to get up, feeling nothing at
all. . . . The pain comes back though . . .

He said to Mrs. Wannop, who was still talking:

"I beg your pardon. I really missed what you said."

Mrs. Wannop said:

"I was saying that that's the best thing I can do for you."

He said:

"I'm really very sorry: it was that that I missed. I'm a little in
trouble you know."

She said:

"I know, I know. The mind wanders; but I wish you'd listen. I've
got to go to work, so have you. I said: after tea you and Valentine
will walk into Rye to fetch your luggage."

Straining his intelligence, for, in his mind, he felt a sudden strong
pleasure: sunlight on pyramidal red roof in the distance: themselves

descending in a long diagonal, a green hill. God, yes, he wanted open air. Tietjens said:

"I see. You take us both under your protection. You'll bluff it out."

Mrs. Wannop said rather coolly:

"I don't know about you both. It's you I'm taking under my protection (it's *your* phrase!). As for Valentine: she's made her bed; she must lie on it. I've told you all that already. I can't go over it again."

She paused, then made another effort:

"It's disagreeable," she said, "to be cut off the Mountby visiting list. They give amusing parties. But I'm too old to care and they'll miss my conversation more than I do theirs. Of course, I back my daughter against the cats and monkeys. Of course, I back Valentine through thick and thin. I'd back her if she lived with a married man or had illegitimate children. But I don't approve, I don't approve of the suffragettes: I despise their aims, I detest their methods. I don't think young girls ought to talk to strange men. Valentine spoke to you and look at the worry it has caused you. I disapprove. I'm a woman, but I've made my own way: other women could do it if they liked or had the energy. I disapprove! But don't believe that I will ever go back on any suffragette, individual, in gangs; my Valentine or any other. Don't believe that I will ever say a word against them that's to be repeated — *you* won't repeat them. Or that I will ever write a word against them. No, I'm a woman and I stand by my sex!"

She got up energetically:

"I must go and write my novel," she said. "I've Monday's instalment to send off by train to-night. You'll go into my study: Valentine will give you paper, ink, twelve different kinds of nibs. You'll find Professor Wannop's books all round the room. You'll have to put up with Valentine typing in the alcove. I've got two serials running, one typed, the other in manuscript."

Tietjens said:

"But *you!*"

"I," she exclaimed, "I shall write in my bedroom on my knee. I'm a woman and can. You're a man and have to have a padded chair and sanctuary. . . . You feel fit to work? Then you've got till five; Valentine will get tea then. At half-past five you'll set off to Rye. You'll be back with your luggage and your friend and your friend's luggage at seven."

She silenced him imperiously with:

"Don't be foolish. Your friend will certainly prefer this house and Valentine's cooking to the pub and the pub's cooking. And he'll save on it. . . . It's *no* extra trouble. I suppose your friend won't inform against that wretched little suffragette girl upstairs." She paused and said: "You're *sure* you can do your work in the time and drive Valentine and her to that place . . . Why it's necessary is that the girl daren't travel by train and we've relations there who've never been connected with the suffragettes. The girl can live hid there for a bit. . . . But sooner than you shouldn't finish your work I'd drive them myself. . . ."

She silenced Tietjens again: this time sharply:

"I tell you it's *no* extra trouble. Valentine and I *always* make our own beds. We don't like servants among our intimate things. We can get three times as much help in the neighbourhood as we want. We're liked here. The extra work you give will be met by extra help. We could have servants if we wanted. But Valentine and I like to be alone in the house together at night. We're very fond of each other."

She walked to the door and then drifted back to say:

"You know I can't get out of my head that unfortunate woman and her husband. We must *all* do what we can for them." Then she started and exclaimed: "But, good heavens, I'm keeping you from your work. The study's in there, through that door."

She hurried through the other doorway and no doubt along a passage, calling out:

"Valentine! Valentine! Go to Christopher in the study. At once . . . at . . ." Her voice died away.

VII

Jumping down from the high step of the dog-cart the girl completely disappeared into the silver: she had on an otter-skin toque, dark, that should have been visible. But she was gone more completely than if she had dropped into deep water, into snow — or through tissue paper. More suddenly, at least! In darkness or in deep water a moving paleness would have been visible for a second, snow or a paper hoop would have left an opening. Here there had been nothing.

The constation interested him. He had been watching her intently and with concern for fear she should miss the hidden lower step, in which case she would certainly bark her shins. But she had jumped clear of the cart with unreasonable pluckiness, in spite of his: "Look out how you get down." He wouldn't have done it himself: he couldn't have faced jumping down into that white solidity . . .

He would have asked: "Are you all right?" but to express more concern than the "look out," which he had expended already, would have detracted from his stolidity. He was Yorkshire and stolid; she south country and soft, emotional, given to such ejaculations as "I hope you're not hurt," when the Yorkshireman only grunts. But soft because she was south country. She was as good as a man — a south country man. She was ready to acknowledge the superior woodenness of the north. . . . That was their convention, so he did not call down: "I hope you're all right," though he had desired to.

Her voice came, muffled, as if from the back of the top of his head. The ventriloquial effect was startling:

"Make a noise from time to time. It's ghostly down here and the lamp's no good at all. It's almost out."

He returned to his constations of the concealing effect of water vapour. He enjoyed the thought of the grotesque appearance he must present in that imbecile landscape. On his right an immense, improbably brilliant horn of a moon, sending a trail as if down the sea, straight to his neck; beside the moon a grotesquely huge star; in an extravagant position above them the Plough, the only constellation that he knew; for, though a mathematician, he despised astronomy. It was not theoretical enough for the pure mathematician and not sufficiently practical for daily life. He had of course calculated the movements of abstruse heavenly bodies, but only from given figures; he had never looked for the stars of his calculations. . . . Above his head and all over the sky were other stars: large and weeping with light, or as the dawn increased, so paling that at times, you saw them, then missed them. Then the eye picked them up again.

Opposite the moon was a smirch or two of cloud; pink below, dark purple above, on the more pallid, lower blue of the limpid sky.

But the absurd thing was this mist! . . . It appeared to spread from his neck, absolutely level, absolutely silver, to infinity on each side of him. At great distances on his right black tree-shapes, in groups — there were four of them — were exactly like coral islands on a silver sea. He couldn't escape the idiotic comparison: there wasn't any other.

Yet it didn't actually spread from his neck; when he now held his

hands, nipple-high, like pallid fish they held black reins which ran
downwards into nothingness. If he jerked the rein, the horse threw its
head up. Two pricked ears were visible in greyness: the horse being
sixteen two and a bit over, the mist might be ten-foot-high. Thereabouts. . . . He wished the girl would come back and jump out of
the cart again. Being ready for it he would watch her disappearance
more scientifically. He couldn't of course ask her to do it again: that
was irritating. The phenomenon would have proved — or it might of
course disprove — his idea of smoke screens. The Chinese of the
Ming dynasty were said to have approached and overwhelmed their
enemies under clouds of — of course, not acrid — vapour. He had
read that the Patagonians, hidden by smoke, were accustomed to approach so near to birds or beasts as to be able to take them by hand.
The Greek under Paleologus the . . .

Miss Wannop's voice said — from beneath the bottom board of
the cart:

"I wish you'd make some noise. It's lonely down here, besides being possibly dangerous. There might be dicks on each side of the
road."

If they were on the marsh there certainly would be dykes — why
did they call ditches "dykes," and why did she pronounce it "dicks"?
— on each side of the road. He could think of nothing to say that
wouldn't express concern and he couldn't do that by the rules of the
game. He tried to whistle "John Peel!" But he was no hand at whistling. He sang:

"D'ye ken, John Peel at the break of day . . ." and felt like a fool.
But he kept on at it, the only tune that he knew. It was the Yorkshire
Light Infantry quick-step: the regiment of his brothers in India. He
wished he had been in the army, but his father hadn't approved of
having more than two younger sons in the army. He wondered if he
would ever run with John Peel's hounds again: he had once or twice.
Or with any of the trencher-fed foot packs of the Cleveland district,
of which there had been still several when he had been a boy. He had
been used to think of himself as being like John Peel with his coat
so grey. "Up through the heather, over Wharton's place, the pack
running wild, the heather dripping; the mist rolling up . . . another
kind of mist than this south country silver sheet. Silly stuff! Magical!
That was the word. A silly word. . . ." South country . . . In the
north the old grey mists rolled together, revealing black hillsides!

He didn't suppose he'd have the wind now: this rotten bureau-cratic life! . . . If he had been in the army like the two brothers, Ernest and James, next above him . . . But no doubt he would not have liked the army. Discipline! He supposed he would have put up with the discipline: a gentleman had to. Because *noblesse oblige*: not for fear of consequences . . . But army officers seemed to him pathetic. They spluttered and roared to make men jump smartly: at the end of apopleptic efforts the men jumped smartly. But there was the end of it. . . .

Actually, this mist was not silver, or was, perhaps, no longer silver: if you looked at it with the eye of the artist . . . With the exact eye! It was smirched with bars of purple, of red, of orange, delicate reflections; dark blue shadows from the upper sky where it formed drifts like snow. . . . The exact eye: exact observation; it was a man's work. The only work for a man. Why then, were artists soft, effeminate, not men at all; whilst the army officer, who had the inexact mind of the schoolteacher, was a manly man? Quite a manly man, until he became an old woman!

And the bureaucrat then? Growing fat and soft like himself, or dry and stringy like Macmaster or old Ingleby? They did men's work: exact observation: return no. 17642 with figures exact. Yet they grew hysterical: they ran about corridors or frantically rang table bells, asking with high voices of querulous eunuchs why form ninety thousand and two wasn't ready. Nevertheless men liked the bureaucratic life: his own brother, Mark, head of the family, heir to Groby. . . . Fifteen years older, a quiet stick, wooden, brown, always in a bowler hat, as often as not with his racing-glasses hung around him. Attending his first-class office when he liked: too good a man for any administration to lose by putting on the screw. . . . But heir to Groby: what would that stick make of the place? . . . Let it, no doubt, and go on pottering from the Albany to race meetings — where he never betted — to Whitehall, where he was said to be indispensable. . . . Why indispensable? Why in heaven's name? That stick who had never hunted, never shot; couldn't tell coulter from plough-handle and lived in his bowler hat! . . . A "sound" man: the archetype of all sound men. Never in his life had anyone shaken his head at Mark and said: "You're *brilliant*!" Brilliant! That stick! No, he was indispensable!

"Upon my soul!" Tietjens said to himself, "that girl down there is the only intelligent living soul I've met for years." A little pronounced in manner sometimes; faulty in reasoning naturally, but quite intelligent, with a touch of wrong accent now and then. But if she was wanted anywhere, there she'd be! Of good stock, of course: on both sides! But, positively, she and Sylvia were the only two human beings he had met for years whom he could respect: the one for sheer efficiency in killing; the other for having the constructive desire and knowing how to set about it. Kill or cure! The two functions of man. If you wanted something killed you'd go to Sylvia Tietjens in the sure faith that she would kill it: emotion, hope, ideal; kill it quick and sure. If you wanted something kept alive you'd go to Valentine: she'd find something to do for it. . . . The two types of mind: remorseless enemy, sure screen, dagger . . . sheath!

Perhaps the future of the world then was to women? Why not? He hadn't in years met a man that he hadn't to talk down to — as you talk down to a child, as he had talked down to General Campion or to Mr. Waterhouse . . . as he always talked down to Macmaster. All good fellows in their way. . . .

But why was he born to be a sort of lonely buffalo outside the herd? Not artist, not soldier, not bureaucrat, not certainly indispensable anywhere; apparently not even sound in the eyes of these dim-minded specialists. An exact observer. . . .

Hardly even that for the last six and a half hours:

> "Die Sommer Nacht hat mirs angethan
> Das war ein schwiegsams Reiten . . ."

he said aloud.

How could you translate that: you couldn't translate it: no one could translate Heine:

> It was the summer night came over me:
> That was silent riding . . .

A voice cut into his warm, drowsy thought:

"Oh, you *do* exist. But you've spoken too late. I've run into the horse." He must have been speaking aloud. He had felt the horse quivering at the end of the reins. The horse, too, was used to her by now. It had hardly stirred . . . He wondered when he had left off singing "John Peel." . . . He said:

"Come along, then; have you found anything?"

The answer came:

"Something . . . But you can't talk in this stuff . . . I'll just . . ."

The voice died away as if a door had shut. He waited, consciously waiting as an occupation! Contritely and to make a noise he rattled the whip-stock in its bucket. The horse started and he had to check in quickly: a damn fool he was. Of course a horse would start if you rattled a whip-stock. He called out:

"Are you all right?" The cart might have knocked her down. He had, however, broken the convention. Her voice came from a great distance:

"I'm all right. Trying the other side . . ."

His last thought came back to him. He had broken their convention; he had exhibited concern, like any other man. . . . He said to himself:

"By God! Why not take a holiday? Why not break all conventions?"

They erected themselves intangibly and irrefragably. He had not known this young woman twenty-four hours, not to speak to, and already the convention existed between them that he must play stiff and cold, she warm and clinging. . . . Yet she was obviously as cool a hand as himself; cooler no doubt, for at bottom he was certainly a sentimentalist.

A convention of the most imbecile type . . . Then break all conventions: with the young woman: with himself above all. For forty-eight hours . . . almost exactly forty-eight hours till he started for Dover. . . .

> And I must to the greenwood go,
> Alone: a banished man!

By the descending moon: it being then just after cockcrow of midsummer night — what sentimentality! — it must be half-past four on Sunday. He had worked out that to catch the morning Ostend boat at Dover he must leave the Wannops' at 5.15 on Tuesday morning, in a motor for the junction. . . . What incredible cross-country train connections! Five hours for not forty miles.

He had then forty-eight and three-quarter hours! Let them be a holiday! A holiday from himself above all; a holiday from his standards, from his convention with himself. From clear observation, from exact thought, from knocking over all the skittles of the exactitudes of others, from the suppression of emotions. . . . From all the weariness that made him intolerable to himself. . . . He felt his limbs lengthen, as if they too had relaxed.

Well, already he had had six and a half hours of it. They had started at 10 and, like any other man, he had enjoyed the drive, though it had been difficult to keep the beastly cart balanced, the girl had had to sit behind with her arm round the other girl who screamed at every oak tree.

But he had — if he put himself to the question — mooned along under the absurd moon that had accompanied them down the heaven, to the scent of hay, to the sound of nightingales, hoarse by now, of course — in June he changes his tune; of corncrakes, of bats, of a heron twice, overhead. They had passed the blue-black shadows of corn stacks, of heavy, rounded oaks, of hop oasts that are half church-tower, half finger-post. And the road silver grey, and the night warm. . . . It was mid-summer night that had done that to him. . . .

Hat mir's angethan.

Das war ein schwiegsames Reiten. . . .

Not absolutely silent of course, but silentish! Coming back from the parson's, where they had dropped the little London sewer rat, they had talked very little. . . . Not unpleasant people the parson's: an uncle of the girl's; three girl cousins, not unpleasant, like the girl, but without the individuality. . . . A remarkably good bite of beef, a truly meritorious Stilton and a drop of whisky that proved the parson to be a man. All in candlelight. A motherly mother of the family to take the rat up some stairs . . . a great deal of laughter of girls . . . then a re-start an hour later than had been scheduled. . . . Well, it hadn't mattered: they had the whole of eternity before them; the good horse — *really* it was a good horse! — putting its shoulders into the work. . . .

They had talked a little at first; about the safeness of the London girl from the police now; about the brickishness of the parson in taking her in. She certainly would never have reached Charing Cross by train. . . .

There had fallen long periods of silences. A bat had whirled very near their off-lamp.

"What a large bat!" she had said. "*Noctilux major* . . ."

He said:

"Where do you get your absurd Latin nomenclature from? Isn't it *phalæna* . . ." She had answered:

"From White . . . *The Natural History of Selborne* is the only natural history I ever read. . . ."

"He's the last English writer that could write," said Tietjens.

"He calls the downs 'those majestic and amusing mountains,'" she said. "Where do you get your dreadful Latin pronunciation from? Phal . . . i . . . i . . . na! To rhyme with Dinah!"

"Its '*sublime* and amusing mountains,' not 'majestic and amusing,'" Tietjens said. "I got my Latin pronunciation, like all public schoolboys of to-day, from the German."

She answered:

"You would! Father used to say it made him sick."

"Cæsar equals Kaiser," Tietjens said. . . .

"Bother your Germans," she said, "they're no ethnologists; they're rotten at philology!" She added: "Father used to say so," to take away from an appearance of pedantry.

A silence then! She had right over her head a rug that her aunt had lent her; a silhouette beside him, with a cocky nose turned up straight out of the descending black mass. But for the square toque she would have had the silhouette of a Manchester cotton-hand: the toque gave it a different line; like the fillet of Diana. It was piquant and agreeable to ride beside a quite silent lady in the darkness of the thick Weald that let next to no moonlight through. The horse's hoofs went clock, clock: a good horse. The near lamp illuminated the russet figure of a man with a sack on his back, pressed into the hedge, a blinking lurcher beside him.

"Keeper between the blankets!" Tietjens said to himself: "All these south country keepers sleep all night. . . . And then you give them a five quid tip for the week-end shoot. . . ." He determined that, as to that too he would put his foot down. No more week-ends with Sylvia in the mansions of the Chosen People. . . .

The girl said suddenly; they had run into a clearing of the deep underwoods:

"I'm not stuffy with you over that Latin, though you were unnecessarily rude. And I'm not sleepy. I'm loving it all."

He hesitated for a minute. It was a silly-girl thing to say. She didn't usually say silly-girl things. He ought to snub her for her own sake. . . .

He had said:

"I'm rather loving it too!" She was looking at him; her nose had disappeared from the silhouette. He hadn't been able to help it; the moon had been just above her head; unknown stars all round her; the night was warm. Besides, a really manly man may condescend at times! He rather owes it to himself. . . .

She said:

"That was nice of you! You might have hinted that the rotten drive was taking you away from your so important work. . . ."

"Oh, I can think as I drive," he said. She said:

"Oh!" and then: "The reason why I'm unconcerned over your rudeness about my Latin is that I know I'm a much better Latinist than you. You can't quote a few lines of Ovid without sprinkling howlers in. . . . It's *vastum*, not *longum* . . . 'Terra tribus scopulis vastum procurrit' . . . It's *alto*, not *caelo* . . . 'Uvidus ex alto desilientis. . . .' How could Ovid have written *ex caelo*? The 'c' after the 'x' sets your teeth on edge."

Tietjens said:

"*Excogitabo!*"

"That's purely canine!" she said with contempt.

"Besides," Tietjen said, "*longum* is much better than *vastum*. I hate cant adjectives like 'vast.' . . ."

"It's like your modesty to correct Ovid," she exclaimed. "Yet you say Ovid and Catullus were the only two Roman poets to *be* poets. That's because they *were* sentimental and used adjectives like *vastum*. . . . What's 'Sad tears mixed with kisses' but the sheerest sentimentality!"

"It ought, you know," Tietjens said with soft dangerousness, "to be 'Kisses mingled with sad tears' . . . 'Tristibus et lacrimis oscula mixta dabis.' . . ."

"I'm hanged if I ever could," she exclaimed explosively. "A man like you could die in a ditch and I'd never come near. You're desiccated even for a man who has learned his Latin from the Germans."

"Oh, well, I'm a mathematician," Tietjens said. "Classics is not my line!"

"It *isn't*," she answered tartly.

A long time afterwards from her black figure came the words:

"You used 'mingled' instead of 'mixed' to translate *mixta*. I shouldn't think you took English at Cambridge, either! Though they're as rotten at that as at everything else, father used to say."

"Your father was Balliol, of course," Tietjens said with the snuffy contempt of a scholar of Trinity College, Cambridge. But having lived most of her life amongst Balliol people she took this as a compliment and an olive branch.

Some time afterwards Tietjens, observing that her silhouette was still between him and the moon, remarked:

"I don't know if you know that for some minutes we've been running nearly due west. We ought to be going south-east by a bit south. I suppose you *do* know this road. . . ."

"Every inch of it," she said, "I've been on it over and over again on my motor-bicycle with mother in the side-car. The next cross road is called Grandfather's Wantways. We've got eleven miles and a quarter still to do. The road turns back here because of the old Sussex iron pits; it goes in and out amongst them, hundreds of them. You know the exports of the town of Rye in the eighteenth century were hops, cannon, kettles and chimney backs. The railings round St. Paul's are made of Sussex iron."

"I knew that, of course," Tietjens said: "I come of an iron county myself. Why didn't you let me run the girl over in the side-car, it would have been quicker?"

"Because," she said, "three weeks ago I smashed up the side-car on the milestone at Hog's Corner: doing forty."

"It must have been a pretty tidy smash!" Tietjens said. "Your mother wasn't aboard?"

"No," the girl said, "suffragette literature. The side-car was full. It *was* a pretty tidy smash. Hadn't you observed I still limp a little? . . ."

A few minutes later she said:

"I haven't the least notion where we really are. I clean forgot to notice the road. And I don't care. . . . Here's a signpost though; pull into it."

The lamps would not, however, shine on the arms of the post; they were burning dim and showing low. A good deal of fog was in the air. Tietjens gave the reins to the girl and got down. He took out the near light and, going back a yard or two to the signpost, examined its bewildering ghostlinesses. . . .

The girl gave a little squeak that went to his backbone; the hoofs clattered unusually; the cart went on. Tietjens went after it; it was astonishing — it had completely disappeared. Then he ran into it: ghostly, reddish and befogged. It must have got much thicker suddenly. The fog swirled all round the near lamp as he replaced it in its socket.

"Did you do that on purpose?" he asked the girl. "Or can't you hold a horse?"

"I can't drive a horse," the girl said; "I'm afraid of them. I can't drive a motor-bike either. I made that up because I *knew* you'd say you'd rather have taken Gertie over in the side-car than driven with me."

"Then do you mind," Tietjens said, "telling me if you know this road at all?"

"Not a bit!" she answered cheerfully. "I never drove it in my life. I looked it up on the map before we started because I'm sick to death of the road we went by. There's a one-horse 'bus from Rye to Tenterden, and I've walked from Tenterden to my uncle's over and over again. . . ."

"We shall probably be out all night then," Tietjens said. "Do you mind? The horse may be tired. . . ."

She said:

"Oh, the poor horse! . . . I *meant* us to be out all night. . . . But the poor horse. What a brute I was not to think of it."

"We're thirteen miles from a place called Brede; eleven and a quarter from a place whose name I couldn't read; six and three-quarters from somewhere called something like Uddlemere. . . ." Tietjens said. "This is the road to Uddlemere."

"Oh, that was Grandfather's Wantways all right," she declared. "I know it well. It's called 'Grandfather's' because an old gentleman used to sit there called Gran'fer Finn. Every Tenterden market day he used to sell fleed cakes from a basket to the carts that went by. Tenterden market was abolished in 1845 — the effect of the repeal of the Corn Laws, you know. As a Tory you ought to be interested in that."

Tietjens sat patiently. He could sympathise with her mood; she had now a heavy weight off her chest; and, if long acquaintance with his wife had not made him able to put up with feminine vagaries, nothing ever would.

"Would you mind," he said then, "telling me . . ."

"If," she interrupted, "that was really Gran'fer's Wantways: midland English. 'Vent' equals four cross-roads: high French *carrefour*. . . . Or, perhaps, that isn't the right word. But it's the way your mind works. . . ."

"You have, of course, often walked from your uncle's to Gran'fer's Wantways," Tietjens said, "with your cousins, taking brandy to the invalid in the old toll-gate house. That's how you know the story of Grandfer. You said you had never driven it; but you *have* walked it. That's the way *your* mind works, isn't it?"

She said: "*Oh!*"

"Then," Tietjens went on, "would you mind telling me — for the sake of the poor horse — whether Uddlemere is or isn't on our road home. I take it you don't know just this stretch of road, but you know whether it is the right road."

"The touch of pathos," the girl said, "is a wrong note. It's you who're in mental trouble about the road. The horse isn't. . . ."

Tietjens let the cart go on another fifty yards; then he said:

"It *is* the right road. The Uddlemere turning *was* the right one. You wouldn't let the horse go another five steps if it wasn't. You're as soppy about horses as . . . as I am."

"There's at least that bond of sympathy between us," she said drily. "Gran'fer's Wantways is six and three-quarters miles from Udimore; Udimore is exactly five from us; total, eleven and three-quarters; twelve and a quarter if you add half a mile for Udimore itself. The name is Udimore, not Uddlemere. Local place-name enthusiasts derive this from 'O'er the mere.' Absurd! Legend as follows: Church builders desiring to put church with relic of St. Rumwold in wrong place, voice wailed: 'O'er the mere.' Obviously absurd! . . . Putrid! 'O'er the' by Grimm's law impossible as 'Udi'; 'mere' not a middle Low German word at all. . . ."

"Why," Tietjens said, "are you giving me all this information?"

"Because," the girl said, "it's the way your mind works. . . . It picks up useless facts as silver after you've polished it picks up sulphur vapour; and tarnishes! It arranges the useless facts in obsolescent patterns and makes Toryism out of them. . . . I've never met a Cambridge Tory man before. I though they were all in museums and you work them up again out of bones. That's what father used to say; he was an Oxford Disraelian Conservative Imperialist. . . ."

"I know of course," Tietjens said.

"Of course you know," the girl said. "You know everything. . . . And you've worked everything into absurd principles. You think father was unsound because he tried to apply tendencies to life. *You* want to be an English country gentleman and spin principles out of the newspapers and the gossip of horse-fairs. And let the country go to hell, you'll never stir a finger except to say I told you so."

She touched him suddenly on the arm:

"*Don't* mind me!" she said. "It's reaction. I'm so happy. I'm so happy."

He said:

"That's all right! That's all right!" But for a minute or two it wasn't really. All feminine claws, he said to himself, are sheathed in velvet; but they can hurt a good deal if they touch you on the sore places of the defects of your qualities — even merely with the velvet. He added: "Your mother works you very hard."

She exclaimed:

"How you *understand*. You're amazing: for a man who tries to be a sea-anemone!" She said: "Yes, this is the first holiday I've had for four solid months; six hours a day typing; four hours a day work for the movement; three, housework and gardening; three, mother reading out her day's work for slips of the pen. And on the top of it the raid and the anxiety. . . . Dreadful anxiety, you know. Suppose mother *had* gone to prison. . . . Oh, I'd have gone mad. . . . Week-days and Sundays. . . ." She stopped: "I'm apoligising, really," she went on. "Of course I ought not to have talked to you like that. You, a great Panjandrum; saving the country with your statistics and all. . . . It *did* make you a rather awful figure, you know . . . and the relief to find you're . . . oh, a man like oneself with feet of clay. I'd dreaded this drive. I'd have dreaded it dreadfully if I hadn't been in such a dread about Gertie and the police. And, if I hadn't let off steam I should have had to jump out and run beside the cart. . . . I could still . . ."

"You couldn't," Tietjens said. "You couldn't see the cart."

They had just run into a bank of solid fog that seemed to encounter them with a soft, ubiquitous blow. It was blinding; it was deadening to sounds; it was in a sense mournful; but it was happy, too, in its romantic unusualness. They couldn't see the gleam of the lamps; they could hardly hear the step of the horse; the horse had fallen at once to a walk. They agreed that neither of them could be responsible for losing the way; in the circumstances that was impossible. Fortunately the horse would take them somewhere; it had belonged to a local higgler: a man that used the roads buying poultry for re-sale. . . . They agreed that they had no responsibilities, and after that went on for unmeasured hours in silence; the mist growing, but very, very gradually, more luminous. . . . Once or twice, at a rise in the road, they saw again the stars and the moon, but mistily. On the fourth occasion they had emerged into the silver lake; like mermen rising to the surface of a tropical sea. . . .

Tietjens had said:

"You'd better get down and take the lamp. See if you can find a milestone; I'd get down myself, but you might not be able to hold the horse. . . ." She had plunged in . . .

And he had sat, feeling he didn't know why, like a Guy Fawkes; up in the light, thinking by no means disagreeable thoughts — intent, like Miss Wannop herself, on a complete holiday of forty-eight hours; till Tuesday morning! He had to look forward to a long and luxurious day of figures; a rest after dinner; half a night more of figures; a Monday devoted to a horse-deal in the market-town where he happened to know the horse-dealer. The horse-dealer, indeed, was known to every hunting man in England! A luxurious, long argument in the atmosphere of stable-hartshorn and slow wranglings couched in ostler's epigrams. You couldn't have a better day; the beer in the pub probably good, too. Or if not that, the claret. . . . The claret in south country inns was often quite good; there was no sale for it so it got well kept. . . .

On Tuesday it would close in again, beginning with the meeting of his wife's maid at Dover. . . .

He was to have, above all, a holiday from himself and to take it like other men; free of his conventions, his strait waistcoatings. . . .

The girl said:

"I'm coming up now! I've found out something. . . ." He watched intently the place where she must appear; it would give him pointers about the impenetrability of mist to the eye.

Her otter skin cap had beads of dew; beads of dew were on her hair beneath; she scrambled up, a little awkwardly, her eyes sparkled with fun; panting a little; her cheeks bright. Her hair was darkened by the wetness of the mist, but she appeared golden in the sudden moonlight.

Before she was quite up, Tietjens almost kissed her. Almost. An all but irresistible impulse! He exclaimed:

"Steady, the Buffs!" in his surprise.

She said:

"Well, you might as well have given me a hand." "I found," she went on, "a stone that had I.R.D.C. on it, and then the lamp went out. We're not on the marsh because we're between quick hedges. That's all I've found. . . . But I've worked out what makes me so tart with you. . . ."

He couldn't believe she could be so absolutely calm: the after-wash of that impulse had been so strong in him that it was as if he had tried to catch her to him and had been foiled by her. She ought to be indignant, amused, even pleased. . . . She ought to show some emotion. . . .

She said:

"It was your silencing me with that absurd non-sequitur about the Pimlico clothing factory. It was an insult to my intelligence."

"You recognised that it was a fallacy!" Tietjens said. He was looking hard at her. He didn't know what had happened to him. She took a long look at him, cool, but with immense eyes. It was as if for a moment destiny, which usually let him creep past somehow, had looked at him. "Can't," he argued with destiny, "a man want to kiss a schoolgirl in a scuffle. . . ." His own voice, a caricature of his own voice, seemed to come to him: "Gentlemen don't . . ." He exclaimed:

"Don't gentlemen? . . ." and then stopped because he realised that he had spoken aloud.

She said:

"Oh, *gentlemen* do!" she said, "use fallacies to glide over tight places in arguments. And they browbeat schoolgirls with them. It's that, that underneath, has been exasperating me with you. You regarded me at that date — three-quarters of a day ago — as a schoolgirl."

Tietjens said:

"I don't now!" He added: "Heaven knows I don't now!"

She said: "No; you don't now!"

He said:

"It didn't need your putting up all that blue stocking erudition to convince me. . . ."

"Blue stocking!" she exclaimed contemptuously. "There's nothing of the blue stocking about me. I know Latin because father spoke it with us. It was your pompous blue socks I was pulling."

Suddenly she began to laugh. Tietjens was feeling sick, physically sick. She went on laughing. He stuttered:

"What is it?"

"The sun!" she said, pointing. Above the silver horizon was the sun; not a red sun: shining, burnished.

"I don't see . . ." Tietjens said.

"What there is to laugh at?" she asked. "It's the day! . . . The longest day's begun . . . and tomorrow's as long. . . . The summer solstice, you know. After to-morrow the days shorten towards winter. But tomorrow's as long. . . . I'm so glad . . ."

"That we've got through the night? . . ." Tietjens asked.

She looked at him for a long time. "You're not so dreadfully ugly, really," she said.

Tietjens said:

"What's that church?"

Rising out of the mist on a fantastically green knoll, a quarter of a mile away, was an unnoticeable place of worship; an oak shingle tower roof that shone grey like lead; an impossibly bright weather-cock, brighter than the sun. Dark elms all round it, holding wetnesses of mist.

"Icklesham!" she cried softly. "Oh, we're nearly home. Just above Mountby. . . . That's the Mountby drive. . . ."

Trees existed, black and hoary with the dripping mist. Trees in the hedgerow and the avenue that led to Mountby; it made a right-angle just before coming into the road and the road went away at right-angles across the gate.

"You'll have to pull to the left before you reach the avenue," the girl said. "Or as like as not the horse will walk right up to the house. The higgler who had him used to buy Lady Claudine's eggs."

Tietjens exclaimed barbarously:

"Damn Mountby. I wish we'd never come near it," and he whipped the horse into a sudden trot. The hoofs sounded suddenly loud. She placed her hand on his gloved driving hand. Had it been his flesh she wouldn't have done it.

She said:

"My dear, it couldn't have lasted for ever . . . But you're a good man. And very clever. . . . You will get through. . . .",

Not ten yards ahead Tietjen saw a tea-tray, the underneath of a black-lacquered tea-tray, gliding towards them, mathematically straight, just rising from the mist. He shouted, mad, the blood in his head. His shout was drowned by the scream of the horse; he had swung it to the left. The cart turned up, the horse emerged from the mist, head and shoulders, pawing. A stone sea-horse from the fountain of Versailles! Exactly that! Hanging in air for an eternity; the girl looking at it, leaning slightly forward.

The horse didn't come over backwards: he had loosened the reins. It wasn't there any more. The damndest thing that *could* happen! He had known it would happen. He said:

"We're all right now!" There was a crash and scraping like twenty tea-trays, a prolonged sound. They must be scraping along the mud-guard of the invisible car. He had the pressure of the horse's mouth; the horse was away, going hell for leather. He increased the pressure. The girl said:

"I know I'm all right with you."

They were suddenly in bright sunlight: cart, horse, commonplace hedgerows. They were going uphill: a steep brae. He wasn't certain she hadn't said: "Dear!" or "My dear!" Was it possible after so short . . . ? But it had been a long night. He was, no doubt, saving her life too. He increased his pressure on the horse's mouth gently, up to all his twelve stone, all his strength. The hill told too. Steep, white road between shaven grass banks!

Stop, damn you! Poor beast . . . The girl fell out of the cart. No! jumped clear! Out to the animal's head. It threw its head up. Nearly off her feet: she was holding the bit. . . . She couldn't! Tender mouth . . . afraid of horses. . . . He said:

"Horse cut!" Her face like a little white blanc-mange!

"Come quick," she said.

"I must hold a minute," he said, "might go off if I let go to get down. Badly cut?"

"Blood running down solid! Like an apron," she said.

He was at last at her side. It was true. But not so much like an apron. More like a red, varnished stocking. He said:

"You've a white petticoat on. Get over the hedge; jump it, and take it off . . ."

"Tear it into strips?" she asked. "Yes!"

He called to her; she was suspended halfway up the bank:

"Tear one half off first. The rest into strips."

She said: "All right!" She didn't go over the quickset as neatly as he had expected. No take off. But she was over. . . .

The horse, trembling, was looking down, its nostrils distended, at the blood pooling from its near foot. The cut was just on the shoulder. He put his left arm right over the horse's eyes. The horse stood it, almost with a sigh of relief. . . . A wonderful magnetism with horses. Perhaps with women too? God knew. He was almost certain she had said "Dear."

She said: "Here." He caught a round ball of whitish stuff. He undid it. Thank God: what sense! A long, strong, white band. What the devil was the hissing? A small, closed car with crumpled mudguards, noiseless nearly, gleaming black . . . God curse it, it passed them, stopped ten yards down . . . the horse rearing back: mad!

Clean mad . . . something like a scarlet and white cockatoo, fluttering out of the small car door . . . a general. In full tog. White feathers! Ninety medals! Scarlet coat! Black trousers with red stripe. Spurs too, by God!

Tietjens said:

"God damn you, you bloody swine. Go away!"

The apparition, past the horse's blinkers, said:

"I can, at least, hold the horse for you. I went past to get you out of Claudine's sight."

"Damn good-natured of you," Tietjens said as rudely as he could. "You'll have to pay for the horse."

The General exclaimed:

"Damn it all! Why should I? You were driving your beastly camel right into my drive."

"You never sounded your horn," Tietjens said.

"I was on private ground," the General shouted. "Besides I did." An enraged, scarlet scarecrow, very thin, he was holding the horse's bridle. Tietjens was extending the half petticoat, with a measuring eye, before the horse's chest. The General said:

"Look here! I've got to take the escort for the Royal party at St. Peter-in-Manor, Dover. They're laying the Buff's colours on the altar or something."

"You never sounded your horn," Tietjens said. "Why didn't you bring your chauffeur? He's a capable man. . . . You talk very big about the widow and child. But when it comes to robbing them of fifty quid by slaughtering their horse . . ."

The General said:

"What the devil were you doing coming into our drive at five in the morning?"

Tietjens, who had applied the half petticoat to the horse's chest, exclaimed:

"Pick up that thing and give it me." A thin roll of linen was at his feet: it had rolled down from the hedge.

"Can I leave the horse?" the General asked.

"Of course you can," Tietjens said. "If I can't quiet a horse better than you can run a car . . ."

He bound the new linen strips over the petticoat: the horse dropped its head, smelling his hand. The General, behind Tietjens, stood back on his heels, grasping his gold-mounted sword. Tietjens went on twisting and twisting the bandage.

"Look here," the General suddenly bent forward to whisper into Tietjens' ear, "what am I tell Claudine? I believe she saw the girl."

"Oh, tell her we came to ask what time you cast off your beastly otter hounds," Tietjens said; "that's a matutinal job. . . ."

The General's voice had a really pathetic intonation:

"On a Sunday!" he exclaimed. Then in a tone of relief he added: "I shall tell her you were going to early communion in Duchemin's church at Pett."

"If you want to add blasphemy to horse-slaughtering as a profession, do," Tietjens said. "But you'll have to pay for the horse."

"I'm damned if I will," the General shouted. "I tell you you were driving into my drive."

"Then I *shall*," Tietjens said, "and you know the construction you'll put on *that*."

He straightened his back to look at the horse.

"Go away," he said, "say what you like. Do what you like! But as you go through Rye send up the horse-ambulance from the vet.'s. Don't forget that. I'm going to save this horse. . . ."

"You know, Chris," the General said, "you're the most wonderful hand with a horse . . . There isn't another man in England . . ."

"I know it," Tietjens said. "Go away. And send up that ambulance. . . . There's your sister getting out of your car. . . ."

The General began:

"I've an awful lot to get explained . . ." But, at a thin scream of: "General! General!" he pressed on his sword hilt to keep it from between his long, black, scarlet-striped legs, and running to the car, pushed back into its door a befeathered, black bolster. He waved his hand to Tietjens:

"I'll send the ambulance," he called.

The horse, its upper leg swathed with criss-crosses of white through which a purple stain was slowly penetrating, stood motionless, its head hanging down, mule-like, under the blinding sun. To ease it Tietjens began to undo the trace. The girl hopped over the hedge and, scrambling down, began to help him.

"Well. *My* reputation's gone," she said cheerfully. "I know what Lady Claudine is. . . . Why did you try to quarrel with the General?"

"Oh, you'd better," Tietjens said wretchedly, "have a law-suit with him. It'll account for . . . for you not going to Mountby . . ."

"You think of everything," she said.

They wheeled the cart backwards off the motionless horse. Tietjens moved it two yards forward — to get it out of sight of its own blood. Then they sat down side by side on the slope of the bank.

"Tell me about Groby," the girl said at last.

Tietjens began to tell her about his home. . . . There was, in front of it, an avenue that turned into the road at right angles. Just like the one at Mountby.

"My great-great-grandfather made it," Tietjens said. "He liked privacy and didn't want the house visible by vulgar people on the road . . . just like the fellow who planned Mountby, no doubt. . . . But it's beastly dangerous with motors. We shall have to alter it . . . just at the bottom of a dip. We can't have horses hurt. . . . You'll see. . . ." It came suddenly into his head that he wasn't perhaps the father of the child who was actually the heir to that beloved place over which generation after generation had brooded. Ever since Dutch William! A damn Nonconformist swine!

On the bank his knees were almost level with his chin. He felt himself slipping down.

"If I ever take you there . . ." he began.

"Oh, but you never will," she said.

The child wasn't his. The heir to Groby! All his brothers were childless . . . There was a deep well in the stable yard. He had meant to teach the child how, if you dropped a pebble in, you waited to count twenty-three. And there came up a whispering roar. . . . But not his child! Perhaps he hadn't even the power to beget children. His married brothers hadn't. . . . Clumsy sobs shook him. It was the dreadful injury to the horse which had finished him. He felt as if the responsibility were his. The poor beast had trusted him and he had smashed it up. Miss Wannop had her arm over his shoulder.

"My dear!" she said, "you won't ever take me to Groby . . . It's perhaps . . . oh . . . short acquaintance; but I feel you're the splendidest . . ."

He thought: "It *is* rather short acquaintance."

He felt a great deal of pain, over which there presided the tall, eel-skin, blonde figure of his wife. . . .

The girl said:

"There's a fly coming!" and removed her arm.

A fly drew up before them with a blear-eyed driver. He said General

Campion had kicked him out of bed, from beside his old woman. He
wanted a pound to take them to Mrs. Wannop's, waked out of his
beauty sleep and all. The knacker's cart was following.

"You'll take Miss Wannop home at once," Tietjens said, "she's
got her mother's breakfast to see to. . . . I shan't leave the horse till
the knacker's van comes."

The fly-driver touched his age-green hat with his whip.

"Aye," he said thickly, putting a sovereign into his waistcoat pocket.
"Always the gentleman . . . a merciful man is merciful also to his
beast. But I wouldn't leave my little wooden 'ut, nor miss my breakfast, for no beast. . . . Some do and some . . . do not."

He drove off with the girl in the interior of his antique conveyance.

Tietjens remained on the slope of the bank, in the strong sunlight,
beside the drooping horse. It had done nearly forty miles and lost, at
last, a lot of blood.

Tietjens said:

"I suppose I could get the governor to pay fifty quid for it. They
want the money. . . ."

He said:

"But it wouldn't be playing the game!"

A long time afterwards he said:

"Damn all principles!" And then:

"But one has to keep on going. . . . Principles are like a skeleton
map of a country — you know whether you're going east or north."

The knacker's cart lumbered round the corner.

Part Two

SYLVIA TIETJENS ROSE from her end of the lunch-table and swayed along it, carrying her plate. She still wore her hair in bandeaux and her skirts as long as she possibly could; she didn't, she said, with her height, intend to be taken for a girl guide. She hadn't, in complexion, in figure or in the languor of her gestures, aged by a minute. You couldn't discover in the skin of her face any deadness; in her eyes the shade more of fatigue than she intended to express, but she had purposely increased her air of scornful insolence. That was because she felt that her hold over men increased to the measure of her coldness. Someone, she knew, had once said of a dangerous woman, that when she entered the room every woman kept her husband on the leash. It was Sylvia's pleasure to think that, before she went out of that room, all the women in it realised with mortification — that they needn't! For if coolly and distinctly she had said on entering: "Nothing doing!" as barmaids will to the enterprising, she couldn't more plainly have conveyed to the other women that she had no use for their treasured rubbish.

Once, on the edge of a cliff in Yorkshire, where the moors come above the sea, during one of the tiresome shoots that are there the fashion, a man had bidden her observe the demeanour of the herring gulls below. They were dashing from rock to rock on the cliff face, screaming, with none of the dignity of gulls. Some of them even let fall the herrings that they had caught and she saw the pieces of silver dropping into the blue motion. The man told her to look up; high, circling and continuing for a long time to circle; illuminated by the sunlight below, like a pale flame against the sky was a bird. The man told her that that was some sort of fish-eagle or hawk. Its normal habit was to chase the gulls which, in their terror, would drop their booty of herrings, whereupon the eagle would catch the fish before it struck the water. At the moment the eagle was not on duty, but the gulls were just as terrified as if it had been.

Sylvia stayed for a long time watching the convolutions of the eagle. It pleased her to see that, though nothing threatened the gulls, they yet screamed and dropped their herrings. . . . The whole affair reminded her of herself in her relationship to the ordinary women of the barnyard. . . . Not that there was the breath of a scandal against herself; that she very well knew, and it was her preoccupation just as turning down nice men — the "really nice men" of commerce — was her hobby.

She practiced every kind of "turning down" on these creatures: the really nice ones, with the Kitchener moustaches, the seal's brown eyes, the honest, thrilling voices, the clipped words, the straight backs and the admirable records — as long as you didn't enquire *too* closely. Once, in the early days of the Great Struggle, a young man — she *had* smiled at him in mistake for someone more trustable — had followed in a taxi, hard on her motor, and flushed with wine, glory and the firm conviction that all women in that lurid carnival had become common property, had burst into her door from the public stairs. . . . She had overtopped him by the forehead and before a few minutes were up she seemed to him to have become ten foot high with a gift of words that scorched his backbone and the voice of a frozen marble statue: a *chaud-froid* effect. He had come in like a stallion, red-eyed, and all his legs off the ground: he went down the stairs like a half-drowned rat, with dim eyes and really looking wet, for some reason or other.

Yet she hadn't really told him more than the way one should behave to the wives of one's brother officers then actually in the line, a point of view that, with her intimates, she daily agreed was pure bosh. But it must have seemed to him like the voice of his mother — when his mother had been much younger, of course — speaking from paradise, and his conscience had contrived the rest of his general wetness. This, however, had been melodrama and war stuff at that: it hadn't, therefore, interested her. She preferred to inflict deeper and more quiet pains.

She could, she flattered herself, tell the amount of empressment which a man would develop about herself at the first glance — the amount and the quality too. And from not vouchsafing a look at all, or a look of the barest and most incurious to some poor devil who even on introduction couldn't conceal his desires, to letting, after dinner, a measured glance travel from the right foot of a late dinner partner, diagonally up the ironed fold of the right trouser to the watch pocket, diagonally still, across the shirt front, pausing at the stud and so, rather more quickly away over the left shoulder, while the poor fellow stood appalled, with his dinner going wrong — from the milder note to the more pronounced she ran the whole gamut of "turnings down." The poor fellows next day would change their bootmakers, their sock merchants, their tailors, the designers of their dress-studs and shirts; they would sigh even to change the cut of their faces, communing seriously with their after-breakfast mirrors. But they knew in their hearts that calamity came from the fact that she hadn't deigned to look into their eyes. . . . Perhaps hadn't dared was the right word!

Sylvia, herself, would have cordially acknowledged that it might have been. She knew that, like her intimates — all the Elizabeths, Alixs, and Lady Moiras of the smooth-papered, be-photographed weekly journals — she was man-mad. It was the condition, indeed, of their intimacy as of their eligibilities for reproduction on hot-pressed paper. They went about in bands with, as it were, a cornfield of feather boas floating above them, though to be sure no one *wore* feather boas; they shortened their hairs and their skirts and flattened, as far as possible, their chest developments, which *does* give, oh, you know . . . a *certain* . . . They adopted demeanours as like as possible — and yet how unlike — to those of waitresses in tea-shops frequented by city men. And one reads in police court reports of raids what *those* are! Probably they were, in action, as respectable as any body of women; *more* respectable, probably, than the great middle class of before the war, and certainly spotless by comparison with their own upper servants whose morals, merely as recorded in the divorce court statistics — *that* she had from Tietjens — would put to shame even those of Welsh or lowland Scotch villages. Her mother was accustomed to say that she was sure her butler would get to heaven, simply because the Recording Angel, being an angel — and, as such, delicately minded — wouldn't have the face to put down, much less read out, the least venial of Morgan's offences.

And, sceptical as she was by nature, Sylvia Tietjens didn't really even believe in the capacity for immoralities of her friends. She didn't believe that any one of them was seriously what the French would call the *maîtresse en titre* of any particular man. Passion wasn't, at least, their strong suit: they left that to more — or to less — august circles. The Duke of A—— and all the little A's might be the children of the morose and passion-stricken Duke of B—— instead of the still more morose but less passionate late Duke of A——. Mr. C, the Tory statesman and late Foreign Minister, might equally be the father of all the children of the Tory Lord Chancellor E——. The Whig front benches, the gloomy and disagreeable Russells and Cavendishes trading off these — again French — *collages sérieux* against the matrimonial divagations of their own Lord F—— and Mr. G——. But those amorous of heavily titled and born front benchers were rather of august politics. The hot-pressed weekly journals never got hold of them: the parties to them didn't, for one thing, photograph well, being old, uglyish and terribly badly dressed. They were matter rather for the memoirs of the indiscreet, already written, but not to see the light for fifty years. . . .

The affairs of her own set, female front benchers of one side or other as they were, were more tenuous. If they ever came to heads, their affairs, they had rather the nature of promiscuity and took place at the country houses where bells rang at five in the morning. Sylvia had heard of such country houses, but she didn't know of any. She imagined that they might be the baronial halls of such barons of the crown as had patronymics ending in schen, stein, and baum. There were getting to be a good many of these, but Sylvia did not visit them. She had in her that much of the papist.

Certain of her more brilliant girl friends certainly made very sudden marriages; but the averages of those were not markedly higher than in the case of the daughters of doctors, solicitors, the clergy, the lord mayors, and common councilmen. They were the product usually of the more informal type of dance, of inexperience and champagne — of champagne of unaccustomed strength or of champagne taken in unusual circumstances — fasting as often as not. They were, these hasty marriages, hardly ever the result of either passion or temperamental lewdness.

In her own case — years ago now — she had certainly been taken advantage of, after champagne, by a married man called Drake. A bit of a brute she acknowledged him now to be. But after the event passion had developed: intense on her side and quite intense enough on his. When, in a scare that had been as much her mother's as her own, she had led Tietjens on and married him in Paris to be out of the way — though it was fortunate that the English Catholic church of the Avenue Hoche had been the scene of her mother's marriage also, thus establishing a precedent and an ostensible reason! — there had been dreadful scenes right up to the very night of the marriage. She had hardly to close her eyes in order to see the Paris hotel bedroom, the distorted face of Drake, who was mad with grief and jealousy, against a background of white things, flowers and the like, sent in overnight for the wedding. She knew that she had been very near death. She had wanted death.

And even now she had only to see the name of Drake in the paper — her mother's influence with the pompous front bencher of the Upper House, her cousin, had put Drake in the way of colonial promotions that were recorded in gazettes — nay, she had only involuntarily to think of that night and she would stop dead, speaking or walking, drive her nails into her palms and groan slightly. . . . She had to invent a chronic stitch in her heart to account for this groan which ended in a mumble and seemed to herself to degrade her. . . .

The miserable memory would come, ghost-like, at any time, anywhere. She would see Drake's face, dark against the white things; she would feel the thin night-gown ripping off her shoulder; but most of all she would seem, in darkness that excluded the light of any room in which she might be, to be transfused by the mental agony that there she had felt: the longing for the brute who had mangled her, the dreadful pain of the mind. The odd thing was that the sight of Drake himself, whom she had seen several times since the outbreak of the war, left her completely without emotion. She had no aversion, but no longing for him. . . . She had, nevertheless, longing, but she knew it was longing merely to experience again that dreadful feeling. And not with Drake. . . .

Her "turnings down" then of the really nice men, if it were a sport, was a sport not without a spice of danger. She imagined that, after a success, she must feel much of the exhilaration that men told her they felt after bringing off a clean right and left, and no doubt she felt some of the emotions that the same young men felt when they were out shooting with beginners. Her personal chastity she now cherished much as she cherished her personal cleanliness and persevered in her Swedish exercises after her baths before an open window, her rides afterwards, and her long nights of dancing which she would pursue in any room that was decently ventilated. Indeed, the two

sides of life were, in her mind, intimately connected: she kept herself
attractive by her skillfully selected exercises and cleanlinesses; and
the same fatigues, healthful as they were, kept her in the mood for
chastity of life. She had done so ever since her return to her husband;
and this not because of any attachment to her husband or to virtue as
such, as because she had made the pact with herself out of caprice
and meant to keep it. She *had* to have men at her feet; that was, as it
were, the price of her — purely social — daily bread as it was the price
of the daily bread of her intimates. She was, and had been for many
years, absolutely continent. And so very likely were, and had been,
all her Moiras, and Megs, and Lady Marjories — but she was perfectly
aware that they had to have, above their assemblies as it were, a light
vapour of the airs and habits of the brothel. The public demanded
that . . . a light vapour, like the slight traces of steam that she had
seen, glutinously adhering to the top of the water in the crocodile-
houses of the Zoo.

It was, indeed, the price; and she was aware that she had been lucky.
Not many of the hastily married young women of her set really kept
their heads above water *in* her set: for a season you would read that
Lady Marjorie and Captain Hunt, after her presentation at Court
on the occasion of her marriage, were to be seen at Roehampton, at
Goodwood, and the like: photographs of the young couple, striding
along with the palings of the Row behind them, would appear for a
month or so. Then the records of their fashionable doings would
transfer themselves to the lists of the attendants and attachés of distant vice-regal courts in tropics bad for the complexion. "And then
no more of he and she," as Sylvia put it.

In her case it hadn't been so bad, but it had been nearish. She had
had the advantage of being an only daughter of a very rich woman;
her husband wasn't just any Captain Hunt to stick on a vice-regal
staff. He was in a first-class office and when Angélique wrote notes
on the young menage she could — Angélique's ideas of these things
being hazy — always refer to the husband as the future Lord Chancellor or Ambassador to Vienna. And their little, frightfully expensive establishment — to which her mother, who had lived with
them had very handsomely contributed — had floated them over the
first dangerous two years. They had entertained like mad, and two
much-canvassed scandals had had their beginnings in Sylvia's small
drawing-room. She had been quite established when she had gone
off with Perowne.

And coming back had not been so difficult. She had expected it would be, but it hadn't. Tietjens had stipulated for large rooms in Gray's Inn. That hadn't seemed to her to be reasonable; but she imagined that he wanted to be near his friend and, though she had no gratitude to Tietjens for taking her back and nothing but repulsion from the idea of living in his house, as they were making a bargain, she owed it to herself to be fair. She had never swindled a railway company, brought dutiable scent past a custom-house, or represented to a second-hand dealer that her clothes were less worn than they were, though with her prestige she could actually have done this. It was fair that Tietjens should live where he wished and live there they did, their very tall windows looking straight into those of Macmaster across the Georgian quadrangle.

They had two floors of a great building, and that gave them a great deal of space, the breakfast-room, in which during the war they also lunched, was an immense room, completely lined with books that were nearly all calf-backed, with an immense mirror over an immense, carved, yellow and white marble mantelpiece, and three windows that, in their great height, with the spideriness of their divisions and their old, bulging glass — some of the panes were faintly violet in age —gave to the room an eighteenth-century distinction. It suited, she admitted, Tietjens, who was an eighteenth-century figure of the Dr. Johnson type — the only eighteenth-century type of which she knew, except for that of the beau something who wore white satin and ruffles, went to Bath, and must have been indescribably tiresome.

Above, she had a great white drawing-room, with fixings that she knew were eighteenth century and to be respected. For Tietjens — again she admitted — had a marvellous gift for old furniture; he despised it as such, but he knew it down to the ground. Once when her friend Lady Moira had been deploring the expense of having her new, little house furnished from top to toe under the advice of Sir John Robertson, the specialist (the Moiras had sold Arlington Street stock, lock and barrel to some American), Tietjens, who had come in to tea and had been listening without speaking, had said, with the soft good nature, rather sentimental in tone, that once in a blue moon he would bestow on her prettiest friends:

"You had better let me do it for you."

Taking a look round Sylvia's great drawing-room, with the white panels, the Chinese lacquer screens, the red lacquer and ormolu cabinets, and the immense blue and pink carpet (and Sylvia knew that if only for the three panels by a fellow called Fragonard, bought just before Fragonards had been boomed by the late King, her draw-ing-room was something remarkable), Lady Moira had said to Tiet-jens, rather flutteringly and almost with the voice with which she be-gan one of her affairs:

"Oh, if you only *would.*"

He had done it, and he had done it for a quarter of the estimate of Sir John Robertson. He had done it without effort, as if with a roll or two of his elephantine shoulders, for he seemed to know what was in every dealer's and auctioneer's catalogue by looking at the green halfpenny stamp on the wrapper. And, still more astonishingly, he had made love to Lady Moira — they had stopped twice with the Moiras in Gloucestershire and the Moiras had three times week-ended with Mrs. Satterthwaite as the Tietjens' *invités*. Tietjens had made love to Lady Moira quite prettily and sufficiently to tide Moira over until she was ready to begin her affair with Sir William Heathly.

For the matter of that, Sir John Robertson, the specialist in old furniture, challenged by Lady Moira to pick holes in her beautiful house, had gone there, poked his large spectacles against cabinets, smelt the varnish of table tops and bitten the backs of chairs in his ancient and short-sighted way, and had then told Lady Moira that Tietjens had bought her nothing that wasn't worth a bit more than he had given for it. This increased their respect for the old fellow: it explained his several millions. For, if the old fellow proposed to make out of a friend like Moira a profit of 300 per cent — limiting it to that out of sheer affection for a pretty woman — what wouldn't he make out of a natural — and national — enemy like a United States senator!

And the old man took a great fancy to Tietjens himself — which Tietjens, to Sylvia's bewilderment, did not resent. The old man would come in to tea and, if Tietjens were present, would stay for hours talking about old furniture. Tietjens would listen without talking. Sir John would expatiate over and over again about this to Mrs. Tietjens. It was extraordinary. Tietjens went purely by instinct: by taking a glance at a thing and chancing its price. According to Sir John one of the most remarkable feats of the furniture trade had been Tietjens' purchase of the Hemingway bureau for Lady Moira. Tiet-jens, in his dislikeful way, had bought this at a cottage sale for £3 10s., and had told Lady Moira it was the best piece she would ever possess: Lady Moira had gone to the sale with him. Other dealers present had

hardly looked at it; Tietjens certainly hadn't opened it. But at Lady
Moira's, poking his spectacles into the upper part of the glazed piece,
Sir John had put his nose straight on the little bit of inserted yellow
wood by a hinge, bearing signature, name, and date: "Jno. Hemingway, Bath, 1784." Sylvia remembered them because Sir John told her
so often. It was a lost "piece" that the furnishing world had been
after for many years.

For that exploit the old man seemed to love Tietjens. That he
loved Sylvia herself, she was quite aware. He fluttered round her
tremulously, gave fantastic entertainments in her honour and was the
only man she had never turned down. He had a harem, so it was said,
in an enormous house at Brighton or somewhere. But it was another
sort of love he bestowed on Tietjens: the rather pathetic love that the
aged bestow on their possible successors in office.

Once Sir John came in to tea and quite formally and with a sort of
portentousness announced that that was his seventy-first birthday,
and that he was a broken man. He seriously proposed that Tietjens
should come into partnership with him with the reversion of the business — not, of course, of his private fortune. Tietjens had listened
amiably, asking a detail or two of Sir John's proposed arrangement.
Then he had said, with the rather caressing voice that he now and
then bestowed on a pretty woman, that he didn't think it would do.
There would be too much beastly money about it. As a career it
would be more congenial to him than his office . . . but there was
too much beastly money about it.

Once more, a little to Sylvia's surprise — but men are queer creatures! — Sir John seemed to see this objection as quite reasonable,
though he heard it with regret and combated it feebly. He went away
with a relieved jauntiness; for, if he couldn't have Tietjens he couldn't;
and he invited Sylvia to dine with him somewhere where they were
going to have something fabulous and very nasty at about two guineas
the ounce on the menu. Something like that! And during dinner Sir
John had entertained her by singing the praises of her husband. He
said that Tietjens was much too great a gentleman to be wasted on
the old-furniture trade: that was why he hadn't persisted. But he
sent by Sylvia a message to the effect that if ever Tietjens *did* come
to be in want of money . . .

Occasionally Sylvia was worried to know why people — as they
sometimes did — told her that her husband had great gifts. To her
he was merely unaccountable. His actions and opinions seemed simply

the products of caprice — like her own; and, since she knew that most
of her own manifestations were a matter of contrariety, she abandoned the habit of thinking much about him.

But gradually and dimly she began to see that Tietjens had, at least,
a consistency of character and a rather unusual knowledge of life.
This came to her when she had to acknowledge that their move to
the Inn of Court had been a social success and had suited herself.
When they had discussed the change at Lobscheid — or rather when
Sylvia had unconditionally given in to every stipulation of Tietjens!
— he had predicted almost exactly what would happen, though it had
been the affair of her mother's cousin's opera box that had most impressed her. He had told her, at Lobscheid, that he had no intention
of interfering with her social level, and he was convinced that he was
not going to. He had thought about it a good deal.

She hadn't much listened to him. She had thought, firstly, that he
was a fool and, secondly, that he *did* mean to hurt her. And she
acknowledged that he had a certain right. If, after she had been off
with another man, she asked this one still to extend to her the honour
of his name and the shelter of his roof, she had no right to object to
his terms. Her only decent revenge on him was to live afterwards with
such equanimity as to let him know the mortification of failure.

But at Lobscheid he had talked a lot of nonsense, as it had seemed
to her: a mixture of prophecy and politics. The Chancellor of the
Exchequer of that date had been putting pressure on the great landlords; the great landlords had been replying by cutting down their
establishments and closing their town houses — not to any great extent, but enough to make a very effective gesture of it, and so as to
raise a considerable clamour from footmen and milliners. The Tietjens — both of them — were of the great landowning class: they
could adopt that gesture of shutting up their Mayfair house and going
to live in a wilderness. All the more if they made their wilderness a
thoroughly comfortable affair!

. He had counselled her to present this aspect of the matter to her
mother's cousin, the morosely portentous Rugeley. Rugeley was a
great landowner — almost the greatest of all; and he was a landowner
obsessed with a sense of his duties both to his dependents and his
even remote relatives. Sylvia had only, Tietjens said, to go to the
Duke and tell him that the Chancellor's exactions had forced them
to this move, but that they had done it partly as a protest, and the
Duke would accept it almost as a personal tribute to himself. *He*

couldn't, even as a protest, be expected to shut up Mexborough or
reduce his expenses. But, if his humbler relatives spiritedly did, he
would almost certainly make it up to them. And Rugeley's favours
were on the portentous scale of everything about him. "I shouldn't
wonder," Tietjens had said, "if he didn't lend you the Rugeley box to
entertain in."

And that is exactly what had happened.

The Duke — who must have kept a register of his remotest cousins
— had, shortly before their return to London, heard that this young
couple had parted with every prospect of a large and disagreeable
scandal. He had approached Mrs. Satterthwaite — tor whom he had
a gloomy affection — and he had been pleased to hear that the rumour was a gross libel. So that, when the young couple actually
turned up again — from Russia! — Rugeley, who perceived that they
were not only together, but to all appearances quite united, was determined not only to make it up to them, but to show, in order to
abash their libellers as signal a mark of his favour as he could without
inconvenience to himself. He, therefore, twice — being a widower
— invited Mrs. Satterthwaite to entertain for him, Sylvia to invite
the guests, and then had Mrs. Tietjens' name placed on the roll of
those who could have the Rugeley box at the opera, on application
at the Rugeley estate office, when it wasn't wanted. This was a very
great privilege and Sylvia had known how to make the most of it.

On the other hand, on the occasion of their conversation at Lobscheid, Tietjens had prophesied what at the time seemed to her a lot
of tosh. It had been two or three years before, but Tietjens had said
that about the time grouse-shooting began, in 1914, a European conflagration would take place which would shut up half the houses in
Mayfair and beggar their inhabitants. He had patiently supported his
prophecy with financial statistics as to the approaching bankruptcy of
various European powers and the growingly acquisitive skill and rapac-
ity of the inhabitants of Great Britain. She had listened to that with
some attention: it had seemed to her rather like the usual nonsense
talked in country houses — where, irritatingly, he never talked. But
she liked to be able to have a picturesque fact or two with which to
support herself when she too, to hold attention, wanted to issue moving statements as to revolutions, anarchies and strife in the offing.
And she had noticed that when she magpied Tietjens' conversations
more serious men in responsible positions were apt to argue with her
and to pay her more attention than before. . . .

And now, walking along the table with her plate in her hand, she could not but acknowledge that, triumphantly — and very comfortably for her! — Tietjens had been right! In the third year of the war it was very convenient to have a dwelling, cheap, comfortable, almost august and so easy to work that you could have, at a pinch, run it with one maid, though the faithful Hullo Central had not let it come to that yet. . . .

Being near Tietjens she lifted her plate, which contained two cold cutlets in aspic and several leaves of salad; she wavered a little to one side and, with a circular motion of her hand, let the whole contents fly at Tietjens' head. She placed the plate on the table and drifted slowly towards the enormous mirror over the fireplace.

"I'm bored," she said. "Bored! Bored!"

Tietjens had moved slightly as she had thrown. The cutlets and most of the salad leaves had gone over his shoulder. But one, couched, very green leaf was on his shoulder-strap, and the oil and vinegar from the plate — Sylvia *knew* that she took too much of all condiments — had splashed from the revers of his tunic to his green staff-badges. She was glad that she had hit him as much as that: it meant that her marksmanship had not been quite rotten. She was glad, too, that she had missed him. She was also supremely indifferent. It had occurred to her to do it and she had done it. Of that she was glad!

She looked at herself for some time in the mirror of bluish depths. She pressed her immense bandeaux with both hands on to her ears. She was all right: high-featured; alabaster complexion — but that was mostly the mirror's doing — beautiful, long, cool hands — what man's forehead wouldn't long for them? . . . And that hair! What man wouldn't think of it, unloosed on white shoulders! . . . Well, Tietjens wouldn't! Or, perhaps, he did . . . she hoped he did, curse him, for he never saw that sight. Obviously sometimes, at night, with a little whiskey taken he must want to!

She rang the bell and bade Hullo Central sweep the plateful from the carpet; Hullo Central, tall and dark, looking with wide-open eyes, motionlessly at nothing.

Sylvia went along the bookshelves, pausing over a book back, "*Vitae Hominum Notiss . . .*" in gilt, irregular capitals pressed deep into the old leather. At the first long window she supported herself by the blind-cord. She looked out and back into the room.

"There's that veiled woman!" she said, "going into eleven. . . . It's two o'clock, of course. . . ."

She looked at her husband's back hard, the clumsy khaki back that was getting round-shouldered now. Hard! She wasn't going to miss a motion or a stiffening.

"I've found out who it is!" she said, "and who she goes to. I got it out of the porter." She waited. Then she added:

"It's the woman you travelled down from Bishop's Auckland with. On the day war was declared."

Tietjens turned solidly round in his chair. She knew he would do that out of stiff politeness, so it meant nothing.

His face was whitish in the pale light, but it was always whitish since he had come back from France and passed his day in a tin hut among dust heaps. He said:

"So you saw me!" But that, too, was mere politeness.

She said:

"Of course the whole crowd of us from Claudine's saw you! It was old Campion who said she was a Mrs. . . . I've forgotten the name."

Tietjens said:

"I imagined he would know her. I saw him looking in from the corridor!"

She said:

"Is she your mistress, or only Macmaster's, or the mistress of both of you? It would be like you to have a mistress in common. . . . She's got a mad husband, hasn't she? A clergyman."

Tietjens said:

"She hasn't!"

Sylvia checked suddenly in her next questions, and Tietjens, who in these discussions never manœuvred for position, said:

"She has been Mrs. Macmaster over six months."

Sylvia said:

"She married him then the day after her husband's death."

She drew a long breath and added:

"I don't care. . . . She has been coming here every Friday for three years. . . . I tell you I shall expose her unless that little beast pays you to-morrow the money he owes you. . . . God knows you need it!" She said then hurriedly, for she didn't know how Tietjens might take that proposition:

"Mrs. Wannop rang up this morning to know who was . . . oh! . . . the evil genius of the Congress of Vienna. Who, by the by, is Mrs. Wannop's secretary? She wants to see you this afternoon. About war babies!"

Tietjens said:

"Mrs. Wannop hasn't got a secretary. It's her daughter who does her ringing-up."

"The girl," Sylvia said, "you were so potty about at that horrible afternoon Macmaster gave. Has she had a war baby by you? They all say she's your mistress."

Tietjens said:

"No, Miss Wannop isn't my mistress. Her mother has had a commission to write an article about war babies. I told her yesterday there weren't any war babies to speak of, and she's upset because she won't be able to make a sensational article. She wants to try and make me change my mind."

Sylvia said:

"It *was* Miss Wannop at that beastly affair of your friend's?" Sylvia asked. "And I suppose the woman who received was Mrs. What's-er-name: your other mistress. An unpleasant show. I don't think much of your taste. The one where all the horrible geniuses in London were? There was a man like a rabbit talked to me about how to write poetry."

"That's no good as an identification of the party," Tietjens said. "Macmaster gives a party every Friday, not Saturday. He has for years. Mrs. Macmaster goes there every Friday. To act as hostess. She has for years. Miss Wannop goes there every Friday after she has done work for her mother. To support Mrs. Macmaster. . . ."

"She has for years!" Sylvia mocked him. "And you go there every Friday! to croodle over Miss Wannop. Oh, Christopher!" — she adopted a mock pathetic voice — "I never did have much opinion of your taste . . . but not *that*! Don't let it be that. Put her back. She's too young for you. . . ."

"All the geniuses in London," Tietjens continued equably, "go to Macmaster's every Friday. He has been trusted with the job of giving away Royal Literary Bounty money: that's why they go. They go: that's why he was given his C.B."

"I should not have thought they counted," Sylvia said.

"Of course they count," Tietjens said. "They write for the Press. They can get anybody anything . . . except themselves!"

"Like you!" Sylvia said; "exactly like you! They're a lot of bribed squits."

"Oh, no," Tietjens said. "It isn't done obviously or discreditably. Don't believe that Macmaster distributes forty-pounders yearly of bounty on condition that he gets advancement. He hasn't, himself, the least idea of how it works, except by his atmosphere."

"I never knew a beastlier atmosphere," Sylvia said. "It *reeked* of rabbit's food."

"You're quite mistaken," Tietjens said; "that is the Russian leather of the backs of the specially bound presentation copies in the *large* bookcase."

"I don't know what you're talking about," Sylvia said. "What *are* presentation copies? I should have thought you'd had enough of the beastly Russian smells Kiev stunk of."

Tietjens considered for a moment.

"No! I don't remember it," he said. "Kiev? . . . Oh, it's where we were . . ."

"You put half your mother's money," Sylvia said, "into the Government of Kiev 12½ per cent. City Tramways. . . ."

At that Tietjens certainly winced, a type of wincing that Sylvia hadn't wanted.

"You're not fit to go out to-morrow," she said. "I shall wire to old Campion."

"Mrs. Duchemin," Tietjens said woodenly. "Mrs. Macmaster that is, also used to burn a little incense in the room before the parties. . . . Those Chinese stinks . . . what do they call them? Well, it doesn't matter"; he added that resignedly. Then he went on: "Don't you make any mistake. Mrs. Macmaster is a very superior woman. Enormously efficient! Tremendously respected. I shouldn't advise even you to come up against her, now she's in the saddle."

Mrs. Tietjens said:

"*That* sort of woman!"

Tietjens said:

"I don't say you ever will come up against her. Your spheres differ. But, if you do, don't. . . I say it because you seem to have got your knife into her."

"I don't like that sort of thing going on under my windows," Sylvia said.

Tietjens said:

"What sort of thing? . . . I was trying to tell you a little about Mrs. Macmaster . . . she's like the woman who was the mistress of the man who burned the other fellow's horrid book. . . . I can't remember the names."

Sylvia said quickly:

"Don't try!" In a slower tone she added: "I don't in the least want to know. . . ."

"Well, she was an Egeria!" Tietjens said. "An inspiration to the distinguished. Mrs. Macmaster is all that. The geniuses swarm round her, and with the really select ones she corresponds. She writes superior letters, about the Higher Morality usually; very delicate in feeling. Scotch naturally. When they go abroad she sends them snatches of London literary happenings; well done, mind you! And then, every now and then, she slips in something she wants Macmaster to have. But with great delicacy. . . . Say it's this C.B. . . . she transfuses into the minds of Genius One, Two and Three the idea of a C.B. for Macmaster. . . . Genius No. One lunches with the Deputy Sub-Patronage Secretary, who looks after literary honours and lunches with geniuses to get the gossip. . . ."

"Why," Sylvia said, "did you lend Macmaster all that money?" Sylvia asked. . . .

"Mind you," Tietjens continued his own speech, "it's perfectly proper. That's the way patronage *is* distributed in this country; it's the way it should be. The only clean way. Mrs. Duchemin backs Macmaster because he's a first-class fellow for his job. And *she* is an influence over the geniuses because she's a first-class person for hers. . . . She represents the higher, nicer morality for really nice Scots. Before long she will be getting tickets stopped from being sent to people for the Academy soirees. She already does it for the Royal Bounty dinners. A little later, when Macmaster is knighted for bashing the French in the eye, she'll have a tiny share in auguster assemblies. . . . Those people have to ask *somebody* for advice. Well, one day you'll want to present some débutante. And you won't get a ticket. . . ."

"Then I'm glad," Sylvia exclaimed, "that I wrote to Brownie's uncle about the woman. I was a little sorry this morning because, from what Glorvina told me, you're in such a devil of a hole. . . ."

"Who's Brownie's uncle?" Tietjens asked. "Lord . . . Lord . . . The banker! I know Brownie's in his uncle's bank."

"Port Scatho!" Sylvia said. "I wish you wouldn't act forgetting people's names. You overdo it."

Tietjens' face went a shade whiter. . . .

"Port Scatho," he said, "is the chairman of the Inn Billeting Committees, of course. And you wrote to him?"

"I'm sorry," Sylvia said. "I mean I'm sorry I said that about your forgetting. . . . I wrote to him and said that as a resident of the Inn I objected to your mistress — he knows the relationship, of course! — creeping in every Friday under a heavy veil and creeping out every Saturday at four in the morning."

"Lord Port Scatho knows about my relationship," Tietjens began.

"He saw her in your arms in the train," Sylvia said. "It upset Brownie so much he offered to shut down your overdraft and return any cheques you had out marked R.D."

"To please you?" Tietjens asked. "Do bankers do that sort of thing? It's a new light on British society."

"I suppose bankers try to please their women friends, like other men," Sylvia said. "I told him very emphatically it wouldn't please me . . . But . . ." She hesitated: "I wouldn't give him a chance to get back on you. I don't want to interfere in your affairs. But Brownie doesn't like you. . . ."

"He wants you to divorce me and marry him?" Tietjens asked.

"How did you know?" Sylvia asked indifferently. "I let him give me lunch now and then because it's convenient to have him manage my affairs, you being away. . . . But of course he hates you for being in the army. All the men who aren't hate all the men that are. And, of course, when there's a woman between them the men who aren't do all they can to do the others in. When they're bankers they have a pretty good pull. . . ."

"I suppose they have," Tietjens said, vaguely; "of course they would have. . . ."

Sylvia abandoned the blind-cord on which she had been dragging with one hand. In order that light might fall on her face and give more impressiveness to her words, for, in a minute or two, when she felt brave enough, she meant really to let him have her bad news! — she drifted to the fireplace. He followed her round, turning on his chair to give her his face.

She said:

"Look here, it's all the fault of this beastly war, isn't it? Can you deny it? . . . I mean that decent, gentlemanly fellows like Brownie have turned into beastly squits!"

"I suppose it is," Tietjens said dully. "Yes, certainly it is. You're quite right. It's the incidental degeneration of the heroic impulse: if the heroic impulse has too even a strain put on it the incidental degeneration gets the upper hand. That accounts for the Brownies . . . all the Brownies . . . turning squits. . . ."

"Then why do you go on with it?" Sylvia said. "God knows I could wangle you out if you'd back me in the least little way."

Tietjens said:

"Thanks! I prefer to remain in it. . . . How else am I to get a living? . . ."

"You know then," Sylvia exclaimed almost shrilly. "You know that they won't have you back in the office if they can find a way of getting you out. . . ."

"Oh, they'll find that!" Tietjens said. . . . He continued his other speech: "When we go to war with France," he said dully. . . . And Sylvia knew he was only now formulating his settled opinion so as not to have his active brain to give to the discussion. He must be thinking hard of the Wannop girl! With her littleness: her tweed-skirtishness. . . . A provincial miniature of herself, Sylvia Tietjens. . . . If she, then, had been miniature, provincial. . . . But Tietjens' words cut her as if she had been lashed with a dog-whip. "We shall behave more creditably," he had said, "because there will be less heroic impulse about it. We shall . . . half of us . . . be ashamed of ourselves. So there will be much less incidental degeneration."

Sylvia who, by that was listening to him, abandoned the consideration of Miss Wannop and the pretence that obsessed her, of Tietjens talking to the girl, against a background of books at Macmaster's party. She exclaimed:

"Good God! What are you talking about? . . ."

Tietjens went on:

"About our next war with France. . . . We're the natural enemies of the French. We have to make our bread either by robbing them or making catspaws of them. . . ."

Sylvia said:

"We can't! We couldn't . . ."

"We've got to!" Tietjens said. "It's the condition of our existence. We're a practically bankrupt, overpopulated, northern country; they're rich southerners, with a falling population. Towards 1930 we shall have to do what Prussia did in 1914. Our conditions will be exactly those of Prussia then. It's the . . . what is it called? . . ."

"But . . ." Sylvia cried out. "You're a Franco-maniac. . . . You're thought to be a French agent. . . . That's what's bitching your career!"

"I am?" Tietjens asked uninterestedly. He added: "Yes, that probably *would* bitch my career. . . ." He went on, with a little more animation and a little more of his mind:

"Ah! *that* will be a war worth seeing. . . . None of their drunken rat-fighting for imbecile boodlers . . ."

"It would drive mother mad!" Sylvia said.

"Oh, no it wouldn't," Tietjens said. "It will stimulate her if she is still alive. . . . Our heroes won't be drunk with wine and lechery; our squits won't stay at home and stab the heroes in the back. Our Minister for Water-closets won't keep two and a half million men in any base in order to get the votes of their women at a General Election — that's been the first evil effects of giving women the vote! With the French holding Ireland and stretching in a solid line from Bristol to Whitehall, we should hang the Minister before he had time to sign the papers. And we should be decently loyal to our Prussian allies and brothers. Our Cabinet won't hate them as they hate the French for being frugal and strong in logic and well-educated and remorselessly practical. Prussians are the sort of fellows you can be hoggish with when you want to. . . ."

Sylvia interjected violently:

"For God's sake stop it. You almost make me believe what you say is true. I tell you mother would go mad. Her greatest friend is the Duchesse Tonnerre Chateaulherault. . . ."

"Well!" Tietjens said. "Your greatest friends are the Med . . . Med . . . the Austrian officers you take chocolates and flowers to. That there was all the row about . . . we're at war with *them* and you haven't gone mad!"

"I don't know," Sylvia said. "Sometimes I think I am going mad!" She drooped. Tietjens, his face very strained, was looking at the table-cloth. He muttered: "Med . . . Met . . . Kos . . ." Sylvia said:

"Do you know a poem called *Somewhere*? It begins: 'Somewhere or other there must surely be . . .'"

Tietjens said:

"I'm sorry. No! I haven't been able to get up my poetry again."

Sylvia said:

"*Don't!*" She added: "You've got to be at the War Office at 4.15, haven't you? What's the time now?" She extremely wanted to give him her bad news before he went; she extremely wanted to put off giving it as long as she could. She wanted to reflect on the matter first; she wanted also to keep up a desultory conversation, or he might leave the room. She didn't want to have to say to him: "Wait a minute, I've something to say to you!" for she might not, at that moment, be in the mood. He said it was not yet two. He could give her an hour and a half more.

To keep the conversation going, she said:

"I suppose the Wannop girl is making bandages or being a Waac. Something forceful."

Tietjens said:

"No; she's a pacifist. As pacifist as you. Not so impulsive; but, on the other hand, she has more arguments. I should say she'll be in prison before the war's over. . . ."

"A nice time you must have between the two of us," Sylvia said. The memory of her interview with the great lady nicknamed Glorvina — though it was not at all a good nickname — was coming over her forcibly.

She said:

"I suppose you're always talking it over with her? You see her every day."

She imagined that that might keep him occupied for a minute or two. He said — she caught the sense of it only — and quite indifferently that he had tea with Mrs. Wannop every day. She had moved to a place called Bedford Park, which was near his office: not three minutes' walk. The War Office had put up a lot of huts on some public green in that neighbourhood. He only saw the daughter once a week, at most. They never talked about the war; it was too disagreeable a subject for the young woman. Or rather, too painful. . . . His talk gradually drifted into unfinished sentences.

They played that comedy occasionally, for it is impossible for two people to live in the same house and not have some common meeting ground. So they would each talk, sometimes talking at great length and with politeness, each thinking his or her thoughts till they drifted into silence.

And, since she had acquired the habit of going into retreat — with an Anglican sisterhood in order to annoy Tietjens, who hated converts and considered that the communions should not mix — Sylvia had acquired also the habit of losing herself almost completely in reveries. Thus she was now vaguely conscious that a greyish lump, Tietjens, sat at the head of a whitish expanse: the lunch-table. There were also books . . . actually she was seeing a quite different figure and other books — the books of Glorvina's husband, for the great lady had received Sylvia in that statesman's library.

Glorvina, who was the mother of two of Sylvia's absolutely most intimate friends, had sent for Sylvia. She wished, kindly and even wittily, to remonstrate with Sylvia because of her complete abstention from any patriotic activity. She offered Sylvia the address of a place in the city where she could buy wholesale and ready-made diapers for babies which Sylvia could present to some charity or other as being her own work. Sylvia said she would do nothing of the sort, and Glorvina said she would present the idea to poor Mrs. Pilsenhauser. She — Glorvina — said she spent some time every day thinking out acts of patriotism for the distressed rich with foreign names, accents or antecedents. . . .

Glorvina was a fiftyish lady with a pointed, grey face and a hard aspect; but when she was inclined to be witty or to plead earnestly she had a kind manner. The room in which they were was over a Belgravia back garden. It was lit by a skylight and the shadows from above deepened the lines of her face, accentuating the rather dusty grey of the hair as well as both the hardness and the kind manner. This very much impressed Sylvia, who was used to seeing the lady by artificial light. . . .

She said, however:

"You don't suggest, Glorvina, that I'm the distressed rich with a foreign name!"

The great lady had said:

"My dear Sylvia; it isn't so much you as your husband. Your last exploit with the Esterhazys and Metternichs has pretty well done for *him*. You forget that the present powers that be are not logical. . . ."

Sylvia remembered that she had sprung up from her leather saddle-back chair, exclaiming:

"You mean to say that those unspeakable swine think that I'm . . ."

Glorvina said patiently:

"My dear Sylvia, I've already said it's not you. It's your husband that suffers. He appears to be too good a fellow to suffer. Mr. Waterhouse says so. I don't know him myself, well."

Sylvia remembered that she had said:

"And who in the world is Mr. Waterhouse?" and, hearing that Mr. Waterhouse was a late Liberal Minister, had lost interest. She couldn't indeed, remember any of the further words of her hostess, as words. The sense of them had too much overwhelmed her. . . .

She stood now, looking at Tietjens and only occasionally seeing him, in her mind completely occupied with the effort to recapture Glorvina's own words in the desire for exactness. Usually she remembered conversations pretty well; but on this occasion her mad fury, her feeling of nausea, the pain of her own nails in her palms, an unrecoverable sequence of emotions had overwhelmed her.

She looked at Tietjens now with a sort of gloating curiosity. How was it possible that the most honourable man she knew should be so overwhelmed by foul and baseless rumours? It made you suspect that honour had, in itself, a quality of the evil eye. . . .

Tietjens, his face pallid, was fingering a piece of toast. He muttered:

"Met . . . Met . . . It's Met . . ." He wiped his brow with a table-napkin, looked at it with a start, threw it on the floor and pulled out a handkerchief. . . . He muttered: "Mett . . . Metter . . . His face illuminated itself like the face of a child listening at a shell.

Sylvia screamed with a passion of hatred:

"For God's sake say *Metternich* . . . you're driving me mad!"

When she looked at him again, his face had cleared and he was walking quickly to the telephone in the corner of the room. He asked her to excuse him and gave a number at Ealing. He said after a moment:

"Mrs. Wannop? Oh! My wife has just reminded me that Metternich was the evil genius of the Congress of Vienna. . . ." He said: "Yes! Yes!" and listened. After a time he said: "Oh, you could put it stronger than that. You could put it that the Tory determination to ruin Napoleon at all costs was one of those pieces of party imbecility that, etc. . . . Yes; Castlereagh. And of course Wellington. . . . I'm very sorry I must ring off. . . . Yes; to-morrow at 8.30 from Waterloo. . . . No; I *shan't* be seeing her again. . . . No; she's made a mistake. . . . Yes; give her my love . . . good-bye." He was reversing the earpiece to hang it up, but a high-pitched series of yelps from the instrument forced it back to his ear: "Oh! W*ar babies!*" he exclaimed. "I've already sent the statistics off to you! No! there *isn't* a marked increase of the illegitimacy rate, except in patches. The rate's appallingly high in the lowlands of Scotland; but it always *is* appallingly high there . . ." He laughed and said good-naturedly: "Oh, you're an old journalist: you won't let fifty quid go for

that . . ." He was breaking off. But: "*Or*," he suddenly exclaimed,
"here's another idea for you. The rate's about the same, probably
because of this: half the fellows who go out to France are reckless
because it's the last chance, as they see it. But the other half are
made twice as conscientious. A decent Tommie thinks twice about
leaving his girl in trouble just before he's killed. The divorce statistics are up, of course, because people will chance making new starts
within the law. Thanks . . . thanks . . ." He hung up the earpiece. . . .

Listening to that conversation had extraordinarily cleared Sylvia's
mind. She said, almost sorrowfully:

"I suppose that that's why you don't seduce that girl." And she
knew — she had known at once from the suddenly changed inflection
of Tietjens' voice when he had said "a decent Tommie thinks twice
before leaving his girl in trouble"! — that Tietjens himself had
thought twice.

She looked at him now almost incredulously, but with great coolness. Why *shouldn't* he, she asked herself, give himself a little pleasure with his girl before going to almost certain death. . . . She felt
a real, sharp pain at her heart. A poor wretch in such a devil of a
hole. . . .

She had moved to a chair close beside the fireplace and now sat
looking at him, leaning interestedly forward, as if at a garden party
she had been finding — *par impossible*! — a pastoral play not so badly
produced. Tietjens was a fabulous monster. . . .

He was a fabulous monster not because he was honourable and
virtuous. She had known several very honourable and very virtuous
men. If she had never known an honourable or virtuous woman except among her French or Austrian friends, that was, no doubt, because virtuous and honourable women did not amuse her or because,
except just for the French and Austrians, they were not Roman
Catholics. . . . But the honourable and virtuous men she had known
had usually prospered and been respected. They weren't the great
fortunes, but they were well-offish: well spoken of, of the country
gentleman type . . . Tietjens. . . .

She arranged her thoughts. To get one point settled in her mind,
she asked:

"What really happened to you in France? What is really the matter
with your memory? Or your brain, is it?"

He said carefully:

"It's half of it, an irregular piece of it, dead. Or rather pale. Without a proper blood supply. . . . So a great portion of it, in the shape of memory, has gone."

She said:

"But *you*! . . . without a brain! . . ." As this was not a question he did not answer.

His going at once to the telephone, as soon as he was in the possession of the name "Metternich," had at last convinced her that he had not been, for the last four months, acting hypochondriacal or merely lying to obtain sympathy or extended sick leave. Amongst Sylvia's friends a wangle known as shell-shock was cynically laughed at and quite approved of. Quite decent and, as far as she knew, quite brave menfolk of her women would openly boast that, when they had had enough of it over there, they would wangle a little leave or get a little leave extended by simulating this purely nominal disease, and in the general carnival of lying, lechery, drink, and howling that this affair was, to pretend to a little shell-shock had seemed to her to be almost virtuous. At any rate if a man passed his time at garden parties — or, as for the last months Tietjens had done, passed his time in a tin hut amongst dust heaps, going to tea every afternoon in order to help Mrs. Wannop with her newspaper articles — when men were so engaged they were, at least, not trying to kill each other.

She said now:

"Do you mind telling me what actually happened to you?"

He said:

"I don't know that I can very well. . . . Something burst — or 'exploded' is probably the right word — near me, in the dark. I expect you'd rather not hear about it? . . ."

"I want to!" Sylvia said.

He said:

"The point about it is that I *don't* know what happened and I don't remember what I did. There are three weeks of my life dead. . . . What I remember is being in a C.C.S. and not being able to remember my own name."

"You *mean* that?" Sylvia asked. "It's not just a way of talking?"

"No, it's not just a way of talking," Tietjens answered. "I lay in bed in the C.C.S. . . . Your friends were dropping bombs on it."

"You might not call them my friends," Sylvia said.

Tietjens said:

"I beg your pardon. One gets into a loose way of speaking. The poor bloody Huns then were dropping bombs from aeroplanes on the hospital huts. . . . I'm not suggesting they knew it was a C.C.S.; it was, no doubt, just carelessness. . . ."

"You needn't spare the Germans for me!" Sylvia said. "You needn't spare any man who has killed another man."

"I was, then, dreadfully worried," Tietjens went on. "I was composing a preface for a book on Arminianism. . . ."

"You haven't written a book!" Sylvia exclaimed eagerly, because she thought that if Tietjens took to writing a book there might be a way of his earning a living. Many people had told her that he ought to write a book.

"No, I hadn't written a book," Tietjens said, "and I didn't know what Arminianism was. . . ."

"You know perfectly well what the Arminian heresy is," Sylvia said sharply; "you explained it all to me years ago."

"Yes," Tietjens exclaimed. "Years ago I could have, but I couldn't then. I could now, but I was a little worried about it then. It's a little awkward to write a preface about a subject of which you know nothing. But it didn't seem to me to be discreditable in an army sense. . . . Still it worried me dreadfully not to know my own name. I lay and worried and worried and thought how discreditable it would appear if a nurse came along and asked me and I didn't know. Of course my name was on a luggage label tied to my collar; but I'd forgotten they did that to casualties. . . . Then a lot of people carried pieces of a nurse down the hut; the Germans' bombs had done that of course. They were still dropping about the place."

"But good heavens," Sylvia cried out, "do you mean they carried a dead nurse past you?"

"The poor dear wasn't dead," Tietjens said. "I wish she had been. Her name was Beatrice Carmichael . . . the first name I learned after my collapse. She's dead now of course. . . . That seemed to wake up a fellow on the other side of the room with a lot of blood coming through the bandages on his head. . . . He rolled out of his bed and, without a word, walked across the hut and began to strangle me. . . ."

"But this isn't believable," Sylvia said. "I'm sorry, but I can't believe it. . . . You were an officer: they *couldn't* have carried a wounded nurse under your nose. They must have known your sister Caroline was a nurse and was killed. . . ."

"Carrie!" Tietjens said, "was drowned on a hospital ship. I thank

God I didn't have to connect the other girl with her. . . . But you don't suppose that in addition to one's name, rank, unit, and date of admission they'd put that I'd lost a sister and two brothers in action and a father — of a broken heart I daresay. . . ."

"But you only lost one brother," Sylvia said. "I went into mourning for him and your sister. . . ."

"No, two," Tietjens said; "but the fellow who was strangling me was what I wanted to tell you about. He let out a number of ear-piercing shrieks and lots of orderlies came and pulled him off me and sat all over him. Then he began to shout 'Faith'! He shouted: 'Faith! . . . Faith! . . . Faith! . . .' at intervals of two seconds, as far as I could tell by my pulse, until four in the morning, when he died. . . . I don't know whether it was a religious exhortation or a woman's name, but I disliked him a good deal because he started my tortures, such as they were. . . . There had been a girl I knew called Faith. Oh, not a love affair: the daughter of my father's head gardener, a Scotsman. The point is that every time he said Faith I asked myself 'Faith . . . Faith what?' I couldn't remember the name of my father's head gardener."

Sylvia, who was thinking of other things, asked:

"What *was* the name?"

Tietjens answered:

"I don't know, I don't know to this day. . . . The point is that when I knew that I didn't know *that* name, I was as ignorant, as *uninstructed*, as a new-born babe and much more worried about it. . . . The Koran says — I've got as far as K in my reading of the Encyclopædia Britannica every afternoon at Mrs. Wannop's — 'The strong man when smitten is smitten in his pride!' . . . Of course I got King's Regs. and the M.M.L. and Infantry Field Training and all the A.C.I.s to date by heart very quickly. And that's all a British officer is really encouraged to know. . . ."

"Oh, Christopher!" Sylvia said. "You read that Encyclopædia; it's pitiful. You used to despise it so."

"That's what's meant by 'smitten in his pride,'" Tietjens said. "Of course what I read or hear now I remember. . . . But I haven't got to M, much less V. That was why I was worried about Metternich and the Congress of Vienna. I *try* to remember things on my own, but I haven't yet done so. You see it's as if a certain area of my brain had been wiped white. Occasionally one name suggests another. You noticed, when I got Metternich it suggested Castlereagh and Wellington — and even other names. . . . But that's what the Department of Statistics will get me on. When they fire me out. The real reason will be that I've served. But they'll pretend it's because I've no more general knowledge than is to be found in the Encyclopædia, or two-thirds or more or less — according to the duration of the war. . . . Or, of course, the real reason will be that I won't fake statistics to dish the French with. They asked me to, the other day, as a holiday task. And when I refused you should have seen their faces."

"Have you *really*," Sylvia asked, "lost two brothers in action?"

"Yes," Tietjens answered. "Curly and Longshanks. You never saw them because they were always in India. And they weren't noticeable. . . ."

"*Two!*" Sylvia said. "I only wrote to your father about one called Edward. And your sister Caroline. In the same letter. . . ."

"Carrie wasn't noticeable either," Tietjens said. "She did Charity Organisation Society work. . . . But I remember: you didn't like her. She was the born old maid. . . ."

"Christopher!" Sylvia asked, "do you still think your mother died of a broken heart because I left you?"

Tietjens said:

"Good God; no. I never thought so and I don't think so. I *know* she didn't."

"*Then!*" Sylvia exclaimed, "she died of a broken heart because I came back. . . . It's no good protesting that you don't think so. I remember your face when you opened the telegram at Lobscheid. Miss Wannop forwarded it from Rye. I remember the postmark. She was born to do me ill. The moment you got it I could see you thinking that you must conceal from me that you thought it was because of me she died. I could see you wondering if it wouldn't be practicable to conceal from me that she was dead. You couldn't, of course, do that because, you remember, we were to have gone to Wiesbaden and show ourselves; and we couldn't do that because we should have to be in mourning. So you took me to Russia to get out of taking me to the funeral."

"I took you to Russia," Tietjens said. "I remember it all now — because I had an order from Sir Robert Ingleby to assist the British Consul-General in preparing a Blue Book statistical table of the Government of Kiev. . . . It appeared to be the most industrially promising region in the world in those days. It isn't now, naturally. I shall never see back a penny of the money I put into it. I thought

I was clever in those days. . . . And of course, yes, the money was my mother's settlement. It comes back . . . yes, of course. . . ."

"Did you," Sylvia asked, "get out of taking me to your mother's funeral because you thought I should defile your mother's corpse by my presence? Or because you were afraid that in the presence of your mother's body you wouldn't be able to conceal from me that you thought I killed her? . . . Don't deny it. And don't get out of it by saying that you can't remember those days. You're remembering now: that I killed your mother; that Miss Wannop sent the telegram — why don't you score it against her that she sent the news? . . . Or, good God, why don't you score it against yourself, as the wrath of the Almighty, that your mother was dying while you and that girl were croodling over each other? . . . At Rye! Whilst I was at Lobscheid. . . ."

Tietjens wiped his brow with his handkerchief.

"Well, let's drop that," Sylvia said. "God knows I've no right to put a spoke in that girl's wheel or in yours. If you love each other you've a right to happiness and I daresay she'll make you happy. I can't divorce you, being a Catholic; but I won't make it difficult for you other ways, and self-contained people like you and her will manage somehow. You'll have learned the way from Macmaster and his mistress. . . . But, oh, Christopher Tietjens, have you ever considered how foully you've used *me!*"

Tietjens looked at her attentively, as if with magpie anguish.

"If," Sylvia went on with her denunciation, "you had once in our lives said to me: 'You whore! You bitch! You killed my mother. May you rot in hell for it. . . .' If you'd only once said something like it . . . about the child! About Perowne! . . . you might have done something to bring us together. . . ."

Tietjens said:

"That's, of course, true!"

"I know," Sylvia said, "you can't help it. . . . But when, in your famous county family pride — though a youngest son! — you say to yourself: And I daresay if . . . Oh, Christ! . . . you're shot in the trenches you'll say it . . . oh, between the saddle and the ground! that you never did a dishonourable action. . . . And, mind you, I believe that no other man save one has ever had more right to say it than you. . . ."

Tietjens said:

"You believe that!"

"As I hope to stand before my Redeemer," Sylvia said, "I believe it. . . . But, in the name of the Almighty, how could any woman live beside you . . . and be for ever forgiven? Or no: not forgiven; ignored! . . . Well, be proud when you die because of your honour. But, God, you be humble about . . . your errors in judgment. *You* know what it is to ride a horse for miles with too tight a curb-chain and its tongue cut almost in half. . . . You remember the groom your father had who had the trick of turning the hunters out like that. . . . And you horse-whipped him, and you've told me you've almost cried ever so often afterwards for thinking of that mare's mouth. . . . Well! Think of *this* mare's mouth sometimes! You've ridden me like that for seven years. . . ."

She stopped and then went on again:

"Don't you know, Christopher Tietjens, that there is only one man from whom a woman could take '*Neither I condemn thee*' and not hate him more than she hates the fiend! . . ."

Tietjens so looked at her that he contrived to hold her attention.

"I'd like you to let me ask you," he said, "how I could throw stones at you? I have never disapproved of your actions."

Her hands dropped dispiritedly to her sides.

"Oh, Christopher," she said, "don't carry on that old play acting. I shall never see you again, very likely, to speak to. You'll sleep with the Wannop girl to-night; you're going out to be killed to-morrow. *Let's* be straight for the next ten minutes or so. And give me your attention. The Wannop girl can spare that much if she's to have all the rest. . . ."

She could see that he was giving her his whole mind.

"As you said just now," he exclaimed slowly, "as I hope to meet my Redeemer I believe you to be a good woman. One that never did a dishonourable thing."

She recoiled a little in her chair.

"Then!" she said, "you're the wicked man I've always made believe to think you, though I didn't."

Tietjens said:

"No! . . . Let me try to put it to you as I see it."

She exclaimed:

"No! . . . I've been a wicked woman. I have ruined you. I am not going to listen to you."

He said:

"I daresay you have ruined me. That's nothing to me. I am completely indifferent."

She cried out:

"Oh! Oh! . . . Oh!" on a note of agony.

Tietjens said doggedly:

"I don't care. I can't help it. Those are — those *should* be — the conditions of life amongst decent people. When our next war comes I hope it will be fought out under those conditions. Let us, for God's sake, talk of the gallant enemy. Always. We have *got* to plunder the French or millions of our people must starve: they have *got* to resist us successfully or be wiped out. . . . It's the same with you and me. . . ."

She exclaimed:

"You mean to say that you don't think I was wicked when I . . . when I trepanned is what mother calls it? . . ."

He said loudly:

"*No!* . . . You had been let in for it by some brute. I have always held that a woman who has been let down by one man has the right — has the duty for the sake of her child — to let down a man. It becomes woman against man: against one man. I happened to be that one man: it was the will of God. But you were within your rights. I will never go back on that. Nothing will make me, ever!"

She said:

"And the others! And Perowne . . . I know you'll say that anyone is justified in doing anything as long as they are open enough about it. . . . But it killed your mother. Do you disapprove of my having killed your mother? Or you consider that I have corrupted the child. . . ."

Tietjens said:

"I don't. . . . I want to speak to you about that."

She exclaimed:

"You *don't*. . . ."

He said calmly:

"You know I don't . . . while I was certain that I was going to be here to keep him straight and an Anglican I fought your influence over him. I'm obliged to you for having brought up of yourself the considerations that I may be killed and that I am ruined. I am, I could not raise a hundred pounds between now and to-morrow. I am, therefore, obviously not the man to have sole charge of the heir of Groby."

Sylvia was saying:

"Every penny I have is at your disposal. . . ." when the maid, Hullo Central, marched up to her master and placed a card in his hand. He said:

"Tell him to wait five minutes in the drawing-room."

Sylvia said:

"Who is it?"

Tietjens answered:

"A man . . . Let's get this settled. I've never thought you corrupted the boy. You tried to teach him to tell white lies. On perfectly straight Papist lines. I have no objection to Papists and no objection to white lies for Papists. You told him once to put a frog in Marchant's bath. I've no objection to a boy's putting a frog in his nurse's bath, as such. But Marchant is an old woman, and the heir to Groby should respect old women always and old family servants in particular. . . . It hasn't, perhaps, struck you that the boy is heir to Groby. . . ."

Sylvia said:

"If . . . if your second brother is killed. . . . But your eldest brother . . ."

"He," Tietjens said, "has got a French woman near Euston station. He's lived with her for over fifteen years, of afternoons, when there were no race meetings. She'll never let him marry and she's past the child-bearing stage. So there's no one else. . . ."

Sylvia said:

"You mean that I may bring the child up as a Catholic."

Tietjens said:

"A *Roman* Catholic. . . . You'll teach him, please, to use that term before myself if I ever see him again. . . ."

Sylvia said:

"Oh, I thank God that he has softened your heart. This will take the curse off this house."

Tietjens shook his head:

"I think not," he said, "off you, perhaps. Off Groby very likely. It was, perhaps, time that there should be a Papist owner of Groby again. You've read Speldon on sacrilege about Groby? . . ."

She said:

"Yes! The first Tietjens who came over with Dutch William, the swine, was pretty bad to the Papist owners. . . ."

"He was a tough Dutchman," Tietjens said, "but let us get on!

There's enough time, but not too much. . . . I've got this man to see."

"Who is he?" Sylvia asked.

Tietjens was collecting his thoughts.

"My dear!" he said. "You'll permit me to call you 'my dear'? We're old enemies enough and we're talking about the future of our child."

Sylvia said:

"You said 'our' child, not 'the' child. . . ."

Tietjens said with a great deal of concern:

"You will forgive me for bringing it up. You might prefer to think he was Drake's child. He can't be. It would be outside the course of nature. . . . I'm as poor as I am because . . . forgive me . . . I've spent a great deal of money on tracing the movements of you and Drake before our marriage. And if it's a relief to you to know . . ."

"It *is*," Sylvia said. "I . . . I've always been too beastly shy to put the matter before a specialist, or even before mother. . . . And we women are so ignorant. . . ."

Tietjens said:

"I know . . . I know you were too shy even to think about it yourself, hard." He went into months and days; then he continued: "But it would have made no difference: a child born in wedlock is by law the father's, and if a man who's a gentleman suffers the begetting of his child he must, in decency, take the consequences; the woman and the child must come before the man, be he who he may. And worse-begotten children than ours have inherited statelier names. And I loved the little beggar with all my heart and with all my soul from the first minute I saw him. That may be the secret clue, or it may be sheer sentimentality. . . . So I fought your influence because it was Papist, while I was a whole man. But I'm not a whole man any more, and the evil eye that is on me might transfer itself to him."

He stopped and said:

"For I must to the greenwood go. Alone a banished man. . . . But have him well protected against the evil eye. . . ."

"Oh, Christopher," she said, "it's true I've not been a bad woman to the child. And I never will be. And I will keep Marchant with him till she dies. You'll tell her not to interfere with his religious instruction, and she won't. . . ."

Tietjens said with a friendly weariness:

"That's right . . . and you'll have Father . . . Father . . . the priest that was with us for a fortnight before he was born to give him his teachings. He was the best man I ever met and one of the most intelligent. It's been a great comfort to me to think of the boy as in his hands.. . ."

Sylvia stood up, her eyes blazing out of a pallid face of stone:

"Father Consett," she said, "was hung on the day they shot Casement. They dare not put it into the papers because he was a priest and all the witnesses Ulster witnesses. . . . And yet I may not say this is an accursed war."

Tietjens shook his head with the slow heaviness of an aged man.

"You may for me . . ." he said. "You might ring the bell, will you? Don't go away. . . ."

He sat with the blue gloom of that enclosed space all over him, lumped heavily in his chair.

"Speldon on sacrilege," he said, "may be right after all. You'd say so from the Tietjenses. There's not been a Tietjens since the first Lord Justice cheated the Papist Loundeses out of Groby, but died of a broken neck or of a broken heart; for all the fifteen thousand acres of good farming land and iron land, and for all the heather on the top of it. . . . What's the quotation: 'Be ye something as something and something and ye shall not escape. . . .' What is it?"

"Calumny!" Sylvia said. She spoke with intense bitterness. . . . "Chaste as ice and cold as . . . as you are. . . ."

Tietjens said:

"Yes! Yes. . . . And mind you none of the Tietjens were ever soft. Not one! They had reason for their broken hearts. . . . Take my poor father. . . ."

Sylvia said:

"*Don't!*"

"Both my brothers were killed in Indian regiments on the same day and not a mile apart. And my sister in the same week, out at sea, not so far from them. . . . Unnoticeable people. But one can be fond of unnoticeable people. . . ."

Hullo Central was at the door. Tietjens told her to ask Lord Port Scatho to step down. . . .

"You must, of course, know these details," Tietjens said, "as the mother to my father's heir. . . . My father got the three notifications on the same day. It was enough to break his heart. He only lived a month. I saw him . . ."

Sylvia screamed piercingly:

"Stop! stop! stop!" She clutched at the mantelpiece to hold herself up. "Your father died of a broken heart," she said, "because your brother's best friend, Ruggles, told him you were a squit who lived on women's money and had got the daughter of his oldest friend with child. . . ."

Tietjens said:

"Oh! Ah! Yes! . . . I suspected that. I knew it, really. I suppose the poor dear knows better now. Or perhaps he doesn't. . . . It doesn't matter."

II

It has been remarked that the peculiarly English habit of self-suppression in matters of the emotions puts the Englishman at a great disadvantage in moments of unusual stresses. In the smaller matters of the general run of life he will be impeccable and not to be moved; but in sudden confrontations of anything but physical dangers he is apt — he is, indeed, almost certain — to go to pieces very badly. This, at least, was the view of Christopher Tietjens, and he very much dreaded his interview with Lord Port Scatho — because he feared that he must be near breaking point.

In electing to be peculiarly English in habits and in as much of his temperament as he could control — for, though no man can choose the land of his birth or his ancestry, he can, if he have industry and determination, so watch over himself as materially to modify his automatic habits — Tietjens had quite advisedly and of set purpose adopted a habit of behaviour that he considered to be the best in the world for the normal life. If every day and all day long you chatter at high pitch and with the logic and lucidity of the Frenchman; if you shout in self-assertion, with your hat on your stomach, bowing from a stiff spine and by implication threaten all day long to shoot your interlocutor, like the Prussian; if you are as lachrymally emotional as the Italian, or as drily and epigrammaticaly imbecile over unessentials as the American, you will have a noisy, troublesome, and thoughtless society without any of the surface calm that should distinguish the atmosphere of men when they are together. You will never have deep arm-chairs in which to sit for hours in clubs thinking of nothing at all — or of the off-theory in bowling. On the other hand, in the face of death — except at sea, by fire, railway accident

or accidental drowning in rivers; in the face of madness, passion, dishonour, or — and particularly — prolonged mental strain, you will
have all the disadvantage of the beginner at any game and may come
off very badly indeed. Fortunately death, love, public dishonour and
the like are rare occurrences in the life of the average man, so that
the great advantage would seem to have lain with English society;
at any rate before the later months of the year 1914. Death for man
came but once: the danger of death so seldom as to be practically
negligible; love of a distracting kind was a disease merely of the weak;
public dishonour for persons of position, so great was the hushing
up power of the ruling class, and the power of absorption of the re-
moter Colonies, was practically unknown.

Tietjens found himself now faced by all these things, coming upon
him cumulatively and rather suddenly, and he had before him an
interview that might cover them all and with a man whom he much
respected and very much desired not to hurt. He had to face these,
moreover, with a brain two-thirds of which felt numb. It was exactly
like that.

It was not so much that he couldn't use what brain he had as
trenchantly as ever: it was that there were whole regions of fact upon
which he could no longer call in support of his argument. His knowledge of history was still practically negligible: he knew nothing whatever of the humaner letters and, what was far worse, nothing at all
of the higher and more sensuous phases of mathematics. And the
comings back of these things was much slower than he had confessed
to Sylvia. It was with these disadvantages that he had to face Lord
Port Scatho.

Lord Port Scatho was the first man of whom Sylvia Tietjens had
thought when she had been considering of men who were absolutely
honourable, entirely benevolent . . . and rather lacking in constructive intelligence. He had inherited the management of one of the
most respected of the great London banks, so that his commercial and
social influences were very extended; he was extremely interested in
promoting Low Church interests, the reform of the divorce laws and
sports for the people, and he had a great affection for Sylvia Tietjens.
He was forty-five, beginning to put on weight, but by no means obese;
he had a large, quite round head, very high-coloured cheeks that shone
as if with frequent ablutions, and uncropped, dark moustache, dark,
very cropped, smooth hair, brown eyes, a very new grey tweed suit, a
very new grey Trilby hat, a black tie in a gold ring and very new

patent leather boots that had white calf tops. He had a wife almost the spit of himself in face, figure, probity, kindliness, and interests, except that for his interest in sports for the people she substituted that for maternity hospitals. His heir was his nephew, Mr. Brownlie, known as Brownie, who would also be physically the exact spit of his uncle, except that, not having put on flesh, he appeared to be taller and that his moustache and hair were both a little longer and more fair. This gentleman entertained for Sylvia Tietjens a gloomy and deep passion that he considered to be perfectly honourable because he desired to marry her after she had divorced her husband. Tietjens he desired to ruin because he wished to marry Mrs. Tietjens and partly because he considered Tietjens to be an undesirable person of no great means. Of this passion Lord Port Scatho was ignorant.

He now came into the Tietjens' dining-room, behind the servant, holding an open letter; he walked rather stiffly because he was very much worried. He observed that Sylvia had been crying and was still wiping her eyes. He looked round the room to see if he could see in it anything to account for Sylvia's crying. Tietjens was still sitting at the head of the lunch-table. Sylvia was rising from a chair beside the fireplace.

Lord Port Scatho said:

"I want to see you, Tietjens, for a minute on business."

Tietjens said:

"I can give you ten minutes. . . ."

Lord Port Scatho said:

"Mrs. Tietjens perhaps . . ."

He waved the open letter towards Mrs. Tietjens. Tietjens said:

"No! Mrs. Tietjens will remain." He desired to say something more friendly. He said: "Sit down."

Lord Port Scatho said:

"I shan't be stopping a minute. But really . . ." and he moved the letter, but not with so wide a gesture, towards Sylvia.

"I have no secrets from Mrs. Tietjens," Tietjens said. "Absolutely none . . ."

Lord Port Scatho said:

"No . . . No, of course not . . . But . . ."

Tietjens said:

"Similarly, Mrs. Tietjens has no secrets from me. Again absolutely none."

Sylvia said:

"I don't, of course, tell Tietjens about my maid's love affairs or what the fish costs every day."

Tietjens said:

"You'd better sit down." He added on an impulse of kindness: "As a matter of fact I was just clearing up things for Sylvia to take over . . . this command." It was part of the disagreeableness of his mental disadvantages that upon occasion he could not think of other than military phrases. He felt intense annoyance. Lord Port Scatho affected him with some of the slight nausea that in those days you felt at contact with the civilian who knew none of your thoughts, phrases, or preoccupations. He added, nevertheless equably:

"One has to clear up. I'm going out."

Lord Port Scatho said hastily:

"Yes; yes. I won't keep you. One has so many engagements in spite of the war. . . ." His eyes wandered in bewilderment. Tietjens could see them at last fixing themselves on the oil stains that Sylvia's salad dressing had left on his collar and green tabs. He said to himself that he must remember to change his tunic before he went to the War Office. He must not forget. Lord Port Scatho's bewilderment at these oil stains was such that he had lost himself in the desire to account for them. . . . You could see the slow thoughts moving inside his square, polished brown forehead. Tietjens wanted very much to help him. He wanted to say: "It's about Sylvia's letter that you've got in your hand, isn't it?" But Lord Port Scatho had entered the room with the stiffness, with the odd, high-collared sort of gait that on formal and unpleasant occasions Englishmen use when they approach each other; braced up, a little like strange dogs meeting in the street. In view of that, Tietjens couldn't say "Sylvia." . . . But it would add to the formality and unpleasantness if he said again "Mrs. Tietjens!" *That* wouldn't help Port Scatho. . . .

Sylvia said suddenly:

"You don't understand, apparently. My husband is going out to the front line. To-morrow morning. It's for the second time."

Lord Port Scatho sat down suddenly on a chair beside the table. With his fresh face and brown eyes suddenly anguished he exclaimed:

"But, my dear fellow! You! Good God!" and then to Sylvia: "I beg your pardon!" To clear his mind he said again to Tietjens: "*You!* Going out to-morrow!" And, when the idea was really there, his face suddenly cleared. He looked with a swift, averted glance at Sylvia's face and then for a fixed moment at Tietjens' oil-stained tunic. Tiet-

jens could see him explaining to himself with immense enlighten-
ment that *that* explained both Sylvia's tears and the oil on the tunic.
For Port Scatho might well imagine that officers went to the conflict
in their oldest clothes. . . .

But, if his puzzled brain cleared, his distressed mind became suddenly distressed doubly. He had to add to the distress he had felt on
entering the room and finding himself in the midst of what he took to
be a highly emotional family parting. And Tietjens knew that during
the whole war Port Scatho had never witnessed a family parting at all.
Those that were not inevitable he would avoid like the plague, and
his own nephew and all his wife's nephews were in the bank. That
was quite proper for, if the ennobled family of Brownlie were not of
the Ruling Class — who had to go! — they were of the Administrative Class, who were privileged to stay. So he had seen no partings.

Of his embarrassed hatred of them he gave immediate evidence.
For he first began several sentences of praise of Tietjens' heroism
which he was unable to finish and then getting quickly out of his
chair exclaimed:

"In the circumstances then . . . the little matter I came about
. . . I couldn't of course think . . ."

Tietjens said:

"No; don't go. The matter you came about — I know all about it
of course — had better be settled."

Port Scatho sat down again; his jaw fell slowly; under his bronzed
complexion his skin became a shade paler. He said at last:

"You know what I came about? But then . . ."

His ingenuous and kindly mind could be seen to be working with
reluctance; his athletic figure drooped. He pushed the letter that he
still held along the table-cloth towards Tietjens. He said, in the voice
of one awaiting a reprieve:

"But you *can't* be . . . aware . . . Not of this letter. . . ."

Tietjens left the letter on the cloth, from there he could read the
large handwriting on the blue-grey paper:

"Mrs. Christopher Tietjens presents her compliments to Lord
Port Scatho and the Honourable Court of Benchers of the Inn. . . ."
He wondered where Sylvia had got hold of that phraseology; he
imagined it to be fantastically wrong. He said:

"I have already told you that I know about this letter, as I have
already told you that I know — and I will add that I approve! — of
all Mrs. Tietjens' actions. . . ." With his hard blue eyes he looked

brow-beatingly into Port Scatho's soft brown orbs, knowing that he was sending the message: "Think what you please and be damned to you!"

The gentle brown things remained on his face; then they filled with an expression of deep pain. Port Scatho cried:

"But good God! Then . . ."

He looked at Tietjens again. His mind, which took refuge from life in the affairs of the Low Church, of Divorce Law Reform, and of Sports for the People, became a sea of pain at the contemplation of strong situations. His eye said:

"For heaven's sake do not tell me that Mrs. Duchemin, the mistress of your dearest friend, is the mistress of yourself, and that you take this means of wreaking a vulgar spite on them."

Tietjens, leaning heavily forward, made his eyes as enigmatic as he could; he said very slowly and very clearly:

"Mrs. Tietjens is, of course, not aware of *all* the circumstances."

Port Scatho threw himself back in his chair.

"I don't understand!" he said. "I do not understand. How am I to act? You do not wish me to act on this letter? You can't!"

Tietjens, who found himself, said:

"You had better talk to Mrs. Tietjens about that. I will say something myself later. In the meantime let me say that Mrs. Tietjens would seem to me to be quite within her rights. A lady, heavily veiled, comes here every Friday and remains until four of the Saturday morning. . . . If you are prepared to palliate the proceeding you had better do so to Mrs. Tietjens. . . ."

Port Scatho turned agitatedly on Sylvia.

"I can't, of course, palliate," he said. "God forbid. . . . But, my dear Sylvia . . . my dear Mrs. Tietjens. . . . In the case of two people so much esteemed! . . . We have, of course, argued the matter of principle. It is a part of a subject I have very much at heart: the granting of divorce . . . civil divorce, at least . . . in cases in which one of the parties to the marriage is in a lunatic asylum. I have sent you the pamphlets of E. S. P. Haynes that we publish. I know that as a Roman Catholic you hold strong views. . . . I do not, I assure you, stand for latitude. . . ." He became then simply eloquent: he really had the matter at heart, one of his sisters having been for many years married to a lunatic. He expatiated on the agonies of this situation all the more eloquently in that it was the only form of human distress which he had personally witnessed.

Sylvia took a long look at Tietjens: he imagined for counsel. He looked at her steadily for a moment, then at Port Scatho, who was earnestly turned to her, then back at her. He was trying to say:

"Listen to Port Scatho for a minute. I need time to think of my course of action!"

He needed, for the first time in his life, time to think of his course of action.

He had been thinking with his under mind ever since Sylvia had told him that she had written her letter to the benchers denouncing Macmaster and his woman; ever since Sylvia had reminded him that Mrs. Duchemin in the Edinburgh to London express of the day before the war had been in his arms, he had seen, with extraordinary clearness a great many north-country scenes though he could not affix names to all the places. The forgetfulness of the names was abnormal: he ought to know the names of places from Berwick down to the vale of York — but that he should have forgotten the incidents was normal enough. They had been of little importance: he preferred not to remember the phases of his friend's love affair; moreover, the events that happened immediately afterwards had been of a nature to make one forget quite normally what had just preceded them. That Mrs. Duchemin should be sobbing on his shoulder in a locked corridor carriage hadn't struck him as in the least important: she was the mistress of his dearest friend; she had had a very trying time for a week or so, ending in a violent, nervous quarrel with her agitated lover. She was, of course, crying off the effects of the quarrel which had been all the more shaking in that Mrs. Duchemin, like himself, had always been almost too self-contained. As a matter of fact he did not himself like Mrs. Duchemin, and he was pretty certain that she herself more than a little disliked him; so that nothing but their common feeling for Macmaster had brought them together. General Campion, however, was not to know that. . . . He had looked into the carriage in the way one does in a corridor just after the train had left. . . . He couldn't remember the name. . . . Doncaster . . . No! . . . Darlington; it wasn't that. At Darlington there was a model of the Rocket . . . or perhaps it isn't the Rocket. An immense clumsy leviathan of a locomotive by . . . by . . . The great gloomy stations of the north-going trains . . . Durham . . . No! Alnwick. . . . No! . . . Wooler . . . By God! Wooler! The junction for Bamborough. . . .

It had been in one of the castles at Bamborough that he and

Sylvia had been staying with the Sandbachs. Then . . . a name had come into his mind spontaneously! . . . Two names! . . . It was, perhaps, the turn of the tide! For the first time . . . To be marked with a red stone . . . after this: some names, sometimes, on the tip of the tongue, might come over! He had, however, to get on. . . .

The Sandbachs, then, and he and Sylvia . . . others too . . . had been in Bamborough since mid-July: Eton and Harrow at Lord's, waiting for the real house parties that would come with the 12th. . . . He repeated these names and dates to himself for the personal satisfaction of knowing that, amongst the repairs effected in his mind, these two remained: Eton and Harrow, the end of the London season: 12th of August, grouse shooting begins. . . . It was pitiful. . . .

When General Campion had come up to rejoin his sister he, Tietjens, had stopped only two days. The coolness between the two of them remained; it was the first time they had met, except in Court, after the accident. . . . For Mrs. Wannop, with grim determination, had sued the General for the loss of her horse. It had lived all right — but it was only fit to draw a lawn-mower for cricket pitches. . . . Mrs. Wannop, then, had gone bald-headed for the General, partly because she wanted the money, partly because she wanted a public reason for breaking with the Sandbachs. The General had been equally obstinate and had undoubtedly perjured himself in Court: not the best, not the most honourable, the most benevolent man in the world would not turn oppressor of the widow and orphan when his efficiency as a chauffeur was impugned or the fact brought to light that at a very dangerous turning he hadn't sounded his horn. Tietjens had sworn that he hadn't, the General that he had. There *could* not be any question of doubt, for the horn was a beastly thing that made a prolonged noise like that of a terrified peacock. . . . So Tietjens had not, till the end of that July, met the General again. It had been quite a proper thing for gentlemen to quarrel over and was quite convenient, though it had cost the General fifty pounds for the horse and, of course, a good bit over for costs. Lady Claudine had refused to interfere in the matter; she was privately of opinion that the General *hadn't* sounded his horn, but the General was both a passionately devoted and explosive brother. She had remained closely intimate with Sylvia, mildly cordial with Tietjens and had continued to ask the Wannops to such of her garden parties as the General did not attend. She was also very friendly with Mrs. Duchemin.

Tietjens and the General had met with the restrained cordiality of English gentlemen who had some years before accused each other of perjury in a motor accident. On the second morning a violent quarrel had broken out between them on the subject of whether the General had or hadn't sounded his horn. The General had ended up by shouting . . . really shouting:

"By God! If I ever get you under my command. . . ."

Tietjens remembered that he had quoted and given the number of a succinct paragraph in King's Regs. dealing with the fate of general or higher field officers who gave their subordinates bad confidential reports because of private quarrels. The General had exploded into noises that ended in laughter.

"What a rag-bag of a mind you have, Chrissie!" he said. "What's King's Regs. to you? And how do you know it's paragraph 66 or whatever you say it is? I don't." He added more seriously: "*What* a fellow you are for getting into obscure rows! What in the world do you do it for?"

That afternoon Tietjens had gone to stop, a long way up in the moors, with his son, the nurse, his sister Effie and her children. They were the last days of happiness he was to know and he hadn't known so many. He was then content. He played with his boy, who thank God, was beginning to grow healthy at last. He walked about the moors with his sister Effie, a large, plain, parson's wife, who had no conversation at all, though at times they talked of their mother. The moors were like enough to those above Groby to make them happy. They lived in a bare, grim farmhouse, drank great quantities of buttermilk and ate great quantities of Wensleydale. It was the hard, frugal life of his desire and his mind was at rest.

His mind was at rest because there was going to be a war. From the first moment of his reading the paragraph about the assassination of the Archduke Franz Ferdinand he had known that, calmly and with assurance. Had he imagined that this country would come in he would not have known a mind at rest. He loved this country for the run of its hills, the shape of its elm trees and the way the heather, running uphill to the skyline, meets the blue of the heavens. War for this country could only mean humiliation, spreading under the sunlight, an almost invisible pall over the elms, the hills, the heather, like the vapour that spread from . . . oh, Middlesbrough! We were fitted neither for defeat nor for victory; we could be true to neither friend nor foe. Not even to ourselves!

But of war for us he had no fear. He saw our Ministry sitting tight till the opportune moment and then grabbing a French channel port or a few German colonies as the price of neutrality. And he was thankful to be out of it; for his back-doorway out — his second! — was the French Foreign Legion. First Sylvia: then that! Two tremendous disciplines, for the soul and for the body.

The French he admired: for their tremendous efficiency, for their frugality of life, for the logic of their minds, for their admirable achievements in the arts, for their neglect of the industrial system, for their devotion, above all, to the eighteenth century. It would be restful to serve, if only as a slave, people who saw clearly, coldly, straight; not obliquely and with hypocrisy only such things as should deviously conduce to the standard of comfort of hogs and to lecheries winked at. . . . He would rather sit for hours on a bench in a barrack-room polishing a badge in preparation for the cruelest of route marches of immense lengths under the Algerian sun.

For, as to the Foreign Legion, he had had no illusion. You were treated not as a hero, but as a whipped dog; he was aware of all the *asticoteries*, the cruelties, the weight of the rifle, the cells. You would have six months of training in the desert and then be hurtled into the line to be massacred without remorse . . . as foreign dirt. But the prospect seemed to him one of deep peace: he had never asked for soft living and now was done with it. . . . The boy was healthy; Sylvia, with the economies they had made, very rich . . . and even at that date he was sure that, if the friction of himself, Tietjens, were removed, she would make a good mother. . . .

Obviously he might survive; but after that tremendous physical drilling what survived would not be himself, but a man with cleaned, sand-dried bones: a clear mind. His private ambition had always been for saintliness: he must be able to touch pitch and not be defiled. That he knew marked him off as belonging to the sentimental branch of humanity. He couldn't help it: Stoic or Epicurean; Caliph in the harem or Dervish desiccating in the sand; one or the other you must be. And his desire was to be a saint of the Anglican variety . . . as his mother had been, without convent, ritual, vows, or miracles to be performed by your relics! That sainthood, truly, the Foreign Legion might give you. . . . The desire of every English gentleman from Colonel Hutchinson upwards. A mysticism. . . .

Remembering the clear sunlight of those naïvetés — though in his

blue gloom he had abated no jot of the ambition — Tietjens sighed
deeply as he came back for a moment to regard his dining-room.
Really, it was to see how much time he had left in which to think
out what to say to Port Scatho. . . . Port Scatho had moved his
chair over to beside Sylvia and, almost touching her, was leaning
over and recounting the griefs of his sister who was married to a
lunatic. Tietjens gave himself again for a moment to the luxury of
self-pity. He considered that he was dull-minded, heavy, ruined, and
so calumniated that at times he believed in his own infamy, for it is
impossible to stand up for ever against the obloquy of your kind and
remain unhurt in the mind. If you hunch your shoulders too long
against a storm your shoulders will grow bowed. . . .

His mind stopped for a moment and his eyes gazed dully at Sylvia's
letter which lay open on the table-cloth. His thoughts came together,
converging on the loosely-written words:

"For the last nine months a woman . . ."

He wondered swiftly what he had already said to Port Scatho: only
that he had known of his wife's letter; not when! And that he approved! Well, on principle! He sat up. To think that one could be
brought down to thinking so slowly!

He ran swiftly over what had happened in the train from Scotland
and before. . . .

Macmaster had turned up one morning beside their breakfast
table in the farmhouse, much agitated, looking altogether too small
in a cloth cap and a new grey tweed suit. He had wanted £50 to pay
his bill with; at some place up the line above . . . above . . . Berwick suddenly flashed into Tietjens' mind. . . .

That was the geographic position. Sylvia was at Bamborough on
the coast (junction Wooler); he, himself, to the north-west, on the
moors. Macmaster to the north-east of him, just over the border, in
some circumspect beauty spot where you did not meet people. Both
Macmaster and Mrs. Duchemin would know that country and gurgle
over its beastly literary associations. . . . The Shirra! Maida! Pet
Marjorie . . . Faugh! Macmaster would, no doubt, turn an honest
penny by writing articles about it and Mrs. Duchemin would hold his
hand. . . .

She had become Macmaster's mistress, as far as Tietjens knew, after
a dreadful scene in the rectory, Duchemin having mauled his wife
like a savage dog, and Macmaster in the house. . . . It was natural:
a Sadic reaction as it were. But Tietjens rather wished they hadn't.

Now it appeared they had been spending a week together . . . or more. Duchemin by that time was in an asylum. . . .

From what Tietjens had made out they had got out of bed early one morning to take a boat and see the sunrise on some lake and had passed an agreeable day together quoting, "Since when we stand side by side only hands may meet" and other poems of Gabriel Charles Dante Rossetti, no doubt to justify their sin. On coming home they had run their boat's nose into the tea-table of the Port Scathos with Mr. Brownlie, the nephew, just getting out of a motor to join them. The Port Scatho group were spending the night at the Macmasters' hotel which backed on to the lake. It was the ordinary damn sort of thing that must happen in these islands that are only a few yards across.

The Macmasters appear to have lost their heads frightfully, although Lady Port Scatho had been as motherly as possible to Mrs. Duchemin; so motherly, indeed, that if they had not been unable to observe anything, they might have recognised the Port Scathos as backers rather than spies upon themselves. It was, no doubt, however, Brownlie who had upset them: he wasn't very civil to Macmaster, whom he knew as a friend of Tietjens. He had dashed up from London in his motor to consult his uncle, who was dashing down from the west of Scotland, about the policy of the bank in that moment of crisis. . . .

Macmaster, anyhow, did not spend the night in the hotel, but went to Jedburgh or Melrose or some such place, turning up again almost before it was light to have a frightful interview about five in the morning with Mrs. Duchemin, who, towards three, had come to a disastrous conclusion as to her condition. They had lost their nerves for the first time in their association, and they had lost them very badly indeed, the things that Mrs. Duchemin said to Macmaster seeming almost to have passed belief. . . .

Thus, when Macmaster turned up at Tietjens' breakfast, he was almost out of his mind. He wanted Tietjens to go over in the motor he had brought, pay the bill at the hotel, and travel down to town with Mrs. Duchemin, who was certainly in no condition to travel alone. Tietjens was also to make up the quarrel with Mrs. Duchemin and to lend Macmaster £50 in cash, as it was then impossible to change cheques anywhere. Tietjens got the money from his old nurse, who, because she distrusted banks, carried great sums in £5 notes in a pocket under her underpetticoat.

Macmaster, pocketing the money, had said:

"That makes exactly two thousand guineas that I owe you. I'm making arrangements to repay you next week. . . ."

Tietjens remembered that he had rather stiffened and had said: "For God's sake don't. I beg you not to. Have Duchemin properly put under trustees in lunacy, and leave his capital alone. I really beg you. You don't know what you'll be letting yourselves in for. You don't owe me anything and you can always draw on me."

Tietjens never knew what Mrs. Duchemin had done about her husband's estate over which she had at that date had a power of attorney; but he had imagined that, from that time on, Macmaster had felt a certain coldness for himself and that Mrs. Duchemin had hated him. During several years Macmaster had been borrowing hundreds at a time from Tietjens. The affair with Mrs. Duchemin had cost her lover a good deal: he had week-ended almost continuously in Rye at the expensive hostel. Moreover, the famous Friday parties for geniuses had been going on for several years now, and these had meant new furnishings, bindings, carpets, and loans to geniuses — at any rate before Macmaster had had the ear of the Royal Bounty. So the sum had grown to £2,000, and now to guineas. And, from that date, the Macmasters had not offered any repayment.

Macmaster had said that he dare not travel with Mrs. Duchemin because all London would be going south by that train. All London had. It pushed in at every conceivable and inconceivable station all down the line — it was the great rout of the 3-8-14. Tietjens had got on board at Berwick, where they were adding extra coaches, and by giving a £5 note to the guard, who hadn't been able to promise isolation for any distance, had got a locked carriage. It hadn't remained locked for long enough to let Mrs. Duchemin have her cry out — but it had apparently served to make some mischief. The Sandbach party had got on, no doubt at Wooler; the Port Scatho party somewhere else. Their petrol had run out somewhere and sales were stopped, even to bankers. Macmaster, who, after all, had travelled by the same train, hidden beneath two bluejackets, had picked up Mrs. Duchemin at King's Cross and that had seemed the end of it.

Tietjens, back in his dining-room, felt relief and also anger. He said:

"Port Scatho. Time's getting short. I'd like to deal with this letter if you don't mind."

Port Scatho came as if up out of a dream. He had found the process of attempting to convert Mrs. Tietjens to divorce law reform very
pleasant — as he always did. He said:

"Yes! . . . Oh, yes!"

Tietjens said slowly:

"If you can listen. . . . Macmaster has been married to Mrs.
Duchemin exactly nine months. . . . Have you got that? Mrs. Tietjens did not know this till this afternoon. The period Mrs. Tietjens complains of in her letter is nine months. She did perfectly
right to write the letter. As such I approve of it. If she had known
that the Macmasters were married she would not have written it.
I didn't know she was going to write it. If I had known she was
going to write it I should have requested her not to. If I had
requested her not to she would, no doubt, not have done so. I did
know of the letter at the moment of your coming in. I had heard
of it at lunch only ten minutes before. I should, no doubt, have
heard of it before, but this is the first time I have lunched at home
in four months. I have to-day had a day's leave as being warned for
foreign service. I have been doing duty at Ealing. To-day is the first
opportunity I have had for serious business conversation with Mrs.
Tietjens. . . . Have you got all that? . . ."

Port Scatho was running towards Tietjens, his hand extended, and
over his whole shining personage the air of an enraptured bridegroom. Tietjens moved his right hand a little to the right, thus elud-
ing the pink, well-fleshed hand of Port Scatho. He went on frigidly:

"You had better, in addition, know as follows: The late Mr.
Duchemin was a scathological — afterwards a homicidal — lunatic.
He had recurrent fits, usually on a Saturday morning. That was because he fasted — not abstained merely — on Fridays. On Fridays
he also drank. He had acquired the craving for drink when fasting,
from finishing the sacramental wine after communion services. That
is a not unknown occurrence. He behaved latterly with great physical
violence to Mrs. Duchemin. Mrs. Duchemin, on the other hand,
treated him with the utmost consideration and concern: she might
have had him certified much earlier, but, considering the pain that
confinement must cause him during his lucid intervals, she refrained.
I have been an eye-witness of the most excruciating heroisms on her
part. As for the behaviour of Macmaster and Mrs. Duchemin, I am
ready to certify — and I believe society accepts — that it has been
most . . . oh, circumspect and right! . . . There has been no se-

cret of their attachment to each other. I believe that their determination to behave with decency during their period of waiting has not been questioned. . . ."

Lord Port Scatho said:

"No! no! Never . . . Most . . . as you say . . . circumspect and, yes . . . right!"

"Mrs. Duchemin," Tietjens continued, "has presided at Macmaster's literary Fridays for a long time; of course since long before they were married. But, as you know, Macmaster's Fridays have been perfectly open — you might almost call them celebrated. . . ."

Lord Port Scatho said:

"Yes! yes! indeed . . . I sh'd be only too glad to have a ticket for Lady Port Scatho. . . ."

"She's only got to walk in," Tietjens said. "I'll warn them: they'll be pleased. . . . If, perhaps, you would look in to-night! They have a special party. . . . But Mrs. Macmaster was always attended by a young lady who saw her off by the last train to Rye. Or I very frequently saw her off myself, Macmaster being occupied by the weekly article that he wrote for one of the papers on Friday nights. . . . They were married on the day after Mr. Duchemin's funeral. . . ."

"You can't blame 'em!" Lord Port Scatho proclaimed.

"I don't propose to," Tietjens said. "The really frightful tortures Mrs. Duchemin had suffered justified — and indeed necessitated — her finding protection and sympathy at the earliest possible moment. They have deferred this announcement of their union partly out of respect for the usual period of mourning, partly because Mrs. Duchemin feels very strongly that, with all the suffering that is now abroad, wedding feasts and signs of rejoicing on the part of non-participants are eminently to be deprecated. Still, the little party of to-night is by way of being an announcement that they are married. . . ." He paused to reflect for a moment.

"I perfectly understand!" Lord Port Scatho exclaimed. "I perfectly approve. Believe me, I and Lady Port Scatho will do everything. . . . Everything! . . . Most admirable people. . . . Tietjens, my dear fellow, your behaviour . . . most handsome. . . ."

Tietjens said:

"Wait a minute. . . . There was an occasion in August, '14. In a place on the border. I can't remember the name. . . ."

Lord Port Scatho burst out:

"My dear fellow . . . I beg you won't . . . I beseech you not to . . ."

Tietjens went on:

"Just before then Mr. Duchemin had made an attack of an un-paralleled violence on his wife. It was that that caused his final incarceration. She was not only temporarily disfigured, but she suffered serious internal injuries and, of course, great mental disturbance. It was absolutely necessary that she should have change of scene. . . . But I think you will bear me out that, in that case too, their behaviour was . . . again, circumspect and right. . . ."

Port Scatho said:

"I know; I know . . . Lady Port Scatho and I agreed — even without knowing what you have just told me — that the poor things almost exaggerated it. . . . He slept, of course, at Jedburgh?"

Tietjens said:

"Yes! They almost exaggerated it. . . . I had to be called in to take Mrs. Duchemin home. . . . It caused, apparently, misunderstandings. . . ."

Port Scatho — full of enthusiasm at the thought that at least two unhappy victims of the hateful divorce laws had, with decency and circumspectness, found the haven of their desires — burst out:

"By God, Tietjens, if I ever hear a man say a word against you. . . . Your splendid championship of your friend. . . . Your . . . your unswerving devotion . . ."

Tietjens said:

"Wait a minute, Port Scatho, will you?" He was unbuttoning the flap of his breast pocket.

"A man who can act so splendidly in one instance," Port Scatho said. . . . "And your going to France. . . . If anyone . . . if *anyone* . . . dares . . ."

At the sight of a vellum-cornered, green-edged book in Tietjens' hand Sylvia suddenly stood up; as Tietjens took from an inner flap a cheque that had lost its freshness she made three great strides over the carpet to him.

"Oh, Chrissie! . . ." she cried out. "He hasn't . . . That beast hasn't . . ."

Tietjens answered:

"He has . . ." He handed the soiled cheque to the banker. Port Scatho looked at it with slow bewilderment.

" 'Account overdrawn,' " he read. "Brownie's . . . my nephew's handwriting. . . . To the club . . . It's . . ."

"You aren't going to take it lying down?" Sylvia said. "Oh, thank goodness, you aren't going to take it lying down."

"No! I'm not going to take it lying down," Tietjens said. "Why should I?" A look of hard suspicion came over the banker's face.

"You appear," he said, "to have been overdrawing your account. People should not overdraw their accounts. For what sum are you overdrawn?"

Tietjens handed his pass-book to Port Scatho.

"I don't understand on what principle you work," Sylvia said to Tietjens. "There are things you take lying down; this you don't."

Tietjens said:

"It doesn't matter, really. Except for the child."

Sylvia said:

"I guaranteed an overdraft for you up to a thousand pounds last Thursday. You can't be overdrawn over a thousand pounds."

"I'm not overdrawn at all," Tietjens said. "I was for about fifteen pounds yesterday. I didn't know it."

Port Scatho was turning over the pages of the pass-book, his face completely blank.

"I simply don't understand," he said. "You appear to be in credit. . . . You appear always to have been in credit except for a small sum now and then. For a day or two."

"I was overdrawn," Tietjens said, "for fifteen pounds yesterday. I should say for three or four hours: the course of a post, from my army agent to your head office. During these two or three hours your bank selected two out of six of my cheques to dishonour — both being under two pounds. The other one was sent back to my mess at Ealing, who won't, of course, give it back to me. That also is marked "account overdrawn," and in the same handwriting."

"But good God," the banker said. "That means your ruin."

"It certainly means my ruin," Tietjens said. "It was meant to."

"But," the banker said — a look of relief came into his face which had begun to assume the aspect of a broken man's — "you must have other accounts with the bank . . . a speculative one, perhaps, on which you are heavily down. . . . I don't myself attend to client's accounts, except the very huge ones, which affect the bank's policy."

"You ought to," Tietjens said. "It's the very little ones you ought to attend to, as a gentleman making his fortune out of them. I have no other account with you. I have never speculated in anything in my life. I have lost a great deal in Russian securities — a great deal for me. But so, no doubt, have you."

"Then . . . betting!" Port Scatho said.

"I never put a penny on a horse in my life," Tietjens said. "I know too much about them."

Port Scatho looked at the faces first of Sylvia, then of Tietjens. Sylvia, at least, was his very old friend. She said:

"Christopher never bets and never speculates. His personal expenses are smaller than those of any man in town. You could say he had *no* personal expenses."

Again the swift look of suspicion came into Port Scatho's open face.

"Oh," Sylvia said, "you couldn't suspect Christopher and me of being in a plot to blackmail you."

"No; I couldn't suspect that," the banker said. "But the other explanation is just as extraordinary. . . . To suspect the bank . . . the *bank.* . . . How do *you* account? . . ." He was addressing Tietjens; his round head seemed to become square, below; emotion worked on his jaws.

"I'll tell you simply this," Tietjens said. "You can then repair the matter as you think fit. Ten days ago I got my marching orders. As soon as I had handed over to the officer who relieved me I drew cheques for everything I owed — to my military tailor, the mess — for one pound twelve shillings. I had also to buy a compass and a revolver, the Red Cross orderlies having annexed mine when I was in hospital. . . ."

Port Scatho said: "Good God!"

"Don't you know they annex things?" Tietjens asked. He went on: "The total, in fact, amounted to an overdraft of fifteen pounds, but I did not think of it as such because my army agents ought to have paid my month's army pay over to you on the first. As you perceive, they have only paid it over this morning, the 13th. But, as you will see from my pass-book, they have always paid about the 13th, not the 1st. Two days ago I lunched at the club and drew that cheque for one pound fourteen shillings and sixpence: one ten for personal expenses and the four and six for lunch. . . ."

"You were, however, actually overdrawn," the banker said sharply. Tietjens said:

"Yesterday, for two hours."

"But then," Port Scatho said, "what do you want done? We'll do what we can."

Tietjens said:

"I don't know. Do what you like. You'd better make what explanation you can to the military authority. If they court martialled me it would hurt you more than me. I assure you of that. There *is* an explanation."

Port Scatho began suddenly to tremble.

"What . . . what . . . what explanation?" he said. "You . . . damn it . . . you draw this out. . . . Do you dare to say my bank. . . ." He stopped, drew his hand down his face and said: "But yet . . . you're a sensible, sound man. . . . I've heard things against you. But I don't believe them. . . . Your father always spoke very highly of you. I remember he said if you wanted money you could always draw on him through us for three or four hundred. . . . That's what makes it so incomprehensible. It's . . . it's . . ." His agitation grew on him. "It seems to strike at the very heart. . . ."

Tietjens said:

"Look here, Port Scatho. . . . I've always had a respect for you. Settle it how you like. Fix the mess up for both our sakes with any formula that's not humiliating for your bank. I've already resigned from the club. . . ."

Sylvia said: "Oh, *no*, Christopher . . . not from the *club!*"

Port Scatho started back from beside the table.

"But if you're in the right!" he said. "You *couldn't* . . . Not resign from the club. . . . I'm on the committee. . . . I'll explain to them, in the fullest, in the most generous . . ."

"You couldn't explain," Tietjens said. "You can't get ahead of rumour. . . . It's half over London at this moment. You know what the toothless old fellows of your committee are. . . . Anderson! ffolliot . . . And my brother's friend, Ruggles. . . ."

Port Scatho said:

"Your brother's friend Ruggles. . . . But look here. . . . He's something about the Court, isn't he? But look here. . . ." His mind stopped. He said: "People shouldn't overdraw. . . . But if your father said you could draw on him I'm really much concerned. . . . You're a first-rate fellow. I can tell that from your pass-book alone. . . . Nothing but cheques drawn to first-class tradesmen for reasonable amounts. The sort of pass-book I liked to see when I was a junior clerk in the bank. . . ." At that early reminiscence feelings of pathos overcame him and his mind once more stopped.

Sylvia came back into the room; they had not perceived her going. She in turn held in her hand a letter.

Tietjens said:

"Look here, Port Scatho, don't get into this state. Give me your word to do what you can when you've assured yourself the facts are as I say. I wouldn't bother you at all, it's not my line, except for Mrs. Tietjens. A man alone can live that sort of thing down, or die. But there's no reason why Mrs. Tietjens should live, tied to a bad hat, while he's living it down or dying."

"But that's not *right*," Port Scatho said, "it's not the right way to look at it. You can't pocket . . . I'm simply bewildered. . . ."

"You've no right to be bewildered," Sylvia said. "You're worrying your mind for expedients to save the reputation of your bank. We know your bank is more to you than a baby. You should look after it better, then."

Port Scatho, who had already fallen two paces away from the table, now fell two paces back, almost on top of it. Sylvia's nostrils were dilated.

She said:

"Tietjens shall not resign from your beastly club. He shall not! Your committee will request him formally to withdraw his resignation. You understand? He will withdraw it. Then he will resign for good. He is too good to mix with people like you. . . ." She paused, her chest working fast. "Do you understand what you've got to do?" she asked.

An appalling shadow of a thought went through Tietjens' mind: he would not let it come into words.

"I don't know . . ." the banker said. "I don't know that I can get the committee . . ."

"You've got to," Sylvia answered. "I'll tell you why . . . Christopher was never overdrawn. Last Thursday I instructed your people to pay a thousand pounds to my husband's account. I repeated the instruction by letter and I kept a copy of the letter witnessed by my confidential maid. I also registered the letter and have the receipt for it. . . . You can see them."

Port Scatho mumbled from over the letter:

"It's to Brownie . . . Yes, a receipt for a letter to Brownie . . ." He examined the little green slip on both sides. He said: "Last

Thursday. . . . To-day's Monday. . . . an instruction to sell North-Western stock to the amount of one thousand pounds and place to the account of . . . Then . . ."

Sylvia said:

"That'll do. . . . You can't angle for time any more. Your nephew has been in an affair of this sort before. . . . I'll tell you. Last Thursday at lunch your nephew told me that Christopher's brother's solicitors had withdrawn all the permissions for overdrafts on the books of the Groby estate. There were several to members of the family. Your nephew said that he intended to catch Christopher on the hop — that's his own expression — and dishonour the next cheque of his that came in. He said he had been waiting for the chance ever since the war and the brother's withdrawal had given it him. I begged him not to . . ."

"But, good God," the banker said, "this is unheard of . . ."

"It isn't," Sylvia said. "Christopher has had five snotty, little, miserable subalterns to defend at court martials for exactly similar cases. One was an exact reproduction of this. . . ."

"But, good God," the banker exclaimed again, "men giving their lives for their country. . . . Do you mean to say Brownlie did this out of revenge for Tietjens' defending at court martials. . . . And then . . . your thousand pounds is not shown in your husband's pass-book. . . ."

"Of course it's not," Sylvia said. "It has never been paid in. On Friday I had a formal letter from your people pointing out that North-Westerns were likely to rise and asking me to reconsider my position. The same day I sent an express telling them explicitly to do as I said. . . . Ever since then your nephew has been on the 'phone begging me not to save my husband. He was there, just now, when I went out of the room. He was also beseeching me to fly with him."

Tietjens said:

"Isn't that enough, Sylvia? It's rather torturing."

"Let them be tortured," Sylvia said. "But it appears to be enough."

Port Scatho had covered his face with both his pink hands. He had exclaimed:

"Oh, my God! Brownie again. . . ."

Tietjens' brother Mark was in the room. He was smaller, browner, and harder than Tietjens and his blue eyes protruded more. He had in one hand a bowler hat, in the other an umbrella, wore a pepper-

and-salt suit and had race-glasses slung across him. He disliked Port Scatho, who detested him. He had lately been knighted. He said:

"Hullo, Port Scatho," neglecting to salute his sister-in-law. His eyes, whilst he stood motionless, rolled a look round the room and rested on a miniature bureau that stood on a writing-table, in a recess, under and between bookshelves.

"I see you've still got that cabinet," he said to Tietjens.

Tietjens said:

"I haven't. I've sold it to Sir John Robertson. He's waiting to take it away till he has room in his collection."

Port Scatho walked, rather unsteadily, round the lunch-table and stood looking down from one of the long windows. Sylvia sat down on her chair beside the fireplace. The two brothers stood facing each other, Christopher suggesting wheat-sacks, Mark, carved wood. All round them, except for the mirror that reflected bluenesses, the gilt backs of books. Hullo Central was clearing the table.

"I hear you're going out again to-morrow," Mark said. "I want to settle some things with you."

"I'm going at nine from Waterloo," Christopher said. "I've not much time. You can walk with me to the War Office if you like."

Mark's eyes followed the black and white of the maid round the table. She went out with the tray. Christopher suddenly was reminded of Valentine Wannop clearing the table in her mother's cottage. Hullo Central was no faster about it. Mark said:

"Port Scatho! As you're there we may as well finish one point. I have cancelled my father's security for my brother's overdraft."

Port Scatho said, to the window, but loud enough:

"We all know it. To our cost."

"I wish you, however," Mark Tietjens went on, "to make over from my own account a thousand a year to my brother as he needs it. Not more than a thousand in any one year."

Port Scatho said:

"Write a letter to the bank. I don't look after clients' accounts on social occasions."

"I don't see why you don't," Mark Tietjens said. "It's the way you make your bread and butter, isn't it?"

Tietjens said:

"You may save yourself all this trouble, Mark. I am closing my account in any case."

Port Scatho spun round on his heel.

"I beg that you won't," he exclaimed. "I beg that we . . . that we may have the honour of continuing to have you draw upon us." He had the trick of convulsively working jaws; his head against the light was like the top of a rounded gate-post. He said to Mark Tietjens: "You may tell your friend, Mr. Ruggles, that your brother is empowered by me to draw on my private account . . . on my personal and private account up to any amount he needs. I say that to show my estimate of your brother; because I know he will incur no obligations he cannot discharge."

Mark Tietjens stood motionless, leaning slightly on the crook of his umbrella on the one side, on the other displaying, at arm's length, the white silk lining of his bowler hat, the lining being the brightest object in the room.

"That's your affair," he said to Port Scatho. "All I'm concerned with is to have a thousand a year paid to my brother's account till further notice."

Christopher Tietjens said, with what he knew was a sentimental voice, to Port Scatho. He was very touched; it appeared to him that with the spontaneous appearance of several names in his memory, and with this estimate of himself from the banker, his tide was turning and that this day might indeed be marked by a red stone:

"Of course, Port Scatho, I won't withdraw my wretched little account from you if you want to keep it. It flatters me that you should." He stopped and added: "I only wanted to avoid these . . . these family complications. But I suppose you can stop my brother's money being paid into my account. I don't want his money."

He said to Sylvia:

"You had better settle the other matter with Port Scatho."

To Port Scatho:

"I'm intensely obliged to you, Port Scatho. . . . You'll get Lady Port Scatho round to Macmaster's this evening if only for a minute; before eleven. . . ." And to his brother:

"Come along, Mark. I'm going down to the War Office. We can talk as we walk."

Sylvia said very nearly with timidity — and again a dark thought went over Tietjens' mind:

"Do we meet again then? . . . I know you're very busy. . . ."

Tietjens said:

"Yes. I'll come and pick you out from Lady Job's, if they don't keep me too long at the War Office. I'm dining, as you know, at Macmaster's; I don't suppose I shall stop late."

"I'd come," Sylvia said, "to Macmaster's, if you thought it was appropriate. I'd bring Claudine Sandbach and General Wade. We're only going to the Russian dancers. We'd cut off early."

Tietjens could settle that sort of thought very quickly.

"Yes, do," he said hurriedly. "It would be appreciated."

He got to the door. He came back; his brother was nearly through. He said to Sylvia, and for him the occasion was a very joyful one:

"I've worried out some of the words of that song. It runs:

> ' Somewhere or other there must surely be
> The face not seen: the voice not heard . . .'

Probably it's 'the voice not ever heard' to make up the metre. . . . I don't know the writer's name. But I hope I'll worry it all out during the day."

Sylvia had gone absolutely white.

"Don't!" she said. "Oh . . . *don't*." She added coldly: "Don't take the trouble," and wiped her tiny handkerchief across her lips as Tietjens went away.

She had heard the song at a charity concert and had cried as she heard it. She had read, afterwards, the words in the programme and had almost cried again. But she had lost the programme and had never come across the words again. The echo of them remained with her like something terrible and alluring: like a knife she would some day take out and with which she would stab herself.

III

THE TWO brothers walked twenty steps from the door along the empty Inn pavements without speaking. Each was completely expressionless. To Christopher it seemed like Yorkshire. He had a vision of Mark, standing on the lawn at Groby, in his bowler hat and with his umbrella, whilst the shooters walked over the lawn, and up the hill to the butts. Mark probably never had done that; but it was so that his image always presented itself to his brother. Mark was considering that one of the folds of his umbrella was disarranged. He seriously debated with himself whether he should unfold it at once and refold it — which was a great deal of trouble to take! — or whether he should leave it till he got to his club, where he would tell the porter to have it done at once. That would mean that he would have to walk for a mile and a quarter through London with a disarranged umbrella, which was disagreeable.

He said:

"If I were you I wouldn't let that banker fellow go about giving you testimonials of that sort."

Christopher said:

"Ah!"

He considered that, with a third of his brain in action, he was over a match for Mark, but he was tired of discussions. He supposed that some unpleasant construction would be put by his brother's friend, Ruggles, on the friendship of Port Scatho for himself. But he had no curiosity. Mark felt a vague discomfort. He said:

"You had a cheque dishonoured at the club this morning?"

Christopher said:

"Yes."

Mark waited for explanations. Christopher was pleased at the speed with which the news had travelled: it confirmed what he had said to Port Scatho. He viewed his case from outside. It was like looking at the smooth working of a mechanical model.

Mark was more troubled. Used as he had been for thirty years to the vociferous south he had forgotten that there were taciturnities still. If at his Ministry he laconically accused a transport clerk of remissness, or if he accused his French mistress — just as laconically — of putting too many condiments on his nightly mutton chop, or too much salt in the water in which she boiled his potatoes, he was used to hearing a great many excuses or negations, uttered with energy and continued for long. So he had got into the habit of considering himself almost the only laconic being in the world. He suddenly remembered with discomfort — but also with satisfaction — that his brother was his brother.

He knew nothing about Christopher, for himself. He had seemed to look at his little brother down avenues, from a distance, the child misbehaving himself. Not a true Tietjens: born very late; a mother's child, therefore, rather than a father's. The mother an admirable woman, but from the South Riding. Soft, therefore, and ample. The elder Tietjens children, when they had experienced failures, had been wont to blame their father for not marrying a woman of their

own Riding. So, for himself, he knew nothing of this boy. He was
said to be brilliant: an un-Tietjens-like quality. Akin to talkativeness!
. . . Well, he wasn't talkative. Mark said:

"What have you done with all the brass our mother left you?
Twenty thousand, wasn't it?"

They were just passing through a narrow way between Georgian
houses. In the next quadrangle Tietjens stopped and looked at his
brother. Mark stood still to be looked at. Christopher said to himself:

"This man has the right to ask these questions!"

It was as if a queer slip had taken place in a moving-picture. This
fellow had become the head of the house: he, Christopher, was the
heir. At that moment, their father, in the grave four months now,
was for the first time dead.

Christopher remembered a queer incident. After the funeral, when
they had come back from the churchyard and had lunched, Mark —
and Tietjens could now see the wooden gesture — had taken out his
cigar-case and, selecting one cigar for himself, had passed the rest
round the table. It was as if people's hearts had stopped beating.
Groby had never, till that day, been smoked in: the father had had
his twelve pipes filled and put in the rose-bushes in the drive. . . .

It had been regarded merely as a disagreeable incident, a piece of
bad taste. . . . Christopher, himself, only just back from France,
would not even have known it as such, his mind was so blank, only
the parson had whispered to him: "And Groby never smoked in till
this day."

But now! It appeared a symbol, and an absolutely right symbol.
Whether they liked it or not, here were the head of the house and
the heir. The head of the house must make his arrangements, the
heir agree or disagree; but the elder brother had the right to have his
enquiries answered.

Christopher said:

"Half the money was settled at once on my child. I lost seven
thousand in Russian securities. The rest I spent. . . ."

Mark said:

"Ah!"

They had just passed under the arch that leads into Holborn.
Mark, in turn, stopped and looked at his brother and Christopher
stood still to be inspected, looking into his brother's eyes. Mark said
to himself:

"The fellow isn't at least afraid to look at you!" He had been convinced that Christopher would be. He said:

"You spent it on women? Or where do you get the money that you spend on women?"

Christopher said:

"I never spent a penny on a woman in my life."

Mark said:

"Ah!"

They crossed Holborn and went by the backways towards Fleet Street.

Christopher said:

"When I say 'woman' I'm using the word in the ordinary sense. Of course I've given women of our own class tea or lunch and paid for their cabs. Perhaps I'd better put it that I've never — either before or after marriage — had connection with any woman other than my wife."

Mark said:

"Ah!"

He said to himself:

"Then Ruggles must be a liar." This neither distressed nor astonished him. For twenty years he and Ruggles had shared a floor of a large and rather gloomy building in Mayfair. They were accustomed to converse whilst shaving in a joint toilet-room, otherwise they did not often meet except at the club. Ruggles was attached to the Royal Court in some capacity, possibly as sub-deputy gold-stick-in-waiting. Or he might have been promoted in the twenty years. Mark Tietjens had never taken the trouble to enquire. Enormously proud and shut in on himself, he was without curiosity of any sort. He lived in London because it was immense, solitary, administrative and apparently without curiosity as to its own citizens. If he could have found, in the north, a city as vast and as distinguished by the other characteristics, he would have preferred it.

Of Ruggles he thought little or nothing. He had once heard the phrase "agreeable rattle," and he regarded Ruggles as an agreeable rattle, though he did not know what the phrase meant. Whilst they shaved Ruggles gave out the scandal of the day. He never, that is to say, mentioned a woman whose virtue was not purchasable, or a man who would not sell his wife for advancement. This matched with Mark's ideas of the south. When Ruggles aspersed the fame of a man of family from the north, Mark would stop him with:

"Oh, no. That's not true. He's a Craister of Wantley Fells," or another name, as the case might be. Half Scotchman, half Jew, Ruggles was very tall and resembled a magpie, having his head almost always on one side. Had he been English, Mark would never have shared his rooms with him; he knew indeed few Englishmen of sufficient birth and position to have that privilege, and, on the other hand, few Englishmen of birth and position would have consented to share rooms so grim and uncomfortable, so furnished with horse-hair seated mahogany, or so lit with ground-glass skylights. Coming up to town at the age of twenty-five, Mark had taken these rooms with a man called Peebles, long since dead, and he had never troubled to make any change, though Ruggles had taken the place of Peebles. The remote similarity of the names had been less disturbing to Mark Tietjens than would have been the case had the names been more different. It would have been very disagreeable, Mark often thought, to share with a man called, say, Granger. As it was he still often called Ruggles Peebles, and no harm was done. Mark knew nothing of Ruggles' origins, then — so that, in a remote way, their union resembled that of Christopher with Macmaster. But whereas Christopher would have given his satellite the shirt off his back, Mark would not have lent Ruggles more than a five-pound note, and would have turned him out of their rooms if it had not been returned by the end of the quarter. But, since Ruggles never had asked to borrow anything at all, Mark considered him an entirely honourable man. Occasionally Ruggles would talk of his determination to marry some widow or other with money, or of his influence with people in exalted stations, but, when he talked like that, Mark would not listen to him and he soon returned to stories of purchasable women and venial men.

About five months ago Mark had said one morning to Ruggles:

"You might pick up what you can about my youngest brother Christopher and let me know."

The evening before that Mark's father had called Mark to him from over the other side of the smoking-room and had said:

"You might find out what you can about Christopher. He may be in want of money. Has it occurred to you that he's the heir to the estate! After you, of course." Mr. Tietjens had aged a good deal after the deaths of his children. He said: "I suppose you won't marry?" and Mark had answered:

"No; I shan't marry. But I suppose I'm a better life than Christopher. He appears to have been a good deal knocked about out there."

Armed then with this commission Mr. Ruggles appears to have displayed extraordinary activity in preparing a Christopher Tietjens dossier. It is not often that an inveterate gossip gets a chance at a man whilst being at the same time practically shielded against the law of libel. And Ruggles disliked Christopher Tietjens with the inveterate dislike of the man who revels in gossip for the man who never gossips. And Christopher Tietjens had displayed more than his usual insolence to Ruggles. So Ruggles' coat-tails flashed round an unusual number of doors and his top-hat gleamed before an unusual number of tall portals during the next week.

Amongst others he had visited the lady known as Glorvina.

There is said to be a book, kept in a holy of holies, in which bad marks are set down against men of family and position in England. In this book Mark Tietjens and his father — in common with a great number of hard-headed Englishmen of county rank — implicitly believed. Christopher Tietjens didn't: he imagined that the activities of gentlemen like Ruggles were sufficient to stop the careers of people whom they disliked. On the other hand, Mark and his father looked abroad upon English society and saw fellows, apparently with every qualification for successful careers in one service or the other; and these fellows got no advancements, orders, titles or preferments of any kind. Just, rather mysteriously, they didn't make their marks. This they put down to the workings of the book.

Ruggles, too, not only believed in the existence of that compilation of the suspect and doomed, but believed that his hand had a considerable influence over the inscriptions in its pages. He believed that if, with more moderation and with more grounds than usual, he uttered denigrations of certain men before certain personages, it would at least do those men a great deal of harm. And, quite steadily and with, indeed, real belief in much of what he said, Ruggles had denigrated Tietjens before these personages. Ruggles could not see why Christopher had taken Sylvia back after her elopement with Perowne; he could not see why Christopher had, indeed, married Sylvia at all when she was with child by a man called Drake — just as he wasn't going to believe that Christopher could get a testimonial out of Lord Port Scatho except by the sale of Sylvia to the banker. He couldn't see anything but money or jobs at the bottom of these things. He couldn't see how Tietjens otherwise got the money to

support Mrs. Wannop, Miss Wannop and her child, and to maintain
Mrs. Duchemin and Macmaster in the style they affected, Mrs.
Duchemin being the mistress of Christopher. He simply could see
no other solution. It is, in fact, asking for trouble if you are more
altruist than the society that surrounds you.

Ruggles, however, hadn't any pointers as to whether or no or to
what degree he had really damaged his room-mate's brother. He had
talked in what he considered to be the right quarters, but he hadn't
any evidence that what he had said had got through. It was to ascertain that that he had called on the great lady, for if anybody knew,
she would.

He hadn't definitely ascertained anything, for the great lady was —
and he knew it — a great deal cleverer than himself. The great lady,
he was allowed to discover, had a real affection for Sylvia, her daughter's close friend, and she expressed real concern to hear that Christopher Tietjens wasn't getting on. Ruggles had gone to visit her
quite openly to ask whether something better couldn't be done for
the brother of the man with whom he lived. Christopher had, it was
admitted, great abilities; yet neither in his office — in which he would
surely have remained had he been satisfied with his prospects — nor
in the army did he occupy anything but a very subordinate position.
Couldn't, he asked, Glorvina do anything for him? And he added:
"It's almost as if he had a bad mark against him. . . ."

The great lady had said, with a great deal of energy, that she could
not do anything at all. The energy was meant to show how absolutely
her party had been downed, outed and jumped on by the party in
power, so that she had no influence of any sort anywhere. That was
an exaggeration; but it did Christopher Tietjens no good, since
Ruggles chose to take it to mean that Glorvina said she could do
nothing because there *was* a black mark against Tietjens in the book
of the inner circle to which — if anyone had — the great lady must
have had access.

Glorvina, on the other hand, had been awakened to concern for
Tietjens. In the existence of a book she didn't believe: she had never
seen it. But that a black mark of a metaphorical nature might have
been scored against him she was perfectly ready to believe and, when
occasion served, during the next five months, she made enquiries
about Tietjens. She came upon a Major Drake, an intelligence officer, who had access to the central depot of confidential reports upon
officers, and Major Drake showed her, with a great deal of readiness,

as a specimen, the report on Tietjens. It was of a most discouraging sort and peppered over with hieroglyphics, the main point being Tietjens' impecuniosity and his predilection for the French; and apparently for the French Royalists. There being at that date and with that Government a great deal of friction with our Allies this characteristic which earlier had earned him a certain number of soft jobs had latterly done him a good deal of harm. Glorvina carried away the definite information that Tietjens had been seconded to the French artillery as a liaison officer and had remained with them for some time, but, having been shell-shocked, had been sent back. After that a mark had been added against him: "Not to be employed as liaison officer again."

On the other hand, Sylvia's visits to Austrian officer-prisoners had also been noted to Tietjens' account and a final note added: "Not to be entrusted with any confidential work."

To what extent Major Drake himself compiled these records the great lady didn't know and didn't want to know. She was acquainted with the relationships of the parties and was aware that in certain dark, full-blooded men the passion for sexual revenge is very lasting, and she let it go at that. She discovered, however, from Mr. Waterhouse — now also in retreat — that he had a very high opinion of Tietjens' character and abilities, and that just before Waterhouse's retirement he had especially recommended Tietjens for very high promotion. That alone, in the then state of Ministerial friendships and enmities, Glorvina knew to be sufficient to ruin any man within range of Governmental influence.

She had, therefore, sent for Sylvia and had put all these matters before her, for she had too much wisdom to believe that, even supposing there should be differences between the young people, of which she had no evidence at all, Sylvia could wish to do anything but promote her husband's material interests. Moreover, sincerely benevolent as the great lady was towards this couple, she also saw that here was a possibility of damaging, at least, individuals of the party in power. A person in a relatively unimportant official position can sometimes make a very nasty stink if he is unjustly used, has determination and a small amount of powerful backing. This Sylvia, at least, certainly had.

And Sylvia had received the great lady's news with so much emotion that no one could have doubted that she was utterly devoted to her husband and would tell him all about it. This Sylvia had not as yet managed to do.

Ruggles in the meantime had collected a very full budget of news and inferences to present to Mark Tietjens whilst shaving. Mark had been neither surprised nor indignant. He had been accustomed to call all his father's children, except the brother immediately next him, "the whelps," and their concerns had been no concerns of his. They would marry, beget unimportant children who would form collateral lines of Tietjens and disappear as is the fate of sons of younger sons. And the deaths of the intermediate brothers had been so recent that Mark was not yet used to thinking of Christopher as anything but a whelp, a person whose actions might be disagreeable but couldn't matter. He said to Ruggles:

"You had better talk to my father about this. I don't know that I could keep all these particulars accurately in my head."

Ruggles had been only too pleased to, and — with to give him weight, his intimacy with the eldest son, who certified to his reliability in money matters and his qualifications for amassing details as to personalities, acts and promotions — that day, at tea at the club, in a tranquil corner, Ruggles had told Mr. Tietjens senior that Christopher's wife had been with child when he had married her; he had hushed up her elopement with Perowne and connived at other love affairs of hers to his own dishonour, and was suspected in high places of being a French agent, thus being marked down as suspect in the great book. . . . All this in order to obtain money for the support of Miss Wannop, by whom he had had a child, and to maintain Macmaster and Mrs. Duchemin on a scale unsuited to their means, Mrs. Duchemin being his mistress. The story that Tietjens had had a child by Miss Wannop was first suggested, and then supported, by the fact that in Yorkshire he certainly had a son who never appeared in Gray's Inn.

Mr. Tietjens was a reasonable man; not reasonable enough to doubt Ruggles' circumstantial history. He believed implicitly in the great book — which has been believed in by several generations of country gentlemen; he perceived that his brilliant son had made no advancement commensurate with either his brilliance or his influence; he suspected that brilliance was synonymous with reprehensible tendencies. Moreover, his old friend, General ffolliott, had definitely told him some days before that he ought to enquire into the goings on of Christopher. On being pressed ffolliott had, also definitely, stated that Christopher was suspected of very dishonourable dealings, both in money and women. Ruggles' allegations came, therefore, as a definite confirmation of suspicions that appeared only too well backed up.

He bitterly regretted that, knowing Christopher to be brilliant, he had turned the boy — as is the usual portion of younger sons — adrift, with what of a competence could be got together, to sink or swim. He had, he said to himself, always wished to keep at home and under his own eyes this boy for whom he had had especial promptings of tenderness. His wife, to whom he had been absolutely attached by a passionate devotion, had been unusually wrapped up in Christopher, because Christopher had been her youngest son, born very late. And, since his wife's death, Christopher had been especially dear to him, as if he had carried about his presence some of the radiance and illumination that had seemed to attach to his mother. Indeed, after his wife's death, Mr. Tietjens had very nearly asked Christopher and his wife to come and keep house for him at Groby, making, of course, special testamentary provision for Christopher in order to atone for his giving up his career at the Department of Statistics. His sense of justice to his other children had prevented him doing this.

What broke his heart was that Christopher should not only have seduced but should have had a child by Valentine Wannop. Very grand seigneur in his habits, Mr. Tietjens had always believed in his duty to patronise the arts and, if he had actually done little in this direction beyond purchasing some chocolate-coloured pictures of the French historic school, he had for long prided himself on what he had done for the widow and children of his old friend, Professor Wannop. He considered, and with justice, that he had made Mrs. Wannop a novelist, and he considered her to be a very great novelist. And his conviction of the guilt of Christopher was strengthened by a slight tinge of jealousy of his son, a feeling that he would not have acknowledged to himself. For, since Christopher — he didn't know how, for he had given his son no introduction — had become an intimate of the Wannop household, Mrs. Wannop had completely given up asking him, Mr. Tietjens, clamourously and constantly for advice. In return she had sung the praises of Christopher in almost extravagant terms. She had, indeed, said that if Christopher had not been almost daily in the house or at any rate at the end of the 'phone she would hardly have been able to keep on working at full pressure. This had not overpleased Mr. Tietjens. Mr. Tietjens entertained for Valentine Wannop an affection of the very deepest, the same qualities appealing to the father as appealed to the son. He had even, in spite of his sixty-odd years, seriously entertained the idea of marrying the girl. She was a lady: she would have managed Groby very well; and, although the entail on the property was very strict indeed, he would, at least, have been able to put her beyond the reach of want after his death. He had thus no doubt of his son's guilt, and he had to undergo the additional humiliation of thinking that not only had his son betrayed this radiant personality, but he had done it so clumsily as to give the girl a child and let it be known. That was unpardonable want of management in the son of a gentleman. And now this boy was his heir with a misbegotten brat to follow. Irrevocably!

All his four tall sons, then, were down. His eldest tied for good to — a quite admirable! — trollop; his two next dead; his youngest worse than dead; his wife dead of a broken heart.

A soberly but deeply religious man, Mr. Tietjens' very religion made him believe in Christopher's guilt. He knew that it is as difficult for a rich man to go to heaven as it is for a camel to go through the gate in Jerusalem called the Needle's Eye. He humbly hoped that his Maker would receive him amongst the pardoned. Then, since he was a rich — an enormously rich — man, his sufferings on this earth must be very great. . . .

From tea-time that day until it was time to catch the midnight train for Bishop's Auckland he had been occupied with his son Mark in the writing-room of the club. They had made many notes. He had seen his son Christopher, in uniform, looking broken and rather bloated, the result, no doubt, of debauch. Christopher had passed through the other end of the room and Mr. Tietjens had avoided his eye. He had caught the train and reached Groby, travelling alone. Towards dusk he had taken out a gun. He was found dead next morning, a couple of rabbits beside his body, just over the hedge from the little churchyard. He appeared to have crawled through the hedge, dragging his loaded gun, muzzle forwards, after him. Hundreds of men, mostly farmers, die from that cause every year in England. . . .

With these things in his mind — or as much of them as he could keep at once — Mark was now investigating his brother's affairs. He

would have let things go on longer, for his father's estate was by no
means wound up, but that morning Ruggles had told him that the
club had had a cheque of his brother's returned and that his brother
was going out to France next day. It was five months exactly since
the death of their father. That had happened in March, it was now
August: a bright, untidy day in narrow, high courts.

Mark arranged his thoughts.

"How much of an income," he said, "do you need to live in comfort? If a thousand isn't enough, how much? Two?"

Christopher said that he needed no money and didn't intend to
live in comfort. Mark said:

"I am to let you have three thousand, if you'll live abroad. I'm
only carrying out our father's instructions. You could cut a hell of a
splash on three thousand in France."

Christopher did not answer.

Mark began again:

"The remaining three thousand then, that was over from our
mother's money. Did you settle it on your girl, or just spend it on
her?"

Christopher repeated with patience that he hadn't got a girl.

Mark said:

"The girl who had a child by you. I'm instructed, if you haven't
settled anything already — but father took it that you would have —
I was to let her have enough to live in comfort. How much do you
suppose she'll need to live in comfort? I allow Charlotte four hundred. Would four hundred be enough? I suppose you want to go on
keeping her? Three thousand isn't a great lot for her to live on with
a child."

Christopher said:

"Hadn't you better mention names?"

Mark said:

"No! I never mention names. I mean a woman writer and her
daughter. I suppose the girl is father's daughter, isn't she?"

Christopher said:

"No. She couldn't be. I've thought of it. She's twenty-seven. We
were all in Dijon for the two years before she was born. Father didn't
come into the estate till next year. The Wannops were also in Canada
at the time. Professor Wannop was principal of a university there.
I forget the name."

Mark said:

"So we were. In Dijon! For my French!" He added: "Then she can't be father's daughter. Its a good thing. I thought, as he wanted to settle money on them, they were very likely his children. There's a son, too. He's to have a thousand. What's he doing?"

"The son," Tietjens said, "is a conscientious objector. He's on a mine-sweeper. A bluejacket. His idea is that picking up mines is saving life, not taking it."

"Then he won't want the brass yet," Mark said, "it's to start him in any business. What's the full name and address of your girl? Where do you keep her?"

They were in an open space, dusty, with half-timber buildings whose demolition had been interrupted. Christopher halted close to a post that had once been a cannon; up against this he felt that his brother could lean in order to assimilate ideas. He said slowly and patiently:

"If you're consulting with me as to how to carry out our father's intentions, and as there's money in it you had better make an attempt to get hold of the facts. I wouldn't bother you if it wasn't a matter of money. In the first place, no money is wanted at this end. I can live on my pay. My wife is a rich woman, relatively. Her mother is a very rich woman. . . ."

"She's Rugeley's mistress, isn't she?" Mark asked.

Christopher said:

"No, she isn't. I should certainly say she wasn't. Why should she be? She's his cousin."

"Then it's your wife who was Rugeley's mistress?" Mark asked. "Or why should she have the loan of his box?"

"Sylvia also is Rugeley's cousin, of course, a degree further removed," Tietjens said. "She isn't anyone's mistress. You can be certain of that."

"They *say* she is," Mark answered. "They say she's a regular tart.
. . . I suppose you think I've insulted you."

Christopher said:

"No, you haven't. . . . It's better to get all this out. We're practically strangers, but you've a right to ask."

Mark said:

"Then you haven't got a girl and don't need money to keep her.
. . . You could have what you liked. There's no reason why a man shouldn't have a girl, and if he has he ought to keep her decently. . . ."

Christopher did not answer. Mark leaned against the half-buried cannon and swung his umbrella by its crook.

"But," he said, "if you don't keep a girl what do you do for . . ." He was going to say "for the comforts of home," but a new idea had come into his mind. "Of course," he said, "one can see that your wife's soppily in love with you." He added: "Soppily . . . one can see that with half an eye. . . ."

Christopher felt his jaw drop. Not a second before — that very second! — he had made up his mind to ask Valentine Wannop to become his mistress that night. It was no good, any more, he said to himself. She loved him, he knew, with a deep, an unshakable passion, just as his passion for her was a devouring element that covered his whole mind as the atmosphere envelopes the earth. Were they, then, to go down to death separated by years, with no word ever spoken? To what end? For whose benefit? The whole world conspired to force them together! To resist became a weariness!

His brother Mark was talking on. "I know all about women," he had announced. Perhaps he did. He had lived with exemplary fidelity to a quite unpresentable woman, for a number of years. Perhaps the complete study of one woman gave you a map of all the rest!

Christopher said:

"Look here, Mark. You had better go through all my pass-books for the last ten years. Or ever since I had an account. This discussion is no good if you don't believe what I say."

Mark said:

"I don't want to see your pass-books. I believe you."

He added, a second later:

"Why the devil shouldn't I believe you? It's either believing you're a gentleman or Ruggles a liar. It's only commonsense to believe Ruggles a liar, in that case. I didn't before because I had no grounds to."

Christopher said:

"I doubt if liar is the right word. He picked up things that were said against me. No doubt he reported them faithfully enough. Things *are* said against me. I don't know why."

"Because," Mark said with emphasis, "you treat these south country swine with the contempt that they deserve. They're incapable of understanding the motives of a gentleman. If you live among dogs they'll think you've the motives of a dog. What other motives can they give you?" He added: "I thought you'd been buried so long under their muck that you were as mucky as they!"

Tietjens looked at his brother with the respect one has to give to a man ignorant but shrewd. It was a discovery that his brother was shrewd.

But, of course, he would be shrewd. He was the indispensable head of a great department. He had to have some qualities. . . . Not cultivated, not even instructed. A savage! But penetrating!

"We must move on," he said, "or I shall have to take a cab." Mark detached himself from his half buried cannon.

"What did you do with the other three thousand?" he asked. "Three thousand is a hell of a big sum to chuck away. For a younger son."

"Except for some furniture I bought for my wife's rooms," Christopher said, "it went mostly in loans."

"Loans!" Mark exclaimed. "To that fellow Macmaster?"

"Mostly to him," Christopher answered. "But about seven hundred to Dicky Swipes, of Cullercoats."

"Good God! Why to him?" Mark ejaculated.

"Oh, because he was Swipes, of Cullercoats," Christopher said, "and asked for it. He'd have had more, only that was enough for him to drink himself to death on."

Mark said:

"I suppose you don't give money to every fellow that asks for it?"

Christopher said:

"I do. It's a matter of principle."

"It's lucky," Mark said, "that a lot of fellows don't know that. You wouldn't have much brass left for long."

"I didn't have it for long," Christopher said.

"You know," Mark said, "you couldn't expect to do the princely patron on a youngest son's portion. It's a matter of taste. I never gave a ha'penny to a beggar myself. But a lot of the Tietjens were princely. One generation to addle brass; one to keep; one to spend. That's all right. . . . I suppose Macmaster's wife *is* your mistress? That'll account for it not being the girl. They keep an arm-chair for you."

Christopher said:

"No. I just backed Macmaster for the sake of backing him. Father lent him money to begin with."

"So he did," Mark exclaimed.

"His wife," Christopher said, "was the widow of Breakfast Duchemin. *You* knew Breakfast Duchemin?"

"Oh, *I* knew Breakfast Duchemin," Mark said. "I suppose Mac-

master's a pretty warm man now. Done himself proud with Duchemin's money."

"Pretty proud!" Christopher said. "They won't be knowing me
long now."

"But damn it all!" Mark said. "You've Groby to all intents and
purposes. *I'm* not going to marry and beget children to hinder you."
Christopher said:

"Thanks. I don't want it."

"Got your knife into me?" Mark asked.

"Yes. I've got my knife into you," Christopher answered. "Into
the whole bloody lot of you, and Ruggles' and ffolliott's and our
father!"

Mark said: "Ah!"

"You don't suppose I wouldn't have?" Christopher asked.

"Oh, *I* don't suppose you wouldn't have," Mark answered. "I
thought you were a soft sort of bloke. I see you aren't."

"I'm as North Riding as yourself!" Christopher answered.

They were in the tide of Fleet Street, pushed apart by foot pas-
sengers and separated by traffic. With some of the imperiousness of
the officer of those days Christopher barged across through motor-
buses and paper lorries. With the imperiousness of the head of a
department Mark said:

"Here, policeman, stop these damn things and let me get over."
But Christopher was over much the sooner and waited for his brother
in the gateway of the Middle Temple. His mind was completely
swallowed up in the endeavour to imagine the embraces of Valentine Wannop. He said to himself that he had burnt his boats.

Mark, coming alongside him, said:

"You'd better know what our father wanted."
Christopher said:

"Be quick then. I must get on." He had to rush through his War
Office interview to get to Valentine Wannop. They would have
only a few hours in which to recount the loves of two lifetimes. He
saw her golden head and her enraptured face. He wondered how
her face would look, enraptured. He had seen on it humour, dismay,
tenderness, in the eyes — and fierce anger and contempt for his,
Christopher's, political opinions. His militarism!

Nevertheless they halted by the Temple fountain. That respect was
due to their dead father. Mark had been explaining. Christopher
had caught some of his words and divined the links. Mr. Tietjens

had left no will, confident that his desires as to the disposal of his immense fortune would be carried out meticulously by his eldest son. He would have left a will, but there was the vague case of Christopher to be considered. Whilst Christopher had been a youngest son you arranged that he had a good lump sum and went, with it, to the devil how he liked. He was no longer a youngest son, by the will of God.

"Our father's idea," Mark said by the fountain, "was that no settled sum could keep you straight. His idea was that if you were a bloody pimp living on women . . . You don't mind?"

"I don't mind your putting it straightforwardly," Christopher said. He considered the base of the fountain that was half full of leaves. This civilisation had contrived a state of things in which leaves rotted by August. Well, it was doomed!

"If you were a pimp living on women," Mark repeated, "it was no good making a will. You might need uncounted thousands to keep you straight. You were to have 'em. You were to be as debauched as you wanted, but on clean money. I was to see how much in all probability that would be and arrange the other legacies to scale. . . . Father had crowds of pensioners. . . ."

"How much did father cut up for?" Christopher asked.

Mark said:

"God knows. . . . You saw we proved the estate at a million and a quarter as far as ascertained. But it might be twice that. Or five times! . . . With steel prices what they have been for the last three years it's impossible to say what the Middlesbrough district property won't produce. . . . The death duties even can't catch it up. And there are all the ways of getting round *them*."

Christopher inspected his brother with curiosity. This brown-complexioned fellow with bulging eyes, shabby on the whole, tightly buttoned into a rather old pepper-and-salt suit, with a badly rolled umbrella, old race-glasses, and his bowler hat the only neat thing about him, was, indeed, a prince. With a rigid outline! All real princes must look like that. He said:

"Well! You won't be a penny the poorer by me."

Mark was beginning to believe this. He said:

"You won't forgive father?"

Christopher said:

"I won't forgive father for not making a will. I won't forgive him for calling in Ruggles. I saw him and you in the writing-room the

night before he died. He never spoke to me. He could have. It was
clumsy stupidity. That's unforgivable."

"The fellow shot himself," Mark said. "You usually forgive a fellow
who shoots himself."

"I don't," Christopher said. "Besides he's probably in heaven and
don't need my forgiveness. Ten to one he's in heaven. He was a
good man."

"One of the best," Mark said. "It was I that called in Ruggles
though."

"I don't forgive you either," Christopher said.

"But you *must*," Mark said — and it was a tremendous concession
to sentimentality — "take enough to make you comfortable."

"By God!" Christopher exclaimed. "I loathe your whole beastly
buttered-toast, mutton-chopped, carpet-slippered, rum-negused comfort as much as I loathe your beastly Riviera-palaced, chauffeured,
hydraulic-lifted, hot-house aired beastliness of fornication. . . ." He
was carried away, as he seldom let himself be, by the idea of his
amours with Valentine Wannop which should take place on the
empty boards of a cottage, without draperies, fat meats, gummy
aphrodisiacs. . . . "You won't," he repeated, "be a penny the poorer
by me."

Mark said:

"Well, you needn't get shirty about it. If you won't you won't.
We'd better move on. You've only just time. We'll say that settles
it. . . . Are you, or aren't you, overdrawn at your bank? I'll make
that up, whatever you damn well do to stop it."

"I'm not overdrawn," Christopher said. "I'm over thirty pounds
in credit, and I've an immense overdraft guaranteed by Sylvia. It was
a mistake of the bank's."

Mark hesitated for a moment. It was to him almost unbelievable
that a bank could make a mistake. One of the great banks. The props
of England.

They were walking down towards the embankment. With his
precious umbrella Mark aimed a violent blow at the railings above
the tennis lawns, where whitish figures, bedrabbled by the dim atmosphere, moved like marionettes practising crucifixions.

"By God!" he said, "this is the last of England. . . . There's only
my department where they never made mistakes. I tell you, if there
were any mistakes made there there would be some backs broken!"
He added: "But don't you think that I'm going to give up comfort,

I'm not. My Charlotte makes better buttered toast than they can at the club. And she's got a tap of French rum that's saved my life over and over again after a beastly wet day's racing. And she does it all on the five hundred I give her and keeps herself clean and tidy on top of it. Nothing like a Frenchwoman for managing. . . . By God, I'd marry the doxy if she wasn't a Papist. It would please her and it wouldn't hurt me. But I couldn't stomach marrying a Papist. They're not to be trusted."

"You'll have to stomach a Papist coming into Groby," Christopher said. "My son's to be brought up as a Papist."

Mark stopped and dug his umbrella into the ground.

"Eh, but that's a bitter one," he said. "Whatever made ye do that? . . . I suppose the mother made you do it. She tricked you into it before you married her." He added: "I'd not like to sleep with that wife of yours. She's too athletic. It'd be like sleeping with a bundle of faggots. I suppose though you're a pair of turtle doves. . . . Eh, but I'd not have thought ye would have been so weak."

"I only decided this morning," Christopher said, "when my cheque was returned from the bank. You won't have read Spelden on Sacrilege, about Groby."

"I can't say I have," Mark answered.

"It's no good trying to explain that side of it then," Christopher said, "there isn't time. But you're wrong in thinking Sylvia made it a condition of our marriage. Nothing would have made me consent then. It has made her a happy woman that I have. The poor thing thought our house was under a curse for want of a Papist heir."

"What made ye consent now?" Mark asked.

"I've told you," Christopher said, "it was getting my cheque returned to the club; that on the top of the rest of it. A fellow who can't do better than that had better let the mother bring up the child. . . . Besides, it won't hurt a Papist boy to have a father with dishonoured cheques as much as it would a Protestant. They're not quite English."

"That's true too," Mark said.

He stood still by the railings of the public garden near the Temple station.

"Then," he said, "if I'd let the lawyers write and tell you the guarantee for your overdraft from the estate was stopped as they wanted to, the boy wouldn't be a Papist? You wouldn't have overdrawn."

"I didn't overdraw," Christopher said. "But if you had warned me I should have made enquiries at the bank and the mistake wouldn't have occurred. Why didn't you?"

"I meant to," Mark said. "I meant to do it myself. But I hate writing letters. I put it off. I didn't much like having dealings with the fellow I thought you were. I suppose that's another thing you won't forgive me for?"

"No. I shan't forgive you for not writing to me," Christopher said. "You ought to write business letters."

"I hate writing 'em," Mark said. Christopher was moving on. "There's one thing more," Mark said. "I suppose the boy is your son?"

"Yes, he's my son," Christopher said.

"Then that's all," Mark said. "I suppose if you're killed you won't mind my keeping an eye on the youngster?"

"I'll be glad," Christopher said.

They strolled along the Embankment side by side, walking rather slowly, their backs erected and their shoulders squared because of their satisfaction of walking together, desiring to lengthen the walk by going slow. Once or twice they stopped to look at the dirty silver of the river, for both liked grim effects of landscape. They felt very strong, as if they owned the land!

Once Mark chuckled and said:

"It's too damn funny. To think of our both being . . . what is it? . . . monogamists? Well, it's a good thing to stick to one woman . . . you can't say it isn't. It saves trouble. And you know where you are."

Under the lugubrious arch that leads into the War Office quadrangle Christopher halted.

"No. I'm coming in," Mark said. "I want to speak to Hogarth. I haven't spoken to Hogarth for some time. About the transport waggon parks in Regent's Park. I manage all those beastly things and a lot more."

"They say you do it damn well," Christopher said. "They say you're indispensable." He was aware that his brother desired to stay with him as long as possible. He desired it himself.

"I damn well am!" Mark said. He added: "I suppose you couldn't do that sort of job in France? Look after transport and horses."

"I could," Christopher said, "but I suppose I shall go back to liaison work."

"I don't think you will," Mark said. "I could put in a word for you with the transport people."

"I wish you would," Christopher said. "I'm not fit to go back into the front line. Besides I'm no beastly hero! And I'm a rotten infantry officer. No Tietjens was ever a soldier worth talking of."

They turned the corner of the arch. Like something fitting in, exact and expected, Valentine Wannop stood looking at the lists of casualties that hung beneath a cheaply green-stained deal shelter against the wall, a tribute at once to the weaker art movements of the day and the desire to save the ratepayers' money.

With the same air of finding Christopher Tietjens fit in exactly to an expected landscape she turned on him. Her face was blue-white and distorted. She ran upon him and exclaimed:

"Look at this horror! And you in that foul uniform can support it!"

The sheets of paper beneath the green roof were laterally striped with little serrated lines. Each line meant the death of a man, for the day.

Tietjens had fallen a step back off the kerb of the pavement that ran round the quadrangle. He said:

"I support it because I have to. Just as you decry it because you have to. They're two different patterns that we see." He added: "This is my brother Mark."

She turned her head stiffly upon Mark: her face was perfectly waxen. It was as if the head of a shopkeeper's lay-figure had been turned. She said to Mark:

"I didn't know Mr. Tietjens had a brother. Or hardly. I've never heard him speak of you."

Mark grinned feebly, exhibiting to the lady the brilliant lining of his hat.

"I don't suppose anyone has ever heard me speak of *him*," he said, "but he's my brother all right!"

She stepped on to the asphalt carriage-way and caught between her fingers and thumb a fold of Christopher's khaki sleeve.

"I must speak to you," she said; "I'm going then."

She drew Christopher into the centre of the enclosed, hard, and ungracious space, holding him still by the stuff of his tunic. She pushed him round until he was facing her. She swallowed hard, it was as if the motion of her throat took an immense time. Christopher looked round the skyline of the buildings of sordid and besmirched stone. He had often wondered what would happen if an air-bomb of some size dropped into the mean, grey stoniness of that cold heart of an embattled world.

The girl was devouring his face with her eyes: to see him flinch. Her voice was hard between her little teeth. She said:

"Were you the father of the child Ethel was going to have? Your wife says you were."

Christopher considered the dimensions of the quadrangle. He said vaguely:

"Ethel? Who's she?" In pursuance of the habits of the painter-poet Mr. and Mrs. Macmaster called each other always "Guggums!" Christopher had in all probability never heard Mrs. Duchemin's Christian names since his disaster had swept all names out of his head.

He came to the conclusion that the quadrangle was not a space sufficiently confined to afford much bursting resistance to a bomb.

The girl said:

"Edith Ethel Duchemin! Mrs. Macmaster that is!" She was obviously waiting intensely. Christopher said with vagueness:

"No! Certainly not! . . . What was said?"

Mark Tietjens was leaning forward over the kerb in front of the green-stained shelter, like a child over a brookside. He was obviously waiting, quite patient, swinging his umbrella by the hook. He appeared to have no other means of self-expression. The girl was saying that when she had rung up Christopher that morning a voice had said, without any preparation at all, the girl repeated, without any preparation at all:

"You'd better keep off the grass if you're the Wannop girl. Mrs. Duchemin is my husband's mistress already. You keep off!"

Christopher said:

"She said that, did she?" He was wondering how Mark kept his balance, really. The girl said nothing more. She was waiting, with an insistence that seemed to draw him, a sort of sucking in of his personality. It was unbearable. He made his last effort of that afternoon.

He said:

"Damn it all. How could you ask such a tomfool question? *You!* I took you to be an intelligent person. The only intelligent person I know. Don't you *know* me?"

She made an effort to retain her stiffening.

"Isn't Mrs. Tietjens a truthful person?" she asked. "I thought she looked truthful when I saw her at Vincent and Ethel's."

He said:

"What she says she believes. But she only believes what she wants to, for the moment. If you call that truthful, she's truthful. I've nothing against her." He said to himself: "I'm not going to appeal to her by damning my wife."

She seemed to go all of a piece, as the hard outline goes suddenly out of a piece of lump sugar upon which you drop water.

"Oh," she said, "it *isn't* true. I *knew* it wasn't true." She began to cry.

Christopher said:

"Come along. I've been answering tomfool questions all day. I've got another tomfool to see here, then I'm through."

She said:

"I can't come with you, crying like this."

He answered:

"Oh, yes you can. This is the place where women cry." He added: "Besides there's Mark. He's a comforting ass."

He delivered her over to Mark.

"Here, look after Miss Wannop," he said. "You want to talk to her anyhow, don't you?" and he hurried ahead of them like a fussy shop-walker into the lugubrious hall. He felt that, if he didn't come soon to an unemotional ass in red, green, blue or pink tabs, who would have fish-like eyes and would ask the sort of questions that fishes ask in tanks, he, too, must break down and cry. With relief! However, that was a place where men cried, too!

He got through at once by sheer weight of personality, down miles of corridors, into the presence of a quite intelligent, thin, dark person with scarlet tabs. That meant a superior staff affair, not dustbins.

The dark man said to him at once:

"Look here! What's the matter with the Command Depots? You've been lecturing a lot of them. In economy. What are all these damn mutinies about? Is it the rotten old colonels in command?"

Tietjens said amiably:

"Look here! I'm not a beastly spy, you know? I've had hospitality from the rotten old colonels."

The dark man said:

"I daresay you have. But that's what you were sent round for. General Campion said you were the brainiest chap in his command.

He's gone out now, worse luck. . . . What's the matter with the
Command Depots? Is it the men? Or is it the officers? You needn't
mention names."

Tietjens said:

"Kind of Campion. It isn't the officers and it isn't the men. It's
the foul system. You get men who think they've deserved well of
their country — and they damn well have! — and you crop their
heads. . . ."

"That's the M.O.s." the dark man said. "They don't want lice."

"If they prefer mutinies . . ." Tietjens said. "A man wants to walk
with his girl and have a properly oiled quiff. They don't like being
regarded as convicts. That's how they are regarded."

The dark man said:

"All right. Go on. Why don't you sit down?"

"I'm a little in a hurry," Tietjens said. "I'm going out to-morrow
and I've got a brother and people waiting below."

The dark man said:

"Oh, I'm sorry. . . . But damn. You're the sort of man we want at
home. Do you want to go? We can, no doubt, get you stopped if you
don't."

Tietjens hesitated for a moment.

"Yes!" he said eventually. "Yes, I want to go."

For the moment he had felt temptation to stay. But it came into
his discouraged mind that Mark had said that Sylvia was in love with
him. It had been underneath his thoughts all the while: it had struck
him at the time like a kick from the hind leg of a mule in his subliminal consciousness. It was the impossible complication. It might
not be true; but, whether or no, the best thing for him was to go and
get wiped out as soon as possible. He meant, nevertheless, fiercely,
to have his night with the girl who was crying downstairs. . . .

He heard in his ear, perfectly distinctly, the lines:

> The voice that never yet . . .
> Made answer to my word . . .

He said to himself:

"That was what Sylvia wanted! I've got that much!"

The dark man had said something. Tietjens repeated:

"I'd take it very unkindly if you stopped my going . . . I want
to go."

The dark man said:

"Some do. Some do not. I'll make a note of your name in case you come back . . . You won't mind going on with your cinder-sifting, if you do? . . . Get on with your story as quick as you can. And get what fun you can before you go. They say it's rotten out there. Damn awful! There's a hell of a strafe on. That's why they want all you."

For a moment Tietjens saw the grey dawn at rail-head with the distant sound of a ceaselessly boiling pot, from miles away! The army feeling redescended upon him. He began to talk about Command Depots, at great length and with enthusiasm. He snorted with rage at the way men were treated in these gloomy places. With ingenious stupidity!

Every now and then the dark man interrupted him with:

"Don't forget that a Command Depot is a place where sick and wounded go to get made fit. We've got to get 'em back as soon as we can."

"And do you?" Tietjens would ask.

"No, we don't," the other would answer. "That's what this enquiry is about."

"You've got," Tietjens would continue, "on the north side of a beastly clay hill nine miles from Southampton three thousand men from the Highlands, North Wales, Cumberland. . . . God knows where, as long as it's three hundred miles from home to make them rather mad with nostalgia. . . . You allow 'em out for an hour a day during the pub's closing time. You shave their heads to prevent 'em appealing to local young women who don't exist, and you don't let 'em carry the swagger-canes! God knows why! To prevent their poking their eyes out, if they fall down, I suppose. Nine miles from anywhere, with chalk down roads to walk on and not a bush for shelter or shade . . . And, damn it, if you get two men, chums, from the Seaforths or the Argylls you don't let them sleep in the same hut, but shove 'em in with a lot of fat Buffs or Welshmen, who stink of leeks and can't speak English. . . ."

"That's the infernal medicals' orders to stop 'em talking all night."

"To make 'em conspire all night not to turn out for parade," Tietjens said. "And there's a beastly mutiny begun. . . . And, damn it, they're fine men. They're first-class fellows. Why don't you — as this is a Christian land — let 'em go home to convalesce with their girls and pubs and friends and a little bit of swank, for heroes? Why in God's name don't you? Isn't there suffering enough?"

"I wish you wouldn't say 'you,' " the dark man said. "It isn't me. The only A.C.I. I've drafted was to give every Command Depot a cinema and a theatre. But the beastly medicals got it stopped . . . for fear of infection. And, of course, the parsons and Nonconformist magistrates . . ."

"Well, you'll have to change it all," Tietjens said, "or you'll just have to say: thank God we've got a navy. You won't have an army. The other day three fellows — Warwicks — asked me at question time, after a lecture, why they were shut up there in Wiltshire whilst Belgian refugees were getting bastards on their wives in Birmingham. And when I asked how many men made that complaint over fifty stood up. All from Birmingham. . . ."

The dark man said:

"I'll make a note of that. . . . Go on."

Tietjens went on; for as long as he stayed there he felt himself a man, doing work that befitted a man, with the bitter contempt for fools that a man should have and express. It was a letting up, a real last leave.

IV

MARK TIETJENS, his umbrella swinging sheepishly, his bowler hat pushed firmly down on to his ears to give him a sense of stability, walked beside the weeping girl in the quadrangle.

"I say," he said, "don't give it to old Christopher too beastly hard about his militarist opinions. . . . Remember, he's going out to-morrow and he's one of the best."

She looked at him quickly, tears remaining upon her cheeks, and then away.

"One of the best," Mark said. "A fellow who never told a lie or did a dishonourable thing in his life. Let him down easy, there's a good girl. You ought to, you know."

The girl, her face turned away, said:

"I'd lay down my life for him!"

Mark said:

"I know you would. I know a good woman when I see one. And think! He probably considers that he *is* . . . offering his life, you know, for you. And me, too, of course! It's a different way of looking at things." He gripped her awkwardly but irresistibly by the upper arm. It was very thin under her blue cloth coat. He said to himself:

"By Jove! Christopher likes them skinny. It's the athletic sort that attracts him. This girl is as clean run as . . ." He couldn't think of anything as clean run as Miss Wannop, but he felt a warm satisfaction at having achieved an intimacy with her and his brother. He said:

"You aren't going away? Not without a kinder word to him. You think! He might be killed. . . . Besides, probably he's never killed a German. He was a liaison officer. Since then he's been in charge of a dump where they sift army dustbins. To see how they can give the men less to eat. That means that the civilians get more. You don't object to his giving civilians more meat? . . . It isn't even helping to kill Germans. . . ."

He felt her arm press his hand against her warm side.

"What's he going to do now?" she asked. Her voice wavered.

"That's what I'm here about," Mark said. "I'm going in to see old Hogarth. You don't know Hogarth? Old General Hogarth? I think I can get him to give Christopher a job with the transport. A safe job. Safeish! No beastly glory business about it. No killing beastly Germans either. . . . I beg your pardon, if you like Germans."

She drew her arm from his hand in order to look him in the face.

"Oh!" she said, "*you* don't want him to have any beastly military glory!" The colour came back into her face: she looked at him open-eyed.

He said:

"No! Why the devil should he?" He said to himself: "She's got enormous eyes; a good neck; good shoulders; good breasts; clean hips; small hands. She isn't knock-kneed; neat ankles. She stands well on her feet. Feet not too large! Five foot four, say! A real good filly!" He went on aloud: "Why in the world should he want to be a beastly soldier? He's the heir to Groby. That ought to be enough for one man."

Having stood still sufficiently long for what she knew to be his critical inspection, she put her hand in turn, precipitately, under his arm and moved him towards the entrance steps.

"Let's be quick then," she said. "Let's get him into your transport at once. Before he goes to-morrow. Then we'll know he's safe."

He was puzzled by her dress. It was very business-like, dark blue and very short. A white blouse with a black silk, man's tie. A wide-awake, with, on the front of the band, a cipher.

"You're in uniform yourself," he said. "Does your conscience let you do war work?"

She said:

"No. We're hard up. I'm taking the gym classes in a great big school to turn an honest penny. . . . *Do* be quick!"

Her pressure on his elbow flattered him. He resisted it a little, hanging back, to make her more insistent. He liked being pleaded with by a pretty woman; Christopher's girl at that.

He said:

"Oh, it's not a matter of minutes. They keep 'em weeks at the base before they send 'em up. . . . We'll fix him up all right, I've no doubt. We'll wait in the hall till he comes down."

He told the benevolent commissionaire, one of two in a pulpit in the crowded grim hall, that he was going up to see General Hogarth in a minute or two. But not to send a bell-boy. He might be some time yet.

He sat himself beside Miss Wannop, clumsily on a wooden bench, humanity surging over their toes as if they had been on a beach. She moved a little to make room for him and that, too, made him feel good. He said:

"You said just now: 'we' are hard up. Does 'we' mean you and Christopher?"

She said:

"I and Mr. Tietjens. Oh, no! I and mother! The paper she used to write for stopped. When your father died, I believe. He found money for it, I think. And mother isn't suited to free-lancing. She's worked too hard in her life."

He looked at her, his round eyes protruding.

"I don't know what that is, free-lancing," he said. "But you've got to be comfortable. How much do you and your mother need to keep you comfortable? And put in a bit more so that Christopher could have a mutton-chop now and then!"

She hadn't really been listening. He said with some insistence:

"Look here! I'm here on business. Not like an elderly admirer forcing himself on you. Though, by God, I do admire you too. . . . But my father wanted your mother to be comfortable. . . ."

Her face, turned to him, became rigid.

"You don't mean . . ." she began. He said:

"You won't get it any quicker by interrupting. I have to tell my stories in my own way. My father wanted your mother to be com-

fortable. He said so that she could write books, not papers. I don't
know what the difference is: that's what he said. He wants you to
be comfortable too. . . . You've not got any encumbrances? Not
. . . oh, say a business! a hat shop that doesn't pay? Some girls
have. . . ."

She said: "No. I just teach . . . oh, *do* be quick. . . ."

For the first time in his life he dislocated the course of his thoughts
to satisfy a longing in some one else.

"You may take it to go on with," he said, "as if my father had left
your mother a nice little plum." He cast about to find his scattered
thoughts.

"He has! He *has*! After all!" the girl said. "Oh, thank God!"

"There'll be a bit for you, if you like," Mark said, "or perhaps
Christopher won't let you. He's ratty with me. And something for
your brother to buy a doctor's business with." He asked: "You
haven't fainted, have you?" She said:

"No. I don't faint. I cry."

"That'll be all right," he answered. He went on: "That's your side
of it. Now for mine. I want Christopher to have a place where he'll
be sure of a mutton-chop and an arm-chair by the fire. And someone
to be good for him. *You're* good for him. I can see that. I know
women!"

The girl was crying, softly and continuously. It was the first moment of the lifting of strain that she had known since the day before
the Germans crossed the Belgian frontier, near a place called Gemmenich.

It had begun with the return of Mrs. Duchemin from Scotland.
She had sent at once for Miss Wannop to the rectory, late at night.
By the light of candles in tall silver sticks, against oak panelling she
had seemed like a mad block of marble, with staring, dark eyes and
mad hair. She had exclaimed in a voice as hard as a machine's:

"How do you get rid of a baby? You've been a servant. You ought
to know!"

That had been the great shock, the turning-point, of Valentine
Wannop's life. Her last years before that had been of great tranquillity, tinged, of course, with melancholy because she loved Christopher Tietjens. But she had early learned to do without, and the
world as she saw it was a place of renunciations, of high endeavour
and sacrifice. Tietjens had to be a man who came to see her mother
and talked wonderfully. She had been happy when he had been in

the house — she in the housemaid's pantry, getting the tea-things.
She had, besides, been very hard-worked for her mother; the weather
had been, on the whole, good, the corner of the country in which
they lived had continued to seem fresh and agreeable. She had had
excellent health, got an occasional ride on the *qui-tamer* with which
Tietjens had replaced Joel's rig; and her brother had done admirably
at Eton, taking such a number of exhibitions and things that, once
at Magdalen, he had been nearly off his mother's hands. An admirable, gay boy, not unlikely to run for, as well as being a credit to,
his university, if he didn't get sent down for his political extrava-
gances. He was a Communist!

And at the rectory there had been the Duchemins, or rather Mrs.
Duchemin and, during most week-ends, Macmaster somewhere about.

The passion of Macmaster for Edith Ethel and of Edith Ethel for
Macmaster had seemed to her one of the beautiful things of life.
They seemed to swim in a sea of renunciations, of beautiful quotations, and of steadfast waiting. Macmaster did not interest her
personally much, but she took him on trust because of Edith Ethel's
romantic passion and because he was Christopher Tietjens' friend.
She had never heard him say anything original; when he used quotations they would be apt rather than striking. But she took it for
granted that he was the right man — much as you take it for granted
the engine of an express train in which you are is reliable. The right
people have chosen it for you. . . .

With Mrs. Duchemin, mad before her, she had the first intimation
that her idolised friend, in whom she had believed as she had believed
in the firmness of the great, sunny earth, had been the mistress of
her lover — almost since the first day she had seen him. . . . And
that Mrs. Duchemin had, stored somewhere, a character of an extreme harshness and great vulgarity of language. She raged up and
down in the candlelight, before the dark oak panelling, screaming
coarse phrases of the deepest hatred for her lover. Didn't the oaf
know his business better than to . . . ? The dirty little Port of Leith
fish-handler. . . .

What, then, were tall candles in silver sticks for? And polished
panelling in galleries?

Valentine Wannop couldn't have been a little ashcat in worn
cotton dresses, sleeping under the stairs, in an Ealing household with
a drunken cook, an invalid mistress and three over-fed men, without
acquiring a considerable knowledge of the sexual necessities and ex-

cesses of humanity. But, as all the poorer helots of great cities hearten
their lives by dreaming of material beauties, elegance, and suave
wealth, she had always considered that, far from the world of Ealing
and its county councillors who over-ate and neighed like stallions,
there were bright colonies of beings, chaste, beautiful in thought,
altruist and circumspect.

And, till that moment, she had imagined herself on the skirts of
such a colony. She presupposed a society of beautiful intellects centr-
ing in London round her friends. Ealing she just put out of her
mind. She considered: she had, indeed once heard Tietjens say that
humanity was made up of exact and constructive intellects on the one
hand and on the other of stuff to fill graveyards. . . . Now, what had
become of the exact and constructive intellects?

Worst of all, what became of her beautiful inclination towards
Tietjens, for she couldn't regard it as anything more? Couldn't her
heart sing any more whilst she was in the housemaid's pantry and he
in her mother's study? And what became, still more, of what she
knew to be Tietjens' beautiful inclination towards her? She asked
herself the eternal question — and she knew it to be the eternal
question — whether no man and woman can ever leave it at the
beautiful inclination. And, looking at Mrs. Duchemin, rushing backwards and forwards in the light of candles, blue-white of face and
her hair flying, Valentine Wannop said: "No! no! The tiger lying in
the reeds will always raise its head!" But tiger . . . it was more like
a peacock.

Tietjens, raising his head from the other side of the tea-table and
looking at her with his long, meditative glance from beside her
mother; ought he then, instead of blue and protruding, to have eyes
divided longitudinally in the blacks of them — that should divide,
closing or dilating, on a yellow ground, with green glowings of furtive light?

She was aware that Edith Ethel had done her an irreparable wrong,
for you cannot suffer a great sexual shock and ever be the same. Or
not for years. Nevertheless she stayed with Mrs. Duchemin until far
into the small hours, when that lady fell, a mere parcel of bones in a
peacock-blue wrapper, into a deep chair and refused to move or
speak; nor did she afterwards slacken in her faithful waiting on her
friend. . . .

On the next day came the war. That was a nightmare of pure
suffering, with never a let-up, day or night. It began on the morning

of the fourth with the arrival of her brother from some sort of Oxford Communist Summer School on the Broads. He was wearing a
German corps student's cap and was very drunk. He had been seeing
German friends off from Harwich. It was the first time she had ever
seen a drunken man, so that was a good present to her.

Next day, and sober, he was almost worse. A handsome, dark boy
like his father, he had his mother's hooked nose and was always a
little unbalanced: not mad, but always overviolent in any views he
happened for the moment to hold. At the Summer School he had
been under very vitriolic teachers of all sorts of notions. That hadn't
hitherto mattered. Her mother had written for a Tory paper; her
brother, when he had been at home, had edited some sort of Oxford
organ of disruption. But her mother had only chuckled.

The war changed that. Both seemed to be filled with a desire for
blood and to torture; neither paid the least attention to the other.
It was as if — so for the rest of those years the remembrance of that
time lived with her — in one corner of the room her mother, aging,
and on her knees, from which she only with difficulty rose, shouted
hoarse prayers to God, to let her, with her own hands, strangle, torture, and flay off all his skin, a being called the Kaiser, and as if, in
the other corner of the room, her brother, erect, dark, scowling, and
vitriolic, one hand clenched above his head, called down the curse
of heaven on the British soldier, so that in thousands, he might die in
agony, the blood spouting from his scalded lungs. It appeared that
the Communist leader whom Edward Wannop affected had had ill-
success in his attempts to cause disaffection among some units or
other of the British army, and had failed rather gallingly, being
laughed at or ignored rather than being ducked in a horse-pond, shot
or otherwise martyrised. That made it obvious that the British man
in the ranks was responsible for the war. If those ignoble hirelings
had refused to fight all the other embattled and terrorised millions
would have thrown down their arms!

Across that dreadful phantasmagoria went the figure of Tietjens.
He was in doubt. She heard him several times voice his doubts to her
mother, who grew every day more vacant. One day Mrs. Wannop
had said:

"What does your wife think about it?"

Tietjens had answered:

"Oh, Mrs. Tietjens is a pro-German. . . . Or no, that isn't exact!
She has German prisoner-friends and looks after them. But she spends

nearly all her time in retreat in a convent reading novels of before the war. She can't bear the thought of physical suffering. I can't blame her."

Mrs. Wannop was no longer listening; her daughter was.

For Valentine Wannop the war had turned Tietjens into far more of a man and far less of an inclination — the war and Mrs. Duchemin between them. He had seemed to grow less infallible. A man with doubts is more of a man, with eyes, hands, the need for food and for buttons to be sewn on. She had actually tightened up a loose glove button for him.

One Friday afternoon at Macmaster's she had had a long talk with him, the first she had had since the drive and the accident.

Ever since Macmaster had instituted his Friday afternoons — and that had been some time before the war — Valentine Wannop had accompanied Mrs. Duchemin to town by the morning train and back at night to the rectory. Valentine poured out the tea, Mrs. Duchemin drifting about the large book-lined room amongst the geniuses and superior journalists.

On this occasion — a November day, very chilly, wet — there had been next to nobody present, the preceding Friday having been unusually full. Macmaster and Mrs. Duchemin had taken a Mr. Spong, an architect, into the dining-room to inspect an unusually fine set of Piranesi's *Views of Rome* that Tietjens had picked up somewhere and had given to Macmaster. A Mr. Jegg and a Mrs. Haviland were sitting close together in the far window-seat. They were talking in low tones. From time to time Mr. Jegg used the word "inhibition." Tietjens rose from the fire-seat on which he had been sitting and came to her. He ordered her to bring her cup of tea over by the fire and talk to him. She obeyed. They sat side by side on the leather fire-seat that stood on polished brass rails, the fire warming their backs. He said:

"Well, Miss Wannop. What have you been doing?" and they drifted into talking of the war. You couldn't not. She was astonished not to find him so loathsome as she had expected, for, just at that time, with the facts that were always being driven into her mind by the pacifist friends of her brother and with continual brooding over the morals of Mrs. Duchemin, she had an automatic feeling that all manly men were lust-filled devils, desiring nothing better than to stride over battlefields, stabbing the wounded with long daggers in frenzies of sadism. She knew that this view of Tietjens was wrong, but she cherished it.

She found him — as subconsciously she knew he was — astonishingly mild. She had too often watched him whilst he listened to her mother's tirades against the Kaiser, not to know that. He did not raise his voice, he showed no emotion. He said at last:

"You and I are like two people . . ." He paused and began again more quickly: "Do you know these soap advertisement signs that read differently from several angles? As you come up to them you read 'Monkey's Soap'; if you look back when you've passed it's 'Needs no Rinsing.' . . . You and I are standing at different angles and though we both look at the same thing we read different messages. Perhaps if we stood side by side we should see yet a third. . . . But I hope we respect each other. We're both honest. I, at least, tremendously respect you and I hope you respect me."

She kept silent. Behind their backs the fire rustled. Mr. Jegg, across the room, said: "The failure to co-ordinate . . ." and then dropped his voice.

Tietjens looked at her attentively.

"You don't respect me?" he asked. She kept obstinately silent.

"I'd have liked you to have said it," he repeated.

"Oh," she cried out, "how can I respect you when there is all this suffering? So much pain! Such torture . . . I can't sleep . . . never . . . I haven't slept a whole night since . . . Think of the immense spaces, stretching out under the night . . . I believe pain and fear must be worse at night. . . ." She knew she was crying out like that because her dread had come true. When he had said: "I'd have liked you to have said it," using the past, he had said his valedictory. Her man, too, was going.

And she knew too: she had always known under her mind and now she confessed it; her agony had been, half of it, because one day he would say farewell to her, like that, with the inflexion of a verb. As, just occasionally, using the word "we" — and perhaps without intention — he had let her know that he loved her.

Mr. Jegg drifted across from the window, Mrs. Haviland was already at the door.

"We'll leave you to have your war talk out," Mr. Jegg said. He added: "For myself, I believe it's one's sole duty to preserve the beauty of things that's preservable. I can't help saying that."

She was alone with Tietjens and the quiet day. She said to herself: "Now he must take me in his arms. He must. He *must*!" The deepest of her instincts came to the surface, from beneath layers of thought hardly known to her. She could feel his arms round her; she had in her nostrils the peculiar scent of his hair — like the scent of the skin of an apple, but very faint. "You must! You *must!*" she said to herself. There came back to her overpoweringly the memory of their drive together and the moment, the overwhelming moment, when, climbing out of the white fog into the blinding air, she had felt the impulse of his whole body towards her and the impulse of her whole body towards him. A sudden lapse, like the momentary dream when you fall. . . . She saw the white disk of the sun over the silver mist and behind them was the long, warm night. . . .

Tietjens sat, huddled rather together, dejectedly, the firelight playing on the silver places of his hair. It had grown nearly dark outside. They had a sense of the large room that, almost week by week, had grown, for its gleams of gilding and hand-polished dark woods, more like the great dining-room at the Duchemins. He got down from the fire-seat with a weary movement, as if the fire-seat had been very high. He said, with a little bitterness, but as if with more fatigue:

"Well, I've got the business of telling Macmaster that I'm leaving the office. That, too, won't be an agreeable affair! Not that what poor Vinnie thinks matters." He added: "It's queer, dear . . ." In the tumult of her emotions she was almost certain that he had said "dear." . . . "Not three hours ago my wife used to me almost the exact words you have just used. Almost the exact words. She talked of her inability to sleep at night for thinking of immense spaces full of pain that was worse at night. . . . And she, too, said that she could not respect me. . . ."

She sprang up.

"Oh," she said, "she didn't mean it. *I* didn't mean it. Almost every man who is a man must do as you are doing. But don't you see it's a desperate attempt to get you to stay: an attempt on moral lines? How can we leave any stone unturned that could keep us from losing our men?" She added, and it was another stone that she didn't leave unturned: "Besides, how can you reconcile it with your sense of duty, even from your point of view? You're more useful — you know you're more useful to your country here than . . ."

He stood over her, stooping a little, somehow suggesting great gentleness and concern.

"I can't reconcile it with my conscience," he said. "In this affair there is nothing that any man can reconcile with his conscience. I don't mean that we oughtn't to be in this affair and on the side we're

on. We ought. But I'll put to you things I have put to no other
soul."

The simplicity of his revelation seemed to her to put to shame any
of the glibnesses she had heard. It appeared to her as if a child were
speaking. He described the disillusionment it had cost him personally
as soon as this country had come into the war. He even described the
sunlit heather landscape of the north, where naïvely he had made his
tranquil resolution to join the French Foreign Legion as a common
soldier and his conviction that that would give him, as he called it,
clean bones again.

That, he said, had been straightforward. Now there was nothing
straightforward, for him or for any man. One could have fought with
a clean heart for a civilisation: if you like for the eighteenth century
against the twentieth, since that was what fighting for France against
the enemy countries meant. But our coming in had changed the aspect at once. It was one part of the twentieth century using the eighteenth as a catspaw to bash the other half of the twentieth. It was
true there was nothing else for it. And as long as we did it in a
decent spirit it was just bearable. One could keep at one's job —
which was faking statistics against the other fellow — until you were
sick and tired of faking and your brain reeled. And then some!

It was probably impolitic to fake - to overstate! — a case against
enemy nations. The chickens would come home to roost in one way
or another, probably. Perhaps they wouldn't. That was a matter for
one's superiors. Obviously! And the first gang had been simple,
honest fellows. Stupid, but relatively disinterested. But now! What
was one to do? . . . He went on, almost mumbling. . . .

She had suddenly a clear view of him as a man extraordinarily clear-
sighted in the affairs of others, in great affairs, but in his own so
simple as to be almost a baby. And gentle! And extraordinarily un-
selfish. He didn't betray one thought of self-interest . . . not one!

He was saying:

"But now, with this crowd of boodlers! . . . Supposing one's
asked to manipulate the figures of millions of pairs of boots in order
to force someone else to send some miserable general and his troops
to, say, Salonika — when they and you and common sense and everyone and everything else, know it's disastrous? . . . And from that to
monkeying with our own forces. . . . Starving particular units for
political . . ." He was talking to himself, not to her. And indeed
he said:

"I can't, you see, talk really before you. For all I know your sympathies, perhaps your activities, are with the enemy nations."

She said passionately:

"They're not! They're not! How dare you say such a thing?"

He answered:

"It doesn't matter . . . No! I'm sure you're not. . . . But, anyhow, these things are official. One can't, if one's scrupulous, even talk about them . . . And then . . . You see it means such infinite deaths of men, such an infinite prolongation . . . all this interference for side-ends! . . . I seem to see these fellows with clouds of blood over their heads. . . . And then . . . I'm to carry out their orders because they're my superiors. . . . But helping them means unnumbered deaths. . . ."

He looked at her with a faint, almost humorous smile:

"You see!" he said, "we're perhaps not so very far apart! You mustn't think you're the only one that sees all the deaths and all the sufferings. All, you see. I, too, am a conscientious objector. My conscience won't let me continue any longer with these fellows. . . ."

She said:

"But isn't there any other . . ."

He interrupted:

"No! There's no other course. One is either a body or a brain in these affairs. I suppose I'm more brain than body. I suppose so. Perhaps I'm not. But my conscience won't let me use my brain in this service. So I've a great, hulking body! I'll admit I'm probably not much good. But I've nothing to live for: what I stand for isn't any more in this world. What I want, as you know, I can't have. So . . ."

She exclaimed bitterly:

"Oh, say it! Say it! Say that your large hulking body will stop two bullets in front of two small anæmic fellows. . . . And how can you say you'll have nothing to live for? You'll come back. You'll do your good work again. You know you did good work . . ."

He said:

"Yes! I believe I did. I used to despise it, but I've come to believe I did. . . . But no! They'll never let me back. They've got me out, with all sorts of bad marks against me. They'll pursue me, systematically. . . . You see in such a world as this, an idealist — or perhaps it's only a sentimentalist — must be stoned to death. He makes the others so uncomfortable. He haunts them at their golf. . . . No, they'll get me, one way or the other. And some fellow — Macmaster

here — will do my jobs. He won't do them so well, but he'll do them
more dishonestly. Or no. I oughtn't to say dishonestly. He'll do them
with enthusiasm and righteousness. He'll fulfil the order of his superiors with an immense docility and unction. He'll fake figures
against our allies with the black enthusiasm of a Calvin and, when
that war comes, he'll do the requisite faking with the righteous wrath
of Jehovah smiting the priest of Baal. And he'll be right. It's all
we're fitted for. We ought never to have come into this war. We
ought to have snaffled other peoples' colonies as the price of neutrality. . . ."

"Oh!" Valentine Wannop said, "how can you so hate your
country?"

He said with great earnestness:

"Don't say it! Don't believe it! Don't even for a moment think it!
I love every inch of its fields and every plant in the hedgerows: com-
frey, mullein, paigles, long red purples, that liberal shepherds give a
grosser name . . . and all the rest of the rubbish — you remember
the field between the Duchemins and your mother's — and we have
always been boodlers and robbers and reivers and pirates and cattle
thieves, and so we've built up the great tradition that we love. . . .
But, for the moment, it's painful. Our present crowd is not more corrupt than Walpole's. But one's too near them. One sees of Walpole
that he consolidated the nation by building up the National Debt;
one doesn't see his methods. . . . My son, or his son, will only see
the glory of the boodle we make out of this show. Or rather out of
the next. He won't know about the methods. They'll teach him at
school that across the counties went the sound of bugles that his
father knew. . . . Though that was another discreditable affair. . . ."

"But you!" Valentine Wannop exclaimed. "You! what will *you*
do! After the war!"

"I!" he said rather bewilderedly. "I! . . . Oh, I shall go into the
old furniture business. I've been offered a job. . . ."

She didn't believe he was serious. He hadn't, she knew, ever
thought about his future. But suddenly she had a vision of his white
head and pale face in the back glooms of a shop full of dusty things.
He would come out, get heavily on to a dusty bicycle and ride off to
a cottage sale. She cried out:

"Why don't you do it at once? Why don't you take the job at
once?" for in the back of the dark shop he would at least be safe.

He said:

"Oh, no! Not at this time! Besides the old furniture trade's probably not itself for the minute. . . ." He was obviously thinking of something else.

"I've probably been a low cad," he said, "wringing your heart with my doubts. But I wanted to see where our similarities come in. We've always been — or we've seemed always to me — so alike in our thoughts. I daresay I wanted you to respect me. . . ."

"Oh, I respect you! I respect you!" she said. "You're as innocent as a child."

He went on:

"And I wanted to get some thinking done. It hasn't been often of late that one has had a quiet room and a fire and . . . you! To think in front of. You *do* make one collect one's thoughts. I've been very muddled till to-day . . . till five minutes ago! Do you remember our drive? You analysed my character. I'd never have let another soul . . . But you see . . . Don't you see?"

She said:

"No! What am I to see? I remember . . ."

He said:

"That I'm certainly not an English country gentleman now; picking up the gossip of the horse markets and saying: let the country go to hell, for me!"

She said:

"Did I say that? . . . Yes, I said that!"

The deep waves of emotion came over her: she trembled. She stretched out her arms. . . . She thought she stretched out her arms. He was hardly visible in the firelight. But she could see nothing, she was blind for tears. She could hardly be stretching out her arms, for she had both hands to her handkerchief on her eyes. He said something: it was no word of love or she would have held it; it began with: "Well, I must be . . ." He was silent for a long time: she imagined herself to feel great waves coming from him to her. But he wasn't in the room. . . .

The rest, till that moment at the War Office, had been pure agony, and unrelenting. Her mother's paper cut down her money, no orders for serials came in; her mother, obviously, was failing. The eternal diatribes of her brother were like lashes upon her skin. He seemed to be praying Tietjens to death. Of Tietjens she saw and heard nothing. At the Macmasters she heard, once, that he had just gone out. It added to her desire to scream when she saw a newspaper. Poverty in-

vaded them. The police raided the house in search of her brother and
his friends. Then her brother went to prison, somewhere in the Mid-
lands. The friendliness of their former neighbours turned to surly
suspicion. They could get no milk. Food became almost unprocurable
without going to long distances. For three days Mrs. Wannop was
clean out of her mind. Then she grew better and began to write a
new book. It promised to be rather good. But there was no publisher.
Edward came out of prison, full of good-humour and boisterousness.
They seemed to have had a great deal to drink in prison. But, hearing
that his mother had gone mad over that disgrace, after a terrible
scene with Valentine, in which he accused her of being the mistress
of Tietjens and therefore militarist, he consented to let his mother
use her influence — of which she had still some — to get him appointed as an A.B. on a mine-sweeper. Great winds became an agony
to Valentine Wannop in addition to the unbearable sounds of firing
that came continuously over the sea. Her mother grew much better,
she took pride in having a son in a service. She was then the more able
to appreciate the fact that her paper stopped payment altogether.
A small mob on the fifth of November burned Mrs. Wannop in
effigy in front of their cottage and broke their lower windows. Mrs.
Wannop ran out and in the illumination of the fire knocked down
two farm labourer hobbledehoys. It was terrible to see Mrs. Wannop's grey hair in the firelight. After that the butcher refused them
meat altogether, ration card or no ration card. It was imperative that
they should move to London.

The marsh horizon became obscured with giant stilts, the air above
it filled with aeroplanes, the roads covered with military cars. There
was then no getting away from the sounds of the war.

Just as they had decided to move Tietjens came back. It was for a
moment heaven to have him in this country. But when, a month
later, Valentine Wannop saw him for a minute, he seemed very
heavy, aged, and dull. It was then almost as bad as before, for it
seemed to Valentine as if he hardly had his reason.

On hearing that Tietjens was to be quartered — or, at any rate,
occupied — in the neighbourhood of Ealing, Mrs. Wannop at once
took a small house in Bedford Park, whilst, to make ends meet — for
her mother made terribly little — Valentine Wannop took a post as
athletic mistress in a great school in a not very near suburb. Thus,
though Tietjens came in for a cup of tea almost every afternoon with
Mrs. Wannop in the dilapidated little suburban house, Valentine

Wannop hardly ever saw him. The only free afternoon she had was the Friday, and on that day she still regularly chaperoned Mrs. Duchemin, meeting her at Charing Cross towards noon and taking her back to the same station in time to catch the last train to Rye. On Saturdays and Sundays she was occupied all day in typing her mother's manuscript.

Of Tietjens, then, she saw almost nothing. She knew that his poor mind was empty of facts and of names; but her mother said he was a great help to her. Once provided with facts his mind worked out sound Tory conclusions — of quite startling and attractive theories — with extreme rapidity. This Mrs. Wannop found of the greatest use to her whenever — though it wasn't now very often — she had an article to write for an excitable newspaper. She still, however, contributed to her failing organ of opinion, though it paid her nothing.

Mrs. Duchemin, then, Valentine Wannop still chaperoned, though there was no bond any more between them. Valentine knew, for instance, perfectly well that Mrs. Duchemin, after she had been seen off by train from Charing Cross, got out at Clapham Junction, took a taxicab back to Gray's Inn after dark and spent the night with Macmaster, and Mrs. Duchemin knew quite well that Valentine knew. It was a sort of parade of circumspection and rightness, and they kept it up even after, at a sinister registry office, the wedding had taken place, Valentine being the one witness and an obscure-looking substitute for the usual pew opener another. There seemed to be, by then, no very obvious reason why Valentine should support Mrs. Macmaster any more on these rather dreary occasions, but Mrs. Macmaster said she might just as well, until they saw fit to make the marriage public. There were, Mrs. Macmaster said, censorious tongues, and even if these were confuted afterwards it is difficult, if not impossible, to outrun scandal. Besides, Mrs. Macmaster was of opinion that the Macmaster afternoons with these geniuses must be a liberal education for Valentine. But, as Valentine sat most of the time at the tea-table near the door, it was the backs and side faces of the distinguished rather than their intellects with which she was most acquainted. Occasionally, however, Mrs. Duchemin would show Valentine, as an enormous privilege, one of the letters to herself from men of genius — usually North British, written, as a rule, from the Continent or more distant and peaceful climates, for most of them believed it their duty in these hideous times to keep alive in the world the only glimmering spark of beauty. Couched in terms so eulogistic

as to resemble those used in passionate love-letters by men more profane, these epistles recounted, or consulted Mrs. Duchemin as to,
their love affairs with foreign princesses, the progress of their ailments
or the progresses of their souls towards those higher regions of
morality in which floated their so beautiful-souled correspondent.

The letters entertained Valentine and, indeed, she was entertained
by that whole mirage. It was only the Macmasters' treatment of her
mother that finally decided Valentine that this friendship had died;
for the friendships of women are very tenacious things, surviving
astonishing disillusionments, and Valentine Wannop was a woman
of more than usual loyalty. Indeed, if she couldn't respect Mrs.
Duchemin on the old grounds, she could very really respect her for
her tenacity of purpose, her determination to advance Macmaster,
and for the sort of ruthlessness that she put into these pursuits.

Valentine's affection had, indeed, survived even Edith Ethel's continued denigrations of Tietjens — for Edith Ethel regarded Tietjens
as a clog round her husband's neck, if only because he was a very unpopular man, grown personally rather unpresentable and always extremely rude to the geniuses on Fridays. Edith Ethel, however, never
made these complaints that grew more and more frequent as more
and more the distinguished flocked to the Fridays, before Macmaster.
And they ceased very suddenly and in a way that struck Valentine
as odd.

Mrs. Duchemin's grievance against Tietjens was that, Macmaster
being a weak man, Tietjens had acted as his banker until, what with
interest and the rest of it, Macmaster owed Tietjens a great sum:
several thousand pounds. And there had been no real reason: Macmaster had spent most of the money either on costly furnishings for
his rooms or on his costly journeys to Rye. On the one hand Mrs.
Duchemin could have found Macmaster all the bric-a-brac he could
possibly have wanted from amongst the things at the rectory, where
no one would have missed them and, on the other, she, Mrs. Duchemin, would have paid all Macmaster's travelling expenses. She had
had unlimited money from her husband, who never asked for accounts. But, whilst Tietjens still had influence with Macmaster, he
had used it uncompromisingly against this course, giving him the
delusion — it enraged Mrs. Duchemin to think! — that it would have
been dishonourable. So that Macmaster had continued to draw upon
him.

And, most enraging of all, at a period when she had had a power of attorney over all Mr. Duchemin's fortune and could, perfectly easily, have sold out something that no one would have missed for the couple of thousand or so that Macmaster owed, Tietjens had very forcibly refused to allow Macmaster to agree to anything of the sort. He had again put into Macmaster's weak head that it would be dishonourable. But Mrs. Duchemin — and she closed her lips determinedly after she had said it — knew perfectly well Tietjen's motive. So long as Macmaster owed him money he imagined that they couldn't close their doors upon him. And their establishment was beginning to be a place where you meet people of great influence who might well get for a person as lazy as Tietjens a sinecure that would suit him. Tietjens, in fact, knew which side his bread was buttered.

For what, Mrs. Duchemin asked, could there have been dishonourable about the arrangement she had proposed? Practically the whole of Mr. Duchemin's money was to come to her: he was by then insane; it was therefore, morally, her own. But immediately after that, Mr. Duchemin having been certified, the estate had fallen into the hands of the Lunacy Commissioners and there had been no further hope of taking the capital. Now, her husband being dead, it was in the hands of trustees, Mr. Duchemin having left the whole of his property to Magdalen College and merely the income to his widow. The income was very large; but where, with their expenses, with the death duties and taxation, which were by then merciless, was Mrs. Duchemin to find the money? She was to be allowed, under her husband's will, enough capital to buy a pleasant little place in Surrey, with rather a nice lot of land — enough to let Macmaster know some of the leisures of a country gentleman's lot. They were going in for shorthorns, and there was enough land to give them a small golf-course and, in the autumn, a little — oh, mostly rough! — shooting for Macmaster to bring his friends down to. It would just run to that. Oh, no ostentation. Merely a nice little place. As an amusing detail the villagers there already called Macmaster "squire" and the women curtsied to him. But Valentine Wannop would understand that, with all these expenses, they couldn't find the money to pay off Tietjens. Besides, Mrs. Macmaster said she wasn't going to pay off Tietjens. He had had his chance once; now he could go without, for her. Macmaster would have to pay it himself and he would never be able to, his contribution to their housekeeping being what it was. And there were going to be complications. Macmaster wondered

about their little place in Surrey, saying that he would consult Tietjens about this and that alteration. But over the doorsill of that place
the foot of Tietjens was never going to go! Never! It would mean a
good deal of unpleasantness; or rather it would mean one sharp:
"C-r-r-unch!" And then: Napoo finny! Mrs. Duchemin sometimes,
and with great effect, condescended to use one of the more picturesque phrases of the day.

To all these diatribes Valentine Wannop answered hardly anything. It was no particular concern of her's; even if, for a moment, she
felt proprietarily towards Christopher as she did now and then, she
felt no particular desire that his intimacy with the Macmasters
should be prolonged, because she knew he could have no particular
desire for its prolongation. She imagined him turning them down
with an unspoken and good-humoured gibe. And, indeed, she agreed
on the whole with Edith Ethel. It *was* demoralising for a weak little
man like Vincent to have a friend with an ever-open purse beside
him. Tietjens ought not to have been princely; it was a defect, a
quality that she did not personally admire in him. As to whether it
would or wouldn't have been dishonourable for Mrs. Duchemin to
take her husband's money and give it to Macmaster, she kept an
open mind. To all intents and purposes the money *was* Mrs. Duchemin's, and if Mrs. Duchemin had then paid Christopher off it would
have been sensible. She could see that later it had become very inconvenient. There were, however, male standards to be considered,
and Macmaster, at least, passed for a man. Tietjens, who was wise
enough in the affairs of others, had, in that, probably been wise; for
there might have been great disagreeablenesses with trustees and
heirs-at-law had Mr. Duchemin's subtraction of a couple of thousand
pounds from the Duchemin estate afterwards come to light. The
Wannops had never been large property owners as a family, but
Valentine had heard enough of collateral wranglings over small
family dishonesties to know how very disagreeable these could be.

So she had made little or no comment; sometimes she had even
faintly agreed as to the demoralisation of Macmaster and that had
sufficed. For Mrs. Duchemin had been certain of her rightness and
cared nothing at all for the opinion of Valentine Wannop, or else
took it for granted.

And when Tietjens had been gone to France for a little time Mrs.
Duchemin seemed to forget the matter, contenting herself with saying that he might very likely not come back. He was the sort of

clumsy man who generally got killed. In that case, since no I.O.U.s or paper had passed, Mrs. Tietjens would have no claim. So that would be all right.

But two days after the return of Christopher — and that was how Valentine knew he had come back! — Mrs. Duchemin with a lowering brow exclaimed:

"That oaf, Tietjens, is in England, perfectly safe and sound. And now the whole miserable business of Vincent's indebtedness . . . Oh!"

She had stopped so suddenly and so markedly that even the stoppage of Valentine's own heart couldn't conceal the oddness from her. Indeed it was as if there were an interval before she completely realised what the news was and as if, during that interval, she said to herself:

"It's very queer. It's exactly as if Edith Ethel has stopped abusing him on my account . . . As if she *knew*!" But how could Edith Ethel know that she loved the man who had returned? It was impossible! She hardly knew herself. Then the great wave of relief rolled over her: he was in England. One day she would see him, there, in the great room. For these colloquies with Edith Ethel always took place in the great room where she had last seen Tietjens. It looked suddenly beautiful and she was resigned to sitting there, waiting for the distinguished.

It was indeed a beautiful room; it had become so during the years. It was long and high — matching the Tietjens'. A great cut-glass chandelier from the rectory hung dimly coruscating in the centre, reflected and re-reflected in convex gilt mirrors, topped by eagles. A great number of books had gone to make place on the white panelled walls for the mirrors, and for the fair orange and brown pictures by Turner, also from the rectory. From the rectory had come the immense scarlet and lapis lazuli carpet, the great brass fire-basket and appendages, the great curtains that, in the three long windows, on their peacock-blue Chinese silk showed parti-coloured cranes ascending in long flights — and all the polished Chippendale arm-chairs. Amongst all these, gracious, trailing, stopping with a tender gesture to rearrange very slightly the crimson roses in the famous silver bowls, still in dark blue silks, with an amber necklace and her elaborate black hair, waved exactly like that of Julia Domna of the Musée Lapidaire at Arles, moved Mrs. Macmaster — also from the rectory. Macmaster had achieved his desire, even to the shortbread cakes and the peculiarly scented tea that came every Friday morning from Princes Street. And, if Mrs. Macmaster hadn't the pawky, relishing humour of the great Scots ladies of past days, she had in exchange her deep aspect of comprehension and tenderness. An astonishingly beautiful and impressive woman: dark hair; dark, straight eyebrows; a straight nose; dark blue eyes in the shadows of her hair and bowed, pomegranate lips in a chin curved like the bow of a Greek boat. . . .

The etiquette of the place on Fridays was regulated as if by a royal protocol. The most distinguished and, if possible, titled person was led to a great walnut-wood fluted chair that stood askew by the fireplace, its back and seat of blue velvet, heaven knows how old. Over him would hover Mrs. Duchemin; or, if he were *very* distinguished, both Mr. and Mrs. Macmaster. The not-so-distinguished were led up by turns to be presented to the celebrity and would then arrange themselves in a half-circle in the beautiful arm-chairs; the less distinguished still, in outer groups in chairs that had no arms; the almost undistinguished stood, also in groups or languished, awestruck on the scarlet leather window seats. When all were there Macmaster would establish himself on the incredibly unique hearthrug and would address wise sayings to the celebrity; occasionally, however, saying a kind thing to the youngest man present — to give him a chance of distinguishing himself. Macmaster's hair, at that date, was still black, but not quite so stiff or so well brushed; his beard had in it greyish streaks and his teeth, not being quite so white, looked less strong. He wore also a single eyeglass, the retaining of which in his right eye gave him a slightly agonized expression. It gave him, however, the privilege of putting his face very close to the face of anyone upon whom he wished to make a deep impression. He had lately become much interested in the drama, so that there were usually several large and, of course, very reputable and serious actresses in the room. On rare occasions Mrs. Duchemin would say across the room in her deep voice:

"Valentine, a cup of tea for his highness," or "Sir Thomas," as the case might be, and when Valentine had threaded her way through the chairs with a cup of tea Mrs. Duchemin, with a kind, aloof smile, would say: "Your highness, this is my little brown bird." But as a rule Valentine sat alone at the tea-table, the guests fetching from her what they wanted.

Tietjens came to the Fridays twice during the five months of his stay at Ealing. On each occasion he accompanied Mrs. Wannop.

In earlier days — during the earliest Fridays — Mrs. Wannop, if she ever came, had always been installed, with her flowing black, in the throne and, like an enlarged Queen Victoria, had sat there whilst suppliants were led up to this great writer. But now: on the first occasion Mrs. Wannop got a chair without arms in the outer ring, whilst a general officer commanding lately in chief somewhere in the East, whose military success had not been considerable, but whose despatches were considered very literary, occupied, rather blazingly, the throne. But Mrs. Wannop had chatted very contentedly all the afternoon with Tietjens, and it had been comforting to Valentine to see Tietjens' large, uncouth, but quite collected figure, and to observe the affection that these two had for each other.

But, on the second occasion, the throne was occupied by a very young woman who talked a great deal and with great assurance. Valentine didn't know who she was. Mrs. Wannop, very gay and distracted, stood nearly the whole afternoon by a window. And even at that, Valentine was contented, quite a number of young men crowding round the old lady and leaving the younger one's circle rather bare.

There came in a very tall, clean run and beautiful, fair woman, dressed in nothing in particular. She stood with extreme — with noticeable — unconcern near the doorway. She let her eyes rest on Valentine, but looked away before Valentine could speak. She must have had an enormous quantity of fair tawny hair, for it was coiled in a great surface over her ears. She had in her hand several visiting cards which she looked at with a puzzled expression and then laid on a card table. She was no one who had ever been there before.

Edith Ethel — it was for the second time! — had just broken up the ring that surrounded Mrs. Wannop, bearing the young men tributary to the young woman in the walnut chair and leaving Tietjens and the older woman high and dry in a window; thus Tietjens saw the stranger, and there was no doubt left in Valentine's mind. He came, diagonally, right down the room to his wife and marched her straight up to Edith Ethel. His face was perfectly without expression.

Macmaster, perched on the centre of the hearthrug, had an emotion that was extraordinarily comic to witness, but that Valentine was quite unable to analyse. He jumped two paces forward to meet Mrs. Tietjens, held out a little hand, half withdrew it, retreated half a step. The eyeglass fell from his perturbed eye: this gave him actu-

ally an expression less perturbed, but, in revenge, the hairs on the
back of his scalp grew suddenly untidy. Sylvia, wavering along beside
her husband, held out her long arm and careless hand. Macmaster
winced almost at the contact, as if his fingers had been pinched in a
vice. Sylvia wavered desultorily towards Edith Ethel, who was suddenly small, insignificant, and relatively coarse. As for the young
woman celebrity in the arm-chair, she appeared to be about the size
of a white rabbit.

A complete silence had fallen on the room. Every women in it was
counting the pleats of Sylvia's skirt and the amount of material in it.
Valentine Wannop knew that because she was doing it herself. If one
had that amount of material and that number of pleats one's skirt
might hang like that. . . . For it was extraordinary: it fitted close
round the hips, and gave an effect of length and swing — yet it did
not descend as low as the ankles. It was, no doubt, the amount of material that did that, like the Highlander's kilt that takes twelve yards
to make. And from the silence Valentine could tell that every woman
and most of the men — if they didn't know that this was Mrs.
Christopher Tietjens — knew that this was a personage of *Illustrated
Weekly*, as who should say of county family, rank. Little Mrs. Swan,
lately married, actually got up, crossed the room and sat down beside
her bridegroom. It was a movement with which Valentine could
sympathise.

And Sylvia, having just faintly greeted Mrs. Duchemin, and completely ignored the celebrity in the arm-chair — in spite of the fact
that Mrs. Duchemin had tried half-heartedly to effect an introduction — stood still, looking round her. She gave the effect of a lady
in a nurseryman's hothouse considering what flower should interest
her, collectedly ignoring the nurserymen who bowed round her. She
had just dropped her eyelashes, twice, in recognition of two staff
officers with a good deal of scarlet streak about them who were
tentatively rising from their chairs. The staff officers who came to the
Macmasters were not of the first vintages; still they had the labels and
passed as such.

Valentine was by that time beside her mother, who had been
standing all alone between two windows. She had dispossessed, in
hot indignation, a stout musical critic of his chair and had sat her
mother in it. And, just as Mrs. Duchemin's deep voice sounded, yet
a little waveringly:

"Valentine . . . a cup of tea for . . ." Valentine was carrying a cup of tea to her mother.

Her indignation had conquered her despairing jealousy, if you could call it jealousy. For what was the good of living or loving when Tietjens had beside him, for ever, the radiant, kind, and gracious perfection. On the other hand, of her two deep passions, the second was for her mother.

Rightly or wrongly, Valentine regarded Mrs. Wannop as a great, an august figure: a great brain, a high and generous intelligence. She had written, at least, one great book, and if the rest of her time had been frittered away in the desperate struggle to live that had taken both their lives, that could not detract from that one achievement that should last and for ever take her mother's name down time. That this greatness should not weigh with the Macmasters had hitherto neither astonished nor irritated Valentine. The Macmasters had their game to play and, for the matter of that, they had their predilections. Their game kept them amongst the officially influential, the semi-official and the officially accredited. They moved with such C.B.s, knights, presidents, and the rest as dabbled in writing or the arts: they went upwards with such reviewers, art critics, musical writers and archæologists as had posts in, if possible, first-class public offices or permanent positions on the more august periodicals. If an imaginative author seemed assured of position and lasting popularity Macmaster would send out feelers towards him, would make himself humbly useful, and sooner or later either Mrs. Duchemin would be carrying on with him one of her high-souled correspondences — or she wouldn't.

Mrs. Wannop they had formerly accepted as permanent leader writer and chief critic of a great organ, but the great organ having dwindled and now disappeared the Macmasters no longer wanted her at their parties. That was the game — and Valentine accepted it. But that it should have been done with such insolence, so obviously meant to be noted — for in twice breaking up Mrs. Wannop's little circle Mrs. Duchemin had not even once so much as said: "How d'ye do?" to the elder lady! — that was almost more than Valentine could, for the moment, bear, and she would have taken her mother away at once and would never have re-entered the house, but for the compensations.

Her mother had lately written and even found a publisher for a book — and the book had showed no signs of failing powers. On the contrary, having been perforce stopped off the perpetual journalism that had dissipated her energies, Mrs. Wannop had turned out something that Valentine knew was sound, sane, and well done. Abstractions caused by failing attention to the outside world are not necessarily in a writer signs of failing, as a writer. It may mean merely that she is giving so much thought to her work that her other contacts suffer. If that is the case her work will gain. That this might be the case with her mother was Valentine's great and secret hope. Her mother was barely sixty: many great works have been written by writers aged between sixty and seventy. . . .

And the crowding of youngish men round the old lady had given Valentine a little confirmation of that hope. The book naturally, in the maelstrom flux and reflux of the time, had attracted little attention, and poor Mrs. Wannop had not succeeded in extracting a penny for it from her adamantine publisher; she hadn't, indeed, made a penny for several months, and they existed almost at starvation point in their little den of a villa — on Valentine's earnings as athletic teacher. . . . But that little bit of attention in that semi-public place had seemed, at least, as a confirmation to Valentine: there probably was something sound, sane, and well done in her mother's work. That was almost all she asked of life.

And, indeed, whilst she stood by her mother's chair, thinking with a little bitter pathos that if Edith Ethel had left the three or four young men to her mother the three or four might have done her poor mother a little good, with innocent puffs and the like — and heaven knew they needed that little good badly enough! — a very thin and untidy young man *did* drift back to Mrs. Wannop and asked, precisely, if he might make a note or two for publication as to what Mrs. Wannop was doing. "Her book," he said, "had attracted so much attention. They hadn't known that they had still writers among them. . . ."

A singular, triangular drive had begun through the chairs from the fireplace. That was how it had seemed to Valentine! Mrs. Tietjens had looked at them, had asked Christopher a question and, immediately, as if she were coming through waist-high surf, had borne down Macmaster and Mrs. Duchemin, flanking her obsequiously, setting aside chairs and their occupants, Tietjens and the two, rather bashfully following staff officers, broadening out the wedge.

Sylvia, her long arm held out from a yard or so away, was giving her hand to Valentine's mother. With her clear, high, unembarrassed voice she exclaimed, also from a yard or so away, so as to be heard by every one in the room:

"You're Mrs. Wannop. The great writer! I'm Christopher Tietjens' wife."

The old lady, with her dim eyes, looked up at the younger woman towering above her.

"You're Christopher's wife!" she said. "I must kiss you for all the kindness he has shown me."

Valentine felt her eyes filling with tears. She saw her mother stand up, place both her hands on the other woman's shoulders. She heard her mother say:

"You're a most beautiful creature. I'm sure you're good!"

Sylvia stood, smiling faintly, bending a little to accept the embrace. Behind the Macmasters, Tietjens, and the staff officers, a little crowd of goggle eyes had ranged itself.

Valentine was crying. She slipped back behind the tea-urns, though she could hardly feel the way. Beautiful! The most beautiful woman she had ever seen! And good! Kind! You could see it in the lovely way she had given her cheek to that poor old woman's lips. . . . And to live all day, for ever, beside him . . . she, Valentine, ought to be ready to lay down her life for Sylvia Tietjens. . . .

The voice of Tietjens said, just above her head:

"Your mother seems to be having a regular triumph," and, with his good-natured cynicism, he added, "it seems to have upset some apple-carts!" They were confronted with the spectacle of Macmaster conducting the young celebrity from her deserted arm-chair across the room to be lost in the horseshoe of crowd that surrounded Mrs. Wannop.

Valentine said:

"You're quite gay to-day. Your voice is different. I suppose you're better?" She did not look at him. His voice came:

"Yes! I'm relatively gay!" It went on: "I thought you might like to know. A little of my mathematical brain seems to have come to life again. I've worked out two or three silly problems. . . ."

She said:

"Mrs. Tietjens will be pleased."

"Oh!" the answer came. "Mathematics don't interest her any more than cock-fighting." With immense swiftness, between word and word, Valentine read into that a hope! This splendid creature did not sympathise with her husband's activities. But he crushed it heavily by saying: "Why should she? She's so many occupations of her own that she's unrivalled at!"

He began to tell her, rather minutely, of a calculation he had made only that day at lunch. He had gone into the Department of Statistics and had had rather a row with Lord Ingleby of Lincoln. A pretty title the fellow had taken! They had wanted him to ask to be seconded to his old department for a certain job. But he had said he'd be damned if he would. He detested and despised the work they were doing.

Valentine, for the first time in her life, hardly listened to what he said. Did the fact that Sylvia Tietjens had so many occupations of her own mean that Tietjens found her unsympathetic? Of their relationships she knew nothing. Sylvia had been so much of a mystery as hardly to exist as a problem hitherto. Macmaster, Valentine knew, hated her. She knew that through Mrs. Duchemin; she had heard it ages ago, but she didn't know why. Sylvia had never come to the Macmaster afternoons; but that was natural. Macmaster passed for a bachelor, and it was excusable for a young woman of the highest fashion not to come to bachelor teas of literary and artistic people. On the other hand, Macmaster dined at the Tietjens quite often enough to make it public that he was a friend of that family. Sylvia, too, had never come down to see Mrs. Wannop. But then it would, in the old days, have been a long way to come for a lady of fashion with no especial literary interests. And no one, in mercy, could have been expected to call on poor them in their dog kennel in an outer suburb. They had had to sell almost all their pretty things.

Tietjens was saying that after his tempestuous interview with Lord Ingleby of Lincoln — she wished he would not be so rude to powerful people! — he had dropped in on Macmaster in his private room, and finding him puzzled over a lot of figures had, in the merest spirit of bravado, taken Macmaster and his papers out to lunch. And, he said, chancing to look, without any hope at all, at the figures, he had suddenly worked out an ingenious mystification. It had just come!

His voice had been so gay and triumphant that she hadn't been able to resist looking up at him. His cheeks were fresh coloured, his hair shining; his blue eyes had a little of their old arrogance — and tenderness! Her heart seemed to sing with joy! He was, she felt, her man. She imagined the arms of his mind stretching out to enfold her.

He went on explaining. He had rather, in his recovered self-confidence, gibed at Macmaster. Between themselves, wasn't it easy to do what the Department, under orders, wanted done? They had wanted to rub into our allies that their losses by devastation had been nothing to write home about — so as to avoid sending reinforcements to their lines! Well, if you took just the bricks and mortar of the devastated districts, you could prove that the loss in bricks, tiles, woodwork and the rest didn't — and the figures with a little manipulation would prove it! — amount to more than a normal year's dilapidations spread over the whole country in peace time. . . . House repairs in a normal year had cost several million sterling. The enemy had only destroyed just about so many million sterling in bricks and mortar. And what was a mere year's dilapidations in house property! You just neglected to do them and did them next year.

So, if you ignored the lost harvests of three years, the lost industrial output of the richest industrial region of the country, the smashed machinery, the barked fruit trees, the three years' loss of four and a half-tenths of the coal output for three years — and the loss of life! — we could go to our allies and say:

"All your yappings about losses are the merest bulls. You can perfectly well afford to reinforce the weak places of your own lines. We intend to send our new troops to the Near East, where lies our true interest!" And, though they might sooner or later point out the fallacy, you would by so much have put off the abhorrent expedient of a single command.

Valentine, though it took her away from her own thoughts, couldn't help saying:

"But weren't you arguing against your own convictions?"

He said:

"Yes, of course I was. In the lightness of my heart! It's always a good thing to formulate the other fellow's objections."

She had turned half round in her chair. They were gazing into each other's eyes, he from above, she from below. She had no doubt of his love: he, she knew, could have no doubt of hers. She said:

"But isn't it dangerous? To show these people how to do it?"

He said:

"Oh, no, no. No! You don't know what a good soul little Vinnie is. I don't think you've ever been quite just to Vincent Macmaster! He'd as soon think of picking my pocket as of picking my brains. The soul of honour!"

Valentine had felt a queer, queer sensation. She was not sure after-

wards whether she had felt it before she had realised that Sylvia
Tietjens was looking at them. She stood there, very erect, a queer
smile on her face. Valentine could not be sure whether it was kind,
cruel, or merely distantly ironic; but she was perfectly sure it showed,
whatever was behind it, that its wearer knew all that there was to
know of her, Valentine's, feelings for Tietjens and for Tietjens' feelings for her. . . . It was like being a woman and man in adultery in
Trafalgar Square.

Behind Sylvia's back, their mouths agape, were the two staff officers. Their dark hairs were too untidy for them to amount to much,
but, such as they were, they were the two most presentable males
of the assembly — and Sylvia had snaffled them.

Mrs. Tietjens said:

"Oh, Christopher! I'm going on to the Basils'."

Tietjens said:

"All right. I'll pop Mrs. Wannop into the tube as soon as she's
had enough of it, and come along and pick you up!"

Sylvia had just drooped her long eyelashes, in sign of salutation,
to Valentine Wannop, and had drifted through the door, followed
by her rather unmilitary military escort in khaki and scarlet.

From that moment Valentine Wannop never had any doubt. She
knew that Sylvia Tietjens knew that her husband loved her, Valentine Wannop, and that she, Valentine Wannop, loved her husband
— with a passion absolute and ineffable. The one thing she, Valentine,
didn't know, the one mystery that remained impenetrable, was
whether Sylvia Tietjens was good to her husband!

A long time afterwards Edith Ethel had come to her beside the
tea-cups and had apologised for not having known, earlier than
Sylvia's demonstration, that Mrs. Wannop was in the room. She
hoped that they might see Mrs. Wannop much more often. She
added after a moment that she hoped Mrs. Wannop wouldn't, in
future, find it necessary to come under the escort of Mr. Tietjens.
They were too old friends for that, surely.

Valentine said:

"Look here, Ethel, if you think that you can keep friends with
mother and turn on Mr. Tietjens after all he's done for you, you're
mistaken. You are really. And mother's a great deal of influence. I
don't want to see you making any mistakes, just at this juncture. It's
a mistake to make nasty rows. And you'd make a very nasty one if you
said anything against Mr. Tietjens to mother. She knows a great deal.

Remember. She lived next door to the rectory for a number of years. And she's got a dreadfully incisive tongue. . . ."

Edith Ethel coiled back on her feet as if her whole body were threaded by a steel spring. Her mouth opened, but she bit her lower lip and then wiped it with a very white handkerchief. She said:

"I hate that man! I detest that man! I shudder when he comes near me."

"I know you do!" Valentine Wannop answered. "But I wouldn't let other people know it if I were you. It doesn't do you any real credit. He's a good man."

Edith Ethel looked at her with a long, calculating glance. Then she went to stand before the fireplace.

That had been five — or at most six — Fridays before Valentine sat with Mark Tietjens in the War Office waiting hall, and, on the Friday immediately before that again, all the guests being gone, Edith Ethel had come to the tea-table and, with her velvet kindness, had placed her right hand on Valentine's left. Admiring the gesture with a deep fervour, Valentine knew that that was the end.

Three days before, on the Monday, Valentine, in her school uniform, in a great store to which she had gone to buy athletic paraphernalia, had run into Mrs. Duchemin, who was buying flowers. Mrs. Duchemin had been horribly distressed to observe the costume. She had said:

"But do you go *about* in that? It's really dreadful."

Valentine had answered:

"Oh, yes. When I'm doing business for the school in school hours I'm expected to wear it. And I wear it if I'm going anywhere in a hurry after school hours. It saves my dresses. I haven't got too many."

"But *anyone* might meet you," Edith Ethel said in a note of agony. "It's very inconsiderate. Don't you *think* you've been very inconsiderate? You might meet any of the people who come to our Fridays!"

"I frequently do," Valentine said. "But they don't seem to mind. Perhaps they think I'm a Waac officer. That would be quite respectable. . . ."

Mrs. Duchemin drifted away, her arms full of flowers and real agony upon her face.

Now, beside the tea-table she said, very softly:

"My dear, we've decided not to have our usual Friday afternoon next week." Valentine wondered whether this was merely a lie to get rid of her. But Edith Ethel went on: "We've decided to have a little evening festivity. After a great deal of thought we've come to the conclusion that we ought, now, to make our union public." She paused to await comment, but Valentine making none she went on: "It coincides very happily — I can't help feeling it coincides very happily! — with another event. Not that *we* set much store by these things. . . . But it has been whispered to Vincent that next Friday. . . . Perhaps, my dear Valentine, you, too, will have heard . . ."

Valentine said:

"No, I haven't. I suppose he's got the O.B.E. I'm very glad."

"The Sovereign," Mrs. Duchemin said, "is seeing fit to confer the honour of knighthood on him."

"Well!" Valentine said. "He's had a quick career. I've no doubt he deserves it. He's worked very hard. I do sincerely congratulate you. It'll be a great help to you."

"It's," Mrs. Duchemin said, "not for mere plodding. That's what makes it so gratifying. It's for a special piece of brilliance, that has marked him out. It's, of course, a secret. But . . ."

"Oh, I know!" Valentine said. "He's worked out some calculations to prove that losses in the devastated districts, if you ignore machinery, coal output, orchard trees, harvests, industrial products and so on, don't amount to more than a year's household dilapidations for the . . ."

Mrs. Duchemin said with real horror:

"But how did you know? How on *earth* did you know? . . ." She paused. "It's such a *dead* secret. . . . That fellow must have told you. . . . But how on earth could *he* know?"

"I haven't see Mr. Tietjens to speak to since the last time he was here," Valentine said. She saw, from Edith Ethel's bewilderment, the whole situation. The miserable Macmaster hadn't even confided to his wife that the practically stolen figures weren't his own. He desired to have a little prestige in the family circle; for once a little prestige! Well! Why shouldn't he have it? Tietjens, she knew, would wish him to have all he could get. She said therefore:

"Oh, it's probably in the air. . . . It's known the Government want to break their claims to the higher command. And anyone who could help them to that would get a knighthood. . . ."

Mrs. Duchemin was more calm.

"It's certainly," she said, "Burke'd, as you call it, those beastly people." She reflected for a moment. "It's probably that," she went on. "It's in the air. Anything that can help to influence public opinion against those horrible people is to be welcomed. That's known pretty widely. . . . No! It could hardly be Christopher Tietjens who thought of it and told you. It wouldn't enter his head. He's their friend! He would be . . ."

"He's certainly," Valentine said, "not a friend of his country's enemies. I'm not myself."

Mrs. Duchemin exclaimed sharply, her eyes dilated.

"What do you mean? What on earth do you dare to mean? I thought you were a pro-German!"

Valentine said:

"I'm not! I'm not! . . . I hate men's deaths. . . . I hate any men's deaths. . . . Any men . . ." She calmed herself by main force. "Mr. Tietjens says that the more we hinder our allies the more we drag the war on and the more lives are lost. . . . More lives, do you understand? . . ."

Mrs. Duchemin assumed her most aloof, tender, and high air: "My poor child," she said, "what possible concern can the opinions of that broken fellow cause anyone? You can warn him from me that he does himself no good by going on uttering these discredited opinions. He's a marked man. Finished! It's no good. Guggums, my husband, trying to stand up for him."

"He *does* stand up for him?" Valentine asked. "Though I don't see why it's needed. Mr. Tietjens is surely able to take care of himself."

"My good child," Edith Ethel said, "you may as well know the worst. There's not a more discredited man in London than Christopher Tietjens, and my husband does himself infinite harm in standing up for him. It's our one quarrel."

She went on again:

"It was all very well whilst that fellow had brains. He was said to have some intellect, though I could never see it. But now that, with his drunkenness and debaucheries, he has got himself into the state he is in; for there's no other way of accounting for his condition! They're striking him, I don't mind telling you, off the roll of his office. . . ."

It was there that, for the first time, the thought went through Valentine Wannop's mind, like a mad inspiration: this woman must at one time have been in love with Tietjens. It was possible, men being what they were that she had even once been Tietjens' mistress.

For it was impossible otherwise to account for this spite, which to Valentine seemed almost meaningless. She had, on the other hand, no impulse to defend Tietjens against accusations that could not have any possible grounds.

Mrs. Duchemin was going on with her kind loftiness:

"Of course a fellow like that—in that condition!—could not understand matters of high policy. It is imperative that these fellows should not have the higher command. It would pander to their insane spirit of militarism. They *must* be hindered. I'm talking, of course, between ourselves, but my husband says that that is the conviction in the very highest circles. To let them have their way, even if it led to earlier success, would be to establish a precedent—so my husband says! — compared with which the loss of a few lives. . . ."

Valentine sprang up, her face distorted.

"For the sake of Christ," she cried out, "as you believe that Christ died for you, try to understand that millions of men's lives are at stake. . . ."

Mrs. Duchemin smiled.

"My poor child," she said, "if you moved in the higher circles you would look at these things with more aloofness. . . ."

Valentine leant on the back of a high chair for support.

"You don't move in the higher circles," she said. "For Heaven's sake — for your own — remember that you are a woman, not for ever and for always a snob. You were a good woman once. You stuck to your husband for quite a long time. . . ."

Mrs. Duchemin, in her chair, had thrown herself back.

"My good girl," she said, "have you gone mad?"

Valentine said:

"Yes, very nearly. I've got a brother at sea; I've had a man I loved out there for an infinite time. You can understand that, I suppose, even if you can't understand how one can go mad merely at the thoughts of suffering at all. . . . And I know, Edith Ethel, that you are afraid of my opinion of you, or you wouldn't have put up all the subterfuges and concealments of all these years. . . ."

Mrs. Duchemin said quickly:

"Oh, my good girl. . . . If you've got personal interests at stake you can't be expected to take abstract views of the higher matters. We had better change the subject."

Valentine said:

"Yes, do. Get on with your excuses for not asking me and mother to your knighthood party."

Mrs. Duchemin, too, rose at that. She felt at her amber beads with long fingers that turned very slightly at the tips. She had behind her all her mirrors, the drops of her lustres, shining points of gilt and of the polish of dark woods. Valentine thought that she had never seen anyone so absolutely impersonate kindness, tenderness, and dignity. She said:

"My dear, I was going to suggest that it was the sort of party to which you might not care to come. . . . The people will be stiff and formal and you probably haven't got a frock."

Valentine said:

"Oh, I've got a frock all right. But there's a Jacob's ladder in my party stockings and that's the sort of ladder you can't kick down." She couldn't help saying that.

Mrs. Duchemin stood motionless and very slowly redness mounted into her face. It was most curious to see against that scarlet background the vivid white of the eyes and the dark, straight eyebrows that nearly met. And, slowly again her face went perfectly white; then her dark blue eyes became marked. She seemed to wipe her long, white hands one in the other, inserting her right hand into her left and drawing it out again.

"I'm sorry," she said in a dead voice. "We had hoped that, if that man went to France — or if other things happened — we might have continued on the old friendly footing. But you yourself must see that, with our official position, we can't be expected to connive . . ."

Valentine said:

"I don't understand!"

"Perhaps you'd rather I didn't go on!" Mrs. Duchemin retorted. "I'd much rather not go on."

"You'd probably better," Valentine answered.

"We had meant," the elder woman said, "to have a quiet little dinner — we two and you, before the party — for auld lang syne. But that fellow has forced himself in, and you see for yourself that we can't have you as well."

Valentine said:

"I don't see why not. I always like to see Mr. Tietjens!"

Mrs. Duchemin looked hard at her.

"I don't see the use," she said, "of your keeping on that mask. It is surely bad enough that your mother should go about with that man and that terrible scenes like that of the other Friday should occur. Mrs. Tietjens was heroic; nothing less than heroic. But you have no right to subject us, your friends, to such ordeals."

Valentine said:

"You mean . . . Mrs. Christopher Tietjens . . ."

Mrs. Duchemin went on:

"My husband insists that I should ask you. But I will not. I simply will not. I invented for you the excuse of the frock. Of course we could have given you a frock if that man is so mean or so penniless as not to keep you decent. But I repeat, with our official position we cannot — we cannot; it would be madness! — connive at this intrigue. And all the more as the wife appears likely to be friendly with us. She has been once: she may well come again." She paused and went on solemnly: "And I warn you, if the split comes — as it must, for what woman could stand it! — it is Mrs. Tietjens we shall support. She will always find a home here."

An extraordinary picture of Sylvia Tietjens standing beside Edith Ethel and dwarfing her as a giraffe dwarfs an emu, came into Valentine's head. She said:

"Ethel! Have I gone mad? Or is it you? Upon my word I can't understand. . . ."

Mrs. Duchemin exclaimed:

"For God's sake hold your tongue, you shameless thing! You've had a child by the man, haven't you?"

Valentine saw suddenly the tall silver candlesticks, the dark polished panels of the rectory and Edith Ethel's mad face and mad hair whirling before them.

She said:

"No! I certainly haven't. Can you get that into your head? I certainly haven't." She made a further effort over immense fatigue. "I assure you — I beg you to believe if it will give you any ease — that Mr. Tietjens has never addressed a word of love to me in his life. Nor have I to him. We have hardly talked to each other in all the time we have known each other."

Mrs. Duchemin said in a harsh voice:

"Seven people in the last five weeks have told me you have had a child by that brute beast: he's ruined because he has to keep you and your mother and the child. You won't deny that he has a child somewhere hidden away? . . ."

Valentine exclaimed suddenly:

"Oh, Ethel, you mustn't . . . you *mustn't* be jealous of me! If you only knew you wouldn't be jealous of me. . . . I suppose the child you were going to have was by Christopher? Men are like that. . . . But not of me! You need never, never. I've been the best friend you can ever have had. . . ."

Mrs. Duchemin exclaimed harshly, as if she were being strangled:

"A sort of blackmail! I knew it would come to that! It always does with your sort. Then do your damnedest, you harlot. You never set foot in this house again! Go you and rot. . . ." Her face suddenly expressed extreme fear and with great swiftness she ran up the room. Immediately afterwards she was tenderly bending over a great bowl of roses beneath the lustre. The voice of Vincent Macmaster from the door had said:

"Come in, old man. Of course I've got ten minutes. The book's in here somewhere. . . ."

Macmaster was beside her, rubbing his hands, bending with his curious, rather abject manner, and surveying her agonisedly with his eyeglass, which enormously magnified his lashes, his red lower lid and the veins on his cornea.

"Valentine!" he said, "my dear Valentine. . . . You've heard? We've decided to make it public. . . . Guggums will have invited you to our little feast. And there will be a surprise, I believe. . . ."

Edith Ethel looked, as she bent, lamentably and sharply, over her shoulder at Valentine.

"Yes," she said bravely, aiming her voice at Edith Ethel, "Ethel has invited me. I'll try to come. . . ."

"Oh, but you must," Macmaster said, "just you and Christopher, who've been so kind to us. For old time's sake. You could not . . ."

Christopher Tietjens was ballooning slowly from the door, his hand tentatively held out to her. As they practically never shook hands at home it was easy to avoid his hand. She said to herself: "Oh! How is it possible! How could he have . . ." And the terrible situation poured itself over her mind: the miserable little husband, the desperately nonchalant lover — and Edith Ethel mad with jealousy! A doomed household. She hoped Edith Ethel had seen her refuse her hand to Christopher.

But Edith Ethel, bent over her rose bowl, was burying her beautiful face in flower after flower. She was accustomed to do this for many minutes on end: she thought that, so, she resembled a picture by the subject of her husband's first little monograph. And so, Valentine thought, she did. She was trying to tell Macmaster that Friday evenings were difficult times for her to get away. But her thoat ached too much. That, she knew, was her last sight of Edith Ethel, whom she had loved very much. That also, she hoped, would be her last sight of Christopher Tietjens — whom also she had loved very much. . . . He was browsing along a bookshelf, very big and very clumsy.

Macmaster pursued her into the stony hall with clamorous repetitions of his invitation. She couldn't speak. At the great iron-lined door he held her hand for an eternity, gazing lamentably, his face close up against hers. He exclaimed in accents of great fear:

"Has Guggums? . . . She hasn't . . ." His face, which when you saw it so closely was a little blotched, distorted itself with anxiety: he glanced aside with panic at the drawing-room door.

Valentine burst a voice through her agonised throat.

"Ethel," she said, "has told me she's to be Lady Macmaster. I'm so glad. I'm so truly glad for you. You've got what you wanted, haven't you?"

His relief let him get out distractedly, yet as if he were too tired to be any more agitated:

"Yes! yes! . . . It's, of course, a secret. . . . I don't want him told till Friday next . . . so as to be a sort of bonne bouche . . . He's practically certain to go out again on Saturday. . . . They're sending out a great batch of them . . . for the big push. . . ." At that she tried to draw her hand from his: she missed what he was saying. It was something to the effect that he would give it all for a happy little party. She caught the rather astonishing words: "Wie der alten schoenen Zeit." She couldn't tell whether it was his or her eyes that were full of tears. She said:

"I believe . . . I believe you're a kind man!"

In the great stone hall, hung with long Japanese paintings on silk, the electric light suddenly jumped; it was at best a sad, brown place. He exclaimed:

"I, too, beg you to believe that I will never abandon . . ." He glanced again at the inner door and added: "You both . . . I will never abandon . . . you both!" he repeated.

He let go her hand: she was on the stone stairs in the damp air. The great door closed irresistibly behind her, sending a whisper of air downwards.

V

MARK TIETJENS' announcement that his father had after all carried out his long-standing promise to provide for Mrs. Wannop in such a way as to allow her to write for the rest of her life only the more lasting kind of work, delivered Valentine Wannop of all her problems except one. That one loomed, naturally and immediately, immensely large.

She had passed a queer, unnatural week, the feeling dominating its numbness having been, oddly, that she would have nothing to do on Friday! This feeling recurred to her whilst she was casting her eyes over a hundred girls all in their cloth jumpers and men's black ties, aligned upon asphalt; whilst she was jumping on trams; whilst she was purchasing the tinned or dried fish that formed the staple diet of herself and her mother; whilst she was washing-up the dinner-things; upbraiding the house agent for the state of the bath, or bending closely over the large but merciless handwriting of the novel of her mother's that she was typing. It came, half as a joy, half mournfully across her familiar businesses; she felt as a man might feel who, luxuriating in the anticipation of leisure, knew that it was obtained by being compulsorily retired from some laborious but engrossing job. There would be nothing to do on Fridays!

It was, too, as if a novel had been snatched out of her hand so that she would never know the end. Of the fairytale she knew the end: the fortunate and adventurous tailor had married his beautiful and be-princessed goose-girl, and was well on the way to burial in Westminster Abbey — or at any rate to a memorial service, the squire being actually buried amongst his faithful villagers. But she would never know whether they, in the end, got together all the blue Dutch tiles they wanted to line their bathroom. . . . She would never know. Yet witnessing similar ambitions had made up a great deal of her life.

And, she said to herself, there was another tale ended. On the surface the story of her love for Tietjens had been static enough. It had begun in nothing and in nothing it had ended. But, deep down in her being — ah! it had progressed enough. Through the agency of two women! Before the scene with Mrs. Duchemin there could, she thought, have been few young women less preoccupied than she with the sexual substrata, either of passion or of life. Her months as a domestic servant had accounted for that, sex, as she had seen it from a back kitchen, having been a repulsive affair, whilst the knowledge of its manifestations that she had thus attained had robbed it of the mystery which caused most of the young women whom she knew to brood upon these subjects.

Her conviction as to the moral incidence of sex were, she knew, quite opportunist. Brought up amongst rather "advanced" young people, had she been publicly challenged to pronounce her views she would probably, out of loyalty to her comrades, have declared that neither morality nor any ethical aspects were concerned in the matter. Like most of her young friends, influenced by the advanced teachers and tendential novelists of the day, she would have stated herself to advocate an, of course, enlightened promiscuity. That, before the revelations of Mrs. Duchemin! Actually she had thought very little about the matter.

Nevertheless, even before that date, had her deeper feelings been questioned she would have reacted with the idea that sexual incontinence was extremely ugly and chastity to be prized in the egg-and-spoon race that life was. She had been brought up by her father — who, perhaps, was wiser than appeared on the surface — to admire athleticism, and she was aware that proficiency of the body calls for chastity, sobriety, cleanliness, and the various qualities that group themselves under the heading of abnegation. She couldn't have lived amongst the Ealing servant-class — the eldest son of the house in which she had been employed had been the defendant in a peculiarly scabrous breach of promise case, and the comments of the drunken cook on this and similar affairs had run the whole gamut from the sentimentally reticent to the extreme of coarseness according to the state of her alcoholic barometer — she couldn't then have lived among the Ealing servant-class and come to any other subliminal conclusion. So that, dividing the world into bright beings on the one hand and, on the other, into the mere stuff to fill graveyards whose actions during life couldn't matter, she had considered that the bright beings must be people whose public advocating of enlightened promiscuity went along with an absolute continence. She was aware that enlightened beings occasionally fell away from these standards in order to become portentous Egerias; but the Mary Wollstone-crafts, the Mrs. Taylors, and the George Eliots of the last century she had regarded humorously as rather priggish nuisances. Indeed,

being very healthy and very hard-worked, she had been in the habit of
regarding the whole matter, if not humorously, then at least good-
humouredly, as a nuisance.

But being brought right up against the sexual necessities of a first-
class Egeria had been for her a horrible affair. For Mrs. Duchemin
had revealéd the fact that her circumspect, continent, and suavely
æsthetic personality was doubled by another at least as coarse as,
and infinitely mōre incisive in expression than, that of the drunken
cook. The language that she had used about her lover — calling him
always "that oaf" or "that beast"! — had seemed literally to pain
the girl internally, as if it had caused so many fallings away of internal
supports at each two or three words. She had hardly been able to
walk home through the darkness from the rectory.

And she had never heard what had become of Mrs. Duchemin's
baby. Next day Mrs. Duchemin had been as suave, as circumspect,
and as collected as ever. Never a word more had passed between them
on the subject. This left in Valentine Wannop's mind a dark patch —
as it were of murder — at which she must never look. And across
the darkened world of her sexual tumult there flitted continually the
quick suspicion that Tietjens might have been the lover of her friend.
It was a matter of the simplest analogy. Mrs. Duchemin had appeared
a bright being: so had Tietjens. But Mrs. Duchemin was a foul
whore. . . . How much more then must Tietjens, who was a man,
with the larger sexual necessities of the male . . . Her mind always
refused to complete the thought.

Its suggestion wasn't to be combated by the idea of Vincent Macmaster himself; he was, she felt, the sort of man that it was almost a
necessity for either mistress or comrade to betray. He seemed to ask
for it. Besides, she once put it to herself, how could any woman, given
the choice and the opportunity — and God knows there was opportunity enough — choose that shadowy, dried leaf, if there were
the splendid masculinity of Tietjens in whose arms to lie. She so
regarded these two men. And that shadowy conviction was at once
fortified and appeased when, a little later, Mrs. Duchemin herself
began to apply to Tietjens the epithets of "oaf" and "beast" — the
very ones that she had used to designate the father of her putative
child!

But then Tietjens must have abandoned Mrs. Duchemin; and,
if he had abandoned Mrs. Duchemin, he must be available for her,
Valentine Wannop! The feeling, she considered, made her ignoble;

but it came from depths of her being that she could not control and, existing, it soothed her. Then, with the coming of the war, the whole problem died out, and between the opening of hostilities and what she had known to be the inevitable departure of her lover, she had surrendered herself to what she thought to be the pure physical desire for him. Amongst the terrible, crashing anguishes of that time, there had been nothing for it but surrender! With the unceasing — the never-ceasing — thought of suffering; with the never-ceasing idea that her lover, too, must soon be so suffering, there was in the world no other refuge. No other!

She surrendered. She waited for him to speak the word, or look the look that should unite them. She was finished. Chastity: napoo finny! Like everything else!

Of the physical side of love she had neither image nor conception. In the old days when she had been with him, if he had come into the room in which she was, or if he had merely been known to be coming down to the village, she had hummed all day under her breath and had felt warmer, little currents passing along her skin. She had read somewhere that to take alcohol was to send the blood into the surface vessels of the body, thus engendering a feeling of warmth. She had never taken alcohol, or not enough to produce recognisably that effect; but she imagined that it was thus love worked upon the body — and that it would stop for ever at that!

But, in these later days, much greater convulsions had overwhelmed her. It sufficed for Tietjens to approach her to make her feel as if her whole body was drawn towards him as, being near a terrible height, you are drawn towards it. Great waves of blood rushed across her being as if physical forces as yet undiscovered or invented attracted the very fluid itself. The moon so draws the tides.

Once before, for a fraction of a second, after the long, warm night of their drive, she had felt that impulsion. Now, years after, she was to know it all the time, waking or half-waking; and it would drive her from her bed. She would stand all night at the open window till the stars paled above a world turned grey. It could convulse her with joy; it could shake her with sobs and cut through her breast like a knife.

The day of her long interview with Tietjens, amongst the amassed beauties of Macmaster furnishings, she marked in the calendar of her mind as her great love scene. That had been two years ago; he had been going into the army. Now he was going out again. From that

she knew what a love scene was. It passed without any mention of
the word "love"; it passed in impulses; warmths; rigors of the skin.
Yet with every word they had said to each other they had confessed
their love; in that way, when you listen to the nightingale you hear
the expressed craving of your lover beating upon your heart.

Every word that he had spoken amongst the amassed beauties of
Macmaster furnishings had been a link in a love-speech. It was not
merely that he had confessed to her as he would have to no other
soul in the world — "To no other soul in the world," he had said! —
his doubts, his misgivings, and his fears; it was that every word he uttered and that came to her, during the lasting of that magic, had
sung of passion. If he had uttered the word "Come," she would have
followed him to the bitter ends of the earth; if he had said, "There
is no hope," she would have known the finality of despair. Having
said neither, she knew: "This is our condition; so we must continue!"
And she knew, too, that he was telling her that he, like her, was . . .
oh, say on the side of the angels. She was then, she knew, so nicely
balanced that, had he said, "Will you to-night be my mistress?" she
would have said "Yes"; for it was as if they had been, really, at the
end of the world.

But his abstention not only strengthened her in her predilection
for chastity; it restored to her her image of the world as a place of
virtues and endeavours. For a time at least she again hummed beneath her breath upon occasion, for it seemed as if her heart sang
within her. And there was restored to her her image of her lover as a
beautiful spirit. She had been able to look at him across the tea-table
of their dog kennel in Bedford Park, during the last months, almost
as she had looked across the more shining table of the cottage near
the rectory. The deterioration that she knew Mrs. Duchemin to have
worked in her mind was assuaged. It could even occur to her that Mrs.
Duchemin's madness had been no more than a scare to be followed
by no necessary crime. Valentine Wannop had re-become her confident self in a world of, at least, straight problems.

But Mrs. Duchemin's outbreak of a week ago had driven the old
phantoms across her mind. For Mrs. Duchemin she had still had a
great respect. She could not regard her Edith Ethel as merely a hypocrite or, indeed, as a hypocrite at all. There was her great achievement of making something like a man of that miserable little creature — as there had been her other great achievement of keeping her
unfortunate husband for so long out of a lunatic asylum. That had

been no mean feat; neither feat had been mean. And Valentine knew that Edith Ethel really loved beauty, circumspection, urbanity. It was no hypocrisy that made her advocate the Atalanta race of chastity. But, also, as Valentine Wannop saw it, humanity has these doublings of strong natures; just as the urbane and grave Spanish nation must find its outlet in the shrieking lusts of the bull-ring or the circumspect, laborious and admirable city typist must find her derivative in the cruder lusts of certain novelists, so Edith Ethel must break down into physical sexualities — and into shrieked coarseness of fishwives. How else, indeed, do we have saints? Surely, alone, by the ultimate victory of the one tendency over the other!

But now after her farewell scene with Edith Ethel a simple rearrangement of the pattern had brought many of the old doubts, at least temporarily, back. Valentine said to herself that, just because of the very strength of her character, Edith Ethel couldn't have been brought down to uttering her fantastic denunciation of Tietjens, the merely mad charges of debauchery and excesses and finally the sexually lunatic charge against herself, except under the sting of some such passion as jealousy. She, Valentine, couldn't arrive at any other conclusion. And, viewing the matter as she believed she now did, more composedly, she considered with seriousness that, men being what they are, her lover respecting, or despairing of, herself had relieved the grosser necessities of his being — at the expense of Mrs. Duchemin, who had, no doubt, been only too ready.

And in certain moods during the past week she had accepted this suspicion; in certain other moods she had put it from her. Towards the Thursday it had no longer seemed to matter. Her lover was going from her; the long pull of the war was on; the hard necessities of life stretched out; what could an infidelity more or less matter in the long, hard thing that life is. And on the Thursday two minor, or major, worries came to disturb her level. Her brother announced himself as coming home for several days' leave, and she had the trouble of thinking that she would have forced upon her a companionship and a point of view that would be coarsely and uproariously opposed to anything that Tietjens stood for — or for which he was ready to sacrifice himself. Moreover she would have to accompany her brother to a number of riotous festivities whilst all the time she would have to think of Tietjens as getting hour by hour nearer to the horrible circumstances of troops in contact with enemy forces. In addition her mother had received an enviably-paid-for commission from one of the more excitable Sunday papers to write a series of articles on extravagant matters connected with the hostilities. They had wanted the money so dreadfully — more particularly as Edward was coming home — that Valentine Wannop had conquered her natural aversion from the waste of time of her mother. . . . It would have meant very little waste of time, and the £60 that it would have brought in would have made all the difference to them for months and months.

But Tietjens, whom Mrs. Wannop had come to rely on as her right-hand man in these matters, had, it appeared, shown an unexpected recalcitrancy. He had, Mrs. Wannop said, hardly seemed himself and had gibed at the two first subjects proposed — that of "war babies" and the fact that the Germans were reduced to eating their own corpses — as being below the treatment of any decent pen. The illegitimacy rate, he had said, had shown very little increase; the French-derived German word "*cadaver*" meant bodies of horses or cattle; *leichnam* being the German for the word "corpse." He had practically refused to have anything to do with the affair.

As to the *cadaver* business Valentine agreed with him, as to the "war babies" she kept a more open mind. If there weren't any war babies it couldn't, as far as she could see, matter whether one wrote about them; it couldn't certainly matter as much as to write about them, supposing the poor little things to exist. She was aware that this was immoral, but her mother needed the money desperately and her mother came first.

There was nothing for it, therefore, but to plead with Tietjens, for Valentine knew that without so much of moral support from him as would be implied by a good-natured, or an enforced sanction of the article, Mrs. Wannop would drop the matter and so would lose her connection with the excitable paper which paid well. It happened that on the Friday morning Mrs. Wannop received a request that she would write for a Swiss review a propaganda article about some historical matter connected with the peace after Waterloo. The pay would be practically nothing, but the employment was at least relatively dignified, and Mrs. Wannop — which was quite in the ordinary course of things! — told Valentine to ring Tietjens up and ask him for some details about the Congress of Vienna at which, before and after Waterloo, the peace terms had been wrangled out.

Valentine rang up — as she had done hundreds of times; it was to her a great satisfaction that she was going to hear Tietjens speak once more at least. The telephone was answered from the other end,

and Valentine gave her two messages, the one as to the Congress of
Vienna, the other as to war babies. The appalling speech came back:
"Young woman! You'd better keep off the grass. Mrs. Duchemin
is already my husband's mistress. You keep off." There was about
the voice no human quality; it was if from an immense darkness the
immense machine had spoken words that dealt blows. She answered;
and it was as if a substratum of her mind of which she knew nothing
must have been prepared for that very speech; so that it was not her
own "she" that answered levelly and coolly:
"You have probably mistaken the person you are speaking to. Perhaps you will ask Mr. Tietjens to ring up Mrs. Wannop when he is
at liberty."
The voice said:
"My husband will be at the War Office at 4.15. He will speak to
you there — about your war babies. But I'd keep off the grass if I
were you!" The receiver at the other end was hung up.
She went about her daily duties. She had heard of a kind of pine
kernel that was very cheap and very nourishing, or at least very filling.
They had come to it that it was a matter of pennies balanced against
the feeling of satiety, and she visited several shops in search of this
food. When she had found it she returned to the dog kennel; her
brother Edward had arrived. He was rather subdued. He brought
with him a piece of meat which was part of his leave ration. He
occupied himself with polishing up his sailor's uniform for a rag-
time party to which they were to go that evening. They were to meet
plenty of conchies, he said. Valentine put the meat — it was a Godsend, though very stringy! — on to stew with a number of chopped
vegetables. She went up to her room to do some typing for her
mother.
The nature of Tietjens' wife occupied her mind. Before, she had
barely thought about her: she had seemed unreal; so mysterious as to
be a myth! Radiant and high-stepping, like a great stag! But she must
be cruel! She must be vindictively cruel to Tietjens himself, or she
could not have revealed his private affairs! Just broadcast; for she
could not, bluff it how she might, have been certain of to whom
she was speaking! A thing that wasn't done! But she had delivered her
cheek to Mrs. Wannop; a thing, too, that wasn't done! Yet so kindly!
The telephone bell rang several times during the morning. She let
her mother answer it.
She had to get the dinner, which took three-quarters of an hour.

It was a pleasure to see her mother eat so well; a good stew, rich and heavy with haricot beans. She herself couldn't eat, but no one noticed, which was a good thing. Her mother said that Tietjens had not yet telephoned, which was very inconsiderate. Edward said: "What! The Huns haven't killed old Feather Bolster yet? But of course he's been found a safe job." The telephone on the sideboard became a terror to Valentine; at any moment his voice might ... Edward went on telling anecdotes of how they bamboozled petty officers on mine-sweepers. Mrs. Wannop listened to him with the courteous, distant interest of the great listening to commercial travellers. Edward desired draught ale and produced a two-shilling piece. He seemed very much coarsened; it was, no doubt, only on the surface. In these days everyone was very much coarsened on the surface.

She went with a quart jug to the jug and bottle department of the nearest public-house — a thing she had never done before. Even at Ealing the mistress hadn't allowed her to be sent to a public-house; the cook had had to fetch her dinner beer herself or have it sent in. Perhaps the Ealing mistress had exercised more surveillance than Valentine had believed; a kind woman, but an invalid. Nearly all day in bed. Blind passion overcame Valentine at the thought of Edith Ethel in Tietjens' arms. Hadn't she got her own eunuch? Mrs. Tietjens had said: "Mrs. Duchemin is his mistress!" *Is!* Then he might be there now!

In the contemplation of that image she missed the thrills of buying beer in a bottle and jug department. Apparently it was like buying anything else, except for the smell of beer on the sawdust. You said: "A quart of the best bitter!" and a fat, quite polite man, with an oily head and a white apron, took your money and filled your jug. . . . But Edith Ethel had abused Tietjens so foully! The more foully the more certain it made it! . . . Draught beer in a jug had little marblings of burst foam on its brown surface. It mustn't be spilt at the kerbs of crossings! — the more certain it made it! Some women did so abuse their lovers after sleeping with them, and the more violent the transports the more frantic the abuse. It was the "*post-dash-tristis*" of the Rev. Duchemin! Poor devil! Tristis! Tristis!

Terra tribus scopulis vastum . . . Not longum!

Brother Edward began communing with himself, long and unintelligibly as to where he should meet his sister at 19.30 and give her a blow-out! The names of restaurants fell from his lips into her panic. He decided hilariously and not quite steadily — a quart is a lot to a

fellow from a mine-sweeper carrying no booze at all! — on meeting
her at 7.20 at High Street and going to a pub he knew; they would go
on to the dance afterwards. In a studio. "Oh, God!" her heart said,
"if Tietjens should want her then!" To be his; on his last night. He
might! Everybody was coarsened then; on the surface. Her brother
rolled out of the house, slamming the door so that every tile on the
jerry-built dog kennel rose and sat down again.

She went upstairs and began to look over her frocks. She couldn't
tell what frocks she looked over; they lay like aligned rags on the
bed, the telephone bell ringing madly. She heard her mother's voice,
suddenly assuaged: "Oh! oh! . . . It's you!" She shut her door and
began to pull open and to close drawer after drawer. As soon as she
ceased that exercise her mother's voice became half audible; quite
audible when she raised it to ask a question. She heard her say: "Not
get her into trouble . . . Of *course!*" then it died away into mere
high sounds.

She heard her mother calling:

"Valentine! Valentine! Come down. . . . Don't you want to speak
to Christopher? . . . Valentine! Valentine! . . ." And then another
burst: "Valentine . . . Valentine . . . *Valentine* . . ." As if she
had been a puppy dog! Mrs. Wannop, thank God, was on the lowest step of the creaky stairs. She had left the telephone. She
called up:

"Come down. I want to tell you! The dear boy has saved me! He
always saves me! What shall I do now he's gone?"

"He saved others: himself he could not save!" Valentine quoted
bitterly. She caught up her wideawake. She wasn't going to prink
herself for him. He must take her as she was. . . . Himself he could
not save! But he did himself proud! With women! . . . Coarsened!
But perhaps only on the surface! She herself! . . . She was running
downstairs!

Her mother had retreated into the little parlour: nine feet by nine;
in consequence, at ten feet it was too tall for its size. But there was
in it a sofa with cushions. . . . With her head upon those cushions,
perhaps. . . . If he came home with her! Late! . . .

Her mother was saying: He's a splendid fellow. . . . A root idea
for a war baby article. . . . If a Tommy was a decent fellow he abstained because he didn't want to leave his girl in trouble. . . . If he
wasn't he chanced it because it might be his last chance. . . .

"A message to me!" Valentine said to herself. "But *which* sentence. . . ." She moved, absently, all the cushions to one end of the sofa. Her mother exclaimed:

"He sent his love! His mother was lucky to have such a son!" and turned into her tiny hole of a study.

Valentine ran down over the broken tiles of the garden path, pulling her wideawake firmly on. She had looked at her wrist watch; it was two and twelve: 14.45. If she was to walk to the War Office by 4.15 — 16.15 — a sensible innovation! — she must step out. Five miles to Whitehall. God knows what, then! Five miles back! Two and a half, diagonally, to High Street Station by half-past 19! Twelve and a half miles in five hours or less. And three hours dancing on the top of it. And to dress! . . . She needed to be fit . . . And, with violent bitterness, she said:

"Well! I'm fit. . . ." She had an image of the aligned hundred of girls in blue jumpers and men's ties keeping whom fit had kept her super-fit. She wondered how many of them would be men's mistresses before the year was out. It was August then. But perhaps none! Because she had kept them fit. . . .

"Ah!" she said, "if I had been a loose woman, with flaccid breasts and a soft body. All perfumed!" . . . But neither Sylvia Tietjens nor Ethel Duchemin were soft. They might be scented on occasion! But they could not contemplate with equanimity doing a twelve-mile walk to save a few pence and dancing all night on top of it! She could! And perhaps the price she paid was just that; she was in such hard condition she hadn't moved him to . . . She perhaps exhaled such an aura of sobriety, chastity, and abstinence as to suggest to him that . . . that a decent fellow didn't get his girl into trouble before going to be killed. . . . Yet if he were such a town bull! . . . She wondered how she knew such phrases. . . .

The sordid and aligned houses seemed to rush past her in the mean August sunshine. That was because if you thought hard time went quicker; or because after you noticed the paper shop at this corner you would be up to the boxes of onions outside the shop of the next corner before you noticed anything else.

She was in Kensington Gardens, on the north side; she had left the poor shops behind. . . . In sham country, with sham lawns, sham avenues, sham streams. Sham people pursuing their ways across the sham grass. Or no! Not sham! In a vacuum! No! "Pasteurised" was the word! Like dead milk. Robbed of their vitamines. . . .

If she saved a few coppers by walking it would make a larger pile to put into the leering — or compassionate — taxi-cabman's hand after he had helped her support her brother into the dog kennel door. Edward would be dead drunk. She had fifteen shillings for the taxi. . . . If she gave a few coppers more it seemed generous. . . . What a day to look forward to still! Some days were lifetimes!

She would rather die than let Tietjens pay for the cab!

Why? Once a taximan had refused payment for driving her and Edward all the way to Chiswick, and she hadn't felt insulted. She had paid him; but she hadn't felt insulted! A sentimental fellow; touched at the heart by the pretty sister — or perhaps he didn't really believe it was a sister — and her incapable bluejacket brother! Tietjens was a sentimental fellow too. . . . What was the difference? . . . And then! The mother a dead, heavy sleeper; the brother dead drunk. One in the morning! He couldn't refuse her! Blackness, cushions! She had arranged the cushions, she remembered. Arranged them subconsciously! Blackness! Heavy sleep; dead drunkenness! . . . Horrible! . . . A disgusting affair! An affair of Ealing. . . . It shall make her one with all the stuff to fill graveyards. . . . Well, what else was she, Valentine Wannop; daughter of her father? And of her mother? Yes! But she herself . . . Just a little nobody!

They were no doubt wirelessing from the Admiralty. . . . But her brother was at home, or getting a little more intoxicated and talking treason. At any rate the flickering intermittences over the bitter seas couldn't for the moment concern him. . . . That 'bus touched her skirt as she ran for the island. . . . It might have been better. . . . But one hadn't the courage!

She was looking at patterned deaths under a little green roof, such as they put over bird shelters. Her heart stopped! Before, she had been breathless! She was going mad. She was dying. . . . All these deaths! And not merely the deaths. . . . The waiting for the approach of death; the contemplation of the parting from life! This minute you were; that, and you weren't! What was it like? Oh heaven, she knew. . . . She stood there contemplating parting from . . . One minute you were; the next . . . Her breath fluttered in her chest. . . . Perhaps he wouldn't come . . .

He was immediately framed by the sordid stones. She ran upon him and said something; with a mad hatred. All these deaths and he and his like responsible! . . . He had apparently a brother, a responsible one too! Browner complexioned! . . . But he! He! He! He! Completely calm; with direct eyes. . . . It wasn't possible. "*Holde*

Lippen: klaare Augen: heller Sinn. . . ." Oh, a little bit wilted, the clear intellect! And the lips? No doubt too. But he couldn't look at you so, unless . . .

She caught him fiercely by the arm; for the moment he belonged — more than to any browner, mere civilian, brother! — to her! She was going to ask him! If he answered: "Yes! I am such a man!" she was going to say: "Then you must take me too! If them, why not me? I must have a child. I too!" She desired a child. She would over-whelm these hateful lodestones with a flood of argument; she imag-ined — she felt — the words going between her lips. . . . She imag-ined her fainting mind; her consenting limbs. . . .

His looks were wandering round the cornice of these stone build-ings. Immediately she was Valentine Wannop again; it needed no word from him. Words passed, but words could no more prove an established innocence than words can enhance a love that exists. He might as well have recited the names of railway stations. His eyes, his unconcerned face, his tranquil shoulders; they were what ac-quitted him. The greatest love speech he had ever and could ever make her was when, harshly and angrily, he said something like:

"Certainly not. I imagined you knew me better" — brushing her aside as if she had been a midge. And, thank God, he had hardly listened to her!

She was Valentine Wannop again; in the sunlight the chaffinches said "Pink! pink!" The seed-heads of the tall grasses were brushing against her skirt. She was clean-limbed, clear-headed. . . . It was just a problem whether Sylvia Tietjens was good to him. . . . Good *for* him was, perhaps, the more exact way of putting it. Her mind cleared, like water that goes off the boil. . . . "Waters stilled at even." Nonsense. It was sunlight, and he had an adorable brother! He could save *his* brother. . . . Transport! There was another mean-ing to the word. A warm feeling settled down upon her; this was *her* brother; the next to the best ever! It was as if you had matched a piece of stuff so nearly with another piece of stuff as to make no odds. Yet just not the real stuff! She must be grateful to this relative for all he did for her; yet, ah, never so grateful as to the other — who had done nothing!

Providence is kind in great batches! She heard, mounting the steps, the blessed word Transport! "They," so Mark said: he and she — the family feeling again — were going to get Christopher into the Trans-port. . . . By the kindness of God the First Line Transport was the

only branch of the services of which Valentine knew anything. Their
charwoman, who could not read and write, had a son, a sergeant in a
line regiment. "Hooray!" he had written to his mother, "I've been
off my feed; recommended for the D.C.M. too. So they're putting
me senior N.C.O. of First Line Transport for a rest; the safest soft
job of the whole bally front line caboodle!" Valentine had had to
read this letter in the scullery amongst black-beetles. Aloud! She had
hated reading it as she had hated reading anything that gave details
of the front line. But charity begins surely with the char. She had
had to. Now she could thank God. The sergeant, in direct, perfectly
sincere language, to comfort his mother, had described his daily work,
detailing horses and G.S. limber wagons for jobs and superintending
the horse-standings. "Why," one sentence ran, "our O.C. Transport
is one of those fishing lunatics. Wherever we go he has a space of
grass cleared out and pegged and b——y hell to the man who walks
across it!" There the O.C. practised casting with trout and salmon
rods by the hour together. "That'll show you what a soft job it is!"
the sergeant had finished triumphantly.

So that there she, Valentine Wannop, sat on a hard bench against
a wall; downright, healthy middle-class — or perhaps upper middle-
class — for the Wannops were, if impoverished, yet of ancient family!
Over her sensible, moccasined shoes the tide of humanity flowed before her hard bench. There were two commissionaires, the one always benevolent, the other perpetually querulous, in a pulpit on one
side of her; on the other, a brown-visaged sort of brother-in-law with
bulging eyes, who in his shy efforts to conciliate her was continually
trying to thrust into his mouth the crook of his umbrella. As if it
had been a knob. She could not, at the moment, imagine why he
should want to conciliate her; but she knew she would know in a
minute.

For just then she was occupied with a curious pattern; almost
mathematically symmetrical. Now she was an English middle-class
girl — whose mother had a sufficient income — in blue cloth, a wide-
awake hat, a black silk tie; without a thought in her head that she
shouldn't have. And with a man who loved her: of crystal purity. Not
ten, not five minutes ago, she had been . . . She could not even
remember what she had been! And he had been, he had assuredly
appeared a town . . . No, she could not think the words. . . . A
raging stallion then! If now he should approach her, by the mere
movement of a hand along the table, she would retreat.

It was a Godsend; yet it was absurd. Like the weather machine of the old man and the old woman on opposite ends of the stick. . . . When the old man came out the old woman went in and it would rain; when the old woman came out . . . It was exactly like that! She hadn't time to work out the analogy. But it was like that. . . . In rainy weather the whole world altered. Darkened! . . . The cat-gut that turned them slackened . . . slackened. . . . But, always, they remained at opposite ends of the stick!

Mark was saying, the umbrella crook hindering his utterance:

"We buy then an annuity of five hundred for your mother. . . ."

It was astonishing, though it spread tranquillity through her, how little this astonished her. It was the merely retarded expected. Mr. Tietjens senior, an honourable man, had promised as much years ago. Her mother, an august genius, was to wear herself out putting, Mr. Tietjens alive, his political views in his paper. He was to make it up to her. He was making it up. In no princely fashion, but adequately, as a gentleman.

Mark Tietjens, bending over, held a piece of paper. A bell-boy came up to him and said: "Mr. Riccardo!" Mark Tietjens said: "No! He's gone!" He continued:

"Your brother. . . . Shelved for the moment. But enough to buy a practice, a good practice! When he's a full-fledged sawbones." He stopped, he directed upon her his atrabilarian eyes, biting his umbrella handle; he was extremely nervous.

"Now you!" he said. "Two or three hundred. A year of course! The capital absolutely your own. . . ." He paused: "But I warn you! Christopher won't like it. He's got his knife into me. I wouldn't grudge you . . . oh, any sum!" He waved his hand to indicate an amount boundless in its figures. "I know you keep Christopher straight," he said. "The only person that could!" He added: "Poor devil!"

She said:

"He's got his knife into you? Why?"

He answered vaguely:

"Oh, there's been all this talk. . . . Untrue, of course."

She said:

"People have been saying things against you? To him? Perhaps because there's been delay in settling the estate."

He said:

"Oh, no! The other way round, in fact!"

"Then they have been saying" she exclaimed, "things against . . . against me. And him!"

He exclaimed in anguish:

"Oh, but I ask you to believe . . . I beg you to believe that I believe . . . *you*! Miss Wannop!" He added grotesquely: "As pure as dew that lies within Aurora's sun-tipped . . ." His eyes stuck out like those of a suffocating fish. He said: "I beg you not on that account to hand the giddy mitten to . . ." He writhed in his tight double collar. "His wife!" he said . . . "She's no good to . . . *for* him! . . . She's soppily in love with him. But no good . . ." He very nearly sobbed. "You're the only . . ." he said, "I *know* . . ."

It came into her head that she was losing too much time in this Salle des Pas Perdus! She would have to take the train home! Fivepence! But what did it matter. Her mother had five hundred a year. . . . Two hundred and forty times five. . . .

Mark said brightly:

"If now we bought your mother an annuity of five hundred. . . . You say that's ample to give Christopher his chop. . . . And settled on her three . . . four . . . I like to be exact . . . hundred a year. . . . The capital of it; with remainder to you . . ." His interrogative face beamed.

She saw now the whole situation with perfect plainness. She understood Mrs. Duchemin's:

"You couldn't expect us, with our official position . . . to connive . . ." Edith Ethel had been perfectly right. She *couldn't* be expected. . . . She had worked too hard to appear circumspect and right! You can't ask people to lay down their whole lives for their friends! . . . It was only of Tietjens you could ask that! She said — to Mark:

"It's as if the whole world had conspired . . . like a carpenter's vice — to force us . . ." she was going to say "together. . . ." But he burst in, astonishingly:

"He must have his buttered toast . . . and his mutton chop . . . and Rhum St. James!" He said: "Damn it all. . . . You were made for him. . . . You can't blame people for coupling you. . . . They're forced to it. . . . If you hadn't existed they'd have had to invent you . . . Like Dante for . . . who was it? . . . Beatrice? There *are* couples like that."

She said:

"Like a carpenter's vice. . . . Pushed together. Irresistibly. Haven't
we resisted?"

His face became panic-stricken; his bulging eyes pushed away
towards the pulpit of the two commissionaires. He whispered:

"You won't . . . because of my ox's hoof . . . desert. . . ."

She said: — she heard Macmaster whispering it hoarsely.

"I ask you to believe that I will never . . . abandon . . ."

It was what Macmaster had said. He must have got it from Mrs.
Micawber!

Christopher Tietjens — in his shabby khaki, for his wife had spoilt
his best uniform — spoke suddenly from behind her back. He had
approached her from beyond the pulpit of the two commissionaires
and she had been turned towards Mark on his bench:

"Come along! Let's get out of this!" He was, she asked herself,
getting out of this! Towards what?

Like mutes from a funeral — or as if she had been, between the
brothers, a prisoner under escort — they walked down steps, half
righted towards the exit arch, one and a half righted to face Whitehall. The brothers grunted inaudible but satisfied sounds over her
head. They crossed, by the islands, Whitehall, where the 'bus had
brushed her skirt. Under an archway —

In a stony, gravelled majestic space the brothers faced each other.
Mark said:

"I suppose you won't shake hands!"

Christopher said:

"No! Why should I?" She herself had cried out to Christopher:

"Oh, *do*!" (The wireless squares overhead no longer concerned her.
Her brother was, no doubt, getting drunk in a bar in Piccadilly. . . .
A surface coarseness!)

Mark said:

"Hadn't you better? You might get killed! A fellow just getting
killed would not like to think he had refused to shake his brother
by the hand!"

Christopher had: "Oh . . . well!"

During her happiness over this hyperborean sentimentality he had
gripped her thin upper arm. He had led her past swans — or possibly
huts; she never remembered which — to a seat that had over it, or
near it, a weeping willow. He had said, gasping, too, like a fish:

"Will you be my mistress to-night? I am going out to-morrow at
8.30 from Waterloo."

She had answered:

"Yes! Be at such and such a studio just before twelve. . . . I have to see my brother home. . . . He will be drunk. . . ." She meant to say: "Oh, my darling, I have wanted you so much. . . ."

She said instead:

"I have arranged the cushions. . . ."

She said to herself:

"Now whatever made me say that? It's as if I had said: 'You'll find the ham in the larder under a plate. . . .' No tenderness about it. . . ."

She went away, up a cockle-shelled path, between ankle-high railings, crying bitterly. An old tramp, with red weeping eyes and a thin white beard, regarded her curiously from where he lay on the grass. He imagined himself the monarch of that landscape.

"That's women!" he said with the apparently imbecile enigmaticality of the old and the hardened. "Some do!" He spat into the grass; said: "Ah!" then added: "Some do not!"

VI

He let himself in at the heavy door; when he closed it behind him, in the darkness, the heaviness of the door sent long surreptitious whisperings up the great stone stairs. These sounds irritated him. If you shut a heavy door on an enclosed space it will push air in front of it and there will be whisperings; the atmosphere of mystery was absurd. He was just a man, returning after a night out. . . . Two-thirds, say, of a night out! It must be half-past three. But what the night had lacked in length it had made up in fantastic aspects. . . .

He laid his cane down on the invisible oak chest and, through the tangible and velvety darkness that had always in it the chill of the stone of walls and stairs, he felt for the handle of the breakfast-room door.

Three long parallelograms existed: pale glimmerings above, cut two-thirds of the way down by the serrations of chimney pot and roof-shadows! Nine full paces across the heavy piled carpet; then he ought to reach his round-backed chair, by the left-hand window. He reached his round-backed chair by the left-hand window. He sank into it; it fitted exactly his back. He imagined that no man had ever

been so tired and that no man had ever been so alone! A small, alive
sound existed at the other end of the room; in front of him existed
one and a half pale parallelograms. They were the reflection of the
windows of the mirror; the sound was no doubt Calton, the cat.
Something alive, at any rate! Possibly Sylvia at the other end of the
room, waiting for him, to see what he looked like. Most likely! It
didn't matter!

His mind stopped! Sheer weariness!

When it went on again it was saying:

"Naked shingles and surges drear . . . " and, "On these debatable
borders of the world!" He said sharply: "Nonsense!" The one was
either *Calais beach* or *Dover sands* of the whiskered man: Arnold.
. . . He would be seeing them both within the twenty-four hours.
. . . But no! He was going from Waterloo. Southampton, Havre,
therefore! . . . The other was by that detestable fellow: "the subject of our little monograph!" . . . What a long time ago! . . . He
saw a pile of shining despatch cases: the inscription *This rack is reserved for* . . .": a coloured — pink and blue! — photograph of Boulogne sands and the held up squares, the proofs of "our little . . ."
What a long time ago! He heard his own voice saying in the new railway carriage, proudly, clearly, and with male hardness:

"*I stand for monogamy and chastity. And for no talking about it.
Of course if a man who's a man wants to have a woman he has her.
And again no talking about it.* . . ." His voice — his own voice —
came to him as if from the other end of a long-distance telephone. A
damn long-distance one! Ten years . . .

If then a man who's a man wants to have a woman. . . . Damn
it, he doesn't! In ten years he had learnt that a Tommie who's a
decent fellow. . . . His mind said at one and the same moment, the
two lines running one over the other like the two subjects of a
fugue:

"Some beguiling virgins with the broken seals of perjury," and:

"Since when we stand side by side, only hands may meet!"

He said:

"But damn it; damn it again! The beastly fellow was wrong! Our
hands didn't meet. . . . I don't believe I've shaken hands. . . . I
don't believe I've touched the girl . . . in my life. . . . Never once!
. . . Not the hand-shaking sort. . . . A nod! . . . A meeting and
parting! . . . English, you know . . . But yes, she put her arm over
my shoulders. . . . On the bank! . . . *On such short acquaintance!*

I said to myself then . . . Well, we've made up for it since then. Or
no! Not made up! . . . Atoned. . . . As Sylvia so aptly put it; at
that moment mother was dying. . . ."

He, his conscious self, said:

"But it was probably the drunken brother. . . . You don't beguile
virgins with the broken seals of perjury in Kensington High Street at
two at night supporting, one on each side, a drunken bluejacket with
intermittent legs. . . ."

"Intermittent!" was the word. "Intermittently functioning!"

At one point the boy had broken from them and run with astonishing velocity along the dull wood paving of an immense empty street.
When they had caught him up he had been haranguing under black
hanging trees, with an Oxford voice, an immobile policeman:

"You're the fellows!" he'd been exclaiming, "who make old England what she is! You keep the peace in our homes! You save us
from the vile excesses. . . ."

Tietjens himself he had always addressed with the voice and accent
of a common seaman; with his coarsened surface voice!

He had the two personalities. Two or three times he had said:

"Why don't you kiss the girl? She's a *nice* girl, isn't she? You're
a poor b——y Tommie, ain't cher? Well, the poor b——y Tommies
ought to have all the nice girls they want! That's straight, isn't
it? . . ."

And, even at that time they hadn't known what was going to happen. . . . There are certain cruelties. . . . They had got a four-
wheel cab at last. The drunken boy had sat beside the driver; he had
insisted. . . . Her little, pale, shrunken face had gazed straight before her. . . . It hadn't been possible to speak; the cab, rattling all
over the road had pulled up with frightful jerks when the boy had
grabbed at the reins. . . . The old driver hadn't seemed to mind;
but they had had to subscribe all the money in their pockets to pay
him after they had carried the boy into the black house. . . .

Tietjens' mind said to him:

"Now when they came to her father's house so nimbly she slipped
in, and said: 'There is a fool without and is a maid within. . . .' "

He answered dully:

"Perhaps that's what it really amounts to. . . ." He had stood at
the hall door, she looking out at him with a pitiful face. Then from
the sofa within the brother had begun to snore; enormous, grotesque
sounds, like the laughter of unknown races from darkness. He had

turned and walked down the path, she following him. He had exclaimed:

"It's perhaps too . . . untidy . . ."

She had said:

"Yes! Yes . . . Ugly . . . Too . . . oh . . . *private!*"

He said, he remembered:

"But . . . for ever . . ."

She said, in a great hurry:

"But when you come back. . . . Permanently. And . . . oh, as if it were in public." . . . "I don't know," she had added. "*Ought we? . . . I'd be ready. . . .*" She added: "I will be ready for anything you ask."

He had said at some time: "But obviously. . . . Not under *this* roof. . . ." And he had added: "We're the sort that . . . *do not!*"

She had answered, quickly too:

"Yes — that's it. We're that sort!" And then she had asked: "And Ethel's party? Was it a great success?" It hadn't, she knew, been an inconsequence. He had answered:

"Ah . . . *That's* permanent. . . . *That's* public. . . . There was Rugeley. The Duke . . . Sylvia brought him. She'll be a great friend! . . . And the President of the Local Government Board, I think . . . and a Belgian . . . equivalent to Lord Chief Justice . . . and, of course, Claudine Sanbach. . . . Two hundred and seventy; all of the best, the modestly-elated Guggumses said as I left! And Mr. Ruggles . . . Yes! . . . They're established. . . . No place for me!"

"Nor for *me!*" she had answered. She added: "But I'm glad!"

Patches of silence ran between them. They hadn't yet got out of the habit of thinking they had to hold up the drunken brother. That had seemed to last for a thousand painful months. . . . Long enough to acquire a habit. The brother seemed to roar: "Haw — Haw — Kuryasch. . . ." And after two minutes: "Haw — Haw — Kuryasch. . . ." Hungarian, no doubt!

He said:

"It was splendid to see Vincent standing beside the Duke. Showing him a first edition! Not of course *quite* the thing for a, after all, wedding party! But how was Rugeley to know that? . . . And Vincent not in the least servile! He even corrected cousin Rugeley over the meaning of the word *colophon!* The first time he ever corrected a superior! . . . Established, you see! . . . And *practically* cousin

Rugeley. . . . Dear Sylvia Tietjens' cousin, so the next to nearest thing! Wife of Lady Macmaster's *oldest* friend. . . . Sylvia going to them in their — quite modest! — little place in Surrey. . . . As for us," he had concluded "they also serve who only stand and wait. . . ."

She said:

"I suppose the rooms looked lovely."

He had answered:

"Lovely. . . . They'd got all the pictures by that beastly fellow up from the rectory study in the dining-room on dark oak panelling. . . . A fair blaze of bosoms and nipples and lips and pomegranates. . . . The tallest silver candlesticks of course. . . . You remember, silver candlesticks and dark oak. . . ."

She said:

"Oh, my dear . . . Don't . . . *Don't!*"

He had just touched the rim of his helmet with his folded gloves. "So we just wash out!" he had said.

She said:

"Would you take this bit of parchment. . . . I got a little Jew girl to write on it in Hebrew: It's "God bless you and keep you: God watch over you at your goings out and at . . ."

He tucked it into his breast pocket.

"The talismanic passage," he said. "Of course I'll wear it. . . ."

She said:

"If we *could* wash out this afternoon. . . . It would make it easier to bear. . . . Your poor mother, you know, she was dying when we last . . ."

He said:

"You remember *that* . . . Even then you . . . And if I hadn't gone to Lobscheid. . . ."

She said:

"From the first moment I set eyes on you. . . ."

He said:

"And I . . . from the first moment . . . I'll tell you . . . if I looked out of a door . . . it was all like sand. . . . But to the half left a little bubbling up of water. That could be trusted. To keep on for ever. . . . You, perhaps, won't understand."

She said:

"Yes! I know!"

They were seeing landscapes. . . . sand dunes; close-cropped. . . .
Some negligible shipping; a stump-masted brig from Archangel. . . ."

"From the first moment," he repeated.

She said:

"If we *could* wash out . . ."

He said, and for the first moment felt grand, tender, protective:

"Yes, you *can*," he said. "You cut out from this afternoon, just before 4.58 it was when I said that to you and you consented . . . I
heard the Horse Guards clock. . . . To now. . . . Cut it out; and
join time up. . . . It *can* be done. . . . You know they do it surgi-
cally; for some illness; cut out a great length of the bowel and join
the tube up. . . . For colitis, I think. . . ."

She said:

"But I *wouldn't* cut it out. . . . It was the first spoken sign."

He said:

"No it wasn't. . . . From the very beginning . . . with every
word. . . ."

She exclaimed:

"You felt that too! . . . We've been pushed, as in a carpenter's
vice. . . . We couldn't have got away. . . ."

He said: "By God! That's it. . . ."

He suddenly saw a weeping willow in St. James's Park; 4.59! He
had just said: "Will you be my mistress to-night?" She had gone
away, half left, her hands to her face. . . . A small fountain; half
left. That could be trusted to keep on for ever. . . .

Along the lake side, sauntering, swinging his crooked stick, his incredibly shiny top-hat perched sideways, his claw-hammer coat tails,
very long, flapping out behind, in dusty sunlight, his magpie pince-
nez gleaming, had come, naturally, Mr. Ruggles. He had looked at
the girl; then down at Tietjens, sprawled on his bench. He had just
touched the brim of his shiny hat. He said:

"Dining at the club to-night? . . ."

Tietjens said: "No; I've resigned."

With the aspect of a long-billed bird chewing a bit of putridity,
Ruggles said:

"Oh, but we've had an emergency meeting of the committee . . .
the committee was sitting . . . and sent you a letter asking you to reconsider. . . ."

Tietjens said:

"I know. . . . I shall withdraw my resignation to-night. And re-sign again to-morrow morning."

Ruggles' muscles had relaxed for a quick second, then they stiffened.

"Oh, I say!" he had said. "Not that. . . . You couldn't do that. . . . Not to the *club*! . . . It's never been done. . . . It's an insult. . . ."

"It's meant to be," Tietjens said. "Gentlemen shouldn't be expected to belong to a club that has certain members on its committee."

Ruggles' deepish voice suddenly grew very high.

"Eh, I say, you know!" he squeaked.

Tietjens had said:

"I'm not vindictive. . . . But I *am* deadly tired: of all old women and their chatter."

Ruggles had said:

"I don't . . ." His face had become suddenly dark brown, scarlet, and then brownish purple. He stood droopingly looking at Tietjens' boots.

"Oh! Ah! Well!" he said at last. "See you at Macmaster's to-night. . . . A great thing his knighthood. First-class man. . . ."

That had been the first Tietjens had heard of Macmaster's knighthood; he had missed looking at the honours' list of that morning. Afterwards, dining alone with Sir Vincent and Lady Macmaster, he had seen, pinned up, a back view of the Sovereign doing something to Vincent; a photo for next morning's papers. From Macmaster's embarrassed hushings of Edith Ethel's explanation that the honour was for special services of a specific kind Tietjens guessed both the nature of Macmaster's service and the fact that the little man hadn't told Edith Ethel who, originally, had done the work. And — just like his girl — Tietjens had let it go at that. He didn't see why poor Vincent shouldn't have that little bit of prestige at home — under all the monuments! But he hadn't — though through all the evening Macmaster, with the solicitude and affection of a cringing Italian greyhound, had hastened from celebrity to celebrity to hang over Tietjens, and although Tietjens knew that his friend was grieved and appalled, like any woman, at his, Tietjens', going out again to France — Tietjens hadn't been able to look Macmaster again in the face. . . . He had felt ashamed. He had felt, for the first time in his life, ashamed!

Even when he, Tietjens, had slipped away from the party — to go to his good fortune! — Macmaster had come panting down the stairs, running after him, through guests coming up. He had said:

"Wait . . . You're not going. . . . I want to . . ." With a miserable and appalled glance he had looked up the stairs; Lady Macmaster might have come out too. His black, short beard quivering and his wretched eyes turned down, he had said:

"I wanted to explain. . . . This miserable knighthood. . . ."

Tietjens patted him on the shoulder, Macmaster being on the stairs above him.

"It's all right, old man," he had said — and with real affection: "We've powdered up and down enough for a little thing like that not to . . . I'm very glad. . . ."

Macmaster had whispered:

"And Valentine. . . . She's not here to-night. . . ."

He had exclaimed:

"By God! . . . If I thought . . ." Tietjens had said: "It's all right. It's all right. She's at another party. . . . I'm going on . . ."

Macmaster had looked at him doubtingly and with misery, leaning over and clutching the clammy banisters.

"Tell her . . ." he said . . . "Good God! You may be killed. . . . I beg you . . . I beg you to believe . . . I will . . . Like the apple of my eye. . . ." In the swift glance that Tietjens took of his face he could see that Macmaster's eyes were full of tears.

They both stood looking down at the stone stairs for a long time. Then Macmaster had said: "Well . . ."

Tietjens had said: "Well . . ." But he hadn't been able to look at Macmaster's eyes, though he had felt his friend's eyes pitiably exploring his own face. . . . "A backstairs way out of it," he had thought; a queer thing that you couldn't look in the face a man you were never going to see again!

"But by God," he said to himself fiercely, when his mind came back again to the girl in front of him, "this isn't going to be another backstairs exit. . . . I must tell her. . . . I'm damned if I don't make an effort. . . ."

She had her handkerchief to her face.

"I'm always crying," she said. . . . "A little bubbling spring that can be trusted to keep on. . . ."

He looked to the right and to the left. Ruggles or General Someone with false teeth that didn't fit *must* be coming along. The street with its sooty boskage was clean empty and silent. She was looking at him. He didn't know how long he had been silent, he didn't know where he had been; intolerable waves urged him towards her.

After a long time he said:

"Well . . ."

She moved back. She said:

"I won't watch you out of sight. . . . It is unlucky to watch any-one out of sight. . . . But I will never . . . I will never cut what you said then out of my memory . . ." She was gone; the door shut. He had wondered what she would never cut out of her memory. That he had asked her that afternoon to be his mistress?

He had caught, outside the gates of his old office, a transport lorry that had given him a lift to Holborn.

No More Parades

For two things my heart is grieved:
A man of war that suffereth from poverty
and men of intelligence
that are counted as refuse.

PROVERBS

Part One

WHEN YOU CAME IN the space was desultory, rectangular, warm after the drip of the winter night, and transfused with a brown-orange dust that was light. It was shaped like the house a child draws. Three groups of brown limbs spotted with brass took dim high-lights from shafts that came from a bucket pierced with holes, filled with incandescent coke and covered in with a sheet of iron in the shape of a funnel. Two men, as if hierarchically smaller, crouched on the floor beside the brazier; four, two at each end of the hut, drooped over tables in attitudes of extreme indifference. From the eaves above the parallelogram of black that was the doorway fell intermittent drippings of collected moisture, persistent, with glass-like intervals of musical sound. The two men squatting on their heels over the brazier — they had been miners — began to talk in a low sing-song of dialect, hardly audible. It went on and on, monotonously, without animation. It was as if one told the other long, long stories to which his companion manifested his comprehension or sympathy with animal grunts. . . .

An immense tea-tray, august, its voice filling the black circle of the horizon, thundered to the ground. Numerous pieces of sheet-iron said, "Pack. Pack. Pack." In a minute the clay floor of the hut shook, the drums of ears were pressed inwards, solid noise showered about the universe, enormous echoes pushed these men — to the right, to the left, or down towards the tables, and crackling like that of flames among vast underwood became the settled condition of the night. Catching the light from the brazier as the head leaned over, the lips of one of the two men on the floor were incredibly red and full and went on talking and talking. . . .

The two men on the floor were Welsh miners, of whom the one came from the Rhondda Valley and was unmarried; the other, from Pontardulais, had a wife who kept a laundry, he having given up going underground just before the war. The two men at the table to the right of the door were sergeants-major; the one came from Suffolk and was a time-serving man of sixteen years' seniority as a sergeant in a line regiment. The other was Canadian of English origin. The two officers at the other end of the hut were captains, the one a young regular officer born in Scotland but educated at Oxford; the other, nearly middle-aged and heavy, came from Yorkshire, and was in a militia battalion. The one runner on the floor was filled with a passionate rage because the elder officer had refused him leave to go home and see why his wife, who had sold their laundry, had not yet received the purchase money from the buyer; the other was thinking about a cow. His girl, who worked on a mountainy farm above Caerphilly, had written to him about a queer cow: a black-and-white Holstein — surely to goodness a queer cow. The English sergeant-major was almost tearfully worried about the enforced lateness of the draft. It would be twelve midnight before they could march them off. It was not right to keep men hanging about like that. The men did not like to be kept waiting, hanging about. It made them discontented. They did not like it. He could not see why the depot quartermaster could not keep up his stock of candles for the hooded lamps. The men had no call to be kept waiting, hanging about. Soon they would have to be having some supper. Quarter would not like that. He would grumble fair. Having to indent for suppers. Put his accounts out, fair, it would. Two thousand nine hundred and thirty-four suppers at a penny half-penny. But it was not right to keep the men hanging about till midnight and no suppers. It made them discontented and them going up the line for the first time, poor devils.

The Canadian sergeant-major was worried about a pig-skin leather pocket-book. He had bought it at the ordnance depot in the town. He imagined himself bringing it out on parade, to read out some return or other to the adjutant. Very smart it would look on parade, himself standing up straight and tall. But he could not remember whether he had put it in his kit-bag. On himself it was not. He felt in his right and left breast pockets, his right and left skirt pockets, in all the pockets of his overcoat that hung from a nail within reach of his chair. He did not feel at all certain that the man who acted as

his batman had packed that pocket-book with his kit, though he declared he had. It was very annoying. His present wallet, bought in
Ontario, was bulging and split. He did not like to bring it out when
Imperial officers asked for something out of a return. It gave them a
false idea of Canadian troops. Very annoying. He was an auctioneer.
He agreed that at this rate it would be half-past one before they had
the draft down to the station and entrained. But it was very annoying
to be uncertain whether that pocket-book was packed or not. He had
imagined himself making a good impression on parade, standing up
straight and tall, taking out that pocket-book when the adjutant
asked for a figure from one return or the other. He understood their
adjutants were to be Imperial officers now they were in France. It was
very annoying.

An enormous crashing sound said things of an intolerable intimacy
to each of those men, and to all of them as a body. After its mortal
vomiting all the other sounds appeared a rushing silence, painful to
ears in which the blood audibly coursed. The young officer stood violently up on his feet and caught at the complications of his belt
hung from a nail. The elder, across the table, lounging sideways,
stretched out one hand with a downwards movement. He was aware
that the younger man, who was the senior officer, was just upon out
of his mind. The younger man, intolerably fatigued, spoke sharp, injurious, inaudible words to his companion. The elder spoke sharp,
short words, inaudible too, and continued to motion downwards with
his hand over the table. The old English sergeant-major said to his
junior that Captain Mackenzie had one of his mad fits again, but
what he said was inaudible and he knew it. He felt arising in his
motherly heart that yearned at the moment over his two thousand
nine hundred and thirty-four nurslings a necessity, like a fatigue, to
extend the motherliness of his functions to the orfcer. He said to the
Canadian that Captain Mackenzie there going temporary off his
nut was the best orfcer in His Majesty's army. And going to make a
bleedin' fool of hisself. The best orfcer in His Majesty's army. Not a
better. Careful, smart, brave as an 'ero. And considerate of his men
in the line. You wouldn't believe . . . He felt vaguely that it was a
fatigue to have to mother an officer. To a lance-corporal, or a young
sergeant, beginning to go wrong you could mutter wheezy suggestions
through your moustache. But to an officer you had to say things slant-
ways. Difficult it was. Thank God they had a trustworthy, cool hand
in the other captain. Old and good, the proverb said.

Dead silence fell.

"Lost the ——, they 'ave," the runner from the Rhondda made his voice startlingly heard. Brilliant illuminations flickered on hut-gables visible through the doorway.

"No reason," his mate from Pontardulais rather whined in his native sing-song, "why the bleedin' searchlights, surely to goodness, should light us up for all the —— 'Un planes to see. I want to see my bleedin' little 'ut on the bleedin' Mumbles again, if they don't."

"Not so much swear words, O Nine Morgan," the sergeant-major said.

"Now, Dai Morgan, I'm telling you," O Nine Morgan's mate continued. "A queer cow it must have been whatever. Black-and-white Holstein it wass. . ."

It was as if the younger captain gave up listening to the conversation. He leant both hands on the blanket that covered the table. He exclaimed:

"Who the hell are you to give me orders? I'm your senior. Who the hell . . . Oh, by God, who the hell . . . Nobody gives me orders . . ." His voice collapsed weakly in his chest. He felt his nostrils to be inordinately dilated so that the air pouring into them was cold. He felt that there was an entangled conspiracy against him, and all round him. He exclaimed: "You and your —— pimp of a general! . . ." He desired to cut certain throats with a sharp trench-knife that he had. That would take the weight off his chest. The "Sit *down*" of the heavy figure lumping opposite him paralysed his limbs. He felt an unbelievable hatred. If he could move his hand to get at his trench-knife . . .

O Nine Morgan said: "The ——'s name who's bought my bleedin' laundry is Williams. . . . If I thought it was Evans Williams of Castell Goch, I'd desert."

"Took a hatred for its cawve," the Rhondda man said. "And look you, before you could say . . ." The conversation of orfcers was a thing to which they neither listened. Officers talked of things that had no interest. Whatever could possess a cow to take a hatred of its calf? Up behind Caerphilly on the mountains? On an autumny morning the whole hillside was covered with spider-webs. They shone down the sun like spun glass. Overlooked the cow must be.

The young captain leaning over the table began a long argument as to relative seniority. He argued with himself, taking both sides in an extraordinarily rapid gabble. He himself had been gazetted after

Gheluvelt. The other not till a year later. It was true the other was in permanent command of that depot, and he himself attached to the unit only for rations and discipline. But that did not include orders to sit down. What the hell, he wanted to know, did the other mean by it? He began to talk, faster than ever, about a circle. When its circumference came whole by the disintegration of the atom the world would come to an end. In the millennium there would be no giving or taking orders. Of course he obeyed orders till then.

To the elder officer, burdened with the command of a unit of unreasonable size, with a scratch headquarters of useless subalterns who were continually being changed, with N.C.O.s all unwilling to work, with rank and file nearly all colonials and unused to doing without things, and with a depot to draw on that, being old established, felt that it belonged exclusively to a regular British unit and resented his drawing anything at all, the practical difficulties of his everyday life were already sufficient, and he had troublesome private affairs. He was lately out of hospital; the sackcloth hut in which he lived, borrowed from the Depot medical officer who had gone to England on leave, was suffocatingly hot with the paraffin-heater going, and intolerably cold and damp without it; the batman whom the M.O. had left in charge of the hut appeared to be half-witted. These German air-raids had lately become continuous. The Base was packed with men, tighter than sardines. Down in the town you could not move in the streets. Draft-finding units were commanded to keep their men out of sight as much as possible. Drafts were to be sent off only at night. But how could you send off a draft at night when every ten minutes you had two hours of lights out for an air-raid? Every man had nine sets of papers and tags that had to be signed by an officer. It was quite proper that the poor devils should be properly documented. But how was it to be done? He had two thousand nine hundred and ninety-four men to send off that night and nine times two thousand nine hundred and ninety-four is twenty-six thousand nine hundred and forty-six. They would not or could not let him have a disc-punching machine of his own, but how was the Depot armourer to be expected to punch five thousand nine hundred and eighty-eight extra identity discs in addition to his regular jobs?

The other captain rambled on in front of him. Tietjens did not like his talk of the circle and the millennium. You get alarmed, if you have any sense, when you hear that. It may prove the beginnings of definite, dangerous lunacy. . . . But he knew nothing about the fel-

low. He was too dark and good-looking, too passionate, probably, to
be a good regular officer on the face of him. But he *must* be a good
officer: he had the D.S.O. with a clasp, the M.C., and some foreign
ribbon up. And the general said he was, with the additional odd piece
of information that he was a Vice-Chancellor's Latin Prize man. . . .
He wondered if General Campion knew what a Vice-Chancellor's
Latin Prize man was. Probably he did not, but had just stuck the
piece of information into his note as a barbaric ornament is used by
a savage chief. Wanted to show that he, General Lord Edward
Campion, was a man of culture. There was no knowing where vanity
would not break out.

So this fellow was too dark and good-looking to be a good officer:
yet he *was* a good officer. That explained it. The repressions of the
passionate drive them mad. He must have been being sober, dis-
ciplined, patient, absolutely repressed ever since 1914 — against a
background of hell-fire, row, blood, mud, old tins. . . . And indeed
the elder officer had a vision of the younger as if in a design for a
full-length portrait — for some reason with his legs astride, against a
background of tapestry scarlet with fire and more scarlet with blood.
. . . He sighed a little; that was the life of all those several millions. . . .

He seemed to see his draft: two thousand nine hundred and
ninety-four men he had had command of for over a couple of months
— a long space of time as that life went — men he and Sergeant-
Major Cowley had looked after with a great deal of tenderness, superintending their morale, their morals, their feet, their digestions,
their impatiences, their desires for women. . . . He seemed to see
them winding away over a great stretch of country, the head slowly
settling down, as in the Zoo you will see an enormous serpent slowly
sliding down into its water-tank. . . . Settling down out there, a
long way away, up against that impassable barrier that stretched from
the depths of the ground to the peak of heaven. . . .

Intense dejection, endless muddles, endless follies, endless villainies.
All these men given into the hands of the most cynically care-free
intriguers in long corridors who made plots that harrowed the hearts
of the world. All these men toys, all these agonies mere occasions for
picturesque phrases to be put into politicians' speeches without heart
or even intelligence. Hundreds of thousands of men tossed here and
there in that sordid and gigantic mud-brownness of midwinter . . .
by God, exactly as if they were nuts wilfully picked up and thrown

over the shoulder by magpies. . . . But men. Not just populations.
Men you worried over there. Each man a man with a backbone, knees,
breeches, braces, a rifle, a home, passions, fornications, drunks, pals,
some scheme of the universe, corns, inherited diseases, a green-
grocer's business, a milk walk, a paper stall, brats, a slut of a wife.
. . . The Men: the Other Ranks! And the poor —— little officers.
God help them. Vice-Chancellor's Latin Prize men. . . .

This particular poor —— Prize man seemed to object to noise. They
ought to keep the place quiet for him. . . .

By God, he was perfectly right. That place was meant for the quiet
and orderly preparation of meat for the shambles. Drafts! A Base is
a place where you meditate, perhaps you should pray; a place where
in peace the Tommies should write their last letters home and describe 'ow the guns are 'owling 'orribly.

But to pack a million and a half of men into and round that small
town was like baiting a trap for rats with a great chunk of rotten
meat. The Hun planes could smell them from a hundred miles away.
They could do more harm there than if they bombed a quarter of
London to pieces. And the air defences there were a joke, a mad joke.
They pooped off, thousands of rounds, from any sort of pieces of
ordnance, like schoolboys bombarding swimming rats with stones.
Obviously your best trained air-defence men would be round your
metropolis. But this was no joke for the sufferers.

Heavy depression settled down more heavily upon him. The distrust of the home Cabinet, felt by then by the greater part of that
army, became like physical pain. These immense sacrifices, this
ocean of mental sufferings, were all undergone to further the private
vanities of men who amidst these hugenesses of landscapes and forces
appeared pigmies! It was the worries of all these wet millions in mud-
brown that worried him. They could die, they could be massacred,
by the quarter million, in shambles. But that they should be massacred without jauntiness, without confidence, with depressed brows,
without parade. . . .

He knew really nothing about the officer in front of him. Apparently the fellow had stopped for an answer to some question.
What question? Tietjens had no idea. He had not been listening.
Heavy silence settled down on the hut. They just waited. The fellow
said with an intonation of hatred:

"Well, what about it? That's what I want to know!"

Tietjens went on reflecting. . . . There were a great many kinds

of madness. What kind was this? The fellow was not drunk. He
talked like a drunkard, but he was not drunk. In ordering him to
sit down Tietjens had just chanced it. There are madmen whose momentarily subconscious selves will respond to a military command as
if it were magic. Tietjens remembered having barked "About . . .
turn," to a poor little lunatic fellow in some camp at home and the
fellow who had been galloping hotfoot past his tent, waving a naked
bayonet with his pursuers fifty yards behind, had stopped dead and
faced about with a military stamp like a guardsman. He had tried it
on this lunatic for want of any better expedient. It had apparently
functioned intermittently. He risked saying:

"What about what?"

The man said as if ironically:

"It seems as if I were not worth listening to by your high and
mightiness. I said: 'What about my foul squit of an uncle?' Your
filthy, best friend."

Tietjens said:

"The general's your uncle? General Campion? What's he done to
you?"

The general had sent this fellow down to him with a note asking
him, Tietjens, to keep an eye in his unit on a very good fellow and
an admirable officer. The chit was in the general's own writing, and
contained the additional information as to Captain Mackenzie's scholastic prowess. . . . It had struck Tietjens as queer that the general
should take so much trouble about a casual infantry company commander. How could the fellow have been brought markedly to his
notice? Of course, Campion was good-natured, like another man. If
a fellow, half dotty, whose record showed that he was a very good
man, was brought to his notice Campion would do what he could
for him. And Tietjens knew that the general regarded himself, Tietjens, as a heavy, bookish fellow, able reliably to look after one of his
protégés. . . . Probably Campion imagined that they had no work
to do in that unit: they might become an acting lunatic ward. But if
Mackenzie was Campion's nephew the thing was explained.

The lunatic exclaimed:

"Campion, *my* uncle? Why, he's *yours!*"

Tietjens said:

"Oh, no, he isn't." The general was not even a connection of his,
but he did happen to be Tietjen's godfather and his father's oldest
friend.

The other fellow answered:

"Then it's damn funny. *Damn* suspicious. . . . Why should he be interested in you if he's not your filthy uncle? You're no soldier. . . . You're no sort of a soldier. . . . A meal sack, that's what you look like. . . ." He paused and then went on very quickly: "They say up at H.Q. that your wife has got hold of the disgusting general. I didn't believe it was true. I didn't believe you were that sort of fellow. I've heard a lot about you!"

Tietjens laughed at this madness. Then, in the dark brownness, an intolerable pang went all through his heavy frame — the intolerable pang of home news to these desperately occupied men, the pain caused by disasters happening in the darkness and at a distance. You could do nothing to mitigate them! . . . The extraordinary beauty of the wife from whom he was separated — for she was extraordinarily beautiful! — might well have caused scandals about her to have penetrated to the general's headquarters, which was a sort of family party! Hitherto there had, by the grace of God, been no scandals. Sylvia Tietjens had been excruciatingly unfaithful, in the most painful manner. He could not be certain that the child he adored was his own. . . . That was not unusual with extraordinarily beautiful — and cruel! — women. But she had been haughtily circumspect.

Nevertheless, three months ago, they had parted. . . . Or he thought they had parted. Almost complete blankness had descended upon his home life. She appeared before him so extraordinarily bright and clear in the brown darkness that he shuddered: very tall, very fair, extraordinarily fit, and clean even. Thorough-bred! In a sheath gown of gold tissue, all illuminated, and her mass of hair, like gold tissue too, coiled round and round in plaits over her ears. The features very clean-cut and thinnish; the teeth white and small; the breasts small; the arms thin, long and at attention at her sides. . . . His eyes, when they were tired, had that trick of reproducing images on their retinas with that extreme clearness, images sometimes of things he thought of, sometimes of things merely at the back of the mind. Well, to-night his eyes were very tired! She was looking straight before her, with a little inimical disturbance of the corners of her lips. She had just thought of a way to hurt terribly his silent personality. . . . The semi-clearness became a luminous blue, like a tiny gothic arch, and passed out of his vision to the right.

He knew nothing of where Sylvia was. He had given up looking at the illustrated papers. She had said she was going into a convent at Birkenhead — but twice he had seen photographs of her. The first showed her merely with Lady Fiona Grant, daughter of the Earl and Countess of Ulleswater — and a Lord Swindon, talked of as next minister for International Finance — a new Business Peer. . . . All three walking straight into the camera in the courtyard of Lord Swindon's castle . . . all three smiling! . . . It announced Mrs. Christopher Tietjens as having a husband at the front.

The sting had, however, been in the second picture — in the description of it supplied by the journal! It showed Sylvia standing in front of a bench in the park. On the bench in profile there extended himself in a guffaw of laughter, a young man in a top hat jammed well on to his head, which was thrown back, his prognathous jaw pointing upwards. The description stated that the picture showed Mrs. Christopher Tietjens, whose husband was in hospital at the Front, telling a good story to the son and heir of Lord Brigham! . . . Another of these pestilential, crooked newspaper-owning financial peers . . .

It had struck him for a painful moment whilst looking at the picture in a dilapidated mess ante-room after he had come out of hospital — that, considering the description, the journal had got its knife into Sylvia. . . . But the illustrated papers do not get their knives into society beauties. They are too precious to the photographers. . . . Then Sylvia must have supplied the information; she desired to cause comment by the contrast of her hilarious companions and the statement that her husband was in hospital at the Front. . . . It had occurred to him that she was on the warpath, but he had put it out of his mind. . . . Nevertheless, brilliant mixture as she was, of the perfectly straight, perfectly fearless, perfectly reckless, of the generous, the kind even — and the atrociously cruel, nothing might suit her better than positively to show contempt — no, not contempt! cynical hatred — for her husband, for the war, for public opinion . . . even for the interest of their child! . . . Yet, it came to him, the image of her that he had just seen had been the image of Sylvia, standing at attention, her mouth working a little, whilst she read out the figures beside the bright filament of mercury in a thermometer. . . . The child had had, with measles, a temperature that, even then, he did not dare think of. And — it was at his sister's in Yorkshire, and the local doctor hadn't cared to take the responsibility — he could still feel the warmth of the little mummy-like body; he had covered the head and face with a flannel, for he didn't care for the sight, and lowered the warm, terrible, fragile weight into a shining surface of crushed ice in water. . . . She had stood at attention, the corners of her mouth moving a little: the thermometer going down as you watched it. . . . So that she mightn't want, in damaging the father, atrociously to damage the child. For there could not be anything worse for a child than to have a mother known as a whore. . . .

Sergeant-Major Cowley was standing beside the table. He said:

"Wouldn't it be a good thing, sir, to send a runner to the depot sergeant cook and tell him we're going to indent for suppers for the draft? We could send the other with the 128's to Quarter. They're neither wanted here for the moment."

The other captain went on incessantly talking — but about his fabulous uncle, not about Sylvia. It was difficult for Tietjens to get what he wanted said. He wanted the second runner sent to the depot quartermaster with a message to the effect that if G.S. candles for hooded lamps were not provided for the use of his orderly room by return of bearer he, Captain Tietjens, commanding Number XVI Casual Battalion, would bring the whole matter of supplies for his battalion that same night before Base Headquarters. They were all three talking at once; heavy fatalism overwhelmed Tietjens at the thought of the stubbornness showed by the depot quartermaster. The big unit beside his camp was a weary obstinacy of obstruction. You would have thought they would have displayed some eagerness to get his men up into the line. Let alone that the men were urgently needed, the more of his men went the more of *them* stayed behind. Yet they tried to stop his meat, his groceries, his braces, his identification discs, his soldiers' small books. . . . Every imaginable hindrance, and not even self-interested common sense! . . . He managed also to convey to Sergeant-Major Cowley that, as everything seemed to have quieted down, the Canadian sergeant-major had better go and see if everything was ready for falling his draft in. . . . If things remained quiet for another ten minutes, the "All Clear" might then be expected. . . . He knew that Sergeant-Major Cowley wanted to get the Other Ranks out of the hut with that captain carrying on like that, and he did not see why the old N.C.O. should not have what he wanted.

It was as if a tender and masculine butler withdrew himself. Cowley's grey walrus moustache and scarlet cheeks showed for a moment beside the brazier, whispering at the ears of the runners, a hand kindly on each of their shoulders. The runners went; the Canadian went. Sergeant-Major Cowley, his form blocking the doorway, surveyed the stars. He found it difficult to realise that the same pinpricks of light through black manifolding paper as he looked at, looked down also on his villa and his elderly wife at Isleworth beside the Thames above London. He knew it to be the fact, yet it was difficult to realise. He imagined the trams going along the High Street, his missus in one of them with her supper in a string bag on her stout knees; the trams lit up and shining. He imagined her having kippers for supper: ten to one it would be kippers; her favourites. His daughter was in the Waac's by now. She had been cashier to Parks's, the big butchers in Brentford, and pretty she had used to look in the glass case. Like as if it might have been the British Museum where they had Pharaohs and others in glass cases. . . . There were threshing machines droning away all over the night. He always said they were like threshing machines. . . . Crikey, if only they were! . . . But they might be our own planes, of course. A good Welsh rarebit he had had for tea.

In the hut, the light from the brazier having fewer limbs on which to fall, a sort of intimacy seemed to descend, and Tietjens felt himself gain in ability to deal with his mad friend. Captain Mackenzie — Tietjens was not sure that the name was Mackenzie: it had looked something like it in the general's hand — Captain Mackenzie was going on about the wrongs he had suffered at the hands of some fabulous uncle. Apparently at some important juncture the uncle had refused to acknowledge acquaintanceship with the nephew. From that all the misfortunes of the nephew had arisen. . . . Suddenly Tietjens said:

"Look here, pull yourself together. Are you mad? Stark, staring? . . . Or only just play-acting?"

The man suddenly sank down on to the bully-beef case that served for a chair. He stammered a question as to what — what — what Tietjens meant.

"If you let yourself go," Tietjens said, "you may let yourself go a tidy sight farther than you want to."

"You're not a mad doctor," the other said. "It's no good your trying to come it over me. I know all about you. I've got an uncle who's done the dirty on me — the dirtiest dirty ever was done on a man. If it hadn't been for him I shouldn't be here now."

"You talk as if the fellow had sold you into slavery," Tietjens said.

"He's your closest friend," Mackenzie seemed to advance as a motive for revenge on Tietjens. "He's a friend of the general's, too. Of your wife's as well. He's in with everyone."

A few desultory, pleasurable "pop-op-ops" sounded from far overhead to the left.

"They imagine they've found the Hun again," Tietjens said. "That's all right; you concentrate on your uncle. Only don't exaggerate his importance to the world. I assure you you are mistaken if you call him a friend of mine. I have not got a friend in the world." He added: "Are you going to mind the noise? If it is going to get on your nerves you can walk in a dignified manner to a dugout, now, before it gets bad. . . ." He called out to Cowley to go and tell the Canadian sergeant-major to get his men back into their shelters if they had come out. Until the "All Clear" went.

Captain Mackenzie sat himself gloomily down at table.

"Damn it all," he said, "don't think I'm afraid of a little shrapnel. I've had two periods solid of fourteen and nine months in the line. I could have got out on to the rotten staff. . . . It's, damn it, it's the beastly row. . . . Why isn't one a beastly girl and privileged to shriek? By God, I'll get even with some of them one of these days. . . ."

"Why not shriek?" Tietjens asked. "You can, for me. No one's going to doubt your courage here."

Loud drops of rain spattered down all round the hut; there was a familiar thud on the ground a yard or so away, a sharp tearing sound above, a sharper knock on the table between them. Mackenzie took the shrapnel bullet that had fallen and turned it round and round between finger and thumb.

"You think you caught me on the hop just now," he said injuriously. "You're damn clever."

Two stories down below some one let two hundred-pound dumbbells drop on the drawing-room carpet; all the windows of the house slammed in a race to get it over; the "pop-op-ops" of the shrapnel went in wafts all over the air. There was again sudden silence that was painful, after you had braced yourself up to bear noise. The runner from the Rhondda came in with a light step bearing two fat candles. He took the hooded lamps from Tietjens and began to press the candles up against the inner springs, snorting sedulously through his nostrils. . . .

"Nearly got me, one of those candlesticks did," he said. "Touched my foot as it fell, it did. I did run. Surely to goodness I did run, cahptn."

Inside the shrapnel shell was an iron bar with a flattened, broad nose. When the shell burst in the air this iron object fell to the ground and, since it came often from a great height, its fall was dangerous. The men called these candlesticks, which they much resembled.

A little ring of light now existed on the puce colour of the blanket-covered table. Tietjens showed, silver-headed, fresh-coloured, and bulky; Mackenzie, dark, revengeful eyes above a prognathous jaw, a very thin man; thirtyish.

"You can go into the shelter with the Colonial troops, if you like," Tietjens said to the runner. The man answered after a pause, being very slow thinking, that he preferred to wait for his mate, O Nine Morgan whatever.

"They ought to let my orderly room have tin hats," Tietjens said to Mackenzie. "I'm damned if they didn't take these fellows' tin hats into store again when they attached to me for service, and I'm equally damned if they did not tell me that, if I wanted tin hats for my own headquarters, I had to write to H.Q. Canadians, Aldershot, or some such place in order to get the issue sanctioned."

"Our headquarters are full of Huns doing the Huns' work," Mackenzie said hatefully. "I'd like to get among them one of these days."

Tietjens looked with some attention at that young man with the Rembrandt shadows over his dark face. He said:

"Do you believe that tripe?"

The young man said:

"No . . . I don't know that I do. I don't know what to think. . . The world's rotten. . . ."

"Oh, the world's pretty rotten, all right," Tietjens answered. And, in his fatigue of mind caused by having to attend to innumerable concrete facts like the providing of households for a thousand men every few days, arranging parade states for an extraordinarily mixed set of troops of all arms with very mixed drills, and fighting the Assistant Provost Marshal to keep his own men out of the clutches of the beastly Garrison Military Police who had got a down on all Canadians, he felt he had not any curiosity at all left. . . . Yet he felt vaguely that, at the back of his mind, there was some reason for trying to cure this young member of the lower middle classes.

He repeated:

"Yes, the world's certainly pretty rotten. But that's not its particular line of rottenness as far as we are concerned. . . . We're tangled up, not because we've got Huns in our orderly rooms, but just because we've got English. That's the bat in our belfry. . . . That Hun plane is presumably coming back. Half a dozen of them. . . ."

The young man, his mind eased by having got off his chest a confounded lot of semi-nonsensical ravings, considered the return of the Hun planes with gloomy indifference. His problem really was: could he stand the —— noise that would probably accompany their return? He had to get really into his head that this was an open space to all intents and purposes. There would not be splinters of stone flying about. He was ready to be hit by iron, steel, lead, copper, or brass shell rims, but not by beastly splinters of stone knocked off house fronts. That consideration had come to him during his beastly, his beastly, his infernal, damnable leave in London, when just such a filthy row had been going on. . . . Divorce leave! . . . Captain McKechnie, second attached ninth Glamorganshires, is granted leave from the 14/11 to the 29/11 for the purpose of obtaining a divorce. . . . The memory seemed to burst inside him with the noise of one of those beastly enormous tin-pot crashes — and it always came when guns made that particular kind of tin-pot crash: the two came together, the internal one and the crash outside. He felt that chimney-pots were going to crash on to his head. You protected yourself by shouting at damned infernal idiots; if you could out-shout the row you were safe. . . . That was not sensible, but you got ease that way! . . .

"In matters of Information they're not a patch on us." Tietjens tried the speech on cautiously, and concluded: "We know what the Enemy rules read in the sealed envelopes beside their breakfast bacon-and-egg plates."

It had occurred to him that it was a military duty to bother himself about the mental equilibrium of this member of the lower classes. So he talked . . . *any* old talk, wearisomely, to keep his mind employed! Captain Mackenzie was an officer of His Majesty the King: the property, body and soul, of His Majesty and His Majesty's War Office. It was Tietjens' duty to preserve this fellow as it was his duty to prevent deterioration in any other piece of the King's property. That was implicit in the oath of allegiance. He went on talking:

The curse of the army, as far as the organisation is concerned, was our imbecile national belief that the game is more than the player.

That was our ruin, mentally, as a nation. We were taught that cricket is more than clearness of mind, so the blasted quartermaster, O.C. Depot Ordnance Stores next door, thought he had taken a wicket if he refused to serve out tin hats to their crowd. That's the Game! And if any of his, Tietjens', men were killed, he grinned and said the game was more than the players of the game. . . . And of course if he got his bowling average down low enough he got promotion. There was a quartermaster in a west-country cathedral city who'd got more D.S.O.s and combatant medals than anyone on active service in France, from the sea to Peronne, or wherever our lines ended. His achievement was to have robbed almost every wretched Tommie in the Western Command of several weeks' separation allowance . . . for the good of the taxpayer, of course. The poor —— Tommies' kids went without proper food and clothing, and the Tommies themselves had been in a state of exasperation and resentment. And nothing in the world was worse for discipline and the army as a fighting machine. But there that quartermaster sat in his office, playing the romantic game over his A.F.B.s till the broad buff sheets fairly glowed in the light of the incandescent gas. "And," Tietjens concluded, "for every quarter of a million sterling for which he bowls out the wretched fighting men he gets a new clasp on his fourth D.S.O. ribbon. . . . The game, in short, is more than the players of the game."

"Oh, damn it!" Captain Mackenzie said. "That's what's made us what we are, isn't it?"

"It is," Tietjens answered. "It's got us into the hole and it keeps us there."

Mackenzie remained dispiritedly looking down at his fingers.

"You may be wrong or you may be right," he said. "It's contrary to everything that I ever heard. But I see what you mean."

"At the beginning of the war," Tietjens said, "I had to look in on the War Office, and in a room I found a fellow . . . What do you think he was doing . . . what the hell do you think he was doing? He was devising the ceremonial for the disbanding of a Kitchener battalion. You can't say we were not prepared in one matter at least. . . . Well, the end of the show was to be: the adjutant would stand the battalion at ease; the band would play *Land of Hope and Glory*, and then the adjutant would say: *There will be no more parades*. . . . Don't you see how symbolical it was — the band playing *Land of Hope and Glory*, and then the adjutant saying *There will be no more parades*? . . . For there won't. There won't, there damn well won't.

. . . No more Hope, no more Glory, no more parades for you and me any more. Nor for the country . . . nor for the world, I dare say . . . None . . . Gone . . . Na poo, finny! No . . . more . . . parades!"

"I dare say you're right," the other said slowly. "But, all the same, what am I doing in this show? I hate soldiering. I hate this whole beastly business. . . ."

"Then why didn't you go on the gaudy Staff?" Tietjens asked. "The gaudy Staff apparently was yearning to have you. I bet God intended you for Intelligence, not for the footslogging department."

The other said wearily:

"I don't know. I was with the battalion. I wanted to stop with the battalion. I was intended for the Foreign Office. My miserable uncle got me hoofed out of that. I was with the battalion. The C.O. wasn't up to much. *Someone* had to stay with the battalion. I was not going to do the dirty on it, taking any soft job. . . ."

"I suppose you speak seven languages and all?" Tietjens asked.

"Five," the other said patiently, "and read two more. And Latin and Greek, of course."

A man, brown, stiff, with a haughty parade step, burst into the light. He said with a high wooden voice:

"'Ere's another bloomin' casualty." In the shadow he appeared to have draped half his face and the right side of his breast with crape. He gave a high, rattling laugh. He bent, as if in a stiff bow, woodenly at his thighs. He pitched, still bent, on to the iron sheet that covered the brazier, rolled off that and lay on his back across the legs of the other runner, who had been crouched beside the brazier. In the bright light it was as if a whole pail of scarlet paint had been dashed across the man's face on the left and his chest. It glistened in the firelight — just like fresh paint, moving! The runner from the Rhondda, pinned down by the body across his knees, sat with his jaw fallen, resembling one girl that should be combing the hair of another recumbent before her. The red viscousness welled across the floor; you sometimes so see fresh water bubbling up in sand. It astonished Tietjens to see that a human body could be so lavish of blood. He was thinking it was a queer mania that that fellow should have, that his uncle was a friend of his, Tietjens. He had no friend in trade, uncle of a fellow who in ordinary times would probably bring you pairs of boots on approval. . . . He felt as he did when you patch up a horse that has been badly hurt. He remembered a horse from a cut on whose chest the blood had streamed down over the off foreleg like a stocking. A girl had lent him her petticoat to bandage it. Nevertheless his legs moved slowly and heavily across the floor.

The heat from the brazier was overpowering on his bent face. He hoped he would not get his hands all over blood, because blood is very sticky. It makes your fingers stick together impotently. But there might not be any blood in the darkness under the fellow's back where he was putting his hand. There was, however: it was very wet.

The voice of Sergeant-Major Cowley said from outside:

"Bugler, call two sanitary lance-corporals and four men. Two sanitary corporals and four men." A prolonged wailing with interruptions transfused the night, mournful, resigned, and prolonged.

Tietjens thought that, thank God, someone would come and relieve him of that job. It was a breathless affair holding up the corpse with the fire burning his face. He said to the other runner:

"Get out from under him, damn you! Are you hurt?" Mackenzie could not get at the body from the other side because of the brazier. The runner from under the corpse moved with short sitting shuffles as if he were getting his legs out from under a sofa. He was saying: "Poor —— O Nine Morgan! Surely to goodness I did not recognice the poor —— Surely to goodness I did not recognice the pore ——"

Tietjens let the trunk of the body sink slowly to the floor. He was more gentle than if the man had been alive. All hell in the way of noise burst about the world. Tietjen's thoughts seemed to have to shout to him between earthquake shocks. He was thinking it was absurd of that fellow Mackenzie to imagine that he could know any uncle of his. He saw very vividly also the face of his girl who was a pacifist. It worried him not to know what expression her face would have if she heard of his occupation, now. Disgust? . . . He was standing with his greasy, sticky hands held out from the flaps of his tunic. . . . Perhaps disgust! . . . It was impossible to think in this row. . . . His very thick soles moved gluily and came up after suction. . . . He remembered he had not sent a runner along to I.B.D. Orderly Room to see how many of his crowd would be wanted for garrison fatigue next day, and this annoyed him acutely. He would have no end of a job warning the officers he detailed. They would all be in brothels down in the town by now. . . . He could not work out what the girl's expression would be. He was never to see her

again, so what the hell did it matter? . . . Disgust, probably! . . .
He remembered that he had not looked to see how Mackenzie was
getting on in the noise. He did not want to see Mackenzie. He was
a bore. . . . How would her face express disgust? He had never seen
her express disgust. She had a perfectly undistinguished face. Fair
. . . O God, how suddenly his bowels turned over! . . . Thinking
of the girl . . . The face below him grinned at the roof — the half
face! The nose was there, half the mouth with the teeth showing
in the firelight. . . . It was extraordinary how defined the peaked
nose and the serrated teeth were in that mess. . . . The eye looked
jauntily at the peak of canvas hut-roof. . . . Gone with a grin.
Singular the fellow should have spoken! After he was dead. He
must have been dead when he spoke. It had been done with the
last air automatically going out of the lungs. A reflex action, probably,
in the dead. . . . If he, Tietjens, had given the fellow the leave he
wanted he would be alive now! . . . Well, he was quite right not to
have given the poor devil his leave. He was, anyhow, better where he
was. And so was he, Tietjens. He had not had a single letter from
home since he had been out this time! Not a single letter. Not even
gossip. Not a bill. Some circulars of old furniture dealers. They never
neglected him! They had got beyond the sentimental stage at home.
Obviously so. . . . He wondered if his bowels would turn over again
if he thought of the girl. He was gratified that they had. It showed
that he had strong feelings. . . . He thought about her deliberately.
Hard. Nothing happened. He thought of her fair, undistinguished,
fresh face that made your heart miss a beat when you thought about
it. His heart missed a beat. Obedient heart! Like the first primrose.
Not *any* primrose. The *first* primrose. Under a bank with the hounds
breaking through the underwood. . . . It was sentimental to say
Du bist wie eine Blume. . . . Damn the German language! But that
fellow was a Jew. . . . One should not say that one's young woman
was like *a* flower, *any* flower. Not even to oneself. That was sentimental. But one might say one special flower. A *man* could say that.
A man's job. She smelt like a primrose when you kissed her. But,
damn it, he had never kissed her. So how did he know how she smelt!
She was a little tranquil, golden spot. He himself must be a ——
eunuch. By temperament. That dead fellow down there must be
one, physically. It was probably indecent to think of a corpse as
impotent. But he was, very likely. That would be why his wife had
taken up with the prize-fighter Red Evans Williams of Castell Coch.

If he had given the fellow leave the prize-fighter would have smashed him to bits. The police of Pontardulais had asked that he should not be let come home — because of the prize-fighter. So he was better dead. Or perhaps not. Is death better than discovering that your wife is a whore and being done in by her cully? *Gwell angau na gwillth*, their own regimental badge bore the words. *"Death is better than dishonour."* . . . No, not death, *angau* means pain. Anguish! Anguish is better than dishonour. The devil it is! Well, that fellow would have got both. Anguish and dishonour. Dishonour from his wife and anguish when the prize-fighter hit him. . . . That was no doubt why his half-face grinned at the roof. The gory side of it had turned brown. Already! Like a mummy of a Pharaoh, *that* half looked. . . . He was born to be a blooming casualty. Either by shell-fire or by the fist of the prize-fighter. . . . Pontardulais! Somewhere in Mid-Wales. He had been through it once in a car, on duty. A long, dull village. Why should anyone want to go back to it? . . .

A tender butler's voice said beside him: "This ain't your job, sir. Sorry you had to do it. . . . Lucky it wasn't you, sir. . . . This was what done it, I should say."

Sergeant-Major Cowley was standing beside him holding a bit of metal that was heavy in his hand and like a candlestick. He was aware that a moment before he had seen the fellow, Mackenzie, bending over the brazier, putting the sheet of iron back. Careful officer, Mackenzie. The Huns must not be allowed to see the light from the brazier. The edge of the sheet had gone down on the dead man's tunic, nipping a bit by the shoulder. The face had disappeared in shadow. There were several men's faces in the doorway.

Tietjens said: "No, I don't believe that did it. Something bigger . . . Say a prize-fighter's fist. . . ."

Sergeant Cowley said:

"No, no prize-fighter's fist would have done that, sir. . . ." And then he added, "Oh, I take your meaning, sir . . . O Nine Morgan's wife, sir. . . ."

Tietjens moved, his feet sticking, towards the sergeant-major's table. The other runner had placed a tin basin with water on it. There was a hooded candle there now, alight; the water shone innocently, a half-moon of translucence wavering over the white bottom of the basin. The runner from Pontardulais said:

"Wash your hands first, sir!"

He said:

"Move a little out of it, cahptn." He had a rag in his black hands.
Tietjens moved out of the blood that had run in a thin stream under
the table. The man was on his knees, his hands rubbing Tietjens'
boot welts heavily, with the rags. Tietjens placed his hands in the
innocent water and watched light purple-scarlet mist diffuse itself
over the pale half-moon. The man below him breathed heavily, sniffing. Tietjens said:

"Thomas, O Nine Morgan was your mate?"

The man's face, wrinkled, dark and ape-like, looked up.

"He was a good pal, pore old ——," he said. "You would not like,
surely to goodness, to go to mess with your shoes all bloody."

"If I had given him leave," Tietjens said, "he would not be dead
now."

"No, surely not," One Seven Thomas answered. "But it is all one.
Evans of Castell Goch would surely to goodness have killed him."

"So you knew, too, about his wife!" Tietjens said.

"We thocht it wass that," One Seven Thomas answered, "or you
would have given him leave, cahptn. You are a good cahptn."

A sudden sense of the publicity that that life was came over Tietjens.

"You knew that," he said. "I wonder what the hell you fellows
don't know and all!" he thought. "If anything went wrong with one
it would be all over the command in two days. Thank God, Sylvia
can't get here!"

The man had risen to his feet. He fetched a towel of the sergeant-
major's, very white with a red border.

"We know," he said, "that your honour is a very goot cahptn. And
Captain McKechnie is a *fery* goot cahptn. And Captain Prentiss, and
Le'tennant Jonce of Merthyr . . ."

Tietjens said:

"That'll do. Tell the sergeant-major to give you a pass to go with
your mate to the hospital. Get someone to wash this floor."

Two men were carrying the remains of O Nine Morgan, the trunk
wrapped in a ground sheet. They carried him in a bandy chair out of
the hut. His arms over his shoulders waved a jocular farewell. There
would be an ambulance stretcher on bicycle wheels outside.

II

THE "ALL CLEAR" went at once after that. Its suddenness was something surprising, the mournful-cheerful, long notes dying regretfully on a night that had only just gone quiet after the perfectly astonishing row. The moon had taken it into its head to rise; begumboiled, jocular, and grotesque, it came from behind the shoulder of one of the hut-covered hills and sent down the lines of Tietjens' huts, long, sentimental rays that converted the place into a slumbering, pastoral settlement. There was no sound that did not contribute to the silence, little dim lights shone through the celluloid casements. Of Sergeant-Major Cowley, his numerals gilded by the moon in the lines of A Company, Tietjens, who was easing his lungs of coke vapours for a minute, asked in a voice that hushed itself in tribute to the moonlight and the now keen frost:

"Where the deuce is the draft?"

The sergeant-major looked poetically down a ribbon of white-washed stones that descended the black downside. Over the next shoulder of hill was the blur of a hidden conflagration.

"There's a Hun plane burning down there. In Twenty-Seven's parade ground. The draft's round that, sir," he said.

Tietjens said:

"Good God!" in a voice of caustic tolerance. He added, "I did think we had drilled some discipline into these blighters in the seven weeks we have had them. . . . You remember the first time when we had them on parade and that acting lance-corporal left the ranks to heave a rock at a sea-gull. . . . And called you 'O₁' Hunkey! . . . Conduct prejudicial to good order and military discipline? Where's that Canadian sergeant-major? Where's the officer in charge of the draft?"

Sergeant-Major Cowley said:

"Sergeant-Major Ledoux said it was like a cattle-stampede on the . . . some river where they come from. You *couldn't* stop them, sir. It was their first German plane. . . . And they going up the line to-night, sir."

"To-night!" Tietjens exclaimed. "Next Christmas!"

The sergeant-major said:

"Poor boys!" and continued to gaze into the distance. "I heard another good one, sir," he said. "The answer to the one about the King saluting a private soldier and he not taking any notice is: when he's dead. . . . But if you marched a company into a field through a gateway and you wanted to get it out again but you did not know any command in the drill book for change of direction, what would you do, sir? . . . You have to get that company out, but you must not use About Turn, or Right or Left Wheel. . . . There's another one, too, about saluting. . . . The officer in charge of draft is Second-Lieutenant Hotchkiss. . . . But he's an A.S.C. officer and turned of sixty. A farrier he is, sir, in civil life. An A.S.C. major was asking me, sir, very civil, if you could not detail someone else. He says he doubts if Second-Lieutenant Hitchcock . . . Hotchkiss could walk as far as the station, let alone march the men, him not knowing anything but cavalry words of command, if he knows them. He's only been in the army a fortnight. . . ."

Tietjens turned from the idyllic scene with the words:

"I suppose the Canadian sergeant-major and Lieutenant Hotchkiss are doing what they can to get their men to come back."

He re-entered the hut.

Captain Mackenzie in the light of a fantastically brilliant hurricane lamp appeared to be bathing dejectedly in a surf of coiling papers spread on the table before him.

"There's all this bumph," he said, "just come from all the headquarters in the bally world."

Tietjens said cheerfully:

"What's it all about?" There were, the other answered, Garrison Headquarter orders, Divisional orders, Lines of Communication orders, half a dozen A.F.B.W. two four two's. A terrific strafe from First Army forwarded from Garrison H.Q. about the draft's not having reach Hazebrouck the day before yesterday. Tietjens said:

"Answer them politely to the effect that we had orders not to send off the draft without its complement of four hundred Canadian Railway Service men — the fellows in furred hoods. They only reached us from Etaples at five this afternoon without blanket or ring papers. Or any other papers for the matter of that."

Mackenzie was studying with increased gloom a small buff memorandum slip:

"This appears to be meant for you privately," he said. "I can't make head or tail of it otherwise. It isn't *marked* private."

He tossed the buff slip across the table.

Tietjens sank down bulkily on to his bully-beef case. He read on the buff at first the initials of the signature, "E.C. Genl.," and then: "For God's sake keep your wife off me. I *will* not have skirts round my H.Q. You are more trouble to me than all the rest of my command put together."

Tietjens groaned and sank more deeply on to his beef case. It was as if an unseen and unsuspected wild beast had jumped on his neck from an overhanging branch. The sergeant-major at his side said in his most admirable butler manner:

"Colour-Sergeant Morgan and Lance-Corporal Trench are obliging us by coming from depot orderly room to help with the draft's papers. Why don't you and the other officer go and get a bit of dinner, sir? The colonel and the padre have only just come in to mess, and I've warned the mess orderlies to keep your food 'ot. . . . Both good men with papers, Morgan and Trench. We can send the soldiers' small books to you at table to sign. . . ."

His feminine solicitude enraged and overwhelmed Tietjens with blackness. He told the sergeant-major that he was to go to hell, for he himself was not going to leave that hut till the draft was moved off. Captain Mackenzie could do as he pleased. The sergeant-major told Captain Mackenzie that Captain Tietjens took as much trouble with his rag-time detachments as if he had been the Coldstream adjutant at Chelsea sending off a draft of Guards. Captain Mackenzie said that that was why they damn well got their details off four days faster than any other I.B.D. in that camp. He *would* say that much, he added grudgingly and dropped his head over his papers again. The hut was moving slowly up and down before the eyes of Tietjens. He might have just been kicked in the stomach. That was how shocks took him. He said to himself that by God he must take himself in hand. He grabbed with his heavy hands at a piece of buff paper and wrote on it in a column of fat, wet letters

a
b
b
a
a
b
b
a and so on.

He said opprobriously to Captain Mackenzie:

"Do you know what a sonnet is? Give me the rhymes for a sonnet. That's the plan of it."

Mackenzie grumbled:

"Of course I know what a sonnet is. What's your game?"

Tietjens said:

"Give me the fourteen end-rhymes of a sonnet and I'll write the lines. In under two minutes and a half."

Mackenzie said injuriously:

"If you do I'll turn it into Latin hexameters in three. In *under* three minutes."

They were like men uttering deadly insults the one to the other. To Tietjens it was as if an immense cat were parading, fascinated and fatal, round that hut. He had imagined himself parted from his wife. He had not heard from his wife since her four-in-the-morning departure from their flat, months and eternities ago, with the dawn just showing up the chimney-pots of the Georgian roof-trees opposite. In the complete stillness of dawn he had heard her voice say very clearly "Paddington" to the chauffeur, and then all the sparrows in the inn waking up in chorus. . . . Suddenly and appallingly it came into his head that it might not have been his wife's voice that had said "Paddington," but her maid's. . . . He was a man who lived very much by rules of conduct. He had a rule: *Never think on the subject of a shock at a moment of a shock.* The mind was then too sensitised. Subjects of shock require to be thought all round. If your mind thinks when it is too sensitised its then conclusions will be too strong. So he exclaimed to Mackenzie:

"Haven't you got your rhymes yet? Damn it *all*!"

Mackenzie grumbled offensively:

"No, I haven't. It's more difficult to get rhymes than to write sonnets. . . . Death, moil, coil, breath . . ." He paused.

"Heath, soil, toil, staggereth," Tietjens said contemptuously. "That's your sort of Oxford young woman's rhyme. . . . Go on . . . *What is it?*"

An extremely age-faded and unmilitary officer was beside the blanketed table. Tietjens regretted having spoken to him with ferocity. He had a grotesquely thin white beard. Positively, white whiskers! He must have gone through as much of the army as he had gone through, with those whiskers, because no superior officer — not even a field-marshal — would have the heart to tell him to take them off!

It was the measure of his pathos. This ghost-like object was apologising for not having been able to keep the draft in hand; he was requesting his superior to observe that these Colonial troops were without any instincts of discipline. None at all. Tietjens observed that he
had a blue cross on his right arm where the vaccination marks are as
a rule. He imagined the Canadians talking to this hero. . . . The
hero began to talk to Major Cornwallis of the R.A.S.C.

Tietjens said apropos of nothing:

"Is there a Major Cornwallis in the A.S.C.? Good God!"

The hero protested faintly:

"The R.A.S.C."

Tietjens said kindly:

"Yes. Yes. The *Royal* Army Service Corps."

Obviously his mind until now had regarded his wife's "*Paddington*" as the definite farewell between his life and hers. . . . He had
imagined her, like Eurydice, tall, but faint and pale, sinking back
into the shades. . . . "*Che faro senz' Eurydice? . . .*" he hummed.
Absurd! And of course it might have been only the maid that had
spoken. . . . She too had a remarkably clear voice. So that the
mystic word "Paddington" might perfectly well be no symbol at all,
and Mrs. Sylvia Tietjens, far from being faint and pale, might perfectly well be playing the very devil with half the general officers commanding in chief from Whitehall to Alaska.

Mackenzie — he *was* like a damned clerk — was transferring the
rhymes that he had no doubt at last found, onto another sheet of
paper. Probably he had a round, copy-book hand. Positively, his
tongue followed his pen round, inside his lips. These were what His
Majesty's regular officers of to-day were. Good God! A damned intelligent, dark-looking fellow. Of the type that is starved in its youth
and takes all the scholarships that the board schools have to offer.
Eyes too big and black. Like a Malay's. . . . Any blasted member of
any subject race.

The A.S.C. fellow had been talking positively about horses. He had
offered his services in order to study the variation of pink-eye that
was decimating all the service horses in the lines. He had been a professor — positively a professor — in some farriery college or other.
Tietjens said that, in that case, he ought to be in the A.V.C. — the
Royal Army Veterinary Corps perhaps it was. The old man said he
didn't know. He imagined that the R.A.S.C. had wanted his service
for their own horses. . . .

Tietjens said:

"I'll tell you what to do, Lieutenant Hitchcock. . . . For, damn it, you're a stout fellow. . . ." The poor old fellow, pushing out at that age from the cloisters of some provincial university . . . He certainly did not look a horsy sportsman. . . .

The old lieutenant said:

"Hotchkiss . . ." And Tietjens exclaimed:

"Of course it's Hotchkiss . . . I've seen your name signing a testimonial to Pigg's Horse Embrocation. . . . Then if you don't want to take this draft up the line . . . Though I'd advise you to . . . It's merely a Cook's Tour to Hazebrouck . . . No, Bailleul . . . And the sergeant-major will march the men for you . . . And you will have been in the First Army Lines and able to tell all your friends you've been on active service at the real front. . . ."

His mind said to himself while his words went on . . .

"Then, good God, if Sylvia is actively paying attention to my career I shall be the laughing-stock of the whole army. I was thinking that ten minutes ago! . . . What's to be done? What in God's name is to be done?" A black crape veil seemed to drop across his vision. . . . Liver . . .

Lieutenant Hotchkiss said with dignity:

"I'm *going* to the front. I'm going to the real front. I was passed A1 this morning. I am going to study the blood reactions of the service-horse under fire."

"Well, you're a damn good chap," Tietjens said. There was nothing to be done. The amazing activities of which Sylvia would be capable were just the thing to send laughter raging like fire through a cachinnating army. She could not, thank God, get into France: to that place. But she could make scandals in the papers that every Tommie read. There was no game of which she was not capable. That sort of pursuit was called "pulling the strings of shower-baths" in her circle of friends. Nothing. Nothing to be done. . . . The beastly hurricane lamp was smoking.

"I'll tell you what to do," he said to Lieutenant Hotchkiss.

Mackenzie had tossed his sheet of rhymes under his nose. Tietjens read: *Death, moil, coil, breath . . . Saith* — "The dirty Cockney!" *Oil, Soil, wraith . . .*

"I'd be blowed," Mackenzie said with a vicious grin, "if I was going to give you rhymes you had suggested yourself . . ."

The officer said:

"I don't of course want to be a nuisance if you're busy."

"It's no nuisance," Tietjens said. "It's what we're for. But I'd suggest that now and then you say 'sir' to the officer commanding your unit. It sounds well before the men. . . . Now you go to No. XVI I.B.D. Mess ante-room . . . the place where they've got the broken bagatelle-table. . . ."

The voice of Sergeant-Major Cowley exclaimed tranquilly from outside:

"Fall in now. Men who've got their ring papers and identity discs — three of them — on the left. Men who haven't, on the right. Any man who has not been able to draw his blankets tell Colour-Sergeant Morgan. Don't forget. You won't get any, where you're going. Any man who hasn't made his will in his Soldier's Small Book or elsewhere and wants to, to consult Captain Tietjens. Any man who wants to draw money, ask Captain Mackenzie. Any R.C. who wants to go to confession after he has got his papers signed can find the R.C. padre in the fourth hut from the left in the Main Line from here. . . . And damn kind it is of his reverence to put himself out for a set of damn blinking mustard-faced red herrings like you who can't keep from running away to the first baby's bonfire you sees. You'll be running the other way before you're a week older, though what good they as asks for you thinks you'll be out there God knows. You *look* like a squad of infants' companions from a Wesleyan Sunday school. That's what you look like and, thank God, we've got a Navy."

Under cover of his voice Tietjens had been writing:

"Now we affront the grinning chops of *Death*," and saying to Lieutenant Hotchkiss: "In the I.B.D. ante-room you'll find any number of dirty little squits of Glamorganshires drinking themselves blind over *La Vie Parisienne*. . . . Ask any one of them you like. . . ." He wrote:

> "And in between our carcass and the *moil*
>   Of marts and cities, toil and moil and *coil* . . ."

"You think this difficult!" he said to Mackenzie. "Why, you've written a whole undertaker's mortuary ode in the rhymes alone," and went on to Hotchkiss: "Ask anyone you like as long as he's a P.B. officer. . . . Do you know what P.B. means? No, not Poor B——y, Permanent Base. Unfit . . . If he'd like to take a draft to Bailleul."

The hut was filling with devious, slow, ungainly men in yellow-brown. Their feet shuffled desultorily; they lumped dull canvas bags along the floor and held in unliterary hands small open books that they dropped from time to time. From outside came a continuing, swelling and descending chant of voices; at times it would seem to be all one laugh, at times one menace, then the motives mingled fugally, like the sea on a beach of large stones. It seemed to Tietjens suddenly extraordinary how shut in on oneself one was in this life. . . . He sat scribbling fast: "Old Spectre blows a cold protecting *breath* . . . Vanity of vanities, the preacher *saith* . . . No more parades, Not any more, no *oil* . . ." He was telling Hotchkiss, who was obviously shy of approaching the Glamorganshires in their ante-room . . . "Unambergris'd our limbs in the naked *soil* . . ." that he did not suppose any P.B. officer would object. They would go on a beanfeast up into the giddy line in a first-class carriage and get draft leave and command pay too, probably . . . "No funeral struments cast before our wraiths . . ." If any fellow does object, you just send his name to me and I will damn well shove it into extra orders. . . .

The advanced wave of the brown tide of men was already at his feet. The extraordinary complications of even the simplest lives . . . A fellow was beside him . . . Private Logan, formerly, of all queer things for a Canadian private, a trooper of the Inniskillings; owner, of all queer things, of a milk-walk or a dairy farm, outside Sydney, which is in Australia. A man of sentimental complications, jauntiness as became an Inniskilling, a Cockney accent such as ornaments the inhabitants of Sydney, and a complete distrust of lawyers. On the other hand, with the completest trust in Tietjens. Over his shoulder — he was blond, upright, with his numerals shining like gold, looked a lumpish, *café-au-lait*, eagle-nosed countenance: a half-caste member of one of the Six Nations, who had been a doctor's errand boy in Quebec. . . . He had his troubles, but was difficult to understand. Behind him, very black-avised with a high colour, truculent eyes, and an Irish accent, was a graduate of McGill University who had been a teacher of languages in Tokyo and had some sort of claim against the Japanese Government. . . . And faces, two and two, in a coil round the hut . . . like dust, like a cloud of dust that would approach and overwhelm a landscape; every one with preposterous troubles and anxieties, even if they did not overwhelm you personally with them . . . Brown dust. . . .

He kept the Inniskilling waiting while he scribbled the rapid sestet to his sonnet which ought to make a little plainer what it all meant. Of course the general idea was that, when you got into the line or near it, there was no room for swank, typified by expensive funerals. As you might say: No flowers by compulsion . . . No more parades! . . . He had also to explain, while he did it, to the heroic veterinary sexagenarian that he need not feel shy about going into the Glamorganshire Mess on a man-catching expedition. The Glamorganshires were bound to lend him, Tietjens, P.B. officers if they had not got other jobs. Lieutenant Hotchkiss could speak to Colonel Johnson, whom he would find in the mess and quite good-natured over his dinner. A pleasant and sympathetic old gentleman who would appreciate Hotchkiss's desire not to go superfluously into the line. Hotchkiss could offer to take a look at the colonel's charger: a Hun horse, captured on the Marne and called Schomburg, that was off its feed. . . . He added: "But don't do anything professional to Schomburg. I ride him myself!"

He threw his sonnet across to Mackenzie, who with a background of huddled khaki limbs and anxious faces was himself anxiously counting out French currency notes and dubious-looking tokens. . . . What the deuce did men want to draw money — sometimes quite large sums of money, the Canadians being paid in dollars converted into local coins — when in an hour or so they would be going up? But they always did and their accounts were always in an incredibly entangled state. Mackenzie might well look worried. As like as not he might find himself a fiver or more down at the end of the evening for unauthorised payments. If he had only his pay and an extravagant wife to keep, that might well put the wind up him. But that was *his* funeral. He told Lieutenant Hotchkiss to come and have a chat with him in his hut, the one next the mess. About horses. He knew a little about horse-illnesses himself. Only empirically, of course.

Mackenzie was looking at his watch.

"You took two minutes and eleven seconds," he said. "I'll take it for granted it's a sonnet . . . I have not read it because I can't turn it into Latin here . . . I haven't got your knack of doing eleven things at once. . . ."

A man with a worried face, encumbered by a bundle and a small book, was studying figures at Mackenzie's elbow. He interrupted Mackenzie in a high American voice to say that he had never drawn fourteen dollars seventy-five cents in Thrasna Barracks, Aldershot.

Mackenzie said to Tietjens:

"You understand. I have not read your sonnet. I shall turn it into

Latin in the mess, in the time stipulated. I don't want you to think
I've read it and taken time to think about it."

The man beside him said:

"When I went to the Canadian Agent, Strand, London, his office
was shut up . . ."

Mackenzie said with white fury:

"How much service have you got? Don't you know better than to
interrupt an officer when he is talking. You must settle your own
figures with your own confounded Colonial paymaster. I've sixteen
dollars thirty cents here for you. Will you take them or leave them?"

Tietjens said:

"I know that man's case. Turn him over to me. It isn't complicated.
He's got his paymaster's cheque, but doesn't know how to cash it and
of course they won't give him another. . . ."

The man with slow, broad, brown features looked from one to the
other officer's face and back again with a keen black-eyed scrutiny as
if he were looking into a wind and dazed by the light. He began a
long story of how he owed Fat-Eared Bill fifty dollars lost at House.
He was perhaps half-Chinese, half-Finn. He continued to talk, being in a state of great anxiety about his money. Tietjens addressed
himself to the cases of the Sydney Inniskilling ex-trooper and the
McGill graduate who had suffered at the hands of the Japanese Educational Ministry. It made altogether a complicated effect. "You
would say," Tietjens said to himself, "that, all together, it ought to
be enough to take my mind up."

The upright trooper had a very complicated sentimental history.
It was difficult to advise him before his fellows. He, however, felt no
diffidence. He discussed the points of the girl called Rosie whom he
had followed from Sydney to British Columbia, of the girl called
Gwen with whom he had taken up in Aberystwyth, of the woman
called Mrs. Hosier with whom he had lived maritally, on a sleeping-
out pass, at Berwick St. James, near Salisbury Plain. Through the
continuing voice of the half-caste Chinaman he discussed them with
a large tolerance, explaining that he wanted them all to have a bit,
as a souvenir, if he happened to stop one out there. Tietjens handed
him the draft of a will he had had written out for him, asked him
to read it attentively and copy it with his own hand into his soldier's
small book. Then Tietjens would witness it for him. He said:

"Do you think this will make my old woman in Sydney part? I

guess it won't. She's a sticker, sir. A regular July bur, God bless her."
The McGill graduate was beginning already to introduce a further
complication into his story of complications with the Japanese Government. It appeared that in addition to his scholastic performances
he had invested a little money in a mineral water spring near Kobe,
the water, bottled, being exported to San Francisco. Apparently his
company had been indulging in irregularities according to Japanese
law, but a pure French Canadian, who had experienced some difficulties in obtaining his baptismal certificate from a mission somewhere in the direction of the Klondike, was allowed by Tietjens to
interrupt the story of the graduate; and several men without complications, but anxious to get their papers signed so as to write
last letters home before the draft moved, overflowed across Tietjens's
table.

The tobacco smoke from the pipes of the N.C.O.s at the other end
of the room hung, opalescent, beneath the wire cages of the brilliant
hurricane lamps hung over each table; buttons and minerals gleamed
in the air that the universal khaki tinge of the limbs seemed to turn
brown, as if into a gas of dust. Nasal voices, throat voices, drawling
voices, melted into a rustle so that the occasional high, sing-song
profanity of a Welsh N.C.O.: Why the *hell* haffn't you got your 124?
Why the —— hell haffn't you got your 124? Don't you *know* you
haff to haff your bleedin' 124's? seemed to wail tragically through a silence. . . . The evening wore on and on. It astounded Tietjens, looking at one time at his watch to discover that it was only 21 hrs. 19.
He seemed to have been thinking drowsily of his own affairs for ten
hours. . . . For, in the end, these were his own affairs. . . . Money,
women, testamentary bothers. Each of these complications from over
the Atlantic and round the world were his own troubles: a world in
labour; an army being moved off in the night. Shoved off. Anyhow.
And over the top. A lateral section of the world. . . .

He had happened to glance at the medical history of a man beside
him and noticed that he had been described as C1. . . . It was obviously a slip of the pen on the part of the Medical Board, or one of
their orderlies. He had written C instead of A. The man was Pte.
197394 Thomas Johnson, a shining-faced lump of beef, an agricultural odd jobman from British Columbia where he had worked on
the immense estates of Sylvia Tietjens' portentous ducal second
cousin Rugeley. It was a double annoyance. Tietjens had not wanted
to be reminded of his wife's second cousin, because he had not

wanted to be reminded of his wife. He had determined to give his
thoughts a field day on that subject when he got warm into his flea-
bag in his hut that smelt of paraffin whilst the canvas walls crackled
with frost and the moon shone. . . . He would think of Sylvia beneath the moon. He was determined not to now! But 197394 Pte.
Johnson, Thomas, was otherwise a nuisance and Tietjens cursed
himself for having glanced at the man's medical history. If this preposterous yokel was C3 he could not go on a draft . . . C1 rather!
It was all the same. That would mean finding another man to make
up the strength and that would drive Sergeant-Major Cowley out of
his mind. He looked up towards the ingenuous, protruding, shining,
liquid, bottle-blue eyes of Thomas Johnson. . . . The fellow had
never had an illness. He could not have had an illness — except from
a surfeit of cold, fat, boiled pork — and for that you would give him
a horse's blue ball and drench which, ten to one, would not remove
the cause of the belly-ache. . . .

His eyes met the non-committal glance of a dark, gentlemanly thin
fellow with a strikingly scarlet hat-band, a lot of gilt about his khaki
and little strips of steel chain-armour on his shoulders. . . . Levin
. . . Colonel Levin, G.S.O. II, or something, attached to General
Lord Edward Campion. . . . How the hell did fellows get into these
intimacies of commanders of units and their men? Swimming in like
fishes into the brown air of a tank and there at your elbow —— spies!
. . . The men had all been called to attention and stood like gasping
codfish. The ever-watchful Sergeant-Major Cowley had drifted to his,
Tietjens', elbow. You protect your orfcers from the gawdy Staff as
you protect your infant daughters in lambswool from draughts. The
dark, bright, cheerful staffwallah said with a slight lisp:

"Busy, I see." He might have been standing there for a century and
have a century of the battalion headquarters' time to waste like that.
"What draft is this?"

Sergeant-Major Cowley, always ready in case his orfcer should not
know the name of his unit or his own name, said:

"No. 16 I.B.D. Canadian First Division Casual Number Four
Draft, sir."

Colonel Levin let air lispingly out between his teeth.

"No. 16 Draft not off yet . . . Dear, dear! Dear, dear! . . . We
shall be strafed to hell by First Army. . . ." He used the word hell as
if he had first wrapped it in eau-de-cologned cotton-wadding.

Tietjens, on his feet, knew this fellow very well: a fellow who had been a very bad Society water-colour painter of good family on the mother's side, hence the cavalry gadgets on his shoulders. Would it then be good . . . say good taste to explode? He let the sergeant-major do it. Sergeant-Major Cowley was of the type of N.C.O. who carried weight because he knew ten times as much about his job as any Staff officer. The sergeant-major explained that it had been impossible to get off the draft earlier. The colonel said:

"But surely, sergeant-majah . . ."

The sergeant-major, now a deferential shopwalker in a lady's store, pointed out that they had had urgent instructions not to send up the draft without the four hundred Canadian Railway Service men who were to come from Etaples. These men had only arrived that evening at 5.30 . . . at the railway station. Marching them up had taken three-quarters of an hour. The colonel said:

"But surely, sergeant-majah . . ."

Old Cowley might as well have said "madam" as "sir" to the red hat-band. . . . The four hundred had come with only what they stood up in. The unit had had to wangle everything: boots, blankets, tooth-brushes, braces, rifles, iron-rations, identity discs out of the depot store. And it was now only twenty-one twenty. . . . Cowley permitted his commanding officer at this point to say:

"You must understand that we work in circumstances of extreme difficulty, sir. . . ."

The graceful colonel was lost in an absent contemplation of his perfectly elegant knees.

"I know, of course. . . ." he lisped. "Very difficult . . ." He brightened up to add: "But you must admit you're unfortunate. . . . You must admit that. . . ." The weight settled, however, again on his mind.

Tietjens said:

"Not, I suppose, sir, any more unfortunate than any other unit working under a dual control for supplies. . . ."

The colonel said:

"What's that? Dual . . . Ah, I see you're there, Mackenzie. . . . Feeling well . . . feeling fit, eh?"

The whole hut stood silent. His anger at the waste of time made Tietjens say:

"If you understand, sir, we are a unit whose principal purpose is drawing things to equip drafts with. . . ." This fellow was delaying them atrociously. He was brushing his knees with a handkerchief!

"I've had," Tietjens said, "a man killed on my hands this afternoon because we have to draw tin-hats for my orderly room from Dublin on an A.F.B. Canadian from Aldershot. . . . Killed here. . . . We've only just mopped up the blood from where you're stand-ing. . . ."

The cavalry colonel exclaimed:

"Oh, good gracious me! . . ." jumped a little and examined his beautiful, shining, knee-high aircraft boots. "Killed! . . . Here! . . . But there'll have to be a court of inquiry. . . . You certainly are *most* unfortunate, Captain Tietjens. . . . Always these mysterious . . . Why wasn't your man in a dug-out? . . . Most unfortunate. . . . We cannot have casualties among the Colonial troops. . . . Troops from the Dominions, I mean. . . ."

Tietjens said grimly:

"The man was from Pontardulais . . . not from any Dominion. . . . One of my orderly room. . . . We are forbidden on pain of court martial to let any but Dominion Expeditionary Force men go into the dug-outs. . . . My Canadians were all there. . . . It's an A.C.I. local of the eleventh of November. . . ."

The Staff officer said:

"It makes, of course, a difference! . . , Only a Glamorganshire? You say . . . Oh, well. . . . But these mysterious . . ."

He exclaimed, with the force of an explosion, and the relief:

"Look here . . . can you spare, possibly ten . . . twenty . . . eh . . . minutes? . . . It's not exactly a service matter . . . so per . . ."

Tietjens exclaimed:

"You see how we're situated, colonel . . ." and, like one sowing grass seed on a lawn, extended both hands over his papers and to-wards his men. . . . He was choking with rage. Colonel Levin had, under the chaperonage of an English dowager, who ran a chocolate store down on the quays in Rouen, a little French piece to whom he was quite seriously engaged. In the most naïve manner. And the young woman, fantastically jealous, managed to make endless in-sults to herself out of her almost too handsome colonel's barbaric French. It was an idyll, but it drove the colonel frantic. At such times Levin would consult Tietjens, who passed for a man of brains and a French scholar as to really nicely turned compliments in a difficult language. . . . And as to how you explained that it was necessary for a G.S.O. II, or whatever the colonel was, to be seen quite frequently in the company of very handsome V.A.D.s and female organisers of

all arms . . . It was the sort of silliness as to which no gentleman
ought to be consulted. . . . And here was Levin with the familiar
feminine-agonised wrinkle on his bronzed-alabaster brow. . . . Like
a beastly soldier-man out of a revue. Why didn't the ass burst into
gesture and a throaty tenor. . . .

Sergeant-Major Cowley naturally saved the situation. Just as Tietjens was as near saying *Go to hell* as you can be to your remarkably
senior officer on parade, the sergeant-major, now a very important solicitor's most confidential clerk, began whispering to the colonel. . . .

"The captain might as well take a spell as not. . . . We're through
with all the men except the Canadian Railway batch, and they can't
be issued with blankets not for half an hour . . . not for three-
quarters. If then! It depends if our runner can find where Quarter's
lance-corporal is having his supper, to issue them. . . ." The sergeant-
major had inserted that last speech deftly. The Staff officer, with a
vague reminiscence of his regimental days, exclaimed:

"Damn it! . . . I wonder you don't break into the depot blanket
store and take what you want. . . ."

The sergeant-major, becoming Simon Pure, exclaimed:

"Oh, no, sir, we could never do that, sir. . . ."

"But the confounded men are urgently needed in the line,"
Colonel Levin said. "Damn it, it's touch and go! We're rushing . . ."
He appreciated the fact again that he was on the gawdy Staff, and
that the sergeant-major and Tietjens, playing like left backs into each
other's hands, had trickily let him in.

"We can only pray, sir," the sergeant-major said, "that these 'ere
bloomin' 'Uns has got quartermasters and depots and issuing departments, same as ourselves." He lowered his voice into a husky
whisper. "Besides, sir, there's a rumour . . . round the telephone in
depot orderly room . . . that there's a W.O. order at 'Edquarters
. . . countermanding this and other drafts. . . ."

Colonel Levin said: "Oh, my God!" and consternation rushed
upon both him and Tietjens. The frozen ditches, in the night, out
there; the agonized waiting for men; the weight upon the mind like a
weight upon the brows; the imminent sense of approaching unthink-
ableness on the right or the left, according as you looked up or down
the trench; the solid protecting earth of the parapet then turns into
pierced mist . . . and no reliefs coming from here. . . . The men
up there thinking naïvely that they were coming, and they not coming. Why not? Good God, why not? Mackenzie said:

"Poor —— old Bird. . . . His crowd had been in eleven weeks last Wednesday. . . . About all they could stick. . . ."

"They'll have to stick a damn lot more," Colonel Levin said. "I'd like to get at some of the brutes. . . ." It was at that date the settled conviction of His Majesty's Expeditionary Force that the army in the field was the tool of politicians and civilians. In moments of routine that cloud dissipated itself lightly; when news of ill omen arrived it settled down again heavily like a cloud of black gas. You hung your head impotently. . . .

"So that," the sergeant-major said cheerfully, "the captain could very well spare half an hour to get his dinner. Or for anything else. . . ." Apart from the domestic desire that Tietjens' digestion should not suffer from irregular meals he had the professional conviction that for his captain to be in intimate private converse with a member of the gawdy Staff was good for the unit. . . . "I suppose, sir," he added valedictorily to Tietjens, "I'd better arrange to put this draft, and the nine hundred men that came in this afternoon to replace them, twenty in a tent. . . . It's lucky we didn't strike them. . . ."

Tietjens and the colonel began to push men out of their way, going towards the door. The Inniskilling-Canadian, a small open brown book, extended deprecatingly stood, modestly obtrusive, just beside the door-post. Catching avidly at Tietjens' "Eh?" he said:

"You'd got the names of the girls wrong in your copy, sir. It was Gwen Lewis I had a child by in Aberystwyth that I wanted to have the lease of the cottage and the ten bob a week. Mrs. Hosier that I lived with in Berwick St. James, she was only to have five guineas for a soovneer. . . . I've took the liberty of changing the names back again. . . ."

Tietjens grabbed the book from him, and bending down at the sergeant-major's table scrawled his signature on the bluish page. He thrust the book back at the man and said:

"There . . . fall out." The man's face shone. He exclaimed:

"Thank you, sir. Thank you kindly, captain. . . . I wanted to get off and go to confession. I did bad. . . ." The McGill graduate with his arrogant black moustache put himself in the way as Tietjens struggled into his British warm.

"You won't forget, sir . . ." he began.

Tietjens said:

"Damn you, I've told you I won't forget. I never forget. You instructed the ignorant Jap in Asaki, but the educational authority is in

Tokyo. And your flagitious mineral-water company had their head-quarters at the Tan Sen spring near Kobe. . . . Is that right? Well, I'll do my best for you."

They walked in silence through the groups of men that hung round the orderly room door and gleamed in the moonlight. In the broad country street of the main line of the camp Colonel Levin began to mutter between his teeth:

"You take enough trouble with your beastly crowd . . . a whole lot of trouble. . . . Yet . . ."

"Well, what's the matter with us?" Tietjens said. "We get our drafts ready in thirty-six hours less than any other unit in this command."

"I know you do," the other conceded. "It's only all these mysterious rows. Now . . ."

Tietjens said quickly:

"Do you mind my asking: Are we still on parade? Is this a strafe from General Campion as to the way I command my unit?"

The other conceded quite as quickly and much more worriedly:

"God forbid." He added more quickly still: "Old bean!" and prepared to tuck his wrist under Tietjens' elbow. Tietjens, however, continued to face the fellow. He was really in a temper.

"Then tell me," he said, "how the deuce you can manage to do without an overcoat in this weather?" If only he could get the chap off the topics of his mysterious rows they might drift to the matter that had brought him up there on that bitter night when he should be sitting over a good wood fire philandering with Mlle Nanette de Bailly. He sank his neck deeper into the sheepskin collar of his British warm. The other, slim, was with all his badges, ribands, and mail, shining darkly in a cold that set all Tietjens' teeth chattering like porcelain. Levin became momentarily animated:

"You should do as I do. . . . Regular hours . . . lots of exercise . . . horse exercise. . . . I do P.T. every morning at the open window of my room . . . hardening. . . ."

"It must be very gratifying for the ladies in the rooms facing yours," Tietjens said grimly. "Is that what's the matter with Mlle Nanette, now? . . . I haven't got time for proper exercise. . . ."

"Good gracious, no," the colonel said. He now tucked his hand firmly under Tietjens' arm and began to work him towards the left hand of the road, in the direction leading out of the camp. Tietjens worked their steps as firmly towards the right and they leant one against the other. "In fact, old bean," the colonel said, "Campy is working so hard to get the command of a fighting army — though he's indispensable here — that we might pack up bag and baggage any day. . . . That is what has made Nanette see reason. . . ."

"Then what am I doing in this show?" Tietjens asked. But Colonel Levin continued blissfully:

"In fact I've got her almost practically for certain to promise that next week . . . or the week after next at latest . . . she'll . . . damn it, she'll name the happy day."

Tietjens said:

"Good hunting! . . . How splendidly Victorian!"

"That's, damn it," the colonel exclaimed manfully, "what I say myself. . . . Victorian is what it is. . . . All these marriage settlements. . . . And what is it . . . *Droits du Seigneur?* . . . And notaires . . . And the Count, having his say . . . and the Marchioness . . . and two old grand-aunts . . . But . . . Hoopla! . . ." He executed with his gloved right thumb in the moonlight a rapid pirouette . . . "Next week . . . or at least the week after . . ." His voice suddenly dropped.

"At least," he wavered, "that was what it was at lunch-time. Since then . . . something happened. . . ."

"You've not been caught in bed with a V.A.D.?" Tietjens asked. The colonel mumbled:

"No, not in bed. . . . Not with a V.A.D. . . . Oh, damn it, at the railway station. . . . With . . . The general sent me down to meet her . . . and Nanny of course was seeing off her grandmother, the Duchesse . . . The giddy cut she handed me out. . . ."

Tietjens became coldly furious.

"Then it *was* over one of your beastly imbecile rows with Miss de Bailly that you got me out here," he exclaimed. "Do you mind going down with me towards the I.B.D. headquarters? Your final orders may have come in there. The sappers won't let me have a telephone, so I have to look in there the last thing. . . ." He felt a yearning towards rooms in huts, warmed by coke-stoves and electrically lit, with acting lance-corporals bending over A.F.B.s on a background of deal pigeon-holes filled with returns on buff and blue paper. You got quiet and engrossment there. It was a queer thing; the only place where he, Christopher Tietjens of Groby, could be absently satisfied was in some orderly room or other. The only place in the world . . . And why? It was a queer thing. . . .

But not queer, really. It was a matter of inevitable selection if you came to think it out. An acting orderly-room lance-corporal was selected for his penmanship, his power of elementary figuring, his trustworthiness amongst innumerable figures and messages, his dependability. For this he differed a hair's breadth in rank from the rank and file. A hair's breadth that was to him the difference between life and death. For, if he proved not to be dependable, back he went — returned to duty! As long as he was dependable he slept under a table in a warm room, his toilette arrangements and washing in a bully-beef case near his head, a billy full of tea always stewing for him on an always burning stove. . . . A paradise! . . . No! Not a paradise; *the* paradise of the Other Ranks! . . . He might be awakened at one in the morning. Miles away the enemy might be beginning a strafe. . . . He would roll out from among the blankets under the table amongst the legs of hurrying N.C.O.s and officers, the telephone going like hell. . . . He would have to manifold innumerable short orders on buff slips, on a typewriter. . . . A bore to be awakened at one in the morning, but not unexciting: the enemy putting up a tremendous barrage in front of the village of Dranoutre; the whole nineteenth division to be moved into support along the Bailleul-Nieppe road. In case . . .

Tietjens considered the sleeping army. . . . That country village under the white moon, all of sack-cloth sides, celluloid windows, forty men to a hut . . . That slumbering Arcadia was one of . . . how many? Thirty-seven thousand five hundred, say for a million and a half of men. . . . But there were probably more than a million and a half in that base. . . . Well, round the slumbering Arcadias were the fringes of virginly glimmering tents. . . . Fourteen men to a tent. . . . For a million . . . Seventy-one thousand four hundred and twenty-one tents round, say, one hundred and fifty I.B.D.s, C.B.D.s, R.E.B.D.s. . . . Base depots for infantry, cavalry, sappers, gunners, airmen, anti-airmen, telephone-men, vets, chiropodists, Royal Army Service Corps men, Pigeon Service men, Sanitary Service men, Women's Auxiliary Army Corps women, V.A.D. women — what in the world did V.A.D. stand for? — canteens, rest-tent attendants, barrack damage superintendents, parsons, priests, rabbis, Mormon bishops, Brahmins, Lamas, Imams, Fanti men, no doubt, for African troops. And all really dependent on the acting orderly-room lance-corporals for their temporal and spiritual salvation. . . . For, if by a slip of the pen a lance-corporal sent a Papist priest to an Ulster regiment, the Ulster men would lynch him, and all go to hell. Or, if by a slip of the tongue at the telephone, or a slip of the typewriter, he sent a division to Westoutre instead of to Dranoutre at one in the morning, the six or seven thousand poor devils in front of Dranoutre might all be massacred and nothing but His Majesty's Navy could save us. . . .

Yet, in the end, all this tangle was satisfactorily unravelled; the drafts moved off, unknotting themselves like snakes, coiling out of inextricable bunches, sliding vertabrately over the mud to dip into their bowls — the rabbis found Jews dying to whom to administer; the vets, spavined mules; the V.A.D.s, men without jaws and shoulders in C.C.S.s; the camp-cookers, frozen beef; the chiropodists, ingrowing toenails; the dentists, decayed molars; the naval howitzers, camouflaged emplacements in picturesquely wooded dingles. . . . Somehow they got there — even to the pots of strawberry jam by the ten dozen!

For if the acting lance-corporal, whose life hung by a hair, made a slip of the pen over a dozen pots of jam, back he went, *Returned to duty* . . . back to the frozen rifle, the ground-sheet on the liquid mud, the desperate suction on the ankle as the foot was advanced, the landscapes silhouetted with broken church towers, the continual drone of the planes, the mazes of duckboards in vast plains of slime, the unending Cockney humour, the great shells labelled *Love to Little Willie.* . . . Back to the Angel with the Flaming Sword. The wrong side of him! . . . So, on the whole, things moved satisfactorily. . . .

He was walking Colonel Levin imperiously between the huts towards the mess quarters, their feet crunching on the freezing gravel, the colonel hanging back a little; but a mere light-weight and without nails in his elegant bootsoles, so he had no grip on the ground. He was remarkably silent. Whatever he wanted to get out he was reluctant to come to. He brought out, however:

"I wonder you don't apply to be returned to duty . . . to your battalion. I jolly well should if I were you."

Tietjens said:

"Why? Because I've had a man killed on me? . . . There must have been a dozen killed to-night."

"Oh, more, very likely," the other answered. "It was one of our own planes that was brought down. . . . But it isn't that. . . . Oh, damn it! . . . Would you mind walking the other way? . . . I've the great-

est respect . . . oh, almost . . . for you personally. You're a man
of intellect. . . ."

Tietjens was reflecting on a nice point of military etiquette.

This lisping, ineffectual fellow — he was a very careful Staff officer or Campion would not have had him about the place! — was
given to moulding himself exactly on his general. Physically, in costume as far as possible, in voice — for his lisp was not his own so
much as an adaptation of the general's slight stutter — and above all
in his uncompleted sentences and point of view. . . . Now, if he
said:

"Look here, colonel . . ." or "Look here, Colonel Levin . . ." or
"Look here, Stanley, my boy . . ." For the one thing an officer may
not say to a superior whatever their intimacy was: "Look here, Levin
. . ." If he said then:

"Look here, Stanley, you're a silly ass. It's all very well for Campion to say that I am unsound because I've some brains. He's my godfather and has been saying it to me since I was twelve, and had more
brain in my left heel than he had in the whole of his beautifully
barbered skull. . . . But when you say it you are just a parrot. You
did not think that out for yourself. You do not even think it. You
know I'm heavy, short in the wind, and self-assertive . . . but you
know perfectly well that I'm as good on detail as yourself. And a
damned sight more. You've never caught me tripping over a return.
Your sergeant in charge of returns may have. But not you. . . ."

If Tietjens should say that to this popinjay, would that be going
farther than an officer in charge of detachment should go with a
member of the Staff set above him, though not on parade and in a
conversation of intimacy? Off parade and in intimate conversation
all His Majesty's poor ——— officers are equals . . . gentlemen having
His Majesty's commission, there can be no higher rank and all that
Bilge! . . . For how off parade could this descendant of an old-clo'
man from Frankfurt be the equal of him, Tietjens of Groby? He
wasn't his equal in any way — let alone socially. If Tietjens hit him
he would drop dead; if he addressed a little sneering remark to Levin,
the fellow would melt so that you would see the old spluttering Jew
swimming up through his carefully arranged Gentile features. He
couldn't shoot as well as Tietjens, or ride, or play a hand at auction.
Why, damn it, he, Tietjens, hadn't the least doubt that he could
paint better water-colour pictures. . . . And, as for returns . . . he
would undertake to tear the guts out of half a dozen new and contra-

dictory A.C.I.s — Army Council Instructions — and write twelve correct Command Orders founded on them, before Levin had lisped out the date and serial number of the first one. . . . He had done it several times up in the room, arranged like a French blue stocking's salon, where Levin worked at Garrison headquarters. . . . He had written Levin's blessed command orders while Levin fussed and fumed about their being delayed for tea with Mlle de Bailly . . . and curled his delicate moustache. . . . Mlle de Bailly, chaperoned by old Lady Sachse, had tea by a clear wood fire in an eighteenth-century octagonal room, with blue-grey tapestried walls and powdering closets, out of priceless porcelain cups without handles. Pale tea that tasted faintly of cinnamon!

Mlle de Bailly was a long, dark, high-coloured Provençale. Not heavy, but precisely long, slow, and cruel; coiled in a deep arm-chair, saying the most wounding, slow things to Levin, she resembled a white Persian cat luxuriating, sticking out a tentative pawful of expanding claws. With eyes slanting pronouncedly upwards and a very thin hooked nose . . . Almost Japanese . . . And with a terrific cortège of relatives, swell in a French way. One brother a chauffeur to a Marshal of France . . . An aristocratic way of shirking!

With all that, obviously even off parade, you might well be the social equal of a Staff colonel, but you jolly well had to keep from showing that you were his superior. Especially intellectually. If you let yourself show a Staff officer that he *was* a silly ass — you could say it as often as you liked as long as you didn't prove it! — you could be certain that you would be for it before long. And quite properly. It was not English to be intellectually adroit. Nay, it was positively un-English. And the duty of field officers is to keep messes as English as possible. . . . So a Staff officer would take it out of such a regimental inferior. In a perfectly creditable way. You would never imagine the hash headquarters warrant officers would make of your returns. Until you were worried and badgered and in the end either you were ejected into, or prayed to be transferred to . . . any other command in the whole service. . . .

And that was beastly. The process, not the effect. On the whole Tietjens did not care where he was or what he did as long as he kept out of England, the thought of that country, at night, slumbering across the Channel, being sentimentally unbearable to him. . . . Still, he was fond of old Campion, and would rather be in his command than any other. He had attached to his staff a very decent set of fellows, as decent as you could be in contact with . . . if you had to be in contact with your kind. . . . So he just said:

"Look here, Stanley, you are a silly ass," and left it at that, without demonstrating the truth of the assertion.

The colonel said:

"Why, what have I been doing now? . . . I *wish* you would walk the other way. . . ."

Tietjens said:

"No, I can't afford to go out of camp. . . . I've got to come to witness your fantastic wedding-contract to-morrow afternoon, haven't I? . . . I can't leave camp twice in one week. . . ."

"You've got to come down to the camp-guard," Levin said. "I hate to keep a woman waiting in the cold . . . though she *is* in the general's car. . . ."

Tietjens exclaimed:

"You've not been . . . oh, extraordinary enough, to bring Miss de Bailly out here? To talk to me?"

Colonel Levin mumbled, so low Tietjens almost imagined that he was not meant to hear:

"It isn't Miss de Bailly!" Then he exclaimed quite aloud: "Damn it all, Tietjens, haven't you had hints enough? . . ."

For a lunatic moment it went through Tietjens' mind that it must be Miss Wannop in the general's car, at the gate, down the hill beside the camp guard-room. But he knew folly when it presented itself to his mind. He had nevertheless turned and they were going very slowly back along the broad way between the huts. Levin was certainly in no hurry. The broad way would come to an end of the hutments; about two acres of slope would descend blackly before them, white stones to mark a sort of coastguard track glimmering out of sight beneath a moon gone dark with the frost. And, down there in the dark forest, at the end of that track, in a terrific Rolls-Royce, was waiting something of which Levin was certainly deucedly afraid. . . .

For a minute Tietjens' backbone stiffened. He didn't intend to interfere between Mlle de Bailly and any married woman Levin had had as a mistress. . . . Somehow he was convinced that what was in that car was a married woman. . . . He did not dare to think otherwise. If it was not a married woman it might be Miss Wannop. If it was, it couldn't be. . . . An immense waft of calm, sentimental happiness had descended upon him. Merely because he had imagined her! He imagined her little, fair, rather pug-nosed face; under a fur cap, he did not know why. Leaning forward she would be, on the seat of the general's illuminated car, glazed in, a regular raree show! Peering out, shortsightedly on account of the reflections on the inside of the glass. . . .

He was saying to Levin:

"Look here, Stanley . . . why I said you are a silly ass is because Miss de Bailly has one chief luxury. It's exhibiting jealousy. Not feeling it; exhibiting it."

"*Ought* you," Levin asked ironically, "to discuss my fiancée before me? As an English gentleman. Tietjens of Groby and all."

"Why, of course," Tietjens said. He continued feeling happy. "As a sort of swollen best man, it's my duty to instruct you. Mothers tell their daughters things before marriage. Best men do it for the innocent Benedict. . . . And you're always consulting me about the young woman. . . ."

"I'm not doing it now," Levin grumbled direly.

"Then what, in God's name, are you doing? You've got a cast mistress, haven't you, down there in old Campion's car? . . ." They were beside the alley that led down to his orderly room. Knots of men, dim, and desultory, still half filled it, a little way down.

"I *haven't*," Levin exclaimed almost tearfully. "I never *had* a mistress. . . ."

"And you're not married?" Tietjens asked. He used on purpose the schoolboy's ejaculation "Lummy!" to soften the jibe. "If you'll excuse me," he said, "I must just go and take a look at my crowd. To see if your orders have come down."

He found no orders in a hut as full as ever of the dull mists and odours of khaki, but he found in revenge a fine upstanding, blond, Canadian-born lance-corporal of old Colonial lineage, with a moving story as related by Sergeant-Major Cowley:

"This man, sir, of the Canadian Railway lot, 'is mother's just turned up in the town, come on from Eetarpels. Come all the way from Toronto where she was bedridden."

Tietjens said:

"Well, what about it? Get a move on."

The man wanted leave to go to his mother who was waiting in a decent estaminet at the end of the tramline, just outside the camp where the houses of the town began.

Tietjens said: "It's impossible. It's absolutely impossible. You know that."

The man stood erect and expressionless; his blue eyes looked confoundedly honest to Tietjens who was cursing himself. He said to the man:

"You can see for yourself that it's impossible, can't you?"

The man said slowly:

"Not knowing the regulations in these circumstances I can't say, sir. But my mother's is a very special case. . . . She's lost two sons already."

Tietjens said:

"A great many people have. . . . Do you understand, if you went absent off my pass I might — I quite possibly might — lose my commission? I'm responsible for you fellows getting up the line."

The man looked down at his feet. Tietjens said to himself that it was Valentine Wannop doing this to him. He ought to turn the man down at once. He was pervaded by a sense of her being. It was imbecile. Yet it was so. He said to the man:

"You said good-bye to your mother, didn't you, in Toronto, before you left?"

The man said:

"No, sir." He had not seen his mother in seven years. He had been up in the Chilkoot when war broke out and had not heard of it for ten months. Then he had at once joined up in British Columbia, and had been sent straight through for railway work, on to Aldershot where the Canadians have a camp in building. He had not known that his brothers were killed till he got there and his mother, being bedridden at the news, had not been able to get down to Toronto when his batch had passed through. She lived about sixty miles from Toronto. Now she had risen from her bed like a miracle and come all the way. A widow, sixty-two years of age. Very feeble.

It occurred to Tietjens as it occurred to him ten times a day that it was idiotic of him to figure Valentine Wannop to himself. He had not the slightest idea where she was: in what circumstances, or even in what house. He did not suppose she and her mother had stayed on in that dog-kennel of a place in Bedford Park. They would be fairly comfortable. His father had left them money. "It is preposterous," he said to himself, "to persist in figuring a person to yourself when you have no idea of where they are." He said to the man:

"Wouldn't it do if you saw your mother at the camp gate, by the guard-room?"

"Not much of a leave-taking, sir," the man said; "she not allowed in the camp and I not allowed out. Talking under a sentry's nose very likely."

Tietjens said to himself:

"What a monstrous absurdity this is of seeing and talking, for a minute or so! You meet and talk . . ." And next day at the same hour. Nothing. . . . As well not to meet or talk. . . . Yet the mere fantastic idea of seeing Valentine Wannop for a minute. . . . She not allowed in the camp and he not going out. Talking under a sentry's nose, very likely. . . . It had made him smell primroses. Primroses, like Miss Wannop. He said to the sergeant-major:

"What sort of a fellow is this?" Cowley, in open-mouthed suspense, gasped like a fish. Tietjens said:

"I suppose your mother is fairly feeble to stand in the cold?"

"A very decent man, sir," the sergeant-major got out, "one of the best. No trouble. A perfectly clean conduct sheet. Very good education. A railway engineer in civil life. . . . Volunteered, of course, sir."

"That's the odd thing," Tietjens said to the man, "that the percentages of absentees is as great amongst the volunteers as the Derby men or the compulsorily enlisted. . . . Do you understand what will happen to you if you miss the draft?"

The man said soberly:

"Yes, sir. Perfectly well."

"You understand that you will be shot? As certainly as that you stand there. And that you haven't a chance of escape."

He wondered what Valentine Wannop, hot pacifist, would think of him if she heard him. Yet it was his duty to talk like that: his human, not merely his military duty. As much his duty as that of a doctor to warn a man that if he drank of typhoid-contaminated water he would get typhoid. But people are unreasonable. Valentine too was unreasonable. She would consider it brutal to speak to a man of the possibility of his being shot by a firing party. A groan burst from him at the thought that there was no sense in bothering about what Valentine Wannop would or would not think of him. No sense. No sense. No sense. . .

The man, fortunately, was assuring him that he knew, very soberly, all about the penalty for going absent off a draft. The sergeant-major, catching a sound from Tietjens, said with admirable fussiness to the man:

"There, there! Don't you hear the officer's speaking? Never interrupt an officer."

"You'll be shot," Tietjens said, "at dawn. . . . Literally at dawn."
Why did they shoot them at dawn? To rub it in that they were never
going to see another sunrise. But they drugged the fellows so that
they wouldn't know the sun if they saw it; all roped in a chair. . . .
It was really the worse for the firing party. He added to the man:

"Don't think I'm insulting you. You appear to be a very decent
fellow. But very decent fellows have gone absent. . . ." He said to
the sergeant-major:

"Give this man a two-hours' pass to go to the . . . whatever's the
name of the estaminet. . . . The draft won't move off for two
hours, will it?" He added to the man: "If you see your draft passing
the pub you run out and fall in. Like mad, you understand. You'd
never get another chance."

There was a mumble like applause and envy of a mate's good luck
from a packed audience that had hung on the lips of simple melodrama . . . an audience that seemed to be all enlarged eyes, the
khaki was so colourless. . . . They came as near applause as they
dared, but there was no sense in worrying about whether Valentine
Wannop would have applauded or not. . . . And there was no
knowing whether the fellow would not go absent, either. As likely as
not there was no mother. A girl very likely. And very likely the man
would desert. . . . The man looked you straight in the eyes. But
a strong passion, like that for escape — or a girl — will give you control over the muscles of the eyes. A little thing that, before a strong
passion! One would look God in the face on the day of judgment
and lie, in that case.

Because what the devil did he want of Valentine Wannop? Why
could he not stall off the thought of her? He could stall off the
thought of his wife . . . or his not-wife. But Valentine Wannop
came wriggling in. At all hours of the day and night. It was an obsession. A madness . . . what those fools called "a complex"! . . . Due,
no doubt, to something your nurse had done, or your parents said to
you. At birth . . . A strong passion . . . or no doubt not strong
enough. Otherwise he, too, would have gone absent. At any rate,
from Sylvia . . . Which he hadn't done. Which he hadn't done. Or
hadn't he? There was no saying. . . .

It was undoubtedly colder in the alley between the huts. A man was
saying: "Hoo . . . Hooo . . . Hoo . . ." A sound like that, and

flapping his arms and hopping . . . "Hand and foot, mark time! . . ." Somebody ought to fall these poor devils in and give them that to keep their circulations going. But they might not know the command. . . . It was a Guards' trick, really. . . . What the devil were these fellows kept hanging about here for? he asked.

One or two voices said that they did not know. The majority said gutturally:

"Waiting for our mates, sir. . . ."

"I should have thought you could have waited under cover," Tietjens said caustically. "But never mind; it's your funeral, if you like it. . . ." This getting together . . . a strong passion. There was a warmed recreation-hut for waiting drafts not fifty yards away. But they stood, teeth chattering and mumbling "Hoo . . . Hooo . . ." rather than miss thirty seconds of gabble. . . . About what the English sergeant-major said and about what the officer said and how many dollars did they give you. . . . And of course about what you answered back. . . . Or perhaps not that. These Canadian troops were husky, serious fellows, without the swank of the Cockney or the Lincolnshire Moonrakers. They wanted, apparently, to learn the rules of war. They discussed anxiously information that they received in orderly rooms, and looked at you as if you were expounding the gospels. . . .

But damn it, he, he himself, would make a pact with Destiny, at that moment, willingly, to pass thirty months in the frozen circle of hell, for the chance of thirty seconds in which to tell Valentine Wannop what he had answered back . . . to Destiny! . . . What was the fellow in the Inferno who was buried to the neck in ice and begged Dante to clear the icicles out of his eyelids so that he could see out of them? And Dante kicked him in the face because he was a Ghibelline. Always a bit of a swine, Dante. . . . Rather like . . . like whom? . . . Oh, Sylvia Tietjens. . . . A good hater! . . . He imagined hatred coming to him in waves from the convent in which Sylvia had immured herself. . . . Gone into retreat. . . . He imagined she had gone into retreat. She had said she was going. For the rest of the war. . . . For the duration of hostilities or life, whichever were the longer. . . . He imagined Sylvia, coiled up on a convent bed. . . . Hating. . . Her certainly glorious hair all round her. . . . Hating. . . Slowly and coldly. . . Like the head of a snake when you examined it. . . . Eyes motionless, mouth closed tight. . . . Looking away into the distance and hating. . . . She was presumably in

Birkenhead. . . . A long way to send your hatred. . . . Across a
country and a sea in an icy night! Over all that black land and water
. . . with the lights out because of air-raids and U-boats. . . . Well,
he did not have to think of Sylvia at the moment. She was well out
of it. . . .

It was certainly getting no warmer as the night drew on. . . .
Even that ass Levin was pacing swiftly up and down in the dusky
moon-shadow of the last hutments that looked over the slope and
the vanishing trail of white stones. . . . In spite of his boasting
about not wearing an overcoat; to catch women's eyes with his pretty
Staff gadgets he was carrying on like a leopard at feeding time.

Tietjens said:

"Sorry to keep you waiting, old man. . . . Or rather your lady.
. . . But there were some men to see to. And, you know . . . 'The
comfort and — what is it? — of the men comes before every — is it
"consideration"? — except the exigencies of actual warfare' . . . My
memory's gone phut these days. . . . And you want me to slide
down this hill and wheeze back again. . . . To see a woman!"

Levin screeched: "Damn you, you ass! It's your wife who's waiting
for you at the bottom there."

III

THE ONE thing that stood out sharply in Tietjens' mind when at
last, with a stiff glass of rum punch, his officer's pocket-book complete
with pencil because he had to draft before eleven a report as to the
desirability for giving his unit special lectures on the causes of the
war, and a cheap French novel on a camp chair beside him he sat in
his flea-bag with six army blankets over him — the one thing that
stood out as sharply as Staff tabs was that that ass Levin was rather
pathetic. His unnailed bootsoles very much cramping his action on
the frozen hillside, he had alternately hobbled a step or two, and,
reduced to inaction, had grabbed at Tietjens' elbow, while he brought
out breathlessly puzzled sentences.

There resulted a singular mosaic of extraordinary, bright-coloured
and melodramatic statements, for Levin, who first hobbled down the
hill with Tietjens and then hobbled back up, clinging to his arm,
brought out monstrosities of news about Sylvia's activities, without

any sequence, and indeed without any apparent aim except for the great affection he had for Tietjens himself. . . . All sorts of singular things seemed to have been going on round him in the vague zone, outside all this engrossed and dust-coloured world — in the vague zone that held . . . Oh, the civilian population, tea-parties short of butter! . . .

And as Tietjens, seated on his hams, his knees up, pulled the soft woolliness of his flea-bag under his chin and damned the paraffin heater for letting out a new and singular stink, it seemed to him that this affair was like coming back after two months and trying to get the hang of battalion orders. . . . You come back to the familiar, slightly battered mess ante-room. You tell the mess orderly to bring you the last two months' orders, for it is as much as your life is worth not to know what is or is not in them. . . . There might be an A.C.I. ordering you to wear your helmet back to the front, or a battalion order that Mills bombs must always be worn in the left breast pocket. Or there might be the detail for putting on a new gas helmet! . . . The orderly hands you a dishevelled mass of faintly typewritten matter, thumbed out of all chance of legibility, with the orders for November 16 fastened inextricably into the middle of those for the 1st of December, and those for the 10th, 15th and 29th missing altogether. . . . And all that you gather is that headquarters has some exceedingly insulting things to say about A Company; that a fellow called Hartopp, whom you don't know, has been deprived of his commission; that at a court of inquiry held to ascertain deficiencies in C Company Captain Wells — poor Wells! — has been assessed at £27 11s. 4d., which he is requested to pay forthwith to the adjutant. . . .

So, on that black hillside, going and returning, what stuck out for Tietjens was that Levin had been taught by the general to consider that he, Tietjens, was an extraordinarily violent chap who would certainly knock Levin down when he told him that his wife was at the camp gates; that Levin considered himself to be the descendant of an ancient Quaker family. . . . (Tietjens had said *Good God!* at that); that the mysterious "rows" to which in his fear Levin had been continually referring had been successive letters from Sylvia to the harried general . . . and that Sylvia had accused him, Tietjens, of stealing two pairs of her best sheets. . . . There was a great deal more. But, having faced what he considered to be the worst of the situation, Tietjens set himself coolly to recapitulate every aspect of his separation from his wife. He had meant to face every aspect, not that merely social one upon which, hitherto, he had automatically imagined their disunion to rest. For, as he saw it, English people of good position consider that the basis of all marital unions or disunions, is the maxim: No scenes. Obviously for the sake of the servants — who are the same thing as the public. No scenes, then, for the sake of the public. And indeed, with him, the instinct for privacy — as to his relationships, his passions, or even as to his most unimportant motives — was as strong as the instinct of life itself. He would, literally, rather be dead than an open book.

And, until that afternoon, he had imagined that his wife, too, would rather be dead than have her affairs canvassed by the other ranks. But that assumption had to be gone over. Revised. . . Of course he might say she had gone mad. But, if he said she had gone mad he would have to revise a great deal of their relationships, so it would be as broad as it was long. . . .

The doctor's batman, from the other end of the hut, said: "Poor —— O Nine Morgan! . . ." in a sing-song, mocking voice. . . .

For though, hours before, Tietjens had appointed this moment of physical ease that usually followed on his splurging heavily down on to his creaking camp-bed in the doctor's lent hut, for the cool consideration of his relations with his wife, it was not turning out a very easy matter. The hut was unreasonably warm: he had invited Mackenzie — whose real name turned out to be McKechnie, James Grant McKechnie — to occupy the other end of it. The other end of it was divided from him by a partition of canvas and a striped Indian curtain. And McKechnie, who was unable to sleep, had elected to carry on a long — an interminable — conversation with the doctor's batman.

The doctor's batman also could not sleep and, like McKechnie, was more than a little barmy on the crumpet — an almost non-English-speaking Welshman from God knows what up-country valley. He had shaggy hair like a Caribbean savage and two dark, resentful wall-eyes; being a miner he sat on his heels more comfortably than on a chair and his almost incomprehensible voice went on in a low sort of ululation, with an occasionally and startlingly comprehensible phrase sticking out now and then.

It was troublesome, but orthodox enough. The batman had been blown literally out of most of his senses and the VIth Battalion of the Glamorganshire Regiment by some German high explosive or other, more than a year ago. But before then, it appeared, he had been in McKechnie's own company in that battalion. It was perfectly in order that an officer should gossip with a private formerly of his own platoon or company, especially on first meeting him after long separation caused by a casualty to one or the other. And McKechnie had first re-met this scoundrel Jonce, or Evanns, at eleven that night — two and a half hours before. So there, in the light of a single candle stuck in a stout bottle they were tranquilly at it: the batman sitting on his heel by the officer's head; the officer, in his pyjamas, sprawling half out of bed over his pillows, stretching his arms abroad, occasionally yawning, occasionally asking: "What became of Company-Sergeant-Major Hoyt?" They might talk till half-past three.

But that was troublesome to a gentleman seeking to recapture what exactly were his relations with his wife.

Before the doctor's batman had interrupted him by speaking startlingly of O Nine Morgan, Tietjens had got as far as what follows with his recapitulation: The lady, Mrs. Tietjens, was certainly without mitigation a whore; he himself equally certainly and without qualification had been physically faithful to the lady and their marriage tie. In law, then, he was absolutely in the right of it. But that fact had less weight than a cobweb. For after the last of her highhanded divagations from fidelity he had accorded to the lady the shelter of his roof and of his name. She had lived for years beside him, apparently on terms of hatred and miscomprehension. But certainly in conditions of chastity. Then, during the tenuous and lugubrious small hours, before his coming out there again to France, she had given evidence of a madly vindictive passion for his person. A physical passion at any rate.

Well, those were times of mad, fugitive emotions. But even in the calmest times a man could not expect to have a woman live with him as the mistress of his house and mother of his heir without establishing some sort of claim upon him. They hadn't slept together. But was it not possible that a constant measuring together of your minds was as proper to give you a proprietary right as the measuring together of the limbs? It was perfectly possible. Well then . . .

What, in the eyes of God, severed a union? . . . Certainly he had imagined — until that very afternoon — that their union had been cut, as the tendon of Achilles is cut in a hamstringing, by Sylvia's clear voice, outside his house, saying in the dawn to a cabman, "Paddington!" He tried to go with extreme care through every detail of their last interview in his still nearly dark drawing-room at the other end of which she had seemed a mere white phosphorescence. . . .

They had, then, parted for good on that day. He was going out to France; she into retreat in a convent near Birkenhead — to which place you go from Paddington. Well then, that was one parting. That, surely, set him free for the girl!

He took a sip from the glass of rum and water on the canvas chair beside him. It was tepid and therefore beastly. He had ordered the batman to bring it him hot, strong, and sweet, because he had been certain of an incipient cold. He had refrained from drinking it because he had remembered that he was to think cold-bloodedly of Sylvia, and he made a practice of never touching alcohol when about to engage in protracted reflection. That had always been his theory; it had been immensely and empirically strengthened by his warlike experience. On the Somme, in the summer, when stand-to had been at four in the morning, you would come out of your dug-out and survey, with a complete outfit of pessimistic thoughts, a dim, grey, repulsive landscape over a dull and much too thin parapet. There would be repellent posts, altogether too fragile entanglements of barbed wire, broken wheels, detritus, coils of mist over the positions of revolting Germans. Grey stillness; grey horrors, in front, and behind amongst the civilian populations! And clear, hard outlines to every thought. . . . Then your batman brought you a cup of tea with a little — quite a little — rum in it. In three or four minutes the whole world changed beneath your eyes. The wire aprons became jolly efficient protections that your skill had devised and for which you might thank God; the broken wheels were convenient landmarks for raiding at night in No Man's Land. You had to confess that, when you had re-erected that parapet, after it had last been jammed in, your company had made a pretty good job of it. And, even as far as the Germans were concerned, you were there to kill the swine; but you didn't feel that the thought of them would make you sick beforehand. . . . You were, in fact, a changed man. With a mind of a different specific gravity. You could not even tell that the roseate touches of dawn on the mists were not really the effects of rum. . . .

Therefore he had determined not to touch his grog. But his throat had gone completely dry; so, mechanically, he had reached out for something to drink, checking himself when he had realised what he was doing. But why should his throat be dry? He hadn't been on the drink. He had not even had any dinner. And why was he in this extraordinary state? . . . For he was in an extraordinary state. It was because the idea had suddenly occurred to him that his parting from his wife had set him free for his girl. . . . The idea had till then never entered his head.

He said to himself: We must go methodically into this! Methodically into the history of his last day on earth. . . .

Because he swore that when he had come out to France this time he had imagined that he was cutting loose from this earth. And during the months that he had been there he had seemed to have no connection with any earthly things. He had imagined Sylvia in her convent and done with; Miss Wannop he had not been able to imagine at all. But she had seemed to be done with.

It was difficult to get his mind back to that night. You cannot force your mind to a deliberate, consecutive recollection unless you are in the mood; then it will do whether you want it to or not. . . . He had had then, three months or so ago, a very painful morning with his wife, the pain coming from a suddenly growing conviction that his wife was forcing herself into an attitude of caring for him. Only an attitude probably, because, in the end, Sylvia was a lady and would not allow herself really to care for the person in the world for whom it would be least decent of her to care. . . . But she would be perfectly capable of forcing herself to take that attitude if she thought that it would enormously inconvenience himself. . . .

But that wasn't the way, wasn't the way, wasn't the way his excited mind said to himself. He was excited because it was possible that Miss Wannop, too, might not have meant their parting to be a permanency. That opened up an immense perspective. Nevertheless, the contemplation of that immense perspective was not the way to set about a calm analysis of his relations with his wife. The facts of the story *must* be stated before the moral. He said to himself that he must put, in exact language, as if he were making a report for the use of garrison headquarters, the history of himself in his relationship to his wife. . . . And to Miss Wannop, of course. "Better put it into writing," he said.

Well then. He clutched at his pocket-book and wrote in large pencilled characters:

"When I married Miss Satterthwaite," — he was attempting exactly to imitate a report to General Headquarters — "unknown to myself, she imagined herself to be with child by a fellow called

Drake. I think she was not. The matter is debatable. I am passionately attached to the child who is my heir and the heir of a family of considerable position. The lady was subsequently, on several occasions, though I do not know how many, unfaithful to me. She left me with a fellow called Perowne, whom she had met constantly at the house of my godfather, General Lord Edward Campion, on whose staff Perowne was. That was long before the war. This intimacy was, of course, certainly unsuspected by the general. Perowne is again on the staff of General Campion, who has the quality of attachment to his old subordinates, but as Perowne is an inefficient officer, he is used only for more decorative jobs. Otherwise, obviously, as he is an old regular, his seniority should make him a general, and he is only a major. I make this diversion about Perowne because his presence in this garrison causes me natural personal annoyance.

"My wife, after an absence of several months with Perowne, wrote and told me that she wished to be taken back into my household. I allowed this. My principles prevent me from divorcing any woman, in particular any woman who is the mother of a child. As I had taken no steps to ensure publicity for the escapade of Mrs. Tietjens, no one, as far as I know, was aware of her absence. Mrs. Tietjens, being a Roman Catholic, is prevented from divorcing me.

"During this absence of Mrs. Tietjens with the man Perowne, I made the acquaintance of a young woman, Miss Wannop, the daughter of my father's oldest friend, who was also an old friend of General Campion's. Our station in Society naturally forms rather a close ring. I was immediately aware that I had formed a sympathetic but not violent attachment for Miss Wannop, and fairly confident that my feeling was returned. Neither Miss Wannop nor myself being persons to talk about the state of our feelings, we exchanged no confidences. . . . A disadvantage of being English of a certain station.

"The position continued thus for several years. Six or seven. After her return from her excursion with Perowne, Mrs. Tietjens remained, I believe, perfectly chaste. I saw Miss Wannop sometimes frequently, for a period, in her mother's house or on social occasions, sometimes not for long intervals. No expression of affection on the part of either of us ever passed. Not one. Ever.

"On the day before my second going out to France I had a very painful scene with my wife, during which, for the first time, we went into the question of the parentage of my child and other matters. In the afternoon I met Miss Wannop by appointment outside the War

Office. The appointment had been made by my wife, not by me. I knew nothing about it. My wife must have been more aware of my feelings for Miss Wannop than was I myself.

"In St. James's Park I invited Miss Wannop to become my mistress that evening. She consented and made an assignation. It is to be presumed that that was evidence of her affection for me. We have never exchanged words of affection. Presumably a young lady does not consent to go to bed with a married man without feeling affection for him. But I have no proof. It was, of course, only a few hours before my going out to France. Those are emotional sorts of moments for young women. No doubt they consent more easily.

"But we didn't. We were together at one-thirty in the morning, leaning over her suburban garden gate. And nothing happened. We agreed that we were the sort of persons who didn't. I do not know how we agreed. We never finished a sentence. Yet it was a passionate scene. So I touched the brim of my cap and said: *So long!* . . . Or perhaps I did not even say *So long*. Or she. . . I don't remember. I remember the thoughts I thought and the thoughts I gave her credit for thinking. But perhaps she did not think them. There is no knowing. It is no good going into them . . . except that I gave her credit for thinking that we were parting for good. Perhaps she did not mean that. Perhaps I could write letters to her. And live . . ."

He exclaimed:

"God, what a sweat I am in! . . ."

The sweat, indeed, was pouring down his temples. He became instinct with a sort of passion to let his thoughts wander into epithets and go about where they would. But he stuck at it. He was determined to get it expressed. He wrote on again:

"I got home towards two in the morning and went into the dining-room in the dark. I did not need a light. I sat thinking for a long time. Then Sylvia spoke from the other end of the room. There was thus an abominable situation. I have never been spoken to with such hatred. She went, perhaps, mad. She had apparently been banking on the idea that if I had physical contact with Miss Wannop I might satisfy my affection for the girl. . . . And feel physical desires for *her*. . . . But she knew, without my speaking, that I had not had physical contact with the girl. She threatened to ruin me; to ruin me in the Army; to drag my name through the mud. . . . I never spoke. I am damn good at not speaking. She struck me in the face. And went away. Afterwards she threw into the room, through the half-open doorway, a gold medallion of St. Michael, the R.C. patron of soldiers in action that she had worn between her breasts. I took it to mean the final act of parting. As if by no longer wearing it she abandoned all prayer for my safety. . . . It might just as well mean that she wished me to wear it myself for my personal protection. . . . I heard her go down the stairs with her maid. The dawn was just showing through the chimney-pots opposite. I heard her say: *Paddington.* Clear, high syllables! And a motor drove off.

"I got my things together and went to Waterloo. Mrs. Satterthwaite, her mother, was waiting to see me off. She was very distressed that her daughter had not come, too. She was of opinion that it meant we had parted for good. I was astonished to find that Sylvia had told her mother about Miss Wannop because Sylvia had always been extremely reticent, even to her mother, . . . Mrs. Satterthwaite, who was *very* distressed — she likes me! — expressed the most gloomy forebodings as to what Sylvia might not be up to. I laughed at her. She began to tell me a long anecdote about what a Father Consett, Sylvia's confessor, had said about Sylvia years before. He had said that if I ever came to care for another woman Sylvia would tear the world to pieces to get at me. . . . Meaning, to disturb my equanimity! . . . It was difficult to follow Mrs. Satterthwaite. The side of an officer's train, going off, is not a good place for confidences. So the interview ended rather untidily."

At this point Tietjens groaned so audibly that McKechnie, from the other end of the hut, asked if he had not said anything. Tietjens saved himself with:

"That candle looks from here to be too near the side of the hut. Perhaps it isn't. These buildings are very inflammable."

It was no good going on writing. He was no writer, and this writing gave no sort of psychological pointers. He wasn't himself ever much the man for psychology, but one ought to be as efficient at it as at anything else. . . . Well then . . . What was at the bottom of all the madness and cruelty that had distinguished both himself and Sylvia on his last day and night in his native country? . . . For, mark! It was Sylvia who had made, unknown to him, the appointment through which the girl had met him. Sylvia had wanted to force him and Miss Wannop into each other's arms. Quite definitely. She had said as much. But she had only said that afterwards. When the game had not come off. She had had too much knowledge of amatory manœuvres to show her hand before. . . .

Why then had she done it? Partly, undoubtedly, out of pity for him. She had given him a rotten time; she had undoubtedly, at one moment, wanted to give him the consolation of his girl's arms. . . . Why, damn it, she, Sylvia, and no one else, had forced out of him the invitation to the girl to become his mistress. Nothing but the infernal cruelty of their interview of the morning could have forced him to the pitch of sexual excitement that would make him make a proposal of illicit intercourse to a young lady to whom hitherto he had spoken not even one word of affection. It was an effect of a Sadic kind. That was the only way to look at it scientifically. And without doubt Sylvia had known what she was doing. The whole morning, at intervals, like a person directing the whiplash to a cruel spot of pain, reiteratedly, she had gone on and on. She had accused him of having Valentine Wannop for his mistress. She had accused him of having Valentine Wannop for his mistress. She had accused him of having Valentine Wannop for his mistress. . . . With maddening reiteration, like that. They had disposed of an estate; they had settled up a number of business matters; they had decided that his heir was to be brought up as a Papist — the mother's religion! They had gone, agonisedly enough, into their own relationships and past history. Into the very paternity of his child. . . . But always, at moments when his mind was like a blind octopus, squirming in an agony of knife-cuts she would drop in that accusation. She had accused him of having Valentine Wannop for his mistress. . . .

He swore by the living God. . . . He had never realised that he had a passion for the girl till that morning; that he had a passion deep and boundless like the sea, shaking like a tremor of the whole world, an unquenchable thirst, a thing the thought of which made your bowels turn over. . . . But he had not been the sort of fellow who goes into his emotions. . . . Why, damn it, even at that moment when he thought of the girl, there, in that beastly camp, in that Rembrandt beshadowed hut, when he thought of the girl he named her to himself Miss Wannop. . . .

It wasn't in that way that a man thought of a young woman whom he was aware of passionately loving. He wasn't aware. He hadn't been aware. Until that morning. . . .

Then . . . that let him out. . . . Undoubtedly that let him out. . . . A woman cannot throw her man, her official husband, into the arms of the first girl that comes along and consider herself as having any further claims upon him. Especially if, on the same day, you part with him, he going out to France! *Did* it let him out? Obviously it did.

He caught with such rapidity at his glass of rum and water that a little of it ran over on to his thumb. He swallowed the lot, being instantly warmed. . . .

What in the world was he doing? Now? With all this introspection? . . . Hang it all, he was not justifying himself. . . . He had acted perfectly correctly as far as Sylvia was concerned. Not perhaps to Miss Wannop. . . . Why, if he, Christopher Tietjens of Groby, had the need to justify himself, what did it stand for to be Christopher Tietjens of Groby? That was the unthinkable thought.

Obviously he was not immune from the seven deadly sins, in the way of a man. One might lie, yet not bear false witness against a neighbour; one might kill, yet not without fitting provocation or for self-interest; one might conceive of theft as reiving cattle from the false Scots which was the Yorkshireman's duty; one might fornicate, obviously, as long as you did not fuss about it unhealthily. That was the right of the Seigneur in a world of Other Ranks. He hadn't personally committed any of these sins to any great extent. One reserved the right so to do and to take the consequences. . . .

But what in the world had gone wrong with Sylvia? She was giving away her own game, and that he had never known her do. But she could not have made more certain, if she had wanted to, of returning him to his allegiance to Miss Wannop than by forcing herself there into his private life, and doing it with such blatant vulgarity. For what she had done had been to make scenes before the servants! All the while he had been in France she had been working up to it. Now she had done it, before the Tommies of his own unit. But Sylvia did not make mistakes like that. It was a game. What game? He didn't even attempt to conjecture! She could not expect that he would in the future even extend to her the shelter of his roof. . . . What then was the game? He could not believe that she could be capable of vulgarity except with a purpose.

She was a thoroughbred. He had always credited her with being that. And now she was behaving as if she had every mean vice that a mare could have. Or it looked like it. Was that, then, because she had been in his stable? But how in the world otherwise could he have run their lives? She had been unfaithful to him. She had never been anything but unfaithful to him, before or after marriage. In a highhanded way so that he could not condemn her, though it was disagreeable enough to himself. He took her back into his house after she had been off with the fellow Perowne. What more could she ask? . . . He could find no answer. And it was not his business!

But even if he did not bother about the motives of the poor beast of a woman, she was the mother of his heir. And now she was running about the world declaiming about her wrongs. What sort of a thing was that for a boy to have happen to him? A mother who made scenes before the servants! That was enough to ruin any boy's life. . . .

There was no getting away from it that that was what Sylvia had been doing. She had deluged the general with letters for the last two months or so, at first merely contenting herself with asking where he, Tietjens, was and in what state of health, conditions of danger, and the like. Very decently, for some time, the old fellow had said nothing about the matter to him. He had probably taken the letters to be the naturally anxious inquiries of a wife with a husband at the front; he had considered that Tietjens' letters to her must have been insufficiently communicative, or concealed what she imagined to be wounds or a position of desperate danger. That would not have been very pleasant in any case; women should not worry superior officers about the vicissitudes of their menfolk. It was not done. Still, Sylvia was very intimate with Campion and his family — more intimate than he himself was, though Campion was his godfather. But quite obviously her letters had got worse and worse.

It was difficult for Tietjens to make out exactly what she had said. His channel of information had been Levin, who was too gentlemanly ever to say anything direct at all. Too gentlemanly, too implicitly trustful of Tietjens' honour . . . and too bewildered by the charms of Sylvia, who had obviously laid herself out to bewilder the poor Staff-wallah. . . . But she had gone pretty far, either in her letters or in her conversation since she had been in that city, to which — it was characteristic — she had come without any sort of passports or papers, just walking past gentlemen in their wooden boxes at pier-heads and the like, in conversation with — of all people in the world! — with Perowne, who had been returning from leave with King's dispatches, or something glorified of the Staff sort! In a special train very likely. That was Sylvia all over.

Levin said that Campion had given Perowne the most frightful dressing down he had ever heard mortal man receive. And it really was *damn* hard on the poor general, who, after happenings to one of his predecessors, had been perfectly rabid to keep skirts out of his headquarters. Indeed it was one of the crosses of Levin's worried life that the general had absolutely refused him, Levin, leave to marry Miss de Bailly if he would not undertake that that young woman should leave France by the first boat after the ceremony. Levin, of course, was to go with her, but the young woman was not to return to France for the duration of hostilities. And a fine row all her noble relatives had raised over that. It had cost Levin another hundred and fifty thousand francs in the marriage settlements. The married wives of officers in any case were not allowed in France, though you could not keep out their unmarried ones. . . .

Campion, anyhow, had dispatched his furious note to Tietjens after receiving, firstly, in the early morning, a letter from Sylvia in which she said that her ducal second-cousin, the lugubrious Rugeley, highly disapproved of the fact that Tietjens was in France at all, and after later receiving, towards four in the afternoon, a telegram, dispatched by Sylvia herself from Havre, to say that she would be arriving by a noon train. The general had been almost as much upset at the thought that his car would not be there to meet Sylvia as by the thought that she was coming at all. But a strike of French railway civilians had delayed Sylvia's arrival. Campion had dispatched, within five minutes, his snorter to Tietjens, who he was convinced knew all about Sylvia's coming, and his car tò Rouen Station with Levin in it.

The general, in fact, was in a fine confusion. He was convinced that Tietjens, as Man of Intellect, had treated Sylvia badly, even to the extent of stealing two pair of her best sheets, and he was also convinced that Tietjens was in close collusion with Sylvia. As Man of Intellect, Campion was convinced, Tietjens was dissatisfied with his lowly job of draft-forwarding officer, and wanted a place of an extravagantly cooshy kind in the general's own entourage. . . . And Levin had said that it made it all the worse that Campion in his bothered heart thought that Tietjens really ought to have more exalted employment. He had said to Levin:

"Damn it all, the fellow ought to be in command of my Intelligence instead of you. But he's unsound. That's what he is, unsound. He's too brilliant. . . . And he'd talk both the hind legs off Sweedlepumpkins." Sweedlepumpkins was the general's favourite charger. The general was afraid of talk. He practically never talked with anyone except about his job — certainly never with Tietjens — without being proved to be in the wrong, and that undermined his belief in himself.

So that altogether he was in a fine fume. And confusion. He was almost ready to believe that Tietjens was at the bottom of every trouble that occurred in his immense command.

But, when all that was gathered, Tietjens was not much farther forward in knowing what his wife's errand in France was.

"She complains," Levin had bleated painfully at some point on the slippery coastguard path, "about your taking her sheets. And about a Miss . . . a Miss Wanostrocht, is it? . . . The general is not inclined to attach much importance to the sheets."

It appeared that a sort of conference on Tietjens' case had taken place in the immense tapestried salon in which Campion lived with the more intimate members of his headquarters, and which was, for the moment, presided over by Sylvia, who had exposed various wrongs to the general and Levin. Major Perowne had excused himself on the ground that he was hardly competent to express an opinion. Really, Levin said, he was sulking, because Campion had accused him of running the risk of getting himself and Mrs. Tietjens "talked about." Levin thought it was a bit thick of the general. Were none of the members of his staff ever to escort a lady anywhere? As if they were sixth-form schoolboys. . . .

"But you . . . you . . . you . . ." he stuttered and shivered together, "certainly *do* seem to have been remiss in not writing to Mrs. Tietjens. The poor lady — excuse me! — really appears to have been out of her mind with anxiety. . . ." That was why she had been waiting in the general's car at the bottom of the hill. To get a glimpse of Tietjens' living body. For they had been utterly unable, up at H.Q., to convince her that Tietjens was even alive, much less in that town.

She hadn't in fact waited even so long. Having apparently convinced herself by conversation with the sentries outside the guard-room that Tietjens actually still existed, she had told the chauffeur-orderly to drive her back to the Hôtel de la Poste, leaving the wretched Levin to make his way back into the town by tram, or as best he might. They had seen the lights of the car below them, turning, with its gaily lit interior, and disappearing among the trees along the road farther down. . . . The sentry, rather monosyllabically and gruffly — you can tell all right when a Tommie has something at the back of his mind! — informed them that the sergeant had turned out the guard so that all his men together could assure the lady that the captain was alive and well. The obliging sergeant said that he had adopted that manœuvre which generally should attend only the visits of general officers and, once a day, for the C.O., because the lady had seemed so distressed at having received no letters from the captain. The guard-room itself, which was unprovided with cells, was decorated by the presence of two drunks who, having taken it into their heads to destroy their clothing, were in a state of complete nudity. The sergeant hoped, therefore, that he had done no wrong. Rightly the Garrison Military Police ought to take drunks picked up outside camp to the A.P.M.'s guard-room, but seeing the state of undress and the violent behaviour of these two, the sergeant had thought right to oblige the Red Caps. The voices of the drunks, singing the martial anthem of the "Men of Harlech" could be heard corroborating the sergeant's opinion as to their states. He added that he would not have turned out the guard if it had not been for its being the captain's lady.

"A damn smart fellow, that sergeant," Colonel Levin had said. "There couldn't have been any better way of convincing Mrs. Tietjens."

Tietjens had said — and even whilst he was saying it he tremendously wished he hadn't:

"Oh, a *damned* smart fellow," for the bitter irony of his tone had given Levin the chance to remonstrate with him as to his attitude towards Sylvia. Not at all as to his actions — for Levin conscientiously stuck to his thesis that Tietjens was the soul of honour — but just as to his tone of voice in talking of the sergeant who had been kind to Sylvia, and, just precisely, because Tietjens' not writing to his wife had given rise to the incident. Tietjens had thought of saying that, considering the terms on which they had parted, he would have considered himself as molesting the lady if he had addressed to her any letter at all. But he said nothing and, for quarter of an hour, the incident resolved itself into a soliloquy on the slippery hillside, delivered by Levin on the subject of matrimony. It was a matter which, naturally, at that moment very much occupied his thoughts. He considered that a man should so live with his wife that she should be able to open all his letters. That was his idea of the idyllic. And when Tietjens remarked with irony that he had never in his life either written or received a letter that his wife might not have read, Levin exclaimed with such enthusiasm as almost to lose his balance in the mist:

"I was sure of it, old fellow. But it enormously cheers me up to hear you say so." He added that he desired as far as possible to model his ideas of life and his behaviour on those of this his friend. For, naturally, about as he was to unite his fortunes with those of Miss de Bailly, that could be considered a turning point of his career.

IV

THEY had gone back up the hill so that Levin might telephone to headquarters for his own car in case the general's chauffeur should not have the sense to return for him. But that was as far as Tietjens got in uninterrupted reminiscence of that scene. . . . He was sitting in his flea-bag, digging idly with his pencil into the squared page of his notebook which had remained open on his knees, his eyes going over and over again the words with which his report on his own case had concluded — the words: *So the interview ended rather untidily.* Over the words went the image of the dark hillside with the lights of the town, now that the air-raid was finished, spreading high up into the sky below them. . . .

But at that point the doctor's batman had uttered, as if with a jocular, hoarse irony, the name:

"Poor —— O Nine Morgan! . . ." and over the whitish sheet of paper on a level with his nose Tietjens perceived thin films of reddish purple to be wavering, then a glutinous surface of gummy scarlet pigment. Moving! It was once more an effect of fatigue, operating on the retina, that was perfectly familiar to Tietjens. But it filled him with indignation against his own weakness. He said to himself: Wasn't the name of the wretched O Nine Morgan to be mentioned in his hearing without his retina presenting him with the glowing image of the fellow's blood? He watched the phenomenon, growing fainter, moving to the right-hand top corner of the paper and turning a faintly luminous green. He watched it with a grim irony.

Was he, he said to himself, to regard himself as responsible for the fellow's death? Was his inner mentality going to present that claim upon him. That would be absurd. The end of the earth! The absurd end of the earth . . . Yet that insignificant ass Levin had that eve-

ning asserted the claim to go into his, Tietjens of Groby's, relations
with his wife. That was an end of the earth as absurd! It was the unthinkable thing, as unthinkable as the theory that the officer can be
responsible for the death of the man. . . . But the idea had certainly
presented itself to him. How could he be responsible for the death?
In fact — in literalness — he was. It had depended absolutely upon
his discretion whether the man should go home or not. The man's
life or death had been in his hands. He had followed the perfectly
correct course. He had written to the police of the man's home town,
and the police had urged him not to let the man come home. . . .
Extraordinary morality on the part of a police force! The man, they
begged, should not be sent home because a prize-fighter was occupying his bed and laundry. . . . Extraordinary common sense, very
likely. They probably did not want to get drawn into a scrap with
Red Evans of the Red Castle. . . .

For a moment he seemed to see . . . he actually saw . . . O Nine
Morgan's eyes, looking at him with a sort of wonder, as they had
looked when he had refused the fellow his leave. . . . A sort of
wonder! Without resentment, but with incredulity. As you might
look at God, you being very small and ten feet or so below His throne
when He pronounced some inscrutable judgment! The Lord giveth
home-leave, and the Lord refuseth. . . . Probably not blessed, but
queer, be the name of God-Tietjens!

And at the thought of the man as he was alive and of him now,
dead, an immense blackness descended all over Tietjens. He said to
himself: *I am very tired.* Yet he was not ashamed. . . . It was the
blackness that descends on you when you think of your dead. . . .
It comes, at any time, over the brightness of sunlight, in the grey of
evening, in the grey of the dawn, at mess, on parade; it comes at the
thought of one man or at the thought of half a battalion that you
have seen, stretched out, under sheeting, the noses making little
pimples; or not stretched out, lying face downwards, half buried. Or
at the thought of dead that you have never seen dead at all. . . .
Suddenly the light goes out. . . . In this case it was because of one
fellow, a dirty enough man, not even very willing, not in the least
endearing, certainly contemplating desertion. . . . But your dead
. . . *yours* . . . your own. As if joined to your own identity by a
black cord. . . .

In the darkness outside, the brushing, swift, rhythmic pacing of an
immense number of men went past, as if they had been phantoms.

A great number of men in fours, carried forward, irresistibly, by the overwhelming will of mankind in ruled motion. The sides of the hut were so thin that it was peopled by an in innumerable throng. A sodden voice, just at Tietjens' head, chuckled: "For God's sake, sergeant-major, stop these ——. I'm too —— drunk to halt them. . . ."

It made for the moment no impression on Tietjens' conscious mind. Men were going past. Cries went up in the camp. Not orders, the men were still marching. Cries.

Tietjens' lips — his mind was still with the dead — said:

"That obscene Pitkins! . . . I'll have him cashiered for this. . . ." He saw an obscene subaltern, small, with one eyelid that drooped.

He came awake at that. Pitkins was the subaltern he had detailed to march the draft to the station and go on to Bailleul under a boozy field officer of sorts.

McKechnie said from the other bed:

"That's the draft back."

Tietjens said:

"Good God! . . ."

McKechnie said to the batman:

"For God's sake go and see if it is. Come back at once. . . ."

The intolerable vision of the line, starving beneath the moon, of grey crowds murderously elbowing back a thin crowd in brown, zigzagged across the bronze light in the hut. The intolerable depression that, in those days, we felt — that all those millions were the playthings of ants busy in the miles of corridors beneath the domes and spires that rise up over the central heart of our comity, that intolerable weight upon the brain and the limbs, descended once more on those two men lying upon their elbows. As they listened their jaws fell open. The long, polyphonic babble, rushing in from an extended line of men stood easy, alone rewarded their ears.

Tietjens said:

"That fellow won't come back. . . . He can never do an errand and come back. . . ." He thrust one of his legs cumbrously out of the top of his flea-bag. He said:

"By God, the Germans will be all over here in a week's time!"

He said to himself:

"If they so betray us from Whitehall that fellow Levin has no right to pry into my matrimonial affairs. It is proper that one's individual feelings should be sacrificed to the necessities of a collective entity. But not if that entity is to be betrayed from above. Not if it hasn't the ten-millionth of a chance. . . ." He regarded Levin's late incursion on his privacy as enquiries set afoot by the general. . . . Incredibly painful to him, like a medical examination into nudities, but perfectly proper. Old Campion had to assure himself that the other ranks were not demoralized by the spectacle of officers' matrimonial infidelities. . . . But such enquiries were not to be submitted to if the whole show were one gigantic demoralization!

McKechnie said, in reference to Tietjens' protruded foot:

"There's no good your going out. . . . Cowley will get the men into their lines. He was prepared." He added: "If the fellows in Whitehall are determined to do old Puffles in, why don't they recall him?"

The legend was that an eminent personage in the Government had a great personal dislike for the general in command of one army — the general being nicknamed Puffles. The Government, therefore, were said to be starving his command of men so that disaster should fall upon his command.

"They can recall generals easy enough," McKechnie went on, "or anyone else!"

A heavy dislike that this member of the lower middle classes should have opinions on public affairs overcame Tietjens. He exclaimed: "Oh, that's all tripe!"

He was himself outside all contact with affairs by now. But the other rumour in that troubled host had it that, as a political manœuvre, the heads round Whitehall — the civilian heads — were starving the army of troops in order to hold over the allies of Great Britain the threat of abandoning altogether the Western Front. They were credited with threatening a strategic manœuvre on an immense scale in the Near East, perhaps really intending it, or perhaps to force the hands of their allies over some political intrigue. These atrocious rumours reverberated backwards and forwards in the ears of all those millions under the black vault of heaven. All their comrades in the line were to be sacrificed as a rear-guard to their departing host. That whole land was to be annihilated as a sacrifice to one vanity. Now the draft had been called back. That seemed proof that the Government meant to starve the line! McKechnie groaned:

"Poor —— old Bird! . . . He's booked. Eleven months in the front line, he's been. . . . Eleven *months*! . . . I was nine, this stretch. With him."

He added:

"Get back into bed, old bean. . . . I'll go and look after the men if it's necessary. . . ."

Tietjens said:

"You don't so much as know where their lines are. . . ." And sat listening. Nothing but the long roll of tongues came to him. He said:

"Damn it! The men ought not to be kept standing in the cold like that. . . ." Fury filled him beneath despair. His eyes filled with tears. "God," he said to himself, "the fellow Levin presumes to interfere in my private affairs. . . . Damn it," he said again, "it's like doing a little impertinence in a world that's foundering. . . ."

The world was foundering.

"I'd go out," he said, "but I don't want to have to put that filthy little Pitkins under arrest. He only drinks because he's shell-shocked. He's not man enough else, the unclean little Nonconformist. . . ."

McKechnie said:

"Hold on! . . . I'm a Presbyterian myself. . . ."

Tietjens answered:

"You would be! . . ." He said: "I beg your pardon. . . . There will be no more parades. . . . The British Army is dishonoured for ever. . . ."

McKechnie said:

"That's all right, old bean. . . ."

Tietjens exclaimed with sudden violence:

"What the hell are you doing in the officers' lines? . . . Don't you know it's a court-martial offence?"

He was confronted with the broad, mealy face of his regimental quartermaster-sergeant, the sort of fellow who wore an officer's cap against the regulations, with a Tommie's silver-plated badge. A man determined to get Sergeant-Major Cowley's job. The man had come in unheard under the role of voices outside. He said:

"Excuse me, sir, I took the liberty of knocking. . . . The sergeant-major is in an epileptic fit. I wanted your directions before putting the draft into the tents with the other men. . . ." Having said that tentatively he hazarded cautiously: "The sergeant-major throws these fits, sir, if he is suddenly woke up. . . . And Second-Lieutenant Pitkins woke him very suddenly. . . ."

Tietjens said:

"So you took on you the job of a beastly informer against both of them. . . . I shan't forget it." He said to himself:

"I'll get this fellow one day . . ." and he seemed to hear with pleasure the clicking and tearing of the scissors as, inside three parts of a hollow square, they cut off his stripes and badges.

McKechnie exclaimed:

"Good God, man, you aren't going out in nothing but your pyjamas. Put your slacks on under your British warm. . . ."

Tietjens said:

"Send the Canadian sergeant-major to me at the double. . . ." to the quarter. "My slacks are at the tailor's, being pressed." His slacks were being pressed for the ceremony of the signing of the marriage contract of Levin, the fellow who had interfered in his private affairs. He continued into the mealy broad face and vague eyes of the quartermaster: "You know as well as I do that it was the Canadian sergeant-major's job to report to me. . . . I'll let you off this time, but, by God, if I catch you spying round the officers' lines again you are for a D.C.M. . . ."

He wrapped a coarse, Red Cross, grey-wool muffler under the turned-up collar of his British warm.

"That swine," he said to McKechnie, "spies on the officers' lines in the hope of getting a commission by catching out —— little squits like Pitkins, when they're drunk. . . . I'm seven hundred braces down. Morgan does not know that I know that I'm that much down. But you can bet he knows where they have gone. . . ."

McKechnie said:

"I wish you would not go out like that. . . . I'll make you some cocoa. . . ."

Tietjens said:

"I can't keep the men waiting while I dress. . . . I'm as strong as a horse."

He was out amongst the bitterness, the mist, and the moongleams on three thousand rifle barrels, and the voices. . . . He was seeing the Germans pour through a thin line, and his heart was leaden. . . . A tall, graceful man swam up against him and said, through his nose, like any American:

"There has been a railway accident, due to the French strikers. The draft is put back till three pip emma the day after to-morrow, sir."

Tietjens exclaimed:

"It isn't countermanded?" breathlessly.

The Canadian sergeant-major said:

"No, sir. . . . A railway accident . . . Sabotage by the French, they say. . . . Four Glamorganshire sergeants, all nineteen-fourteen men, killed, sir, going home on leave. But the draft is not cancelled. . . ." Tietjens said:

"Thank God!"

The slim Canadian with his educated voice said:

"You're thanking God, sir, for what's very much to our detriment. Our draft was ordered for Salonika till this morning. The sergeant in charge of draft returns showed me the name *Salonika* scored off in his draft roster. Sergeant-Major Cowley had got hold of the wrong story. Now it's going up the line. The other would have been a full two months' more life for us."

The man's rather slow voice seemed to continue for a long time. As it went on Tietjens felt the sunlight dwelling on his nearly coverless limbs, and the tide of youth returning to his veins. It was like champagne. He said:

"You sergeants get a great deal too much information. The sergeant in charge of returns had no business to show you his roster. It's not your fault, of course. But you are an intelligent man. You can see how useful that news might be to certain people, people that it's not to your own interest should know these things. . . ." He said to himself: "A landmark in history . . ." And then: "Where the devil did my mind get hold of that expression at this moment?"

They were walking in mist, down an immense lane, one hedge of which was topped by the serrated heads and irregularly held rifles that showed here and there. He said to the sergeant-major: "Call 'em to attention. Never mind their dressing, we've got to get 'em into bed. Roll-call will be at nine to-morrow."

His mind said:

"If this means the single command. . . . And it's bound to mean the single command, it's the turning point. . . . Why the hell am I so extraordinarily glad? What's it to me?"

He was shouting in a round voice:

"Now then, men, you've got to go six extra in a tent. See if you can fall out six at a time at each tent. It's not in the drill book, but see if you can do it for yourselves. You're smart men: use your intelligences. The sooner you get to bed the sooner you'll be warm. I wish I was. Don't disturb the men who're already in the tents. They've got to be up for fatigues to-morrow at five, poor devils. You can lie soft till three hours after that. . . . The draft will move to the left in

fours. . . . Form fours . . . Left . . ." Whilst the voices of the
sergeants in charge of companies yelped varyingly to a distance in the
quick march order he said to himself:

"Extraordinarily glad . . . A strong passion . . . How damn well
these fellows move! . . . Cannon fodder . . . Cannon fodder . . .
That's what their steps say. . . ." His whole body shook in the grip
of the cold that beneath his loose overcoat gnawed his pyjamaed
limbs. He could not leave the men, but cantered beside them with
the sergeant-major till he came to the head of the column in the open
in time to wheel the first double company into a line of ghosts that
were tents, silent and austere in the moon's very shadowy light. . . .
It appeared to him a magic spectacle. He said to the sergeant-major:
"Move the second company to B line, and so on," and stood at the
side of the men as they wheeled, stamping, like a wall in motion. He
thrust his stick half-way down between the second and third files.
"Now then, a four and half a four to the right; remaining half-four
and next four to the left. Fall out into first tents to right and left.
. . ." He continued saying "First four and half, this four to the
right. . . . Damn you, by the left! How can you tell which beastly
four you belong to if you don't march by the left. . . . Remember
you're soldiers, not new-chum lumbermen. . . ."

It was sheer exhilaration to freeze there on the downside in the
extraordinarily pure air with the extraordinarily fine men. They came
round, marking time with the stamp of guardsmen. He said, with
tears in his voice: .

"Damn it all, I·gave them that extra bit of smartness. . . . Damn
it all, there's something I've done. . . ." Getting cattle into condition
for the slaughterhouse. . . . They were as eager as bullocks running
down by Camden Town to Smithfield Market. . . . Seventy per cent
of them would never come back. . . . But it's better to go to heaven
with your skin shining and master of your limbs than as a hulking
lout. . . . The Almighty's orderly room will welcome you better in
all probability. . . . He continued exclaiming monotonously: "Remaining half-four and next four to the left. . . . Hold your beastly
tongues when you fall out. I can't hear myself give orders. . . ." It
lasted a long time. Then they were all swallowed up.

He staggered, his knees wooden-stiff with the cold, and the cold
more intense now the wall of men no longer sheltered him from the
wind, out along the brink of the plateau to the other lines. It gave
him satisfaction to observe that he had got his men into their lines

seventy-five per cent quicker than the best of the N.C.O.s who had
had charge of the other lines. Nevertheless, he swore bitingly at the
sergeants; their men were in knots round the entrance to the alleys of
ghost-pyramids. . . . Then there were no more, and he drifted with
regret across the plain towards his country street of huts. One of them
had a coarse evergreen rose growing over it. He picked a leaf, pressed
it to his lips and threw it up into the wind. . . . "That's for Valentine," he said meditatively. "Why did I do that? . . . Or perhaps it's
for England. . . ." He said: "Damn it all, this is patriotism! . . .
This is patriotism. . . ." It wasn't what you took patriotism as a rule
to be. There were supposed to be more parades about that job! . . .
But this was just a broke to the wide, wheezy, half-frozen Yorkshireman, who despised everyone in England not a Yorkshireman, or
from more to the North, at two in the morning picking a leaf from
a rose-tree and slobbering over it, without knowing what he was doing. And then discovering that it was half for a pug-nosed girl whom
he presumed, but didn't know, to smell like a primrose; and half for
. . . England! At two in the morning with the thermometer ten
degrees below zero. . . . Damn, it was cold! . . .

And why these emotions? . . . Because England, not before it was
time, had been allowed to decide not to do the dirty on her associates!
. . . He said to himself: "It is probably because a hundred thousand
sentimentalists like myself commit similar excesses of the subcon-
scious that we persevere in this glorious but atrocious undertaking.
All the same, I didn't know I had it in me!" A strong passion! . . .
For his girl and his country! . . . Nevertheless, his girl was a pro-
German. . . . It was a queer mix-up! . . . Not of course a pro-
German, but disapproving of the preparation of men, like bullocks,
with sleek healthy skins for the abattoirs in Smithfield. . . . Agree-
ing presumably with the squits who had been hitherto starving the
B.E.F. of men. . . . A queer mix-up. . . .

At half-past one the next day, in chastened winter sunlight, he
mounted Schomburg, a coffin-headed, bright chestnut, captured from
the Germans on the Marne, by the second battalion of the Glamorganshires. He had not been on the back of the animal two minutes
before he remembered that he had forgotten to look it over. It was
the first time in his life that he had ever forgotten to look at an
animal's hoofs, fetlocks, knees, nostrils, and eyes, and to take a pull
at the girth before climbing into the saddle. But he had ordered the

horse for a quarter to one and, even though he had bolted his cold lunch like a cannibal in haste, there he was three-quarters of an hour late, and with his head still full of teasing problems. He had meant to clear his head by a long canter over the be-hutted downs, dropping down into the city by a bypath.

But the ride did not clear his head — rather, the sleeplessness of the night began for the first time then to tell on him after a morning of fatigues, during which he had managed to keep the thought of Sylvia at arm's length. He had to wait to see Sylvia before he could see what Sylvia wanted. And morning had brought the common-sense idea that probably she wanted to do nothing more than pull the string of the showerbath — which meant committing herself to the first extravagant action that came into her head — and exulting in the consequences.

He had not managed to get to bed at all the night before. Captain McKechnie, who had had some cocoa — a beverage Tietjens had never before tasted — hot and ready for him on his return from the lines, had kept him till past half-past four, relating with a male fury his really very painful story. It appeared that he had obtained leave to go home and divorce his wife, who, during his absence in France, had been living with an Egyptologist in Government service. Then, acting under conscientious scruples of the younger school of the day, he had refrained from divorcing her. Campion had in consequence threatened to deprive him of his commission. . . . The poor devil — who had actually consented to contribute to the costs of the household of his wife and the Egyptologist — had gone raving mad and had showered an extraordinary torrent of abuse at the decent old fellow that Campion was . . . a decent old fellow, really. For the interview, being delicate, had taken place in the general's bedroom and the general had not felt it necessary, there being no orderlies or junior officers present, to take any official notice of McKechnie's outburst. McKechnie was a fellow with an excellent military record; you could in fact hardly have found a regimental officer with a better record. So Campion had decided to deal with the man as suffering from a temporary brain-storm and had sent him to Tietjen's unit for rest and recuperation. It was an irregularity, but the general was of a rank to risk what irregularities he considered to be of use to the service.

It had turned out that McKechnie was actually the nephew of Tietjens' very old intimate, Sir Vincent Macmaster, of the Department of Statistics, being the son of his sister who had married the assistant to the elder Macmaster, a small grocer in the Port of Leith in Scotland. . . . That indeed had been why Campion had been interested in him. Determined as he was to show his godson no unreasonable military favours, the general was perfectly ready to do a kindness that he thought would please Tietjens. All these pieces of information Tietjens had packed away in his mind for future consideration and, it being after four-thirty before McKechnie had calmed himself down, Tietjens had taken the opportunity to inspect the breakfasts of the various fatigues ordered for duty in the town, these being detailed for various hours from a quarter to five to seven. It was a matter of satisfaction to Tietjens to have seen to the breakfasts, and inspected his cook-houses, since he did not often manage to make the opportunity and he could by no means trust his orderly officers.

At breakfast in the depot mess-hut he was detained by the colonel in command of the depot, the Anglican padre, and McKechnie; the colonel, very old, so frail that you would have thought that a shudder or a cough would have shaken his bones one from another, had yet a passionate belief that the Greek Church should exchange communicants with the Anglican; the padre, a stout, militant Churchman, had a gloomy contempt for Orthodox theology. McKechnie from time to time essayed to define the communion according to the Presbyterian rite. They all listened to Tietjens whilst he dilated on the historic aspects of the various schisms of Christianity and accepted his rough definition to the effect that, in transubstantiation, the host actually became the divine presence, whereas in consubstantiation the substance of the host, as if miraculously become porous, was suffused with the presence as a sponge is with water. . . . They all agreed that the breakfast bacon supplied from store was uneatable and agreed to put up half a crown a week a piece to get better for their table.

Tietjens had walked in the sunlight down the lines, past the hut with the evergreen climbing rose, in the sunlight, thinking in an interval, good-humouredly about his official religion: about the Almighty as, on a colossal scale, a great English Landowner, benevolently awful, a colossal duke who never left his study and was thus invisible, but knowing all about the estate down to the last hind at the home farm and the last oak; Christ, an almost too benevolent Land-Steward, son of the Owner, knowing all about the estate down to the last child at the porter's lodge, apt to be got round by the more detrimental tenants; the Third Person of the Trinity, the spirit of the estate, the Game as it were, as distinct from the players of the game; the atmosphere of the estate, that of the interior of Winchester Cathedral just after a Handel anthem has been finished, a perpetual Sunday, with, probably, a little cricket for the young men. Like Yorkshire of a Saturday afternoon; if you looked down on the whole broad county you would not see a single village green without its white flannels. That was why Yorkshire always leads the averages. . . . Probably by the time you got to heaven you would be so worn out by work on this planet that you would accept the English Sunday, for ever, with extreme relief!

With his belief that all that was good in English literature ended with the seventeenth century, his imaginations of heaven must be materialist — like Bunyan's. He laughed good-humouredly at his projection of a hereafter. It was probably done with. Along with cricket. There would be no more parades of that sort. Probably they would play some beastly yelping game. . . . Like baseball or Association football. . . . And heaven? . . . Oh, it would be a revival meeting on a Welsh hillside. Or Chatauqua, wherever that was. . . . And God? A Real Estate Agent, with Marxist views. . . . He hoped to be out of it before the cessation of hostilities, in which case he might be just in time for the last train to the old heaven. . . .

In his orderly hut he found an immense number of papers. On the top an envelope marked *Urgent, Private* with a huge rubber stamp, from Levin. Levin, too, must have been up pretty late. It was not about Mrs. Tietjens, or even Miss de Bailly. It was a private warning that Tietjens would probably have his draft on his hands another week or ten days, and very likely another couple of thousand men extra as well. He warned Tietjens to draw all the tents he could get hold of as soon as possible. . . . Tietjens called to a subaltern with pimples who was picking his teeth with a pen-nib at the other end of the hut: "Here, you! . . . Take two companies of the Canadians to the depot store and draw all the tents you can get up to two hundred and fifty. . . . Have 'em put alongside my D lines. . . . Do you know how to look after putting up tents? . . . Well then, get Thompson . . . no, Pitkins, to help you. . . ." The subaltern drifted out sulkily. Levin said that the French railway strikers, for some political reason, had sabotaged a mile of railway, the accident of the night before had completely blocked up all the lines, and the French civilians would not let their own breakdown gangs make any repairs. German prisoners had been detailed for that fatigue, but probably Tietjens' Canadian railway corps would be wanted. He had better hold them in readiness. The strike was said to be a manœuvre for forcing our hands — to get us to take over more of the line. In that case they had jolly well dished themselves, for how could we take over more of the line without more men, and how could we send up more men without the railway to send them by? We had half-a-dozen army corps all ready to go. Now they were all jammed. Fortunately the weather at the front was so beastly that the Germans could not move. He finished up, "Four in the morning, old bean, *à tantôt!*" the last phrase having been learned from Mlle de Bailly. Tietjens grumbled that if they went on piling up the work on him like this he could never get down to the signing of that marriage contract.

He called the Canadian sergeant-major to him.

"See," he said, "that you keep the Railway Service Corps in camp with their arms ready, whatever their arms are. Tools, I suppose. Are their tools all complete? And their muster roll?"

"Girtin has gone absent, sir," the slim dark fellow said, with an air of destiny. Girtin was the respectable man with the mother to whom Tietjens had given the two hours' leave the night before.

Tietjens answered:

"He would have!" with a sour grin. It enhanced his views of strictly respectable humanity. They blackmailed you with lamentable and pathetic tales and then did the dirty on you. He said to the sergeant-major:

"You will be here for another week or ten days. See that you get your tents up all right and the men comfortable. I will inspect them as soon as I have taken my orderly room. Full marching order. Captain McKechnie will inspect their kits at two."

The sergeant-major, stiff but graceful, had something at the back of his mind. It came out:

"I have my marching orders for two-thirty this afternoon. The notice for inserting my commission in depot orders is on your table. I leave for the O.T.C. by the three train. . . ."

Tietjens said:

"Your commission! . . ." It was a confounded nuisance.

The sergeant-major said:

"Sergeant-Major Cowley and I applied for our commissions three months ago. The communications granting them are both on your table together. . . ."

Tietjens said:

"Sergeant-Major Cowley. . . . Good God! Who recommended you?"

The whole organization of his confounded battalion fell to pieces. It appeared that a circular had come round three months before — before Tietjens had been given command of that unit — asking for experienced first-class warrant officers capable of serving as instructors in Officers' Training Corps, with commissions. Sergeant-Major Cowley had been recommended by the colonel of the depot, Sergeant-Major Ledoux by his own colonel. Tietjens felt as if he had been let down — but of course he had not been. It was just the way of the army, all the time. You got a platoon, or a battalion, or, for the matter of that, a dug-out or a tent, by herculean labours into good fettle. It ran all right for a day or two, then it all fell to pieces, the personnel scattered to the four winds by what appeared merely wanton orders, coming from the most unexpected headquarters, or the premises were smashed up by a chance shell that might just as well have fallen somewhere else. . . . The finger of Fate!

But it put a confounded lot more work on him. . . . He said to Sergeant-Major Cowley, whom he found in the next hut where all the paper work of the unit was done:

"I should have thought you would have been enormously better off as regimental sergeant-major than with a commission. I know I would rather have the job." Cowley answered — he was very pallid and shaken — that with his unfortunate infirmity, coming on at any moment of shock, he would be better in a job where he could slack off, like an O.T.C. He had always been subject to small fits, over in a minute, or couple of seconds even. . . . But getting too near a H.E. shell — after Noircourt which had knocked out Tietjens himself — had brought them on, violent. There was also, he finished, the gentility to be considered. Tietjens said:

"Oh, the gentility! That's not worth a flea's jump. . . . There won't be any more parades after this war. There aren't any now. Look at who your companions will be in an officer's quarters; you'd be in a great deal better society in any self-respecting sergeants' mess." Cowley answered that he knew the service had gone to the dogs. All the same his missis liked it. And there was his daughter Winnie to be considered. She had always been a bit wild, and his missis wrote that she had gone wilder than ever, all due to the war. Cowley thought that the bad boys would be a little more careful how they monkeyed with her if she was an officer's daughter. . . . There was probably something in that!

Coming out into the open, confidentially with Tietjens, Cowley dropped his voice huskily to say:

"Take Quartermaster-Sergeant Morgan for R.S.M., sir."

Tietjens said explosively:

"I'm damned if I will." Then he asked: "Why?" The wisdom of old N.C.O.s is a thing no prudent officer neglects.

"He can do the work, sir," Cowley said. "He's out for a commission, and he'll do his best. . . ." He dropped his husky voice to a still greater depth of mystery:

"You're over two hundred — I should say nearer three hundred — pounds down in your battalion stores. I don't suppose you want to lose a sum of money like that?"

Tietjens said:

"I'm damned if I do. . . . But I don't see. . . . Oh, yes, I do. . . . If I make him sergeant-major he has to hand over the stores all complete. . . . To-day . . . Can he do it?"

Cowley said that Morgan could have till the day after to-morrow. He would look after things till then.

"But you'll want to have a flutter before you go," Tietjens said. "Don't stop for me."

Cowley said that he would stop and see the job through. He had thought of going down into the town and having a flutter. But the girls down there were a common sort, and it was bad for his complaint. . . . He would stop and see what could be done with Morgan. Of course it was possible that Morgan might decide to face things out. He might prefer to stick to the money he'd got by disposing of Tietjens' stores to other battalions that were down, or to civilian contractors. And stand a court martial! But it wasn't likely. He was a Nonconformist deacon, a pew-opener, or even a minister possibly, at home in Wales. . . . From near Denbigh! And Cowley had got a very good man, a first-class man, an Oxford professor, now a lance-corporal at the depot, for Morgan's place. The colonel would lend him to Tietjens and would get him rated acting quartermaster-sergeant unpaid. . . . Cowley had it all arranged. . . . Lance-Corporal Caldicott was a first-class man, only he could not tell his right hand from his left on parade. Literally could not tell them. . . .

So the battalion settled itself down. . . . Whilst Cowley and he were at the colonel's orderly room arranging for the transfer of the professor — he was really only a fellow of his college — who did not know his right hand from his left, Tietjens was engaged in the remains of the colonel's furious argument as to the union of the Anglican and Eastern rites. The colonel — he was a full colonel — sat in his lovely private office, a light, gay compartment of a tin-hutment, the walls being papered in scarlet, with, on the purplish, thick, soft baize of his table-cover, a tall glass vase from which sprayed out pale Riviera roses, the gift of young lady admirers amongst the V.A.D.s in the town because he was a darling, and an open, very gilt and leather-bound volume of a biblical encyclopædia beneath his delicate septuagenarian features. He was confirming his opinion that a union between the Church of England and the Greek Orthodox Church was the only thing that could save civilization. The whole war turned on that. The Central Empires represented Roman Catholicism, the Allies Protestantism and Orthodoxy. Let them unite. The papacy was a traitor to the cause of civilization. Why had the Vatican not protested with no uncertain voice about the abominations practiced on the Belgian Catholics? . . .

Tietjens pointed out languidly objections to this theory. The first thing our ambassador to the Vatican had found out on arriving in Rome and protesting about massacres of Catholic laymen in Belgium was that the Russians before they had been a day in Austrian Poland had hanged twelve Roman Catholic bishops in front of their palaces.

Cowley was engaged with the adjutant at another table. The colonel ended his theologico-political tirade by saying:

"I shall be very sorry to lose you, Tietjens. I don't know what we shall do without you. I never had a moment's peace with your unit until you came."

Tietjens said:

"Well, you aren't losing me, sir, as far as I know."

The colonel said:

"Oh, yes, we are. You are going up the line next week. . . ." He added: "Now, don't get angry with me. . . . I've protested very strongly to old Campion — General Campion — that I cannot do without you." And he made, with his delicate, thin, hairy-backed, white hands a motion as of washing.

The ground moved under Tietjens' feet. He felt himself clambering over slopes of mud with his heavy legs and labouring chest. He said:

"Damn it all! . . . I'm not fit. . . . I'm C3. . . . I was ordered to live in an hotel in the town. . . . I only mess here to be near the battalion."

The colonel said with some eagerness:

"Then you can protest to Garrison. . . . I hope you will. . . . But I suppose you are the sort of fellow that won't."

Tietjens said:

"No, sir. . . . Of course I cannot protest. . . . Though it's probably a mistake of some clerk. . . . I could not stand a week in the line. . . ." The profound misery of brooding apprehension in the line was less on his mind than, precisely, the appalling labour of the lower limbs when you live in mud to the neck. Besides, whilst he had been in hospital, practically the whole of his equipment had disappeared from his kitbag — including Sylvia's two pair of sheets! — and he had no money with which to get more. He had not even any trench-boots. Fantastic financial troubles settled on his mind.

The colonel said to the adjutant at the other purple baize-covered table:

"Show Captain Tietjens those marching orders of his. . . . They're from Whitehall, aren't they? . . . You never know where these things come from nowadays. I call them the arrow that flieth by night!"

The adjutant, a diminutive, a positively miniature gentleman with Coldstream badges up and a dreadfully worried brow, drifted a quarto sheet of paper out of a pile, across his table-cloth towards Tietjens. His tiny hands seemed about to fall off at the wrists; his temples shuddered with neuralgia. He said:

"For God's sake do protest to Garrison if you feel you can. . . . We *can't* have more work shoved on us. . . . Major Lawrence and Major Halkett left the whole of the work of your unit to us. . . ."

The sumptuous paper, with the royal arms embossed at the top, informed Tietjens that he would report to his VIth battalion on the Wednesday of next week in preparation for taking up the duties of divisional transport officer to the XIXth division. The order came from room G 14 R, at the War Office. He asked what the deuce G 14 R was, of the adjutant, who in an access of neuralgic agony, shook his head miserably, between his two hands, his elbows on the table-cloth.

Sergeant-Major Cowley, with his air of a solicitor's clerk, said the room G 14 R was the department that dealt with civilian requests for the services of officers. To the adjutant who asked what the devil a civilian request for the employment of officers could have to do with sending Captain Tietjens to the XIXth division, Sergeant-Major Cowley presumed that it was because of the activities of the Earl of Beichan. The Earl of Beichan, a Levantine financier and race-horse owner, was interesting himself in army horses, after, a short visit to the lines of communication. He also owned several newspapers. So they had been waking up the army transport-animals' department to please him. The adjutant would no doubt have observed a Veterinary-Lieutenant Hotchkiss or Hitchcock. He had come to them through G 14 R at the request of Lord Beichan, who was personally interested in Lieutenant Hotchkiss's theories. He was to make experiments on the horses of the Fourth Army — in which the XIXth division was then to be found. . . . "So," Cowley said, "you'll be under him as far as your horse lines go. If you go up." Perhaps Lord Beichan was a friend of Captain Tietjens and had asked for him, too: Captain Tietjens was known to be wonderful with horses.

Tietjens, his breath rushing through his nostrils, swore he would not go up the line at the bidding of a hog like Beichan, whose real name was Stavropolides, formerly Nathan.

He said the army was reeling to its base because of the continual interference of civilians. He said it was absolutely impossible to get through his programmes of parades because of the perpetual extra drills that were forced on them at the biddings of civilians. Any fool who owned a newspaper, nay, any fool who could write to a newspaper, or any beastly little squit of a novelist could frighten the Government and the War Office into taking up one more hour of the men's parade time for patent manœuvres with jampots or fancy underclothing. Now he was asked if his men wanted lecturing on the causes of the war and whether he — he, good God! — would not like to give the men cosy chats on the nature of the Enemy nations.

The colonel said:

"There, there, Tietjens! . . . There, there! . . . We all suffer alike. *We've* got to lecture our men on the uses of a new patent saw-dust stove. If you don't want that job, you can easily get the general to take you off it. They say you can turn him round your little finger. . . ."

"He's my godfather," Tietjens thought it wise to say. "I never asked him for a job, but I'm damned if it isn't his duty as a Chris-

tian to keep me out of the clutches of this Greek-'Ebrew pagan peer.
. . . He's not even Orthodox, colonel. . . ."

The adjutant here said that Colour-Sergeant Morgan of their orderly room wanted a word with Tietjens. Tietjens said he hoped to
goodness that Morgan had some money for him! The adjutant said
he understood that Morgan had unearthed quite a little money that
ought to have been paid to Tietjens by his agents and hadn't.

Colour-Sergeant Morgan was the regimental magician with figures.
Inordinately tall and thin, his body whilst his eyes peered into distant columns of cyphers, appeared to be always parallel with the surface of his table and, as he always answered the several officers whom
he benefited without raising his head, his face was very little known
to his superiors. He was, however, in appearance a very ordinary,
thin, N.C.O. whose spidery legs, when very rarely he appeared on
a parade, had the air of running away with him as a race-horse might
do. He told Tietjens that, pursuant to his instructions and the A.C.P.
i 96 b that Tietjens had signed, he had ascertained that command
pay at the rate of two guineas a day and supplementary fuel and
light allowance at the rate of 6s. 8d. was being paid weekly by the
Paymaster-General's Department to his, Tietjens', account at his
agents'. He suggested that Tietjens should write to his agents that if
they did not immediately pay to his account the sum of £194 13s. 4d.,
by them received from the Paymaster's Department, he would proceed against the Crown by Petition of Right. And he strongly recommended Tietjens to draw a cheque on his own bank for the whole of
the money because, if by any chance the agents had not paid the
money in, he could sue them for damages and get them cast in
several thousand pounds. And serve the devils right. They must have
a million or so in hand in unpaid command and detention allow-
ances due to officers. He only wished he could advertise in the papers
offering to recover unpaid sums due by agents. He added that he had
a nice little computation as to variations in the course of Gunter's
Second Comet that he would like to ask Tietjens' advice about one
of these days. The colour-sergeant was an impassioned amateur as-
tronomer.

So Tietjens' morning went up and down. . . . The money at the
moment, Sylvia being in that town, was of tremendous importance to
him and came like an answer to prayer. It was not so agreeable, however, even in a world in which, never, never, never for ten minutes did
you know whether you stood on your head or your heels, for Tietjens,

on going back to the colonel's private office, to find Sergeant-Major Cowley coming out of the next room in which, on account of the adjutant's neuralgia, the telephone was kept. Cowley announced to the three of them that the general had the day before ordered his correspondence-corporal to send a very emphatic note to Colonel Gillum to the effect that he was informing the competent authority that he had no intention whatever of parting with Captain Tietjens, who was invaluable in his command. The correspondence-corporal had informed Cowley that neither he nor the general knew who was the competent authority for telling Room G 14 R at the War Office to go to hell, but the matter would be looked up and put all right before the chit was sent off. . . .

That was good as far as it went. Tietjens was really interested in his present job, and although he would have liked well enough to have the job of looking after the horses of a division, or even an army, he felt that he would rather it was put off till the spring, given the weather they were having and the state of his chest. And the complication of possible troubles with Lieutenant Hotchkiss who, being a professor, had never really seen a horse — or not for ten years! — was something to be thought about very seriously. But all this appeared quite another matter when Cowley announced that the civilian authority who had asked for Tietjens' transfer was the permanent secretary to the Ministry of Transport. . . .

Colonel Gillum said:

"That's your brother, Mark. . . ." And indeed the permanent secretary to the Ministry of Transport was Tietjens' brother Mark, known as the Indispensable Official. Tietjens felt a real instant of dismay. He considered that his violent protest against the job would appear rather a smack in the face for poor old wooden-featured Mark who had probably taken a good deal of trouble to get him the job. Even if Mark should never hear of it, a man should not slap his brother in the face! Moreover, when he came to think of his last day in London, he remembered that Valentine Wannop, who had exaggerated ideas as to the safety of First Line Transport, had begged Mark to get him a job as divisional officer. . . . And he imagined Valentine's despair if she heard that he — Tietjens — had moved heaven and earth to get out of it. He saw her lower lip quivering and the tears in her eyes. But he probably had got that from some novel, because he had never seen her lower lip quiver. He had seen tears in her eyes!

He hurried back to his lines to take his orderly room. In the long hut McKechnie was taking that miniature court of drunks and defaulters for him and, just as Tietjens reached it, he was taking the case of Girtin and two other Canadian privates. . . . The case of Girtin interested him, and when McKechnie slid out of his seat Tietjens occupied it. The prisoners were only just being marched in by a Sergeant Davis, an admirable N.C.O. whose rifle appeared to be part of his rigid body and who executed an amazing number of stamps in seriously turning in front of the C.O.'s table. It gave the impression of an Indian war dance. . . .

Tietjens glanced at the charge sheet, which was marked as coming from the Provost-Marshal's Office. Instead of the charge of absence from draft he read that of conduct prejudicial to good order and military discipline in that. . . . The charge was written in a very illiterate hand; an immense beery lance-corporal of Garrison Military Police, with a red hat-band, attended to give evidence. . . . It was a tenuous and disagreeable affair. Girtin had not gone absent, so Tietjens had to revise his views of the respectable, at any rate of the respectable Colonial private soldier with mother complete. For there really had been a mother, and Girtin had been seeing her into the last tram down into the town. A frail old lady. Apparently, trying to annoy the Canadian, the beery lance-corporal of the Garrison Military Police had hustled the mother. Girtin had remonstrated; very moderately, he said. The lance-corporal had shouted at him. Two other Canadians returning to camp had intervened and two more police. The police had called the Canadians —— conscripts, which was almost more than the Canadians could stand, they being voluntarily enlisted 1914 or 1915 men. The police — it was an old trick — had kept the men talking until two minutes after the last post had sounded and then had run them in for being absent off pass — and for disrespect to their red hat-bands.

Tietjens, with a carefully measured fury, first cross-examined and then damned the police witness to hell. Then he marked the charge sheets with the words "Case explained," and told the Canadians to go and get ready for his parade. It meant he was aware of a frightful row with the provost-marshal, who was a port-winey old general called O'Hara and loved his police as if they had been ewe-lambs.

He took his parade, the Canadian troops looking like real soldiers in the sunlight, went round his lines with the new Canadian sergeant-major, who had his appointment, thank goodness, from his own authorities; wrote a report on the extreme undesirability of lecturing his men on the causes of the war, since his men were either graduates of one or other Canadian university and thus knew twice as much about the causes of the war as any lecturer the civilian authorities could provide, or else they were half-breed Micamuc Indians, Esquimaux, Japanese, or Alaskan Russians, none of whom could understand any English lecturer. . . . He was aware that he would have to re-write his report so as to make it more respectful to the newspaper-proprietor peer who, at that time, was urging on the home Government the necessity of lecturing all the subjects of His Majesty on the causes of the war. But he wanted to get that grouse off his chest and its disrespect would pain Levin, who would have to deal with these reports if he did not get married first. Then he lunched off army sausage-meat and potatoes, mashed with their skins complete, watered with an admirable 1906 brut champagne which they bought themselves, and an appalling Canadian cheese — at the headquarters table to which the colonel had invited all the subalterns who that day were going up the line for the first time. They had some h's in their compositions, but in revenge they must have boasted of a pint of adenoid growths between them. There was, however, a charming young half-cast Goa second-lieutenant, who afterwards proved of an heroic bravery. He gave Tietjens a lot of amusing information as to the working of the purdah in Portuguese India.

So, at half-past one Tietjens sat on Schomburg, the coffin-headed, bright chestnut from the Prussian horse-raising establishment near Celle. Almost a pure thoroughbred, this animal had usually the paces of a dining-room table, its legs being fully as stiff. But to-day its legs might have been made of cotton-wool, it lumbered over frosty ground breathing stertorously and, at the jumping-ground of the Deccan Horse, a mile above and behind Rouen, it did not so much refuse a very moderate jump as come together in a lugubrious crumple. It was, in the light of a red, jocular sun, like being mounted on a broken-hearted camel. In addition, the fatigues of the morning beginning to tell, Tietjens was troubled by an obsession of O Nine Morgan which he found tiresome to have to stall off.

"What the hell," he asked of the orderly, a very silent private on a roan beside him, "what the hell is the matter with his horse? . . . Have you been keeping him warm?" He imagined that the clumsy paces of the animal beneath him added to his gloomy obsessions.

The orderly looked straight in front of him over a valley full of hutments. He said:

"No, sir." The 'oss 'ad been put in the 'oss-standings of G depot. By the orders of Lieutenant 'Itchcock. 'Osses, Lieutenant 'Itchcock said, 'ad to be 'ardened.

Tietjens said:

"Did you tell him that it was my orders that Schomburg was to be kept warm? In the stables of the farm behind No. XVI I.B.D."

"The lieutenant," the orderly explained woodenly, "said as 'ow henny departure f'm 'is orders would be visited by the extreme displeasure of Lord Breech'em, K.C.V.O., K.C.B., etcetera." The orderly was quivering with rage.

"You will," Tietjens said very carefully, "when you fall out with the horses at the Hôtel de la Poste, take Schomburg and the roan to the stables of La Volonté Farm, behind No. XVI I.B.D." The orderly was to close all the windows of the stable, stopping up any chinks with wadding. He would procure, if possible, a sawdust stove, new pattern, from Colonel Gillum's store and light it in the stables. He was also to give Schomburg and the roan oatmeal and water warmed as hot as the horses would take it. . . . And Tietjens finished sharply, "If Lieutenant Hotchkiss makes any comments, you will refer him to me. As his C.O."

The orderly seeking information as to horse-ailments, Tietjens said:

"The school of horse-copers, to which Lord Beichan belongs, believes in the hardening of all horse-flesh other than racing cattle." They bred racing-cattle. Under six blankets apiece! Personally Tietjens did not believe in the hardening process and would not permit any animal over which he had control to be submitted to it. . . . It had been observed that if any animal was kept at a lower temperature than of its normal climatic condition it would contract diseases to which ordinarily it was not susceptible. . . . If you keep a chicken for two days in a pail of water it will contract human scarlet-fever or mumps if injected with either bacillus. If you remove the chicken from the water, dry it, and restore it to its normal conditions, the scarlet-fever or the mumps will die out of the animal. . . . He said to the orderly: "You are an intelligent man. What deduction do you draw?"

The orderly looked away over the valley of the Seine.

"I suppose, sir," he said, "that our 'osses, being kept alwise cold in their standings, 'as hillnesses they wouldn't otherwise 'ave."

"Well then," Tietjens said, "keep the poor animals warm."

He considered that here was the makings of a very nasty row for himself if, by any means, his sayings came round to the ears of Lord Beichan; but that he had to chance. He could not let a horse for which he was responsible be martyred. . . . There was too much to think about . . . so that nothing at all stood out to be thought of. The sun was glowing. The valley of the Seine was blue-grey, like a Gobelin tapestry. Over it all hung the shadow of a deceased Welsh soldier. An odd skylark was declaiming over an empty field behind the incinerators' headquarters. . . . An odd lark. For as a rule larks do not sing in December. Larks sing only when courting, or over the nest. . . . The bird must be oversexed. O Nine Morgan was the other thing, that accounting for the prize-fighter!

They dropped down a mud lane between brick walls into the town. . . .

Part Two

I<small>N THE ADMIRABLY APPOINTED</small>, white-enamelled, wickerworked, be-mirrored lounge of the best hotel of that town Sylvia Tietjens sat in a wickerwork chair, not listening rather abstractedly to a staff-major who was lachrymosely and continuously begging her to leave her bedroom door unlocked that night. She said:

"I don't know. . . . Yes, perhaps. . . . I don't know. . . ." And looked distantly into a bluish wall-mirror that, like all the rest, was framed with white-painted cork bark. She stiffened a little and said:

"There's Christopher!"

The staff-major dropped his hat, his stick, and his gloves. His black hair, which was without parting and heavy with some preparation of a glutinous kind, moved agitatedly on his scalp. He had been saying that Sylvia had ruined his life. Didn't Sylvia know that she had ruined his life? But for her he might have married some pure young thing. Now he exclaimed:

"But what does he want? . . . Good God! . . . what does he want?"

"He wants," Sylvia said, "to play the part of Jesus Christ."

Major Perowne exclaimed:

"Jesus Christ! But he's the most foul-mouthed officer in the general's command. . . ."

"Well," Sylvia said, "if you had married your pure young thing she'd have . . . what is it? . . . cuckolded you within nine months. . . ."

Perowne shuddered a little at the word. He mumbled:

"I don't see. . . . It seems to be the other way . . ."

"Oh, no, it isn't," Sylvia said. "Think it over. . . . Morally, *you're* the husband. . . . *Im*morally, I should say. . . . Because he's the man I want. . . . He looks ill. . . . Do hospital authorities always tell wives what is the matter with their husbands?"

From his angle in the chair from which he had half-emerged Sylvia seemed to him to be looking at a blank wall.

"I don't see him," Perowne said.

"I can see him in the glass," Sylvia said. "Look! From here you can see him."

Perowne shuddered a little more.

"I don't want to see him. . . . I have to see him sometimes in the course of duty. . . . I don't like to. . . ."

Sylvia said:

"*You*," in a tone of very deep contempt. "You only carry chocolate boxes to flappers. . . . How can he come across you in the course of duty? . . . You're not a *soldier!*"

Perowne said:

"But what are we going to do? What will *he* do?"

"I," Sylvia answered, "shall tell the page-boy when he comes with his card to say that I'm engaged. . . . I don't know what *he'll* do. Hit you, very likely. He's looking at your back now. . . ."

Perowne became rigid, sunk into his deep chair.

"But he *couldn't!*" he exclaimed agitatedly. "You said that he was playing the part of Jesus Christ. Our Lord wouldn't hit people in an hotel lounge. . . ."

"Our Lord!" Sylvia said contemptuously. "What do you know about our Lord? Our Lord was a gentleman. . . . Christopher is playing at being our Lord calling on the woman taken in adultery. . . . He's giving me the social backing that his being my husband seems to him to call for."

A one-armed, bearded *maître d'hôtel* approached them through groups of arm-chairs arranged for *tête-à-tête*. He said:

"Pardon . . . I did not see madame at first. . . ." And displayed a card on a salver. Without looking at it, Sylvia said:

"*Dîtes à ce monsieur* . . . that I am occupied." The *maître d'hôtel* moved austerely away.

"But he'll smash me to pieces . . ." Perowne exclaimed. "What am I to do? . . . What the deuce am I to do?" There would have been no way of exit for him except across Tietjens' face.

With her spine very rigid and the expression of a snake that fixes a bird, Sylvia gazed straight in front of her and said nothing until she exclaimed:

"For God's sake leave off trembling. . . . He would not do anything to a girl like you. He's a man. . . ." The wickerwork of Pcrowne's chair had been crepitating as if it had been in a railway car. The sound ceased with a jerk. . . . Suddenly she clenched both her hands and let out a hateful little breath of air between her teeth.

"By the immortal saints," she exclaimed, "I swear I'll make his wooden face wince yet."

In the bluish looking-glass, a few minutes before, she had seen the agate-blue eyes of her husband, thirty feet away, over arm-chairs and between the fans of palms. He was standing, holding a riding-whip, looking rather clumsy in the uniform that did not suit him. Rather clumsy and worn out, but completely expressionless! He had looked straight into the reflection of her eyes and then looked away. He moved so that his profile was towards her, and continued gazing motionless at an elk's head that decorated the space of wall above glazed doors giving into the interior of the hotel. The hotel servant approaching him, he had produced a card and had given it to the servant, uttering three words. She saw his lips move in the three words: Mrs. Christopher Tietjens. She said, beneath her breath:

"Damn his chivalry! . . . Oh, God damn his chivalry!" She knew what was going on in his mind. He had seen her, with Perowne, so he had neither come towards her nor directed the servant to where she sat. For fear of embarrassing her! He would leave it to her to come to him if she wished.

The servant, visible in the mirror, had come and gone deviously back, Tietjens still gazing at the elk's head. He had taken the card and restored it to his pocket-book and then had spoken to the servant. The servant had shrugged his shoulders with the formal hospitality of his class and, with his shoulders still shrugged and his one hand pointing towards the inner door, had preceded Tietjens into the hotel. Not one line of Tietjens' face had moved when he had received back his card. It had been then that Sylvia had sworn that she would yet make his wooden face wince. . . .

His face was intolerable. Heavy; fixed. Not insolent, but simply gazing over the heads of all things and created beings, into a world too distant for them to enter. And yet it seemed to her, since he was so clumsy and worn out, almost not sporting to persecute him. It was like whipping a dying bulldog. . . .

She sank back into her chair with a movement almost of discouragement. She said:

"He's gone into the hotel. . . ."

Perowne lurched agitatedly forward in his chair. He exclaimed
that he was going. Then he sank discouragedly back again:

"No, I'm not," he said, "I'm probably much safer here. I might
run against him going out."

"You've realised that my petticoats protect you," Sylvia said contemptuously. "Of course, Christopher would never hit anyone in my
presence."

Major Perowne was interrupting her by asking:

"What's he going to do? What's he doing in the hotel?"

Mrs. Tietjens said:

"Guess!" She added: "What would you do in similar circumstances?"

"Go and wreck your bedroom," Perowne answered with prompti-
tude. "It's what I did when I found you had left Yssingueux."

Sylvia said:

"Ah, that was what the place was called."

Perowne groaned:

"You're callous," he said. "There's no other word for it. Callous.
That's what you are."

Sylvia asked absently why he called her callous at just that juncture. She was imagining Christopher stumping clumsily along the
hotel corridor looking at bedrooms, and then giving the hotel servant
a handsome tip to ensure that he should be put on the same floor as
herself. She could almost hear his not disagreeable male voice that
vibrated a little from the chest and made her vibrate.

Perowne was grumbling on. Sylvia was callous because she had forgotten the name of the Brittany hamlet in which they had spent
three blissful weeks together, though she had left it so suddenly that
all her outfit remained in the hotel.

"Well, it wasn't any kind of a beanfeast for me," Sylvia went on,
when she again gave him her attention. "Good heavens! . . .
Do you think it *would* be any kind of a beanfeast with you, *pour
tout potage*? Why should I remember the name of the hateful
place?"

Perowne said:

"Yssingueux-les-Pervenches, such a pretty name," reproachfully.

"It's no good," Sylvia answered, "your trying to awaken sentimental memories in me. You will have to make me forget what you were like if you want to carry on with me. . . . I'm stopping here and listening to your corncrake of a voice because I want to wait until Christopher goes out of the hotel . . . Then I am going to my room to tidy up for Lady Sachse's party and you will sit here and wait for me."

"I'm *not*," Perowne said, "going to Lady Sachse's. Why, *he* is going to be one of the principal witnesses to sign the marriage contract. And Old Campion and all the rest of the staff are going to be there. . . . You don't catch *me*. . . . An unexpected prior engagement is my line. No fear."

"You'll come with me, my little man," Sylvia said, "if you ever want to bask in my smile again. . . . I'm not going to Lady Sachse's alone, looking as if I couldn't catch a man to escort me, under the eyes of half the French house of peers. . . . If they've got a house of peers! . . . You don't catch *me*. . . . No fear!" she mimicked his creaky voice. "You can go away as soon as you've shown yourself as my escort. . . ."

"But, good God!" Perowne cried out, "that's just what I mustn't do. Campion said that if he heard any more of my being seen about with you he would have me sent back to my beastly regiment. And my beastly regiment is in the trenches. . . . You don't see *me* in the trenches, do you?"

"I'd rather see you there than in my own room," Sylvia said. "Any day!"

"Ah, there you are!" Perowne exclaimed with animation. "What guarantee have I that if I do what you want I shall bask in your smile as you call it? I've got myself into a most awful hole, bringing you here without any papers. You never told me you hadn't any papers. General O'Hara, the P.M., has raised a most awful strafe about it. And what have I got for it? . . . Not the ghost of a smile. . . . And you should see old O'Hara's purple face! . . . Someone woke him from his afternoon nap to report to him about your heinous case and he hasn't recovered from the indigestion yet. . . . Besides, he hates Tietjens . . . Tietjens is always chipping away at his military police . . . O'Hara's lambs. . . ."

Sylvia was not listening, but she was smiling a slow smile at an inward thought. It maddened him.

"What's your game?" he exclaimed. "Hell and hounds, what's your game? . . . You can't have come here to see . . . *him*. You don't come here to see me, as far as I can see. Well then . . ."

Sylvia looked round at him with all her eyes, wide open as if she had just awakened from a deep sleep.

"I didn't know I was coming," she said. "It came into my head to come suddenly. Ten minutes before I started. And I came. I didn't know papers were wanted. I suppose I could have got them if I had wanted them. . . . You never asked me if I had any papers. You just froze on to me and had me into your special carriage. . . . I didn't know you were coming."

That seemed to Perowne the last insult. He exclaimed:

"Oh, damn it, Sylvia! you *must* have known. . . . You were at the Quirks' squash on Wednesday evening. And *they* knew. My best friends."

"Since you ask for it," she said, "I didn't know. . . . And I would not have come by that train if I had known you would be going by it. You force me to say rude things to you." She added: "Why can't you be more conciliatory?" to keep him quiet for a little. His jaw dropped down.

She was wondering where Christopher had got the money to pay for a bed at the hotel. Only a very short time before she had drawn all the balance of his banking account, except for a shilling. It was the middle of the month and he could not have drawn any more pay. . . . That, of course, was a try on her part. He might be forced into remonstrating. In the same way she had tried on the accusation that he had carried off her sheets. It was sheer wilfulness, and when she looked again at his motionless features she knew that she had been rather stupid. . . . But she was at the end of her tether: she had before now tried making accusations against her husband, but she had never tried inconveniencing him. . . . Now she suddenly realised the full stupidity of which she had been guilty. He would know perfectly well that those petty frightfulnesses of hers were not in the least in her note; so he would know, too, that each of them was just a try-on. He would say: "She is trying to make me squeal. I'm damned if I will!"

She would have to adopt much more formidable methods. She said: "He shall . . . he shall . . . he *shall* come to heel."

Major Perowne had now closed his jaw. He was reflecting. Once he mumbled: "More *conciliatory*! Holy smoke!"

She was feeling suddenly in spirits; it was the sight of Christopher had done it, the perfect assurance that they were going to live under the same roof again. She would have betted all she possessed and her immortal soul on the chance that he would not take up with the Wannop girl. And it would have been betting on a certainty! . . . But she had had no idea what their relations were to be, after the war. At first she had thought that they had parted for good when she had gone off from their flat at four o'clock in the morning. It had seemed logical. But, gradually, in retreat at Birkenhead, in the still, white, nun's room, doubt had come upon her. It was one of the disadvantages of living as they did that they seldom spoke their thoughts. But that was also at times an advantage. She had certainly meant their parting to be for good. She had certainly raised her voice in giving the name of her station to the taxi-man with the pretty firm conviction that he would hear her; and she had been pretty well certain that he would take it as a sign that the breath had gone out of their union. . . . Pretty certain. But not quite! . . .

She would have died rather than write to him; she would die, now, rather than give any inkling that she wanted them to live under the same roof again. . . . She said to herself:

"Is he writing to that girl?" And then: "No! . . . I'm certain that he isn't." She had had all his letters stopped at the flat, except for a few circulars that she let dribble through to him, so that he might imagine that all his correspondence was coming through. From the letters to him that she did read she was pretty sure that he had given no other address than the flat in Gray's Inn. . . . But there had been no letters from Valentine Wannop. . . . Two from Mrs. Wannop, two from his brother Mark, one from Port Scatho, one or two from brother officers and some officials' chits. . . . She said to herself that, if there *had* been any letters from that girl, she would have let all his letters go through, including the girl's. . . . Now she was not so certain that she would have.

In the glass she saw Christopher marching woodenly out of the hotel, along the path that led from door to door behind her. It came to her with extraordinary gladness — the absolute conviction that he was not corresponding with Miss Wannop. The absolute conviction. . . . If he had come alive enough to do that he would have looked different. She did not know how he would have looked. But different . . . alive! Perhaps self-conscious; perhaps . . . satisfied . . .

For some time the major had been grumbling about his wrongs. He said that he followed her about all day, like a lap-dog, and got

nothing for it. Now she wanted him to be conciliatory. She said she
wanted to have a man on show as escort. Well then, an escort got
something. . . . At just this moment he was beginning again with:

"Look here . . . will you let me come to your room to-night or
will you not?"

She burst into high, loud laughter. He said:

"Damn it all, it isn't any laughing matter! . . . Look here! You
don't know what I risk. . . . There are A.P.M.s and P.M.s and
deputy sub-acting A.P.M.s walking about the corridors of all the
hotels in this town, all night long. . . . It's as much as my job is'
worth. . . ."

She put her handkerchief to her lips to hide a smile that she knew
would be too cruel for him not to notice. And even when she took it
away, he said:

"Hang it all, what a cruel-looking fiend you are! . . . Why the
devil do I hang around you? . . . There's a picture that my mother's
got, by Burne-Jones . . . A cruel-looking woman with a distant
smile . . . some vampire . . . La belle Dame sans Merci. That's
what you're like."

She looked at him suddenly with considerable seriousness. . . .

"See here, Potty . . ." she began. He groaned:

"I believe you'd like me to be sent to the beastly trenches. . . .
Yet a big, distinguished-looking chap like me wouldn't have a chance.
. . . At the first volley the Germans fired, they'd pick me off. . . ."

"Oh, Potty," she exclaimed, "try to be serious for a minute. . . .
I tell you I'm a woman who's trying . . . who's desperately wanting
. . . to be reconciled to her husband! I would not tell that to another soul. . . . I would not tell it to myself. . . . But one owes
something . . . a parting scene, if nothing else. . . . Well, something . . . to a man one's been in bed with. . . . I didn't give you
a parting scene at .   . ah, Yssingueux-les-Pervenches . . . so I give
you this tip instead. . . ."

He said:

"Will you leave your bedroom door unlocked, or won't you?"

She said:

"If that man would throw his handkerchief to me, I would follow
him round the world in my shift! Look here . . . see me shake when
I think of it. . . ." She held out her hand at the end of her long arm:
hand and arm trembled together, minutely, then very much. . . .
"Well," she finished, "if you see that and still want to come to my

room . . . your blood be on your own head. . . ." She paused for a breath or two and then said:

"You can come. . . . I won't lock my door. But I don't say that you'll get anything . . . or that you'll like what you get. . . . That's a fair tip. . . ." She added suddenly: "You *sale fat* . . . take what you get and be damned to you! . . ."

Major Perowne had suddenly taken to twirling his moustaches; he said:

"Oh, I'll chance the A.P.M.s. . . ."

She suddenly coiled her legs into her chair.

"I know now what I came here for," she said.

Major Wilfrid Fosbrooke Eddicker Perowne of Perowne, the son of his mother, was one of those individuals who have no history, no strong proclivities, nothing; his knowledge seemed to be bounded by the contents of his newspaper for the immediate day. At any rate, his conversation never went any farther. He was not bold, he was not shy; he was neither markedly courageous nor markedly cowardly. His mother was immoderately wealthy, owned an immense castle that hung over crags, above a western sea, much as a bird-cage hangs from a window of a high tenement building, but she received few or no visitors, her cuisine being indifferent and her wine atrocious. She had strong temperance opinions and, immediately after the death of her husband, she had emptied the contents of his cellar, which were almost as historic as his castle, into the sea, a shudder going through county-family and no, or almost no, characteristics. He had done England. But even this was not enough to make Perowne himself notorious.

His mother allowed him — after an eyeopener in early youth — the income of a junior royalty, but he did nothing with it. He lived in a great house in Palace Gardens, Kensington, and he lived all alone with rather a large staff of servants who had been selected by his mother, but they did nothing at all, for he ate all his meals, and even took his bath and dressed for dinner at the Bath Club. He was otherwise parsimonious.

He had, after the fashion of his day, passed a year or two in the army when young. He had been first gazetted to His Majesty's Forty-second Regiment, but on the Black Watch proceeding to India he had exchanged into the Glamorganshires, at that time commanded by General Campion and recruiting in and around Lincolnshire. The

general had been an old friend of Perowne's mother, and, on being
promoted to brigadier, had taken Perowne on to his staff as his galloper, for, although Perowne rode rather indifferently, he had a certain social knowledge and could be counted on to know how correctly to address a regimental invitation to a dowager countess who
had married a viscount's third son. . . . As a military figure otherwise he had a very indifferent word of command, a very poor drill and
next to no control of his men, but he was popular with his batmen,
and in a rather stiff way was presentable in the old scarlet uniform
or the blue mess jacket. He was exactly six foot, to a hairbreadth,
in his stockings, had very dark eyes, and a rather grating voice; the
fact that his limbs were a shade too bulky for his trunk, which was
not at all corpulent, made him appear a little clumsy. If in a club
you asked what sort of a fellow he was your interlocutor would tell
you, most probably, that he had or was supposed to have warts on
his head, this to account for his hair which all his life he had combed
back, unparted from his forehead. But as a matter of fact he had no
warts on his head.

He had once started out on an expedition to shoot big game in
Portuguese East Africa. But on its arrival his expedition was met with
the news that the natives of the interior were in revolt, so Perowne
had returned to Kensington Palace Gardens. He had had several
mild successes with women, but, owing to his habits of economy and
fear of imbroglios, until the age of thirty-four, he had limited the
field of his amours to young women of the lower social orders. . . .

His affair with Sylvia Tietjens might have been something to boast
about, but he was not boastful, and indeed he had been too hard hit
when she had left him even to bear to account lyingly for the employment of the time he had spent with her in Brittany. Fortunately no
one took sufficient interest in his movements to wait for his answer to
their indifferent questions as to where he had spent the summer.
When his mind reverted to her desertion of him moisture would
come out of his eyes, undemonstratively, as water leaves the surface
of a sponge. . . .

Sylvia had left him by the simple expedient of stepping without
so much as a reticule on to the little French tramway that took you to
the main railway line. From there she had written to him in pencil
on a closed correspondence card that she had left him because she
simply could not bear either his dullness or his craking voice. She
said they would probably run up against each other in the course of

the autumn season in town and, after purchase of some night things, had made straight for the German spa to which her mother had retreated.

At the later date Sylvia had no difficulty in accounting to herself for her having gone off with such an oaf: she had simply reacted in a violent fit of sexual hatred, from her husband's mind. And she could not have found a mind more utterly dissimilar than Perowne's in any decently groomed man to be found in London. She could recall, even in the French hotel lounge, years after, the almost painful emotion of joyful hatred that had visited her when she had first thought of going off with him. It was the self-applause of one who has just hit upon an excruciatingly inspiring intellectual discovery. In her previous transitory infidelities to Christopher she had discovered that, however presentable the man with whom she might have been having an affair, and however short the affair, even if it were only a matter of a week-end, Christopher had spoilt her for the other man. It was the most damnable of his qualities that to hear any other man talk of any subject — any, any subject — from stable form to the balance of power, or from the voice of a given opera singer to the recurrence of a comet — to have to pass a week-end with any other man and hear his talk after having spent the inside of the week with Christopher, hate his ideas how you might, was the difference between listening to a grown man and, with an intense boredom, trying to entertain an inarticulate schoolboy. As beside him, other men simply did not seem ever to have grown up. . . .

Just before, with an extreme suddenness, consenting to go away with Perowne, the illuminating idea had struck her: if I did go away with him it would be the most humiliating thing I could do to Christopher. . . . And just when the idea *had* struck her, beside her chair in the conservatory at a dance given by the general's sister, Lady Claudine Sandbach, Perowne, his voice rendered more throaty and less disagreeable than usual by emotion, had been going on and on begging her to elope with him. . . . She had suddenly said:

"Very well . . . let's. . . ."

His emotion had been so unbridled in its astonishment that she had, even at that, almost been inclined to treat her own speech as a joke and to give up the revenge. . . . But the idea of the humiliation that Christopher must feel proved too much for her. For, for your wife to throw you over for an attractive man is naturally humiliating, but that she should leave you publicly for a man of hardly any intelligence at all, you priding yourself on your brains, must be nearly as mortifying a thing as can happen to you.

But she had hardly set out upon her escapade before two very serious defects in her plan occurred to her with extreme force: the one that, however humiliated Christopher might feel she would not be with him to witness his humiliation; the other that, oaf as she had taken Perowne to be in casual society, in close daily relationship he was such an oaf as to be almost insufferable. She had imagined that he would prove a person out of whom it might be possible to make *something* by a judicious course of alternated mothering and scorn; she discovered that his mother had already done for him almost all that woman could do. For, when he had been an already rather backward boy at a private school, his mother had kept him so extremely short of pocket-money that he had robbed other boys' desks of a few shillings here and there — in order to subscribe towards a birthday present for the head master's wife. His mother, to give him a salutary lesson, had given so much publicity to the affair that he had become afflicted with a permanent bent towards shyness that rendered him by turns very mistrustful of himself or very boastful and, although he repressed manifestations of either tendency towards the outside world, the continual repression rendered him almost incapable of any vigorous thought or action. . . .

That discovery did not soften Sylvia towards him: it was, as she expressed it, *his* funeral and, although she would have been ready for any normal job of smartening up a roughish man, she was by no means prepared to readjust other women's hopeless maternal misfits.

So she had got no farther than Ostend, where they had proposed to spend a week or so at the tables, before she found herself explaining to some acquaintances whom she met that she was in that gay city merely for an hour or two, between trains, on the way to join her mother in a German health resort. The impulse to say that had come upon her by surprise, for, until that moment, being completely indifferent to criticism, she had intended to cast no veil at all over her proceedings. But, quite suddenly, on seeing some well-known English faces in the casino it had come over her to think that, however much she imagined Christopher to be humiliated by her going off with an oaf like Perowne, that humiliation must be as nothing compared with that which she might be expected to feel at having found no one better than an oaf like Perowne to go off with. Moreover . . . she began to miss Christopher.

These feelings did not grow any less intense in the rather stuffy but inconspicuous hotel in the Rue St. Roque in Paris to which she immediately transported the bewildered but uncomplaining Perowne, who had imagined that he was to be taken to Wiesbaden for a course of light gaieties. And Paris, when you avoid the more conspicuous resorts, and when you are unprovided with congenial companionship can prove nearly as overwhelming as is, say, Birmingham on a Sunday.

So that Sylvia waited for only just long enough to convince herself that her husband had no apparent intention of applying for an immediate divorce and had, indeed, no apparent intention of doing anything at all. She sent him, that is to say, a postcard saying that letters and other communications would reach her at her inconspicuous hotel — and it mortified her not a little to have to reveal the fact that her hotel was so inconspicuous. But, except that her own correspondence was forwarded to her with regularity, no communications at all came from Tietjens.

In an air-resort in the centre of France to which she next removed Perowne, she found herself considering rather seriously what it might be expected that Tietjens *would* do. Through indirect and unsuspecting allusions in letters from her personal friends she found that if Tietjens did not put up, he certainly did not deny, the story that she had gone to nurse or be with her mother, who was supposed to be seriously ill. . . . That is to say, her friends said how rotten it was that her mother, Mrs. Satterthwaite, should be so seriously ill; how rotten it must be for her to be shut up in a potty little German kur-ort when the world could be so otherwise amusing, and how well Christopher whom they saw from time to time seemed to be getting on considering how rotten it must be for him to be left all alone. . . .

At about this time Perowne began to become, if possible, more irritating than ever. In their air-resort, although the guests were almost entirely French, there was a newly opened golf-course, and at the game of golf Perowne displayed an inefficiency and at the same time a morbid conceit that were surprising in one naturally lymphatic. He would sulk for a whole evening if either Sylvia or any Frenchman beat him in a round, and, though Sylvia was by then completely indifferent to his sulking, what was very much worse was that he became gloomily and loud-voicedly quarrelsome over his games with foreign opponents.

Three events, falling within ten minutes of each other, made her determined to get as far away from that air-resort as was feasible. In the first place she observed at the end of the street some English people called Thurston, whose faces she faintly knew, and the emotion she suddenly felt let her know how extremely anxious she was that she should let it remain feasible for Tietjens to take her back. Then, in the golf club-house, to which she found herself fiercely hurrying in order to pay her bill and get her clubs, she overheard the conversation of two players that left no doubt in her mind that Perowne had been detected in little meannesses of moving his ball at golf or juggling with his score. . . . This was almost more than she could stand. And, at the same moment, her mind, as it were, condescended to let her remember Christopher's voice as it had once uttered the haughty opinion that no man one could speak to would ever think of divorcing any woman. If he could not defend the sanctity of his hearth he must lump it unless the woman wanted to divorce him. . . .

At the time when he had said it her mind — she had been just then hating him a good deal — had seemed to take no notice of the utterance. But now that it presented itself forcibly to her again it brought with it the thought: Supposing he wasn't really only talking through his hat!

She dragged the wretched Perowne off his bed where he had been lost in an after-lunch slumber and told him that they must both leave that place at once, and, that as soon as they reached Paris or some larger town where he could find waiters and people to understand his French, she herself was going to leave him for good. They did not, in consequence, get away from the air-resort until the six o'clock train next morning. Perowne's passion of rage and despair at the news that she wished to leave him took an inconvenient form, for instead of announcing any intention of committing suicide, as might have been expected, he became gloomily and fantastically murderous. He said that unless Sylvia swore on a little relic of St. Anthony she carried that she had no intention of leaving him he would incontinently kill her. He said, as he said for the rest of his days, that she had ruined his life and caused great moral deterioration in himself. But for her he might have married some pure young thing. Moreover, influencing him against his mother's doctrines, she had forced him to drink wine, by an effect of pure scorn. Thus he had done harm, he was convinced, both to his health and to his manly proportions. . . . It was indeed for Sylvia one of the most unbearable things about this man — the way he took wine. With every glass he put to his lips he would exclaim with an unbearable titter some such imbecility as: Here is another nail in my coffin. And he had taken to wine, and even to stronger liquor, very well.

Sylvia had refused to swear by St. Anthony. She definitely was not going to introduce the saint into her amorous affairs, and she definitely was not going to take on any relic an oath that she meant to break at an early opportunity. There was such a thing as playing it too low down; there are dishonours to which death is preferable. So getting hold of his revolver at a time when he was wringing his hands, she dropped it into the water-jug and then felt reasonably safe.

Perowne knew no French and next to nothing about France, but he had discovered that the French did nothing to you for killing a woman who intended to leave you. Sylvia, on the other hand, was pretty certain that, without a weapon, he could not do much to her. If she had had no other training at her very expensive school she had had so much drilling in calisthenics as to be singularly mistress of her limbs, and, in the interests of her beauty she had always kept herself very fit. . . .

She said at last:

"Very well. We will go to Yssingueux-les-Pervenches. . . ."

A rather pleasant French couple in the hotel had spoken of this little place in the extreme west of France as a lonely paradise, they having spent their honeymoon there. . . . And Sylvia wanted a lonely paradise if there was going to be any scrapping before she got away from Perowne.

She had no hesitation as to what she was going to do. The long journey across half France by miserable trains had caused her an agony of home-sickness! Nothing less! . . . It was a humiliating disease from which to suffer. But it was unavoidable, like mumps. You had to put up with it. Besides, she even found herself wanting to see her child, whom she imagined herself to hate, as having been the cause of all her misfortunes. . . .

She therefore prepared, after great thought, a letter telling Tietjens that she intended to return to him. She made the letter as nearly as possible like one she would write announcing her return from a country house to which she should have been invited for an indefinite period, and she added some rather hard instructions about her maid, these being intended to remove from the letter any possible trace of emotion. She was certain that, if she showed any emotion at all,

Christopher would never take her under his roof again. She was pretty certain that no gossip had been caused by her escapade. Major Thurston had been at the railway station when they had left, but they had not spoken — and Thurston was a very decentish, brown-moustached fellow, of the sort that does not gossip.

It had proved a little difficult to get away, for Perowne during several weeks watched her like an attendant in a lunatic asylum. But at last the idea presented itself to him that she would never go without her frocks, and, one day, in a fit of intense somnolence after a lunch, washed down with rather a large quantity of the local and fiery cordial, he let her take a walk alone. . . .

She was by that time tired of men, or she imagined that she was; for she was not prepared to be certain, considering the muckers she saw women coming all round her over the most unpresentable individuals. Men, at any rate, never fulfilled expectations. They might, upon acquaintance, turn out more entertaining than they appeared; but almost always taking up with a man was like reading a book you had read when you had forgotten that you had read it. You had not been for ten minutes in any sort of intimacy with any man before you said: "But I've read all this before. . . ." You knew the opening, you were already bored by the middle, and, especially, you knew the end. . . .

She remembered, years ago, trying to shock her mother's spiritual adviser, Father Consett, whom they had lately murdered in Ireland, along with Casement. . . . The poor saint had not in the least been shocked. He had gone her one better. For when she had said something like that her idea of a divvy life — they used in those days to say divvy — would be to go off with a different man every week-end, he had told her that after a short time she would be bored already by the time the poor dear fellow was buying the railway tickets. . . .

And, by heavens, he had been right. . . . For when she came to think of it, from the day that poor saint had said that thing in her mother's sitting-room in the little German spa — Lobscheid, it must have been called — in the candle-light, his shadow denouncing her from all over the walls, to now when she sat in the palmish wicker-work of that hotel that had been new-whitely decorated to celebrate hostilities, never once had she sat in a train with a man who had any right to look upon himself as justified in mauling her about. . . . She wondered if, from where he sat in heaven, Father Consett would be satisfied with her as he looked down into that lounge. . . . Perhaps it was really he that had pulled off that change in her.

Never once till yesterday . . . For perhaps the unfortunate Perowne might just faintly have had the right yesterday to make himself for about two minutes — before she froze him into a choking, pallid snowman with goggle eyes — the perfectly loathsome thing that a man in a railway train becomes. . . . Much too bold and yet stupidly awkward with the fear of the guard looking in at the window, the train doing over sixty, without corridors. . . . No, never again for *me,* father, she addressed her voice towards the ceiling. . . .

Why in the world couldn't you get a man to go away with you and be just — oh, light comedy — for a whole, a whole blessed week-end. For a whole blessed life . . . Why not? . . . Think of it. . . . A whole blessed life with a man who was a good sort and yet didn't go all gurgly in the voice, and cod-fish-eyed and all-overish — to the extent of not being able to find the tickets when asked for them. . . . Father, dear, she said again upwards, if I could find men like that, that would be just heaven . . . where there is no marrying. . . . But, of course, she went on almost resignedly, he would not be faithful to you. . . . And then, one would have to stand it. . . .

She sat up so suddenly in her chair that beside her, too, Major Perowne nearly jumped out of his wickerwork, and asked if *he* had come back. . . . She explained:

"No, I'd be damned if I would. . . . I'd be damned, I'd be damned, I'd be damned if I would. . . . Never. Never. By the living God!"

She asked fiercely of the agitated major:

"Has Christopher got a girl in this town? . . . You'd better tell me the truth!"

The major mumbled:

"He . . . no, he's too much of a stick. . . . He never even goes to Suzette's. . . . Except once to fetch out some miserable little squit of a subaltern who was smashing up Mother Hardelot's furniture. . . ."

He grumbled:

"But you shouldn't give a man the jumps like that! . . . Be conciliatory, you said. . . ." He went on to grumble that her manners had not improved since she had been at Yssingueux-les-Pervenches, and then went on to tell her that in French the words *yeux des pervenches* meant eyes of periwinkle blue. And that was the only French

he knew, because a Frenchman he had met in the train had told him
so and he had always thought that if *her* eyes had been periwinkle
blue . . . "But you're not listening. . . . Hardly polite, I call it,"
he had mumbled to a conclusion. . . .

She was sitting forward in her chair still clenching her hand under
her chin at the thought that perhaps Christopher had Valentine
Wannop in that town. That was perhaps why he elected to remain
there. She asked:

"Why does Christopher stay on in this God-forsaken hole? . . .
The inglorious base, they call it. . . ."

"Because he's jolly well got to. . . ." Major Perowne said. "He's
got to do what he's told. . . ."

She said: "Christopher! . . . You mean to say they'd keep a man
like *Christopher* anywhere he didn't want to be. . . ."

"They'd jolly well knock spots off him if he went away," Major
Perowne exclaimed. . . . "What the deuce do you think your blessed
fellow is? . . . The King of England? . . ." He added with a sudden sombre ferocity: "They'd shoot him like anybody else if he
bolted. . . . What do *you* think?"

She said: "But all that wouldn't prevent his having a girl in this
town?"

"Well, he hasn't got one," Perowne said. "He sticks up in that
blessed old camp of his like a blessed she-chicken sitting on addled
eggs. . . . That's what they say of him. I don't know anything about
the fellow. . . ."

Listening vindictively and indolently, she thought she caught in
his droning tones a touch of the homicidal lunacy that had used to
underlie his voice in the bedroom at Yssingueux. The fellow had undoubtedly about him a touch of the dull, mad murderer of the police-
courts. With a sudden animation she thought:

"Suppose he tried to murder Christopher. . . ." And she imagined
her husband breaking the fellow's back across his knee, the idea going
across her mind as fire traverses the opal. Then, with a dry throat, she
said to herself:

"I've got to find out whether he has that girl in Rouen. . . ."
Men stuck together. The fellow Perowne might well be protecting
Tietjens. It would be unthinkable that any rules of the service could
keep Christopher in that place. They could not shut up the upper
classes. If Perowne had any sense he would know that to shield Tiet-

jens was the way not to get her. . . . But he had no sense. . . .
Besides, sexual solidarity was a terribly strong thing. She knew that
she herself would not give a woman's secrets away in order to get her
man. Then . . . how was she to ascertain whether the girl was not in
that town? How? . . . She imagined Tietjens going home every
night to her. . . . But he was going to spend that night with herself.
. . . She knew that. . . . Under that roof. . . . Fresh from the
other. . . .

She imagined him there, now. . . . In the parlour of one of the
little villas you see from the tram on the top of the town. They were
undoubtedly, now, discussing her. . . . Her whole body writhed,
muscle on muscle, in her chair. She must discover. . . . But how do
you discover? Against a universal conspiracy. . . . This whole war
was an agapemone. . . . You went to war when you desired to rape
innumerable women. It was what war was for. . . . All these men,
crowded in this narrow space. . . . She stood up:

"I'm going," she said, "to put on a little powder for Lady Sachse's
feast. . . . You needn't stay if you don't want to. . . ." She was
going to watch every face she saw until it gave up the secret of where
in that town Christopher had the Wannop girl hidden. . . . She
imagined her freckled, snubnosed face pressed — squashed was the
word — against his cheek. . . . She was going to investigate. . . .

II

SHE found an early opportunity to carry on her investigations. For, at
dinner that night, she found herself, Tietjens having gone to the
telephone with a lance-corporal, opposite what she took to be a small
tradesman, with fresh-coloured cheeks, and a great, grey, forward-
sprouting moustache, in a uniform so creased that the creases resembled the veins of a leaf. . . . A very trustworthy small tradesman:
the grocer from round the corner whom, sometimes, you allow to
supply you with paraffin. . . . He was saying to her:

"If, ma'am, you multiply two-thousand nine hundred and something by ten you arrive at twenty-nine thousand odd. . . ."

And she had exclaimed:

"You really mean that my husband, Captain Tietjens, spent yes-

terday afternoon in examining twenty-nine thousand toe-nails. . . .
And two thousand nine hundred toothbrushes. . . ."

"I told him," her interlocutor answered with deep seriousness,
"that these being Colonial troops it was not so necessary to examine
their toothbrushes. . . . Imperial troops *will* use the brush they clean
their buttons with for their teeth so as to have a clean toothbrush
to show the medical officer. . . ."

"It sounds," she said with a little shudder, "as if you were all schoolboys playing a game. . . . And you say my husband really occupies
his mind with such things. . . ."

Second-Lieutenant Cowley, dreadfully conscious that the shoulder-
strap of his Sam Browne belt, purchased that afternoon at the Ordnance, and therefore brand-new, did not match the abdominal part
of the belt that he had had for nearly ten years — a splendid bit of
leather, that! — answered nevertheless stoutly:

"Madam! If the brains of an army aren't, the life of an army *is* . . .
in its feet. . . . And nowadays, the medical officers say, in its teeth.
. . . Your husband, ma'am, is an admirable officer. . . . He says that
no draft he turns out shall . . ."

She said:

"He spent three hours in . . . You say, foot and kit inspection. . . ."

Second-Lieutenant Cowley said:

"Of course he had other officers to help him with the kit . . . but
he looked at every foot himself. . . ."

She said:

"That took him from two till five. . . . Then he had tea, I suppose. . . . And went to . . . What is it? . . . The papers of the
draft. . . ."

Second-Lieutenant Cowley said, muffledly through his moustache:

"If the captain is a little remiss in writing letters . . . I *have* heard.
. . . You might, madam . . . I'm a married man myself . . . with
a daughter. . . . And the army is not very good at writing letters.
. . . You might say, in that respect, that thank God we have got a
navy, ma'am. . . ."

She let him stagger on for a sentence or two, imagining that, in his
confusion, she might come upon traces of Miss Wannop in Rouen.
Then she said handsomely:

"Of course you have explained everything, Mr. Cowley, and I am
very much obliged. . . . Of course my husband would not have time

to write very full letters. . . . He is not like the giddy young subalterns who run after . . ."

He exclaimed in a great roar of laughter:

"The captain run after skirts. . . . Why, I can number on my hands the times he's been out of my sight since he's had the battalion!"

A deep wave of depression went over Sylvia.

"Why," Lieutenant Cowley laughed on, "if we *had* a laugh against him it was that he mothered the lot of us as if he was a hen sitting on addled eggs. . . . For it's only a rag-time army, as the saying is, when you've said the best for it that you can. . . . And look at the other commanding officers we've had before we had him. . . . There was Major Brooks. . . . Never up before noon, if then, and out of camp by two-thirty. Get your returns ready for signing before then or never get 'em signed. . . . And Colonel Potter . . . Bless my soul . . . 'e wouldn't sign any blessed papers at all. . . . He lived down here in this hotel, and we never saw him up at the camp at all. . . . But the captain . . . We always say that if 'e was a Chelsea adjutant getting off a draft of the Second Coldstreams . . ."

With her indolent and gracious beauty — Sylvia knew that she was displaying indolent and gracious beauty — Sylvia leaned over the table-cloth listening for items in the terrible indictment that, presently, she was going to bring against Tietjens. . . . For the morality of these matters is this: If you have an incomparably beautiful woman on your hands you must occupy yourself solely with her. . . . Nature exacts that of you . . . until you are unfaithful to her with a snub-nosed girl with freckles; that, of course, being a reaction, is still in a way occupying yourself with your woman! . . . But to betray her with a battalion . . . That is against decency, against Nature. . . . And for him, Christopher Tietjens, to come down to the level of the men you met here! . . .

Tietjens, mooning down the room between tables, had more than his usually aloof air since he had just come out of a telephone box. He slipped, a weary mass, into the polished chair between her and the lieutenant. He said:

"I've got the washing arranged for . . ." and Sylvia gave to herself a little hiss between the teeth, of vindictive pleasure! This was indeed betrayal to a battalion. He added: "I shall have to be up in camp before four-thirty to-morrow morning. . . ."

Sylvia could not resist saying:

"Isn't there a poem . . . '*Ah me, the dawn, the dawn, it comes too soon!*' . . . said of course by lovers in bed? . . . Who was the poet?"

Cowley went visibly red to the roots of his hair and evidently beyond. Tietjens finished his speech to Cowley, who had remonstrated against his going up to the camp so early by saying that he had not been able to get hold of an officer to march the draft. He then said in his leisurely way:

"There were a great many poems with that refrain in the Middle Ages. . . . You are probably thinking of an aubade by Arnaut Daniel, which someone translated lately. . . . An aubade was a song to be sung at dawn when, presumably, no one but lovers would be likely to sing. . . ."

"Will there," Sylvia asked, "be anyone but you singing up in your camp to-morrow at four?"

She could not help it. . . . She knew that Tietjens had adopted his slow pomposity in order to give the grotesque object at the table with them time to recover from his confusion. She hated him for it. What right had he to make himself appear a pompous ass in order to shield the confusion of anybody?

The second-lieutenant came out of his confusion to exclaim, actually slapping his thigh:

"There you are, madam. . . . Trust the captain to know everything! . . . I don't believe there's a question under the sun you could ask him that he couldn't answer. . . . They say up at the camp . . ." He went on with long stories of all the questions Tietjens *had* answered up at the camp. . . .

Emotion was going all over Sylvia . . . at the proximity of Tietjens. She said to herself: "Is this to go on for ever?" Her hands were ice-cold. She touched the back of her left hand with the fingers of her right. It *was* ice-cold. She looked at her hands. They were bloodless. . . . She said to herself: "It's pure sexual passion . . . it's pure sexual passion . . . God! Can't I get over this? Father! . . . You used to be fond of Christopher. . . . *Get* our Lady to get me over this. . . . It's the ruin of him and the ruin of me. But, oh *damn*, don't! . . . For it's all I have to live for. . . . When he came mooning back from the telephone I thought it was all right. . . . I thought what a heavy wooden-horse he looked. . . . For two minutes. . . . Then it's all over me again. . . . I want to swallow my saliva and I can't. My throat won't work. . . ."

She leaned one of her white bare arms on the table-cloth towards the walrus-moustache that was still snuffling gloriously:

"They used to call him Old Sol at school," she said. "But there's one question of Solomon's he could not answer. . . . The one about the way of a man with . . . Oh, a maid! . . . Ask him what happened before the dawn ninety-six — no, ninety-eight days ago. . . ."

She said to herself: "I can't help it. . . . Oh, I *can't* help it. . . ."

The ex-sergeant-major was exclaiming happily:

"Oh, no one ever said the captain was one of these thought-readers. . . . It's real solid knowledge of men and things he has. . . . Wonderful how he knows the men considering he was not born in the service. . . . But there, your born gentleman mixes with men all his days and knows them. Down to the ground and inside their puttees. . . ."

Tietjens was looking straight in front of him, his face perfectly expressionless.

"But I bet I got him," she said to herself and then to the sergeant-major:

"I suppose now an army officer — one of your born gentlemen — when a back-from-leave train goes out from any of the great stations — Paddington, say — to the front. . . . He knows how all the men are feeling. . . . But not what the married women think . . . or the . . . the girl. . . ."

She said to herself: "Damn it, how clumsy I am getting! . . . I used to be able to take his hide off with a word. Now I take sentences at a time. . . ."

She went on with her uninterrupted sentence to Cowley:

"Of course he may never be going to see his only son again, so it makes him sensitive. . . . The officer at Paddington, I mean. . . ."

She said to herself: "By God, if that beast does not give in to me to-night he never *shall* see Michael again. . . . Ah, but I got him. . . ." Tietjens had his eyes closed, round each of his high-coloured nostrils a crescent of whiteness was beginning. And increasing. . . . She felt a sudden alarm and held the edge of the table with her extended arm to steady herself. . . . Men went white at the nose like that when they were going to faint. . . . She did not want him to faint. . . . But he *had* noticed the word Paddington. . . . Ninety-eight days before. . . . She had counted every day since. . . . She had got that much information. . . . She had said *Paddington* outside the house at dawn and he had taken it as a farewell. He *had* . . .

He had imagined himself free to do what he liked with the girl. . . .
Well, he wasn't. . . . That was why he was white about the
gills. . . .

Cowley exclaimed loudly:

"Paddington! . . . It isn't from there that back-from-leave trains
go. Not for the front: the B.E.F. . . . Not from Paddington. . . .
The Glamorganshires go from there to the depot. . . . And the
Liverpools . . . They've got a depot at Birkenhead. . . . Or is that
the Cheshires? . . ." He asked of Tietjens: "Is it the Liverpools or
the Cheshires that have a depot at Birkenhead, sir? . . . You remember we recruited a draft from there when we were at Penhally. . . .
At any rate, you go to Birkenhead from Paddington. . . . I was
never there myself. . . . They say it's a nice place. . . ."

Sylvia said — she did not want to say it:

"It's quite a nice place . . . but I should not think of staying there
for ever. . . ."

Tietjens said:

"The Cheshires have a training camp — not a depot — near Birkenhead. And of course there are R.G.A.s there. . . ." She had been
looking away from him. . . . Cowley exclaimed:

"You were nearly off, sir," hilariously. "You had your peepers
shut. . . ." Lifting a champagne glass, he inclined himself towards
her. "You must excuse the captain, ma'am," he said. "He had no
sleep last night. . . . Largely owing to my fault. . . . Which is what
makes it so kind of him. . . . I tell you, ma'am, there are few things
I would not do for the captain. . . ." He drank his champagne and
began an explanation: "You may not know, ma'am, this is a great
day for me. . . . And you and the captain are making it the greatest
day of my life. . . ." Why, at four this morning there hadn't been a
wretcheder man in Ruin town. And now . . . He must tell her that
he suffered from an unfortunate — a miserable — complaint. . . .
One that makes one have to be careful of celebrations. . . . And to-
day was a day that he had to celebrate. . . . But he dare not have
done it where Sergeant-Major Ledoux is along with a lot of their old
mates. . . . "I dare not . . . I dussn't!" he finished. "So I might
have been sitting, now, at this very moment, up in the cold camp.
. . . But for you and the captain. . . . Up in the cold camp . . .
You'll excuse me, ma'am. . . ."

Sylvia felt that her lids were suddenly wavering:

"I might have been myself," she said, "in a cold camp, too . . .

if I hadn't thrown myself on the captain's mercy! . . . At Birkenhead, you know. . . . I happened to be there till three weeks ago. . . . It's strange that you mentioned it. . . . There *are* things like signs . . . but you're not a Catholic! They could hardly be coincidences. . . ."

She was trembling. . . . She looked, fumblingly opening it, into the little mirror of her powder-box — of chased, very thin gold with a small blue stone, like a forget-me-not in the centre of the concentric engravings. . . . Drake — the possible father of Michael — had given it to her. . . . The first thing he had ever given her. She had brought it down to-night out of defiance. She imagined that Tietjens disliked it. She said breathlessly to herself: "Perhaps the damn thing is an ill omen. . . ." Drake had been the first man who had ever . . . A hot-breathed brute! . . . In the little glass her features were chalk-white. . . . She looked like . . . she looked like . . . She had a dress of golden tissue. . . . The breath was short between her white set teeth. . . . Her face was as white as her teeth. . . . And . . . Yes! Nearly! Her lips. . . . What was her face like? . . . In the chapel of the convent of Birkenhead there was a tomb all of alabaster. . . . She said to herself:

"He was near fainting. . . . I'm near fainting. . . . What's this beastly thing that's between us? . . . If I let myself faint . . . But it would not make that beast's face any less wooden! . . ."

She leaned across the table and patted the ex-sergeant-major's black-haired hand:

"I'm sure," she said, "you're a very good man. . . ." She did not try to keep the tears out of her eyes, remembering his words: "Up in the cold camp." . . . "I'm glad the captain, as you call him, did not leave you in the cold camp. . . . You're devoted to him, aren't you? . . . There are others he does leave . . . up in . . . the cold camp. . . . For punishment, you know. . . ."

The ex-sergeant-major, the tears in his eyes too, said:

"Well, there *is* men you 'as to give the C.B. to. . . . C.B. means confined to barracks. . . ."

"Oh, there are!" she exclaimed. "There are! . . . And women, too. . . . Surely there are women, too? . . ."

The sergeant-major said:

"Waacs, per'aps . . . I don't know. . . . They say women's discipline is much like ours. . . . Founded on hours!"

She said:

"Do you know what they used to say of the captain? . . ." She said to herself: "I pray to God the stiff, fatuous beast likes sitting here listening to this stuff. . . . Blessed Virgin, mother of God, make him take me. . . . Before midnight. Before eleven. . . . As soon as we get rid of this . . . No, he's a decent little man. . . . Blessed Virgin!" . . . "Do you know what they used to say of the captain? . . . I heard the warmest banker in England say it of him. . . ."

The sergeant-major, his eyes enormously opened, said:

"Did you know the warmest banker in England? . . . But there, we always knew the captain was well connected. . . ." She went on:

"They said of him. . . . He was always helping people." . . . "Holy Mary, mother of God! . . . He's my *husband*. It's not a sin. . . . Before midnight. . . . Oh, give me a sign. . . . Or before . . . the termination of hostilities. . . . If you give me a sign I could wait." . . . "He helped virtuous Scotch students, and broken-down gentry. . . . And women taken in adultery. . . . All of them. . . . Like . . . You know Who. . . . That is his model. . . ." She said to herself: "Curse him! . . . I hope he likes it. . . . You'd think the only thing he thinks about is the beastly duck he's wolfing down." And then aloud: "They used to say: 'He saved others; himself he could not save. . . .' "

The ex-sergeant-major looked at her gravely:

"Ma'am," he said, " we couldn't say exactly that of the captain. . . . For I fancy it was said of our Redeemer. . . . But we 'ave said that if ever there was a poor bloke the captain could 'elp, 'elp 'im 'e would. . . . Yet the unit was always getting 'ellish strafe from headquarters. . . ."

Suddenly Sylvia began to laugh. . . . As she began to laugh she had remembered . . . The alabaster image in the nun's chapel at Birkenhead the vision of which had just presented itself to her, had been the recumbent tomb of an honourable Mrs. Tremayne-Warlock. . . . She was said to have sinned in her youth and her husband had never forgiven her. That was what the nuns said. . . . She said aloud:

"A sign . . ." Then to herself: "Blessed Mary! You've given it me in the neck. . . . Yet you could not name a father for your child, and I can name two. . . . I'm going mad. . . . Both I and he are going to go mad. . . ."

She thought of dashing an enormous patch of red upon either cheek. Then she thought it would be rather melodramatic. . . .

She made in the smoking-room, whilst she was waiting for both Tietjens and Cowley to come back from the telephone, another pact, this time with Father Consett in heaven! She was fairly sure that Father Consett — and quite possibly other of the heavenly powers — wanted Christopher not to be worried, so that he could get on with the war — or because he was a good sort of dullish man such as the heavenly authorities are apt to like. . . . Something like that. . . .

She was by that time fairly calm again. You cannot keep up fits of emotion by the hour. At any rate, with her, the fits of emotion were periodical and unexpected, though her colder passion remained always the same. . . . Thus, when Christopher had come into Lady Sachse's that afternoon, she had been perfectly calm. He had mooned through a number of officers, both French and English, in a great octagonal, bluish salon where Lady Sachse gave her teas, and had come to her side with just a nod — the merest inflexion of the head! . . . Perowne had melted away somewhere behind the disagreeable duchess. The general, very splendid and white-headed and scarlet-tipped and gilt, had also borne down upon her at that. . . . At the sight of Perowne with her he had been sniffing and snorting whilst he talked to the young nobleman — a dark fellow in blue with a new belt who seemed just a shade too theatrical, he being chauffeur to a marshal of France and first cousin and nearest relative, except for parents and grandparents, of the prospective bride.

The general had told her that he was running the show pretty strong on purpose because he thought it might do something to cement the Entente Cordiale. But it did not seem to be doing it. The French — officers, soldiers, and women — kept pretty well all on the one side of the room — the English on the other. The French were as a rule more gloomy than men and women are expected to be. A marquis of sorts — she understood that these were all Bonapartist nobility — having been introduced to her had distinguished himself no more than by saying that, for his part, he thought the duchess was right, and by saying that to Perowne who, knowing no French, had choked exactly as if his tongue had suddenly got too big for his mouth.

She had not heard what the duchess — a very disagreeable duchess who sat on a sofa and appeared savagely careworn — had been saying, so that she had inclined herself, in the courtly manner that at school she had been taught to reserve for the French legitimist nobility, but that she thought she might expend upon a rather state function even for the Bonapartists, and had replied that without the least doubt the duchess had the right of the matter. . . . The marquis had given her from dark eyes one long glance, and she had returned it with a long cold glance that certainly told him she was meat for his masters. It extinguished him. . . .

Tietjens had staged his meeting with herself remarkably well. It was the sort of lymphatic thing he *could* do, so that, for the fifth of a minute, she wondered if he had any feelings or emotions at all. But she knew that he had. . . . The general, at any rate, bearing down upon them with satisfaction, had remarked:

"Ah, I see you've seen each other before to-day. . . . I thought perhaps you wouldn't have found time before, Tietjens. Your draft must be a great nuisance. . . ."

Tietjens said without expression:

"Yes, we have seen each other before. . . . I made time to call at Sylvia's hotel, sir."

It was at Tietjens' terrifying expressionlessness, at that completely being up to a situation, that the first wave of emotion had come over her. . . . For, till that very moment, she had been merely sardonically making the constatation that there was not a single presentable man in the room. . . . There was not even one that you could call a gentleman . . . for you cannot size up the French . . . ever! But, suddenly, she was despairing! . . . How, she said to herself, could she ever move, put emotion into, this lump! It was like trying to move an immense mattress filled with feathers. You pulled at one end, but the whole mass sagged down and remained immobile until you seemed to have no strength at all. Until virtue went out from you. . . .

It was as if he had the evil eye, or some special protector. He was so appallingly competent, so appallingly always in the centre of his own picture.

The general said, rather joyfully:

"Then you can spare a minute, Tietjens, to talk to the duchess! About coal! . . . For goodness' sake, man, save the situation! I'm worn out. . . ."

Sylvia bit the inside of her lower lip — she never bit her lip itself! — to keep herself from exclaiming aloud. It was just exactly what should not happen to Tietjens at that juncture. . . . She heard the general explaining to her in his courtly manner, that the duchess was holding up the whole ceremony because of the price of coal. The general loved her desperately. Her, Sylvia! In quite a proper manner for an elderly general. . . . But he would go to no small extremes in her interests! So would his sister!

She looked hard at the room to get her senses into order again. She said:

"It's like a Hogarth picture. . . ."

The undissolvable air of the eighteenth century that the French contrive to retain in all their effects kept the scene singularly together. On a sofa sat the duchess, relatives leaning over her. She was a duchess with one of those impossible names: Beauchain-Radigutz or something like it. The bluish room was octagonal and vaulted, up to a rosette in the centre of the ceiling. English officers and V.A.D.s of some evident presence opened out to the left, French military and very black-clothed women of all ages, but all apparently widows, opened out to the right, as if the duchess shone down a sea at sunset. Beside her on the sofa you did not see Lady Sachse; leaning over her you did not see the prospective bride. This stoutish, unpresentable, coldly venomous woman, in black clothes so shabby that they might have been grey tweed, extinguished other personalities as the sun conceals planets. A fattish, brilliantined personality, in mufti, with a scarlet rosette, stood sideways to the duchess's right, his hands extended forward as if in an invitation to a dance; an extremely squat lady, also apparently a widow, extended, on the left of the duchess, both her black-gloved hands, as if she too were giving an invitation to the dance.

The general, with Sylvia beside him, stood glorious in the centre of the clearing that led to the open doorway of a much smaller room. Through the doorway you could see a table with a white damask cloth; a silver-gilt inkpot, fretted, like a porcupine with pens, a fat, flat leather case for the transportation of documents, and two notaires: one in black, fat, and bald-headed; one in blue uniform, with a shining monocle, and a brown moustache that he continued to twirl.

Looking round that scene Sylvia's humour calmed her and she heard the general say:

"She's supposed to walk on my arm to that table and sign the settlement. . . . We're supposed to be the first to sign it together. . . . But she won't. Because of the price of coal. It appears that she has hothouses in miles. And she thinks the English have put up the price

of coal as if . . . damn it you'd think we did it just to keep her hot-
house stoves out."

The duchess had delivered, apparently, a vindictive, cold, calm and
uninterruptible oration on the wickedness of her country's allies as
people who should have allowed France to be devastated, and the
flower of her youth slain in order that they might put up the price of
a comestible that was absolutely needed in her life. There was no arguing with her. There was no British soul there who both knew anything about economics and spoke French. And there she sat, apparently immovable. She did not refuse to sign the marriage contract.
She just made no motion to go to it and, apparently, the resulting
marriage would be illegal if that document were brought to her! . . .

The general said:

"Now, what the deuce will Christopher find to say to her? He'll
find something because he could talk the hind legs off anything. But
what the deuce will it be? . . ."

It almost broke Sylvia's heart to see how exactly Christopher did
the right thing. He walked up that path to the sun and made in front
of the duchess a little awkward nick with his head and shoulders that
was rather more like a curtsy than a bow. It appeared that he knew
the duchess quite well . . . as he knew everybody in the world quite
well. He smiled at her and then became just suitably grave. Then
he began to speak an admirable, very old-fashioned French with an
atrocious English accent. Sylvia had no idea that he knew a word of
the language — that she herself knew very well indeed. She said to
herself that upon her word it was like hearing Chateaubriand talk —
if Chateaubriand had been brought up in an English hunting country. . . . Of course Christopher *would* cultivate an English accent
to show that he was an English county gentleman. And he would
speak correctly — to show that an English Tory can do anything in
the world if he wants to. . . .

The British faces in the room looked blank; the French faces
urned electrically upon him. Sylvia said:

"Who would have thought? . . ." The duchess jumped to her feet
and took Christopher's arm. She sailed with him imperiously past the
general and past Sylvia. She was saying that that was just what she
would have expected of a *milor Anglais*. . . . *Avec un spleen tel que
vous l'avez!*

Christopher, in short, had told the duchess that as his family
owned almost the largest stretch of hothouse coal-burning land in

England and her family the largest stretch of hothouses in the sister-country of France, what could they do better than make an alliance? He would instruct his brother's manager to see that the duchess was supplied for the duration of hostilities and as long after as she pleased with all the coal needed for her glass at the pit-head prices of the Middlesbrough-Cleveland district as the prices were on the 3rd of August, nineteen fourteen. . . . He repeated: "The pit-head price . . . *livrable au prix de l'houille-maigre dans l'enceinte des puits de ma campagne.*" Much to the satisfaction of the duchess, who knew all about prices.

A triumph for Christopher was at that moment so exactly what Sylvia thought she did not want that she decided to tell the general that Christopher was a Socialist. That might well take him down a peg or two in the general's esteem . . . for the general's arm-patting admiration for Tietjens, the man who did not argue but acted over the price of coal, was as much as she could bear. . . . But, thinking it over in the smoking-room after dinner, by which time she was a good deal more aware of what she did want, she was not so certain that she *had* done what she wanted. Indeed, even in the octagonal room during the economical festivities that followed the signatures, she had been far from certain that she had not done almost exactly what she did not want. . . .

It had begun with the general's exclaiming to her:

"You know your man's the most unaccountable fellow. . . . He wears the damn-shabbiest uniform of any officer I ever have to talk to. He's said to be unholily hard up. . . . I even heard he had a cheque sent back to the club. Then he goes and makes a princely gift like that — just to get Levin out of ten minutes' awkwardness. . . . I wish to goodness I could understand the fellow. . . . He's got a positive genius for getting all sorts of things out of the most beastly muddles. . . . Why he's even been useful to me. . . . And then he's got a positive genius for getting into the most disgusting messes. . . . You're too young to have heard of Dreyfus. . . . But I always say that Christopher is a regular Dreyfus. . . . I shouldn't be astonished if he didn't end by being drummed out of the army . . . which heaven forfend!"

It had been then that Sylvia had said:

"Hasn't it ever occurred to you that Christopher was a Socialist?"

For the first time in her life Sylvia saw her husband's godfather look grotesque. . . . His jaw dropped down, his white hair became disarrayed and he dropped his pretty cap with all the gold oakleaves and the scarlet. When he rose from picking it up his thin old face was purple and distorted. She wished she hadn't said it; she wished she hadn't said it. He exclaimed:

"Christopher! . . . A So . . ." He gasped as if he could not pronounce the word. He said: "Damn it all! . . . I've loved that boy. . . . He's my only godson. . . . His father was my best friend. . . . I've watched over him. . . . I'd have married his mother if she would have had me. . . . Damn it all, he's down in my will as residuary legatee after a few small things left to my sister and my collection of horns to the regiment I commanded. . . ."

Sylvia — they were sitting on the sofa the duchess had left — patted him on the forearm and said:

"But general . . . godfather. . . ."

"It explains everything," he said with a mortification that was painful. His white moustache drooped and trembled. "And what makes it all the worse — he's never had the courage to tell me his opinions." He stopped, snorted and exclaimed: "By God, I *will* have him drummed out of the service. . . . By God, I will. I can do that much. . . ."

His grief so shut him in on himself that she could say nothing to him. . . .

"You tell me he seduced the little Wannop girl. . . . The last person in the world he should have seduced. . . . Ain't there millions of other women? He got you sold up, didn't he? . . . Along with keeping a girl in a tobacco-shop. . . . By jove, I almost lent him . . . offered to lend him money on that occasion. . . . You can forgive a young man for doing wrong with women. We all do. . . . We've all set up girls in tobacco-shops in our time. . . . But, damn it all, if the fellow's a Socialist it puts a different complexion. . . . I could forgive him even for the little Wannop girl, if he wasn't . . . But . . . Good God, isn't it just the thing that a dirty-minded Socialist would do? . . . To seduce the daughter of his father's oldest friend, next to me. . . . Or perhaps Wannop was an older friend than me. . . ."

He had calmed himself a little — and he was not such a fool. He looked at her now with a certain keenness in his blue eyes that showed no sign of age. He said:

"See here, Sylvia . . . You aren't on terms with Christopher for all the good game you put up here this afternoon. . . . I shall have to go into this. It's a serious charge to bring against one of His Majesty's officers. . . . Women do say things against their husbands when they are not on good terms with them. . . ." He went on to say that he did not say she wasn't justified. If Christopher had seduced the little Wannop girl it was enough to make her wish to harm him. He had always found her the soul of honour, straight as a die, straight as she rode to hounds. And if she wished to nag against her husband, even if in little things it wasn't quite the truth, she was perhaps within her rights as a woman. She had said, for instance, that Tietjens had taken two pair of her best sheets. Well, his own sister, her friend, raised Cain if he took anything out of the house they lived in. She had made an atrocious row because he had taken his own shaving-glass out of his own bedroom at Mountsby. Women liked to have sets of things. Perhaps, she, Sylvia had sets of pairs of sheets. His sister had linen sheets with the date of the battle of Waterloo on them. . . . Naturally you would not want a set spoiled. But this was another matter. He ended up very seriously:

"I have not got time to go into this now. . . . I ought not to be another minute away from my office. These are very serious days. . . ." He broke off to utter against the Prime Minister and the Cabinet at home a series of violent imprecations. He went on:

"But this will have to be gone into. . . . It's heart-breaking that my time should be taken up by matters like this in my own family. . . . But these fellows aim at sapping the heart of the army. . . . They say they distribute thousands of pamphlets recommending the rank and file to shoot their officers and go over to the Germans. . . . Do you seriously mean that Christopher belongs to an organization? What is it you are going on? What evidence have you? . . ."

She said:

"Only that he is heir to one of the biggest fortunes in England, for a commoner, and he refuses to touch a penny. His brother Mark tells me Christopher could have . . . oh, a fabulous sum a year. . . . But he has made over Groby to me. . . ."

The general nodded his head as if he were ticking off ideas.

"Of course, refusing property is a sign of being one of these fellows. By Jove, I must go. . . . But as for his not going to live at Groby. . . . If he is setting up house with Miss Wannop. . . . Well, he could not flaunt her in the face of the county. . . . And, of course, those sheets! . . . As you put it it looked as if he'd beggared himself with his dissipations. . . . But of course, if he is refusing

money from Mark, it's another matter. . . . Mark would make up
a couple of hundred dozen pairs of sheets without turning a hair.
. . . Of course there are the extraordinary things Christopher says.
I've often heard you complain of the immoral way he looks at the
serious affairs of life. . . . You said he once talked of lethal-cham-
bering unfit children."

He exclaimed:

"I must go. There's Thurston looking at me. . . . But what then
is it that Christopher has said? Hang it all, what *is* at the bottom of
that fellow's mind? . . ."

"He desires," Sylvia said, and she had no idea when she said it,
"to model himself upon our Lord. . . ."

The general leant back in the sofa. He said almost indulgently:

"Who's that . . . our *Lord*?"

Sylvia said:

"Upon our Lord Jesus Christ. . . ."

He sprang to his feet as if she had stabbed him with a hatpin.

"Our . . ." he exclaimed. "Good God! . . . I always knew he had
a screw loose. . . . But . . ." He said briskly: "Give all his goods
to the poor! . . . But He wasn't a . . . Not a Socialist! What was
it He said: Render under Cæsar . . . It wouldn't be necessary to
drum Him out of the army . . ." He said: "Good Lord! . . . Good
Lord! . . . Of course his poor dear mother was a little . . . But,
hang it! . . . The Wannop girl! . . ." Extreme discomfort overcame
him. . . . Tietjens was half-way across from the inner room, coming towards them.

He said:

"Major Thurston is looking for you, sir. Very urgently. . . ." The
general regarded him as if he had been the unicorn of the royal arms,
come alive. He exclaimed:

"Major Thurston! . . . Yes! Yes! . . ." and, Tietjens saying to
him:

"I wanted to ask you, sir . . ." He pushed Tietjens away as if he
dreaded an assault and went off with short, agitated steps.

So sitting there, in the smoking-lounge of the hotel which was
cram-jam full of officers, and no doubt perfectly respectable, but
over-giggling women — the sort of place and environment which she
had certainly never expected to be called upon to sit in; and waiting
for the return of Tietjens and the ex-sergeant-major — who again was

certainly not the sort of person that she had ever expected to be asked
to wait for, though for long years she had put up with Tietjens'
protégé, the odious Sir Vincent Macmaster, at all sorts of meals and
all sorts of places . . . but of course that was only Christopher's
rights . . . to have in his own house, which, in the circumstances,
wasn't morally hers, any snuffling, nervous, walrus-moustached or
orientally obsequious protégé that he chose to patronize. And she
quite believed that Tietjens, when he had invited the sergeant-major
to celebrate his commission with himself at dinner, hadn't expected
to dine with her. . . . It was the sort of obtuseness of which he was
disconcertingly capable, though at other times he was much more
disconcertingly capable of reading your thoughts to the last hair's
breadth. . . . And, as a matter of fact, she objected much less to
dining with the absolute lower classes than with merely snuffly little
official critics like Macmaster, and the sergeant-major had served her
turn very well when it had come to flaying the hide off Christopher.
. . . So, sitting there, she made a new pact, this time with Father
Consett in heaven.

Father Consett was very much in her mind, for she was very much
in the midst of the British military authorities who had hung him.
. . . She had never seemed before to be so in the midst of these
negligible, odious, unpresentable, horse-laughing schoolboys. It an-
tagonized her, and it was a weight upon her, for hitherto she had
completely ignored them; in this place they seemed to have a coherence, a mass . . . almost a life. . . . They rushed in and out of
rooms occupied, as incomprehensibly, as unpresentably, with things
like boots, washing, vaccination certificates. Even with old tins! . . .
A man with prematurely white hair and a pasty face, with a tunic that
bulged both above and below his belt, would walk into the drawing-
room of a lady who superintended all the acid-drop and cigarette
stalls of that city and remark to a thin-haired, deaf man with an
amazingly red nose — a nose that had a perfectly definite purple and
scarlet diagonal demarcation running from the bridge to the upper
side of the nostrils — that he had got his old tins off his hands at last.
He would have to repeat it in a shout because the red-nosed man, his
head hanging down, would have heard nothing at all. The deaf man
would say Humph! Humph! Snuffle. The woman giving the tea — a
Mrs. Hemmerdine, of Tarbolton, whom you might have met at home,
would be saying that at last she had got twelve reams of notepaper
with forget-me-nots in the top corners when the deaf-faced man

would begin, gruffly and uninterruptedly, a monologue on his urgent
need for twenty thousand tons of sawdust for the new slow-burning
stoves in the men's huts.

It was undeniably like something moving.. . . . All these things
going in one direction. . . . A disagreeable force set in motion by
gawky schoolboys — but schoolboys of the Sixth Form, sinister,
hobbledehoy, waiting in the corners of playgrounds to torture someone, weak and unfortunate. . . . In one or other corner of their
world-wide playground they had come upon Father Consett and
hanged him. No doubt they tortured him first. And, if he made an
offering of his sufferings, then and there to Heaven, no doubt he was
already in paradise. Or, if he was not yet in heaven, certain of the
souls in purgatory were yet listened to in the midst of their torments. . . .

So she said:

"Blessed and martyred father, I know that you loved Christopher
and wish to save him from trouble. I will make this pact with you.
Since I have been in this room I have kept my eyes in the boat — almost in my lap. I will agree to leave off torturing Christopher and I
will go into retreat in a convent of Ursuline Dames Nobles — for I
can't stand the nuns of that other convent — for the rest of my life.
. . . And I know that will please you, too, for you were always anxious for the good of my soul. . . ." She was going to do that if
when she raised her eyes and really looked round the room she saw
in it one man that looked presentable. She did not ask that he should
more than look presentable, for she wanted nothing to do with the
creature. He was to be a sign, not a prey!

She explained to the dead priest that she could not go all the
world over to see if it contained a presentable man, but she could not
bear to be in a convent for ever, and have the thought that there
wasn't, for other women, one presentable man in the world. . . .
For Christopher would be no good to them. He would be mooning
for ever over the Wannop girl. Or her memory. That was all one . . .
He was content with LOVE. . . . If he knew that the Wannop girl
was loving him in Bedford Park, and he in the Khyber States with the
Himalayas between them, he would be quite content. That would be
correct in its way, but not very helpful for other women. . . . Besides, if he were the only presentable man in the world, half the
women would be in love with him. . . . And that would be disas-

trous, because he was no more responsive than a bullock in a fat-
ting pen.

"So, father," she said, "work a miracle. . . . It's not very much of
a little miracle. Even if a presentable man doesn't exist you could put
him there. . . . I'll give you ten minutes before I look. . . ."

She thought it was pretty sporting of her, for, she said to herself,
she was perfectly in earnest. If in that long, dim, green-lamp-shaded,
and of course be-palm-leaved, badly-proportioned, glazed, ignoble public room, there appeared one decentish man, as decentish men went
before this beanfeast began, she would go into retreat for the rest of
her life. . . .

She fell into a sort of dim trance after she had looked at her
watch. Often she went into these dim trances . . . ever since she
had been a girl at school with Father Consett for her spiritual adviser! She seemed to be aware of the father moving about the room,
lifting up a book and putting it down. . . . Her ghostly friend! . . .
Goodness, he was unpresentable enough, with his broad, open face
that always looked dirtyish, his great dark eyes, and his great mouth.
. . . But a saint and a martyr. . . . She felt him there. . . . What
had they murdered him for? Hung at the word of a half-mad, half-
drunk subaltern, because he had heard the confession of some of the
rebels the night before they were taken. . . . He was over in the far
corner of the room. . . . She heard him say: They had not understood, the men that had hanged him. That is what you would say,
father . . . Have mercy on them, for they know not what they
do. . . .

Then have mercy on me, for half the time I don't know what I'm
doing! . . . It was like a spell you put on me. At Lobscheid. Where
my mother was, when I came back from that place without my
clothes. . . . You said, didn't you, to mother, but she told me afterwards: The real hell for that poor boy, meaning Christopher, will
come when he falls in love with some young girl — as, mark me, he
will. . . . For she, meaning me, will tear the world down to get at
him. . . . And when mother said she was certain I would never do
anything vulgar you obstinately did not agree. You knew me. . . .

She tried to rouse herself and said: He *knew* me. . . . Damn it,
he knew me! . . . What's vulgarity to me, Sylvia Tietjens, born
Satterthwaite? I do what I want and that's good enough for anyone.
Except a priest. Vulgarity! I wonder mother could be so obtuse. If

I am vulgar I'm vulgar with a purpose. Then it's not vulgarity. It may be vice. Or viciousness. . . . But if you commit a mortal sin with your eyes open it's not vulgarity. You chance hell fire for ever. . . . Good enough!

The weariness sank over her again and the sense of the father's presence. . . . She was back again in Lobscheid, thirty-six hours free of Perowne with the father and her mother in the dim sitting-room, all antlers, candle-lit, with the father's shadow waving over the pitch-pine walls and ceilings. . . . It was a bewitched place, in the deep forests of Germany. The father himself said it was the last place in Europe to be Christianised. Or perhaps it was never Christianised. . . . That was perhaps why those people, the Germans, coming from those deep, devil-infested woods, did all these wickednesses. Or maybe they were not wicked. . . . One would never know properly. . . . But maybe the father had put a spell on her. . . . His words had never been out of her mind, much. At the back of her brain, as the saying was. . . .

Some man drifted near her and said:

"How do you do, Mrs. Tietjens? Who would have thought of seeing you here?"

She answered:

"I have to look after Christopher now and then." He remained hanging over her with a schoolboy grin for a minute, then he drifted away as an object sinks into deep water. . . . Father Consett again hovered near her. She exclaimed:

"But the real point is, father. . . . Is it sporting? . . . Sporting or whatever it is?" And Father Consett breathed: "Ah! . . ." with his terrible power of arousing doubts. . . . She said:

"When I saw Christopher . . . Last night? . . . Yes, it *was* last night. . . . Turning back to go up that hill. . . . And I had been talking about him to a lot of grinning private soldiers. . . . To *madden* him. . . . You *mustn't* make scenes before the servants. . . . A heavy man, tired . . . come down the hill and lumbering up again. . . . There was a searchlight turned on him just as he turned. . . . I remembered the white bulldog I thrashed on the night before it died. . . . A tired, silent beast . . . With a fat white behind. . . . Tired out . . . You couldn't see its tail because it was turned down, the stump. . . . A great, silent beast. . . . The vet said it had been poisoned with red lead by burglars. . . . It's beastly to die of red lead. . . . It eats up the liver. . . . And you think you're getting

better for a fortnight. And you're always cold . . . freezing in
blood-vessels. . . . And the poor beast had left its kennel to try a
be let into the fire. . . . And I found it at the door when I came
from a dance without Christopher. . . . And got the rhinoceros whi
and lashed into it. There's a pleasure in lashing into a naked whit
beast. . . . Obese and silent, like Christopher. . . . I thought Christopher might . . . That night . . . It went through my head . . . It
hung down its head. . . . A great head, room for a whole British
encyclopædia of misinformation, as Christopher used to put it. It
said: 'What a hope!' . . . As I hope to be saved, though I never
shall be, the dog said: 'What a hope!' . . . Snow-white in quite
black bushes. . . . And it went under a bush. They found it dead
there in the morning. You can't imagine what it looked like, with
its head over its shoulder, as it looked back and said: 'What a hope!'
to me. . . . Under a dark bush. An eu . . . eu . . . euonymus,
isn't it? . . . In thirty degrees of frost with all the blood-vessels exposed on the naked surface of the skin. . . . It's the seventh circle
of hell, isn't it? The frozen one . . . The last stud-white bulldog of
that breed. . . . As Christopher is the last stud-white hope of the
Groby Tory breed. . . . Modelling himself on our Lord. . . . But
our Lord was never married. He never touched on topics of sex. Good
for Him. . . ."

She said: "The ten minutes is up, father . . ." and looked at the
round, starred surface between the diamonds of her wrist watch.
She said: "Good God! . . . Only one minute. . . . I've thought
all that in only a minute. . . . I understand how hell can be an
eternity. . . ."

Christopher, very weary, and ex-Sergeant-Major Cowley, very talkative by now, loomed down between palms. Cowley was saying: "It's
infamous! . . . It's past bearing. . . . To re-order the draft at
eleven. . . ." They sank into chairs. Sylvia extended towards Tietjens a small packet of letters. She said: "You had better look at these.
. . . I had your letters sent to me from the flat as there was so much
uncertainty about your movements. . . ." She found that she did not
dare, under Father Consett's eyes, to look at Tietjens as she said that.
She said to Cowley: "We might be quiet for a minute or two while
the captain reads his letters. . . . Have another liqueur? . . ."

She then observed that Tietjens just bent open the top of the
letter from Mrs. Wannop and then opened that from his brother
Mark:

it," she said, "I've given him what he wants! . . . He . . . He's seen the address . . . that they're still in Bedford . . . He can think of the Wannop girl as there. . . . He has . . . n able to know, till now, where she is. . . . He'll be imagin- . . . nself in bed with her there. . . ."

. . . her Consett, his broad, unmodelled dark face full of intelligence with the blissful unction of the saint and martyr, was leaning . . . r Tietjens' shoulder. . . . He must be breathing down Christo- . . . ler's back as, her mother said, he always did when she held a hand . . . t auction and he could not play because it was between midnight and his celebrating the holy mass.

She said:

"No, I am not going mad. . . . This is an effect of fatigue on the optic nerves. . . . Christopher has explained that to me . . . He says that when his eyes have been very tired with making one of his senior wrangler's calculations he has often seen a woman in an eight- eeth-century dress looking into a drawer in his bureau. . . . Thank God, I've had Christopher to explain things to me. . . . I'll never let him go. . . . Never, never, let him go. . . ."

It was not, however, until several hours later that the significance of the father's apparition came to her and those intervening hours were extraordinarily occupied — with emotions, and even with action. To begin with, before he had read the fewest possible words of his brother's letter, Tietjens looked up over it and said:

"Of course you will occupy Groby. . . . With Michael. . . . Nat- urally the proper business arrangements will be made. . . ." He went on reading the letter, sunk in his chair under the green shade of a lamp. . . .

The letter, Sylvia knew, began with the words: "Your —— of a wife has been to see me with the idea of getting any allowance I might be minded to make you transferred to herself. Of course she can have Groby, for I shan't let it, and could not be bothered with it myself. On the other hand, you may want to live at Groby with that girl and chance the racket. I should if I were you. You would probably find the place worth the — what is it? ostracism, if there was any. But I'm forgetting that the girl is not your mistress unless anything has happened since I saw you. And you probably would want Michael to be brought up at Groby, in which case you couldn't keep the girl there, even if you camouflaged her as governess. At least I think that kind of arrangement always turns out badly: there's bound to be a stink, though Crosby of Ulick did it and nobody much minded. But it was mucky for the Crosby children. Of course if you want your wife to have Groby she must have enough to run it with credit, and expenses are rising damnably. Still, our incomings rise not a little, too, which is not the case with some. The only thing I insist on is that you make plain to that baggage that whatever I allow her, even if it's no end of a hot income, not one penny of it comes out of what I wish you would allow me to allow you. I mean I want you to make plain to that rouged piece — or perhaps it's really natural, my eyes are not what they were — that what you have is absolutely independent of what she sucks up as the mother of our father's heir and to keep our father's heir in the state of life that is his due. I hope you feel satisfied that the boy is your son, for it's more than I should be, looking at the party. But even if he is not he is our father's heir all right and must be so treated.

"But be plain about that, for the trollop came to me, if you please, with the proposal that I should dock you of any income I might propose to allow you — and to which of course you are absolutely entitled under our father's will, though it is no good reminding you of that! — as a token from me that I disapproved of your behaviour when, damn it, there is not an action of yours that I would not be proud to have to my credit. At any rate in this affair, for I cannot help thinking that you could be of more service to the country if you were anywhere else but where you are. But you know what your conscience demands of you better than I and I dare say these hellcats have so mauled you that you are glad to be able to get away into any hole. But don't let yourself die in your hole. Groby will have to be looked after, and even if you do not live there you can keep a strong hand on Sanders, or whoever you elect to have as manager. That monstrosity you honour with your name — which is also mine, thank you! — suggested that if I consented to let her live at Groby she would have her mother to live with her, in which case her mother would be good to look after the estate. I dare say she would, though she has had to let her own place. But then almost everyone else has. She seems anyhow a notable woman, with her head screwed on the right way. I did not tell the discreditable daughter that she — her mother — had come to see me at breakfast immediately after seeing you off, she was so upset. And she *keawert ho down i' th' ingle and had a gradely pow.* You remember how Gobbles the gardener used to say that. A good chap, though he came from Lancasheere! The mother has no illusions about the daughter and is heart and soul for you. She was dreadfully upset at your going, the more so as she believes that it's her offspring has driven you out of the country and that you purpose — isn't stopping one the phrase? Don't do that.

"I saw your girl yesterday. She looked peaky. But of course I have seen her several times, and she always looks peaky. I do not understand why you do not write to them. The mother is clamorous because you have not answered several letters and have not sent her military information she wants for some article she is writing for a Swiss magazine. . . ."

Sylvia knew the letter almost by heart as far as that because in the unbearable white room of the convent near Birkenhead she had twice begun to copy it out, with the idea of keeping the copies for use in some sort of publicity. But, at that point, she had twice been overcome by the idea that it was not a very sporting thing to do, if you really think about it. Besides, the letter after that — she *had* glanced through it — occupied itself almost entirely with the affairs of Mrs. Wannop. Mark, in his naïve way, was concerned that the old lady, although now enjoying the income from the legacy left her by their father, had not immediately settled down to write a deathless novel; although, as he added, he knew nothing about novels. . . .

Christopher was reading away at his letters beneath the green-shaded lamp; the ex-quartermaster had begun several sentences and dropped into demonstrative silence at the reminder that Tietjens was reading. Christopher's face was completely without expression; he might have been reading a return from the office of statistics in the old days at breakfast. She wondered, vaguely, if he would see fit to apologize for the epithets that his brother had applied to her. Probably he would not. He would consider that she having opened the letter must take the responsibility of the contents. Something like that. Thumps and rumbles began to exist in the relative silence. Cowley said: "They're coming again then!" Several couples passed them on the way out of the room. Amongst them there was certainly no presentable man; they were all either too old or too hobbledehoy, with disproportionate noses and vacant, half-opened mouths.

Accompanying Christopher's mind, as it were, whilst he read his letter had induced in her a rather different mood. The pictures in her own mind were rather of Mark's dingy breakfast-room in which she had had her interview with him — and of the outside of the dingy house in which the Wannops lived, at Bedford Park. . . . But she was still conscious of her pact with the father and, looking at her wrist watch, saw that by now six minutes had passed. . . . It was astonishing that Mark, who was a millionaire at least, and probably a good deal more, should live in such a dingy apartment — it had for its chief decoration the hoofs of several deceased race-winners, mounted as ink-stands, as pen-racks, as paper-weights — and afford himself only such a lugubrious breakfast of fat slabs of ham over which bled pallid eggs. . . . For she too, like her mother, had looked in on Mark at breakfast-time — her mother because she had just seen Christopher off to France, and she because, after a sleepless night — the third of a series — she had been walking about St. James's Park and, passing under Mark's windows, it had occurred to her that she might do Christopher some damage by putting his brother wise about the entanglement with Miss Wannop. So, on the spur of the moment, she had invented a desire to live at Groby with the accompanying necessity for additional means. For, although she was a pretty wealthy woman, she was not wealthy enough to live at Groby and keep it up. The immense old place was not so immense because of its room-space, though, as far as she could remember, there must be anything between forty and sixty rooms, but because of the vast old grounds, the warren of stabling, wells, rose-walks, and fencing. . . . A man's place, really, the furniture very grim and the corridors on the ground floor all slabbed with great stones. So she had looked in on Mark, reading his correspondence with his copy of *The Times* airing on a chair-back before the fire — for he was just the man to retain the eighteen-forty idea that you can catch cold by reading a damp news-paper. His grim, tight, brown-wooden features that might have been carved out of an old chair, had expressed no emotion at all during the interview. He had offered to have up some more ham and eggs for her and had asked one or two questions as to how she meant to live at Groby if she went there. Otherwise he had said nothing about the information she had given him as to the Wannop girl having had a baby by Christopher — for purposes of conversation she had adhered to that old story, at any rate till that interview. He had said nothing at all. Not one word. . . . At the end of the interview, when he had risen and produced from an adjoining room a bowler hat and a um-brella, saying that he must now go to his office, he had witthout any expression pretty well what stood in in as business was concerned. He said that she could h she must understand that, his father being now dead an

official, without children and occupied in London with work that
suited him, Groby was practically Christopher's property to do what
he liked with as long as — which he certainly would — he kept it in
proper style. So that, if she wished to live there, she must produce
Christopher's authorization to that effect. And he added, with an
equableness so masking the proposition that it was not until she was
well out of the house and down the street that its true amazingness
took her breath away:

"Of course, Christopher, if what you say is true, might want to
live at Groby with Miss Wannop. In that case he would have to."
And he had offered her an expressionless hand and shepherded her,
rather fussily, through his dingy and awkward front passages that
were lit only from ground-glass windows giving apparently on to his
bathroom. . . .

It wasn't until that moment, really, that, at once with exhilaration
and also with a sinking at the heart, she realised what she was up
against in the way of a combination. For, when she had gone to
Mark's, she had been more than half-maddened by the news that
Christopher at Rouen was in hospital and, although the hospital authorities had assured her, at first by telegram and then by letter, that
it was nothing more than his chest, she had not had any knowledge of
to what extent Red Cross authorities did or did not mislead the relatives of casualties.

So it had seemed natural that she should want to inflict on him
all the injuries that she could at the moment, the thought that he was
probably in pain making her wish to add all she could to that pain.
Otherwise, of course, she would not have gone to Mark's. . . . For
it was a mistake in strategy. But then she said to herself: "Confound
it! . . . What strategy was it a mistake in? What do I care about
strategy? What am I out for? . . ." She did what she wanted to, on
the spur of the moment! . . .

Now she certainly realised. How Christopher had got round Mark
she did not know or much care, but there Christopher certainly was,
although his father had certainly died of a broken heart at the
rumours that were going round about his son — rumours she, almost
as efficiently as the man called Ruggles and more irresponsible gossips, had set going about Christopher. They had been meant to
smash Christopher: they had smashed his father instead. . . . But
Christopher had got round Mark, whom he had not seen for ten
s. . . . Well, he probably would. Christopher was perfectly im-

maculate, that was a fact, and Mark, though he appeared half-witted in a North Country way, was no fool. He could not be a fool. He was a really august public official. And, although as a rule Sylvia gave nothing at all for any public official, if a man like Mark had the position by birth amongst presentable men that he certainly ought to have and was also the head of a department and reputed absolutely indispensable — you could not ignore him. . . . He said, indeed, in the later, more gossipy parts of his letter that he had been offered a baronetcy, but he wanted Christopher to agree with his refusing it. Christopher would not want the beastly title after his death, and for himself he would be rather struck with the pip than let that harlot — meaning herself — become Lady T. by any means of his. He had added, with his queer solicitude, "Of course if you thought of divorcing — which I wish to God you would, though I agree that you are right not to — and the title would go to the girl after my decease I'd take it gladly, for a title is a bit of a help after a divorce. But as it is I propose to refuse it and ask for a knighthood, if it won't too sicken you to have me a Sir. For I hold no man ought to refuse an honour in times like these, as has been done by certain sickening intellectuals because it is like slapping the sovereign in the face and bound to hearten the other side, which no doubt was what was meant by those fellows."

There was no doubt that Mark — with the possible addition of the Wannops — made a very strong backing for Christopher if she decided to make a public scandal about him. . . . As for the Wannops . . . the girl was negligible. Or possibly not, if she turned nasty and twisted Christopher round her fingers. But the old mother was a formidable figure — with a bad tongue, and viewed with a certain respect in places where people talked . . . both on account of her late husband's position and of the solid sort of articles she wrote. . . . She, Sylvia, had gone to take a look at the place where these people lived . . . a dreary street in an outer suburb, the houses — she knew enough about estates to know — what is called tile-healed, the upper parts of tile, the lower flimsy brick and the tiles in bad condition. Oldish houses really, in spite of their sham artistic aspect, and very much shadowed by old trees that must have been left to add to the picturesqueness. The rooms poky, and they must be very dark. . . . The residence of extreme indigence, or of absolute poverty. . . . She understood that the old lady's income had so fallen off during the war that they had nothing to live on but what the girl

made as a school-teacher, or a teacher of athletics in a girls' school.
She had walked two or three times up and down the street with the
idea that the girl might come out, then it had struck her that that
was rather an ignoble proceeding, really. . . . It was, for the matter
of that, ignoble that she should have a rival who starved in an ashbin.
. . . But that was what men were like; she might think herself lucky
that the girl did not inhabit a sweetshop. . . . And the man, Macmaster, said that the girl had a good head and talked well, though the
woman Macmaster said that she was a shallow ignoramus. . . . That
last probably was not true; at any rate the girl had been the Macmaster woman's most intimate friend for many years — as long as
they were sponging on Christopher and until, lower middle-class
snobs as they were, they began to think they could get into Society
by carneying to herself. . . . Still, the girl probably was a good talker
and, if little, yet physically uncommonly fit. A good homespun article. . . . She wished her no ill!

What was incredible was that Christopher should let her go on
starving in such a poverty-stricken place when he had something like
the wealth of the Indies at his disposal. . . . But the Tietjens were
hard people! You could see that in Mark's rooms . . . and Christopher would lie on the floor as lief as in a goose-feather bed. And
probably the girl would not take his money. She was quite right. That
was the way to keep him. . . . She herself had no want of comprehension of the stimulation to be got out of parsimonious living. . . .
In retreat at her convent she lay as hard and as cold as any anchorite,
and rose to the nuns' matins at four.

It was not, in fact, their fittings or food that she objected to — it
was that the lay-sisters, and some of the nuns, were altogether too
much of the lower classes for her to like to have always about her.
. . . That was why it was to the Dames Nobles that she would go, if
she had to go into retreat for the rest of her life, according to contract.

A gun manned by exhilarated anti-aircraft fellows, and so close
that it must have been in the hotel garden, shook her physically at
almost the same moment as an immense maroon popped off on the
quay at the bottom of the street in which the hotel was. She was
filled with annoyance at these schoolby exercises. A tall, purple-faced,
white-moustached general of the more odious type, appeared in the
doorway and said that all the lights but two must be extinguished
and, if they took his advice, they would go somewhere else. There

were good cellars in the hotel. He loafed about the room extinguishing the lights, couples and groups passing him on the way to the door. . . . Tietjens looked up from his letter — he was now reading one of Mrs. Wannop's — but seeing that Sylvia made no motion he remained sunk in his chair.

The old general said:

"Don't get up, Tietjens. . . . Sit down, lieutenant. . . . Mrs. Tietjens, I presume. . . . But of course I know you are Mrs. Tietjens. . . . There's a portrait of you in this week's . . . I forget the name. . . ." He sat down on the arm of a great leather chair and told her of all the trouble her escapade to that city had caused him. . . . He had been awakened immediately after a good lunch by some young officer on his staff who was scared to death by her having arrived without papers. His digestion had been deranged ever since. . . . Sylvia said she was very sorry. He should drink hot water and no alcohol with his lunch. She had had very important business to discuss with Tietjens, and she had really not understood that they wanted papers of grown-up people. The general began to expatiate on the importance of his office and the number of enemy agents his perspicacity caused to be arrested every day in that city and the lines of communication. . . .

Sylvia was overwhelmed at the ingenuity of Father Consett. She looked at her watch. The ten minutes were up, but there did not appear to be a soul in the dim place. . . . The father had — and no doubt as a Sign that there could be no mistaking! — completely emptied that room. It was like his humour!

To make certain, she stood up. At the far end of the room, in the dimness of the one other reading lamp that the general had not extinguished, two figures were rather indistinguishable. She walked towards them, the general at her side extending civilities all over her. He said that she need not be under any apprehension there. He adopted that device of clearing the room in order to get rid of the beastly young subalterns who would use the place to spoon in when the lights were turned down. She said she was only going to get a timetable from the far end of the room. . . .

The stab of hope that she had that one of the two figures would turn out to be the presentable man died. . . . They were a young mournful subaltern, with an incipient moustache and practically tears in his eyes, and an elderly, violently indignant bald-headed man in civilian evening clothes that must have been made by a country tailor. He was smacking his hands together to emphasize what, with great agitation, he was saying.

The general said that it was one of the young cubs on his own staff getting a dressing down from his dad for spending too much money. The young devils would get amongst the girls — and the old ones too. There was no stopping it. The place was a hotbed of . . . He left the sentence unfinished. She would not believe the trouble it gave him. . . . That hotel itself . . . The scandals . . .

He said she would excuse him if he took a little nap in one of the arm-chairs too far away to interfere with their business talk. He would have to be up half the night. He seemed to Sylvia a blazingly contemptible personage — too contemptible really for Father Consett to employ as an agent, in clearing the room. . . . But the omen was given. She had to consider her position. It meant — or did it? — that she had to be at war with the heavenly powers! . . . She clenched her hands. . . .

In passing by Tietjens in his chair the general boomed out the words:

"I got your chit of this morning, Tietjens. . . . I must say . . ."

Tietjens lumbered out of his chair and stood at attention, his leg-of-mutton hands stiffly on the seams of his breeches.

"It's pretty strong," the general said, "marking a charge-sheet sent down from *my* department: *Case explained.* We don't lay charges without due thought. And Lance-Corporal Berry is a particularly reliable N.C.O. I have difficulty enough to get them. Particularly after the late riots. It takes courage, I can tell you."

"If," Tietjens said, "you would see fit, sir, to instruct the G.M.P. not to call Colonial troops damned conscripts, the trouble would be over. . . . We're instructed to use special discretion, as officers, in dealing with troops from the Dominions. They are said to be very susceptible of insult. . . ."

The general suddenly became a boiling pot from which fragments of sentences came away: *damned* insolence; court of inquiry; damned conscripts they were too. He calmed enough to say:

"They *are* conscripts, your men, aren't they? They give me more trouble . . . I should have thought you would have wanted . . ."

Tietjens said:

"No, sir. I have not a man in my unit, as far as it's Canadian or British Columbian, that is not voluntarily enlisted. . . ."

The general exploded to the effect that he was bringing the whole matter before the G.O.C.I.C.'s department. Campion could deal with it how he wished: it was beyond himself. He began to bluster away from them, stopped, directed a frigid bow to Sylvia who was not looking at him, shrugged his shoulders and stormed off.

It was difficult for Sylvia to get hold again of her thoughts in the smoking-room, for the evening was entirely pervaded with military effects that seemed to her the pranks of schoolboys. Indeed, after Cowley, who had by now quite a good skinful of liquor, had said to Tietjens: "By Jove, I would not like to be you and a little bit on if old Blazes caught sight of you to-night," she said to Tietjens with real wonder:

"You don't mean to say that a gaga old fool like that could have any possible influence over you . . . *You!*"

Tietjens said:

"Well, it's a troublesome business, all this. . . ."

She said that it so appeared to be, for before he could finish his sentence an orderly was at his elbow extending, along with a pencil, a number of dilapidated papers. Tietjens looked rapidly through them, signing one after the other and saying intermittently:

"It's a trying time."

"We're massing troops up the line as fast as we can go."

"And with an endlessly changing personnel. . . ." He gave a snort of exasperation and said to Cowley: "That horrible little Pitkins has got a job as bombing instructor. He can't march the draft. . . . Who the deuce am I to detail? Who the deuce is there? . . . You know all the little . . ." He stopped because the orderly could hear. A smart boy. Almost the only smart boy left him.

Cowley barged out of his seat and said he would telephone to the mess to see who was there. . . . Tietjens said to the boy:

"Sergeant-Major Morgan made out these returns of religions in the draft?"

The boy answered: "No, sir, I did. They're all right." He pulled a slip of paper out of his tunic pocket and said shyly:

"If you would not mind signing this, sir . . . I can get a lift on an A.S.C. trolley that's going to Boulogne to-morrow at six. . . ."

Tietjens said:

"No, you can't have leave. I can't spare you. What's it for?"

The boy said almost inaudibly that he wanted to get married.

Tietjens, still signing, said: "Don't. . . . Ask your married pals what it's like!"

The boy, scarlet in his khaki, rubbed the sole of one foot on the instep of the other. He said that saving madam's presence it was urgent. It was expected any day now. She was a real good gel. Tietjens signed the boy's slip and handed it to him without looking up. The boy stood with his eyes on the ground. A diversion came from the telephone, which was at the far end of the room. Cowley had not been able to get on to the camp because an urgent message with regard to German espionage was coming through to the sleeping general.

Cowley began to shout: "For goodness' sake hold the line. . . . For goodness' sake hold the line. . . . I'm not the general. . . . I'm *not* the general. . . ." Tietjens told the orderly to awaken the sleeping warrior. A violent scene at the mouth of the quiescent instrument took place. The general roared to know who was the officer speaking. Captain Bubbleyjocks. . . . Captain Cuddlestocks . . . what in hell's name! And who was he speaking for? . . . Who? Himself? . . . Urgent was it? . . . Didn't he know the proper procedure was by writing? . . . Urgent damnation! . . . Did he not know where he was? . . . In the First Army by the Cassell Canal. . . . Well then . . . But the spy was in L. of C. territory, across the canal. . . . The French civilian authorities were very concerned. . . . They were, damn them! . . . And damn the officer. And damn the French *maire*. And damn the horse the supposed spy rode upon. . . . And when the officer was damned let him write to First Army Headquarters about it and attach the horse and the bandoliers as an exhibit.

There was a great deal more of it. Tietjens reading his papers still, intermittently explained the story as it came in fragments over the telephone in the general's repetitions. . . . Apparently the French civilian authorities of a place called Warendonck had been alarmed by a solitary horseman in English uniform who had been wandering desultorily about their neighbourhood for several days, seeming to want to cross the canal bridges, but finding them guarded. There was an immense artillery dump in the neighbourhood, said to be the largest in the world, and the Germans dropped bombs as thick as peas all over those parts in the hopes of hitting it. . . . Apparently the officer speaking was in charge of the canal bridgehead guards; but, as he was in First Army country, it was obviously an act of the utmost impropriety to awaken a general in charge of the spy-catching apparatus on the other side of the canal. . . . The general, returning past them to an arm-chair farther from the telephone, emphasized this point of view with great vigour.

The orderly had returned; Cowley went once more to the telephone, having consumed another liqueur brandy. Tietjens finished his papers and went through them rapidly again. He said to the boy: "Got anything saved up?" The boy said: "A fiver and a few bob." Tietjens said: "How many bob?" The boy: "Seven, sir." Tietjens, fumbling clumsily in an inner pocket and a little pocket beneath his belt, held out one leg-of-mutton fist and said: "There! That will double it. Ten pounds fourteen! But it's very improvident of you. See that you save up a deuced lot more against the next one. Accouchements are confoundedly expensive things, as you'll learn, and ring money doesn't stretch for ever! . . ." He called out to the retreating boy: "Here, orderly, come back. . . ." He added: "Don't let it get all over camp. I can't afford to subsidise all the seven-months children in the battalion. . . . I'll recommend you for paid lance-corporal when you return from leave if you go on as well as you have done." He called the boy back again to ask him why Captain McKechnie had not signed the papers. The boy stuttered and stammered that Captain McKechnie was . . . He was . . .

Tietjens muttered: "Good God!" beneath his breath. He said: "The captain has had another nervous breakdown. . . ." The orderly accepted the phrase with gratitude. That was it. A nervous breakdown. They say he had been very queer at mess. About divorce. Or the captain's uncle. A barrow-night! Tietjens said: "Yes, yes." He half rose in his chair and looked at Sylvia. She exclaimed painfully.

"You can't go. I insist that you can't go." He sank down again and muttered wearily that it was very worrying. He had been put in charge of this officer by General Campion. He ought not to have left the camp at all, perhaps. But McKechnie had seemed better. A great deal of the calmness of her insolence had left her. She had expected to have the whole night in which luxuriously to torment the lump opposite her. To torment him and to allure him. She said:

"You have settlements to come to now and here that will affect your whole life. Our whole lives! You propose to abandon them because a miserable little nephew of your miserable little friend. . . ." She added in French: "Even as it is you cannot pay any attention to these serious matters, because of these childish preoccupations of yours. That is to be intolerably insulting to me!" She was breathless.

Tietjens asked the orderly where Captain McKechnie was now. The orderly said he had left the camp. The colonel of the depot had sent a couple of officers as a search-party. Tietjens told the orderly to go and find a taxi. He could have a ride himself up to camp. The orderly said taxis would not be running on account of the air-raid. Could he order the G.M.P. to requisition one on urgent military service? The exhilarated air-gun pooped off thereupon three times from the garden. For the next hour it went off every two or three minutes. Tietjens said: "Yes! Yes!" to the orderly. The noises of the air-raid became more formidable. A blue express letter of French civilian make was handed to Tietjens. It was from the duchess to inform him that coal for the use of greenhouses was forbidden by the French Government. She did not need to say that she relied on his honour to ensure her receiving her coal through the British military authority, and she asked for an immediate reply. Tietjens expressed real annoyance while he read this. Distracted by the noise, Sylvia cried out that the letter must be from Valentine Wannop in Rouen. Did not the girl intend to let him have an hour in which to settle the whole business of his life? Tietjens moved to the chair next to hers. He handed her the duchess's letter.

He began a long, slow, serious explanation with a long, slow, serious apology. He said he regretted very much that when she should have taken the trouble to come so far in order to do him the honour to consult him about a matter which she would have been perfectly at liberty to settle for herself, the extremely serious military position should render him so liable to interruption. As far as he was concerned Groby was entirely at her disposal with all that it contained. And of course a sufficient income for the upkeep.

She exclaimed in an access of sudden and complete despair:

"That means that you do not intend to live there." He said that that must settle itself later. The war would no doubt last a good deal longer. While it lasted there could be no question of his coming back. She said that that meant that he intended to get killed. She warned him that, if he got killed, she should cut down the great cedar at the south-west corner of Groby. It kept all the light out of the principal drawing-room and the bed-rooms above it. . . . He winced; he certainly winced at that. She regretted that she had said it. It was along other lines that she desired to make him wince.

He said that, apart from his having no intention of getting himself killed, the matter was absolutely out of his hands. He had to go where he was ordered to go and do what he was told to do.

She exclaimed:

"You! *You!* Isn't it ignoble. That you should be at the beck and call of these ignoramuses. You!"

He went on explaining seriously that he was in no great danger — in no danger at all unless he was sent back to his battalion. And he was not likely to be sent back to his battalion unless he disgraced himself or showed himself negligent where he was. That was unlikely. Besides his category was so low that he was not eligible for his battalion, which, of course, was in the line. She ought to understand that everyone that she saw employed there was physically unfit for the line. She said:

"That's why they're such an awful lot. . . . It is not to this place that one should come to look for a presentable man. . . . Diogenes with his lantern was nothing to it."

He said:

"There's that way of looking at it. . . . It is quite true that most of . . . let's say *your* friends . . . were killed off during the early days, or if they're still going they're in more active employments." What she called presentableness was very largely a matter of physical fitness. . . . The horse, for instance, that he rode was rather a crock. . . . But though it was German and not thoroughbred it contrived to be up to his weight. . . . Her friends, more or less, of before the war were professional soldiers or of the type. Well, they were gone: dead or snowed under. But on the other hand, this vast town full of crocks did keep the thing going, if it could be made to go. It was not they that hindered the show; if it was hindered, that was done by her much less presentable friends, the ministry who, if they were professionals at all were professional boodlers.

She exclaimed with bitterness:

"Then why didn't you stay at home to check them, if they *are* boodlers." She added that the only people at home who kept social matters going at all with any life were precisely the more successful political professionals. When you were with them you would not know there was any war. And wasn't that what was wanted? Was the *whole* of life to be given up to ignoble horseplay? . . . She spoke with increased rancour because of the increasing thump and rumble of the air-raid. . . . Of course the politicians were ignoble beings that, before the war, you would not have thought of having in your house. . . . But whose fault was that, if not that of the better classes, who had gone away leaving England a dreary wilderness of fellows without consciences or traditions or manners? And she added some details of the habits at a country house of a member of the Government whom she disliked. "And," she finished up, "it's your fault. Why aren't *you* Lord Chancellor, or Chancellor of the Exchequer, instead of whoever is, for I am sure I don't know? You could have been, with your abilities and your interests. Then things would have been efficiently and honestly conducted. If your brother Mark, with not a tithe of your abilities can be a permanent head of a department, what could you not have risen to with your gifts, and your influence . . . and your integrity?" And she ended up: "Oh, Christopher!" on almost a sob.

Ex-Sergeant-Major Cowley, who had come back from the telephone, and during an interval in the thunderings, had heard some of Sylvia's light cast on the habits of members of the home Government, so that his jaw had really hung down, now, in another interval, exclaimed:

"Hear, hear! Madam! . . . There is nothing the captain might not have risen to. . . . He is doing the work of a brigadier now on the pay of an acting captain. . . . And the treatment he gets is scandalous. . . . Well, the treatment we all get is scandalous, tricked and defrauded as we are all at every turn. . . . And look at this new start with the draft. . . ." They had ordered the draft to be ready and countermanded it, and ordered it to be ready and countermanded it, until no one knew whether he stood on 'is 'ed or 'is 'eels. . . . It was to have gone off last night: when they'd 'ad it marched down to the station they 'ad it marched back and told them all it would not be wanted for six weeks. . . . Now it was to be got ready to go before daylight to-morrow morning in motor-lorries to the rail Ondekoeter way, the rail here 'aving been sabotaged! . . . Before daylight so that the enemy aeroplanes should not see it on the road. . . . Wasn't that a thing to break the 'earts of men *and* horderly rooms? It was outrageous. Did they suppose the 'Uns did things like that?

He broke off to say with husky enthusiasm of affection to Tietjens: "Look 'ere old . . . I mean, sir . . . There's *no* way of getting hold of an officer to march the draft. Them as are eligible gets to 'ear of what drafts is going and they've all bolted into their burries. Not a man of 'em will be back in camp before five to-morrow morning. Not when they 'ears there's a draft to go at four of mornings like this. . . . Now . . ." His voice became husky with emotion as he offered to take the draft hisself to oblige Captain Tietjens. And the captain knew he could get a draft off pretty near as good as himself, or very near. As for the draft-conducting major he lived in that hotel and he, Cowley, 'ad seen 'im. No four in the morning for 'im. He was going to motor to Ondekoeter Station about seven. So there was no sense in getting the draft off before five, and it was still dark then — too dark for the 'Un planes to see what was moving. He'd be glad if the captain would be up at the camp by five to take a final look and to sign any papers that only the commanding officer could sign. But he knew the captain had had no sleep the night before because of his, Cowley's, infirmity, mostly, so he couldn't do less than give up a day and a half of his leave to taking the draft. Besides, he was going home for the duration and he would not mind getting a look at the old places they'd seen in 'fourteen, for the last time as a Cook's tourist. . . .

Tietjens, who was looking noticeably white, said:

"Do you remember O Nine Morgan at Noircourt?"

Cowley said:

"No. . . . Was 'e there? In your company, I suppose? . . . The man you mean that was killed yesterday. Died in your arms owing to my oversight. I ought to have been there." He said to Sylvia with the gloating idea N.C.O.s had that wives liked to hear of their husband's near escapes: "Killed within a foot of the captain, 'e was. An 'orrible shock it must 'ave been for the captain." A horrible mess . . . The captain held him in his arms while he died, as if he'd been a baby. Wonderful tender, the captain was! Well, you're apt to be when it's one of your own men. . . . No rank then! "Do you know the only time the King must salute a private soldier and the private takes no notice? . . . When 'e's dead. . . ."

Both Sylvia and Tietjens were silent — and silvery white in the greenish light from the lamp. Tietjens indeed had shut his eyes. The old N.C.O. went on rejoicing to have the floor to himself. He had got on his feet preparatory to going up to camp, and he swayed a little. . . .

"No," he said and he waved his cigar gloriously, "I don't remember O Nine Morgan at Noircourt. . . . But I remember . . ."

Tietjens, with his eyes still shut, said:

"I only thought he might have been a man. . . ."

"No," the old fellow went on imperiously, "I don't remember 'im. . . . But, Lord, I remember what happened to *you!*" He looked

down gloriously upon Sylvia: "The captain caught 'is foot in. . . .
You'd never believe what 'e caught 'is foot in! Never! . . . A pretty
quiet affair it was, with a bit of moonlight. Nothing much in the
way of artillery. . . . Perhaps we surprised the 'Uns proper, perhaps
they were wanting to give up their front-line trenches for a purpose. . . . There was next to no one in 'em. . . . I know it made
me nervous. . . . My heart was fair in my boots, because there was
so little doing! It was when there was little doing that the 'Uns
could be expected to do their worst. . . . Of course there was some
machine-gunning. . . . There was one in particular away to the
right of us. . . . And the moon, it was shining in the early morning. Wonderful peaceful. And a little mist . . . and frozen hard
. . . hard as you wouldn't believe. . . . Enough to make the shells
dangerous."

Sylvia said:

"It's not always mud, then?" and Tietjens, to her: "He'll stop if
you don't like it." She said monotonously: "No . . . I want to hear."

Cowley drew himself up for his considerable effect:

"Mud!" he said. "Not then . . . Not by half. . . . I tell you,
ma'am, we trod on the frozen faces of dead Germans as we doubled.
. . . A terrible lot of Germans we'd killed a day or so before. . . .
That was no doubt the reason they give up the trenches so easy;
difficult to attack from, they was. . . . Anyhow, they left the dead for
us to bury, knowing probably they were going, with a better 'eart!
. . . But it fair put the wind up me anyhow to think of what their
counter-attack was going to be. . . . The counter-attack is always
ten times as bad as the preliminary resistance. They 'as you with
the rear of their trenches — the parados, we call it — as your front
to boot. So I was precious glad when the moppers-up and supports
come and went through us. Laughing, they was — Wiltshires. . . .
My missus comes from that county. . . . Mrs. Cowley, I mean. . . .
So I'd seen the captain go down earlier on and I'd said: 'There's
another of the best stopped one. . . .'" He dropped his voice a little;
he was one of the noted yarners of the regiment: "Caught 'is foot,
'e 'ad, between two 'ands . . . Sticking up out of the frozen ground
. . . As it might be in prayer . . . like this!" He elevated his two
hands, the cigar between the fingers, the wrists close together and
the fingers slightly curled inwards: "Sticking up in the moonlight.
. . . Poor devil!"

Tietjens said:

"I thought perhaps it was O Nine Morgan I saw that night.
. . . Naturally I looked dead. . . . I hadn't a breath in my body.
. . . And I saw a Tommy put his rifle to his pal's upper arm and
fire. . . . As I lay on the ground. . . ."

Cowley said:

"Ah, you saw that . . . I heard the men talking of it. . . . But
they naturally did not say who and where!"

Tietjens said with a negligence that did not ring true:

"The wounded man's name was Stilicho. . . . A queer name . . .
I suppose it's Cornish. . . . It was B Company in front of us."

"You didn't bring 'em to a court martial?" Cowley asked. Tietjens
said: No. He could not be quite certain. Though he *was* certain.
But he had been worrying about a private matter. He had been
worrying about it while he lay on the ground and that rather obscured his sense of what he saw. Besides, he said faintly, an officer
must use his judgment. He had judged it better in this case not to
have seen the . . . His voice had nearly faded away. It was clear
to Sylvia that he was coming to a climax of some mental torture.
Suddenly he exclaimed to Cowley:

"Supposing I let him off one life to get him killed two years
after. My God! That would be too beastly!"

Cowley snuffled in Tietjens' ear something that Sylvia did not
catch — consolatory and affectionate. That intimacy was more than
she could bear. She adopted her most negligent tone to ask:

"I suppose the one man had been trifling with the other's girl. Or
wife!"

Cowley exploded: "God bless you, no! They'd agreed upon it between them. To get one of them sent 'ome and the other, at any
rate, out of *that* 'ell, leading him back to the dressing-station." She
said:

"You mean to say that a man would do *that*, to get out of it? . . ."

Cowley said:

"God bless you, ma'am, with the *'ell* the Tommies 'as of it. . . .
For it's in the line that the difference between the Other Ranks' life
and the officers' comes in. . . . I tell you, ma'am, old soldier as I
am, and I've been in seven wars one with another . . . there were
times in this war when I could have shrieked, holding my right
hand down. . . ."

He paused and said: "It was my idea. . . . And it's been a good
many others', that if I 'eld my 'and up over the parapet with perhaps

my hat on it, in two minutes there would be a German sharpshooter's bullet through it. And then me for Blighty, as the soldiers say. . . . And if that could happen to me, a regimental sergeant-major, with twenty-three years in the service . . ."

The bright orderly came in, said he had found a taxi, and melted into the dimness.

"A man," the sergeant-major said, "would take the risk of being shot for wounding his pal. . . . They get to love their pals, passing the love of women. . . ." Sylvia exclaimed: "Oh!" as if at a pang of toothache. "They do, ma'am," he said, "it's downright touch-ing. . . ."

He was by now very unsteady as he stood, but his voice was quite clear. That was the way it took him. He said to Tietjens:

"It's queer, what you say about home worries taking up your mind. . . . I remember in the Afghan campaign, when we were in the devil of a hot corner, I got a letter from my wife, Mrs. Cowley, to say that our Winnie had the measles. . . . And there was only one difference between me and Mrs. Cowley: I said that a child must have flannel next its skin, and she said flannelette was good enough. Wiltshire doesn't hold by wool as Lincolnshire does. Long fleeces the Lincolnshire sheep have. . . . And dodging the Afghan bullets all day among the boulders as we was, all I could think of . . . For you know, ma'am, being a mother yourself, that the great thing with measles is to keep a child warm. . . . I kep' saying to myself — 'arf crying I was — 'If she only keeps wool next Winnie's skin! If she only keeps wool next Winnie's skin!' . . . But you know that, being a mother yourself. I've seen your son's photo on the captain's dressing-table. Michael, 'is name is. . . . So you see, the captain doesn't forget you and 'im."

Sylvia said in a clear voice:

"Perhaps you would not go on!"

Distracted as she was by the anti-air-gun in the garden, though it was on the other side of the hotel and permitted you to get in a sentence or two before splitting your head with a couple of irregular explosions, she was still more distracted by a sudden vision — a re-membrance of Christopher's face when their boy had had a tem-perature of 105° with the measles, up at his sister's house in York-shire. He had taken the responsibility, which the village doctor would not face, of himself placing the child in a bath full of split ice. . . . She saw him bending, expressionless in the strong lamp-light, with the child in his clumsy arms over the glittering, rubbled surface of the bath. He was just as expressionless then as now. . . . He reminded her now of how he had been then: some strain in the lines of the face perhaps that she could not analyse. . . . Rather as if he had a cold in the head — a little suffocating, with suppressing his emotions, of course; his eyes looking at nothing. You would not have said that he even saw the child — heir to Groby and all that! . . . Something had said to her, just in between two crashes of the gun "It's his own child. He went as you might say down to hell to bring it back to life. . . ." She knew it was Father Consett saying that. She knew it was true: Christopher had been down to hell to bring the child back. . . . Fancy facing its pain in that dreadful bath! . . . The thermometer had dropped, running down under their eyes. . . . Christopher had said: "A good heart, he's got! A good plucked one!" and then held his breath, watching the thin filament of bright mercury drop to normal. . . . She said now, between her teeth: "The child is his property as much as the damned estate. . . . Well, I've got them both. . . ."

But it wasn't at this juncture that she wanted him tortured over that. So, when the second gun had done its crash, she had said to the bibulous old man:

"I wish you would not go on!" And Christopher had been prompt to the rescue of the *convenances* with:

"Mrs. Tietjens does not see eye to eye with us in some matters!"

She said to herself: "Eye to eye! My God! . . ." The whole of this affair, the more she saw of it, overwhelmed her with a sense of hatred. . . . And of depression! She saw Christopher buried in this welter of fools, playing a schoolboy's game of make-believe. But of a make-believe that was infinitely formidable and infinitely sinister. . . . The crashings of the gun and of all the instruments for making noise seemed to her so atrocious and odious because they were, for her, the silly pomp of a schoolboy-man's game. . . . Campion, or some similar schoolboy, said: "Hullo! Some German airplanes about . . . That lets us out on the air-gun! Let's have some pops!" . . . As they fire guns in the park on the King's birthday. It was sheer insolence to have a gun in the garden of an hotel where people of quality might be sleeping or wishing to converse!

At home she had been able to sustain the conviction that it was such a game. . . . Anywhere: at the house of a minister of the Crown, at dinner, she had only to say: "Do let us leave off talking

of these odious things. . . ." And immediately there would be ten
or a dozen voices, the minister's included, to agree with Mrs. Tietjens of Groby that they had altogether too much of it.

But here! . . . She seemed to be in the very belly of the ugly
affair. . . . It moved and moved, under your eyes dissolving, yet
always there. As if you should try to follow one diamond of pattern
in the coil of an immense snake that was in irrevocable motion. . . .
It gave her a sense of despair: the engrossment of Tietjens, in common with the engrossment of this disreputable toper. She had never
seen Tietjens put his head together with any soul before; he was
the lonely buffalo. . . . Now! Anyone, any fatuous staff-officer, whom
at home he would never so much as have spoken to; any trustworthy beer-sodden sergeant, any street urchin dressed up as orderly.
. . . They had only to appear and all his mind went into a close-
headed conference over some ignoble point in the child's game: the
laundry, the chiropody, the religions, the bastards . . . of millions
of the indistinguishable. . . . Or their deaths as well! But, in
heaven's name what hypocrisy, or what inconceivable chicken-
heartedness was this? They promoted this beanfeast of carnage for
their own ends; they caused the deaths of men in inconceivable holo-
causts of pain and terror. Then they had crises of agony over the
death of one single man. For it was plain to her that Tietjens was
in the middle of a full nervous breakdown. Over one man's death!
She had never seen him so suffer; she had never seen him so appeal
for sympathy — him, a cold fiend of reticence! Yet he was now in
an agony! *Now!* . . . And she began to have a sense of the infinitely
spreading welter of pain, going away to an eternal horizon of night.
. . . 'Ell for the Other Ranks! Apparently it was hell for the officers as well.

The real compassion in the voice of that snuffling, half-drunken
old man had given her a sense of that enormous wickedness. . . .
These horrors, these infinities of pain, this atrocious condition of the
world had been brought about in order that men should indulge
themselves in orgies of promiscuity. That in the end was at the bottom of male honour, of male virtue, observance of treaties, up-
holding of the flag. . . . An immense warlock's carnival of appetites,
lusts, ebrieties. . . . And once set in motion there was no stopping
it. This state of things would never cease. . . . Because once they
had tasted of the joy — the blood — of this game, who would let it
end? These men talked of these things that occupied them there

with the lust of men telling dirty stories in smoking-rooms. . . .
That was the only parallel!

There was no stopping it, any more than there was any stopping
the by now all but intoxicated ex-sergeant-major. He was off! With,
as might be expected, advice to a young couple with differences of
opinion! The wine had made him bold!

In the depth of her pictures of these horrors, snatches of his wisdom penetrated to her intelligence. . . . Queer snatches. . . . She
was getting it certainly in the neck! . . . Someone, to add to the
noise, had started some mechanical musical instrument in an adja-
cent hall.

> "Corn an' lasses
> Served by Ras'us!"

a throaty voice proclaimed,

> "I'd be tickled to death to know that I could go
> And stay right there . . ."

The ex-sergeant-major was adding to her knowledge the odd detail
that when he, Sergeant-Major Cowley, went to the wars — seven of
them — his missus, Mrs. Cowley spent the first three days and nights
unpicking and re-hemstitching every sheet and pillow-slip in the
'ouse. To keep 'erself f'm thinking . . . This was apparently meant
as a reproof or an exhortation to her, Sylvia Tietjens. . . . Well, he
was all right! Of the same class as Father Consett, and with the
same sort of wisdom.

The gramophone howled; a new note of rumbling added itself
to the exterior tumult and continued through six mitigated thumps
of the gun in the garden. . . . In the next interval, Cowley was in
the midst of a valedictory address to her. He was asking her to remember that the captain had had a sleepless night before.

There occurred to her irreverent mind a sentence of one of the
Duchess of Marlborough's letters to Queen Anne. The duchess had
visited the general during one of his campaigns in Flanders. "My
Lord," she wrote, "did me the honour three times in his boots!" . . .
The sort of thing she would remember. . . . She would — she *would*
— have tried it on the sergeant-major, just to see Tietjens' face, for
the sergeant-major would not have understood. . . . And who cared
if he did! . . . He was bibulously skirting round the same idea.

But the tumult increased to an incredible volume: even the thrill-ings of the near-by gramophone of two hundred horse-power, or whatever it was, became mere shimmerings of a gold thread in a drab fabric of sound. She screamed blasphemies that she was hardly aware of knowing. She had to scream against the noise; she was no more responsible for the blasphemy than if she had lost her identity under an anæsthetic. She *had* lost her identity. . . . She was one of this crowd!

The general woke in his chair and gazed malevolently at their group as if they alone were responsible for the noise. It dropped. Dead! You only knew it, because you caught the tail end of a belated woman's scream from the hall and the general shouting: "For God's sake don't start that damned gramophone again!" In the blessed silence, after preliminary wheezings and guitar noises an astonishing voice burst out:

> "Less than the dust . . .
> Before thy char . . ."

And then, stopping after a murmur of voices, began:

> "Pale hands I loved . . ."

The general sprang from his chair and rushed to the hall. . . . He came back crestfallenly.

"It's some damned civilian big-wig. . . . A novelist, they say. . . . I can't stop *him*. . . ." He added with disgust: "The hall's full of young beasts and harlots. . . . *Dancing!*" The melody had indeed, after a buzz, changed to a languorous and interrupted variation of a waltz. "Dancing in the dark!" the general said with enhanced disgust. . . . "And the Germans may be here at any moment. . . . If they knew what I know! . . ."

Sylvia called across to him:

"Wouldn't it be fun to see the blue uniform with the silver buttons again and some decently set-up men? . . ."

The general shouted:

"*I'd* be glad to see them. . . . I'm sick to death of these. . . ."

Tietjens took up something he had been saying to Cowley. What it was Sylvia did not hear, but Cowley answered, still droning on with an idea Sylvia thought they had got past:

"I remember when I was sergeant in Quetta, I detailed a man — called Herring — for watering the company horses, after he begged off it because he had a fear of horses. . . . A horse got him down in the river and drowned 'im. . . . Fell with him and put its foot on his face. . . . A fair sight he was. . . . It wasn't any good my saying anything about military exigencies. . . . Fair put me off my feed, it did. . . . Cost me a fortune in Epsom salts. . . ."

Sylvia was about to scream out that if Tietjens did not like men being killed it ought to sober him in his war-lust, but Cowley continued meditatively:

"Epsom salts they say is the cure for it. . . . For seeing your dead . . . And of course you should keep off women for a fortnight. . . . I know I did. Kept seeing Herring's face with the hoof-mark. And . . . there was a piece, a decent bit of goods in what we called the Government Compound. . . ."

He suddenly exclaimed:

"Saving your . . . Ma'am, I'm . . ." He stuck the stump of the cigar into his teeth and began assuring Tietjens that he could be trusted with the draft next morning, if only Tietjens would put him into the taxi.

He went away, leaning on Tietjens' arm, his legs at an angle of sixty degrees with the carpet. . . .

"He can't . . ." Sylvia said to herself, "he can't, not . . . if he's a gentleman. . . . After all that old fellow's hints. . . . He'd be a damn coward if he kept off. . . . For a fortnight . . . And who else is there not a public . . ." She said: "O God! . . ."

The old general, lying in his chair, turned his face aside to say:

"I wouldn't, madam, not if I were you, talk about the blue uniform with silver buttons here. . . . We, of course, understand. . . ."

To herself she said: "You see . . . even that extinct volcano . . . He's undressing me with his eyes full of blood veins. . . . Then why can't *he*? . . ."

She said aloud:

"Oh, but even you, general, said you were sick of your companions!"

She said to herself:

"Hang it! . . . I will have the courage of my convictions. . . . No man shall say I am a coward. . . ."

She said:

"Isn't it saying the same thing as you, general, to say that I'd rather be made love to by a well-set-up man in blue and silver — or anything else! — than by most of the people one sees here! . . ."

The general said:

"Of course, if you put it that way, madam. . . ."

She said:

"What other way should a woman put it?" . . . She reached to the table and filled herself a lot of brandy. The old general was leering towards her:

"Bless me," he said, "a lady who takes liquor like that . . ."

She said:

"You're a Papist, aren't you? With the name of O'Hara and the touch of the brogue you have . . . And the devil you no doubt are with . . . You know what. . . . Well, then . . . It's with a special intention! . . . As you say your Hail, Maries . . ."

With the liquor burning inside her she saw Tietjens loom in the dim light.

The general, to her bitter amusement, said to him:

"Your friend was more than a bit on. . . . Not the society surely for madam!"

Tietjens said:

"I never expected to have the pleasure of dining with Mrs. Tietjens to-night. . . . That officer was celebrating his commission and I could not put him off. . . ." The general said: "Oh, ah! . . . Of course not. . . . I dare say . . ." and settled himself again in his chair.

Tietjens was overwhelming her with his great bulk. She had still lost her breath. . . . He stooped over and said: It was the luck of the half-drunk:

"They're dancing in the lounge. . . ."

She coiled herself passionately into her wickerwork. It had dull blue cushions. She said:

"Not with anyone else. . . . I don't want any introductions. . . ." Fiercely! . . . He said:

"There's no one there that I could introduce you to. . . ."

She said:

"Not if it's a charity!"

He said:

"I thought it might be rather dull. . . . It's six months since I danced. . . ." She felt beauty flowing over all her limbs. She had a gown of gold tissue. Her matchless hair was coiled over her ears. She was humming Venusberg music; she knew music if she knew nothing else. . . .

She said: "You call the compounds where you keep the

Waacs Venusberg's, don't you? Isn't it queer that Venus should be your own? . . . Think of poor Elisabeth!"

The room where they were dancing was very dark. . . . It was queer to be in his arms. . . . She had known better dancers. . . . He had looked ill. . . . Perhaps he was. . . . Oh, poor Valentine-Elisabeth. . . . What a funny position! . . . The good gramophone played. . . . *Destiny!* . . . . You see, father! . . . In his arms! Of course, dancing is not really. . . . But so near the real thing! So near! . . . "Good luck to the special intention! . . ." She had almost kissed him on the lips. . . . All but! . . . *Effleurer,* the French call it. . . . But she was not as humble. . . . He had pressed her tighter. . . . All these months without . . . My lord did me honour . . . Good for Malbrouck *s'en va-t-en guerre.* . . . He *knew* she had almost kissed him on the lips. . . . And that his lips had almost responded. . . . The civilian, the novelist, had turned out the last light. . . . Tietjens said, "Hadn't we better talk? . . ." She said: "In my room, then! I'm dog-tired. . . . I haven't slept for six nights. . . . In spite of drugs. . . ." He said: "Yes. Of course! Where else? . . ." Astonishingly. . . . Her gown of gold tissue was like the colobium sidonis the King wore at the coronation. . . . As they mounted the stairs she thought what a fat tenor Tannhäuser always was! . . . The Venusberg music was dinning in her ears. . . . She said: "Sixty-six inexpressibles! I'm as sober as a judge . . . I need to be!"

Part Three

A SHADOW — the shadow of the General Officer Commanding
in Chief — falling across the bar of light that the sunlight
threw in at his open door seemed providentially to awaken
Christopher Tietjens, who would have thought it extremely disagreeable to be found asleep by that officer. Very thin, graceful, and
gay with his scarlet and gilt oak-leaves, and ribbons, of which he had
many, the general was stepping attractively over the sill of the door,
talking backwards over his shoulder, to someone outside. So, in the
old days, Gods had descended! It was, no doubt, really the voices
from without that had awakened Tietjens, but he preferred to think
the matter a slight intervention of Providence, because he felt in
need of a sign of some sort! Immediately upon awakening he was not
perfectly certain of where he was, but he had sense enough to answer
with coherence the first question that the general put to him and
to stand stiffly on his legs. The general had said:

"Will you be good enough to inform me, Captain Tietjens, why
you have no fire-extinguishers in your unit? You are aware of the
extremely disastrous consequences that would follow a conflagration
in your lines?"

Tietjens said stiffly:

"It seems impossible to obtain them, sir."

The general said:

"How is this? You have indented for them in the proper quarter.
Perhaps you do not know what the proper quarter is?"

Tietjens said:

"If this were a British unit, sir, the proper quarter would be the

444

Royal Engineers." When he had sent his indent in for them to the
Royal Engineer they informed him that this being a unit of troops
from the Dominions, the quarter to which to apply was the Ordnance. On applying to the Ordnance, he was informed that no provision was made of fire-extinguishers for troops from the Dominions
under Imperial officers, and that the proper course was to obtain
them from a civilian firm in Great Britain, charging them against
barrack damages. . . . He had applied to several firms of manufacturers, who all replied that they were forbidden to sell these articles
to anyone but to the War Office direct. . . . "I am still applying
to civilian firms," he finished.

The officer accompanying the general was Colonel Levin, to whom,
over his shoulder, the general said: "Make a note of that, Levin,
will you? And get the matter looked into." He said again to Tietjens:

"In walking across your parade-ground I noticed that your officer
in charge of your physical training knew conspicuously nothing
about it. You had better put him on to cleaning out your drains. He
was unreasonably dirty."

Tietjens said:

"The sergeant-instructor, sir, is quite competent. The officer is
an R.A.S.C. officer. I have at the moment hardly any infantry officers in the unit. But officers have to be on these parades — by A.C.I.
They give no orders."

The general said drily:

"I was aware from the officer's uniform of what arm he belonged
to. I am not saying you do not do your best with the material at
your command." From Campion on parade this was an extraordinary graciousness. Behind the general's back Levin was making signs
with his eyes which he meaningly closed and opened. The general,
however, remained extraordinarily dry in manner, his face having its
perfectly expressionless air of studied politeness which allowed no
muscle of its polished-cherry surface to move. The extreme politeness
of the extremely great to the supremely unimportant!

He glanced round the hut markedly. It was Tietjens' own office
and contained nothing but the blanket-covered tables and, hanging
from a strut, an immense calendar on which days were roughly
crossed out in red ink and blue pencil. He said:

"Go and get your belt. You will go round your cook-houses with
me in a quarter of an hour. You can tell your sergeant-cook. What
sort of cooking arrangements have you?"

Tietjens said:

"Very good cook-houses, sir."

The general said:

"You're extremely lucky, then. Extremely lucky! . . . Half the units like yours in this camp haven't anything but company cookers and field ovens in the open. . . ." He pointed with his crop at the open door. He repeated with extreme distinctness "Go and get your belt!" Tietjens wavered a very little on his feet. He said:

"You are aware, sir, that I am under arrest."

Campion imported a threat into his voice:

"I gave you," he said, "an order. To perform a duty!"

The terrific force of the command from above to below took Tietjens staggering through the door. He heard the general's voice say: "I'm perfectly aware he's not drunk." When he had gone four paces, Colonel Levin was beside him.

Levin was supporting him by the elbow. He whispered:

"The general wishes me to go with you if you are feeling unwell. You understand you are released from arrest!" He exclaimed with a sort of rapture: "You're doing splendidly. . . . It's amazing. Everything I've ever told him about you . . . Yours is the only draft that got off this morning. . . ."

Tietjens grunted:

"Of course I understand that if I'm given an order to perform a duty, it means I am released from arrest." He had next to no voice. He managed to say that he would prefer to go alone. He said: "He's forced my hand. . . . The last thing I want is to be released from arrest. . . ."

Levin said breathlessly:

"You *can't* refuse. . . . You can't upset him. . . . Why, you *can't*. . . . Besides, an officer cannot demand a court martial."

"You look," Tietjens said, "like a slightly faded bunch of wall-flowers. . . . I'm sure I beg your pardon. . . . It came into my head!" The colonel drooped intangibly, his moustache a little ragged, his eyes a little rimmed, his shaving a little ridged. He exclaimed:

"Damn it! . . . Do you suppose I don't *care* what happens to you? . . . O'Hara came storming into my quarters at half-past three. . . . I'm not going to tell you what he said. . . ." Tietjens said gruffly:

"No, don't! I've all I can stand for the moment. . . ."

Levin exclaimed desperately:

"I want you to understand. . . . It's impossible to believe anything against . . ."

Tietjens faced him, his teeth showing like a badger's. He said:

"Whom? . . . Against whom? Curse you!"

Levin said pallidly:

"Against . . . against . . . either of you. . . ."

"Then leave it at that!" Tietjens said. He staggered a little until he reached the main lines. Then he marched. It was purgatory. They peeped at him from the corners of huts and withdrew. . . . But they always did peep at him from the corners of huts and withdraw! That is the habit of the Other Ranks on perceiving officers. The fellow called McKechnie also looked out of a hut door. He too withdrew. . . . There was no mistaking that! He had the news. . . . On the other hand, McKechnie too was under a cloud. It might be his, Tietjens', duty, to strafe McKechnie to hell for having left camp last night. So he might be avoiding him. . . . There was no knowing . . . He lurched infinitesimally to the right. The road was rough. His legs felt like detached and swollen objects that he dragged after him. He must master his legs. He mastered his legs. A batman carrying a cup of tea ran against him. Tietjens said: "Put that down and fetch me the sergeant-cook at the double. Tell him the general's going round the cook-houses in a quarter of an hour." The batman ran, spilling the tea in the sunlight.

In his hut, which was dim and profusely decorated with the doctor's ideals of female beauty in every known form of pictorial reproduction, so that it might have been lined with peach-blossom, Tietjens had the greatest difficulty in getting into his belt. He had at first forgotten to remove his hat, then he put his head through the wrong opening; his fingers on the buckles operated like sausages. He inspected himself in the doctor's cracked shaving-glass: he was exceptionally well shaved.

He had shaved that morning at six-thirty, five minutes after the draft had got off. Naturally, the lorries had been an hour late. It was providential that he had shaved with extra care. An insolently calm man was looking at him, the face divided in two by the crack in the glass: a naturally white-complexioned double-half of a face, a patch of high colour on each cheekbone; the pepper-and-salt hair ruffled, the white streaks extremely silver. He had gone very silver lately. But he swore he did not look worn. Not careworn. McKechnie said from behind his back:

"By Jove, what's this all about. The general's been strafing me to hell for not having my table tidy!"

Tietjens, still looking in the glass, said:

"You should keep your table tidy. It's the only strafe the battalion's had."

The general, then, must have been in the orderly room of which he had put McKechnie in charge. McKechnie went on, breathlessly:

"They say you knocked the general. . . ."

Tietjens said:

"Don't you know enough to discount what they say in this town?" He said to himself: "That was all right!" He had spoken with a cool edge on a contemptuous voice.

He said to the sergeant-cook who was panting — another heavy, grey-moustached, very senior N.C.O.:

"The general's going round the cook-houses. . . . You be damn certain there's no dirty cook's clothing in the lockers!" He was fairly sure that otherwise his cook-houses would be all right. He had gone round them himself the morning of the day before yesterday. Or was it yesterday? . . .

It was the day after he had been up all night because the draft had been countermanded. . . . It didn't matter. He said:

"I wouldn't serve out white clothing to the cooks. . . . I bet you've got some hidden away, though it's against orders."

The sergeant looked away into the distance, smiled all-knowingly over his walrus moustache.

"The general likes to see 'em in white," he said, "and he won't know the white clothing has been countermanded."

Tietjens said:

"The snag is that the beastly cooks always will tuck some piece of beastly dirty clothing away in a locker rather than take the trouble to take it round to their quarters when they've changed."

Levin said with great distinctness:

"The general has sent me to you with this, Tietjens. Take a sniff of it if you're feeling dicky. You've been up all night on end two nights running." He extended in the palm of his hand a bottle of smelling-salts in a silver section of tubing. He said the general suffered from vertigo now and then. Really he himself carried that restorative for the benefit of Miss de Bailly.

Tietjens asked himself why the devil the sight of that smelling-salts container reminded him of the brass handle of the bedroom door moving almost imperceptibly . . . and incredibly. It was, of course, because Sylvia had on her illuminated dressing-table, reflected by the glass, just such another smooth, silver segment of tubing. . . . Was everything he saw going to remind him of the minute movement of that handle?

"You can do what you please," the sergeant-cook said, "but there will always be one piece of clothing in a locker for a G.O.C.I.C.'s inspection. And the general always walks straight up to that locker and has it opened. I've seen General Campion do it three times."

"If there's any found this time, the man it belongs to goes for a D.C.M.," Tietjens said. "See that there's a clean diet-sheet on the messing board."

"The generals really like to find dirty clothing," the sergeant-cook said; "it gives them something to talk about if they don't know anything else about cook-houses. . . . I'll put up my own diet-sheet, sir. . . . I suppose you can keep the general back for twenty minutes or so? It's all I ask."

Levin said towards his rolling, departing back:

"That's a damn smart man. Fancy being as confident as that about an inspection. . . . Ugh! . . ." and Levin shuddered in remembrance of inspections through which in his time he had passed.

"He's a damn smart man!" Tietjens said. He added to McKechnie:

"You might take a look at dinners in case the general takes it into his head to go round them."

McKechnie said darkly:

"Look here, Tietjens, are you in command of this unit or am I?"

Levin exclaimed sharply, for him:

"What's that? What the . . ."

Tietjens said:

"Captain McKechnie complains that he is the senior officer and should command this unit."

Levin ejaculated:

"Of all the . . ." He addressed McKechnie with vigour: "My man, the command of these units is an appointment at disposition of headquarters. Don't let there be any mistake about that!"

McKechnie said doggedly:

"Captain Tietjens asked me to take the battalion this morning. I understood he was under . . ."

"You," Levin said, "are attached to this unit for discipline and rations. You damn well understand that if some uncle or other of yours were not, to the general's knowledge, a protégé of Captain Tietjens', you'd be in a lunatic asylum at this moment. . . ."

McKechnie's face worked convulsively, he swallowed as men are said to swallow who suffer from hydrophobia. He lifted his fist and cried out:

"My un . . ."

Levin said:

"If you say another word you go under medical care the moment it's said. I've the order in my pocket. Now, fall out. At the double!"

McKechnie wavered on the way to the door. Levin added:

"You can take your choice of going up the line tonight. Or a court of inquiry for obtaining divorce leave and then not getting a divorce. Or the other thing. And you can thank Captain Tietjens for the clemency the general has shown you!"

The hut now reeling a little, Tietjens put the opened smelling bottle to his nostrils. At the sharp pang of the odour the hut came to attention. He said:

"We can't keep the general waiting."

"He told me," Levin said, "to give you ten minutes. He's sitting in your hut. He's tired. This affair has worried him dreadfully. O'Hara is the first C.O. he ever served under. A useful man, too, at his job."

Tietjens leaned against his dressing-table of meat-cases.

"You told that fellow McKechnie off, all right," he said. "I did not know you had it in you. . . ."

"Oh," Levin said, "it's just being with *him*. . . . I get his manner and it does all right. Of course I don't often hear him have to strafe anybody in that manner. There's nobody really to stand up to him. Naturally. . . . But just this morning I was in his cabinet doing private secretary, and he was talking to Pe . . . Talking while he shaved. And he said exactly that: You can take your choice of going up the line to-night or a court martial! . . . So naturally I said as near the same as I could to your little friend. . . ."

Tietjens said:

"We'd better go now."

In the winter sunlight Levin tucked his arm under Tietjens', leaning towards him gaily and not hurrying. The display was insufferable to Tietjens, but he recognized that it was indispensable. The bright day seemed full of things with hard edges — a rather cruel definiteness. . . . Liver! . . .

The little depot adjutant passed them going very fast, as if before a wind. Levin just waved his hand in acknowledgment of his salute and went on, being enraptured in Tietjens' conversation. He said:

"You and . . . and Mrs. Tietjens are dining at the general's to-night. To meet the G.O.C.I.C. Western Division. And General O'Hara. . . . We understand that you have definitely separated from Mrs. Tietjens. . . ." Tietjens forced his left arm to violence to restrain it from tearing itself from the colonel's grasp.

His mind had become a coffin-headed, leather-jawed charger, like Schomburg. Sitting on his mind was like sitting on Schomburg at a dull water-jump. His lips said: "Bub-bub-bub-bub!" He could not feel his hands. He said:

"I recognize the necessity. If the general sees it in that way. I saw it in another way myself." His voice was intensely weary. "No doubt," he said, "the general knows best!"

Levin's face exhibited real enthusiasm. He said:

"You decent fellow! You awfully decent fellow! We're all in the same boat. . . . Now, will you tell me? For *him*. Was O'Hara drunk last night or wasn't he?"

Tietjens said:

"I think he was not drunk when he burst into the room with Major Perowne. . . . I've been thinking about it! I think he became drunk. . . . When I first requested and then ordered him to leave the room he leant against the doorpost. . . . He was certainly then — in disorder! . . . I then told him that I should order him under arrest, if he didn't go. . . ."

Levin said:

"Mm! Mm! Mm!"

Tietjens said:

"It was my obvious duty. . . . I assure you that I was perfectly collected. . . . I beg to assure you that I was perfectly collected. . . ."

Levin said: "I am not questioning the correctness. . . . But . . . we are all one family. . . . I admit the atrocious . . . the unbearable nature. . . . But you understand that O'Hara had the right to enter your room. . . . As P.M.! . . ."

Tietjens said:

"I am not questioning that it was his right. I was assuring you that I was perfectly collected because the general had honoured me by asking my opinion on the condition of General O'Hara. . . ."

They had by now walked far beyond the line leading to Tietjens' office and, close together, were looking down upon the great tapestry of the French landscape.

"*He*," Levin said, "is anxious for your opinion. It really amounts to as to whether O'Hara drinks too much to continue in his job! . . . And he says he will take your word. . . . You could not have a greater testimonial. . . ."

"He could not," Tietjens said studiedly, "do anything less. Knowing me."

Levin said:

"Good heavens, old man, you rub it in!" He added quickly: "He wishes me to dispose of this side of the matter. He will take my word and yours. You will forgive . . ."

The mind of Tietjens had completely failed; the Seine below looked like an S on fire in an opal. He said: "Eh?" And then: "Oh, yes! I forgive. . . . It's painful. . . . You probably don't know what you are doing."

He broke off suddenly:

"By God! . . . Were the Canadian Railway Service to go with my draft? They were detailed to mend the line here to-day. Also to go . . . I kept them back. . . . Both orders were dated the same day and hour. I could not get on to headquarters either from the hotel or from here. . . ."

Levin said:

"Yes, that's all right. He'll be immensely pleased. He's going to speak to you about *that*!" Tietjens gave an immense sigh of relief.

"I remembered that my orders were conflicting just before. . . . It was a terrible shock to remember. . . . If I sent them up in the lorries, the repairs to the railway might be delayed. . . . If I didn't, you might get strafed to hell. . . . It was an intolerable worry. . . ."

Levin said:

"You remember it just as you saw the handle of your door moving. . . ."

Tietjens said from a sort of a mist:

"Yes. You know how beastly it is when you suddenly remember you have forgotten something in orders. As if the pit of your stomach had. . . ."

Levin said:

"All I ever thought about if I'd forgotten anything was what would be a good excuse to put up to the adjutant. . . . When I was a regimental officer . . ."

Suddenly Tietjens said insistently:

"How did you know that? . . . About the door handle? Sylvia could not have seen it. . . ." He added: "And she could not have known what I was thinking. . . . She had her back to the door. . . . And to me . . . Looking at me in the glass. . . . She was not even aware of what had happened. . . . So she could not have seen the handle move!"

Levin hesitated:

"I . . ." he said. "Perhaps I ought not to have said that. . . . You've told us. . . . That is to say, you've told . . ." He was pale in the sunlight. He said: "Old man . . . Perhaps you don't know. . . . Didn't you perhaps ever, in your childhood? . . ."

Tietjens said:

"Well . . . what is it?"

"That you talk . . . when you're sleeping!" Levin said.

Astonishingly, Tietjens said:

"What of that? . . . It's nothing to write home about! With the overwork I've had and the sleeplessness . . ."

Levin said, with a pathetic appeal to Tietjens' omniscience:

"But doesn't it mean . . . We used to say when we were boys . . . that if you talk in your sleep . . . you're . . . in fact a bit dotty?"

Tietjens said without passion:

"Not necessarily. It means that one has been under mental pressure, but all mental pressure does not drive you over the edge. Not by any means. . . . Besides, what does it matter?"

Levin said:

"You mean you don't care. . . . Good God!" He remained looking at the view, drooping, in intense dejection. He said: "This *beastly* war! This *beastly* war! . . . Look at all that view. . . ."

Tietjens said:

"It's an encouraging spectacle, really. The beastliness of human nature is always pretty normal. We lie and betray and are wanting in imagination and deceive ourselves, always, at about the same rate. In peace and in war! But, somewhere in that view there are enormous bodies of men. . . . If you got a still more extended range of view over this whole front you'd have still more enormous bodies of men. Seven to ten million. . . . All moving towards places towards which they desperately don't want to go. Desperately! Every one of them is desperately afraid. But they go on. An immense blind will forces them in the effort to consummate the one decent action that humanity has to its credit in the whole of recorded history; the one we are engaged in. That effort is the one certain creditable fact in all their lives. . . . But the *other* lives of all those men are dirty, potty and discreditable little affairs. . . . Like yours . . . Like mine. . . ."

Levin exclaimed:

"Just heavens! *What* a pessimist you are!"

Tietjens said: "Can't you see that that is optimism?"

"But," Levin said, "we're being beaten out of the field. . . . You don't know how desperate things are."

Tietjens said:

"Oh, I know pretty well. As soon as this weather really breaks we're probably done."

"We can't," Levin said, "possibly hold them. Not possibly."

"But success or failure," Tietjens said, "have nothing to do with the credit of a story. And a consideration of the virtues of humanity does not omit the other side. If we lose, they win. If success is necessary to your idea of virtue — *virtus* — they then provide the success instead of ourselves. But the thing is to be able to stick to the integrity of your character, whatever earthquake sets the house tumbling over your head. . . . That, thank God, we're doing. . . ."

Levin said:

"I don't know. . . . If you knew what is going on at home . . ."

Tietjens said:

"Oh, I know. . . . I know that ground as I know the palm of my hand. I could invent that life if I knew nothing at all about the facts."

Levin said:

"I believe you could." He added: "Of course you could. . . . And yet the only use we can make of you is to martyrise you because two drunken brutes break into your wife's bedroom. . . ."

Tietjens said:

"You betray your non-Anglo-Saxon origin by being so vocal. . . . And by your illuminative exaggerations!"

Levin suddenly exclaimed:

"What the devil were we talking about?"

Tietjens said grimly:

"I am here at the disposal of the competent military authority — you! — that is inquiring into my antecedents. I am ready to go on belching platitudes till you stop me."

Levin answered:

"For goodness' sake help me. This is horribly painful. *He* — the general — has given me the job of finding out what happened last night. He won't face it himself. He's attached to you both."

Tietjens said:

"It's asking too much to ask me to help you. . . . What did I say in my sleep? What has Mrs. Tietjens told the general?"

"The general," Levin said, "has not seen Mrs. Tietjens. He could not trust himself. He knew she would twist him round her little finger."

Tietjens said:

"He's beginning to learn. He was sixty last July, but he's beginning."

"So that," Levin said, "what we do know we learnt in the way I have told you. And from O'Hara of course. The general would not let Pe . . ., the other fellow, speak a word, while he was shaving. He just said: 'I won't hear you. I won't hear you. You can take your choice of going up the line as soon as there are trains running or being broke on my personal application to the King in Council.'"

"I didn't know," Tietjens said, "that he could talk as straight as that."

"He's dreadfully hard hit," Levin answered; "if you and Mrs. Tietjens separate — and still more if there's anything real against either of you — it's going to shatter all his illusions. And . . ." He paused: "Do you know Major Thurston? A gunner? Attached to our anti-aircraft crowd? . . . The general is very thick with him. . . ."

Tietjens said:

"He's one of the Thurstons of Lobden Moorside. . . . I don't know him personally. . . ."

Levin said:

"He's upset the general a good deal. . . . With something he told him. . . ."

Tietjens said:

"Good God!" And then: "He can't have told the general anything against me. . . . Then it must be against . . ."

Levin said:

"Do you want the general always to be told things against you in contradistinction to things about . . . another person."

Tietjens said:

"We shall be keeping the fellows in my cook-house a confoundedly long time waiting for inspections. . . . I'm in your hands as regards the general. . . ."

Levin said:

"The general's in your hut, thankful to goodness to be alone. He never is. He said he was going to write a private memorandum for the Secretary of State, and I could keep you any time I liked as long as I got everything out of you. . . ."

Tietjens said:

"Did what Major Thurston allege take place . . . Thurston has lived most of his life in France. . . . But you had better not tell me. . . ."

Levin said:

"He's our anti-craft liaison officer with the French civilian authorities. Those sort of fellows generally have lived in France a good deal. A very decentish, quiet man. He plays chess with the general and they talk over the chess. . . . But the general is going to talk about what he said to you himself. . . ."

Tietjens said:

"Good God! . . . He going to talk as well as you. . . . You'd say the coils were closing in. . . ."

Levin said:

"We can't go on like this. . . . It's my own fault for not being more direct. But this can't last all day. We could neither of us stand it. . . . I'm pretty nearly done. . . ."

Tietjens said:

"Where *did* your father come from, really? Not from Frankfurt? . . ."

Levin said:

"Constantinople. . . . His father was financial agent to the Sultan; my father was his son by an Armenian presented to him by the Selamlik along with the Order of the Medjidje, first class."

"It accounts for your very decent manner, and for your common sense. If you had been English I should have broken your neck before now."

Levin said:

"Thank you! I hope I always behave like an English gentleman. But I am going to be brutally direct now. . . ." He went on: "The really queer thing is that you should always address Miss Wannop in the language of the Victorian *Correct Letter-Writer*. You must excuse my mentioning the name: it shortens things. You said 'Miss Wannop' every two or three half-minutes. It convinced the general more than any possible assertions that your relations were perfectly . . ."

Tietjens, his eyes shut, said:

"I talked to Miss Wannop in my sleep. . . ."

Levin, who was shaking a little, said:

"It was very queer. . . . Almost ghostlike. . . . There you sat, your arms on the table. Talking away. You appeared to be writing a letter to her. And the sunlight streaming in at the hut. I was going to wake you, but he stopped me. He took the view that he was on detective work, and that he might as well detect. He had got it into his mind that you were a Socialist."

"He would," Tietjens commented. "Didn't I tell you he was beginning to learn things? . . ."

Levin exclaimed:

"But you aren't a So . . ."

Tietjens said:

"Of course, if your father came from Constantinople and his mother was a Georgian, it accounts for your attractiveness. You *are* a most handsome fellow. And intelligent. . . . If the general has put you on to inquire whether I am a Socialist I will answer your questions."

Levin said:

"No. . . . That's one of the questions he's reserving for himself to ask. It appears that if you answer that you are a Socialist he intends to cut you out of his will. . . ."

Tietjens said:

"His will! . . . Oh, yes, of course, he might very well leave me something. But doesn't that supply rather a motive for me to say that I *am*? I don't want his money."

Levin positively jumped a step backwards. Money, and particularly money that came by way of inheritance, being one of the sacred things of life for him, he exclaimed:

"I don't see that you *can* joke about such a subject!"

Tietjens answered good-humouredly:

"Well, you don't expect me to play up to the old gentleman in order to get his poor old shekels." He added "Hadn't we better get it over?"

Levin said:

"You've got hold of yourself?"

Tietjens answered:

"Pretty well. . . . You'll excuse my having been emotional so far. You aren't English, so it won't have embarrassed you."

Levin exclaimed in an outraged manner:

"Hang it, I'm English to the backbone! What's the matter with me?"

Tietjens said:

"Nothing. . . . Nothing in the world. That's just what makes you un-English. We're all . . . well, it doesn't matter what's wrong with *us*. . . . What did you gather about my relations with Miss Wannop?"

The question was so unemotionally put and Levin was still so concerned as to his origins that he did not at first grasp what Tietjens had said. He began to protest that he had been educated at Winchester and Magdalen. Then he exclaimed, *"Oh!"* And took time for reflection.

"If," he said finally, "the general had not let out that she was young and attractive . . . at least, I suppose attractive . . . I should have thought that you regarded her as an old maid. . . . You know, of course, that it came to me as a shock, the thought that there was anyone. . . . That you had allowed yourself . . . Anyhow . . . I suppose I'm simple. . . ."

Tietjens said:

"What did the general gather?"

"He . . ." Levin said, "he stood over you with his head held to one side, looking rather cunning . . . like a magpie listening at a hole it's dropped a nut into. . . . First he looked disappointed, then quite glad. A simple kind of gladness. Just glad, you know. . . . When we got outside the hut he said 'I suppose in *vino veritas,*' and then he asked me the Latin for 'sleep.' . . . But I had forgotten it too. . . ."

Tietjens said:

"What did I say?"

"It's . . ." Levin hesitated, "extraordinarily difficult to say what you *did* say. . . . I don't profess to remember long speeches to the letter. . . . Naturally it was a good deal broken up. . . . I tell you, you were talking to a young lady about matters you don't generally talk to young ladies about. . . . And obviously you were trying to let your . . . Mrs. Tietjens, down easily. . . . You were trying to explain also why you had definitely decided to separate from Mrs. Tietjens. . . . And you took it that the young lady might be troubled . . . at the separation. . . ."

Tietjens said carelessly:

"This is rather painful. Perhaps you would let me tell you exactly what *did* happen last night. . . ."

Levin said:

"If you only would!" He added rather diffidently: "If you would not mind remembering that I am a military court of inquiry. It makes it easier for me to report to the general if you say things dully and in the order they happened."

Tietjens said:

"Thank you . . ." and after a short interval, "I retired to rest with my wife last night at. . . . I cannot say the hour exactly. Say half-past one. I reached this camp at half-past four, taking rather over half an hour to walk. What happened, as I am about to relate, took place therefore before four."

"The hour," Levin said, "is not material. We know the incident occurred in the small hours. General O'Hara made his complaint to me at three-thirty-five. He probably took five minutes to reach my quarters."

Tietjens asked:

"The exact charge was . . ."

"The complaints," Levin answered, "were very numerous indeed. . . . I could not catch them all. The succinct charge was at first being drunk and striking a superior officer, then merely that of conduct prejudicial in that you struck . . . There is also a subsidiary charge of conduct prejudicial in that you improperly marked a charge-sheet in your orderly room. . . . I did not catch what all that was about. . . . You appear to have had a quarrel with him about his red-caps. . . ."

"That," Tietjens said, "is what it is really all about." He asked: "The officer I was said to have struck was? . . ."

Levin said:

"Perowne . . ." dryly.

Tietjens said:

"You are sure it was not himself. I am prepared to plead guilty to striking General O'Hara."

"It is not," Levin said, "a question of pleading guilty. There is no charge to that effect against you, and you are perfectly aware that you

are not under arrest. . . . An order to perform any duty after you
have been placed under arrest in itself releases you and dissolves the
arrest."

Tietjens said coolly:

"I am perfectly aware of that. And that that was General Campion's intention in ordering me to accompany him round my cook-
houses. . . . But I doubt . . . I put it to you for your serious attention whether that is the best way to hush this matter up. . . . I
think it would be more expedient that I should plead guilty to a
charge of striking General O'Hara. And naturally to being drunk. An
officer does not strike a general when he is sober. That would be a
quite inconspicuous affair. Subordinate officers are broken every day
for being drunk."

Levin had said "Wait a minute," twice. He now exclaimed with a
certain horror:

"Your mania for sacrificing yourself makes you lose all . . . all
sense of proportion. You forget that General Campion is a gentleman. Things cannot be done in a hole-and-corner manner in this
command. . . ."

Tietjens said:

"They're done unbearably. . . . It would be nothing to me to be
broke for being drunk, but raking up all this is hell."

Levin said:

"The general is anxious to know exactly what has happened. You
will kindly accept an order to relate exactly what happened."

Tietjens said:

"That is what is perfectly damnable. . . ." He remained silent for
nearly a minute, Levin slapping his leggings with his riding-crop in
a nervously passionate rhythm. Tietjens stiffened himself and began:

"General O'Hara came to my wife's room and burst in the door.
I was there. I took him to be drunk. But from what he exclaimed I
have since imagined that he was not so much drunk as misled. There
was another man lying in the corridor where I had thrown him.
General O'Hara exclaimed that this was Major Perowne. I had not
realised that this was Major Perowne. I do not know Major Perowne
very well and he was not in uniform. I had imagined him to be a
French waiter coming to call me to the telephone. I had seen only his
face round the door: he was looking round the door. My wife was in
a state . . . bordering on nudity. I had put my hand under his chin
and thrown him through the doorway. I am physically very strong

and I exercised all my strength. I am aware of that. I was excited, but not more excited than the circumstances seemed to call for. . . ."

Levin exclaimed:

"But . . . At three in the morning! The telephone!"

"I was ringing up my headquarters and yours. All through the night. The O.I.C. draft, Lieutenant Cowley, was also ringing me up. I was anxious to know what was to be done about the Canadian railway men. I had three times been called to the telephone since I had been in Mrs. Tietjens' room, and once an orderly had come down from the camp. I was also conducting a very difficult conversation with my wife as to the disposal of my family's estates, which are large, so that the details were complicated. I occupied the room next door to Mrs. Tietjens and till that moment, the communicating door between the rooms being open, I had heard when a waiter or an orderly had knocked at my own door in the corridor. The night porter of the hotel was a dark, untidy, surly sort of fellow. . . . Not unlike Perowne."

Levin said:

"Is it necessary to go into all this? We . . ."

Tietjens said:

"If I am to make a statement it seems necessary. I would prefer you to question me . . ."

Levin said:

"Please go on. . . . We accept the statement that Major Perowne was not in uniform. He states that he was in his pyjamas and dressing-gown. Looking for the bathroom."

Tietjens said: "Ah!" and stood reflecting. He said:

"May I hear the . . . the purport of Major Perowne's statement?"

"He states," Levin said, "what I have just said. He was looking for the bathroom. He had not slept in the hotel before. He opened a door and looked round it, and was immediately thrown with great violence down into the passage with his head against the wall. He says that this dazed him so that, not really appreciating what had happened, he shouted various accusations against the person who had assaulted him. . . . General O'Hara then came out of his room."

Tietjens said:

"What accusations did Major Perowne shout?"

"He doesn't . . ." Levin hesitated, "eh! . . . elaborate them in his statement."

Tietjens said:

"It is, I imagine, material that I should know what they are. . . ." Levin said:

"I don't know that. . . . If you'll forgive me . . . Major Perowne came to see me, reaching me half an hour after General O'Hara. He was very . . . extremely nervous and concerned. I am bound to say . . . for Mrs. Tietjens. . . . And also very concerned to spare yourself! . . . It appears that he had shouted out just anything. . . . As it might be 'Thieves!' or 'Fire!' . . . But when General O'Hara came out he told him, being out of himself, that he had been invited to your wife's room, and that . . . Oh, excuse me. . . . I'm under great obligations to you . . . the very greatest . . . that you had attempted to blackmail him!"

Tietjens said:

"Well! . . ."

"You understand," Levin said, and he was pleading, "that that is what he said to General O'Hara in the corridor. He even confessed it was madness. . . . He did not maintain the accusation to me. . . ."

Tietjens said:

"Not that Mrs. Tietjens had given him leave? . . ."

Levin said with tears in his eyes:

"I'll not go on with this. . . . I will rather resign my commission than go on tormenting you. . . ."

"You can't resign your commission," Tietjens said.

"I can resign my appointment," Levin answered. He went on sniffling: "This beastly war! . . . This beastly war! . . ."

Tietjens said:

"If what is distressing you is having to tell me that you believe Major Perowne came with my wife's permission I know it's true. It's also true that my wife expected me to be there. She wanted some fun: not adultery. But I am also aware — as Major Thurston appears to have told General Campion — that Mrs. Tietjens was with Major Perowne. In France. At a place called Yssingueux-les-Pervenches. . . ."

"That wasn't the name," Levin blubbered. "It was Saint . . . Saint . . . Saint something. In the Cevennes. . . ."

Tietjens said:

"Don't, there! . . . Don't distress yourself. . . ."

"But I'm . . ." Levin went on, "under great obligations to you. . . ."

"I'd better," Tietjens said, "finish this matter myself."

Levin said:

"It will break the general's heart. He believes so absolutely in Mrs. Tietjens. Who wouldn't? . . . How the devil could you guess what Major Thurston told him?"

"He's the sort of brown, trustworthy man who always does know that sort of thing," Tietjens answered. "As for the general's belief in Mrs. Tietjens, he's perfectly justified. . . . Only there will be no more parades. Sooner or later it has to come to that for us all. . . ." He added with a little bitterness: "Only not for you. Being a Turk or a Jew you are a simple, Oriental, monogamous, faithful soul. . . ." He added again: "I hope to goodness the sergeant-cook has the sense not to keep the men's dinners back for the general's inspection. . . . But of course he will not. . . ."

Levin said:

"What in the world would that matter?" fiercely. "He keeps men waiting as much as three hours. On parade."

"Of course," Tietjens said, "if that is what Major Perowne told General O'Hara it removes a good deal of my suspicions of the latter's sobriety. Try to get the position. General O'Hara positively burst in the little sneck of the door that I had put down and came in shouting: 'Where is the —— blackmailer?' And it was a full three minutes before I could get rid of him. I had had the presence of mind to switch off the light and he persisted in asking for another look at Mrs. Tietjens. You see, if you consider it, he is a very heavy sleeper. He is suddenly awakened after, no doubt, not a few pegs. He hears Major Perowne shouting about blackmail and thieves. . . . I dare say this town has its quota of blackmailers. O'Hara might well be anxious to catch one in the act. He hates me, anyhow, because of his red-caps. I'm a shabby-looking chap he doesn't know much about. Perowne passes for being a millionaire. I dare say he is: he's said to be very stingy. That would be how he got hold of the idea of blackmail and hypnotised the general with it. . . ."

He went on again:

"But I wasn't to know that. . . . I had shut the door on Perowne and didn't even know he was Perowne. I really thought he was the night porter coming to call me to the telephone. I only saw a roaring satyr. I mean that was what I thought O'Hara was. . . . And I assure you I kept my head. . . . When he persisted in leaning against the doorpost and asking for another look at Mrs. Tietjens, he kept on saying: 'the woman' and 'the hussy.' Not 'Mrs. Tietjens.' . . . I thought then that there was something queer. I said: 'This is my wife's room,' several times. He said something to the effect of how could he know she was my wife, and . . . that she had made eyes at himself in the lounge, so it might have been himself as well as Perowne. . . . I dare say he had got it into his head that I had imported some tart to blackmail someone. . . . But you know. . . . I grew exhausted after a time. . . . I saw outside in the corridor one of the little subalterns he has on his staff, and I said: 'If you do not take General O'Hara away I shall order you to put him under arrest for drunkenness.' That seemed to drive the general crazy. I had gone closer to him, being determined to push him out of the door, and he decidedly smelt of whisky. Strongly. . . . But I dare say he was thinking himself outraged, really. And perhaps also coming to his senses. As there was nothing else for it, I pushed him gently out of the room. In going he shouted that I was to consider myself under arrest. I so considered myself. . . . That is to say that, as soon as I had settled certain details with Mrs. Tietjens, I walked up to the camp, which I took to be my quarters, though I am actually under the M.O.'s orders to reside in this hotel owing to the state of my lungs. I saw the draft off, that not necessitating my giving any orders. I went to my sleeping quarters, it being then about six-thirty, and towards seven awakened McKechnie, whom I asked to take my adjutant's and battalion parade and orderly-room. I had breakfast in my hut, and then went into my private office to await developments. I think I have now told you everything material. . . ."

II

GENERAL LORD EDWARD CAMPION, G.C.B., K.C.M.G., (military), D.S.O., etc., sat, radiating glory and composing a confidential memorandum to the Secretary of State for War, on a bully-beef case, leaning forward over a military blanket that covered a deal table. He was for the moment in high good humour on the surface, though his subordinate minds were puzzled and depressed. At the end of each sentence that he wrote — and he wrote with increasing satisfaction! — a mind that he was not using said: "What the devil am I going to do with that fellow?" Or: "How the devil is that girl's name to be kept out of this mess?"

Having been asked to write a confidential memorandum for the information of the home authorities as to what, in his opinion, was the cause of the French railway strike, he had hit on the ingenious device of reporting what was the opinion of the greater part of the forces under his command. This was a dangerous line to take, for he might well come into conflict with the home Government. But he was pretty certain that any inquiries that the home Government could cause to be made amongst the local civilian population would confirm what he was writing — which he was careful to state was not to be taken as a communication of his own opinion. In addition, he did not care what the Government did to him.

He was satisfied with his military career. In the early part of the war, after materially helping mobilisation, he had served with great distinction in the East, in command mostly of mounted infantry. He had subsequently so distinguished himself in the organising and transporting of troops coming and going overseas that, on the part of the lines of communication where he now commanded becoming of great importance, he knew that he had seemed the only general that could be given that command. It had become of enormous importance — these were open secrets! — because, owing to divided opinions in the Cabinet, it might at any moment be decided to move the bulk of H.M. Forces to somewhere in the East. The idea underlying this — as General Campion saw it — had at least some relation to the necessities of the British Empire and strategy embracing world politics as well as military movements — a fact which is often forgotten. There was this much to be said for it: the preponderance of British Imperial interests might be advanced as lying in the Middle and Far Easts — to the east, that is to say, of Constantinople. This might be denied, but it was a feasible proposition. The present operations on the Western front, arduous, and even creditable, as they might have been until relatively lately, were very remote from our Far-Eastern possessions and mitigated from, rather than added to, our prestige. In addition, the unfortunate display in front of Constantinople in the beginning of the war had almost eliminated our prestige with the Mohammedan races. Thus a demonstration in enormous force in any region between European Turkey and the northwestern frontiers of India might point out to Mohammedans, Hindus,

and other Eastern races, what overwhelming forces Great Britain,
were she so minded, could put into the field. It is true that that would
mean the certain loss of the war on the Western front, with corresponding loss of prestige in the West. But the wiping out of the
French republic would convey little to the Eastern races, whereas we
could no doubt make terms with the enemy nations, as a price for
abandoning our allies that might well leave the Empire, not only intact, but actually increased in colonial extent, since it was unlikely
that the enemy empires would wish to be burdened with colonies for
some time.

General Campion was not overpoweringly sentimental over the
idea of the abandonment of our allies. They had won his respect as
fighting organisations and that, to the professional soldier, is a great
deal; but still he *was* a professional soldier, and the prospect of widen-
ing the bounds of the British Empire could not be contemptuously
dismissed at the price of rather sentimental dishonour. Such bargains had been struck before during wars involving many nations,
and doubtless such bargains would be struck again. In addition, votes
might be gained by the Government from the small but relatively
noisy and menacing part of the British population that favoured the
enemy nations.

But when it came to tactics — which it should be remembered concerns itself with the movement of troops actually in contact with
enemy forces — General Campion had no doubt that that plan was
the conception of the brain of a madman. The dishonour of such a
proceeding must of course be considered — and its impracticability
was hopeless. The dreadful nature of what would be our debacle did
we attempt to evacuate the Western front might well be unknown
to, or might be deliberately ignored by, the civilian mind. But the
general could almost see the horrors as a picture — and, professional
soldier as he was, his mind shuddered at the picture. They had by
now in the country enormous bodies of troops who had hitherto not
come into contact with the enemy forces. Did they attempt to withdraw these in the first place the native population would at once
turn from a friendly into a bitterly hostile factor, and moving troops
through hostile country is to the nth power a more lengthy matter
than moving them through territory where the native populations
lend a helping hand, or are at least not obstructive. They had in addition this enormous force to ration, and they would doubtless have
to supply them with ammunition on the almost certain breaking

through of the enemy forces. It would be impossible to do this without the use of the local railways — and the use of these would at once be prohibited. If, on the other hand, they attempted to begin the evacuation by shortening the front, the operation would be very difficult with troops who, by now, were almost solely men trained only in trench warfare, with officers totally unused to that keeping up of communications between units which is the life and breath of a retreating army. Training, in fact, in that element had been almost abandoned in the training camps where instruction was almost limited to bomb-throwing, the use of machine-guns, and other departments which had been forced on the War Office by eloquent civilians — to the almost complete neglect of the rifle. Thus at the mere hint of a retreat the enemy forces must break through and come upon the vast, unorganised, or semi-organised bodies of troops in the rear. . . .

The temptation for the professional soldier was to regard such a state of things with equanimity. Generals have not infrequently enormously distinguished themselves by holding up retreats from the rear when vanguard commanders have disastrously failed. But General Campion resisted the temptation of even hoping that this chance of distinguishing himself might offer itself. He could not contemplate with equanimity the slaughter of great bodies of men under his command, and not even a successful retreating action of that description could be carried out without horrible slaughter. And he would have little hope of conducting necessarily delicate and very hurried movements with an army that, except for its rough training in trench warfare, was practically civilian in texture. So that although, naturally, he had made his plans for such an eventuality, having indeed in his private quarters four enormous paper-covered blackboards upon which he had changed daily the names of units according as they passed from his hands or came into them and became available, he prayed specifically every night before retiring to bed that the task might not be cast upon his shoulders. He prized very much his universal popularity in his command, and he could not bear to think of how the eyes of the Army would regard him as he put upon them a strain so appalling and such unbearable sufferings. He had, moreover, put that aspect of the matter very strongly in a memorandum that he had prepared in answer to a request from the home Government for a scheme by which an evacuation might be effected. But he considered that the civilian element in the Government was so entirely indifferent to the sufferings of the men engaged in these operations, and was so completely ignorant of what are military exigencies, that the words he had devoted to that department of the subject were merely wasted. . . .

So everything pushed him into writing confidentially to the Secretary of State for War a communication that he knew must be singularly distasteful to a number of the gentlemen who would peruse it. He chuckled indeed as he wrote, the open door behind him and the sunlight pouring in on his radiant figure. He said:

"Sit down, Tietjens. Levin, I shall not want you for ten minutes," without raising his head, and went on writing. It annoyed him that, from the corner of his eye, he could see that Tietjens was still standing, and he said rather irritably: "Sit down, sit down. . . ."

He wrote:

"It is pretty generally held here by the native population that the present very serious derangement of traffic, if not actively promoted, is at least winked at by the Government of this country. It is, that is to say, intended to give us a taste of what would happen if I took any measures here for returning any large body of men to the home country or elsewhere, and it is said also to be a demonstration in favour of a single command — a measure which is here regarded by a great weight of instructed opinion as indispensable to the speedy and successful conclusion of hostilities. . . ."

The general paused over that sentence. It came very near the quick. For himself he was absolutely in favour of a single command, and in his opinion, too, it was indispensable to any sort of conclusion of hostilities at all. The whole of military history, in so far as it concerned allied operations of any sort — from the campaigns of Xerxes and operations during the wars of the Greeks and Romans, to the campaigns of Marlborough and Napoleon and the Prussian operations of 1866 and 1870 — pointed to the conclusion that a relatively small force acting homogeneously was, to the nth power again, more effective than vastly superior forces of allies acting only imperfectly in accord or not in accord at all. Modern developments in arms had made no shade at all of difference to strategy and had made differences merely of time and numbers to tactics. To-day, as in the days of the Greek Wars of the Allies, success depended on apt timing of the arrival of forces at given points, and it made no difference whether your lethal weapons acted from a distance of thirty miles or were held and operated by hand; whether you dealt death from above or below the surface of the ground, through the air by dropped missiles or by mephitic and torturing vapours. What won combats, campaigns, and, in the end, wars, was the brain which timed the arrival of forces at given points — and that must be one brain which could command their presence at these points, not a half-dozen authorities requesting each other to perform operations which might or might not fall in with the ideas or the prejudices of any one or other of the half-dozen. . . .

Levin came in noiselessly, slid a memorandum slip on to the blanket beside the paper on which the general was writing. The general read: *T. agrees completely, sir, with your diagnosis of the facts, except that he is much more ready to accept General O'H.'s acts as reasonable. He places himself entirely in your hands.*

The general heaved an immense sigh of relief. The sunlight streaming in became very bright. He had had a real sinking at the heart when Tietjens had boggled for a second over putting on his belt. An officer may not demand or insist on a court martial. But he, Campion, could not in decency have refused Tietjens his court martial if he stood out for it. He had a right to clear his character publicly. It would have been impossible to refuse him. Then the fat would have been in the fire. For, knowing O'Hara through pretty nearly twenty-five years — or it must be thirty! — of service Campion was pretty certain that O'Hara had made a drunken beast of himself. Yet he was very attached to O'Hara — one of the old type of rough-diamond generals who swore your head off, but were damn capable men! . . . It was a tremendous relief.

He said sharply:

"Sit down, can't you, Tietjens! You irritate me by standing there!" He said to himself: "An obstinate fellow. . . . Why, he's gone!" and his mind and eyes being occupied by the sentence he had last written, the sense of irritation remained with him. He re-read the closing clause: ". . . a single command — a measure which is here regarded by a great weight of instructed opinion as indispensable to the speedy and successful termination of hostilities. . . ."

He looked at this, whistling beneath his breath. It was pretty thick. He was not asked for his opinion as to the single command, yet he decidedly wanted to get in and was pretty well prepared to stand the consequences. The consequences might be something pretty bad: he might be sent home. That was quite possible. That, even, was better than what was happening to poor Puffles, who was being starved of men. He had been at Sandhurst with Puffles, and they had got their commissions on the same day to the same regiment. A damn good soldier, but too hot-tempered. He was making an extraordinarily good thing of it in spite of his shortage of men; which was the talk of the army. But it must be damn agonising for him, and a very improper strain on his men. One day — as soon as the weather broke — the enemy *must* break through. Then he, Puffles, would be sent home. That was what the fellows at Westminster and in Downing Street wanted. Puffles had been a great deal too free with his tongue. They would not send him home before he had a disaster because, unless he were in disgrace, he would be a thorn in their sides; whereas if he were disgraced no one much would listen to him. It was smart practice. . . . *Sharp* practice!

He tossed the sheet on which he had been writing across the table and said to Tietjens:

"Look at that, will you?" In the centre of the hut Tietjens was sitting bulkily on a bully-beef case that had been brought in ceremoniously by a runner. "He *does* look beastly shabby," the general said. "There are three . . . four grease stains on his tunic. He ought to get his hair cut!" He added: "It's a perfectly damnable business. No one but this fellow would have got into it. He's a firebrand. That's what he is. A regular firebrand!"

Tietjens' troubles had really shaken the general not a little. He was left up in the air. He had lived the greater part of his life with his sister, Lady Claudine Sandbach, and the greater part of the remainder of his life at Groby, at any rate after he came home from India and during the reign of Tietjens' father. He had idolised Tietjens' mother, who was a saint! What indeed there had been of the idyllic in his life had really all passed at Groby, if he came to think of it. India was not so bad, but one had to be young to enjoy that. . . .

Indeed, only the day before yesterday he had been thinking that if this letter that he was thinking out did result in his being sent back, he should propose to stand for the half of the Cleveland Parliamentary Division in which Groby stood. What with the Groby influence and his nephew's in the country districts, though Castlemaine had not much land left up there, and with Sandbach's interest in the ironworking districts, he would have an admirable chance of getting in. Then he would make himself a thorn in the side of certain persons.

He had thought of quartering himself on Groby. It would have been easy to get Tietjens out of the army and they could all — he,

Tietjens, and Sylvia — live together. It would have been his ideal of a home and of an occupation. . . .

For, of course, he was getting old for soldiering: unless he got a fighting army there was not much more to it as a career for a man of sixty. If he *did* get an army he was pretty certain of a peerage and hefty political work could still be done in the Lords. He would have a good claim on India and that meant dying a Field-Marshal.

On the other hand, the only command that was at all likely to be going — except for deaths, and the health rate amongst army commanders was pretty high! — was poor Puffles'. And that would be no pleasant command — with the men all hammered to pieces. He decided to put the whole thing to Tietjens. Tietjens, like a meal-sack, was looking at him over the draft of the letter that he had just finished reading. The general said:

"Well?"

Tietjens said:

"It's splendid, sir, to see you putting the matter so strongly. It must be put strongly, or we're lost."

The general said:

"You think that?"

Tietjens said:

"I'm sure of it, sir. . . . But unless you are prepared to throw up your command and take to politics. . . ."

The general exclaimed:

"You're a most extraordinary fellow. . . . That was exactly what I was thinking about this very minute."

"It's not so extraordinary," Tietjens said. "A really active general thinking as you do is very badly needed in the House. As your brother-in-law is to have a peerage whenever he asks for it, West Cleveland will be vacant at any moment, and with his influence and Lord Castlemaine's — your nephew's not got much land, but the name is immensely respected in the country districts. . . . And, of course, using Groby for your headquarters. . . ."

The general said:

"That's pretty well botched, isn't it?"

Tietjens said without moving a muscle:

"Why, no, sir. Sylvia is to have Groby and you would naturally make it your headquarters. . . . You've still got your hunters there. . . ."

The general said:

"Sylvia is really to have Groby. . . . Good God!"

Tietjens said:

"So it was no great conjuring trick, sir, to see that you might not mind. . . ."

The general said:

"Upon my soul, I'd as soon give up my chance of heaven . . . no, not heaven, but India, as give up Groby."

"You've got," Tietjens said, "an admirable chance of India. . . . The point is: which way? If they give you the sixteenth section. . . ."

"I hate," the general said, "to think of waiting for poor Puffles' shoes. I was at Sandhurst with him. . . ."

"It's a question, sir," Tietjens said, "of which is the best way. For the country and yourself. I suppose if one were a general one would like to have commanded an army on the Western front. . . ."

The general said:

"I don't know. . . . It's the logical end of a career. . . . But I don't feel that my career is ending. . . . I'm as sound as a roach. And in ten years' time what difference will it make?"

"One would like," Tietjens said, "to see you doing it. . . ."

The general said:

"No one will know whether I commanded a fighting army or this damned Whiteley's outfitting store. . . ."

Tietjens said:

"I know that, sir. . . . But the sixteenth section will desperately need a good man if General Perry is sent home. And particularly a general who has the confidence of all ranks. . . . It will be a wonderful position. You will have every man that's now on the Western front at your back after the war. It's a certain peerage. . . . It's certainly a sounder proposition than that of a free-lance — which is what you'd be — in the House of Commons."

The general said:

"Then what am I to do with my letter? It's a damn good letter. I don't like wasting letters."

Tietjens said:

"You want it to show through that you back the single command for all you are worth, yet you don't want them to put their finger on your definitely saying so yourself?"

The general said:

"That's it. That's just what I do want. . . ." He added: "I suppose you take my view of the whole matter. The Government's pretence of evacuating the Western front in favour of the Middle East is probably only a put-up job to frighten our Allies into giving up the single command. Just as this railway strike is a counterdemonstration by way of showing what would happen to us if we did begin to evacuate. . . ."

Tietjens said:

"It looks like that. . . . I'm not, of course, in the confidence of the Cabinet. I'm not even in contact with them as I used to be. . . . But I should put it that the section of the Cabinet that is in favour of the Eastern expedition is very small. It's said to be a one-man party — with hangers-on — but arguing him out of it has caused all this delay. That's how I see it."

The general exclaimed:

"But, good God! . . . How is such a thing possible? That man must walk along his corridors with the blood of a million — I mean it, of a million — men round his head. He could not stand up under it. . . . That fellow is prolonging the war indefinitely by delaying us now. And men being killed all the time! . . . I can't. . . ." He stood up and paced, stamping up and down the hut. . . . "At Bonderstrom," he said, "I had half a company wiped out under me. . . . By my own fault, I admit. I had wrong information. . . ." He stopped and said: "Good God! . . . Good God! . . . I can see it now. . . . And it's unbearable! After eighteen years. I was a brigadier then. It was your own regiment — the Glamorganshires. They were crowded into a little nullah and shelled to extinction. . . . I could see it going on and we could not get on to the Boer guns with ours to stop 'em. . . . That's hell," he said, "that's the real hell. . . . I never inspected the Glamorganshires after that for the whole war. I could not bear the thought of facing their eyes. . . . Buller was the same. . . . Buller was worse than I. . . . He never held up his head again after. . . ."

Tietjens said:

"If you would not mind, sir, not going on . . ."

The general stamped to a halt in his stride. He said:

"Eh? . . . What's that? What's the matter with you?"

Tietjens said:

"I had a man killed on me last night. In this very hut; where I'm sitting is the exact spot. It makes me . . . It's a sort of . . . complex, they call it now. . . ."

The general exclaimed:

"Good God! I beg your pardon, my dear boy. . . . I ought not to have . . . I have never behaved like that before another soul in the world. . . . Not to Buller. . . . Not to Gatacre, and they were my closest friends. Even after Spion Kop I never. . . ." He broke off and said: "But those old memories won't interest you. . . ." He said: "I've such an absolute belief in your trustworthiness. I *know* you won't betray what you've seen. . . . What I've just said . . ." He paused and tried to adopt the air of the listening magpie. He said: "I was called Butcher Campion in South Africa, just as Gatacre was called Backacher. I don't want to be called anything else because I've made an ass of myself before you. . . . No, damn it all, not an ass. I was immensely attached to your sainted mother. . . ." He said: "It's the proudest tribute any commander of men can have. . . . To be called Butcher and have your men follow you in spite of it. It shows confidence, and it gives you, as commander, confidence! . . . One has to be prepared to lose men in hundreds at the right minute in order to avoid losing them in tens of thousands at the wrong! . . ." He said: "Successful military operations consist not in taking or retaining positions, but in taking or retaining them with a minimum sacrifice of effectives. . . . I wish to God you civilians would get that into your heads. The men have it. They know that I will use them ruthlessly — but that I will not waste one life. . . ." He exclaimed: "Damn it, if I had ever thought I should have such troubles, in your father's days . . ." He said: "Let's get back to what we were talking about. . . . My memorandum to the secretary . . ." He burst out: "My God! . . . *What* can that fellow think when he reads Shakespeare's *When all those heads, legs, arms, joined together on the Last Day shall* . . . How does it run? Henry V's address to his soldiers . . . *Every subject's body is the king's* . . . *but every subject's soul is his own*. . . . *And there is no king, be his cause ever so just*. . . . My God! My God! . . . *as can try it out with all unspotted soldiers*. . . . Have you ever thought of that?"

Alarm overcame Tietjens. The general was certainly in disorder. But over what? There was not time to think. Campion was certainly dreadfully overworked. . . . He exclaimed:

"Sir, hadn't you better! . . ." He said: "If we could get back to your memorandum . . . I am quite prepared to write a report to the effect of your sentence as to the French civilian population's attitude. That would throw the onus on me. . . ."

The general said agitatedly:

"No! No! . . . You've got quite enough on your back as it is. Your confidential report states that you are suspected of having too great common interests with the French. That's what makes the whole position so impossible. . . . I'll get Thurston to write something. He's a good man, Thurston. Reliable. . . ." Tietjens shuddered a little. The general went on astonishingly:

> "But at my back I always hear
> Time's winged chariot hurrying near:
> And yonder all before me lie
> Deserts of vast eternity! . . .

That's a general's life in this accursed war. . . . You think all generals are illiterate fools. But I have spent a great deal of time in reading, though I never read anything written later than the seventeenth century."

Tietjens said:

"I know, sir. . . . You made me read Clarendon's *History of the Great Rebellion* when I was twelve."

The general said:

"In case we . . . I shouldn't like . . . In short . . ." He swallowed: it was singular to see him swallow. He was lamentably thin when you looked at the man and not the uniform.

Tietjens thought:

"What's he nervous about? He's been nervous all the morning."

The general said:

"I am trying to say — it's not much in my line — that in case we never met again, I do not wish you to think me an ignoramus."

Tietjens thought:

"He's not ill . . . and he can't think me so ill that I'm likely to die. . . . A fellow like that doesn't really know how to express himself. He's trying to be kind and he doesn't know how to. . . ."

The general had paused. He began to say:

"But there are finer things in Marvell than that. . . ."

Tietjens thought:

"He's trying to gain time. . . . Why on earth should he? . . . What is this all about?" His mind slipped a notch. The general was looking at his finger-nails on the blanket. He said:

"There's, for instance:

> *The grave's a fine and secret place*
> *But none I think do there embrace. . . .*"

At those words it came to Tietjens suddenly to think of Sylvia,
with the merest film of clothing on her long, shining limbs. . . .
She was working a powder-puff under her armpits in a brilliant illumination from two electric lights, one on each side of her dressing-
table. She was looking at him in the glass with the corners of her
lips just moving. A little curled. . . . He said to himself:

"One is going to that fine and secret place. . . . Why not have?"
She had emanated a perfume founded on sandalwood. As she worked
her swansdown powder-puff over those intimate regions he could
hear her humming. Maliciously! It was then that he had observed the
handle of the door moving minutely. She had incredible arms,
stretched out amongst a wilderness of be-silvered cosmetics. Extraordinarily lascivious! Yet clean! Her gilded sheath gown was about her
hips on the chair. . . .

Well! She had pulled the strings of one too many shower-baths!
Shining; radiating glory but still shrivelled so that he reminded
Tietjens of an old apple inside a damascened helmet; the general had
seated himself once more on the bully-beef case before the blanketed
table. He fingered his very large, golden fountain-pen. He said:

"Captain Tietjens, I should be glad of your careful attention!"
Tietjens said:

"Sir!" His heart stopped.

The general said that that afternoon Tietjens would receive a
movement order. He said stiffly that he must not regard this new
movement order as a disgrace. It was promotion. He, Major-General
Campion, was requesting the colonel commanding the depot to in-
scribe the highest possible testimonial in his, Tietjens', small-book.
He, Tietjens, had exhibited the most extraordinary talent for finding
solutions for difficult problems. The colonel was to write that! In
addition he, General Campion, was requesting his friend, General
Perry, commanding the sixteenth section . . .

Tietjens thought:

"Good God. I am being sent up the line. He's sending me to
Perry's Army. . . . That's certain death!"

. . . To give Tietjens the appointment of second in command
of the VIth Battalion of his regiment!

Tietjens said, but he did not know where the words came from:

"Colonel Partridge will not like that. He's praying for McKechnie
to come back!"

To himself he said:

"I shall fight this monstrous treatment of myself to my last breath."

The general suddenly called out:

"There you are. . . . There is another of your infernal worries. . . ."

He put a strong check on himself, and, drily, like the very great speaking to the very unimportant, asked:

"What's your medical category."

Tietjens said:

"Permanent base, sir. My chest's rotten!"

The general said:

"I should forget that, if I were you. . . . The second in command of a battalion has nothing to do but sit about in arm-chairs waiting for the colonel to be killed." He added: "It's the best I can do for you. . . . I've thought it out very carefully. It's the best I can do for you."

Tietjens said:

"I shall, of course, forget my category, sir. . . ."

Of course he would never fight any treatment of himself! . . .

There it was then: the natural catastrophe! As when, under thunder, a dam breaks. His mind was battling with the waters. What would it pick out as the main terror? The mud, the noise, dread always at the back of the mind? Or the worry! The worry! Your eyebrows always had a slight tension on them. . . . Like eye-strain!

The general had begun, soberly:

"You will recognise that there is nothing else that I can do."

His answering:

"I recognise, naturally, sir, that there is nothing else that you can do . . ." seemed rather to irritate the general. He wanted opposition—he *wanted* Tietjens to argue the matter. He was the Roman father counselling suicide to his son; but he wanted Tietjens to expostulate so that he, General Campion, might absolutely prove that he, Tietjens, was a disgraceful individual. . . . It could not be done. Tietjens was not going to give him the opportunity. The general said:

"You will understand that I can't—no commander could!—have such things happening in my command. . . ."

Tietjens said:

"I must accept that, if you say it, sir."

The general looked at him under his eyebrows. He said:

"I have already told you that this is promotion. I have been much impressed by the way you have handled this command. You are, of course, no soldier, but you will make an admirable officer for the militia, that is all that our troops now are. . . ." He said: "I will emphasise what I am saying. . . . No officer could — without being militarily in the wrong — have a private life that is as incomprehensible and embarrassing as yours. . . ."

Tietjens said:

"He's hit it! . . ."

The general said:

"An officer's private life and his life on parade are as strategy to tactics. . . . I don't want, if I can avoid it, to go into your private affairs. It's extremely embarrassing. . . . But let me put it to you that . . . I wish to be delicate. But you are a man of the world! . . . Your wife is an extremely beautiful woman. . . . There has been a scandal . . . I admit not of your making. . . . But if, on the top of that, I appeared to show favouritism to you . . ."

Tietjens said:

"You need not go on, sir. . . . I understand. . . ." He tried to remember what the brooding and odious McKechnie had said . . . only two nights ago. . . . He couldn't remember. . . . It was certainly a suggestion that Sylvia was the general's mistress. It had then, he remembered, seemed fantastic. . . . Well, what else *could* they think? He said to himself: "It absolutely blocks out my staying here!" He said aloud: "Of course, it's my own fault. If a man so handles his womenfolk that they get out of hand, he has only himself to blame."

The general was going on. He pointed out that one of his predecessors had lost that very command on account of scandals about women. He had turned the place into a damned harem!

He burst out, looking at Tietjens with a peculiar goggle-eyed intentness:

"If you think I'd care about losing my command over Sylvia or any other damned Society woman. . . ." He said: "I beg your pardon . . ." and continued reasoningly:

"It's the men that have to be considered. They think — and they've every right to think it if they wish to — that a man who's a wrong 'un over women isn't the man they can trust their lives in the hands of. . . ." He added: "And they're probably right. . . . A man who's a real wrong 'un. . . . I don't mean who sets up a gal in a tea-shop. . . . But one who sells his wife, or . . . At any rate, in *our* army. . . . The French may be different! . . . Well, a man like that

usually has a yellow streak when it comes to fighting. . . . Mind,
I'm not saying always. . . . Usually. . . . There was a fellow
called . . ."

He went off into an anecdote. . . .

Tietjens recognised the pathos of his trying to get away from the
agonising present moment, back to an India where it was all real
soldiering and good leather and parades that had been parades. But
he did not feel called upon to follow. He could not follow. He was
going up the line. . . .

He occupied himself with his mind. What was it going to do? He
cast back along his military history: what had his mind done in similar moments before? . . . But there had never been a similar moment! There had been the sinister or repulsive businesses of going
up, getting over, standing to — even of the casualty clearing-station!
But he had always been physically keener, he had never been so depressed or overwhelmed.

He said to the general:

"I recognise that I cannot stop in this command. I regret it, for
I have enjoyed having this unit. . . . But does it necessarily mean
the VIth Battalion?"

He wondered what was his own motive at the moment. Why had
he asked the general that! . . . The thing presented itself as pictures: getting down bulkily from a high French train, at dawn. The
light picked out for you the white of large hunks of bread — half-
loaves — being handed out to troops themselves duskily invisible.
. . . . The ovals of light on the hats of English troops; they were
mostly West Countrymen. They did not seem to want the bread
much. . . . A long ridge of light above a wooded bank, then suddenly, pervasively, a sound! . . . For all the world as, sheltering
from rain in a cottager's washhouse on the moors, you hear the cottager's clothes boiling in a copper . . . Bubble . . . bubble . . .
bubbubbub . . . bubble . . . Not terribly loud — but terribly de-
manding attention! . . . The Great Strafe! . . .

The general had said:

"If I could think of anything else to do with you, I'd do it. . . .
But all the extraordinary rows you've got into. . . . They block me
everywhere. . . . Do you realise that I have requested General
O'Hara to suspend his functions until now? . . ."

It was amazing to Tietjens how the general mistrusted his subordinates — as well as how he trusted them! . . . It was probably that

made him so successful an officer. Be worked for by men that
. trust: but distrust them all the time — along certain lines of
.ilty; liquor, women, money! . . . Well, he had long knowledge
i men!

He said:

"I admit, sir, that I misjudged General O'Hara. I have said as
much to Colonel Levin and explained why."

The general said with a gloating irony:

"A damn pretty pass to come to. . . . You put a general officer
under arrest. . . Then you say you had misjudged him! . . . I am
not saying you were not performing a duty. . . ." He went on to recount the classical case of a subaltern, cited in King's Regulations,
temp. William IV, who was court martialled and broken for not putting under arrest his colonel who came drunk on to parade. . . . He
was exhibiting his sensuous delight in misplaced erudition.

Tietjens heard himself say with great slowness:

"I absolutely deny, sir, that I put General O'Hara under arrest!
I have gone into the matter very minutely with Colonel Levin."

The general burst out:

"By God! I had taken that woman to be a saint. . . . I swear she
is a saint. . . ."

Tietjens said:

"There is no accusation against Mrs. Tietjens, sir!"

The general said:

"By God, there is!"

Tietjens said:

"I am prepared to take all the blame, sir."

The general said:

"You shan't. . . . I am determined to get to the bottom of all
this. . . . You have treated your wife damn badly. . . . You admit
that. . . ."

Tietjens said:

"With great want of consideration, sir. . . ."

The general said:

"You have been living practically on terms of separation from her
for a number of years? You don't deny that that was on account of
your own misbehaviour. For how many years?"

Tietjens said:

"I don't know, sir. . . . Six or seven!"

The general said sharply:

"Think, then. . . . It began when you admitted to me that y‹
had been sold up because you kept a girl in a tobacco-shop? Th
was at Rye in 1912. . . ."

Tietjens said:

"We have not been on terms since 1912, sir."

The general said:

"But why? . . . She's a most beautiful woman. She's adorable
What could you want better? . . . She's the mother of you‹
child. . . ."

Tietjens said:

"Is it necessary to go into all this, sir? . . . Our differences were
caused by . . . by differences of temperament. She, as you say, is a
beautiful and reckless woman. . . . Reckless in an admirable way. I,
on the other hand . . ."

The general exclaimed:

"Yes! that's just it. . . . What the hell are you? . . . You're not
a soldier. You've got the makings of a damn good soldier. You amaze
me at times. Yet you're a disaster; you are a disaster to every one
who has to do with you. You are as conceited as a hog; you are as
obstinate as a bullock. . . . You drive me mad. . . . And you have
ruined the life of that beautiful woman. . . . For I maintain she
once had the disposition of a saint. . . . Now! I'm waiting for your
explanation!"

Tietjens said:

"In civilian life, sir, I was a statistician. Second secretary to the Department of Statistics. . . ."

The general exclaimed convictingly:

"And they've thrown you out of that! Because of the mysterious
rows you made. . . ."

Tietjens said:

"Because, sir, I was in favour of the single command. . . ."

The general began a long wrangle: "But why were you? What the
hell had it got to do with you?" Couldn't Tietjens have given the
Department the statistics they wanted — even if it meant faking
them? What was discipline for if subordinates were to act on their
consciences? The home Government had wanted statistics faked in
order to dish the Allies. . . . Well . . . Was Tietjens French or English? Every damn thing Tietjens did . . . every *damn* thing, made it
more impossible to do anything for him! With his attainments he
ought to be attached to the staff of the French Commander-in-Chief.

was forbidden in his, Tietjens', confidential report. There
nderlined note in it to that effect. Where else, then, in
name, could Tietjens be sent to? He looked at Tietjens with
lue eyes:

ere else, in God's name . . . I am not using the Almighty's
blasphemously . . . *can* you be sent to? I *know* it's probably
to send you up the line — in your condition of health. And to
'erry's Army. The Germans will be through it the minute the
er breaks."

began again: "You understand: I'm not the War Office. I
send any officer anywhere. I can't send you to Malta or India,
o other commands in France. I can send you home — in disgrace,
in send you to your own battalion. On promotion! . . . Do you
derstand my situation? . . . I have no alternative."

Tietjens said:

"Not altogether, sir."

The general swallowed and wavered from side to side. He said:

"For God's sake, try to . . . I am genuinely concerned for you.
I won't — I'm damned if I will! — let it appear that you're disgraced.
. . . If you were McKechnie himself I wouldn't! The only really good
jobs I've got to give away are on my own staff. I can't have you
there. Because of the men. At the same time . . ."

He paused and said with a ponderous shyness:

"I believe there's a God. . . . I believe that, though wrong may
flourish, right will triumph in the end! . . . If a man is innocent,
his innocence will one day appear. . . . In a humble way I want to
. . . help Providence. . . . I want some one to be able one day to
say: '*General Campion, who knew the ins and outs of the affair* . . .'
promoted you! In the middle of it. . . ." He said: "It isn't much.
But it's not nepotism. I would do as much for any man in your
position."

Tietjens said:

"It's at least the act of a Christian gentleman!"

A certain lack-lustre joy appeared in the general's eyes. He said:

"I'm not used to this sort of situation. . . . I hope I've always
tried to help my junior officers. . . . But a case like this . . ." He
said:

"Damn it. . . . The general commanding the 9th French Army
is an intimate friend of mine. . . . But in face of your confidential
report — I *can't* ask him to ask for you. That's blocked!"

Tietjens said:

"I do not propose, sir, at any rate in your eyes, to pass as putting the interests of any power before those of my own country. If you examine my confidential report you will find that the unfavourable insertions are initialled G. D. . . . They are the initials of a Major Drake. . . ."

The general said bewilderingly:

"Drake . . . Drake . . . I've heard the name."

Tietjens said:

"It doesn't matter, sir. . . . Major Drake's a gentleman who doesn't like me. . . ."

The general said:

"There are so many. You don't try to make yourself popular, I must say!"

Tietjens said to himself:

"The old fellow feels it! . . . But he can hardly expect me to tell him that Sylvia thinks Drake was the father of my own son, and desires my ruin!" But of course the old man *would* feel it. He, Tietjens, and his wife Sylvia, were as near a son and daughter as the old man had. The obvious answer to make to the old man's query as to where he, Tietjens, ought to be sent was to remind him that his brother Mark had had an order put through to the effect that Tietjens was to be put in command of divisional transport. . . . *Could* he remind the old man of that? Was it a thing one could do?

Yet the idea of commanding divisional transport was like a vision of Paradise to Tietjens. For two reasons: it was relatively safe, being concerned with a lot of horses . . . and the knowledge that he had that employment would put Valentine Wannop's mind at rest.

Paradise! . . . But *could* one wangle out of a hard into a soft job? Some other poor devil very likely wanted it. On the other hand — think of Valentine Wannop! He imagined her torture of mind, wandering about London, thinking of him in the very worst spot of a doomed army. She would get to hear of that. Sylvia would tell her! He would bet Sylvia would ring her up and tell her. Imagine, then, writing to Mark to say that he was with the transport! Mark would pass it on to the girl within half a minute. Why . . . he, Tietjens, would wire. He imagined himself scribbling the wire while the general talked and giving it to an orderly the moment the talk was over. . . . But *could* he put the idea into the old man's head? *Is* it done? . . . Would, say . . . say, an Anglican saint do it?

And then . . . was he up to the job? What about the accursed
obsession of O Nine Morgan that intermittently jumped on him?
All the while he had been riding Schomburg the day before, O Nine
Morgan had seemed to be just before the coffin-headed brute's off-
shoulder. The animal must fall! . . . He had had the passionate impulse to pull up the horse. And all the time a dreadful depression!
A weight! In the hotel last night he had nearly fainted over the
thought that Morgan might have been the man whose life he had
spared at Noircourt. . . . It was getting to be a serious matter! It
might mean that there was a crack in his, Tietjens', brain. A lesion!
If that was to go on . . . O Nine Morgan, dirty as he always was,
and with the mystified eyes of the subject races on his face, rising up
before his horse's off-shoulder! But alive, not with half his head cut
away. . . . If that was to go on he would not be fit to deal with
transport, which meant a great deal of riding.

But he would chance that. . . . Besides, some damn fool of a
literary civilian had been writing passionate letters to the papers
insisting that all horses and mules must be abolished in the army.
. . . Because of their pestilence-spreading dung! . . . It might be
decreed by A.C.I. that no more horses were to be used! . . . Imagine
taking battalion supplies down by night with motor lorries, which
was what that genius desired to see done! . . .

He remembered once or twice — it must have been in September,
'16 — having had the job of taking battalion transport down from
Locre to B.H.Q., which were in the Château of Kemmell village.
. . . You muffled every bit of metal you could think of: bits, trace-
chains, axles . . . and *yet*, whilst you hardly breathed, in the thick
darkness some damn thing would always chink and jolt, beef tins
made a noise of old iron. . . . And *bang*, after the long whine, would
come the German shell, registered exactly on to the corner of the
road where it went down by the shoulder of the hill; where the
placards were ordering you not to go more than two men together.
. . . Imagine doing it with lorries, that could be heard five miles
away! . . . The battalion would go pretty short of rations! . . . The
same anti-chevaline genius had emitted the sentiment that he had
rather the Allies lost the war than that cavalry should distinguish
themselves in any engagement! . . . A wonderful passion for the
extermination of dung . . . ! Or perhaps this hatred of the horse was
social. . . . Because the cavalry wear long moustaches dripping with
Macassar oil and breakfast off caviare, chocolate and Pommery

Greno they must be abolished! . . . Something like that. . . . He exclaimed: "By God! How my mind wanders! How long will it go on?" He said: "I am at the end of my tether." He had missed what the general had said for some time.

The general said:

"Well. Has he?"

Tietjens said:

"I didn't catch, sir?"

"Are you deaf?" the general asked. "I'm sure I speak plain enough. You've just said there are no horses attached to this camp. I asked you if there is not a horse for the colonel commanding the depot. . . . A German horse, I understand!"

Tietjens said to himself:

"Great heavens! I've been talking to him. What in the world about?" It was as if his mind were falling off a hillside. He said:

"Yes, sir . . . Schomburg. But as that's a German prisoner, captured on the Marne, it is not on our strength. It is the private property of the colonel. I ride it myself. . . ."

The general exclaimed drily:

"You *would*. . . ." He added more drily still: "Are you aware that there is a hell of a strafe put in against you by a R.A.S.C. second-lieutenant called Hotchkiss? . . ."

Tietjens said quickly:

"If it's over Schomburg, sir . . . it's a washout. Lieutenant Hotchkiss has no more right to give orders about him than as to where I shall sleep. . . . And I would rather die than subject any horse for which I am responsible to the damnable torture Hotchkiss and that swine Lord Beichan want to inflict on service horses. . . ."

The general said maleficently:

"It looks as if you damn well will die on that account!"

He added: "You're perfectly right to object to wrong treatment of horses. But in this case your objection blocks the only other job open to you." He quietened himself a little. "You are probably not aware," he went on, "that your brother Mark . . ."

Tietjens said:

"Yes, I am aware . . ."

The general said: "Do you know that the 19th Division to which your brother wants you sent is attached to Fourth Army now — and it's Fourth Army horses that Hotchkiss is to play with? . . . How could I send you there to be under his orders?"

Tietjens said:

"That's perfectly correct, sir. There is nothing else that you can do. . . ." He was finished. There was now nothing left but to find out how his mind was going to take it. He wished they could go to his cook-houses!

The general said:

"What was I saying? . . . I'm dreadfully tired. . . . No one could stand this. . . ." He drew from inside his tunic a lapis-lazuli coloured, small be-coroneted note-case and selected from it a folded paper that he first looked at and then slipped between his belt and his tunic. He said: "On top of all the responsibility I have to bear!" He asked: "Has it occurred to you that, if I'm of any service to the country, your taking up my energy — *sapping* my energy over your affairs! — is aiding your country's enemies? . . . I can only afford four hours' sleep as it is. . . . I've got some questions to ask you. . . ." He referred to the slip of paper from his belt, folded it again and again slipped it into his belt.

Tietjens' mind missed a notch again. . . . It *was* the fear of the mud that was going to obsess him. Yet, curiously, he had never been under heavy fire in mud. . . . You would think that that would not have obsessed him. But in his ear he had just heard uttered in a whisper of intense weariness, the words: *Es ist nicht zu ertragen; es ist das dasz uns verloren hat* . . . words in German, of utter despair, meaning: It is unbearable: it is that that has ruined us. . . . The mud! . . . He had heard those words, standing amidst volcano craters of mud, amongst ravines, monstrosities of slime, cliffs and distances, all of slime. . . . He had been going, for curiosity or instruction, from Verdun where he had been attached to the French — on a holiday afternoon when nothing was doing, with a guide, to visit one of the outlying forts. . . . Deamont? No, Douaumont. . . . Taken from the enemy about a week before. . . . When would that be? He had lost all sense of chronology. . . . In November. . . . A beginning of some November. . . . With a miracle of sunshine; not a cloud, the mud towering up shut you in intimately with a sky that ached for limpidity. . . . And the slime had moved . . . following a French bombardier who was strolling along eating nuts, disreputably, his shoulders rolling. . . . *Déserteurs.* . . . The moving slime was German deserters. . . . You could not see them: the leader of them — an officer! — had his glasses so thick with mud that you could not see the colour of his eyes, and his half-dozen

decorations were like the beginnings of swallows' nests, his beard
like stalactites. . . . Of the other men you could only see the eyes
— extraordinarily vivid: mostly blue like the sky! . . . Deserters!
Led by an officer! Of the Hamburg Regiment! As if an officer of the
Buffs had gone over! It was incredible. . . . And that was what the
officer had said as he passed, not shamefacedly, but without any
humanity left in him. . . . *Done!* . . . Those moving saurians com-
pacted of slime kept on passing him afterwards, all the afternoon.
. . . And he could not help picturing their immediate antecedents
for two months. . . . In advanced pill-boxes. . . . No, they didn't
have pill-boxes then. In advanced pockets of mud, in dreadful solitude amongst those ravines . . . suspended in eternity, at the last
day of the world. And it had horribly shocked him to hear again the
German language a rather soft voice, a little suety, like an obscene
whisper. . . . The voice obviously of the damned; hell could hold
nothing curious for those poor beasts. . . . His French guide had
said sardonically: *On dirait l'Inferno de Dante!* . . . Well, those
Germans were getting back on him. They were now to become an obsession! A complex, they said nowadays. . . . The general said coolly:

"I presume you refuse to answer?"

That shook him cruelly.

He said desperately:

"I had to end what I took to be an unbearable position for both
parties. In the interests of my son!" Why in the world had he said
that? . . . He was going to be sick. It came back to him that the
general had been talking of his separation from Sylvia. Last night
that had happened. He said: "I may have been right: I may have
been wrong. . . ."

The general said icily:

"If you don't choose to go into it. . . ."

Tietjens said:

"I would prefer not to. . . ."

The general said:

"There is no end to this. . . . But there are questions it's my
duty to ask. . . . If you do not wish to go into your marital relations, I cannot force you. . . . But, damn it, are you sane? Are you
responsible? Do you intend to get Miss Wannop to live with you before the war is over? Is she, perhaps, here, in this town, now? Is
that your reason for separating from Sylvia? Now, of all times in the
world!"

Tietjens said:

"No, sir. I ask you to believe that I have absolutely no relations with that young lady. None! I have no intention of having any. None! . . ."

The general said:

"I believe that!"

"Circumstances last night," Tietjens said, "convinced me suddenly, there, on the spot, that I had been wronging my wife. . . . I had been putting a strain on the lady that was unwarrantable. It humiliates me to have to say it! I had taken a certain course for the sake of the future of our child. But it was an atrociously wrong course. We ought to have separated years ago. It has led to the lady's pulling the strings of all these shower-baths. . . ."

The general said:

"Pulling the . . ."

Tietjens said:

"It expresses it, sir. . . . Last night was nothing but pulling the string of a shower-bath. Perfectly justifiable. I maintain that it was perfectly justifiable."

The general said:

"Then why have you given her Groby? . . . You're not a little soft, are you? . . . You don't imagine you've . . . say, got a mission? Or that you're another person? . . . That you have to . . . to forgive. . . ." He took off his pretty hat and wiped his forehead with a tiny cambric handkerchief. He said: "Your poor mother was a little . . ."

He said suddenly:

"To-night when you are coming to my dinner . . . I hope you'll be decent. Why do you so neglect your personal appearance? Your tunic is a disgusting spectacle. . . ."

Tietjens said:

"I had a better tunic, sir . . . but it has been ruined by the blood of the man who was killed here last night. . . ."

The general said:

"You don't say you have only two tunics? . . . Have you no mess clothes?"

Tietjens said:

"Yes, sir, I've my blue things. I shall be all right for to-night. . . . But almost everything else I possessed was stolen from my kit when I was in hospital. . . . Even Sylvia's two pair of sheets. . . ."

"But hang it all," the general exclaimed, "you don't mean to say you've spaffled all your father left you?"

Tietjens said:

"I thought fit to refuse what my father left me owning to the way it was left. . . ."

The general said:

"But, good God! . . . Read that!" He tossed the small sheet of paper at which he had been looking across the table. It fell face downwards. Tietjens read, in the minute handwriting of the general's:

"Colonel's horse: Sheets: Jesus Christ: Wannop girl: Socialism?"

The general said irritably:

"The other side . . . the other side. . . ."

The other side of the paper displayed the words in large capitals: WORKERS OF THE WORLD, a wood-cut of a sickle and some other objects. Then high treason for a page.

The general said:

"Have you ever seen anything like that before? Do you know what it is?"

Tietjens answered:

"Yes, sir. I sent that to you. To your Intelligence. . . ."

The general thumped both his fists violently on the army blanket:

"You . . ." he said. "It's incomprehensible. . . . It's incredible. . . ."

Tietjens said:

"No, sir. . . . You sent out an order asking commanders of units to ascertain what attempts were being made by Socialists to undermine the discipline of their other ranks. . . . I naturally asked my sergeant-major, and he produced this sheet, which one of the men had given to him as a curiosity. It had been handed to the man in the street in London. You can see my initials on the top of the sheet!"

The general said:

"You . . . you'll excuse me, but you're not a Socialist yourself? . . ."

Tietjens said:

"I knew you were working round to that, sir. But I've no politics that did not disappear in the eighteenth century. You, sir, prefer the seventeenth!"

"Another shower-bath, I suppose," the general said.

"Of course," Tietjens said, "if it's Sylvia that called me a Socialist, it's not astonishing. I'm a Tory of such an extinct type that she might take me for anything. The last megatherium. She's absolutely to be excused. . . ."

The general was not listening. He said:

"What was wrong with the way your father left his money to you? . . ."

"My father," Tietjens said — the general saw his jaw stiffen — "committed suicide because a fellow called Ruggles told him that I was . . . what the French called *maquereau* . . . I can't think of the English word. My father's suicide was not an act that can be condoned. A gentleman does not commit suicide when he has descendants. It might influence my boy's life very disastrously. . . ."

The general said:

"I can't . . . I *can't* get to the bottom of all this. . . . What in the world did Ruggles want to go and tell your father that for? . . . What are you going to do for a living after the war? They won't take you back into your office, will they?"

Tietjens said:

"No, sir. The Department will not take me back. Everyone who has served in this war will be a marked man for a long time after it is over. That's proper enough. *We're* having our fun now."

The general said:

"You say the wildest things."

Tietjens answered:

"You generally find the things I say come true, sir. Could we get this over? Ruggles told my father what he did because it is not a good thing to belong to the seventeenth or eighteenth centuries in the twentieth. Or really, because it is not good to have taken one's public school's ethical system seriously. I am really, sir, the English public schoolboy. That's an eighteenth-century product. What with the love of truth that — God help me! — they rammed into me at Clifton and the belief Arnold forced upon Rugby that the vilest of sins — the vilest of all sins — is to peach to the head master! That's me, sir. Other men get over their schooling. I never have. I remain adolescent. These things are obsessions with me. Complexes, sir!"

The general said:

"All this seems to be very wild. . . . What's this about peaching to a head master?"

Tietjens said:

"For a swan-song, it's not wild, sir. You're asking for a swan-song. I am to go up into the line so that the morals of the troops in your command may not be contaminated by the contemplation of my marital infelicities."

The general said:

"You don't want to go back to England, do you?"

Tietjens exclaimed:

"Certainly not! Very certainly not! I can never go home. I have to go underground somewhere. If I went back to England there would be nothing for me but going underground by suicide."

The general said:

"You see all that? I can give you testimonials. . . ."

Tietjens asked:

"Who couldn't see that it's impossible?"

The general said:

"But . . . suicide! You won't do that. As you said: think of your son."

Tietjens said:

"No, sir. I shan't do that. But you see how bad for one's descendants suicide is. That is why I do not forgive my father. Before he did it I should never have contemplated the idea. Now I have contemplated it. That's a weakening of the moral fibre. It's contemplating a fallacy as a possibility. For suicide is no remedy for a twisted situation of a psychological kind. It is for bankruptcy. Or for military disaster. For the man of action, not for the thinker. Creditors' meetings wipe the one out. Military operations sweep on. But my problem will remain the same whether I'm here or not. For it's insoluble. It's the whole problem of the relations of the sexes."

The general said:

"Good God! . . ."

Tietjens said:

"No, sir, I've not gone off my chump. That's my problem! . . . But I'm a fool to talk so much. . . . It's because I don't know what to say."

The general sat staring at the tablecloth; his face was suffused with blood. He had the appearance of a man in monstrous ill-humour. He said:

"You had better say what you want to say. What the devil do you mean? . . . What's this all about? . . ."

Tietjens said:

"I'm enormously sorry, sir. It's difficult to make myself plain."

The general said:

"Neither of us do. What is language for? What the *hell* is language for? We go round and round. I suppose I'm an old fool who cannot understand your modern ways . . . But you're not modern. I'll do you *that* justice. . . . That beastly little McKechnie is modern. . . . I shall ram him into your divisional-transport job, so that he won't incommode you in your battalion. . . . Do you understand what the little beast did? He got leave to go and get a divorce. And then did not get a divorce. *That's* modernism. He said he had scruples. I understand that he and his wife and . . . some dirty other fellow . . . slept three in a bed. That's modern scruples. . . ."

Tietjens said:

"No, sir, it's not really. . . . But what is a man to do if his wife is unfaithful to him?"

The general said as if it were an insult:

"Divorce the harlot! Or live with her! . . ." Only a beast, he went on, would expect a woman to live all her life alone in a cockloft! She's bound to die. Or go on the streets. . . . What sort of a fellow wouldn't see that? Was there any sort of beast who'd expect a woman to live . . . with a man beside her. . . . Why, she'd . . . she'd be bound to. . . . He'd have to take the consequences of whatever happened. The general repeated: "Whatever happened! If she pulled all the strings of all the shower-baths in the world!"

Tietjens said:

"Still, sir . . . there are . . . there used to be . . . in families of . . . position . . . a certain . . ." He stopped.

The general said:

"Well . . ."

Tietjens said:

"On the part of the man . . . a certain . . . Call it . . . parade!"

The general said:

"Then there had better be no more parades. . . ." He said: "Damn it! . . . Beside us, all women are saints. . . . Think of what childbearing is. I know the world. . . . Who would stand that? . . . You? . . . I . . . I'd rather be the last poor devil in Perry's lines!"

He looked at Tietjens with a sort of injurious cunning:

"Why *don't* you divorce?" he asked.

Panic came over Tietjens. He knew it would be his last panic of that interview. No brain could stand more. Fragments of scenes of fighting, voices, names, went before his eyes and ears. Elaborate problems. . . . The whole map of the embattled world ran out in front of him — as large as a field. An embossed map in greenish *papier mâché* — a ten-acre field of embossed *papier mâché*, with the blood of O Nine Morgan blurring luminously over it. Years before . . . How many months? . . . Nineteen, to be exact, he had sat on some tobacco plants on the Mont de Kats. . . . No, the Montagne Noire. In Belgium. . . . What had he been doing? . . . Trying to get the lie of the land. . . . No. . . . Waiting to point out positions to some fat home general who had never come. The Belgian proprietor of the tobacco plants had arrived, and had screamed his head off over the damaged plants. . . .

But, up there you saw the whole war. . . . Infinite miles away, over the sullied land that the enemy forces held; into Germany proper. Presumably you could breathe in Germany proper. . . . Over your right shoulder you could see a stump of a tooth. The Cloth Hall at Ypres, at an angle of 50° below. . . . Dark lines behind it. . . . The German trenches before Wytschaete! . . .

That was before the great mines had blown Wytschaete to hell.

But — every half-minute by his wrist-watch — white puffs of cotton-wool existed on the dark lines — the German trenches before Wytschaete. Our artillery practice. . . . Good shooting. Jolly good shooting!

Miles and miles away to the left . . . beneath the haze of light that, on a clouded day, the sea threw off, a shaft of sunlight fell, and was reflected in a grey blur. . . . It was the glass roofs of a great airplane shelter!

A great plane, the largest he had then seen, was moving over, behind his back, with four little planes as an escort. . . . Over the vast slag-heaps by Béthune. . . . High, purplish-blue heaps, like the steam domes of engines or the breasts of women. . . . Bluish-purple. More blue than purple. . . . Like all Franco-Belgian Gobelin tapestry. . . . And all quiet. . . . Under the vast pall of quiet cloud! . . .

There were shells dropping in Poperinghe. . . . Five miles out, under his nose the shells dropped. White vapour rose and ran away in plumes. . . . What sort of shells? . . . There were twenty different kinds of shells. . . .

The Huns were shelling Poperinghe! A senseless cruelty. It was five miles behind the line! Prussian brutality . . . There were two

girls who kept a tea-shop in Poperinghe. . . . High coloured. . . .
General Plumer had liked them . . . a fine old general. The shells
had killed them both . . . Any man might have slept with either
of them with pleasure and profit. . . . Six thousand of H.M. officers
must have thought the same about those high-coloured girls. Good
girls! . . . But the Hun shells got them. . . . What sort of fate
was that? . . . To be desired by six thousand men and smashed into
little gobbets of flesh by Hun shells?

It appeared to be mere Prussianism — the senseless cruelty of the
Hun! — to shell Poperinghe. An innocent town with a tea-shop five
miles behind Ypres. . . . Little noiseless plumes of smoke rising
under the quiet blanketing of the pale maroon skies, with the haze
from the aeroplane shelters, and the great aeroplanes over the
Béthune slag-heaps. . . . What a dreadful name — Béthune. . . .

Probably, however, the Germans had heard that we were massing
men in Poperinghe. It was reasonable to shell a town where men were
being assembled. . . . Or we might have been shelling one of their
towns with an Army H.Q. in it. So they shelled Poperinghe in the
silent grey day. . . .

That was according to the rules of the service. . . . General Campion, accepting with equanimity what German airplanes did to the
hospitals, camps, stables, brothels, theatres, boulevards, chocolate
stalls, and hotels of his town would have been vastly outraged if
Hun planes had dropped bombs on his private lodgings. . . . The
rules of war! . . . You spare, mutually, each other's headquarters
and blow to pieces girls that are desired by six thousand men
apiece. . . .

That had been nineteen months before! . . . Now, having lost
so much emotion, he saw the embattled world as a map. . . . An
embossed map of greenish *papier mâché*. The blood of O Nine Morgan was blurring luminously over it. At the extreme horizon was territory labelled *White Ruthenians*! Who the devil were *those* poor
wretches?

He exclaimed to himself: "By heavens! Is this epilepsy?" He
prayed: "Blessed saints, get me spared that!" He exclaimed: "No,
it isn't! . . . I've complete control of my mind. My uppermost
mind." He said to the general:

"I can't divorce, sir. I've no grounds."

The general said:

"Don't lie. You know what Thurston knows. Do you mean that

you have been guilty of contributory misconduct. . . . Whatever it
is? And can't divorce! I don't believe it."

Tietjens said to himself:

"*Why* the devil am I so anxious to shield that whore? It's not
reasonable. It is an obsession!"

White Ruthenians are miserable peoples to the south of Lithuania.
You don't know whether they incline to the Germans or to the Poles.
The Germans don't even know. . . . The Germans were beginning
to take their people out of the line where we were weak; they were
going to give them proper infantry training. That gave him, Tietjens,
a chance. They would not come over strong for at least two months.
It meant, though, a great offensive in the spring. Those fellows had
sense. In the poor, beastly trenches the Tommies knew nothing but
how to chuck bombs. Both sides did that. But the Germans were
going to cure it! Stood chucking bombs at each other from forty
yards. The rifle was obsolete! Ha! ha! Obsolete! . . . The civilian
psychology!

The general said:

"No I don't believe it. I know you did not keep any girl in any
tobacco-shop. I remember every word you said at Rye in 1912. I
wasn't sure then. I am now. You tried to let me think it. You had
shut up your house because of your wife's misbehaviour. You let me
believe you had been sold up. You weren't sold up at all."

. . . *Why* should it be the civilian psychology to chuckle with
delight, uproariously, when the imbecile idea was promulgated that
the rifle was obsolete? *Why* should public opinion force on the War
Office a training-camp course that completely cut out any thorough
instruction in the rifle and communication drill? It was queer. . . .
It was of course disastrous. Queer. Not altogether mean. Pathetic,
too. . . .

"Love of truth!" the general said. "Doesn't that include a hatred
for white lies? No; I suppose it doesn't, or your servants could not
say you were not at home. . . ."

. . . Pathetic! Tietjens said to himself. Naturally the civilian population wanted soldiers to be made to look like fools, and to be done
in. They wanted the war won by men who would at the end be
either humiliated or dead. Or both. Except, naturally, their own
cousins or fiancées' relatives. That was what it came to. That was
what it meant when important gentlemen said that they had rather
the war were lost than that cavalry should gain any distinction in it!

. . . But it was partly the simple, pathetic illusion of the day that great things could only be done by new inventions. You extinguished the Horse, invented something very simple and became God! That is the real pathetic fallacy. You fill a flower-pot with gunpowder and chuck it in the other fellow's face, and heigh presto! the war is won. *All* the soldiers fall down dead! And You: you who forced the idea on the reluctant military, are the Man that Won the War. You deserve all the women in the world. And . . . you get them! Once the cavalry are out of the way! . . .

The general was using the words:

"Head master!" It brought Tietjens completely back.

He said collectedly:

"Really, sir, why this strafe of yours is so terribly long is that it embraces the whole of life."

The general said:

"You're not going to drag a red herring across the trail. . . . I say you regarded me as a head master in 1912. Now I am your commanding officer — which is the same thing. You must not peach to me. That's what you call the Arnold of Rugby touch. . . . But who was it said: *Magna est veritas et prev* . . . *Prev* something?"

Tietjens said:

"I don't remember, sir."

The general said:

"What was the secret grief your mother had? In 1912? She died of it. She wrote to me just before her death and said she had great troubles. And begged me to look after you, very specially! Why did she do that?" He paused and meditated. He asked: "How do you define Anglican sainthood? The other fellows have canonisations, all shipshape like Sandhurst examinations. But us Anglicans . . . I've heard fifty persons say your mother was a saint. She was. But why?"

Tietjens said:

"It's the quality of harmony, sir. The quality of being in harmony with your own soul. God having given you your own soul you are then in harmony with Heaven."

The general said:

"Ah, that's beyond me. . . . I suppose you will refuse any money I leave you in my will?"

Tietjens said:

"Why, no, sir."

The general said:

"But you refused your father's money. Because he believed things against you. What's the difference?"

Tietjens said:

"One's friends ought to believe that one is a gentleman. Automatically. That is what makes one and them in harmony. Probably your friends are your friends because they look at situations automatically as you look at them. . . . Mr. Ruggles knew that I was hard up. He envisaged the situation. If he were hard up, what would he do? Make a living out of the immoral earnings of women. . . . That translated into the Government circles in which he lives means selling your wife or mistress. Naturally he believed that I was the sort of fellow to sell my wife. So that's what he told my father. The point is, my father should not have believed him."

"But I . . ." the general said.

Tietjens said:

"You never believed anything against me, sir."

The general said:

"I know I've damn well worried myself to death over you . . ."

Tietjens was sentimentally at rest, still with wet eyes. He was walking near Salisbury in a grove, regarding long pastures and ploughlands running to dark, high elms from which, embowered . . . Embowered was the word! — peeped the spire of George Herbert's church. One ought to be a seventeenth-century parson at the time of the renaissance of Anglican saintliness . . . who wrote, perhaps, poems. No, not poems. Prose. The statelier vehicle!

That was home-sickness! . . . He himself was never to go home!

The general said:

"Look here . . . Your father . . . I'm concerned about your father. . . . Didn't Sylvia perhaps tell him some of the things that distressed him?"

Tietjens said distinctly:

"No, sir. That responsibility cannot be put on to Sylvia. My father chose to believe things that were said against me by a perfect — or a nearly perfect — stranger. . . ." He added: "As a matter of fact, Sylvia and my father were not on any sort of terms. I don't believe they exchanged two words for the last five years of my father's life."

The general's eyes were fixed with an extreme hardness on Tietjens'. He watched Tietjens' face, beginning with the edges round the nostrils, go chalk white. He said: "He knows he's given his wife away! . . . Good God!" With his face colourless, Tietjens' eyes of porcelain-blue stuck out extraordinarily. The general thought: "What an ugly fellow! His face is all crooked!" They remained looking at each other.

In the silence the voices of men talking over the game of House came as a murmur to them. A rudimentary card game monstrously in favour of the dealer. When you heard voices going on like that you knew they were playing House. . . . So they had had their dinners.

The general said:

"It isn't Sunday, is it?"

Tietjens said:

"No, sir; Thursday, the seventeenth, I think, of January. . . ."

The general said:

"Stupid of me. . . ."

The men's voices had reminded him of church bells on a Sunday. And of his youth. . . . He was sitting beside Mrs. Tietjens' hammock under the great cedar at the corner of the stone house at Groby. The wind being from the east-north-east the bells of Middlesbrough came to them faintly. Mrs. Tietjens was thirty; he himself thirty; Tietjens — the father — thirty-five or so. A most powerful, quiet man; a wonderful landowner, like his predecessors for generations. It was not from him that this fellow got his . . . his . . . his what? . . . Was it mysticism? . . . Another word! He himself home on leave from India, his head full of polo. Talking for hours about points in ponies with Tietjens' father, who was a wonderful hand with a horse. . . . But this fellow was much more wonderful! . . . Well, he got that from the sire, not the dam! . . . He and Tietjens continued to look at each other. It was as if they were hypnotised. The men's voices went on in a mournful cadence. The general supposed that he too must be pale. He said to himself: "This fellow's mother died of a broken heart in 1912. The father committed suicide five years after. He had not spoken to the son's wife for four or five years! That takes us back to 1912. . . . Then, when I strafed him in Rye, the wife was in France with Perowne."

He looked down at the blanket on the table. He intended again to look up at Tietjens' eyes with ostentatious care. That was his technique with men. He was a successful general because he knew men. He knew that all men will go to hell over three things: alcohol, money . . . and sex. This fellow apparently hadn't. Better for him if he had! He thought:

"It's all gone . . . mother! Father! Groby! This fellow's down and out. It's a bit thick."

He thought:

"But he's right to do as he is doing."

He prepared to look at Tietjens. . . . He stretched out a sudden, ineffectual hand. Sitting on his beef-case, his hands on his knees, Tietjens had lurched. A sudden lurch — as an old house lurches when it is hit by a H.E. shell. It stopped at that. Then he righted himself. He continued to stare direct at the general. The general looked carefully back. He said — very carefully too:

"In case I decide to contest West Cleveland, it is your wish that I should make Groby my headquarters?"

Tietjens said:

"I beg, sir, that you will!"

It was as if they both heaved an enormous sigh of relief. The general said:

"Then I need not keep you. . . ."

Tietjens stood on his feet, wanly, but with his heels together.

The general also rose, settling his belt. He said:

". . . You can fall out."

Tietjens said:

"My cook-houses, sir. . . . Sergeant-Cook Case will be very disappointed. . . . He told me that you couldn't find anything wrong if I gave him ten minutes to prepare. . . ."

The general said:

"Case. . . . Case. . . . Case was in the drums when we were at Delhi. He ought to be at least Quartermaster by now. . . . But he had a woman he called his sister . . ."

Tietjens said:

"He still sends money to his sister."

The general said:

"He went absent over her when he was colour-sergeant and was reduced to the ranks. . . . Twenty years ago that must be! . . . Yes, I'll see your dinners!"

In the cook-houses, brilliantly accompanied by Colonel Levin, the cook-houses spotless with limed walls and mirrors that were the tops of camp-cookers, the general, Tietjens at his side, walked between goggle-eyed men in white who stood to attention holding ladles. Their eyes bulged, but the corners of their lips curved because they liked the general and his beautifully unconcerned companions. The cook-house was like a cathedral's nave, aisles being divided off by the pipes of stoves. The floor was of coke-brise shining under french polish and turpentine.

The building paused, as when a godhead descends. In breathless focusing of eyes the godhead, frail and shining, walked with short steps up to a high-priest who had a walrus moustache and, with seven medals on his Sunday tunic, gazed away into eternity. The general tapped the sergeant's Good Conduct ribbon with the heel of his crop. All stretched ears heard him say:

"How's your sister, Case? . . ."

Gazing away, the sergeant said:

"I'm thinking of making her Mrs. Case . . ."

Slightly leaving him, in the direction of high, varnished, pitch-pine panels, the general said:

"I'll recommend you for a Quartermaster's commission any day you wish. . . . Do you remember Sir Garnet inspecting field kitchens at Quetta?"

All the white tubular beings with global eyes resembled the pierrots of a child's Christmas nightmare. The general said: "Stand at ease, men. . . . Stand easy!" They moved as white objects move in a childish dream. It was all childish. Their eyes rolled.

Sergeant Case gazed away into infinite distance.

"My sister would not like it, sir," he said. "I'm better off as a first-class warrant officer!"

With his light step the shining general went swiftly to the varnished panels in the eastern aisle of the cathedral. The white figure beside them became instantly tubular, motionless, and global-eyed. On the panels were painted: TEA! SUGAR! SALT! CURRY PDR! FLOUR! PEPPER!

The general tapped with the heel of his crop on the locker-panel labelled PEPPER: the top, right-hand locker-panel. He said to the tubular, global-eyed white figure beside it: "Open that, will you, my man? . . ."

To Tietjens this was like the sudden bursting out of the regimental quick-step, as after a funeral with military honours the band and drums march away, back to barracks.

A Man Could
Stand Up—

Part One

S LOWLY, AMIDST INTOLERABLE NOISES from, on the one hand the
street and, on the other, from the large and voluminously echoing playground, the depths of the telephone began, for Valentine, to assume an aspect that, years ago it had used to have — of being a part of the supernatural paraphernalia of inscrutable Destiny.

The telephone, for some ingeniously torturing reason, was in a
corner of the great schoolroom without any protection and, called im-
peratively, at a moment of considerable suspense, out of the asphalt
playground where, under her command ranks of girls had stood electrically only just within the margin of control, Valentine with the receiver at her ear was plunged immediately into incomprehensible
news uttered by a voice that she seemed half to remember. Right in
the middle of a sentence it hit her:

". . . that he ought presumably to be under control, which you
mightn't like!"; after that the noise burst out again and rendered the
voice inaudible.

It occurred to her that probably at that minute the whole population of the world needed to be under control; she knew she herself
did. But she had no male relative that the verdict could apply to in
especial. Her brother? But he was on a mine-sweeper. In dock at the
moment. And now . . . safe for good! There was also an aged great-
uncle that she had never seen. Dean of somewhere. . . . Hereford?
Exeter? . . . Somewhere . . . Had she just said *safe*? *She* was shaken
with joy!

She said into the mouthpiece:

"Valentine Wannop speaking. . . . Physical Instructress at this
school, you know!"

She had to present an appearance of sanity . . . a sane voice at the very least!

The tantalisingly half-remembered voice in the telephone now got in some more incomprehensibilities. It came as if from caverns and as if with exasperated rapidity it exaggerated its "s"s with an effect of spitting vehemence.

"His brothers.s.s got pneumonia, so his mistress.ss.ss even is unavailable to look after . . ."

The voice disappeared; then it emerged again with:

"They're said to be friends now!"

It was drowned then, for a long period in a sea of shrill girls' voices from the playground, in an ocean of factory-hooter's ululations, amongst innumerable explosions that trod upon one another's heels. From where on earth did they get explosives, the population of squalid suburban streets amidst which the school lay? For the matter of that where did they get the spirits to make such an appalling row? Pretty drab people! Inhabiting liver-coloured boxes. Not on the face of it an imperial race.

The sibillating voice in the telephone went on spitting out spitefully that the porter said he had no furniture at all; that he did not appear to recognise the porter. . . . Improbable-sounding pieces of information half-extinguished by the external sounds, but uttered in a voice that seemed to mean to give pain by what it said.

Nevertheless it was impossible not to take it gaily. The thing, out there, miles and miles away must have been signed — a few minutes ago. She imagined along an immense line sullen and disgruntled cannon sounding for a last time.

"I haven't," Valentine Wannop shouted into the mouthpiece, "the least idea of what you want or who you are."

She got back a title. . . . Lady someone or other. . . . It might have been Blastus. She imagined that one of the lady governoresses of the school must be wanting to order something in the way of school sports organised to celebrate the auspicious day. A lady governoress or other was always wanting something done by the School to celebrate something. No doubt the Head who was not wanting in a sense of humour — not *absolutely* wanting! — had turned this lady of title onto Valentine Wannop after having listened with patience to her for half an hour. The Head had certainly sent out to where in the playground they all had stood breathless, to tell Valentine Wannop that there was someone on the telephone that she — Miss

Wanostrocht, the said Head — thought that she, Miss Wannop, ought to listen to. . . . Then: Miss Wanostrocht must have been able to distinguish what had been said by the now indistinguishable lady of title. But of course that had been ten minutes ago. . . . Before the maroons or the sirens, whichever it had been, had sounded. . . . "The porter said he had no furniture at all. . . . He did not appear to recognise the porter. . . . Ought presumably to be under control!" Valentine's mind thus recapitulated the information that she had from Lady (provisionally) Blastus. She imagined now that the Lady must be concerned for the superannuated drill-sergeant the school had had before it had acquired her, Valentine, as physical instructor. She figured to herself the venerable, mumbling gentleman, with several ribbons on a black commissionaire's tunic. In an almhouse, probably. Placed there by the Governors of the school. Had pawned his furniture no doubt. . . .

Intense heat possessed Valentine Wannop. She imagined indeed her eyes flashing. Was this the moment?

She didn't even know whether what they had let off had been maroons or aircraft guns or sirens. It had happened — the noise, whatever it was — whilst she had been coming through the underground passage from the playground to the schoolroom to answer this wicked telephone. So she had not heard the sound. She had missed the sound for which the ears of a world had waited for years, for a generation. For an eternity. No sound. When she had left the playground there had been dead silence. All waiting: girls rubbing one ankle with the other rubber sole. . . .

Then. . . . For the rest of her life she was never to be able to remember the greatest stab of joy that had ever been known by waiting millions. There would be no one but she who would not be able to remember that. . . . Probably a stirring of the heart that was like a stab; probably a catching of the breath that was like the inhalation of flame! It was over now; they were by now in a situation; a condition, something that would affect certain things in certain ways. . . .

She remembered that the putative ex-drill sergeant had a brother who had pneumonia and thus an unavailable mistress. . . .

She was about to say to herself:

"That's just my luck!" When she remembered good-humouredly that her luck was not like that at all. On the whole she had had good luck — ups and downs. A good deal of anxiety at one time — but who hadn't had! But good health; a mother with good health;

a brother safe . . . Anxieties, yes! But nothing that had gone so very
wrong. . . .

This then was an exceptional stroke of bad luck! Might it be an
omen — to the effect that things in future *would* go wrong: to the
effect that she would miss other universal experiences. Never marry,
say; or never know the joy of childbearing, if it was a joy! Perhaps it
was; perhaps it wasn't. One said one thing, one another. At any rate
might it not be an omen that she would miss some universal and
necessary experience! . . . Never see Carcassonne, the French said.
. . . Perhaps she would never see the Mediterranean. You could not
be a proper man if you had never seen the Mediterranean; the sea
of Tibullus, of the Anthologists, of Sappho, even . . . Blue: incredibly blue!

People would be able to travel now. It was incredible! Incredible!
Incredible! But you *could*. Next week you would be able to! You
could call a taxi! And go to Charing Cross! And have a porter! A
whole porter! . . . The wings, the wings of a dove; then would I flee
away, flee away and eat pomegranates beside an infinite washtub of
Reckitt's blue. Incredible, but you *could*!

She felt eighteen again. Cocky! She said, using the good, metallic,
Cockney bottoms of her lungs that she had used for shouting back
at interrupters at Suffrage meetings before . . . before this . . . she
shouted blatantly into the telephone:

"I say, whoever you are! I suppose they have *done* it; did they announce it in your parts by maroons or sirens?" She repeated it three
times, she did not care for Lady Blastus or Lady Blast Anybody else.
She was going to leave that old school and eat pomegranates in the
shadow of the rock where Penelope, wife of Ulysses, did her washing.
With lashings of blue in the water! Was all your underlinen bluish
in those parts owing to the colour of the sea? She could! She could!
She *could*! Go with her mother and brother and all to where you
could eat . . . Oh, new potatoes! In December, the sea being blue.
. . . *What songs the sirens sang and whether* . . .

She was not going to show respect for any Lady anything
ever again. She had had to hitherto, independent young woman of
means though she were, so as not to damage the school and Miss
Wanostrocht with the Governoresses. Now . . . She was never
going to show respect for anyone ever again. She had been through
the mill: the whole world had been through the mill! No more
respect!

As she might have expected she got it in the neck immediately afterwards — for overcockiness!

The hissing, bitter voice from the telephone enunciated the one address she did not want to hear:

"Lincolnss.s.s . . . Inn!"

Sin! . . . Like the Devil!

It hurt.

The cruel voice said:

"I'm s.s.peaking from there!"

Valentine said courageously:

"Well; it's a great day. I suppose you're bothered by the cheering like me. I can't hear what you want. I don't care. Let 'em cheer!"

She felt like that. She should not have.

The voice said:

"You remember your Carlyle. . . ."

It was exactly what she did not want to hear. With the receiver hard at her ear she looked round at the great schoolroom — the Hall, made to let a thousand girls sit silent while the Head made the speeches that were the note of the school. Repressive! . . . The place was like a nonconformist chapel, high, bare walls with Gothic windows running up to a pitch-pine varnished roof. Repression, the note of the place; the place, the very place not to be in to-day . . . You *ought* to be in the streets, hitting policemen's helmets with bladders. This was Cockney London: that was how Cockney London expressed itself. Hit policeman innocuously because policemen were stiff, embarrassed at these tributes of affection, swayed in rejoicing mobs over whose heads they looked remotely, like poplar trees jostled by vulgarer vegetables!

But she was there, being reminded of the dyspepsia of Thomas Carlyle!

"*Oh!*" she exclaimed into the instrument, "You're Edith Ethel!" Edith Ethel Duchemin, now of course Lady Macmaster! But you weren't used to thinking of her as Lady Somebody.

The last person in the world, the very last! Because, long ago she had made up her mind that it was all over between herself and Edith Ethel. She certainly could not make any advance to the ennobled personage who vindictively disapproved of all things made — with a black thought in a black shade, as you might say. Of all things that were not being immediately useful to Edith Ethel!

And, æsthetically draped and meagre, she had sets of quotations

for appropriate occasions. Rossetti for Love; Browning for optimism
— not frequent that; Walter Savage Landor to show acquaintance
with more esoteric prose. And the unfailing quotation from Carlyle
for damping off saturnalia: for New Year's Day, Te Deums, Vic-
tories, anniversaries, celebrations. . . . It was coming over the wire
now, that quotation:

". . . And then I remembered that it was the birthday of their
Redeemer!"

How well Valentine knew it: how often with spiteful conceit had
not Edith Ethel intoned that. A passage from the diary of the Sage
of Chelsea who lived near the Barracks.

"To-day," the quotation ran, "I saw that the soldiers by the public
house at the corner were more than usually drunk. And then I remembered that it was the birthday of their Redeemer!"

How superior of the Sage of Chelsea not to remember till then
that that had been Christmas Day! Edith Ethel, too, was trying to
show how superior she was. She wanted to prove that until she, Valentine Wannop, had reminded her, Lady Macmaster, that that day
had about it something of the popularly festival she, Lady Mac, had
been unaware of the fact. Really quite unaware, you know. She lived
in her rapt seclusion along with Sir Vincent — the critic, you know;
their eyes fixed on the higher things, they disregarded maroons and
had really a quite remarkable collection, by now, of first editions,
official-titled friends and At Homes to their credit.

Yet Valentine remembered that once she had sat at the feet of
the darkly mysterious Edith Ethel Duchemin — where had *that* all
gone? — and had sympathised with her marital martyrdoms, her impressive taste in furniture, her large rooms, and her spiritual adulteries. So she said good-humouredly to the instrument:

"Aren't you just the same, Edith Ethel? And what can I do for
you?"

The good-natured patronage in her tone astonished her, and she
was astonished, too, at the ease with which she spoke. Then she
realised that the noises had been going away, silence was falling, the
cries receded. They were going towards a cumulation at a distance.
The girls' voices in the playground no longer existed: the Head must
have let them go. Naturally, too, the local population wasn't going
to go on letting off crackers in side streets. . . . She was alone, cloistered with the utterly improbable!

Lady Macmaster had sought her out and here was she, Valentine

Wannop, patronising Lady Macmaster! Why? What could Lady Macmaster want her to do? She *couldn't* — but of course she jolly well could! — be thinking of being unfaithful to Macmaster and be wanting her, Valentine Wannop, to play the innocent, the virginal gooseberry or Disciple. Or alibi. Whatever it was. Goose was the most appropriate word . . . Obviously Macmaster was the sort of person to whom any Lady Macmaster would want — would have — to be unfaithful. A little, dark-bearded, drooping, deprecatory fellow. A typical Critic! All Critics' wives were probably unfaithful to them. They lacked the creative gift. What did you call it? A word unfit for a young lady to use!

Her mind ran about in this unbridled Cockney school-girl's vein. There was no stopping it. It was in honour of the DAY! She was temporarily inhibited from bashing policemen on the head, so she was mentally disrespectful to constituted authority — to Sir Vincent Macmaster, Principal Secretary to H.M. Department of Statistics, author of Walter Savage Landor, a Critical Monograph, and of twenty-two other Critical Monographs in the Eminent Bores' Series. . . . *Such* books! And she was being disrespectful and patronising to Lady Macmaster, Egeria to innumerable Scottish Men of Letters! No more respect! Was that to be a lasting effect of the cataclysm that had involved the world? The *late* cataclysm! Thank God, since ten minutes ago they could call it the late cataclysm!

She was positively tittering in front of the telephone from which Lady Macmaster's voice was now coming in earnest, cajoling tones — as if she knew that Valentine was not paying very much attention, saying:

"Valentine! V*a*lentine! V*a*lentine!"

Valentine said negligently:

"I'm listening!"

She wasn't really. She was really reflecting on whether there had not been more sense in the Mistress's Conference that that morning, solemnly, had taken place in the Head's private room. Undoubtedly what the Mistresses with the Head at their head had feared was that if they, Headmistresses, Mistresses, Masters, Pastors — by whom I was made etcetera! — should cease to be respected because saturnalia broke out on the sounding of a maroon the world would go to pieces! An awful thought! The Girls no longer sitting silent in the nonconformist hall while the Head addressed repressive speeches to them. . . .

She had addressed a speech, containing the phrase: "the credit of a Great Public School," in that Hall only last afternoon in which, fair, thin woman, square-elbowed, with a little of sunlight really still in her coiled fair hair, she had seriously requested the Girls not again to repeat the manifestations of joy of the day before. The day before there had been a false alarm and the School — horribly — had sung:

> "Hang Kaiser Bill from the hoar apple tree
> And Glory, Glory, Glory till it's tea-time!"

The Head, now, making her speech was certain that she had now before her a chastened School, a School that anyhow felt foolish because the rumour of the day before had turned out to be a canard. So she impressed on the Girls the nature of the joy they ought to feel, a joy repressed that should send them silent home. Blood was to cease to be shed: a fitting cause for home-joy — as it were a home-lesson. But there was to be no triumph. The very fact that you had ceased hostilities precluded triumph . . .

Valentine, to her surprise, had found herself wondering when you *might* feel triumph? . . . You couldn't whilst you were still contending; you must not when you had won! Then when? The Head told the girls that it was their province as the future mothers of England — nay, of reunited Europe! — to — well, in fact, to go on with their home-lessons and not run about the streets with effigies of the Great Defeated! She put it that it was their function to shed further light of womanly culture — that there, Thank Heaven, they had never been allowed to forget! — athwart a re-illumined Continent. . . . As if you could light up now there was no fear of submarines or raids!

And Valentine wondered why, for a mutinous moment, she had wanted to feel triumph . . . had wanted *someone* to feel triumph. Well, he . . . they . . . had wanted it so much. Couldn't they have it just for a moment — for the space of one Benkollerdy! Even if it were wrong? or vulgar? something human, someone had once said is dearer than a wilderness of decalogues!

But at the Mistress's Conference that morning Valentine had realised that what was really frightening them was the other note. A quite definite fear. If, at this parting of the ways, at this crack across the table of History, the School — the World, the future mothers of Europe — got out of hand, would they ever come back? The Authorities — Authority all over the world — was afraid of that; more afraid of that than of any other thing. Wasn't it a possibility that there was to be no more Respect? None for constituted Authority and consecrated Experience?

And, listening to the fears of those careworn, faded, ill-nourished gentlewomen, Valentine Wannop had found herself speculating.

"No more respect . . . For the Equator! For the Metric system. For Sir Walter Scott! Or George Washington! Or Abraham Lincoln! Or the Seventh Commandment!"

And she had a blushing vision of fair, shy, square-elbowed Miss Wanostrocht — the head! — succumbing to some specious-tongued beguiler! . . . That was where the shoe really pinched! You had to keep them — the Girls, the Populace, everybody! — in hand now, for once you let go there was no knowing where They, like waters parted from the seas, mightn't carry You. Goodness knew! You might arrive anywhere — at county families taking to trade; gentlefolk selling for profit! All the unthinkable sorts of things!

And with a little inward smirk of pleasure Valentine realised that that Conference was deciding that the Girls were to be kept in the playground that morning — at Physical Jerks. She hadn't ever put up with *much* in the way of patronage from the rather untidy-haired bookish branch of the establishment. Still, accomplished Classicist as she once had been, she had had to acknowledge that the bookish branch of a School was what you might call the Senior Service. She was there only to oblige — because her distinguished father had insisted on paying minute attention to her physique which was vital and admirable. She had been there, for some time past only to oblige — War Work and all that — but still she had always kept her place and had never hitherto raised her voice at a Mistress's Conference. So it was indeed the World Turned Upside Down — already! — when Miss Wanostrocht hopefully from behind her desk decorated with two pale pink carnations said:

"The idea is, Miss Wannop, that They should be kept — that you should keep them, please — as nearly as possible — isn't it called? — at attention until the — eh — noises . . . announce the . . . well, *you* know. Then we suppose they will have to give, say, three cheers. And then perhaps you could get them — in an orderly way — back to their classrooms. . . ."

Valentine felt that she was by no means certain that she *could.* It was not really practicable to keep every one of six hundred aligned girls under your eye. Still she was ready to have a shot. She was ready to concede that it might not be altogether — oh, expedient! — to turn six hundred girls stark mad with excitement into the streets already filled with populations that would no doubt be also stark mad with excitement. You had better keep them in if you could. She would have a shot. And she was pleased. She felt fit: amazingly fit! Fit to do the quarter in . . . oh, in any time? And to give a clump on the jaw to any large, troublesome Jewish type of maiden — or Anglo-Teutonic — who should try to break ranks. Which was more than the Head or any one of the other worried and underfed ones could do. She was pleased that they recognised it. Still she was also generous and recognising that the world ought not really to be turned upside down at any rate until the maroons went, she said:

"Of course I will have a shot at it. But it would be a reinforcement, in the way of keeping order, if the Head — you Miss Wanostrocht — and one or two others of the Mistresses would be strolling about. In relays, of course; not all of the staff all the morning . . ."

That had been two and a half hours or so ago: before the world changed, the Conference having taken place at eight-thirty. Now here she was, after having kept those girls pretty exhaustingly jumping about for most of the intervening time — here she was treating with disrespect obviously constituted Authority. For whom *ought* you to respect if not the wife of the Head of a Department, with a title, a country place, and most highly attended Thursday afternoons?

She was not really listening to the telephone because Edith Ethel was telling her about the condition of Sir Vincent: so overworked, poor man, over Statistics that a nervous breakdown was imminently to be expected. Worried over money, too. Those dreadful taxes for this iniquitous affair . . . .

Valentine took leisure to wonder why — why in the world! — Miss Wanostrocht who must know at the least the burden of Edith Ethel's story had sent for her to hear this farrago? Miss Wanostrocht must know: she had obviously been talked to by Edith Ethel for long enough to form a judgment. Then the matter must be of importance. Urgent even, since the keeping of discipline in the playground was of such utter importance to Miss Wanostrocht; a crucial point in the history of the School and the mothers of Europe.

But to whom, then, could Lady Macmaster's communication be of life and death importance? To her, Valentine Wannop? It could not be: there were no events of importance that could affect her life outside the playground, her mother safe at home and her brother safe on a mine-sweeper in Pembroke Dock . . .

Then . . . of importance to Lady Macmaster herself? But how? What could she do for Lady Macmaster? Was she wanted to teach Sir Vincent to perform physical exercises so that he might avoid his nervous breakdown and, in excess of physical health, get the mortgage taken off his country place which she gathered was proving an overwhelming burden on account of iniquitous taxes the result of a war that ought never to have been waged?

It was absurd to think that she could be wanted for that? An absurd business . . . There she was, bursting with health, strength, good-humour, perfectly *full* of beans — there she was, ready in the cause of order to give Leah Heldenstamm, the large girl, no end of a clump on the side of the jaw or, alternatively, for the sake of all the beanfeastishnesses in the world to assist in the amiable discomfiture of the police. There she was in a sort of nonconformist cloister. Nun-like! Positively nunlike! At the parting of the ways of the universe!

She whistled slightly to herself.

"By Jove," she exclaimed coolly, "I hope it does not mean an omen that I'm to be — oh, nunlike — for the rest of my career in the reconstructed world!"

She began for a moment seriously to take stock of her position — of her whole position in life. It had certainly been hitherto rather nunlike. She was twenty-threeish, rising twenty-four. As fit as a fiddle; as clean as a whistle. Five foot in her gym shoes. And no one had ever wanted to marry her. No doubt that was because she was so clean and fit. No one even had ever tried to seduce her. That was *certainly* because she was so clean-run. She didn't obviously offer — what was it the fellow called it? — promise of pneumatic bliss to the gentlemen with sergeant-majors' horse-shoe moustaches and gurglish voices! She never would. Then perhaps she would never marry. And never be seduced!

Nunlike! She would have to stand at an attitude of attention beside a telephone all her life; in an empty schoolroom with the world shouting from the playground. Or not even shouting from the playground any more. Gone to Piccadilly!

But, hang it all, she wanted some fun! Now!

For years now she had been — oh, yes, nunlike! — looking after the lungs and limbs of the girls of the adenoidy, nonconformitish — really undenominational or so little Established as made no difference! — Great Public Girl's School. She had had to worry about impossible but not repulsive little Cockney creatures' breathing when they had their arms extended . . . You *mustn't* breath rhythmically with your movements. No. No. *No!* . . . *Don't* breathe out with the first movement and in with the second! Breathe naturally! Look at me! . . . She breathed perfectly!

Well, for years, that! War-work for a b——y Pro-German. Or Pacifist. Yes, that too she had been for years. She hadn't liked being it because it was the attitude of the superior and she did not like being superior. Like Edith Ethel!

But now! Wasn't it manifest? She could put her hand wholeheartedly into the hand of any Tom, Dick or Harry. And wish him luck! Whole-heartedly! Luck for himself and for his enterprise. She came back, into the fold, into the Nation even. She could open her mouth! She could let out the good little Cockney yelps that were her birthright. She could be free, independent!

Even her dear, blessed, muddle-headed, tremendously eminent mother by now had a depressed-looking Secretary. She, Valentine Wannop, didn't have to sit up all night typing after all day enjoining perfection of breathing in the playground. . . . By Jove they could go all, brother, mother in untidy black and mauve, secretary in untidy black without mauve, and she, Valentine, out of her imitation Girl Scout's uniform and in — oh, white muslin or Harris tweeds — and with Cockney yawps discuss the cooking under the stone-pines of Amalfi. By the Mediterranean. . . . No one, then, would be able to say that she had never seen the sea of Penelope, the Mother of the Gracchi, Delia, Lesbia, Nausicaä, Sappho . . .

"*Saepe te in somnis vidi!*"

She said:

"Good . . . God!"

Not in the least with a Cockney intonation but like a good Tory English gentleman confronted by an unspeakable proposition. Well, it was an unspeakable proposition. For the voice from the telephone had been saying to her inattention, rather crawlingly, after no end of details as to the financial position of the house of Macmaster:

"So I thought, my dear Val, in remembrance of old times, that . . . If in short I were the means of bringing you together again. . . . For I believe you have not been corresponding. . . . You might in return. . . . You can see for yourself that at this moment the sum would be absolutely *crushing* . . ."

II

TEN minutes later she was putting to Miss Wanostrocht, firmly if without ferocity, the question:

"Look here, Head, what did that woman say to you. I don't like her; I don't approve of her and I didn't really listen to her. But I want to hear!"

Miss Wanostrocht, who had been taking her thin, black cloth coat from its peg behind the highly varnished pitch-pine door of her own private cell, flushed, hung up her garment again and turned from the door. She stood, thin, a little rigid, a little flushed, faded, and a little as it were at bay.

"You must remember," she began, "that I am a schoolmistress." She pressed, with a gesture she constantly had, the noticeably golden plait of her dun-coloured hair with the palm of her thin left hand. None of the gentlewomen of that school had had quite enough to eat — for years now. "It's," she continued, "an instinct to accept any means of knowledge. I like you so much, Valentine — if in private you'll let me call you that. And it seemed to me that if you were in . . ."

"In what?" Valentine asked, "Danger? . . . Trouble?"

"You understand," Miss Wanostrocht replied, "That . . . person seemed as anxious to communicate to me facts about yourself as to give you — that was her ostensible reason for ringing you up — news about a . . . another person. With whom you once had . . . relations. And who has reappeared."

"Ah," Valentine heard herself exclaim. "He has reappeared, has he? I gathered as much." She was glad to be able to keep herself under control to that extent.

Perhaps she did not have to trouble. She could not say that she felt changed from what she had been — just before ten minutes ago, by the reappearance of a man she hoped she had put out of her mind. A man who had "insulted" her. In one way or the other he had insulted her!

But probably all her circumstances had changed. Before Edith Ethel had uttered her impossible sentence in that instrument her complete prospects had consisted of no more than the family picnic, under fig-trees, beside an unusually blue sea — and the prospect had

seemed as near — as near as kiss your finger! Mother in black and
purple; mother's secretary in black without adornments. Brother?
Oh, a romantic figure; slight, muscular, in white flannels with a Leghorn hat and — well, why *not* be romantic over one's brother — with
a broad scarlet sash. One foot on shore and one . . . in a light skiff
that gently bobbed in the lapping tide. Nice boy; nice little brother.
Lately employed nautically, so up to managing a light skiff. They
were going tomorrow . . . but why not that very afternoon by
the 4.20?

> "They'd got the ships, they'd got the men,
> They'd got the money too!"

Thank goodness they'd got the money!
The ships, Charing Cross to Vallambrosa, would no doubt run in
a fortnight. The men — the porters — would also be released. You
can't travel in any comfort with mother, mother's secretary, and
brother — with your whole world and its baggage — without lots of
porters . . . Talk about rationed butter! What was that to trying to
get on without porters?
Once having begun it her mind went on singing the old eighteen-
fiftyish, or seventyish, martial, British, and anti-Russian patriotic song
that one of her little friends had unearthed lately — to prove the historic ferocity of his countrymen:

> "We've fought the Bear before,
> And so we will again!
> The Russians shall not have Constantino . . ."

She exclaimed suddenly: "*Oh!*"
She had been about to say: "Oh, *Hell!*" but the sudden recollection
that the War had been over a quarter of an hour made her leave it
at "*Oh!*" You would have to drop war-time phraseology! You became again a Young Lady. Peace, too, has its Defence of the Realm
Acts. Nevertheless, she had been thinking of the man who had once
insulted her as the Bear, whom she would have to fight again! But
with warm generosity she said:
"It's a shame to call him the Bear!" Nevertheless he was — the man
who was said to have "reappeared" — with his problems and all,
something devouring. . . . Overwhelming, with rolling grey shoulders that with their intolerable problems pushed you and your own
problems out of the road. . . .

She had been thinking all that whilst still in the School Hall, before she had gone to see the Head, immediately after Edith Ethel, Lady Macmaster had uttered the *intolerable* sentence.

She had gone on thinking there for a long time. . . . Ten minutes!

She formulated for herself summarily the first item of a period of nasty worries of a time she flattered herself she had nearly forgotten. Years ago, Edith Ethel, out of a clear sky, had accused her of having had a child by that man. But she hardly thought of him as a man. She thought of him as a ponderous, grey, intellectual mass who now, presumably, was mooning, obviously dotty, since he did not recognise the porter, behind the closed shutters of an empty house in Lincoln's Inn. . . . Nothing less, I assure you! She had never been in that house, but she figured him, with cracks of light coming between the shutters, looking back over his shoulder at you in the doorway, grey, super-ursine. . . . Ready to envelop you in suffocating bothers!

She wondered how long it had been since the egregious Edith Ethel·had made that assertion . . . with, naturally, every appearance of indignation for the sake of the man's Wife with whom, equally naturally, Edith Ethel had "sided." (Now she was trying to "bring you together again." . . . The Wife, presumably, did not go to Edith Ethel's tea-parties often enough, or was too brilliantly conspicuous when there. Probably the latter!). How many years ago? Two? Not so much! Eighteen months, then? Surely more! . . . surely, surely more! . . . When you thought of Time in those days your mind wavered impotently like eyes tired by reading too small print. . . . He went out surely in the autumn of . . . No, it had been the first time he went that he went in the autumn. It was her brother's friend, Ted, that went in '16. Or the other . . . Malachi. So many going out and returning, and going out and perhaps not returning. Or only bits: the nose gone . . . or both eyes. Or — or Hell! oh, Hell! and she clenched her fists, her nails into her palms — no mind!

You'd think it must be that from what Edith Ethel had said. He hadn't recognised the porter; he was reported to have no furniture. Then . . . She remembered. . . .

She was then — ten minutes before she interviewed Miss Wanostrocht, ten seconds after she had been blown out of the mouth of the telephone — sitting on a varnished pitch-pine bench that had black iron, clamped legs against the plaster wall, nonconformishistically distempered in torpedo-grey; and she had thought all that in ten seconds. . . . But that had been *really* how it had been!

The minute Edith Ethel had finished saying the words:

"The sum would be absolutely *crushing*. . . ." Valentine had realised that she had been talking about a debt owed by her miserable husband to the one human being she, Valentine, could not bear to think about. It had naturally at the same moment flashed upon her that Edith Ethel had been giving her his news: He was in new troubles; broken down, broken up, broke to the wide. . . . Anything in the world but broken in. . . . But broken . . . And alone. And calling for her!

She could not afford — she could not bear! — to recall even his name or to so much as bring up before her mind, into which, nevertheless, they were continually forcing themselves, his grey-blond face, his clumsy, square, reliable feet; his humpish bulk; his calculatedly wooden expression; his perfectly overwhelming, but authentic omniscience. . . . His masculinity. His . . . his Frightfulness!

Now, through Edith Ethel — you would have thought that even *he* would have found someone more appropriate — he was calling to her again to enter into the suffocating web of his imbroglios. Not even Edith Ethel would have dared to speak to her again of him without his having taken the first step. . . .

It was unthinkable; it was intolerable; and it had been as if she had been lifted off her feet and deposited on that bench against the wall by the mere sound of the offer. . . . What was the offer?

"I thought that you might, if I were the means of bringing you together . . ." She might . . . what?

Intercede with that man, that grey mass not to enforce the pecuniary claim that it had against Sir Vincent Macmaster. No doubt she and . . . the grey mass! . . . would then be allowed the Macmaster drawing-room to . . . to discuss the ethics of the day in! Just like that!

She was still breathless; the telephone continued to quack. She wished it would stop, but she felt too weak to get up and hang the receiver on its hook. She wished it would stop; it gave her the feeling that a strand of Edith Ethel's hair, say, was penetrating nauseously to her torpedo-grey cloister. Something like that!

The grey mass never would enforce its pecuniary claim. . . . Those people had sponged mercilessly on him for years and years without

ever knowing the kind of object upon which they sponged. It made
them the more pitiful. For it *was* pitiful to clamour to be allowed to
become a pimp in order to evade debts that would never be re-
claimed. . . .

Now, in the empty rooms at Lincoln's Inn — for that was probably what it came to! — that man was a grey ball of mist! a grey bear
rolling tenebrously about an empty room with closed shutters. A
grey problem, calling to *her*!

A hell of a lot . . . Beg pardon, she meant a remarkably great
deal! . . . to have thought of in ten minutes! Eleven, by now, probably. Later she realised that that was what thought was. In ten
minutes after large, impressive arms had carried you away from a
telephone and deposited you on a clamped bench against a wall of
the peculiar coldness of torpedo-grey distempered plaster, the sort of
thing rejoiced in by Great Public (Girls') Schools . . . in those ten
minutes you found you thought out more than in two years. Or it was
not as long ago as that.

Perhaps that was not astonishing. If you had not thought about,
say, washable distemper for two years and then thought about it for
ten minutes you could think a hell of a lot about it in those ten minutes. Probably all there was to think. Still, of course, washable distemper was not like the poor — always with you. At least it always
was in those cloisters, but not spiritually. On the other hand you always *were* with yourself.

But perhaps you were not always with yourself spiritually; you went
on explaining how to breathe without thinking of how the life you
were leading was influencing your . . . What? Immortal soul? Aura?
Personality? . . . Something!

Well, for two years. . . . Oh, *call* it two years, for goodness' sake,
and get it over! . . . she must have been in . . . well, call *that* a
"state of suspended animation" and get that over too! A sort of what
they called inhibition. She had been inhibiting — *pro*hibiting — herself from thinking about herself. Well, hadn't she been right? What
had a b——y Pro-German to think about in an embattled, engrossed,
clamouring nation, especially when she had not much liked her
brother-Pro's! A solitary state, only to be dissolved by . . . maroons!
In suspension!

But . . . Be conscientious with yourself, my good girl! *When that
telephone blew you out of its mouth you knew really that for two*

years you had been avoiding wondering whether you had not been insulted! Avoiding wondering that. And nothing else! No other qualified thing!

She had, of course, been, not in suspension, but in suspense. Because, if he made a sign — "I understand," Edith Ethel had said, "that you have not been in correspondence" . . . or had it been "in communication" that she had said? . . . Well, they hadn't been either. . . .

Anyhow, if that grey Problem, that ravelled ball of grey knitting worsted, had made a sign she would have known that she had not been insulted. Or was there any sense in that?

Was it really true that if a male and female of the same species were alone in a room together and the male didn't . . . then it was an insult? That was an idea that did not exist in a girl's head without someone to put it there, but once it had been put there it became a luminous veracity! It had been put into her, Valentine Wannop's head, naturally by Edith Ethel, who equally naturally said that she did not believe it, but that it was a tenet of . . . oh, the man's wife! Of the idle, surpassing-the-Lily-and-Solomon-too, surprisingly svelte, tall, clean-run creature who for ever on the shining paper of illustrated journals advanced towards you with improbable strides along the railings of the Row, laughing, in company with the Honourable Somebody, second son of Lord Some-one-or-other. . . . Edith Ethel was more refined. She had a title, whereas the other hadn't, but she was pensive. She showed you that she had read Walter Savage Landor, and had only very lately given up wearing opaque amber beads, as affected by the later pre-Raphaelites. She was practically never in the illustrated papers, but she held more refined views. She held that there were some men who were not like that — and those, all of them, were the men to whom Edith Ethel accorded the *entrée* to her Afternoons. She was their Egeria! A refining influence!

The Husband of the Wife, then? Once he had been allowed in Edith Ethel's drawing-room: now he wasn't! . . . Must have deteriorated!

She said to herself sharply, in her "No nonsense, there" mood:

"Chuck it. You're in love with a married man who's a Society wife and you're upset because the Titled Lady has put into your head the idea that you might 'come together again.' After ten years!"

But immediately she protested:

"No. *No*. No! It isn't that. It's all right the habit of putting things incisively, but it's misleading to put things too crudely."

What was the coming together that was offered her? Nothing, on the face of it, but being dragged again into that man's intolerable worries as unfortunate machinists are dragged into wheels by belts — and all the flesh torn off their bones! Upon her word that had been her first thought. She was afraid, afraid, afraid! She suddenly appreciated the advantages of nunlike seclusion. Besides she wanted to be bashing policemen with bladders in celebration of Eleven Eleven!

That fellow — he had no furniture; he did not appear to recognise the hall porter. . . . Dotty. Dotty and too morally deteriorated to be admitted to drawing-room of titled lady, the frequenters of which could be trusted not to make love to you on insufficient provocation, if left alone with you. . . .

Her generous mind reacted painfully.

"Oh, that's not *fair!*" she said.

There were all sorts of sides to the unfairness. Before this War, and, of course, before he had lent all his money to Vincent Macmaster that — that grey grizzly had been perfectly fit for the country-parsonage drawing-room of Edith Ethel Duchemin: he had been welcomed there with effusion! . . . After the War and when his money was — presumably — exhausted, and his mind exhausted, for he had no furniture and did not know the porter . . . After the War, then, and when his money was exhausted he was not fit for the Salon of Lady Macmaster — the only Lady to have a Salon in London.

It was what you called kicking down your ladder!

Obviously it had to be done. There were such a lot of these bothering War heroes that if you let them all into your Salon it would cease to be a Salon, particularly if you were under obligations to them! . . . That was already a pressing national problem; it was going to become an overwhelming one now — in twenty minutes' time; after those maroons. The impoverished War Heroes would all be coming back. Innumerable. You would have to tell your parlourmaid that you weren't at home to . . . about seven million!

But wait a minute. . . . Where did they just stand?

He . . . But she could not go on calling him just "he" like a school-girl of eighteen, thinking of her favourite actor . . . in the purity of her young thoughts. What was she to call him? She had never — even when they had known each other — called him anything other than Mr. So and So. . . . She could not bring herself to let her mental lips frame his name. . . . She had never used anything but his surname to this grey thing, familiar object of her mother's study, seen frequently at tea-parties. . . . Once she had been out with it for a whole night in a dog cart! Think of that! . . . And they had spouted Tibullus one to another in moon-lit mist. And she had certainly wanted it to kiss her — in the moon-lit mists a practically, a really completely strange bear!

It couldn't be done, of course, but she remembered still how she had shivered. . . . Ph . . . Ph . . . Ph. . . . Shivering.

She shivered.

Afterwards they had been run into by the car of General Lord Edward Campion, V. C., P. G. Heaven knows what! Godfather of the man's Society Wife, then taking the waters in Germany. . . . Or perhaps not *her* Godfather. The man's rather; but her especial champion, in shining armour. In these days they had worn broad red stripes down the outsides of their trousers, Generals. What a change! *How* significant of the times!

That had been in 1912. . . . Say the first of July; she could not remember exactly. Summer weather, anyhow, before haymaking or just about. The grass had been long in Hogg's Forty Acre, when they had walked through it, discussing Woman's Suffrage. She had brushed the seed-tops of the heavy grass with her hands as they walked. . . . Say the 1/7/12.

Now it was Eleven Eleven. . . . What? Oh, Eighteen, of course!

Six years ago! What changes in the world! What cataclysms! What Revolutions! . . . She heard all the newspapers, all the halfpenny paper journalists in creation crying in chorus!

But hang it, it was true! If, six years ago she had kissed the . . . the greyish lacuna of her mind then sitting beside her on the dog-cart seat it would have been the larkish freak of a school-girl; if she did it to-day — as per invitation presumably of Lady Macmaster, bringing them together, for, of course, it could not be performed from a distance or without correspondence — no, communication! . . . If, then, she did it to-day . . . to-day . . . to-day — the Eleven Eleven! Oh, what a day to-day would be. . . . Not her sentiments those; quotation from Christina, sister of Lady Macmaster's favorite poet. . . . Or, perhaps, since she had had a title she would have found poets more . . . more chic! The poet who was killed at Gallipoli . . . Gerald Osborne, was it? Couldn't remember the name!

But for six years then she had been a member of that . . . triangle.

You couldn't call it *ménage à trois*, even if you didn't know French. They hadn't lived together! . . . They had d——d near died together when the general's car hit their dog-cart! D——d near! (You *must* not use those War-time idioms. *Do* break yourself of it! Remember the maroons!)

An oafish thing to do! To take a school-girl, just . . . oh, just past the age of consent, out all night in a dog-cart and then get yourself run into by the car of the V. C., P. G., champion-in-red-trouserstripe of your Legitimate! You'd think any man who *was* a man would have avoided that!

Most men knew enough to know that the Woman Pays . . . the school-girl too!

But they get it both ways. . . . Look here: when Edith Ethel Duchemin, then, just — or perhaps not quite, Lady Macmaster! At any rate, her husband was dead and she had just married that miserable little . . . (Mustn't use that word!) She, Valentine Wannop, had been the only witness of the marriage — as of the previous, discreet, but so praiseworthy adultery! . . . When, then, Edith Ethel had . . . It must have been on the very day of the knighthood, because Edith Ethel made it an excuse not to ask her to the resultant Party. . . . Edith Ethel had accused her of having had a baby by . . . oh, Mr. So and So. . . . And heaven was her, Valentine Wannop's, witness that, although Mr. So and So was her mother's constant adviser, she, Valentine Wannop, was still in such a state of acquaintance with him that she still called him by his surname. . . . When Lady Macmaster, spitting like the South American beast of burden called a llama, had accused her of having had a baby by her mother's adviser — to her natural astonishment, but, of course, it had been the result of the dog-cart and the motor and the General, and the General's sister, Lady Pauline Something — or perhaps it was Claudine? Yes, Lady Claudine! — who had been in the car and the Society Wife, who was always striding along the railings of the Row. . . . When she had been so accused out of the blue, her first thought — and, confound it, her enduring thought! — had not been concern for her own reputation but for *his*. . . .

That was the *quality* of his entanglements, their very essence. He got into appalling messes, unending and unravellable — no, she meant un-unravellable! — messes and other people suffered for him whilst he mooned on — into more messes! The General charging the dog-cart was symbolical of him. He was perfectly on his right side and all, but it was like him to be in a dog-cart when flagitious automobiles carrying Generals were running a-muck! Then . . . the Woman Paid! . . . She really did, in this case. It had been her mother's horse they had been driving and, although they had got damages out of the General, the costs were twice that. . . . And her, Valentine's, reputation had suffered from being in a dog-cart at dawn, alone with a man. . . . It made no odds that he had — or was it hadn't? — "insulted" her in any way all through that — oh, that delicious, delirious night. . . . She had to be said to have a baby by him, and then she had to be dreadfully worried about *his* poor old reputation. . . . Of course it *would* have been pretty rotten of him — she so young and innocent, daughter of so preposterously eminent, if so impoverished a man, his father's best friend and all. "He hadn't oughter'er done it!" He hadn't really oughter. . . . She heard them all saying it, still!

Well, he hadn't! . . . But she?

That magic night. It was just before dawn, the mists nearly up to their necks as they drove; the sky going pale in a sort of twilight. And one immense star! She remembered only one immense star, though, historically, there had been also a dilapidated sort of moon. But the star was *her* best boy — what her wagon was hitched on to. . . . And they had been quoting — quarrelling over, she remembered:

> *Flebis et arsuro me, Delia, lecto*
> *Tristibus et . . .*

She exclaimed suddenly:

> "Twilight and evening star
>   And one clear call for me
> And may there be no moaning at the bar
>   When I . . ."

She said:

"Oh, but you *oughtn't* to, my dear! That's *Tennyson!*" Tennyson, with a difference!

She said:

"All the same, that would have been an inexperienced school-girl's prank. . . . But if I let him kiss me now I should be. . . ." She would be a what was it . . . a fornicatress? . . . *trix!* Fornicatrix is preferable! Very preferable. Then why not adultrix? You couldn't: you had to be a "cold-blooded adultress!" or morality was not avenged.

Oh, but surely not cold-blooded! . . . Deliberate, then! . . . That wasn't, either, the word for the process. Of osculation! . . . Comic things, words, as applied to states of feelings!

But if she went now to Lincoln's Inn and the Problem held out its arms. . . . That would be "deliberate." It would be asking for it in the fullest sense of the term.

She said to herself quickly:

"This way madness lies!" And then:

"What an imbecile thing to say!"

She had had an Affair with a man, she made her mind say to her, two years ago. That was all right. There could not be a, say, a schoolmistress rising twenty-four or twenty-five, in the world who hadn't had *some* affair, even if it were no more than a gentleman in a teashop who every afternoon for a week had gazed at her disrespectfully over a slice of plum-cake. . . . And then disappeared . . . But you had to have had at least a might-have-been or you couldn't go on being a schoolmistress or a girl in a ministry or a dactylographer of respectability. You packed *that* away in the bottom of your mind and on Sunday mornings before the perfectly insufficient Sunday dinner, you took it out and built castles in Spain in which you were a castanetted heroine turning on wonderful hips, but casting behind you inflaming glances. . . . Something like that!

Well, she had had an affair with this honest, simple creature! So good! So unspeakably GOOD. . . . Like the late Albert, prince consort! The very, helpless, immobile sort of creature that she ought not to have tempted. It had been like shooting tame pigeons! Because he had had a Society wife always in the illustrated papers whilst he sat at home and evolved Statistics or came to tea with her dear, tremendous, distracted mother, whom he helped to get her articles accurate. So a woman tempted him and he did . . . No; he didn't quite eat!

But why? . . . Because he was GOOD?

Very likely.

Or was it . . . That was the intolerable thought that she shut up within her along with the material for castles in the air! Was it because he had been really indifferent?

They had revolved round each other at tea-parties — or rather he had revolved round her, because at Edith Ethel's affairs she always sat, a fixed starlet, behind the tea-urn and dispensed cups. But he would moon round the room, looking at the backs of books; occasionally laying down the law to some guest; and always drifting in the end to her side where he would say a trifle or two. . . . And the beautiful — the quite excruciatingly beautiful wife — striding along the Row with the second son of the Earl of Someone at her side. . . . Asking for it. . . .

So it had been from the 1/7/12, say, to the 4/8/14!

After that, things had become more rubbled — mixed up with alarums. Excursions on his part to unapproved places. And trouble. He was quite damnably in trouble. With his Superiors; with, so unnecessarily, Hun projectiles, wire, mud; over Money; politics; mooning on without a good word from anyone. . . . Unravellable muddles that never got unravelled but that somehow got you caught up in them. . . .

Because he needed her moral support! When, during the late Hostilities, he hadn't been out there, he had drifted to the tea-table much earlier of an afternoon and stayed beside it much longer, till after everyone else had gone and they could go and sit on the tall fender side by side, and argue . . . about the rights and wrongs of the War!

Because she was the only soul in the world with whom he could talk. . . . They had the same sort of good, bread-and-butter brains; without much of the romantic. . . . No doubt a touch . . . in him. Otherwise he would not have always been in these muddles. He gave all he possessed to anyone who asked for it. That was all right. But that those who sponged on him should also involve him in intolerable messes. . . . That was not proper. One ought to defend oneself against that!

Because . . . if you do not defend yourself against that, look how you let in your nearest and dearest — those who have to sympathise with you in your confounded troubles whilst you moon on, giving away more and more and getting into more troubles! In this case it was she who was his Nearest and Dearest. . . . Or had been! At that her nerves suddenly got the better of her and her mind went mad. . . . Supposing that that fellow, from whom she had not heard for two years, *hadn't* now communicated with her. . . . Like an ass she had taken it for granted that he had *asked* Lady . . . Blast her! . . . to "bring them together again"! She had imagined that even Edith Ethel would not have had the cheek to ring her up if he hadn't asked her to!

But she had nothing to go on. . . . Feeble, oversexed ass that she was, she had let her mind jump at once to the conclusion, the moment the mere mention of him seemed implied — jump to the conclusion that he was asking her again to come and be his mistress. . . . Or nurse him through his present muddle till he should be fit to . . .

Mind, she did not say that she would have succumbed. But if she had not jumped at the idea that it was he, really, speaking through Edith Ethel, she would never have permitted her mind to dwell on . . . on his blasted, complacent perfections!

Because she had taken it for granted that if he had had her rung up he would not have been monkeying with other girls during the two years he hadn't written to her. . . . Ah, but hadn't he?

Look here! *Was* it reasonable? Here was a fellow who had all but . . . all BUT . . . "taken advantage of her" one night just before going out to France, say, two years ago. . . . And not another word from him after that! . . . It was all very well to say that he was portentous, looming, luminous, loony: John Peel with his coat so grey, the English Country Gentleman *pur sang*, and then some; saintly, Godlike, Jesus Christ-like. . . . He was all that. But you don't seduce, as near as can be, a young woman and then go off to Hell, leaving her, God knows, in Hell, and not so much as send her, in two years, a picture-postcard with MIZPAH on it. You don't. You don't!

Or if you do you have to have your character revised. You have to have it taken for granted that you were only monkeying with her and that you've been monkeying ever since with Waacs in Rouen or some other Base. . . .

Of course, if you ring your young woman up when you come back . . . or have her rung up by a titled lady. . . . That might restore you in the eyes of the world, or at least in the eyes of the young woman if she was a bit of a softie. . . .

But *had* he? *Had* he? It was absurd to think that Edith Ethel hadn't had the face to do it unasked! To save three thousand, two hundred pounds, not to mention interest — which was what Vincent owed *him*! — Edith Ethel with the sweetest possible smile would beg the pillows off a whole hospital ward full of dying. . . . She was

quite right. She had to save her man. You go to any depths of ig
nominy to save your man.

But that did not help her, Valentine Wannop!

She sprang off the bench; she clenched her nails into her palms;
she stamped her thin-soled shoes into the coke-brise floor that was
singularly unresilient. She exclaimed:

"Damn it all, he didn't ask her to ring me up. He didn't ask her
to. He didn't ask her to!" still stamping about.

She marched straight at the telephone that was by now uttering
long, tinny, night-jar's calls and, with one snap, pulled the receiver
right off the twisted, green-blue cord. . . . Broke it! With incidental
satisfaction.

Then she said:

"Steady the Buffs!" not out of repentance for having damaged
School Property, but because she was accustomed to call her thoughts
The Buffs because of their practical, unromantic character as a rule.
. . . A fine regiment, the Buffs!

Of course, if she had not broken the telephone she could have rung
up Edith Ethel and have asked her whether he had or hadn't asked
to . . . to be brought together again. . . . It was like her, Valentine
Wannop, to smash the only means of resolving a torturing
doubt. . . .

It wasn't, really, in the least like her. *She* was practical enough;
none of the "under the ban of fatality" business about her. She had
smashed the telephone because it had been like smashing a connection with Edith Ethel; or because she hated tinny night-jars; or
because she had smashed it. For nothing in the world; for nothing,
nothing, nothing in the world would she ever ring up Edith Ethel
and ask her:

"Did *he* put you up to ringing me up?"

That would be to let Edith Ethel come between their intimacy.

A subconscious volition was directing her feet towards the great
doors at the end of the Hall, varnished, pitch-pine doors of Gothic
architecture; economically decorated as if with straps and tin-lids
of Brunswick-blacked cast iron.

She said:

"Of course if it's his wife who has removed his furniture that would
be a reason for his wanting to get into communication. They would
have split. . . . But he does not hold with a man divorcing a woman,
and she won't divorce."

As she went through the sticky postern — all that woodwork seemed sticky on account of its varnish! — beside the great doors she said:

"Who cares!"

The great thing was . . . but she could not formulate what the great thing was. You had to settle the preliminaries.

III

SHE said eventually to Miss Wanostrocht who had sat down at her table behind two pink carnations:

"I didn't consciously want to bother you but a spirit in my feet has led me who knows how. . . . That's Shelley, isn't it?"

And indeed a quite unconscious but shrewd mind had pointed out to her whilst still in the School Hall and even before she had broken the telephone, that Miss Wanostrocht very probably would be able to tell her what she wanted to know and that if she didn't hurry she might miss her, since the Head would probably go now the girls were gone. So she had hurried through gauntish corridors whose Decorated Gothic windows positively had bits of pink glass here and there interspersed in their lattices. Nevertheless a nearly deserted, darkish, locker-lined dressing-room being a short cut, she had paused in it before the figure of a clumsyish girl, freckled, in black and, on a stool, desultorily lacing a dull black boot, an ankle on her knee. She felt an impulse to say: "Goodbye, Pettigul!" she didn't know why.

The clumsy, fifteenish, bumpy-faced girl was a symbol of that place — healthyish, but not over healthy; honestish but with no craving for intellectual honesty; big-boned in unexpected places . . . and uncomelily blubbering so that her face appeared dirtyish. . . . It was in fact all "ishes" about that Institution. They were all healthy-ish, honestish, clumsyish, twelve-to-eighteenish, and big-boned in unexpected places because of the late insufficient feeding. . . . Emotionalish, too; apt to blubber rather than to go into hysterics.

Instead of saying good-bye to the girl she said:

"Here!" and roughly, since she was exhibiting too much leg, pulled down the girl's shortish skirt and set to work to lace the unyielding boot on the unyielding shin-bone. . . . After a period of youthful bloom, which would certainly come and as certainly go, this girl would, normally, find herself one of the Mothers of Europe, marriage being due to the period of youthful bloom. . . . Normally that is to say according to a normality that that day might restore. Of course it mightn't!

A tepid drop of moisture fell on Valentine's right knuckle.

"My cousin Bob was killed the day before yesterday," the girl's voice said above her head. Valentine bent her head still lower over the boot with the patience that, in educational establishments, you must, if you want to be businesslike and shrewd, acquire and display in face of unusual mental vagaries. . . . This girl had never had a cousin Bob, or anything else. Pettigul and her two sisters, Pettiguls Two and Three, were all in that Institution at extremely reduced rates precisely because they had not got, apart from their widowed mother, a discoverable relative. The father, a half-pay major, had been killed early in the war. All the mistresses had had to hand in reports on the moral qualities of the Pettiguls, so all the mistresses had this information.

"He gave me his puppy to keep for him before he went out," the girl said. "It doesn't seem just!"

Valentine, straightening herself, said:

"I should wash my face if I were you, before I went out. Or you might get yourself taken for a German!" She pulled the girl's clumsyish blouse straight on her shoulders.

"Try," she added, "to imagine that you've got someone just come back! It's just as easy and it will make you look more attractive!"

Scurrying along the corridors she said to herself:

"Heaven help me, does it make *me* look more attractive?"

She caught the Head, as she had anticipated, just on the point of going to her home in Fulham, an unattractive suburb but near a bishop's palace nevertheless. It seemed somehow appropriate. The lady was episcopally minded, but experienced in the vicissitudes of suburban children: very astonishing some of them unless you took them very much in the lump.

Miss Head had stood behind her table for the first three questions and answers in an attitude of someone who is a little at bay, but she had sat down just before Valentine had quoted her Shelley at her, and she had now the air of one who is ready to make a night of it. Valentine continued to stand.

"This," Miss Wanostrocht said very gently, "is a day on which

one might . . . take steps . . . that might influence one's whole
life."

"That's," Valentine answered, "exactly why I've come to you. I
want to know what that woman said to you so as to know where
I stand before I take a step."

The Head said:

"I had to let the girls go. I don't mind saying that you are very
valuable to me. The Governors — I had an express from Lord
Boulnois — ordered them to be given a holiday to-morrow. It's very
inconsistent. But that makes it all the . . ."

She stopped. Valentine said to herself:

"By Jove, I don't know anything about men; but how little I know
about women. What's she getting at?"

She added:

"She's nervous. She must be wanting to say something she thinks
I won't like!"

She said chivalrously:

"I don't believe anybody could have kept those girls in to-day. It's
a thing one has no experience of. There's never been a day like this
before."

Out there in Piccadilly there would be mobs shoulder to shoulder;
she had never seen the Nelson column stand out of a solid mass.
They might roast oxen whole in the Strand. Whitechapel would be
seething, enamelled iron advertisements looking down on millions of
bowler hats. All sordid and immense London stretched out under her
gaze. She felt herself *of* London as the grouse feels itself of the
heather, and there she was in an emptied suburb looking at two pink
carnations. Dyed probably: offering of Lord Boulnois to Miss
Wanostrocht! You never saw a natural-grown carnation that shade!

She said:

"I'd be glad to know what that woman — Lady Macmaster — told
you."

Miss Wanostrocht looked down at her hands. She had the little-
fingers hooked together, the hands back to back; it was a demoded
gesture. . . . Girton of 1897, Valentine thought; indulged in by the
thoughtfully blonde. . . . Fair girl graduates the sympathetic comic
papers of those days had called them. It pointed to a long sitting.
Well, she, Valentine, was not going to brusque the issue! . . .
French-derived expression that. But how would you put it otherwise?

Miss Wanostrocht said:

"I sat at the feet of your father!"

"You see!" Valentine said to herself. "But she must then have gone to Oxford, not Newnham!" She could not remember whether there had been woman's colleges at Oxford as early as 1895 or 1897. There must have been.

"The greatest Teacher . . . The greatest influence in the world," Miss Wanostrocht said.

It was queer, Valentine thought: This woman had known all about her — at any rate all about her distinguished descent all the time she, Valentine, had been Physical Instructress at that Great Public School (Girls'). Yet except for an invariable courtesy such as she imagined Generals might show to non-commissioned officers, Miss Wanostrocht had hitherto taken no more notice of her than she might have taken of a superior parlourmaid. On the other hand she had let Valentine arrange her physical training exactly as she liked, without any interference.

"We used to hear," Miss Wanostrocht said, "how he spoke Latin with you and your brother from the day of your births. . . . He used to be regarded as eccentric, but how *right*! . . . Miss Hall says that you are the most remarkable Latinist she has ever so much as imagined."

"It's not true," Valentine said, "I can't *think* in Latin. You cannot be a real Latinist unless you do that. He did of course."

"It was the last thing you would think of him as doing," the Head answered with a pale gleam of youth. "He was such a thorough man of the world. So awake!"

"We ought to be a queer lot, my brother and I," Valentine said. "With such a father . . . And mother of course!"

Miss Wanostrocht said:

"Oh . . . your *mother* . . ."

And immediately Valentine conjured up the little, adoring female clique of Miss Wanostrocht's youth, all spying on her father and mother in their walks under the Oxford Sunday trees, the father so jaunty and awake, the mother so trailing, large, generous, unobservant. And all the little clique saying: If only he had *us* to look after him. . . . She said with a little malice:

"You don't read my mother's novels, I suppose. . . . It was she who did all my father's writing for him. He couldn't write, he was too impatient!"

Miss Wanostrocht exclaimed:

"Oh, you *shouldn't* say that!" with almost the pain of someone defending her own personal reputation.

"I don't see why I shouldn't," Valentine said. "He was the first person to say it about himself."

"He shouldn't have said it either," Miss Wanostrocht answered with a sort of soft unction. "He should have taken care more of his own reputation for the sake of his Work!"

Valentine considered this thin, ecstatic spinster with ironic curiosity.

"Of course, if you've sat . . . if you're still sitting at father's feet as much as all that," she conceded, "it gives you a certain right to be careful about his reputation. . . . All the same I wish you would tell me what that person said on the phone!"

The bust of Miss Wanostrocht moved with a sudden eagerness further towards the edge of her table.

"It's precisely because of that," she said, "that I want to speak to you first. . . . That I want you to consider. . . ."

Valentine said:

"Because of my father's reputation. . . . Look here, did that person — Lady Macmaster! — speak to you as if you were me? Our names are near enough to make it possible."

"You're," Miss Wanostrocht said, "as one might say, the fine fruit of the product of his views on the education of women. And if you . . . It's been such a satisfaction to me to observe in you such a . . . a sound, instructed head on such a . . . oh, you know, sane body. . . . And then . . . An earning capacity. A commercial value. Your father, of course, never minced words. . . ." She added:

"I'm bound to say that my interview with Lady Macmaster . . . who surely isn't a lady of whom you could say that you disapprove. I've read her husband's work. It surely — you'd say, wouldn't you? — conserves some of the ancient fire."

"He," Valentine said, "hasn't a word of Latin to his tail. He makes his quotations out, if he uses them, by means of school-cribs. . . . I know his methods of work, you know."

It occurred to Valentine to think that if Edith Ethel really *had* at first taken Miss Wanostrocht for herself there might pretty obviously be some cause for Miss Wanostrocht's concern for her father's reputation as an intimate trainer of young women. She figured Edith Ethel suddenly bursting into a description of the circumstances of that man who was without furniture and did not appear to recognise the porter. The relations she might have described as having existed between her and him might well worry the Head of a Great Public School for Middle Class Girls. She had no doubt been described as having had a baby. A disagreeable and outraged current invaded her feelings. . . .

It was suddenly obscured by a recrudescence of the thought that had come to her only incidentally in the hall. It rushed over her with extraordinary vividness now, like a wave of warm liquid. . . . If it *had* really been that fellow's wife who had removed his furniture what *was* there to keep them apart? He couldn't have pawned or sold or burnt his furniture whilst he had been with the British Expeditionary Force in the Low Countries! He couldn't have without extraordinary difficulty! Then . . . What *should* keep them apart? . . . Middle Class Morality? A pretty gory carnival that had been for the last four years! Was this then Lent, pressing hard on the heels of Saturnalia? Not so hard as that, surely! So that if one hurried. . . . What on earth did she want, unknown to herself?

She heard herself saying, almost with a sob, so that she was evidently in a state of emotion:

"Look here, I disapprove of this whole thing: of what my father has brought me to! Those people . . . the brilliant Victorians talked all the time through their hats. They evolved a theory from anywhere and then went brilliantly mad over it. Perfectly recklessly. . . . Have you noticed Pettigul One? . . . Hasn't it occurred to you that you *can't* carry on violent physical jerks and mental work side by side? I ought not to be in this school and I ought not to be what I am!"

At Miss Wanostrocht's perturbed expression she said to herself:

"What on earth am I saying all this for? You'd think I was trying to cut loose from this school! Am I?"

Nevertheless her voice was going on:

"There's too much oxygenation of the lungs, here. It's unnatural. It affects the brain, deleteriously. Pettigul One is an example of it. She's earnest with me and earnest with her books. Now she's gone dotty. Most of them it only stupefies."

It was incredible to her that the mere imagination that that fellow's wife had left him should make her spout out like this — for all the world like her father spouting out one of his ingenious theories! . . . It had really occurred to her once or twice to think that you could not run a dual physical and mental existence without some risk. The military physical developments of the last four years had been responsible for a real exaggeration of physical values. She was aware that in that Institution, for the last four years, she had been regarded as supplementing if not as actually replacing both the doctor and the priest. . . . But from that to evolving a complete theory that the Pettigul's lie was the product of an overoxygenated brain was going pretty far. . . .

Still, she was prevented from taking part in national rejoicings; pretty certainly Edith Ethel had been talking scandal about her to Miss Wanostrocht. She had the right to take it out in some sort of exaggerated declamation!

"It appears," Miss Wanostrocht said, "for we can't now go into the question of the whole curriculum of the school, though I am inclined to agree with you. What by the by is the matter with Pettigul One? I thought her rather a solid sort of girl. But it appears that the wife of a friend . . . perhaps it's only a former friend of yours, is in a nursing home."

Valentine exclaimed:

"Oh, he . . . But that's too ghastly!"

"It appears," Miss Wanostrocht said, "to be rather a mess." She added: "That appears to be the only expression to use."

For Valentine, that piece of news threw a blinding light upon herself. She was overwhelmingly appalled because that woman was in a nursing home. Because in that case it would not be sporting to go and see the husband!

Miss Wanostrocht went on:

"Lady Macmaster was anxious for your advice. . . . It appears that the only other person that could look after the interests of . . . of your friend: his brother . . ."

Valentine missed something out of that sentence. Miss Wanostrocht talked too fluently. If people wanted you to appreciate items of sledge-hammering news they should not use long sentences. They should say:

"He's mad and penniless. His brother's dying, his wife's just been operated on." Like that! Then you could take it in; even if your mind was rioting about like a cat in a barrel.

"The brother's . . . female companion," Miss Wanostrocht was wandering on, "though it appears that she would have been willing is therefore not available. . . . The theory is that he — he himself, your friend, has been considerably unhinged by his experiences in the war. Then . . . Who in your opinion should take the responsibility of looking after his interests?"

Valentine heard herself say:

"Me!"

She added:

"Him! Looking after him. I don't know that he has any . . . interests!"

He didn't appear to have any furniture, so how could he have the other things. She wished Miss Wanostrocht would leave off using the word "appear." It was irritating . . . and infectious. Could the lady not make a direct statement? But then, no one ever made clear statements and this no doubt appeared to that anæmic spinster a singularly tenebrous affair.

As for clear statements . . . If there had ever been any in precisely this tenebrous mess she, Valentine, would know how she stood with that man's wife. For it was part of the preposterous way in which she herself and all her friends behaved that they never made clear statements — except for Edith Ethel who had the nature of a female costermonger and could not tell the truth, though she could be clear enough. But even Edith Ethel had never hitherto said anything about the way the wife in this case treated the husband. She had given Valentine very clearly to understand that she "sided" with the wife — but she had never gone as far as to say that the wife was a good wife. If she — Valentine — could only know that.

Miss Wanostrocht was asking:

"When you say 'Me,' do you mean that you would propose to look after that man yourself? I trust not."

. . . Because, obviously, if she were a good wife, she, Valentine couldn't butt in . . . not generously. As her father's and still more her mother's daughter. . . . On the face of it you would say that a wife who was always striding along the palings of the Row, or the paths of other resorts of the fashionable could not be a good — a domestic — wife of a Statistician. On the other hand he was a pretty smart man, Governing class, county family, and the rest of it — so he might like his wife to figure in Society; he might even exact it. He was quite capable of that. Why, for all she knew, the wife might be a retiring, shy person whom he thrust out into the hard world. It was not likely, but it was as possible as anything else.

Miss Wanostrocht was asking:

"Aren't there Institutions . . . Military Sanatoria . . . for cases precisely like that of this Captain Tietjens. It appears to be the war that has broken him down, not merely evil living."

"It's precisely," Valentine said, "because of that that one should want . . . shouldn't one . . . Because it's because of the War. . . ."

The sentence would not finish itself.

Miss Wanostrocht said:

"I thought . . . It has been represented to me . . . that you were a Pacifist. Of an extreme type!"

It had given Valentine a turn — like the breaking out of sweat in a case of fever — to hear the name, coldly, "Captain Tietjens," for it was like a release. She had been irrationally determined that hers should not be the first tongue to utter that name.

And apparently from her tone Miss Wanostrocht was prepared to detest that Captain Tietjens. Perhaps she detested him already.

She was beginning to say:

"If one is an extreme Pacifist because one cannot bear to think of the sufferings of men isn't that a precise reason why one should wish that a poor devil, all broken up . . .

But Miss Wanostrocht had begun one of her own long sentences. Their voices went on together, like trains dragging along ballast — disagreeably. Miss Wanostrocht's organ, however, won out with the words:

". . . behaved very badly indeed."

Valentine said hotly:

"You ought not to believe anything of the sort — on the strength of anything said by a woman like Lady Macmaster."

Miss Wanostrocht appeared to have been brought to a complete stop: she leaned forward in her chair; her mouth was a little open. And Valentine said: "Thank Goodness!" to herself.

She had to have a moment to herself to digest what had the air of being new evidence of the baseness of Edith Ethel; she felt herself to be infuriated in regions of her own being that she hardly knew. That seemed to her to be a littleness in herself. She had not thought that she had been as little as that. It ought not to matter what people said of you. She was perfectly accustomed to think of Edith Ethel as telling whole crowds of people very bad things about her, Valentine Wannop. But there was about this a recklessness that was hardly believable. To tell an unknown person, encountered by chance

on the telephone, derogatory facts about a third party who might
be expected to come to the telephone herself in a minute or two —
and, not only that — who must in all probability hear what had been
said very soon after, from the first listener. . . . That was surely
a recklessness of evil-speaking that almost outpassed sanity. . . .
Or else it betrayed a contempt for her, Valentine Wannop, and
what she could do in the way of reprisals that was extremely hard
to bear!

She said suddenly to Miss Wanostrocht:

"Look here! Are you speaking to me as a friend to my father's
daughter or as a Headmistress to a Physical Instructor?"

A certain amount of blood came into the lady's pinkish features.
She had certainly been ruffled when Valentine had permitted her
voice to sound so long alongside her own; for, although Valentine
knew next to nothing about the Head's likes or dislikes she had once
or twice before seen her evince marked distaste on being interrupted
in one of her formal sentences.

Miss Wanostrocht said with a certain coldness:

"I'm speaking at present . . . I'm allowing myself the liberty —
as a much older woman — in the capacity of a friend of your father.
I have been, in short, trying to recall to you all that you owe to
yourself as being an example of his training!"

Involuntarily Valentine's lips formed themselves for a low whistle
of incredulity. She said to herself:

"By Jove! I am in the middle of a nasty affair. . . . This is a sort
of professional cross-examination."

"I am in a way glad," the lady was now continuing, "that you take
that line. . . . I mean of defending Mrs. Tietjens with such heat
against Lady Macmaster. Lady Macmaster appears to dislike Mrs.
Tietjens, but I am bound to say that she appears to be in the right
of it. I mean of her dislike. Lady Macmaster is a serious personality
and, even on her public record Mrs. Tietjens appears to be very
much the reverse. No doubt you wish to be loyal to your . . .
friends, but . . ."

"We appear," Valentine said, "to be getting into an extraordinary
muddle."

She added:

"I haven't, as you seem to think, been defending Mrs. Tietjens. I
would have. I would at any time. I have always thought of her as
beautiful and kind. But I heard you say the words: *'has been behav-*

ing very badly,' and I thought you meant that Captain Tietjens had. I denied it. If you meant that his wife has, I deny it, too. She's an admirable wife . . . and mother . . . that sort of thing, for all I know. . . ."

She said to herself:

"Now why do I say that? What's Hecuba to me?" and then:

"It's to defend *his* honour, of course . . . I'm trying to present Captain Tietjens as English Country Gentleman complete with admirably arranged establishment, stables, kennels, spouse, offspring. . . . That's a queer thing to want to do!"

Miss Wanostrocht who had breathed deeply said now:

"I'm extremely glad to hear that. Lady Macmaster certainly said that Mrs. Tietjens was — let us say — at least a neglectful wife. . . . Vain, you know; idle; overdressed. . . . All that. . . . And you appeared to defend Mrs. Tietjens."

"She's a smart woman in smart Society," Valentine said, "but it's with her husband's concurrence. She has a right to be. . . ."

"We shouldn't," Miss Wanostrocht said, "be in the extraordinary muddle to which you referred if you did not so continually interrupt me. I was trying to say that, for you, an inexperienced girl, brought up in a sheltered home, no pitfall could be more dangerous than a man with a wife who neglected her duties!"

Valentine said:

"You will have to excuse my interrupting you. It *is*, you know, rather more my funeral than yours."

Miss Wanostrocht said quickly:

"You can't say that. You don't know how ardently . . ."

Valentine said:

"Yes, yes. . . . Your *schwaerm* for my father's memory and all. But my father couldn't bring it about that I should lead a sheltered life. . . . I'm about as experienced as any girl of the lower classes. . . . No doubt it was his doing, but don't make any mistakes."

She added:

"Still, it's I that's the corpse. You're conducting the inquest. So it's more fun for you."

Miss Wanostrocht had grown slightly pale:

"I, if . . ." she stammered slightly, "by 'experience' you mean . . ."

"I don't," Valentine exclaimed, "and you have no right to infer that I do on the strength of a conversation you've had, but shouldn't

have had, with one of the worst tongues in London. . . . I mean
that my father left us so that I had to earn my and my mother's living as a servant for some months after his death. That was what his
training came to. But I can look after myself. . . . In consequence . . ."

Miss Wanostrocht had thrown herself back in her chair.

"But . . ." she exclaimed; she had grown completely pale — like
discoloured wax. "There was a subscription. . . . We . . ." she began: "We knew that he hadn't . . ."

"You subscribed," Valentine said, "to purchase his library and
presented it to his wife . . . who had nothing to eat but what my
wages as a tweeny maid got for her." But before the pallor of the
other lady she tried to add a touch of generosity: "Of course the
subscribers wanted, very naturally, to preserve as much as they could
of his personality. A man's books are very much himself. That was
all right." She added: "All the same I had that training: in a suburban basement. So you cannot teach me a great deal about the shady
in life. I was in the family of a Middlesex County Councillor. In
Ealing."

Miss Wanostrocht said faintly:

"This is very dreadful!"

"It isn't really!" Valentine said. "I wasn't badly treated as tweeny
maids go. It would have been better if the Mistress hadn't been a
constant invalid and the cook constantly drunk. . . . After that I
did a little office work. For the suffragettes. That was after old Mr.
Tietjens came back from abroad and gave mother some work on a
paper he owned. We scrambled along then, somehow. Old Mr. Tietjens was father's greatest friend, so father's side, as you might say,
turned up trumps — if you like to think that to console you. . . ."

Miss Wanostrocht was bending her face down over her table,
presumably to hide a little of it from Valentine or to avoid the girl's
eyes.

Valentine went on:

"One knows all about the conflict between a man's private duties
and his public achievements. But with a very little less of the flam-
boyant in his life my father might have left us very much better
off. It isn't what I *want* — to be a cross between a sergeant in the
army and an upper housemaid. Any more than I wanted to be an
under one."

Miss Wanostrotch uttered an "Oh!" of pain. She exclaimed rapidly:

"It was your moral rather than your mere athletic influence that made me so glad to have you here. . . . It was because I felt that you did not set such a high value on the physical. . . ."

"Well, you aren't going to have me here much longer," Valentine said. "Not an instant more than I can in decency help. I'm going to . . ."

She said to herself:

"What on earth am I going to do? . . . What do I want?"

She wanted to lie in a hammock beside a blue, tideless sea and think about Tibullus . . . There was no nonsense about her. She did not want to engage in intellectual pursuits herself. She had not the training. But she intended to enjoy the more luxurious forms of the intellectual products of others. . . . That appeared to be the moral of the day!

And, looking rather minutely at Miss Wanostrocht's inclined face, she wondered if, in the history of the world, there had ever been such another day. Had Miss Wanostrocht, for instance, ever known what it was to have a man come back. Ah, but amid the tumult of a million other men coming back! A collective impulse to slacken off! Immense! Softening!

Miss Wanostrocht had apparently loved her father. No doubt in company with fifty damsels. Did they ever get a collective kick out of that affair? It was even possible that she had spoken as she had . . . *pour cause*. Warning her, Valentine, against the deleterious effect of being connected with a man whose wife was unsatisfactory. . . . Because the fifty damsels had all, in duty bound, thought that her mother was an unsatisfactory wife for the brilliant, grey-black-haired Eminence with the figure of a stripling that her father had been. . . . They had probably thought that, without the untidy figure of Mrs. Wannop as a weight upon him, he might have become . . . Well, with one of *them*! . . . anything! Any sort of figure in the councils of the nation. Why not Prime Minister? For along with his pedagogic theories he had had political occupations. He had certainly had the friendship of Disraeli. He supplied — it was historic! — materials for eternally famous, meretricious speeches. He would have been head-trainer of the Empire's pro-consuls if the other fellow, at Balliol, had not got in first. . . . As it was he had

had to specialise in the Education of Women. Building up Primrose Dames. . . .

So Miss Wanostrocht warned her against the deleterious effect of neglected wives upon young, attached virgins! It probably *was* deleterious. Where would she, Valentine Wannop, have been by now if she had thought that Sylvia Tietjens was really a bad one?

Miss Wanostrocht said, as if with sudden anxiety:

"You are going to do what? You propose to do what?"

Valentine said:

"Obviously after your conversation with Edith Ethel you won't be so glad to have me here. My moral influence has not been brightened in aspect!" A wave of passionate resentment swept over her.

"Look here," she said, "if you think that I am prepared to . . ."

She stopped however, "No," she said, "I am not going to introduce the housemaid note. But you will probably see that this is irritating." She added: "I would have the case of Pettigul One looked into, if I were you. It might become epidemic in a big school like this. And we've no means of knowing where we stand nowadays!"

Part Two

Months and months before Christopher Tietjens had stood extremely wishing that his head were level with a particular splash of purposeless whitewash. Something behind his mind forced him to the conviction that, if his head — and of course the rest of his trunk and lower limbs — were suspended by a process of levitation to that distance above the duckboard on which, now, his feet were, he would be in an inviolable sphere. These waves of conviction recurred continually: he was constantly glancing aside and upwards at that splash; it was in the shape of the comb of a healthy rooster; it gleamed, with five serrations, in the just-beginning light that shone along the thin, unroofed channel in the gravel slope. Wet half-light, just flickering; more visible there than in the surrounding desolation because the deep, narrow channel framed a section of just-illuminated rift in the watery eastwards!

Twice he had stood up on a rifleman's step enforced by a bully-beef case to look over — in the last few minutes. Each time, on stepping down again, he had been struck by that phenomenon: the light seen from the trench seemed if not brighter, then more definite. So, from the bottom of a pit-shaft in broad day you can see the stars. The wind was light, but from the north-west. They had there the weariness of a beaten army, the weariness of having to begin always new days again. . . .

He glanced aside and upwards: that cockscomb of phosphorescence. . . . He felt waves of some X force propelling his temples towards it. He wondered if perhaps the night before he had not observed that that was a patch of reinforced concrete, therefore more

543

resistant. He might of course have observed that and then forgotten it. He hadn't! It was therefore irrational.

If you are lying down under fire — flat under pretty smart fire — and you have only a paper bag in front of your head for cover you feel immeasurably safer than you do without it. You have a mind at rest. This must be the same thing.

It remained dark and quiet. It was forty-five minutes. It became forty-four . . . Forty-three . . . Forty-two minutes and thirty seconds before a crucial moment and the slate grey cases of miniature metal pineapples had not come from the bothering place. . . . Who knew if there was anyone in charge there?

Twice that night he had sent runners back. No results yet. That bothering fellow might quite well have forgotten to leave a substitute. That was not likely. A careful man. But a man with a mania might forget. Still it was not likely! . . .

Thoughts menaced him as clouds threaten the heads of mountains, but for the moment they kept away. It was quiet; the wet cool air was agreeable. They had autumn mornings that felt like that in Yorkshire. The wheels of his physique moved smoothly; he was more free in the chest than he had been for months.

A single immense cannon, at a tremendous distance said something. Something sulky. Aroused in its sleep and protesting. But it was not a signal to begin anything. Too heavy. Firing at something at a tremendous distance. At Paris, maybe, or the North Pole, or the moon! They were capable of that, those fellows!

It would be a tremendous piece of frightfulness to hit the moon. Great gain in prestige. And useless. There was no knowing what they would not be up to, as long as it was stupid and useless. And, naturally, boring. . . . And it was a mistake to be boring. One went on fighting to get rid of those bores — as you would to get rid of a bore in a club.

It was more descriptive to call what had spoken a cannon than a gun — though it was not done in the best local circles. It was all right to call 75's or the implements of the horse artillery "guns"; they were mobile and toy-like. But those immense things were cannons; the sullen muzzles always elevated. Sullen, like cathedral dignitaries or butlers. The thickness of barrel compared to the bore appeared enormous as they pointed at the moon, or Paris, or Nova Scotia.

Well, that cannon had not announced anything except itself! It was not the beginning of any barrage; our own fellows were not pooping off to shut it up. It had just announced itself, saying protestingly, "CAN . . . NON," and its shell soaring away to an enormous height caught the reflection of the unrisen sun on its base. A shining disc, like a halo in flight. . . . Pretty! A pretty motive for a decoration, tiny pretty planes up on a blue sky amongst shiny, flying haloes! Dragon-flies amongst saints. . . . No, "with angels and archangels!" . . . Well, one had seen it!

Cannon. . . . Yes, that was the right thing to call them. Like the up-ended, rusted things that stuck up out of parades when one had been a child.

No, not the signal for a barrage! A good thing! One might as well say "Thank Goodness," for the later they began the less long it lasted. . . . Less long it lasted was ugly alliteration. Sooner it was over was better. . . . No doubt half-past eight or at half-past eight to the stroke those boring fellows would let off their usual offering, probably plump, right on top of that spot. . . . As far as one could tell three salvoes of a dozen shells each at half-minute intervals between the salvoes. Perhaps salvoes was not the right word. Damn all artillery, anyhow!

Why did those fellows do it! Every morning at half-past eight; every afternoon at half-past two. Presumably just to show that they were still alive, and still boring. They were methodical. That was their secret. The secret of their boredom. Trying to kill them was like trying to shut up Liberals who would talk party politics in a non-political club. . . . Had to be done, though! Otherwise the world was no place for . . . Oh, post-prandial naps! . . . Simple philosophy of the contest! . . . Forty minutes! And he glanced aside and upwards at the phosphorescent cockscomb! Within his mind something said that if he were only suspended up there. . . .

He stepped once more on to the rifle-step and on to the bully-beef-case. He elevated his head cautiously: grey desolation sloped down and away F.R.R.R.r.r.r.! A gentle purring sound!

He was automatically back, on the duckboard, his breakfast hurting his chest. He said:

"By Jove! I got the fright of my life!" A laugh was called for; he managed it, his whole stomach shaking. And cold!

A head in a metal pudding-basin — a Suffolk type of blond head, pushed itself from a withdrawn curtain of sacking in the gravel wall beside him, at his back. A voice said with concern:

"There ain't no beastly snipers, is there, sir. I did 'ope there would'n be henny beastly snipers 'ere. It gives such a beastly lot of extra trouble warning the men."

Tietjens said it was a beastly skylark that almost walked into his mouth. The acting sergeant-major said with enthusiasm that them 'ere skylarks could fair scare the guts out of you. He remembered a raid in the dark, crawling on 'is 'ands 'n knees wen 'e put 'is 'and on a skylark on its nest. Never left 'is nest till 'is 'and was on 'im! Then it went up and fair scared the wind out of 'im. Cor! Never would 'e forget that!

With an air of carefully pulling parcels out of a carrier's cart he produced from the cavern behind the sacking two blinking assemblages of tubular khaki-clad limbs. They wavered to erectness, pink cheeses of faces yawning beside tall rifles and bayonets. The sergeant said:

"Keep yer 'eds down as you go along. You never knows!"

Tietjens told the lance-corporal of that party of two that his confounded gas-mask nozzle was broken. Hadn't he seen that for himself? The dismembered object bobbed on the man's chest. He was to go and borrow another from another man and see the other drew a new one at once.

Tietjens' eyes were drawn aside and upwards. His knees were still weak. If he were levitated to the level of that thing he would not have to use his legs for support.

The elderly sergeant went on with enthusiasm about skylarks. Wonderful the trust they showed in hus 'uman beens! Never left ther nesteses till you trod on them tho hall 'ell was rockin' around them.

An appropriate skylark from above and before the parapet made its shrill and heartless noise heard. No doubt the skylark that Tietjens had frightened — that had frightened him.

"Therd bin," the sergeant went on still enthusiastically, pointing a hand in the direction of the noise, skylarks singing on the mornin' of every straf'e'd ever bin in! Woner'ful trust in yumanity! Woner'ful hinstinck set in the fethered brest by the Halmighty! for 'oo was goin' to 'it a skylark on a battlefield?

The solitary Man dropped beside his long, bayonetted rifle that was muddied from stock to bayonet attachment. Tietjens said mildly that he thought the sergeant had got his natural history wrong. He must divide the males from the females. The females sat on the nest through obstinate attachment to their eggs; the males obstinately soared above the nests in order to pour out abuse at other male skylarks in the vicinity.

He said to himself that he must get the doctor to give him a bromide. A filthy state his nerves had got into unknown to himself. The agitation communicated to him by that bird was still turning his stomach round. . . .

"Gilbert White of Shelbourne," he said to the sergeant "called the behaviour of the female 'storge': a good word for it." But, as for trust in humanity, the sergeant might take it that larks never gave us a thought. We were part of the landscape and if what destroyed their nests whilst they sat on them was a bit of H.E. shell or the coulter of a plough it was all one to them.

The sergeant said to the rejoined lance corporal whose box now hung correctly on his muddied chest:

"Now its HAY post you gotter wait at!" They were to go along the trench and wait where another trench ran into it and there was a great A in whitewash on a bit of corrugated iron that was half-buried. "You can tell a great HAY from a bull's foot as well as another, can't you Corporal?" patiently.

"Wen they Mills bombs come 'e was to send 'is Man into Hay Cumpny dugout fer a fatigue to bring 'em along 'ere, but Hay Cumpny could keep '*is* little lot fer 'isself."

"An if they Mills bombs did'n' come the corporal'd better manufacture them on 'is own. An not make no mistakes!"

The lance-corporal said "Yes sargint, no sargint!" and the two went desultorily wavering along the duckboards, grey silhouettes against the wet bar of light, equilibrating themselves with hands on the walls of the trench.

"Ju 'eer what the orfcer said, Corporal," the one said to the other. "Wottever'll 'e say next! Skylarks not trust 'uman beens in battles! Cor!" The other grunted and, mournfully, the voices died out.

The cockscomb-shaped splash became of overwhelming interest momentarily to Tietjens; at the same time his mind began upon abstruse calculation of chances. Of his chances! A bad sign when the mind takes to doing that. Chances of direct hits by shells, by rifle bullets, by grenades, by fragments of shells or grenades. By any fragment of metal impinging on soft flesh. He was aware that he was going to be hit in the soft spot behind the collar-bone. He was conscious of that spot — the right-hand one; he felt none of the rest of his body. It is bad when the mind takes charge like that. A bromide was needed. The doctor must give him one. His mind felt pleasure at the thought of the M.O. A pleasant little fellow of the no-account order that knows his job. And carried liquor cheerfully. Confoundedly cheerfully!

He saw the doctor — plainly! It was one of the plainest things he could see of this whole show. . . . The doctor, a slight figure, vault on to the parapet, like a vaulting horse for height; stand up in the early morning sun. . . . Blind to the world, but humming *Father O'Flynn*. And stroll in the sunlight, a swagger cane of all things in the world, under his arms, right straight over to the German trench. . . . Then throw his cap down into that trench. And walk back! Delicately avoiding the strands in the cut apron of wire that he had to walk through!

The doctor said he had seen a Hun — probably an officer's batman — cleaning a top-boot with an apron over his knees. The Hun had shied a boot-brush at him and he had shied his cap at the Hun. The blinking Hun, he called him! No doubt the fellow had blinked!

No doubt you could do the unthinkable with impunity!

No manner of doubt: if you were blind drunk and all! . . . And however you strained, in an army you fell into routine. Of a quiet morning you do not expect drunken doctors strolling along your parapet. Besides, the German front lines were very thinly held. Amazingly! There might not have been a Hun with a gun within half a mile of that boot-black!

If he, Tietjens, stood in space, his head level with that cockscomb, he would be in an inviolable vacuum — as far as projectiles were concerned!

He was asking desultorily of the sergeant whether he often shocked the men by what he said and the sergeant was answering with blushes: Well, you do *say* things, sir! Not believing in skylarks now! If there was one thing the men believed hit was in the hinstincks of them little creatures!

"So that," Tietjens said, "they look at me as a sort of an atheist."

He forced himself to look over the parapet again, climbing heavily to his place of observation. It was sheer impatience and purely culpable technically. But he was in command of the regiment, of an establishment of a thousand and eighteen men, or that used to be the establishment of a battalion; of a strength of three hundred and thirty-three. Say seventy-five per company. And two companies in command of second lieutenants, one just out. . . . The last four days . . . There ought to be, say, eighty pairs of eyes surveying what he was going to survey. If there were fifteen it was as much as there were! . . . Figures were clean and comforting things. The chance against being struck by a shell-fragment that day, if the Germans came in any force, was fourteen-to-one against. There were battalions worse off than they. The sixth had only one one six left!

The tortured ground sloped down into mists. Say a quarter of a mile away. The German front lines were just shadows, like the corrugations of photographs of the moon: the paradoses of our own trenches two nights ago! The Germans did not seem to have troubled to chuck up much in the way of parapets. They didn't. They were coming on. Anyhow they held their front lines always very sparsely. . . . Was that the phrase? Was it even English?

Above the shadows the mist behaved tortuously, mounting up into umbrella shapes. Like snow-covered umbrella pines.

Disagreeable to force the eye to examine that mist. His stomach turned over. . . . That was the sacks. A flat, slightly disordered pile of wet sacks, half-right at two hundred yards. No doubt a shell had hit a G.S. wagon coming up with sacks for trenching. Or the bearers had bolted, chucking the sacks down. His eyes had fallen on that scattered pile four times already that morning. Each time his stomach had turned over. The resemblance to prostrate men was appalling. The enemy creeping up . . . Christ! Within two hundred yards. So his stomach said. Each time, in spite of the preparation.

Otherwise the ground had been so smashed that it was flat; went down into holes but did not rise up into mounds. That made it look gentle. It sloped down, to the untidiness. They appeared mostly to lie on their faces; why? Presumably they were mostly Germans pushed back in the last counter-attack. Anyhow you saw mostly the seats of their trousers. When you did not, how profound was their repose! You must phrase it a little like that — rhetorically. There was no other way to get the effect of that profoundness. Call it profundity!

It was different from sleep; flatter. No doubt when the appalled soul left the weary body, the panting lungs. . . . Well, you can't go on with a sentence like that. . . . But you collapsed inwards. Like the dying pig they sold on trays in the street. Painter fellows doing battlefields never got that *intimate* effect. Intimate to them there. Unknown to the corridors in Whitehall. . . . Probably because they — the painters — drew from living models or had ideas as to the human form. . . . But these were not limbs, muscles, torsi. Collections of tubular shapes in field-grey or mud-colour they were. Chucked about by Almighty God? As if He had dropped them from on high to make them flatten into the earth. . . . Good gravel soil, that slope and relatively dry. No dew to speak of. The night had been covered . . .

Dawn on the battlefield. '. . . Damn it all, why sneer? It *was* dawn on the battlefield. . . . The trouble was that *this* battle was not over. By no means over. There would be a hundred and eleven years, nine months, and twenty-seven days of it still. . . . No, you could not get the effect of that endless monotony of effort by numbers. Nor yet by saying "Endless monotony of effort." . . . It was like bending down to look into darkness of corridors under dark curtains. Under clouds . . . Mist . . .

At that, with dreadful reluctance his eyes went back to the spectral mists over the photographic shadows. He forced himself to put his glasses on the mists. They mopped and mowed, fantastically; grey, with black shadows; dropping like the dishevelled veils of murdered bodies. They were engaged in fantastic and horrifying laying out of corpses of vast dimensions; in silence, but in accord, they performed unthinkable tasks. They were the Germans. This was fear. This was the intimate fear of black, quiet nights, in dugouts where you heard the obscene suggestions of the miners' picks below you: tranquil, engrossed. Infinitely threatening. . . . But not FEAR.

It was in effect the desire for privacy. What he dreaded at those normal times when fear visited him at lunch; whilst seeing that the men got their baths or when writing, in a trench, in support, a letter to his bank-manager, was finding himself unhurt, surrounded by figures like the brothers of the Misericordia, going unconcerned about their tasks, noticing him hardly at all. . . . Whole hillsides, whole stretches of territory, alive with myriads of whitish-grey, long cagoules, with slits for eyeholes. Occasionally one would look at him through the eye-slits in the hoods. . . . The prisoner!

He would be the prisoner, liable to physical contracts — to being handled and being questioned. An invasion of his privacy!

As a matter of fact that wasn't so far out; not so dotty as it sounded. If the Huns got him — as they precious near had the night before last! — they would be — they had then been — in gas-masks of various patterns. They must be short of these things, but they looked, certainly, like goblin pigs with sore eyes, the hood with the askew, blind-looking eyeholes and the mouthpiece or the other nose

attachment going down into a box, astonishingly like snouts! . . .
Mopping and mowing — no doubt shouting through the masks!

They had appeared with startling suddenness and as if with a supernatural silence, beneath a din so overwhelming that you could not
any longer bother to notice it. They were there, as it were, under a
glass dome of silence that sheltered beneath that dark tumult, in
the white illumination of Verey lights that went on. They were there,
those of them that had already emerged from holes — astonishingly
alert hooded figures with the long rifles that always looked rather
amateurish — though, Hell, they weren't. The hoods and the white
light gave them the aspects of Canadian trappers in snow; made them
no doubt look still more husky fellows as against our poor rats of
Derby men. The heads of goblin pigs were emerging from shell-holes,
from rifts in the torn earth, from old trenches. . . . This ground had
been fought over again and again. Then the counter-attack had come
through his, Tietjens' own crowd. One disorderly mob, as you might
think, going through a disordered crowd that was damn glad to let
them through, realising slowly, in the midst of a general not knowing
what was going to happen, that the fellows were reliefs. They shot
past you clumsily in a darkness spangled with shafts of light coming
from God knows where and appeared going forward, whilst you at
least had the satisfaction that, by order, you were going back. In an
atmosphere of questioning. What was happening? What was going
to happen? . . . What the bloody hell. . . . What . . .

Tidy-sized shells began to drop among them saying: "Wee . . .
ee . . . ry. . . . Whack!" Some fellow showed Tietjens the way
through an immense apron of wire that was beginning to fly about.
He, Tietjens, was carrying a hell of a lot of paper folders and books.
They ought to have evacuated an hour ago; or the Huns ought not
to have got out of their holes for an hour. . . . But the Colonel had
been too . . . too exalted. Call it too exalted. He was not going to
evacuate for a pack of . . . damn orders! . . . The fellow McKechnie, had at last had to beg Tietjens to give the order. . . . Not that
the order mattered. The men could not have held ten minutes longer.
The ghostly Huns would have been in the trenches. But the Company Commanders knew that there was a Divisional Order to retire,
and no doubt they had passed it on to their subalterns before getting
killed. Still, that Bn. H.Q. should have given the order made it better
even if there was no one to take it to the companies. It turned a
practical expulsion into an officially strategic retreat. . . . And damn

good divisional staff work at that. They had been fitted into beautiful, clean, new trenches, all ready for them — like chessmen fitting into their boxes. Damn good for a beaten army that was being forced off the face of the earth. Into the English Channel. . . . What made them stick it? What the devil made the men stick it? They were unbelievable.

There was a stroking on his leg. A gentle, timid stroking! Well, he *ought* to get down: it was setting a bad example. The admirable trenches were perfectly efficiently fitted up with spy-holes. For himself he always disliked them. You thought of a rifle bullet coming smack through them and guided by the telescope into your right eye. Or perhaps you would not have a telescope. Anyhow you wouldn't know. . . .

There were still the three wheels, a-tilt, attached to slanting axles, in a haze of disintegrated wire, that, be-dewed, made profuse patterns like frost on a window. There was their own apron — a perfect village! — of wire over which he looked. Fairly intact. The Germans had put up some of their own in front of the lost trenches, a quarter of a mile off, over the reposing untidinesses. In between there was a perfect maze: their own of the night before last. How the deuce had it not been *all* mashed to pieces by the last Hun barrage? Yet there were three frosty erections — like fairy sheds, half-way between the two lines. And, suspended in them, as there would have to be, three bundles of rags and what appeared to be a very large, squashed crow. How the devil had that fellow managed to get smashed into that shape? It was improbable. There was also — suspended, too, a tall melodramatic object, the head cast back to the sky. One arm raised in the attitude of, say, a Walter Scott Highland officer waving his men on. Waving a sword that wasn't there. . . . That was what wire did for you. Supported you in grotesque attitudes, even in death! The beastly stuff! The men said that was Lieutenant Constantine. It might well be. The night before last he, Tietjens, had looked round at all the officers that were in H.Q. dug-out, come for a last moment conference. He had speculated on which of them would be killed. Ghostly! Well, they had all been killed, and more on to that. But his premonition hadn't run to thinking that Constantine would get caught up in the wire. But perhaps it was not Constantine. Probably they would never know. The Huns would be where he stood by lunchtime, if the attack of which Brigade H.Q. had warned them came off. But it mightn't. . . .

As a final salute to the on the whole not thrilling landscape, he wetted his forefinger by inserting it in his mouth and held it in the air. It was comfortingly chilly on the exterior, towards his back. Light airs were going right in the other fellows' faces. It might be only the dawn wind. But if it stiffened a very little or even held, those blessed Wurtembergers would never that day get out of their trenches. They couldn't come without gas. They were probably pretty well weakened, too. . . . You were not traditionally supposed to think much of Wurtembergers. Mild, dull creatures they were supposed to be. With funny hats. Good Lord! Traditions were going by the board!

He dropped down into the trench. The rather reddish soil with flakes of flint and little, pinkish nodules of pebbles was a friendly thing to face closely.

That sergeant was saying:

"You hadn't ought to do it, sir. Give me the creeps." He added rather lachrymosely that they couldn't do without superior officers *al*together. Odd creatures these Derby N.C.O.'s! They tried to get the tone of the old, time-serving N.C.O. They couldn't; all the same you couldn't say they weren't creditable achievements.

Yes, it was friendly, the trench face. And singularly unbellicose. When you looked at it you hardly believed that it was part of this affair. . . . Friendly! You felt at peace looking at its flints and pebbles. Like being in the butts up above Groby on the moor, waiting for the grouse to come over. The soil was not of course like those butts which were built of turfs. . . .

He asked, not so much for information, as to get the note of this fellow:

Why? What difference did it make whether there were senior officers or not? Anyone above eighteen would do, wouldn't they? They would keep on going on. It was a young man's war!

"It hasn't got that comfortable feeling, sir!" the sergeant expressed it. The young officers were very well for keeping you going through wire and barrages. But when you looked at them you didn't feel they knew so well what you were doing it for, if he might put it that way.

Tietjens said:

"Why? What are you doing it for?"

It wanted thirty-two minutes to the crucial moment. He said:

"Where are those bloody bombs?"

A trench cut in gravel wasn't, for all its friendly reddish-orange coloration, the ideal trench. Particularly against rifle-fire. There were rifts, presumably alongside flakes of flint that a rifle-bullet would get along. Still, the chances against a hit by a rifle-bullet were eighty thousand-to-one in a deep gravel trench like that. And he had had poor Jimmy Johns killed beside him by a bullet like that. So that gave him, say 140,000 chances-to-one against. He wished his mind would not go on and on figuring. It did it whilst you weren't looking. As a well-trained dog will do when you tell it to stay in one part of a room and it prefers another. It prefers to do figuring. Creeps from the rug by the door to the hearth-rug, its eyes on your unconscious face. . . . That was what your mind was like. Like a dog!

The sergeant said:

"They do say the first consignment of bombs was it not smashed. Hin a gully; well behind the line. Another was coming down."

"Then you'd better whistle," Tietjens said, "Whistle for all you're worth."

The sergeant said:

"Fer a wind, sir? Keep the 'Uns' beck, sir?"

Looking up at the whitewash cockscomb Tietjens lectured the sergeant on Gas. He always *had* said, and he said now, that the Germans had ruined themselves with their gas.

He went on lecturing that sergeant on gas. . . . He considered his mind: it was alarming him. All through the war he had had one dread — that a wound, the physical shock of a wound, would cause his mind to fail. He was going to be hit behind the collar-bone. He could feel the spot; not itching, but the blood pulsing just a little warmer. Just as you can become conscious of the end of your nose if you think about it!

The sergeant said that 'e wished 'e could *feel* the Germans 'ad ruined theirselves: they seemed to be drivin' us into the Channel. Tietjens gave his reasons. They were driving us. But not fast enough. Not fast enough. It was a race between our disappearance and their endurance. They had been hung up yesterday by the wind, they were as like as not going to be held up to-day. . . . They were not going fast enough. They could not keep it up.

The sergeant said 'e wished, sir, you'd tell the men that. That was what the men ought to be told; not the stuff that was hin Divisional Comic Cuts and the 'ome pipers. . . .

A key-bugle of singular sweetness — at least Tietjens supposed it to be a key-bugle, for he knew the identities of practically no wind-instruments; it was certainly not a cavalry bugle, for there were no cavalry and even no Army Service Corps at all near — a bugle, then, of astounding sweetness made some remarks to the cool, wet dawn. It induced an astonishingly melting mood. He remarked:

"Do you mean to say, then, that your men, Sergeant, are really damned heroes? I suppose they are!"

He said "your men," instead of "our" or even "the" men, because he had been till the day before yesterday merely the second-in-command — and was likely to be to-morrow again merely the perfectly inactive second-in-command of what was called a rag-time collection that was astonishingly a clique and mutely combined to regard him as an outsider. So he really regarded himself as rather a spectator; as if a railway passenger had taken charge of a locomotive whilst the engine-driver had gone to have a drink.

The sergeant flushed with pleasure. "Hit was," he said, "good to 'ave prise from Regular officers." Tietjens said that he was not a Regular. The sergeant stammered:

"*Hain't* you, sir, a Ranker. The men all thinks you are a promoted Ranker."

No, Tietjens said, he was not a promoted Ranker. He added, after consideration, that he was a militiaman. The men would have, by the will of chance, to put up with his leadership for at least that day. They might as well feel as good about it as they could — as settled in their stomachs! It certainly made a difference that the men should feel assured about their officers; what exact difference there was no knowing. This crowd was not going to get any satisfaction out of being led by a "gentleman." They did not know what a gentleman was: a quite un-feudal crowd. Mostly Derby men. Small drapers, rate-collectors' clerks, gas-inspectors. There were even three music-hall performers, two scene shifters and several milkmen.

It was another tradition that was gone. Still, they desired the companionship of elder, heavier men who had certain knowledges. A militiaman probably filled the bill! Well, he was that, officially!

He glanced aside and upwards at the whitewash cockscomb. He regarded it carefully and with amusement. He knew what it was that had made his mind take the particular turn it had insisted on taking. . . . The picks going in the dark under the H.Q. dug-out in the Cassenoisette section. The men called it Crackerjack.

He had been all his life familiar with the idea of picks going in the dark, underground. There is no North Country man who is not.

All through that country, if you awake at night you hear the sound,
and always it appears supernatural. You know it is the miners, at the
pit-face, hundred and hundreds of feet down.

But just because it was familiar, it was familiarly rather dreadful.
Haunting. And the silence had come at a bad moment. After a perfect hell of noise; after so much of noise that he had been forced to
ascend the slippery clay stairs of the dug-out. . . . And heaven knew
if there was one thing that on account of his heavy-breathing chest
he loathed, it was slippery clay . . . he had been forced to pant up
those slippery stairs. . . . His chest had been much worse, then . . .
two months ago!

Curiosity had forced him up. And no doubt FEAR. The large
battle fear; not the constant little, haunting misgivings. God knew!
Curiosity or fear. In terrific noise; noise like the rushing up of innumerable noises determined not to be late, whilst the earth rocks or
bumps or quakes or protests, you cannot be very coherent about your
thoughts. So it might have been cool curiosity or it might have been
sheer panic at the thought of being buried alive in that dug-out, its
mouth sealed up. Anyhow, he had gone up from the dug-out where in
his capacity of second-in-command, detested as an interloper by his
C.O., he had sat ignominiously in that idleness of the second-in-
command that it is in the power of the C.O. to inflict. He was to sit
there till the C.O. dropped dead: then, however much the C.O. might
detest him, to step into his shoes. Nothing the C.O. could do could
stop that. In the meantime, as long as the C.O. existed, the second-
in-command must be idle; he would be given nothing to do. For fear
he got kudos!

Tietjens flattered himself that he cared nothing about kudos. He
was still Tietjens of Groby; no man could give him anything, no man
could take anything from him. He flattered himself that he in no way
feared death, pain, dishonour, the afterdeath, feared very little disease — except for choking sensations! . . . But his Colonel got in
on him.

He had no disagreeable feelings, thinking of the Colonel. A good
boy, as boys go; perfectly warranted in hating his second-in-command.
. . . There are positions like that! But the fellow got in on him. He
shut him up in that reeling cellar. And, of course, you might lose
control of your mind in a reeling cellar where you cannot hear your
thoughts. If you cannot hear your thoughts how the hell are you going to tell what your thoughts are doing?

You couldn't hear. There was an orderly with fever or shell-shock or something — a rather favourite orderly of the orderly room — asleep on a pile of rugs. Earlier in the night Orderly Room had asked permission to dump the boy in there because he was making such a beastly row in his sleep that they could not hear themselves speak and they had a lot of paper work to do. They could not tell what had happened to the boy, whom they liked. The acting sergeant-major thought he must have got at some methylated spirits.

Immediately, that *strafe* had begun. The boy had lain, his face to the light of the lamp, on his pile of rugs — army blankets, that is to say. . . . A very blond boy's face, contorted in the strong light, shrieking — positively shrieking obscenities at the flame. But with his eyes shut. And two minutes after that *strafe* had begun you could see his lips move, that was all.

Well, he, Tietjens, had gone up. Curiosity or fear? In the trench you could see nothing and noise rushed like black angels gone mad; solid noise that swept you off your feet. . . . Swept your brain off its feet. Something else took control of it. You became second-in-command of your own soul. Waiting for its C.O. to be squashed flat by the direct hit of a four point two before you got control again.

There was nothing to see; mad lights whirled over the black heavens. He moved along the mud of the trench. It amazed him to find that it was raining. In torrents. You imagined that the heavenly powers in decency suspended their activities at such moments. But there was positively lightning. They didn't! A Verey light or something extinguished *that* — not very efficient lightning, really. Just at that moment he fell on his nose at an angle of forty-five degrees against some squashed earth where, as he remembered, the parapet had been revetted. The trench had been squashed in, level with the outside ground. A pair of boots emerged from the pile of mud. How the deuce did the fellow get into that position?

Broadside on to the hostilities in progress! . . . But, naturally, he had been running along the trench when that stuff buried him. Clean buried, anyhow. The obliging Verey light showed to Tietjens, just level with his left hand, a number of small smoking fragments. The white smoke ran level with the ground in a stiff breeze. Other little patches of smoke added themselves quickly. The Verey light went out. Things were coming over. Something hit his foot; the heel of his boot. Not unpleasantly, a smarting feeling as if his sole had been slapped.

It suggested itself to him, under all the noise, that there being no parapet there. . . . He got back into the trench towards the dug-out, skating in the sticky mud. The duckboards were completely sunk in it. In the whole affair it was the slippery mud he hated most. Again a Verey light obliged, but the trench being deep there was nothing to see except the backside of a man. Tietjens said:

"If he's wounded . . . Even if he's dead one ought to pull him down. . . . And get the Victoria Cross!"

The figure slid down into the trench. Speedily, with drill-movements, engrossed, it crammed two clips of cartridges into a rifle correctly held at the loading angle. In a rift of the noise, like a crack in the wall of a house, it remarked:

"Can't reload lying up there, sir. Mud gets into your magazine." He became again merely the sitting portion of a man, presenting to view the only part of him that was not caked with mud. The Verey light faded. Another reinforced the blinking effect. From just overhead.

Round the next traverse after the mouth of their dug-out a rapt face of a tiny subaltern, gazing upwards at a Verey illumination, with an elbow on an inequality of the trench and the forearm pointing upwards suggested — the rapt face suggested The Soul's Awakening! . . . In another rift in the sound the voice of the tiny subaltern stated that he had to economise the Verey cartridges. The battalion was very short. At the same time it was difficult to time them so as to keep the lights going. . . . This seemed fantastic! The Huns were just coming over.

With the finger of his upward pointing hand the tiny subaltern pulled the trigger of his upward pointing pistol. A second later more brilliant illumination descended from above. The subaltern pointed the clumsy pistol to the ground in the considerable physical effort — for such a tiny person! — to reload the large implement. A very gallant child — name of Aranjuez. Maltese, or Portuguese, or Levantine — in origin.

The pointing of the pistol downwards revealed that he had practically coiled around his little feet, a collection of tubular, dead, khaki limbs. It didn't need any rift in the sound to make you understand that his loader had been killed on him. . . . By signs and removing his pistol from his grasp Tietjens made the subaltern — he was only two days out from England — understand that he had better go and get a drink and some bearers for the man who might not be dead.

He was, however. When they removed him a little to make room for Tietjens' immensely larger boots his arms just flopped in the mud, the tin hat that covered the face, to the sky. Like a lay figure, but a little less stiff. Not yet cold.

Tietjens became like a solitary statute of the Bard of Avon, the shelf for his elbow being rather low. Noise increased. The orchestra was bringing in *all* the brass, *all* the strings, *all* the wood-wind, all the percussion instruments. The performers threw about biscuit tins filled with horse-shoes; they emptied sacks of coal on cracked gongs, they threw down forty-storey iron houses. It was comic to the extent that an operatic orchestra's crescendo is comic. Crescendo! . . . Crescendo! CRRRRRESC. . . . The Hero *must* be coming! He didn't!

Still like Shakespeare contemplating the creation of, say, Cordelia, Tietjens leaned against his shelf. From time to time he pulled the trigger of the horse-pistol; from time to time he rested the butt on his ledge and rammed a charge home. When one jammed he took another. He found himself keeping up a fairly steady illumination.

The Hero arrived. Naturally, he was a Hun. He came over, all legs and arms going, like a catamount; struck the face of the parados, fell into the trench on the dead body, with his hands to his eyes, sprang up again and danced. With heavy deliberation Tietjens drew his great trench-knife rather than his revolver. Why? The butcher instinct? Or trying to think himself with the Exmoor stag-hounds. The man's shoulders had come heavily on him as he had rebounded from the parados-face. He felt outraged. Watching that performing Hun he held the knife pointed and tried to think of the German for *Hands Up*. He imagined it to be *Hoch die Haende!* He looked for a nice spot in the Hun's side.

His excursion into a foreign tongue proved supererogatory. The German threw his arm abroad, his — considerably mashed! — face to the sky.

Always dramatic, Cousin Fritz! Too dramatic, really.

He fell, crumbling, into his untidy boot. Nasty boots, all crumpled too, up the calves! But he didn't say *Hoch der Kaiser*, or *Deutschland über alles*, or anything valedictory.

Tietjens fired another light upwards and filled in another charge, then, down on his hams in the mud he squatted over the German's head, the fingers of both hands under the head. He could feel the great groans thrill his fingers. He let go and felt tentatively for his brandy flask.

But there was a muddy group round the traverse end. The noise reduced itself to half. It was bearers for the corpse. And the absurdly wee Aranjuez and a new loader. . . . In those days they had not been so short of men! Shouts were coming along the trench. No doubt other Huns were in.

Noise reduced itself to a third. A bumpy diminuendo. Bumpy! Sacks of coal continued to fall down the stairs with a regular cadence; more irregularly, Bloody Mary, who was just behind the trench, or seemed like it, shook the whole house as you might say and there were other naval howitzers or something, somewhere.

Tietjens said to the bearers:

"Take the Hun first. He's alive. Our man's dead." He was quite remarkably dead. He hadn't, Tietjens had observed, when he bent over the German, really got what you might call a head, though there was something in its place. What had done that?

Aranjuez, taking his place beside the trench-face, said:

"Damn cool you were, sir. Damn cool. I never saw a knife drawn so slow!" They had watched the Hun do the *danse du ventre*! The poor beggar had had rifles and the young feller's revolver turned on him all the time. They would probably have shot him some more but for the fear of hitting Tietjens. Half a dozen Germans had jumped into that sector of trenches in various places. As mad as March hares! . . . That fellow had been shot through both eyes, a fact that seemed to fill the little Aranjuez with singular horror. He said he would go mad if he thought he would be blinded, because there was a girl in the teashop at Bailleul, and a fellow called Spofforth of the Wiltshires would get her if his, Aranjuez's, beauty was spoiled. He positively whimpered at the thought and then gave the information that this was considered to be a false alarm, he meant a feigned attack to draw off troops from somewhere else where the real attempt was being made. There must be pretty good hell going on somewhere else, then.

It looked like that. For almost immediately all the guns had fallen silent except for one or two that bumped and grumped. . . . It had all been just for fun, then!

Well, they were damn near Bailleul now. They would be driven

past it in a day or two. On the way to the Channel. Aranjuez would
have to hurry to see his girl. The little devil! He had overdrawn his
confounded little account over his girl, and Tietjens had had to
guarantee his overdraft — which he could not afford to do. Now the
little wretch would probably overdraw still more — and Tietjens
would have to guarantee still more of an overdraft.

But that night, when Tietjens had gone down into the black
silence of his own particular branch of a cellar — they really had
been in wine-cellars at that date, cellars stretching for hundreds of
yards under chalk with strata of clay which made the mud so particularly sticky and offensive — he had found the sound of the pick-
axes beneath his flea-bag almost unbearable. They were probably our
own men. Obviously they were our own men. But it had not made
much difference, for, of course, if they were there they would be an
attraction, and the Germans might just as well be below them,
counter-mining.

His nerves had been put in a bad way by that rotten *strafe* — that
had been just for fun. He knew his nerves were in a bad way because he had a ghostly visit from O Nine Morgan, a fellow whose
head had been smashed, as it were, on his, Tietjens', own hands, just
after Tietjens had refused him home leave to go and get killed by a
prize-fighter who had taken up with his, O Nine Morgan's, wife. It
was complicated, but Tietjens wished that fellows who wished to
fall on him when they were stopping things would choose to stop
things with something else than their heads. That wretched Hun
dropping on his shoulder, when, by the laws of war, he ought to
have been running back to his own lines, had given him a jar that
still shook his whole body. And, of course, a shock. The fellow
had looked something positively Apocalyptic, his whitey-grey arms
and legs spread abroad. . . . And it had been an imbecile affair,
with no basis of real fighting. . . .

That thin surge of whitey-grey objects of whom not more than
a dozen had reached the line — Tietjens knew that, because, with
a melodramatically drawn revolver and the fellows who would have
been really better employed carrying away the unfortunate Hun
who had had in consequence to wait half an hour before being attended to — with those fellows loaded up with Mills bombs like people carrying pears, he had dodged, revolver first, round half a dozen
traverses, and in quite enough of remains of gas to make his lungs unpleasant. . . . Like a child playing a game of "I spy!" Just like that.

. . . But only to come on several lots of Tommies standing round unfortunate objects who were either trembling with fear and wet and sweat, or panting with their nice little run.

This surge then of whitey-grey objects, sacrificed for fun, was intended . . . was intended ulti . . . ultim . . . then . . .

A voice, just under his camp-bed, said:

"*Bringt dem Hauptmann eine Kerze . . . .*" As who should say: "Bring a candle for the Captain. . . ." Just like that! A dream!

It hadn't been as considerable of a shock as you might have thought to a man just dozing off. Not really as bad as the falling dream, but quite as awakening. . . . His mind had resumed that sentence.

The handful of Germans who had reached the trench had been sacrificed for the stupid sort of fun called Strategy, probably. Stupid! . . . It was, of course, just like German spooks to go mining by candle-light. Obsoletely Nibelungen-like. Dwarfs probably! . . . They had sent over that thin waft of men under a blessed lot of barrage and stuff. . . . A lot! A *whole* lot! It had been really quite an artillery *strafe*. Ten thousand shells as like as not. Then, somewhere up the line they had probably made a demonstration in force. Great bodies of men, an immense surge. And twenty to thirty thousand shells. Very likely some miles of esplanade, as it were, with the sea battering against it. And only a demonstration in force. . . .

It could not be real fighting. They had not been ready for their spring advance.

It had been meant to impress somebody imbecile. . . . Somebody imbecile in Wallachia, or Sofia, or Asia Minor. Or Whitehall, very likely. Or the White House! . . . Perhaps they had killed a lot of Yankees — to make themselves Trans-Atlantically popular. There were no doubt, by then, whole American Army Corps in the line somewhere. By then! Poor devils, coming so late into such an accentuated hell. Damnably accentuated. . . . The sound of even that little bit of fun had been portentously more awful than even quite a big show say in '15. It was better to have been in then and got used to it. . . . If it hadn't broken you, just by duration . . .

Might be to impress anybody. . . . But, who was going to be impressed? Of course, our legislators with the stewed-pear brains running about the ignoble corridors with coke-brize floors and mahogany doors . . . might be impressed. . . . You must not rhyme!

. . Or, of course, our own legislators might have been trying a nice little demonstration in force, equally idiotic somewhere else, to impress someone just as unlikely to be impressed. . . . This, then, would be the answer! But no one ever would be impressed again. We all had each other's measures. So it was just wearisome. . . .

It was remarkably quiet in that thick darkness. Down below, the picks continued their sinister confidences in each other's ears. . . . It was really like that. Like children in the corner of a schoolroom whispering nasty comments about their masters, one to the other. . . . Girls, for choice. . . . Chop, chop, chop, a pick whispered. Chop? another asked in an undertone. The first said Chopchop-chop. Then *Chup*. . . . And a silence of irregular duration. . . . Like what happens when you listen to typewriting and the young woman has to stop to put in another page. . . .

Nice young women with typewriters in Whitehall had very likely taken from dictation, on hot-pressed, square sheets with embossed royal arms, the plan for that very *strafe*. . . . Because, obviously it might have been dictated from Whitehall almost as directly as from Unter den Linden. We might have been making a demonstration in force on the Dwolologda in order to get the Huns to make a counter-demonstration in Flanders. Hoping poor old Puffles would get it in the neck. For they were trying still to smash poor old General Puffles and stop the single command. . . . They might very well be hoping that our losses through the counter-demonstration would be so heavy that the country would cry out for the evacuation of the Western Front. . . . If they could get half a million of us killed perhaps the country might . . . They, no doubt, thought it worth trying. But it was wearisome: those fellows in Whitehall never learned. Any more than Brother Boche. . . .

Nice to be in poor old Puffles' army. Nice but wearisome. . . . Nice girls with typewriters in well-ventilated offices. Did they still put paper cuffs on to keep their sleeves from ink? He would ask Valen . . . Valen . . . It was warm and still. . . . On such a night . . .

"*Bringt dem Hauptmann eine Kerze!*" A voice from under his camp bed! He imagined that the Hauptmann spark must be myopic; short-sightedly examining a tamping fuse. . . . If they used tamping fuses or if that was what they called them in the army!

He could not see the face or the spectacles of the Hauptmann any more than he could see the faces of his men. Not through his flea-bag and shins! They were packed in the tunnel; whitish-grey, tubular agglomerations. . . . Large! Like the maggots that are eaten by Australian natives. . . . Fear possessed him!

He sat up in his flea-bag, dripping with icy sweat.

"By jove, I'm for it!" he said. He imagined that his brain was going; he was mad and seeing himself go mad. He cast about in his mind for some subject about which to think so that he could prove to himself that he had not gone mad.

II

THE KEY-BUGLE remarked with singular distinctness to the dawn:

<pre>
                    dy
    I know a la   fair   kind
                    and
        Was never face
                    so   mind
                pleased my
                    y
</pre>

A sudden waft of pleasure at the seventeenth-century air that the tones gave to the landscape went all over Tietjens. . . . Herrick and Purcell! . . . Or it was perhaps a modern imitation. Good enough. He asked:

"What the devil's that row, Sergeant?"

The sergeant disappeared behind the muddied sacking curtain. There was a guard-room in there. The key-bugle said:

<pre>
        Fair   kind. . . .
            and
        Fair   Fair   Fair
                                kind. . . .
            and . . .   and . . .   and . . .
</pre>

It might be two hundred yards off along the trenches. Astonishing pleasure came to him from that seventeenth-century air and the remembrance of those exact, quiet words. . . . Or perhaps he had not got them right. Nevertheless, they were exact and quiet. As efficient working beneath the soul as the picks of miners in the dark.

The sergeant returned with the obvious information that it was O Nine Griffiths practising on the cornet. Captain McKechnie 'ad promised to 'ear 'im after breakfast 'n recommend 'im to the Divisional Follies to play at the concert to-night, if 'e likes 'im.

Tietjens said:

"Well, I hope Captain McKechnie likes him!"

He hoped McKechnie, with his mad eyes and his pestilential accent, would like that fellow. That fellow spread seventeenth-century atmosphere across the landscape over which the sun's rays were beginning to flood a yellow wash. Then, might the seventeenth century save the fellow's life, for his good taste! For his life would probably be saved. He, Tietjens, would give him a pass back to Division to get ready for the concert. So he would be out of the *strafe*. . . . Probably none of them would be alive after the *strafe* that Brigade reported to be coming in. . . . Twenty-seven minutes, by now! Three hundred and twenty-eight fighting men against . . . say, a Division. Any preposterous number. . . . Well, the seventeenth century might as well save one man!

What had become of the seventeenth century? And Herbert and Donne and Crashaw and Vaughan, the Silurist? . . . Sweet day so cool, so calm, so bright, the bridal of the earth and sky! . . . By Jove, it was that! Old Campion, flashing like a popinjay in the scarlet and gilt of the major-general, had quoted that in the base camp, years ago. Or was it months? Or wasn't it: "But at my back I always hear Time's winged chariots hurrying near," that he had quoted?

Anyhow, not bad for an old general!

He wondered what had become of that elegant collection of light yellow, scarlet, and gilt. . . . Somehow he always thought of Campion as in light yellow, rather than khaki, so much did he radiate light. . . . Campion and his, Tietjens', wife, radiating light together — she in a golden gown!

Campion was about due in these latitudes. It was astonishing that he had not turned up before. But poor old Puffles with his abominably weakened Army had done too jolly well to be replaced. Even at the request of the Minister who hated him. Good for him!

It occurred to him that if he . . . call it "stopped one" that day, Campion would probably marry his, Tietjens', widow. . . . Sylvia in crêpe. With perhaps a little white about it!

The cornet — obviously it was not a key-bugle — remarked:

: her pass   by . . .
                    ing
   I did but view . . .

and then stopped to reflect. After a moment it added meditatively:

            .her . . .
            •   •
And   •   •
    now   •   •
        I   •   •
        love   *.till*
                     I die!

That would scarcely refer to Sylvia. . . . Still, perhaps in crêpe, with a touch of white, passing by, very tall. . . . Say, in a seventeenth-century street. . . .

The only satisfactory age in England! . . . Yet what chance had it to-day. Or, still more, to-morrow. In the sense that the age of, say, Shakespeare had a chance. Or Pericles! Or Augustus!

Heaven knew, we did not want a preposterous drum-beating such as the Elizabethans produced — and received. Like lions at a fair. . . . But what chance had quiet fields, Anglican sainthood, accuracy of thought, heavy-leaved, timbered hedge-rows, slowly creeping plough-lands moving up the slopes? . . . Still, the land remains. . . .

The land remains. . . . It remains! . . . At that same moment the dawn was wetly revealing; over there in George Herbert's parish . . . What was it called? . . . What the devil was its name? Oh, Hell! . . . Between Salisbury and Wilton. . . . The tiny church . . . But he refused to consider the plough-lands, the heavy groves, the slow high-road above the church that the dawn was at that moment wetly revealing — until he could remember that name. . . . He refused to consider that, probably even to-day, that land ran to . . . produced the stock of . . . Anglican sainthood. The quiet thing!

But until he could remember the name he would consider nothing. . . .

He said:

"Are those damned Mills bombs coming?"

The sergeant said:

"In ten minutes they'll be 'ere, sir. HAY Cumpny had just telephoned that they were coming in now."

It was almost a disappointment; in an hour or so, without bombs, they might all have been done with. As quiet as the seventeenth century: in heaven. . . . The beastly bombs would have to explode before that, now! They might, in consequence, survive. . . . Then what was he, Tietjens, going to do! Take orders! It was thinkable. . . .

He said:

"Those bloody imbeciles of Huns are coming over in an hour's time, Brigade says. Get the beastly bombs served out, but keep enough in store to serve as an emergency ration if we should want to advance. . . . Say a third. For C and D Companies. . . . Tell the Adjutant I'm going along all the trenches and I want the Assistant-Adjutant, Mr. Aranjuez, and Orderly-Corporal Colley to come with me. . . . As soon as the bombs come for certain! . . . I don't want the men to think they've got to stop a Hun rush without bombs. . . . They're due to begin their barrage in fourteen minutes, but they won't really come over without a hell of a lot of preparation. . . . I don't know how Brigade knows all this!"

The name *Bemerton* suddenly came on to his tongue. Yes, Bemerton, Bemerton, Bemerton was George Herbert's parsonage. Bemerton, outside Salisbury. . . . The cradle of the race as far as our race was worth thinking about. He imagined himself standing up on a little hill, a lean contemplative parson, looking at the land sloping down to Salisbury spire. A large, clumsily bound seventeenth-century testament, Greek, beneath his elbow. . . . Imagine standing up on a hill! It was the unthinkable thing there!

The sergeant was lamenting, a little wearily, that the Huns were coming.

"Hi did think them bleeding 'uns, 'xcuse me, sir, wasn' per'aps coming this morning. . . . Giv us a rest an' a chance to clear up a bit. . . ." He had the tone of a resigned schoolboy saying that the Head *might* have given the school a holiday on the Queen's birthday. But what the devil did that man think about his approaching dissolution?

That was the unanswerable question. He, Tietjens, had been asked several times what death was like. . . . Once, in a cattle-truck under a bridge, near a Red-Cross Clearing Station, by a miserable fellow called Perowne. In the presence of the troublesome lunatic called

McKechnie. You would have thought that even a Movement Order
Officer would have managed to send up the line that triangle differently arranged. Perowne was known to have been his wife's lover;
he, Tietjens, against his will, had been given the job, as second-in-
command of the battalion, that McKechnie wanted madly. And indeed he had a right to it. They *ought* not to have been sent up together.

But there they had been — Perowne broken down, principally at
the thought that he was not going to see his, Tietjens', wife ever
again in a golden gown. . . . Unless, perhaps, with a golden harp
on a cloud, for he looked at things like that. . . . And, positively,
as soon as that baggage-car — it had been a baggage-car, not a cattle-
truck! — had discharged the deserter with escort and the three
wounded Cochin-Chinese platelayers whom the French authorities
had palmed off on them . . . And where the devil had they all been
going? Obviously up into the line, and already pretty near it: near
Division Headquarters. But where? . . . God knew? Or when? God
knew too! . . . A fine-ish day with a scanty remains of not quite
melted snow in the cutting and the robins singing in the coppice
above. Say February. . . . Say St. Valentine's Day, which, of
course, would agitate Perowne some more. . . . Well, positively as
soon as the baggage-car had discharged the wounded who had
groaned, and the sheepish escort who did not know whether they
ought to be civil to the deserter in the presence of the orfcers, and
the deserter who kept on defiantly — or if you like broken-heartedly,
for there was no telling the difference — asking the escort questions
as to the nature of their girls, or volunteering information as to
the intimate behaviour of *his.* . . . The deserter a gipsyfied, black-
eyed fellow with an immense jeering mouth; the escort a corporal
and two Tommies, blond and blushing East Kents, remarkably
polished about the buttons and brass numerals, with beautifully
neatly-put-on puttees: obviously Regulars, coming from behind the
lines; the Cochin-Chinese, with indistinguishable broad yellow faces,
brown poetic eyes, furred topboots and blue furred hoods over their
bandaged heads and swathed faces. Seated, leaning back against the
side of the box-truck and groaning now and then and shivering all
the time . . .

Well, the moment they had been cleared out at the Deputy Sub.
R.T.O.'s tin shed by the railway bridge, the fellow Perowne with his
well-padded presence and his dark babu-Hindooish aspect had bub-

bled out with questions as to the hereafter according to Tietjens and as to the nature of Death; the immediate process of dissolution: dying. . . . And in between Perowne's questions McKechnie, with his unspeakable intonation and his dark eyes as mad as a cat's, had asked Tietjens how he dared get himself appointed second-in-command of his, McKechnie's, own battalion. . . . "You're no soldier," he would burst out. "Do you think you are a b——y infantryman? You're a mealsack, and what the devil's to become of *my* battalion. . . . Mine. . . . My battalion! *Our* battalion of pals!"

That had been in, presumably, February, and, presumably, it was now April. The way the dawn came up looked like April. . . . What did it matter? . . . That damned truck had stayed under that bridge for two hours and a half . . . in the process of the eternal waiting that is War. You hung about and you hung about, and you kicked your heels and you kicked your heels: waiting for Mills bombs to come, or for jam, or for generals, or for the tanks, or transport, or the clearance of the road ahead. You waited in offices under the eyes of somnolent orderlies, under fire on the banks of canals, you waited in hotels, dug-outs, tin sheds, ruined houses. There will be no man who survives of His Majesty's Armed Forces that shall not remember those eternal hours when Time itself stayed still as the true image of bloody War! . . .

Well, in that case Providence seemed to have decreed a waiting just long enough to allow Tietjens to persuade the unhappy mortal called Perowne that death was not a very dreadful affair. . . . He had enough intellectual authority to persuade the fellow with his glued-down black hair that Death supplied His own anæsthetics. That was the argument. On the approach of Death all the faculties are so numbed that you feel neither pain nor apprehension. . . . He could still hear the heavy, authoritative words that, on that occasion, he had used.

The Providence of Perowne! For, when he was dug out after, next night having been buried in going up into the trenches, they said, he had a smile like a young baby's on his face. He didn't have long to wait and died with a smile on his face . . . nothing having so much become him during the life as . . . well, a becoming smile! During life he had seemed a worried, fussing sort of chap.

Bully for Perowne. . . . But what about him, Tietjens? Was that the sort of thing that Providence ought to do to one? . . . That's Tempting God!

The sergeant beside him said:

"Then a man could stand hup on an 'ill. . . . You really mean to say, sir, that you think a man will be able to stand up on a bleedin' 'ill. . . ."

Presumably Tietjens had been putting heart into that acting temporary sergeant-major. He could not remember what he had been saying to the N.C.O. because his mind had been so deeply occupied with the image of Perowne. . . . He said:

"You're a Lincolnshire man, aren't you? You come from a Fen country. What do you want to stand up on a hill for?"

The man said:

"Ah, but you *do*, sir!"

He added:

"You want to stand up! Take a look around . . ." He struggled for expression: "Like as if you wanted to breathe deep after bein' in a stoopin' posture for a long time!"

Tietjens said:

"Well, you can do that here. With discretion. I did it just now. . . ."

The man said:

"You, sir . . . You're a law hunto yourself!"

It was the most considerable shock that Tietjens received in the course of his military career. And the most considerable reward.

There were all these inscrutable beings: the Other Ranks, a brownish mass, spreading underground, like clay strata in the gravel, beneath all this waving country that the sun would soon be warming; they were in holes, in tunnels, behind sack cloth curtains, carrying on . . . carrying on some sort of life, conversing, breathing, desiring. But completely mysterious, in the mass. Now and then you got a glimpse of a passionate desire: "A man could stand up on a bleedin' 'ill"; now and then you got — though you knew that they watched you eternally and knew the minutest gestures of your sleep — you got some sort of indication as to how they regarded you: "You are a law unto yourself!"

That must be hero-worship: an acting temporary regimental sergeant-major, without any real knowledge of his job, extemporising, not so long ago a carrier in an eastern county of remarkable flatness does not tell his Acting Commanding Officer that he is a law unto himself without meaning it to be a flattering testimony: a certificate, as far as it went, of trustworthiness. . . .

They were now crawling out into the light of day; from behind the sacking, six files that he had last night transferred from C to D Coy., D having been reduced to forty-three rank and file. They shuffled out, an extraordinary Falstaff's battalion of muddy odd-come shorts, fell into some sort of alignment in the trench, shuffled an inch further this way, an inch further that; pushed up their chin-straps and pulled them down; humped up their packs by hunching their shoulders and jerking; adjusted their water bottles and fell into some sort of immobility, their rifles, more or less aligned, poked out before them. In that small company they were men of all sorts of sizes, of all sorts of disparities and grotesquenesses of physique. Two of them were music-hall comedians and the whole lot looked as if they made up a knock-about turn. . . . The Rag-Time Army at its vocation, living and breathing.

The sergeant called them to attention and they wavered back and forward. The sergeant said:

"The Commandin' Officer's lookin' at you. FIX . . . B'ts!"

And, positively, a dwarf concealed under a pudding basin shuffled a foot-length and a half forward in the mud, protruded his rifle-muzzle between his bent knees, jerked his head swiftly to strain his sight along the minute line. . . . It was like a blurred fairy-tale! Why did that dwarf behave in a smart and soldierly manner? Through despair? It wasn't likely!

The men wavered like the edge of a field of tall grass with the wind running along it; they felt round themselves for their bayonet-handles, like women attempting difficult feats with their skirts. . . . The dwarf cut his hand smartly away to his side, as the saying is, the men pulled their rifles up into line. Tietjens exclaimed:

"Stand at ease, stand easy," negligently enough, then he burst out in uncontrollable irritation: "For *God's* sake, put your beastly hats straight!" The men shuffled uneasily, this being no order known to them, and Tietjens explained: "No, this isn't drill. It's only that your hats all at sixes and sevens give me the pip!" And the whispers of the men went down the little line:

"You 'eer the orfcer. . . . Gives 'im the pip, we do! . . . Goin' for a wawk in the pawk wiv our gels, we are. . . ." They glanced nevertheless aside and upwards at each other's tin-hat rims and said: "Shove 'im a shade forward, 'Orace. . . . You tighten your mar-tingale, 'Erb!" They were gaily rueful and impenitently profane; they had let thirty-six hours of let-off. A fellow louder-than-hummed:

> "As I wawk erlong ther Bor dee Berlong
>   Wiv an indipendent air . . .
>   W'ere's me swegger-kine, you fellers!"

Tietjens addressed him:

"Did you ever hear Coborn sing that, Runt?" and Runt replied:

"Yes, sir. I was the hind legs of the elephant when he sung it in the Old Drury panto!" A little, dark, beady-eyed Cockney, his enormous mouth moved lip on lip as if he were chewing a pebble in pride at the reminiscence. The men's voices went on: "'Ind legs 'f the elephink! . . . good ol' Helefink. . . . I'll go 'n see 'n elephink first thing I do in Blighty!"

Tietjens said:

"I'll give every man of you a ticket for Drury Lane next Boxing Day. We'll all be in London for the next Boxing Day. Or Berlin!"

They exclaimed polyphonically and low:

"Oo-er! Djee 'eer 'im? Di'djee 'eer the orfcer? The noo C.O.?"

A hidden man said:

"Mike it the old Shoreditch Empire, sir, 'n we'll thenk you!"

Another:

"I never keered fer the Lane meself! Give me the old Balliam for Boxing Day." The sergeant made the sounds for them to move off.

They shuffled off up the trench. An unseen man said:

"Better'n a bleedin' dipso!" Lips said "Shhh!"

The sergeant shouted — with an astonishing, brutal panic:

"You shut your bleedin' mouth, you man, or I'll shove you in the b——y clink!" He looked nevertheless at Tietjens with calm satisfaction a second later.

"A good lot of chaps, sir," he said. "The best!" He was anxious to wipe out the remembrance of the last spoken word. "Give 'em the right sort of officers 'n they'll beat the world!"

"Do you think it makes any difference to them what officers they have?" Tietjens asked. "Wouldn't it be all the same if they had just anyone?"

The sergeant said:

"No, sir. They bin frightened these last few days. Now they're better."

This was just exactly what Tietjens did not want to hear. He hardly knew why. Or he did. . . . He said:

"I should have thought these men knew their job so well — for this sort of thing — that they hardly needed orders. It cannot make much difference whether they receive orders or not."

The sergeant said:

"It *does* make a difference, sir," in a tone as near that of cold obstinacy as he dare attain to; the feeling of the approaching *strafe* was growing on them. It hung over them.

McKechnie stuck his head out from behind the sacking. The sacking had the lettering P X L in red and the word *Minn* in black. McKechnie's eyes were blazing maniacally, jumping maniacally in his head. They always were jumping maniacally in his head. He was a tiring fellow. He was wearing not a tin hat, but an officer's helmet. The gilt dragon on it glittered. The sun was practically up, somewhere. As soon as its disc cleared the horizon, the Huns, according to Brigade, were to begin sending over their wearisome stuff. In thirteen and a half minutes.

McKechnie gripped Tietjens by the arm, a familiarity that Tietjens detested. He hissed — he really hissed because he was trying to speak under his breath:

"Come past the next traverse. I want to speak to you."

In correctly prepared trenches, made according to order as these had been to receive them in retreat, by a regular battalion acting under the orders of the Royal Engineers, you go along a straight ditch of trench for some yards, then you find a square block of earth protruding inwards from the parapet round which you must walk; then you come to another straight piece, then to another traverse, and so on to the end of the line, the lengths and dimensions varying to suit the nature of the terrain or the character of the soil. These outjuttings were designed to prevent the lateral spreading of fragments of shell bursting in the trench which would otherwise serve as a funnel, like the barrel of a gun to direct those parts of missiles into men's bodies. It was also exciting — as Tietjens expected to be doing before the setting of the not quite risen sun — to crouch rapidly along past one of them, the heart moving very disagreeably, the revolver protruded well in advance, with half a dozen careless fellows with grenades of sorts just behind you. And you not knowing whether, crouching against the side that was just round the corner you would or would not find a whitish, pallid, dangerous object that you would have no time to scrutinise closely.

Past the nearest of these McKechnie led Tietjens. He was portentous and agitated.

At the end of the next stretch of trench, leaning, as it were, against a buttress in an attitude of intense fatigue was a mud-coloured, very thin, tall fellow; squatting dozing on his heels in the mud just beside that one's foot was another, a proper Glamorganshire man of whom not many more than ten were left in the battalion. The standing man was leaning like that to look through a loophole that had been placed very close to the buttress of raw earth. He grunted something to his companion and continued looking intently. The other man grunted too.

McKechnie withdrew precipitately into the recessed pathway. The column of earth in their faces gave a sense of oppression. He said:

"Did you put that fellow up to saying that damnable thing? . . ." He repeated: "That perfectly damnable thing! Damnable!" Besides hating Tietjens he was shocked, pained, femininely lachrymose. He gazed into Tietjens' eyes like a forsaken mistress fit to do a murder, with a sort of wistful incredulity of despair.

To that Tietjens was accustomed. For the last two months Mc-Kechnie whispering in the ear of the C.O. wherever Battalion Head-quarters might happen to be — McKechnie, with his arms spread abroad on the table and his chin nearly on the cloth that they had always managed to retain in spite of three precipitate moves, Mc-Kechnie, with his mad eyes every now and then moving in the direc-tion of Tietjens, had been almost the most familiar object of Tiet-jens' night landscapes. They wanted him gone so that McKechnie might once again become Second in Command of that body of pals. . . . That indeed was what they were . . . with the addition of a great deal too much of what they called 'Ooch.

Tietjens obviously could not go. There was no way of managing it: he had been put there by old Campion and there he must re-main. So that by the agreeable irony of Providence there was Tiet-jens who had wanted above all McKechnie's present relatively bucolic job hated to hell by half a dozen quite decent if trying young squits — the pals — because Tietjens was in his, McKechnie's, desired posi-tion. It seemed to make it all the worse that they were all, with the exception of the Commanding Officer himself, of the little, dark, Cockney type and had the Cockney's voice, gesture, and intonation, so that Tietjens felt himself like a blond Gulliver with hair very silver in patches, rising up amongst a lot of Lilliputian brown creatures. . . . Portentous and unreasonably noticeable.

A large cannon, nearer than the one that had lately spoken, but as it were with a larger but softer voice, remarked: "Phohhhhhhhh," the sound wandering round the landscape for a long while. After a time about four coupled railway-trains hurtled jovially amongst the clouds and went a long way away — four in one. They were probably trying to impress the North Sea.

It might of course be the signal for the German barrage to begin. Tietjens' heart stopped; his skin on the nape of the neck began to prickle; his hands were cold. That was fear: the Battle Fear, experienced in *strafes*. He might not again be able to hear himself think. Not ever. What did he want of life? . . . Well, just not to lose his reason. One would pray. Not that. . . . Otherwise, perhaps a nice parsonage might do. It was just thinkable. A place in which for ever to work at the theory of waves. . . . But of course it was not thinkable. . . .

He was saying to McKechnie:

"You ought not to be here without a tin hat. You will have to put a tin hat on if you mean to stop here. I can give you four minutes if that is not the *strafe* beginning. Who's been saying what?"

McKechnie said.

"I'm not stopping here. I'm going back, after I've given you a piece of my mind, to the beastly job you have got me defiled with."

Tietjens said:

"Well, you'll put on a tin hat to go there, please. And don't ride your horse, if you've got it here, till after you're a hundred yards, at least, down a communication trench."

McKechnie asked how Tietjens dared give him orders and Tietjens said: Fine he would look with Divisional Transport dead in his lines at five in the morning in a parade hat. McKechnie with objurgations said that the Transport Officer had the right to consult the C.O. of a battalion he supplied. Tietjens said:

"I'm commanding here. You've not consulted me."

It appeared to him queer that they should be behaving like that when you could hear . . . oh, say, the wings of the angel of death. . . . You can "almost hear the very rustling of his wings" was the quotation. Good enough rhetoric. But of course that was how armed men would behave. . . . At all times!

He had been trying the old trick of the military, clipped voice on the half-dotty subject. It had before then reduced McKechnie to some sort of military behaviour.

It reduced him in this case to a maudlin state. He exclaimed with a sort of lachrymose agony:

"This is what it has come to with the old battalion . . . the b——y; b——w, b——y old battalion of z——rs!" Each imprecation was a sob. "How we worked at it. . . . And now . . . *you've* got it!"

Tietjens said:

"Well, you were Vice-Chancellor's Latin Prize-man once. It's what we get reduced to." He added: "*Vos mellificatis apes!*"

McKechnie said with gloomy contempt:

"You. . . . You're no Latinist!"

By now Tietjens had counted two hundred and eighty since the big cannon had said "Phooooh." Perhaps then it was not the signal for the barrage to begin. . . . Had it been it would have begun before now; it would have come thumping along on the heels of the "Phoooh." His hands and the nape of his neck were preparing to become normal.

Perhaps the *strafe* would not come at all that day.

There was the wind. If anything it was strengthening. Yesterday he had suspected that the Germans hadn't got any tanks handy. Perhaps the ugly, senseless armadillos — and incapable at that! underengined! — had all got stuck in the marshes in front of G section. Perhaps the heavy artillery fire of ours that had gone on most of yesterday had been meant to pound the beastly things to pieces. Moving, they looked like slow rats, their noses to the ground, snouting crumbs of garbage. When they were still they looked merely pensive!

Perhaps the *strafe* would not come. He hoped it would not. He did not want a *strafe* with himself in command of the battalion. He did not know what to do, what he ought to do by the book. He knew what he would do. He would stroll about along those deep trenches. Stroll. With his hands in his pockets. Like General Gordon in pictures. He would say contemplative things as the time dragged on. . . . A rather abominable sort of Time, really. . . . But that would introduce into the Battalion a spirit of calm that it had lately lacked. . . . The night before last the C.O. with a bottle in each hand had hurled them both at Huns who did not materialise for an hour and a half. Even the Pals had omitted to laugh. After that he, Tietjens, had taken command. With lots of the Orderly Room papers under both arms. They had had to be in a hurry, at night;

with men suggesting pale grey Canadian trappers coming out of holes!

He did not want to command in a *strafe*, or at any other time! He hoped the unfortunate C.O. would get over his trouble by the evening. . . . But he supposed that he, Tietjens, would get through it all right if he had to. Like the man who had never tried playing the violin!

McKechnie had suddenly become lachrymosely feminine, like a woman pleading, large-eyed, for her lover, his eyes explored Tietjens' face for signs of treachery, for signs that what he said was not what he meant in his heart. He said:

"What are you going to do about Bill? Poor old Bill that has sweated for his Battalion as you never . . ." He began again:

"Think of poor old Bill! You can't be *thinking* of doing the dirty on him. . . . *No* man could be such a swine!"

It was curious how those circumstances brought out the feminine that was in man. What was that ass of a German Professor's theory . . . formula? M^y *plus* W^x equals Man? . . . Well, if God hadn't invented woman men would have had to do so. In that sort of place. You grew sentimental. He, Tietjens, was growing sentimental. He said:

"What does Terence say about him this morning?"

The nice thing to have said would have been:

"Of course, old man, I'll do all I can to keep it dark!" Terence was the M.O. — the man who had chucked his cap at the Hun orderly.

McKechnie said:

"That's the damnable thing! Terence is ratty with him. He won't take a pill!"

Tietjens said:

"What's that? What's that?"

McKechnie wavered; his desire for comfort became overpowering. He said:

"Look here! *Do* the decent thing! You know how poor Bill has worked for us! Get Terence not to report him to Brigade!"

This was wearisome, but it had to be faced.

A very minute subaltern — Aranjuez — in a perfectly impossible tin hat peered round the side of the bank. Tietjens sent him away for a moment. . . . These tin hats were probably all right, but they

were the curse of the army. They bred distrust! How could you trust
a man whose incapable hat tumbled forward on his nose? Or another,
with his hat on the back of his head, giving him the air of a ruined
gambler? Or a fellow who had put on a soap-dish, to amuse the
children — not a serious proceeding. . . . The Germans' things were
better — coming down over the nape of the neck and rising over the
brows. When you saw a Hun sideways he looked something: a serious
proposition. Full of ferocity. A Hun up against a Tommie looked like
a Holbein *lansknecht* fighting a music-hall turn. It made you feel
that you were indeed a rag-time army. Rubbed it in!

McKechnie was reporting that the C.O. had refused to take a pill
ordered him by the M.O. Unfortunately the M.O. was ratty that
morning — too much hooch overnight! So he said he should report
the C.O. to Brigade. Not as being unfit for further service, for he
wasn't. But for refusing to take the pill. It was damnable. Because if
Bill wouldn't take a pill he wouldn't. . . . The M.O. said that if
he took a pill, and stayed in bed that day — without hooch of course!
— he would be perfectly fit on the morrow. He had been like that
often enough before. The C.O. had always been given the dose before as a drench. He swore he would not take it as a ball. Sheer contrariety!

Tietjens was accustomed to think of the C.O. as a lad — a good
lad, but young. They were, all the same, much of an age, and, for
the matter of that, because of his deeply-lined forehead the Colonel
looked the older often enough. But when he was fit he was fine. He
had a hooked nose, a forcible, grey moustache, like two badger-
haired paintbrushes joined beneath the nose, pink skin as polished
as the surface of a billiard ball, a noticeably narrow but high forehead, an extremely piercing glance from rather colourless eyes; his
hair was black and most polished in slight waves. He was a soldier.

He was, that is to say, the ranker. Of soldiering in the English
sense — the real soldiering of peace-time, parades, social events, spit
and polish, hard-worked summers, leisurely winters, India, the Ba-
hamas, Cairo seasons, and the rest he only knew the outside, having
looked at it from the barrack windows, the parade ground and, luckily for him, from his Colonel's house. He had been a most admirable batman to that Colonel, had — in Simla — married the Colonel's
memsahib's lady's maid, had been promoted to the orderly-room,
to the corporals' and sergeants' messes, had become a Musketry-
colour sergeant and, two months before the war had been given

a commission. He would have gained this before but for a slight —
a very slight — tendency to overdrinking, which had given on occa,
sion a similarly slight tone of insolence to his answers to field-officers.
Elderly field-officers on parade are apt to make slight mistakes in
their drill; giving the command to move to the right when technically, though troops are moving to the right, the command should
be: "Move to the left!"; and the officer's left being the troops' right,
on a field-day, after lunch, field-officers of a little rustiness are apt to
grow confused. It then becomes the duty of warrant-officers present
if possible to rectify, or if not, to accept the responsibility for the resultant commotion. On two occasions during his brilliant career, being slightly elated, this war-time C.O. had neglected this military
duty, the result being subsequent Orderly Room *strafes* which remained as black patches when he looked back on his past life and
which constantly embittered his remembrances. Professional soldiers
are like that.

In spite of an exceptionally fine service record he remained bitter,
and upon occasion he became unreasonable. Being what the men —
and for the matter of that the officers of the battalion, too — called
a b——y h——ll of a pusher, he had brought his battalion up to a great
state of efficiency; he had earned a double string of ribbons and by
pushing his battalion into extremely tight places, by volunteering it
for difficult services which, even during trench warfare did present
themselves, and by extricating what remained of it with singular skill
during the first battle of the Somme on an occasion — perhaps the
most lamentable of the whole war — when an entire division commanded by a political rather than a military general had been wiped
out, he had earned for his battalion a French decoration called a
Fourragère which is seldom given to other than French regiments.
These exploits and the spirit which dictated them were perhaps less
appreciated by the men under his command than was imagined by
the C.O. and his bosom friend Captain McKechnie who had loyally
aided him, but they *did* justify the two in attaching to the battalion
the sort of almost maudlin sentimentality that certain parents will
bestow upon their children.

In spite, however, of the appreciation that his services had received, the C.O. remained embittered. He considered that, by this
time, he ought at least to have been given a brigade, if not a division,
and he considered that, if that was not the case, it was largely due to
the two black marks against him as well as to the fact of his low so-

cial origin. And, when he had taken a little liquor these obsessions exaggerated themselves very quickly to a degree that very nearly endangered his career. It was not that he soaked — but there were occasions during that period of warfare when the consumption of a certain amount of alcohol was a necessity if the human being were to keep on carrying on and through rough places. Then, happy was the man who carried his liquor well.

Unfortunately the C.O. was not one of these. Worn out by continual attention to papers — at which he was no great hand — and by fighting that would continue for days on end, he would fortify himself with whisky and immediately his bitternesses would overwhelm his mentality, the aspect of the world would change and he would rail at his superiors in the army and sometimes would completely refuse to obey orders, as had been the occasion a few nights before, when he had refused to let his battalion take part in the concerted retreat of the Army Corps. Tietjens had had to see to this.

Now, exasperated by the aftereffects of several day's great anxieties and alcoholisms, he was refusing to take a pill. This was a token of his contempt for his superiors, the outcome of his obsession of bitterness.

III

AN ARMY — especially in peace time — is a very complex and nicely adjusted affair, and though active operations against an enemy force are apt to blunt nicenesses and upset compensations — as they might for a chronometer — and although this of ours, according to its own computation was only a rag-time aggregation, certain customs of times when this force was also Regular had an enormous power of survival.

It may seem a comic affair that a Colonel commanding a regiment in the midst of the most breathless period of hostilities, should refuse to take a pill. But the refusal, precisely like a grain of sand in the works of a chronometer, may cause the most singular perturbations. It was so in this case.

A sick officer of the very highest rank is the subordinate of his doctor the moment he puts himself into the M.O.'s hands: he must obey orders as if he were a Tommy. A Colonel whole and in his senses may obviously order his M.O. to go here and there and to perform this or that duty; the moment he becomes sick the fact that his body is the property of His Majesty the King, comes forcibly into operation, and the M.O. is the representative of the sovereign in so far as bodies are concerned. This is very reasonable and proper, because sick bodies are not only of no use to the King, but are enormously detrimental to the army that has to cart them about.

In the case that Tietjens had perforce to worry over, the matter was very much complicated in the first place by the fact of the great personal dislike that the C.O. had manifested — though always with a sort of field-officer's monumental courtesy — towards himself, and then because Tietjens had a very great respect for the abilities of the Commanding Officer as Commanding Officer. His rag-time battalion of a rag-time army was as nearly on the level of an impeccable regular battalion as such a unit with its constantly changing personnel could possibly be. Nothing had much more impressed Tietjens in the course of even the whole war, than the demeanour of the soldier whom the other night he had seen firing engrossedly into invisibility. The man had fired with care, had come down to re-load with exact drill movements — which are the quickest possible. He had muttered some words which showed that his mind was entirely on his job like a mathematician engrossed in an abstruse calculation. He had climbed back on to the parapet; continued to fire engrossedly into invisibility; had returned and re-loaded and had again climbed back. He might have been firing off a tie at the butts!

It was a very great achievement to have got men to fire at moments of such stress with such complete tranquillity. For discipline works in two ways: in the first place it enables the soldier in action to get through his movements in the shortest possible time; and then the engrossment in the exact performance begets a great indifference to danger. When, with various-sized pieces of metal flying all round you, you go composedly through efficient bodily movements, you are not only wrapped up in your task, but you have the knowledge that that exact performance is every minute decreasing your personal danger. In addition you have the feeling that Providence ought to — and very frequently does — specially protect you. It would not be right that a man exactly and scrupulously performing his duty to his sovereign, his native land and those it holds dear, should not be protected by a special Providence. And he is!

It is not only that that engrossed marksman might — and very probably did — pick off an advancing enemy with every second shot, and thus diminish his personal danger to that extent, it is that the regular and as if mechanical falling of comrades spreads disproportionate dismay in advancing or halted troops. It is no doubt terrible to you to have large numbers of your comrades instantaneously annihilated by the explosion of some huge engine, but huge engines are blind and thus accidental; a slow, regular picking off of the men beside you is evidence that human terribleness that is not blind or accidental is cold-bloodedly and unshakably turning its attention to a spot very near you. It may very shortly turn its attention to yourself.

Of course, it is disagreeable when artillery is bracketting across your line: a shell falls a hundred yards in front of you, another a hundred yards behind you; the next will be half-way between, and you are half-way between. The waiting wrings your soul; but it does not induce panic or the desire to run — at any rate to nearly the same extent. Where, in any event, could you run to?

But from coldly and mechanically advancing and firing troops you *can* run. And the C.O. was accustomed to boast that on the several occasions when imitating the second battalion of the regiment he had been able to line his men up on tapes before letting them go in an attack and had insisted that they should advance at a very slow double indeed, and in exact alignment, his losses had been not only less than those of every other battalion in the Division, but they had been almost farcically negligible. Faced with troops advancing remorselessly and with complete equanimity the good Wurtembergers had fired so wildly and so high that you could hear their bullets overhead like a flock of wild-geese at night. The effect of panic is to make men fire high. They pull too sharply on their triggers.

These boasts of their Old Man naturally reached the men; they would be uttered before warrant officers and the orderly room staff; and the men — than whom in this matter none are keener mathematicians — were quick to see that the losses of their battalion until lately, at any rate, had been remarkably smaller than those of other units engaged in the same places. So that hitherto, though the men had regarded their Colonel with mixed feelings, he had certainly come out on top. That he was a b——y h—ll of a pusher did not elate them; they would have preferred to be reserved for less dangerous enterprises than those by which the battalion gained its remarkable prestige. On the other hand, though they were constantly being pushed into nasty scrapes, they lost less than units in quieter positions, and that pleased them. But they still asked themselves: "If the

Old Man let us be quiet shouldn't we lose proportionately still less? No one at all?"

That had been the position until very lately: until a week or so, or even a day or so before.

But for more than a fortnight this Army had been what amounted to on-the-run. It retreated with some personal stubbornness and upon prepared positions, but these prepared positions were taken with such great speed and method by the enormous forces attacking it, that hostilities had assumed the aspect almost of a war of movement. For this these troops were singularly ill-adapted, their training having been almost purely that suited for the process of attrition known as trench-warfare. In fact, though good with bombs and even with the bayonet, and though courageous and composed when not in motion, these troops were singularly inept when it was a matter of keeping in communication with the units on either side of them, or even within their own unit, and they had practically no experience in the use of the rifle when in motion. To both these branches the Enemy had devoted untiring attention all through the period of relative inaction of the winter that had now closed and in both particulars their troops, though by now apparently inferior in morale, were remarkably superior. So it appeared to be merely a matter of waiting for a period of easterly winds for this Army to be pushed into the North Sea. The easterly winds were needed for the use of the gas without which, in the idea of the German leaders, it was impossible to attack.

The position, nevertheless, had been desperate and remained desperate, and standing there in the complete tranquillity and inaction of an April morning with a slight westerly breeze, Tietjens realised that he was experiencing what were the emotions of an army practically in flight. So at least he saw it. The use of gas had always been extremely disliked by the enemy's men, and its employment in cylinders had long since been abandoned. But the German Higher Staff persisted in preparing their attacks by dense screens of gas put over by huge plasterings of shells. These screens the enemy forces refused to enter if the wind blew in their direction.

There had come in, then, the factor which caused him himself to feel particular discomfort.

The fact that the battalion was remarkably ably commanded and unusually well-disciplined had not, of course, been overlooked by either brigade or division. And the brigade, too, happened to be admirable. Thus — these things did happen even in the confused periods that preceded the final breaking up of trench warfare — the brigade was selected to occupy positions where the enemy divisions might be expected to be hottest in attack, the battalion was selected to occupy the hottest points in that hottest sector of the line. The chickens of the C.O.'s efficiency had come home to roost.

It had been, as Tietjens felt all over his body, nearly more than flesh and blood could stand. Do what the C.O. had been able to do to husband his men, and, do what discipline could do to aid in the process, the battalion was reduced to not more than a third of what would have been a reasonable strength for the position it had had to occupy — and to abandon. And it was small comfort to the men that the Wiltshires on their right and the Cheshires on their left were in far worse case. So the aspect of the Old Man as a b——y h—ll of a pusher became foremost in their considerations.

To a sensitive officer — and all good officers in this respect are sensitive — the psychology of the men makes itself felt in innumerable ways. He can afford to be blind to the feelings of his officers, for officers have to stand so much at the hands of their seniors before the rules of the service give them a chance to retaliate, that it takes a really bad Colonel to put his own mess in a bad way. As officer you *have* to jump to your C.O.'s orders, to applaud his sentiments, to smile at his lighter witticisms and to guffaw at those that are more gross. That is the Service. With the Other Ranks it is different. A discreet warrant-officer will discreetly applaud his officer's eccentricities and good humours, as will a sergeant desirous of promotion; but the rank and file are under no such compulsion. As long as a man comes to attention when spoken to that is all that can be expected of him. He is under no obligation to understand his officer's witticisms so he can still less be expected to laugh at or to repeat them with gusto. He need not even come very smartly to attention. . . .

And for some days the rank and file of the battalion had gone dead, and the C.O. was aware that it had gone dead. Of the various types of field-officer upon whom he could have modelled himself as regards the men, he had chosen that of the genial, rubicund, slightly whiskyfied C.O. who finishes every sentence with the words: "Eh, what?" In him it was a perfectly cold-blooded game for the benefit of the senior non-commissioned officers and the Other Ranks, but it had gradually become automatic.

For some days now, this mannerism had refused to work. It was as if Napoleon the Great had suddenly found that the device of pinching the ear of a grenadier on parade, had suddenly become ineffective. After the "Eh, what!" like a pistol shot the man to whom it was addressed had not all but shuffled nor had any other men within earshot tittered and whispered to their pals. They had all remained just loutish. And it is a considerable test of courage to remain loutish under the Old Man's eyes!

All this the C.O. knew by the book, having been through it. And Tietjens knew that the C.O. knew it; and he half suspected that the C.O. knew that he, Tietjens, knew it. . . . And that the Pals and the Other Ranks also knew: that, in fact, everyone knew that everyone knew. It was like a nightmare game of bridge with all hands exposed and all the players ready to snatch pistols from their hip-pockets.

And Tietjens, for his sins, now held the trump card and was in play!

It was a loathsome position. He loathed having to decide the fate of the C.O. as he loathed the prospect of having to restore the *morale* of the men — if they survived.

And he was faced now by the conviction that he could do it. If he hadn't felt himself get his hand in with that dozen of disreputable tramps he would not have felt that he could do it. Then he must have used his moral authority with the doctor to get the Old Man patched up, drugged up, bucked up, sufficiently to carry the battalion at least to the end of the retreat of the next few days. It was obvious that that must be done if there was no one else to take command — no one else that was pretty well certain to handle the men all right. But if there *was* anyone else to take over didn't the C.O.'s condition make it too risky to let him remain in authority? Did it, or didn't it? Did it, or didn't it?

Looking at McKechnie coolly as if to see where next he should plant his fist he had thus speculated. And he was aware that, at the most dreadful moment of his whole life his besetting sin, as the saying is, was getting back on him. With the dreadful dread of the approaching *strafe* all over him, with a weight on his forehead, his eyebrows, his heavily labouring chest, he had to take . . . Responsibility. And to realise that he was a fit person to take responsibility.

He said to McKechnie:

"The M.O. is the person who has to dispose of the Colonel."

McKechnie exclaimed:

"By God, if that drunken little squit dares . . ."

Tietjens said:

"Terry will act along the lines of my suggestions. He doesn't have to take orders from me. But he has said that he will act along the lines of my suggestions. I shall accept the moral responsibility."

He felt the desire to pant, as if he had just drunk at a draft a too great quantity of liquid. He did not pant. He looked at his wristwatch. Of the time he had decided to give McKechnie, thirty seconds remained.

McKechnie made wonderful use of the time. The Germans sent over several shells. Not such very long-distance shells either. For ten seconds McKechnie went mad. He was always going mad. He was a bore. If that were only the German customary popping off. . . . But it was heavier. Unusual obscenities dropped from the lips of McKechnie. There was no knowing where the German projectiles were going. Or aimed at. A steam laundry in Bailleul as like as not. He said:

"Yes! Yes! Aranjuez!"

The tiny subaltern had peeped again, with his comic hat, round the corner of the pinkish gravel buttress. . . . A good, nervous boy. Imagining that the fact that he had reported had not been noticed! The gravel certainly looked more pink now the sun was come up . . . It was rising on Bemerton! Or perhaps not so far to the west yet. The parsonage of George Herbert, author of *Sweet day so cool, so calm, so bright, the bridal of the earth and sky!*

It was odd where McKechnie who was still shouting got his words for unnatural vice. He had been Latin Prize Man. But he was probably quite pure. The words very likely meant nothing to him. . . . As to the Tommies! . . . Then, why did they use them?

The German artillery thumped on! Heavier than the usual salvoes with which methodically they saluted the dawn. But there were no shells falling in that neighbourhood. So it might not be the barrage opening the Great *Strafe!* Very likely they were being visited by some little German Prince and wanted to show him what shooting was. Or by Field Marshal Count von Brunkersdorf! Who had ordered them to shoot down the chimney of the Bailleul steam laundry. Or it might be sheer irresponsibility such as distinguished all gunners. Few Germans were imaginative enough to be irresponsible, but no doubt their gunners were more imaginative than other Germans.

He remembered being up in the artillery O.P. — what the devil was its name? — before Albert. On the Albert-Bécourt-Bécordel Road! What the *devil* was its name? A gunner had been looking through his glasses. He had said to Tietjens: "Look at that fat! . . ." And through the glasses lent him, Tietjens had seen, on a hillside in the direction of Martinpuich, a fat Hun, in shirt and trousers, carrying in his right hand a food tin from which he was feeding himself with his left. A fat, lousy object, suggesting an angler on a quiet day. The gunner had said to Tietjens:

"Keep your glass on him!"

And they had chased that miserable German about that naked hillside, with shells, for ten minutes. Whichever way he bolted, they put a shell in front of him. Then they let him go. His action, when he had realised that they were really attending to him, had been exactly that of a rabbit dodging out of the wheat the reapers have just reached. At last he just lay down. He wasn't killed. They had seen him get up and walk off later. Still carrying his bait can!

His antics had afforded those gunners infinite amusement. It afforded them almost more when all the German artillery on that front, imagining that God knew what was the matter, had awakened and plastered heaven and earth and everything between for a quarter of an hour with every imaginable kind of missile. And had then, abruptly, shut up. Yes . . . Irresponsible people, gunners!

The incident had really occurred because Tietjens had happened to ask that gunner how much he imagined it had cost in shells to smash to pieces an indescribably smashed field of about twenty acres that lay between Bazentin-le-petit and Mametz Wood. The field was unimaginably smashed, pulverised, powdered. . . . The gunner had replied that with shells from all the forces employed it might have cost three million sterling. Tietjens asked how many men the gunner imagined might have been killed there. The gunner said he didn't begin to know. None at all, as like as not! No one was very likely to have been strolling about there for pleasure, and it hadn't contained any trenches. It was just a field. Nevertheless, when Tietjens had remarked that in that case two Italian labourers with a steam plough could have pulverised that field about as completely for, say, thirty shillings, the gunner had taken it quite badly. He had made his men poop off after that inoffensive Hun with the bait can, just to show what artillery can *do*.

. . . At that point Tietjens had remarked to McKechnie:

"For my part, I shall advise the M.O. to recommend that the Colonel should be sent back on sick leave for a couple of months. It is within his power to do that."

McKechnie had exhausted all his obscene expletives. He was thus
sane. His jaw dropped:

"Send the C.O. back!" he exclaimed lamentably. "At the very moment when . . ."

Tietjens exclaimed:

"Don't be an ass. Or don't imagine that I'm an ass. No one is going
to reap any glory in this Army. Here and now!"

McKechnie said:

"But what price the money? Command pay! Nearly four quid a
day. You could do with two-fifty quid at the end of his two months!"

Not so very long ago it would have seemed impossible that any
man *could* speak to him about either his private financial affairs or his
intimate motives.

He said:

"I have obvious responsibilities . . ."

"Some say," McKechnie went on, "that you're a b——y millionaire.
One of the richest men in England. Giving coal mines to duchesses.
So they say. Some say you're such a pauper that you hire your wife
out to generals. . . . Any generals. That's how you get your jobs."

To that Tietjens had had to listen before. . . .

Max Redoubt . . . It had come suddenly on to his tongue — just
as, before, the name of Bemerton had come, belatedly. The name of
the artillery observation post between Albert and Bécourt-Bécordel
had been Max Redoubt! During the intolerable waitings of that half-
forgotten July and August the name had been as familiar on his lips
as . . . say, as Bemerton itself. . . . When I forget thee, oh, my
Bemerton . . . or, oh, my Max Redoubt . . . may my right hand
forget its cunning! . . . The unforgettables! . . . Yet he had forgotten them!

If only for a time he had forgotten them. Then, his right hand
might forget its cunning. If only for a time. . . . But even that
might be disastrous, might come at a disastrous moment. . . . The
Germans had suppressed themselves. Perhaps they had knocked down
the laundry chimney. Or hit some G.S. wagons loaded with coal. . . .
At any rate, that was not the usual morning *strafe*. That was to come.
Sweet day so cool — began again.

McKechnie hadn't suppressed himself. He was going to get suppressed. He had just been declaring that Tietjens had not displayed
any chivalry in not reporting the C.O. if he, Tietjens, considered him
to be drunk — or even chronically alcoholic. No chivalry. . . .

This was like a nightmare! . . . No it wasn't. It was like fever when things appear stiffly unreal. . . . And exaggeratedly real! Stereoscopic, you might say!

McKechnie with an accent of sardonic hate begged to remind Tietjens that if he considered the C.O. to be a drunkard he ought to have him put under arrest. King's Regs. exacted that. But Tietjens was too cunning. He meant to have that two-fifty quid. He might be a poor man and need it. Or a millionaire, and mean. They said that was how millionaires became millionaires: by snapping up trifles of money that, God knows, would be godsends to people like himself, McKechnie.

It occurred to Tietjens that two hundred and fifty pounds after this was over, might be a godsend to himself in a manner of speaking. And then he thought:

"Why the devil shouldn't I earn it?"

What was he going to do? After this was over.

And it was going over. Every minute the Germans were not advancing they were losing. Losing the power to advance. . . . Now, this minute! It was exciting.

"No!" McKechnie said. "You're too cunning. If you got poor Bill cashiered for drunkenness you'd have no chance of commanding. They'd put in another pukka colonel. As a stop-gap, whilst Bill's on sick leave, you're pretty certain to get it. That's why you're doing the damnable thing you're doing."

Tietjens had a desire to go and wash himself. He felt physically dirty.

Yet what McKechnie said was true enough! It was true! . . . The mechanical impulse to divest himself of money was so strong that he began to say:

"In that case . . ." He was going to finish: "I'll *get* the damned fellow cashiered." But he didn't.

He was in a beastly hole. But decency demanded that he shouldn't act in panic. He had a mechanical, normal panic that made him divest himself of money. Gentlemen don't earn money. Gentlemen, as a matter of fact, don't do anything. They exist. Perfuming the air like Madonna lilies. Money comes into them as air through petals and foliage. Thus the world is made better and brighter. And, of course, thus political life can be kept clean! . . . So you can't make money.

But look here: This unit was the critical spot of the whole affair.

The weak spots of Brigade, Division, Army, British Expeditionary
Force, Allied Forces. . . . If the Hun went through there . . . *Fuit
Ilium et magna gloria.* . . . Not much glory!

He was bound to do his best for that unit. That poor b——y unit.
And for the b——y knockabout comedians to whom he had lately
promised tickets for Drury Lane at Christmas. . . . The poor devils
had said they preferred the Shoreditch Empire or the old Balham.
That was typical of England. The Lane was the *locus classicus* of the
race, but those rag-time . . . heroes, call them heroes! — preferred
Shoreditch and Balham!

An immense sense of those grimy, shuffling, grouching, dirty-nosed
pantomime-supers came over him and an intense desire to give them
a bit of luck, and he said:

"Captain McKechnie, you can fall out. And you will return to duty.
Your own duty. In proper head-dress."

McKechnie, who had been talking, stopped with his head on one
side like a listening magpie. He said:

"What's this? What's this?" stupidly. Then he remarked:

"Oh, well, I suppose if you're in command . . ."

Tietjens said:

"It's usual to say 'sir,' when addressing a senior officer on parade.
Even if you don't belong to his unit."

McKechnie said:

"Don't belong! . . . *I* don't . . . To the poor b——y old
pals! . . ."

Tietjens said:

"You're attached to Division Headquarters, and you'll get back to
it! Now! At once! . . . And you won't come back here. Not while I'm
in command. . . . Fall out. . . ."

That was really a duty — a feudal duty! — performed for the sake
of the rag-time fellows. They wanted to be rid — and at once! — of
dipsomaniacs in command of that unit and having the disposal of
their lives. . . . Well, the moment McKechnie had uttered the
words: "To the poor b——y old pals," an illuminating flash had
presented Tietjens with the conviction that, alone, the C.O. was too
damn good an officer to appear a dipsomaniac, even if he were ob-
servably drunk quite often. But, seen together with this fellow
McKechnie, the two of them must present a formidable appearance
of being alcoholic lunatics!

The rest of the poor b——y old pals didn't really any more exist.

They were a tradition — of ghosts! Four of them were dead: four in hospital, two awaiting court martial for giving worthless cheques. The last of them, practically, if you excepted McKechnie, was the collection of putrescence and rags at that moment hanging in the wire apron. . . . The whole complexion of Headquarters would change with the going of McKechnie.

He considered with satisfaction that he would command a very decent lot. The Adjutant was so inconspicuous you did not even notice him. Beady-eyed, like a bird! Always preoccupied. And little Aranjuez, the signalling officer! And a fat fellow called Dunne, who had represented Intelligence since the Night Before Last! "A" Company Commander was fifty, thin as a pipe-stem, and bald; "B" was a good, fair boy, of good family; "C" and "D" were subalterns, just out. But clean. . . . Satisfactory!

What a handful of frail grass with which to stop an aperture in the dam of — of the Empire! Damn the Empire! It was England! It was Bemerton Parsonage that mattered! What did we want with an Empire! It was only a jerry-building Jew like Disraeli that could have provided us with that jerry-built name! The Tories said they had to have someone to do their dirty work. . . . Well, they'd had it!

He said to McKechnie:

"There's a fellow called Bemer — I mean Griffiths, O Nine — Griffiths, I understand you're interested in for the Divisional Follies. I'll send him along to you as soon as he's had his breakfast. He's first-rate with the cornet."

McKechnie said:

"Yes, sir," saluted rather limply and took a step.

That was McKechnie all over. He never brought his mad fists to a crisis. That made him still more of a bore. His face would be distorted like that of a wildcat in front of its kittens' hole in a stone wall. But he became the submissive subordinate. Suddenly! Without rhyme or reason!

Tiring people! Without manners! . . . They would presumably run the world now. It would be a tiresome world.

McKechnie, however, was saluting. He held a sealed envelope, rather small and crumpled, as if from long carrying. He was talking in a controlled voice after permission asked. He desired Tietjens to observe that the seal on the envelope was unbroken. The envelope contained "The Sonnet."

McKechnie must, then, have gone mad! His eyes, if his voice was quiet, though with an Oxford-Cockney accent — his prune-coloured eyes were certainly mad. . . . Hot prunes!

Men shuffled along the trenches, carrying by rope-handles very heavy, lead-coloured wooden cases; two men to each case. Tietjens said:

"You're 'D' Company . . . Get a move on!"

McKechnie, however, wasn't mad. He was only pointing out that he could pit his Intellect and his Latinity against those of Tietjens; that he could do it when the great day came!

The envelope, in fact, contained a sonnet. A sonnet Tietjens, for distraction, had written to rhymes dictated by McKechnie . . . for distraction in a moment of stress.

Several moments of stress they had been in together. It ought to have formed a bond between them. It hadn't. . . . Imagine having a bond with a Highland-Oxford-Cockney!

Or perhaps it had! There was certainly the sonnet. Tietjens had written it in two and a half minutes, he remembered, to stave off the thought of his wife who was then being a nuisance. . . . Two and a half minutes of forgetting Sylvia! A bit of luck! . . . But McKechnie had insisted on regarding it as a challenge. A challenge to his Latinity. He had then and there undertaken to turn that sonnet into Latin hexameters in two minutes. Or perhaps four. . . .

But things had got in the way. A fellow called O Nine Morgan had got himself killed over their feet. In the hut. Then they had been busy with the Draft!

Apparently McKechnie had sealed up that sonnet in an envelope. In *that* envelope. Then and there. Apparently McKechnie had been inspired with a blind, Celtic, snorting rage to prove that he was better as a Latinist than Tietjens as a sonneteer. Apparently he was still so inspired. He was mad to engage in competition with Tietjens.

It was perhaps that that made him not quite mad. He kept sane in order to be fit for this competition. He was now repeating, holding out the envelope, seal upwards:

"I suppose you believe I have not read your sonnet, sir. I suppose you believe I have not read your sonnet, sir. . . . To prepare myself to translate it more quickly."

Tietjens said:

"Yes! No! . . . I don't care."

He couldn't tell the fellow that the idea of a competition was loathsome to him. Any sort of competition was loathsome to Tietjens. Even competitive games. He liked playing tennis. Real tennis. But he very rarely played because he couldn't get fellows to play with, that beating would not be disagreeable. . . . And it would be loathsome to be drawn into any sort of competition with this Prize Man. . . . They were moving very slowly along the trench, McKechnie retreating sideways and holding out the seal.

"It's your seal, sir!" he was repeating. "Your own seal. You see, it isn't broken. . . . You don't perhaps imagine that I read the sonnet quickly and made a copy from memory?"

. . . The fellow wasn't even a decent Latinist. Or verse-maker, though he was always boasting about it to the impossible, adenoidy, Cockney subalterns who made up the battalion's mess. He would translate their chits into Latin verse. . . . But it was always into tags. Generally from the Æneid. Like:

"*Conticuere omnes,* or *Vino somnoque sepultum!*"

That was, presumably, what Oxford of just before the War was doing.

He said:

"I'm not a beastly detective. . . . Yes, of course, I quite believe it."

He thought of emerging into the society of little Aranjuez who was some sort of gentle earnest Levantine. Think of thinking of a Levantine with pleasure! He said:

"Yes. It's all right, McKechnie."

He felt himself solid. He was really in a competition with this fellow. It was deterioration. He, Tietjens, was crumpling up morally. He had accepted responsibility; he had thought of two hundred and fifty pounds with pleasure; now he was competing with a Cockney-Celtic-Prize Man. He was reduced to that level. . . . Well, as like as not he would be dead before the afternoon. And no one would know.

Think of thinking about whether any one would know or no! . . . But it was Valentine Wannop that wasn't to know. That he had deteriorated under the strain! . . . That enormously surprised him. He said to his subconscious self:

"What! Is *that* still there?"

That girl was at least an admirable Latinist. He remarked, with a sort of sardonic glee that, years before, in a dog-cart, emerging from mist, somewhere in Sussex — Udimore! — she had made him look silly. Over Catullus! Him, Tietjens! . . . Shortly afterwards old

Campion had run into them with his motor that he couldn't drive but *would* drive.

McKechnie, apparently assuaged, said:

"I don't know if you know, sir, that General Campion is to take over this Army the day after to-morrow. . . . But, of course, you would know."

Tietjens said:

"No. I didn't. . . . You fellows in touch with Headquarters get to hear of things long before us." He added:

"It means that we shall be getting reinforcements. . . . It means the Single Command."

IV

It MEANT that the end of the war was in sight.

In the next sector, in front of the Headquarters' dug-out sacking they found only Second-Lieutenant Aranjuez and Lance-Corporal Duckett of the Orderly Room. Both good boys, the lance-corporal, with very long graceful legs. He picked up his feet well, but continually moved his ankles with his soles when he talked earnestly. Somebody's bastard.

McKechnie plunged at once into the story of the sonnet. The lance-corporal had, of course, a large number of papers for Tietjens to sign. An untidy, buff and white sheaf, so McKechnie had time to talk. He wished to establish himself as on a level with the temporary C.O. At least intellectually.

He didn't. Aranjuez kept on exclaiming:

"The Major wrote a sonnet in two and a half minutes! The Major! Who would have thought it!" Ingenuous boy!

Tietjens looked at the papers with some attention. He had been so kept out of contact with the affairs of the battalion, that he wanted to know. As he had suspected, the paper business of the unit was in a shocking state. Brigade, Division, even Army and, positively, Whitehall were *strafing* for information about everything imaginable from jam, toothbrushes and braces, to religions, vaccination, and barrack damages. . . . This was interesting matter. A relief to contemplate.
. . . You would almost think all-wise Authority snowed under and broke the backs of Commanding Officers with papers in order to re-

lieve their minds of affording alternative interests . . . alternative to the exigencies of active hostilities! It was certainly a relief whilst waiting for a *strafe* to come to the right stage — to have to read a violent enquiry about P.R.I. funds, whilst the battalion had been resting near a place called Béhencourt. . . .

It appeared that Tietjens might well be thankful that he had not been allowed to handle the P.R.I. funds.

The second-in-command is the titular administrator of the Regimental Institute: he is the President, supposed to attend to the men's billiard tables, almanacks, backgammon boards, football boots. But the C.O. had preferred to keep these books in his own hands. Tietjens regarded that as a slight. Perhaps it had not been!

It went quickly through his head that the C.O. perhaps had financial difficulties — though that was no real affair of his. . . . The House Guards was pressingly interested in the pre-enlistment affairs of a private called 64 Smith. They asked violently and for the third time for particulars of his religion, previous address and real name. That was no doubt the espionage branch at work. . . . But Whitehall was also more violently interested in answers to queries about the disposal of regimental funds of a training camp in January, 1915. . . . As long ago as that! The mills of God grind slowly. . . . That query was covered by a private note from the Brigadier saying that he wished for goodness' sake the C.O. would answer these queries or there would have to be a Court of Enquiry.

These particular two papers ought not to have been brought to Tietjens. He held them between the thumb and forefinger of his left hand and the query upon 64 Smith — which seemed rather urgent — between his first and second, and so handed them to Lance-Corporal Duckett. That nice, clean, fair boy was, at the moment, talking in intimate undertones to Second-Lieutenant Aranjuez about the resemblances between the Petrarchan and the Shakespearean sonnet form. . . .

This was what His Majesty's Expeditionary Force had come to. You had four of its warriors, four minutes before the zero of a complete advance of the whole German line, all interested in sonnets. . . . Drake and his game of bowls — in fact repeated itself! Differently, of course! But times change.

He handed the two selected papers to Duckett.

"Give this one to the Commanding Officer," he said, "and tell the Sergeant-Major to find what Company 64 Smith is in and have him brought to me, wherever I am. . . . I'm going right along the trenches now. Come after me when you've been to the C.O. and the Sergeant-Major. Aranjuez will make notes of what I want done about revetting, you can put down anything about the personnel of the companies. . . . Get a move on!"

He told McKechnie amiably to be out of those lines forthwith. He didn't want him killed on his hands.

The sun was now shining into the trench.

He looked again through Brigade's morning communication concerning dispositions the unit was to make in the event of the expected German attack. . . . Due to begin — the preparatory artillery at least — in three minutes' time.

Don't we say prayers before battle? . . . He could not imagine himself doing it. . . . He just hoped that nothing would happen that would make him lose control of his mind. . . . Otherwise he found that he was meditating on how to get the paper affair of the unit into a better state. . . . "*Who sweeps a room as for Thy cause . . .*" It was the equivalent of prayer probably.

He noted that Brigade's injunctions about the coming fight were not only endorsed with earnestness by Division but also by very serious exhortations from Army. The chit from Brigade was in handwriting, that from Division in fairly clear typescript, that from Army in very pale type characters. . . . It amounted to this: that they were that day to stick it till they burst. . . . That meant that there was nothing behind their backs — from there to the North Sea! . . . The French were hurrying along probably. . . . He imagined a lot of little blue fellows in red breeches trotting along pink, sunlit plains.

(You cannot control your imagination's pictures. Of course the French no longer wore red trousers.) He saw the line breaking just where the blue section came to; the rest, swept back into the sea. He saw the whole of the terrain behind them. On the horizon was a glistening haze. That was where they were going to be swept to. Or of course they would not be swept. They would be lying on their faces, exposing the seats of their breeches. Too negligible for the large dust-pan and broom. . . . What was death like — the immediate process of dissolution? He stuffed the papers into his tunic pocket.

He remembered with grim amusement that one chit promised him reinforcements. Sixteen men! Sixteen! Worcesters! From a Worcester training camp. . . . Why the deuce weren't they sent to the Worcester battalion just next door? Good fellows, no doubt. But they hadn't got the drill quiffs of our lot; they were not pals with our men; they did not know the officers by name. There would be no welcome to cheer them. . . . It was a queer idea, the deliberate destruction of regimental esprit de corps that the Home Authorities now insisted on. It was said to be imitated at the suggestion of a civilian of advanced social views from the French who in turn had imitated it from the Germans. It is of course lawful to learn of the Enemy; but is it sensible?

Perhaps it is. The Feudal Spirit was broken. Perhaps it would therefore be harmful to Trench-Warfare. It used to be comfortable and cosy. You fought beside men from your own hamlet under the leadership of the parson's son. Perhaps that was not good for you?

At any rate, as at present arranged, dying was a lonely affair.

He, Tietjens, and little Aranjuez there, if something hit them would die — a Yorkshire territorial magnate's son and the son of, positively, an Oporto Protestant minister, if you can imagine such a thing! — the dissimilar souls winging their way to heaven side by side. You'd think God would find it more appropriate if Yorkshiremen went with other North Country fellows, and Dagoes with other Papists. For Aranjuez, though the son of a Non-conformist of sorts, had reverted to the faith of his fathers.

He said:

"Come along, Aranjuez. . . . I want to see that wet bit of trench before the Hun shells hit it."

Well. . . . They were getting reinforcements. The Home Authorities had awakened to their prayers. They sent them sixteen Worcesters. They would be three hundred and forty-four — no, forty-three, because he had sent back O Nine Griffiths, the fellow with the cornet — three hundred and forty-three lonely souls against . . . say two Divisions! Against about eighteen thousand, very likely. And they were to stick it till they burst. Reinforced!

Reinforced. Good God! . . . Sixteen Worcesters!

What was at the bottom of it all?

Campion was going to command that Army. That meant that real reinforcements had been promised from the millions of men that filled the base camps. And it meant the Single Command! Campion would not have consented to take the command of that Army if he had not had those very definite promises.

But it would take time. Months! Anything like adequate reinforcements would take months.

And at that moment, in the most crucial point of the line of the Army, of the Expeditionary Force, the Allied Forces, the Empire, the Universe, the Solar System, they had three hundred and sixty-six men commanded by the last surviving Tory. To face wave on wave of the Enemy.

In one minute the German barrage was due.

Aranjuez said to him:

"You can write a sonnet in two and a half minutes, sir. . . . And your siphon works like anything in that damp trench. . . . It took my mother's great-uncle, the canon of Oporto, fifteen weeks to finish his celebrated sonnet. I know because my mother told me. . . . But you oughtn't to be here, sir."

Aranjuez then was the nephew of the author of the *Sonnet to Night*. He could be. You had to have that sort of oddity to make up this world. So naturally he was interested in sonnets.

And, having got hold of a battalion with a stretch of damp trench, Tietjens had had the opportunity of trying a thing he had often thought of — of drying out vertically cut, damp soil by means of a siphon of soil-pipes put in, not horizontally, but vertically. Fortunately Hackett, the commander of B Company, that had the wet trench, had been an engineer in civil life. Aranjuez had been along, out of sheer hero-worship, to B trenches to see how his hero's siphons had worked. He reported that they worked like a dream.

Little Aranjuez said:

"These trenches are like Pompeii, sir."

Tietjens had never seen Pompeii, but he understood that Aranjuez was referring to the empty square-cut excavations in the earth. Particularly to their emptiness. And to the deadly stillness in the sunlight. . . . Admirable trenches. Made to hold an establishment of several thousand men. To bustle with Cockney life. Now dead empty. They passed three sentries in the pinkish gravel passage and two men, one with a pick, the other with a shovel. They were exactly squaring the juncture of the wall and the path, as they might have done in Pompeii. Or in Hyde Park! A perfect devil for tidiness, "A" Company Commander. But the men seemed to like it. They were sniggering, though they stopped that, of course, when Tietjens passed. . . .

A nice, dark, tiny boy, Aranjuez; his adoration was charming. From the very first — and naturally, frightened out of his little life, he had clung to Tietjens as a child clings to an omnipotent father. Tietjens, all-wise, could direct the awful courses of war and decree safety for the frightened! Tietjens needed that sort of worship. The boy said it would be awful to have anything happen to your eyes. Your girl naturally would not look at you. Not more than three miles away, Nancy Truefitt was now. Unless they had evacuated her. Nancy was his flame. In a tea-shop at Bailleul.

A man was sitting outside the mouth of "A" dug-out, just after they passed the mouth of the communication trench. . . . Comforting that channel in the soil looked, running uphill. You could saunter away up there, out of all this. . . . But you couldn't! There was no turning here either to the right or to the left!

The man writing in a copy-book had his tin hat right over his eyes. Engrossed, he sat on a gravel-step, his copy-book on his knees. His name was Slocombe and he was a dramatist. Like Shakespeare. He made fifty pounds a time writing music-hall sketches, for the outer halls. The outer halls were the cheap music-halls that go in a ring round the suburbs of London. Slocombe never missed a second, writing in his copy-books. If you fell the men out for a rest when marching, Slocombe would sit by the roadside — and out would come his copy-book and his pencil. His wife would type out what he sent home. And write him grumbling letters if the supply of copy failed. How was she to keep up the Sunday best of George and Flossie if he did not keep on writing one-act sketches? Tietjens had this information through censoring one of the man's letters containing manuscript. . . . Slocombe was slovenly as a soldier, but he kept the other men in a good humour, his mind being a perfect repertoire of Cockney jests at the expense of Big and Little Willy and Brother Fritz. Slocombe wrote on, wetting his pencil with his tongue.

The sergeant in the mouth of "A" Company headquarters dug-out started to turn out some sort of a guard, but Tietjens stopped him. "A" Company ran itself on the lines of regulars in the depôt. The O.C. had a conduct sheet-book as neat as a ledger! The old, bald, grim fellow. Tietjens asked the sergeant questions. Had they their Mills bombs all right? They weren't short of rifles — first-class order? . . . But how could they be! Were there any sick? . . . Two! . . . Well, it was a healthy life! . . . Keep the men under cover until the Hun barrage began. It was due now.

It was due now. The second hand of Tietjens' watch, like an animated pointer of hair, kicked a little on the stroke of the minute. . . . "Crumb!" said the punctual, distant sound.

Tietjens said to Aranjuez:

"It's presumably coming now!" Aranjuez pulled at the chin strap of his tin hat.

Tietjen's mouth filled itself with a dreadful salty flavour, the back of his tongue being dry. His chest and heart laboured heavily. Aranjuez said:

"If I stop one, sir, you'll tell Nancy Truefitt that . . ."

Tietjens said:

"Little nippers like you don't stop things. . . . Besides, feel the wind!"

They were at the highest point of the trenches that ran along a hillside. So they were exposed. The wind had undoubtedly freshened, coming down the hill. In front and behind, along the trench, they could see views. Land, some green; greyish trees.

Aranjuez said:

"You think the wind will stop them, sir," appealingly.

Tietjens exclaimed with gruffness:

"Of course it will stop them. They won't work without gas. Yet their men hate to have to face the gas-screens. It's our great advantage. It saps their *morale*. Nothing else would. They can't put up smoke-screens either."

Aranjuez said:

"I know you think their gas has ruined them, sir. . . . It was wicked of them to use it. You can't do a wicked thing without suffering for it, can you, sir?"

It remained indecently quiet. Like Sunday in a village with the people in church. But it was not pleasurable.

Tietjens wondered how long physical irregularities would inconvenience his mind. You cannot think well with a parched back to your tongue. This was practically his first day in the open during a *strafe*. His first whole day for quite a time. Since Noircourt! . . . How long ago? . . . Two years? . . . Maybe! . . . Then he had nothing to go on to tell him how long he would be inconvenienced!

It remained indecently quiet! Running footsteps, at first on duckboards, then on the dry path of trench! They made Tietjens start violently, inside himself. The house must be on fire!

He said to Aranjuez:

"Some one is in a hurry!"

The lad's teeth chattered. They must have made him feel bad, too, the footsteps. The knocking on the gate in *Macbeth*!

They began. It had come. Pam . . . Pamperi . . . Pam! Pam!
. . . Pa . . . Pamperi . . . Pam! Pam! . . . Pampamperipampam-
pam . . . Pam . . . They were the ones that sound like drums.
They continued incessantly. Immensely big drums, the ones that go
at it with real zest . . . You know how it is, looking at an opera orchestra when the fellow with the big drum-sticks really begins. Your
own heart beats like hell. Tietjens' heart did. The drummer appears
to go mad.

Tietjens was never much good at identifying artillery by the sound.
He would have said that these were anti-aircraft guns. And he remembered that, for some minutes, the drone of plane engines had
pervaded the indecent silence. . . . But that drone was so normal
it was part of the silence. Like your own thoughts. A filtered and
engrossed sound, drifting down from overhead. More like fine dust
than noise.

A familiar noise said: "We . . . e . . . e . . . ry!" Shells always
appeared tired of life. As if after a long, long journey they said:
"Weary!" Very much prolonging the "e" sound. Then "Whack!"
when they burst.

This was the beginning of the *strafe*. . . . Though he had been
convinced the *strafe* was coming he had hoped for a prolongation of
the . . . say Bemerton! . . . conditions. The life Peaceful. And Contemplative. But here it was beginning. "Oh well . . ."

This shell appeared heavier and to be more than usually tired.
Desultory. It seemed to pass within six feet over the heads of Aranjuez and himself. Then, just twenty yards up the hill it said, in-
visibly, "Dud!" . . . And it *was* a dud!

It had not, very likely, been aimed at their trench at all. It was
probably just an air-craft shrapnel shell that had not exploded. The
Germans were firing a great number of duds — these days.

So it might not be a sign of the beginning! It was tantalising. But
as long as it ended the right way one could bear it.

Lance-Corporal Duckett, the fair boy, ran to within two foot of
Tietjens' feet and pulled up with a Guardee's stamp and a terrific
salute. There was life in the old dog yet. Meaning that a zest for spit
and polish survived in places in these rag-time days.

The boy said, panting — it might have been agitation, or that he
had run so fast. . . . But why had he run so fast if he were not agitated:

"If you please, sir," . . . Pant. . . . "Will you come to the Colo-

nel?" . . . Pant. "With as little delay as possible!" He remained
panting.

It went through Tietjens' mind that he was going to spend the
rest of that day in a comfortable, dark hole. Not in the blinding daylight. . . . Let us be thankful!

Leaving Lance-Corporal Duckett . . . it came suddenly into his
head that he liked that boy because he suggested Valentine Wannop!
. . . to converse in intimate tones with Aranjuez and so to distract
him from the fear of imminent death or blindness that would mean
the loss of his girl, Tietjens went smartly back along the trenches.
He didn't hurry. He was determined that the men should not see
him hurry. Even if the Colonel should refuse to be relieved of the
command, Tietjens was determined that the men should have the
consolation of knowing that Headquarters numbered one cool, sauntering soul amongst its members.

They had had, when they took over the Trasna Valley trenches before the Mametz Wood affair, a rather good Major who wore an eyeglass and was of good family. He had something the matter with
him, for he committed suicide later. . . . But, as they went in, the
Huns, say fifty yards, began to shout various national battle-cries of
the Allies or the melodies of regimental quicksteps of British regiments. The idea was that if they heard, say: *"Some talk of Alexander. . . ."* resounding from an opposite trench, H.M. Second
Grenadier Guards would burst into cheers and Brother Hun would
know what he had before him.

Well, this Major Grosvenor shut his men up, naturally, and stood
listening with his eyeglass screwed into his face and the air of a
connoisseur at a quartette party. At last he took his eyeglass out,
threw it in the air and caught it again.

"Shout *Banzai!* men," he said.

That, on the off-chance, might give the enemy a scunner at the
thought that we had Japanese troops in the line in front of them, or
it would show them that we were making game of them, a form of
offensive that sent these owlish fellows mad with rage. . . . So the
Huns shut up!

That was the sort of humour in an officer that the men still liked.
. . . The sort of humour Tietjens himself had not got; but he could
appear unconcernedly reflective and all there — and he could tell
them, at trying moments that, say, their ideas about skylarks were all
wrong. . . . That was tranquillising.

Once he had heard a Papist Padre preaching in a barn, under shell-fire. At any rate shells were going overhead and pigs underfoot. The Padre had preached about very difficult points in the doctrine of the Immaculate Conception, and the men had listened raptly. He said that was common sense. They didn't want lachrymose or mortuary orations. They wanted their minds taken off . . . So did the Padre!

Thus you talk to the men, just before the event, about skylarks, or the hind-legs of the elephant at the old Lane! And you don't hurry when the Colonel sends for you.

He walked along, for a moment or two, thinking nothing. The pebbles in the gravel of the trench grew clear and individual. Some one had dropped a letter. Slocombe, the dramatist, was closing his copy-book. Sighing, apparently, he reached for his rifle. "A" Company Sergeant-Major was turning out some men of sorts. He said: "Get a move on!" Tietjens said as he passed: "Keep them under cover as much as you can, Sergeant-Major."

It occurred to him suddenly that he had committed a military misdemeanour in leaving Lance-Corporal Duckett with Aranjuez. An officer should not walk along a stretch of lonely trench without escort. Some Hun offering might hit him and there would be loss of property to His Majesty. No one to fetch a doctor or stretcher-bearers while you bled to death. That was the Army. . . .

Well, he had left Duckett with Aranjuez to comfort him. That minute subaltern was suffering. God knew what little agonies ran about in his little mind, like mice! He was as brave as a lion when *strafes* were on: when they weren't, his little, blackamoor, nobbly face quivered as the thought visited him. . . .

He had really left Valentine Wannop with Aranjuez! That, he realised, was what he had really done. The boy Duckett *was* Valentine Wannop. Clean, blond, small, with the ordinary face, the courageous eyes, the obstinately, slightly peaked nose. . . . It was just as if, Valentine Wannop being in his possession, they had been walking along a road and seen someone in distress. And he, Tietjens, had said:

"I've got to get along. You stop and see what you can do!"

And, amazingly, he was walking along a country road beside Valentine Wannop, being silent, with the quiet intimacy that comes with possession. She belonged to him. . . . Not a mountain road: not Yorkshire. Not a valley road: not Bemerton. A country parsonage was not for him. So he wouldn't take orders!

A dawn-land road, with some old thorn trees. They only grew really in Kent. And the sky coming down on all sides. The flat top of a down!

Amazing! He had not thought of that girl for over a fortnight now, except in moments of great *strafes*, when he had hoped she would not be too worried if she knew where he was. Because he had the sense that, all the time she knew where he was. He had thought of her less and less. At longer intervals. . . . As with his nightmare of the mining Germans who desired that a candle should be brought to the Captain. At first, every night, three or four times every night, it had visited him. . . . Now it came only once every night. . . .

The physical semblance of that boy had brought the girl back to his mind. That was accidental, so it was not part of any psychological rhythm. It did not show him, that is to say, whether, in the natural course of events and without accidents she was ceasing to obsess him.

She was certainly now obsessing him! Beyond bearing or belief. His whole being was overwhelmed by her . . . by her mentality, really. For of course the physical resemblance of the lance-corporal was mere subterfuge. Lance-corporals do not resemble young ladies. . . . And, as a matter of fact, he did not remember exactly what Valentine Wannop looked like. Not vividly. He had not that sort of mind. It was words that his mind found that let him know that she was fair, snub-nosed, rather broad-faced, and square on her feet. As if he had made a note of it and referred to it when he wanted to think of her. His mind didn't make any mental picture; it brought up a sort of blur of sunlight.

It was the mentality that obsessed him: the exact mind, the impatience of solecisms and facile generalisations! . . . A queer catalogue of the charms of one's lady love! . . . But he wanted to hear her say: "Oh, chuck it, Edith Ethel!" when Edith Ethel Duchemin, now of course Lady Macmaster, quoted some of the opinions expressed in Macmaster's critical monograph about the late Mr. Rossetti. . . . How *very* late now!

It would rest him to hear that. She was, in effect, the only person in the world that he wanted to hear speak. Certainly the only person in the world that he wanted to talk to. The only clear intelligence! . . . The repose that his mind needed from the crackling of thorns under all the pots of the world. . . . From the eternal, imbecile "Pampamperipam Pam Pamperi Pam Pam!" of the German guns that all the while continued.

Why couldn't they chuck that? What good did it do them to keep that mad drummer incessantly thundering on his stupid instrument? . . . Possibly they might bring down some of our planes, but they generally didn't. You saw the black ball of their shells exploding and slowly expand like pocket-handkerchiefs about the unconcerned planes, like black peas aimed at dragon-fleas, against the blue; the illuminated, pinkish, pretty things! . . . But his dislike of those guns was just dislike — a Tory prejudice. They were probably worth while. Just . . .

You naturally tried every argument in the unseen contest of wills that went on across the firmament. "Ho!" says our Staff, "they are going to attack in force at such an hour ackemma," because naturally the staff thought in terms of ackemma years after the twenty-four-hour day had been established. "Well, we'll send out a million machine-gun planes to wipe out any men they've got moving up into support!"

It was of course unusual to move bodies of men by daylight. But this game had only two resources: you used the usual; or the unusual. *Usually* you didn't begin your barrage after dawn and launch your attack at ten-thirty or so. So you might do it — the Huns might be trying it on — as a surprise measure.

On the other hand, our people might be sending over the planes, whose immense droning was then making your very bones vibrate, in order to tell the Huns that we were ready to be surprised, that the time had now about come round when we might be expecting the Hun brain to think out a surprise. So we sent out those deathly, dreadful things to run along just over the tops of the hedgerows, in spite of all the guns! For there was nothing more terrifying in the whole war than that span of lightness, swaying, approaching a few feet above the heads of your column of men: instinct with wrath, dispensing the dreadful rain! So we had sent them. In a moment they would be tearing down. . . .

Of course if this were merely a demonstration; if, say, there were no reinforcements moving, no troops detraining at the distant railhead, the correct Hun answer would be to hammer some of our trenches to hell with all the heavy stuff they could put into them. That was like saying sardonically:

"God, if you interfere with our peace and quiet on a fine day we'll interfere with yours!" And . . . Kerumph . . . the wagons of coal would fly over until we recalled our planes and all went to sleep again over the chess-board. . . . You would probably be just as well off if you refrained from either demonstration or counter-demonstration. But Great General Staff liked to exchange these witticisms in iron. And a little blood!

A sergeant of sorts approached him from Bn.H.2 way, shepherding a man with a head wound. His tin hat, that is to say, was perched jauntily forward over a bandage. He was Jewish-nosed, appeared not to have shaved, though he had, and appeared as if he ought to have worn pince-nez to complete his style of Oriental manhood. Private Smith. Tietjens said:

"Look here, what was your confounded occupation before the war?"

The man replied with an agreeable, cultured throaty intonation: "I was a journalist, sir. On a Socialist paper. Extreme Left!"

"And what," Tietjens asked, "was your agreeable name? . . . I'm obliged to ask you that question. I don't want to insult you."

In the old regular army it was an insult to ask a private if he was not going under his real name. Most men enlisted under false names. The man said:

"Eisenstein, sir!"

Tietjens asked if the man were a Derby recruit or compulsorily enlisted. He said he had enlisted voluntarily. Tietjens said: "Why?" If the fellow was a capable journalist and on the right side he would be more useful outside the army. The man said he had been foreign correspondent of a Left paper. Being correspondent of a Left paper with a name like Eisenstein deprived one of one's chance of usefulness. Besides he wanted to have a whack at the Prussians. He was of Polish extraction. Tietjens asked the sergeant if the man had a good record. The Sergeant said: "First-class man. First-class soldier." He had been recommended for the D.C.M., Tietjens said:

"I shall apply to have you transferred to the Jewish regiment. In the meantime you can go back to the First Line Transport. You shouldn't have been a Left journalist and have a name like Eisenstein. One or the other. Not both." The man said the name had been inflicted on his ancestry in the Middle Ages. He would prefer to be called Esau, as a son of that tribe. He pleaded not to be sent to the Jewish regiment, which was believed to be in Mesopotamia, just when the fighting there was at its most interesting.

"You're probably thinking of writing a book," Tietjens said. "Well, there are all Abanar and Pharpar to write about. I'm sorry. But you're intelligent enough to see that I can't take . . ." He stopped, fearing that if the sergeant heard any more the men might make it hot for the fellow as a suspect. He was annoyed at having asked his name before the sergeant. He appeared to be a good man. Jews could fight. . . . And hunt! . . . But he wasn't going to take any risks. The man, dark-eyed and erect, flinched a little, gazing into Tietjens' eyes.

"I suppose you can't, sir," he said. "It's a disappointment. I'm not writing anything. I want to go on in the Army. I like the life."

Tietjens said:

"I'm sorry, Smith. I can't help it. Fall out!" He was sorry. He believed the fellow. But responsibility hardens the heart. It must. A very short time ago he would have taken trouble over that fellow. A great deal of trouble, very likely. Now he wasn't going to. . . .

A large capital "A" in whitewash decorated the piece of corrugated iron that was derelictly propped against a channel at right angles to the trench. To Tietjens' astonishment a strong impulse like a wave of passion influenced his being towards the left — up that channel. It wasn't funk: it wasn't any sort of funk. He had been rather irritatedly wrapped up in the case of Private Smith-Eisenstein. It had undeniably irritated him to have to break the chances of a Jew and Red Socialist. It was the sort of thing one did not do if one were omnipotent — as he was. Then . . . this strong impulse? . . . It was a passionate desire to go where you could find exact intellect: rest.

He thought he suddenly understood. For the Lincolnshire sergeant-major the word Peace meant that a man could stand up on a hill. For him it meant someone to talk to.

V

The Colonel said:

"Look here, Tietjens, lend me two hundred and fifty quid. They say you're a damn beastly rich fellow. My accounts are all out. I've got a loathsome complaint. My friends have all gone back on me. I shall have to face a Court of Enquiry if I go home. But my nerve's gone. I've got to go home."

He added:

"I daresay you knew all that."

From the sudden fierce hatred that he felt at the thought of giving money to this man, Tietjens knew that his inner mind based all its calculations on the idea of living with Valentine Wannop . . . when men could stand up on hills.

He had found the Colonel in his cellar — it really, actually was a cellar, the remains of a farm — sitting on the edge of his camp-bed, in his shorts, his khaki shirt very open at the neck. His eyes were a little bloodshot, but his cropped, silver-grey hair was accurately waved, his grey moustache beautifully pointed. His silver-backed hair-brushes and a small mirror were indeed on the table in front of him. By the rays of the lamp that, hung overhead, rendered that damp stone place faintly nauseating, he looked keen, clean, and resolute. Tietjens wondered how he would look by daylight. He had remarkably seldom seen the fellow by daylight. Beside the mirror and the brushes lay, limply, an unfilled pipe, a red pencil and the white buff papers from Whitehall that Tietjens had already read.

He had begun by looking at Tietjens with a keen, hard, bloodshot glance. He had said:

"You think you can command this battalion? Have you had any experience? It appears you suggest that I take two months' leave."

Tietjens had expected a violent outbreak. Threats even. None had come. The Colonel had continued to regard him with intentness, nothing more. He sat motionless, his long arms, bare to the elbow, dependent over each of his knees, which were far apart. He said that if he decided to go he didn't want to leave his battalion to a man that would knock it about. He continued staring hard at Tietjens. The phrase was singular in that place and at that hour, but Tietjens understood it to mean that he did not want his battalion discipline to go to pieces.

Tietjens answered that he did not think he would let the discipline go to pieces. The Colonel had said:

"How do you know? You're no soldier, are you?"

Tietjens said he had commanded in the line a Company at full strength — nearly as large as the battalion and, out of it, a unit of exactly eight times its present strength. He did not think any complaints had been made of him. The Colonel said, frostily:

"Well! I know nothing about you." He had added:

"You seem to have moved the battalion all right the night before last. I wasn't in a condition to do it myself. I'm not well. I'm obliged to you. The men appear to like you. They're tired of me."

Tietjens felt himself on tenterhooks. He had, now, a passionate desire to command that battalion. It was the last thing he would have expected of himself. He said:

"If it becomes a question of a war of motion, sir, I don't know that I should have much experience."

The Colonel answered:

"It won't become a war of motion before I come back. If I ever do come back."

Tietjens said:

"Isn't it rather like a war of motion now, sir?" It was perhaps the first time in his life he had ever asked for information from a superior in rank — with an implicit belief that he would get an exact answer. The Colonel said:

"No. This is only falling back on prepared positions. There will be positions prepared for us right back to the sea. If the Staff has done its work properly. If it hasn't, the war's over. We're done, finished, smashed, annihilated, non-existent."

Tietjens said:

"But if the great *strafe* that, according to Division, is due now . . ."

The Colonel said: "What?" Tietjens repeated his words and added:

"We might get pushed beyond the next prepared position."

The Colonel appeared to withdraw his thoughts from a great distance.

"There isn't going to be any great *strafe*," he said. He was beginning to add: "Division has got. . . ." A considerable thump shook the hill behind their backs. The Colonel sat listening without much attention. His eyes gloomily rested on the papers before him. He said, without looking up:

"Yes, I don't want my battalion knocked about!" He went on reading again — the communication from Whitehall. He said: "You've read this?" and then:

"Falling back on prepared positions isn't the same as moving in the open. You don't have to do more than you do in a trench-to-trench attack. I suppose you can get your direction by compass all right. Or get someone to, for you."

Another considerable Crump of sound shook the earth, but from a little further away. The Colonel turned the sheet of paper from Whitehall over. Pinned to the back of it was the private note of the Brigadier. He perused this also with gloomy and unsurprised eyes.

"Pretty stiff, all this," he said, "you've read it? I shall have to go back and see about this."

He exclaimed:

"It's rough luck. I should have liked to leave my battalion to some-one that knew it. I don't suppose you do. Perhaps you do, though."

An immense collection of fire-irons: all the fire-irons in the world fell just above their heads. The sound seemed to prolong itself in echoes, though of course it could not have; it was repeated.

The Colonel looked upwards negligently. Tietjens proposed to go to see. The Colonel said:

"No, don't. Notting will tell us if anything's wanted. . . . Though nothing can be wanted!" Notting was the beady-eyed Adjutant in the adjoining cellar. "How could they expect us to keep accounts straight in August 1914? How can they expect me to remember what happened? At the Depot. Then!" He appeared listless, but without resentment. "Rotten luck . . ." he said. "In the battalion and . . . with this!" He rapped the back of his hand on the papers. He looked up at Tietjens.

"I suppose I could get rid of you; with a bad report," he said. "Or perhaps I couldn't . . . General Campion put you here. You're said to be his bastard."

"He's my god-father," Tietjens said. "If you put in a bad report of me I should not protest. That is, if it were on the grounds of lack of experience. I should go to the Brigadier over anything else."

"It's the same thing," the Colonel said. "I mean a god-son. If I had thought you were General Campion's bastard, I should not have said it. . . . No; I don't want to put in a bad report of you. It's my own fault if you don't know the battalion. I've kept you out of it. I didn't want you to see what a rotten state the papers are in. They say you're the devil of a paper soldier. You used to be in a Government office, didn't you?"

Heavy blows were being delivered to the earth with some regularity on each side of the cellar. It was as if a boxer of the size of a moun-tain were delivering rights and lefts in heavy alternation. And it made hearing rather difficult.

"Rotten luck," the Colonel said. "And McKechnie's dotty. Clean dotty." Tietjens missed some words. He said that he would probably be able to get the paper work of the battalion straight before the Colonel came back.

The noise rolled down hill like a heavy cloud. The Colonel continued talking and Tietjens, not being very accustomed to his voice, lost a good deal of what he said but, as if in a rift, he did hear:

"I'm not going to burn my fingers with a bad report on you that may bring a General on my back — to get back McKechnie who's dotty. . . . Not fit to . . ."

The noise rolled in again. Once the Colonel listened to it, turning his head on one side and looking upwards. But he appeared satisfied with what he heard and recommenced his perusal of the Horse Guards letter. He took the pencil, underlined words and then sat idly stabbing the paper with the point.

With every minute Tietjens' respect for him increased. This man at least knew his job — as an engine-driver does, or the captain of a steam tramp. His nerves might have gone to pieces. They probably had; probably he could not go very far without stimulants: he was probably under bromides now.

And, all things considered, his treatment of Tietjens had been admirable and Tietjens had to revise his view of it. He realised that it was McKechnie who had given him the idea that the Colonel hated him, but he would not have said anything. He was too old a hand in the Army to give Tietjens a handle by saying anything definite. . . . And he had always treated Tietjens with the sort of monumental deference that, in a Mess, the Colonel should bestow on his chief assistant. Going through a door at meal-times, for instance, if they happened to be side by side, he would motion with his hand for Tietjens to go first, naturally though, taking his proper precedence when Tietjens halted. And here he was, perfectly calm. And quite ready to be instructive.

Tietjens was not calm: he was too much bothered by Valentine Wannop and by the thought that, if the *strafe* was on, he ought to be seeing about his battalion. And of course, by the bombardment. But the Colonel said, when Tietjens with the aid of signs again made proposals to take a look around:

"No. Stop where you are. This isn't the *strafe*. There is not going to be a *strafe*. This is only a little extra Morning Hate. You can tell by the noise. That's only four point twos. There's nothing really heavy. The really heavies don't come so fast. They'll be turning on to the Worcesters now and only giving us one every half-minute. . . .

That's their game. If you don't know that, what are you doing here?"
He added! "You hear?" pointing his forefinger to the roof. The noise
shifted. It went away to the right as a slow coal-wagon might. He
went on:

"This is your place. Not doing things up above. They'll come and
tell you if they want things. And you've got a first-rate Adjutant in
Notting and Dunne's a good man. . . . The men are all under
cover: that's an advantage in having your strength down to three
hundred. There's dug-outs for all and to spare. . . . All the same,
this is no place for you. Nor for me. This is a young man's war. We're
old 'uns. Three and a half years of it have done for me. Three and a
half months will do for you."

He looked gloomily at his reflection in the mirror that stood before him.

"You're a gone coon!" he said to it. Then he took it and, holding it
for a moment poised at the end of a bare white arm, flung it violently
at the rough stones of the wall behind Tietjens. The fragments
tinkled to the ground.

"There's seven years' bad luck," he said. "God take 'em, if they can
give me seven years worse than this last I'd find it instructive!"

He looked at Tietjens with infuriated eyes.

"Look here you!" he said. "You're an educated man. . . . What's
the worst thing about this war? What's the *worst* thing? Tell me
that!" His chest began to heave. "It's that they won't let us alone.
Never! Not one of us! If they'd let us alone we could fight. But
never. . . . No one! It's not only the beastly papers of the battalion,
though I'm no good with papers. Never was and never shall be. . . .
But it's the people at home. One's own people. God help us, you'd
think that when a poor devil was in the trenches they'd let him
alone. . . . Damn it: I've had solicitors' letters about family quarrels
when I was in hospital. Imagine that! . . . Imagine it! I don't mean
tradesmen's dunnings. But one's own people. I haven't even got a
bad wife as McKechnie has and they say you have. My wife's a bit
extravagant and the children are expensive. That's worry enough.
. . . But my father died eighteen months ago. He was in partnership with my uncle. A builder. And they tried to do his estate out of
his share of the business and leave my old mother with nothing. And
my brother and sister threw the estate into Chancery in order to get
back the little bit my father spent on my wife and children. My wife
and children lived with my father whilst I was in India. . . . And

out here. . . . My solicitor says they can get it out of my share: the cost of their keep. He calls it the doctrine of ademption. . . . Ademption . . . Doctrine of. . . . I was better off as a sergeant," he added gloomily. "But sergeants don't get let alone. They've always got women after them. Or their wives take up with Belgians and they get written to about it. Sergeant Cutts of 'D' Company gets an anonymous letter every week about his wife. How's he to do his duty! But he does. So have I till now. . . ." He added with renewed violence:

"Look here. You're an educated man, aren't you? The sort of man that could write a book. You write a book about that. You write to the papers about it. You'd be more use to the Army doing that than being here. I daresay you're a good enough officer. Old Campion is too keen a commander to stick a rotten officer into this job, godson or no god-son. . . . Besides, I don't believe the whole story about you. If a General wanted to give a soft god-son's job to a fellow, it would be a soft job and a fat one. He wouldn't send him here. So take the battalion with my blessing. You won't worry over it more than I have: the poor bloody Glamorgans."

So he had his battalion! He drew an immense breath. The bumps began to come back along the line. He figured those shells as being like sparrow-hawks beating along a hedge. They were probably pretty accurate. The Germans were pretty accurate. The trenches were probably being knocked about a good deal, the pretty, pinkish gravel falling about in heaps as it would lie in a park, ready to be spread on paths. He remembered how he had been up on the Montagne Noire, still, thank God, behind where they were now. Why did he thank God? Did he really care where the Army was. Probably! But enough to say "thank God" about? Probably too. . . . But as long as they kept on at the job did anything matter? Anything else? It was keeping on that mattered. From the Montagne Noire he had seen our shells bursting on a thinnish line in the distance, in shining weather. Each shell existing in a white puff, beautifully. Forward and backward along the line. . . . Under Messines village. He had felt exhilaration to think that our gunners were making such good practice. Now some Hun on a hill was feeling exhilaration over puffs of smoke in our line. But he, Tietjens, was . . . Damn it, he was going to make two hundred and fifty quid towards living with Valentine Wannop — when you really *could* stand up on a hill . . . anywhere!

The Adjutant, Notting, looked in and said:

"Brigade wants to know if we're suffering any, sir?"

The Colonel surveyed Tietjens with irony:

"Well, what are you going to report?" he asked. . . . "This officer is taking over from me," he said to Notting. Notting's beady eyes and red-varnished cheeks expressed no emotions.

"Oh, tell Brigade," the Colonel said, "that we're all as happy as sand-boys. We could stand this till Kingdom Come." He asked: "We *aren't* suffering any, are we?"

Notting said: "No, not in particular. 'C' Company was grumbling that all its beautiful revetments had been knocked to pieces. The sentry near their own dug-out complained that the pebbles in the gravel were nearly as bad as shrapnel."

"Well, tell Brigade what I said. With Major Tietjens' compliments, not mine. He's in command."

". . . You may as well make a cheerful impression to begin with," he added to Tietjens.

It was then that, suddenly, he burst out with:

"Look here! Lend me two hundred and fifty quid!"

He remained staring fixedly at Tietjens with an odd air of a man who has just asked a teasing, jocular conundrum. . . .

Tietjens had recoiled — really half an inch. The man said he was suffering from a loathsome disease: it was being near something dirty. You don't contract loathsome diseases except from the cheapest kind of women or through being untidy-minded. . . . The man's pals had gone back on him. That sort of man's pals do go back on him! His accounts were all out. . . . He was in short the sort of swindling, unclean scoundrel to whom one lent money. . . . Irresistibly!

A crash of the sort that you couldn't ignore, as is the case with certain claps in thunderstorms, sent a good deal of gravel down their cellar steps. It crashed against their shaky door. They heard Notting come out of his cellar and tell someone to shovel the beastly stuff back again where it had come from.

The Colonel looked up at the roof. He said that had knocked their parapet about a bit. Then he resumed his fixed glaze at Tietjens.

Tietjens said to himself:

"I'm losing my nerve. . . . It's the damned news that Campion is coming. . . . I'm becoming a wretched, irresolute Johnny."

The Colonel said:

"I'm not a beastly sponger. I never borrowed before!" His chest heaved. . . . It really expanded and then got smaller again, the orifice in the khaki at his throat contracting. Perhaps he never had borrowed before. . . .

After all, it didn't matter what kind of man this was, it was a question of what sort of a man Tietjens was becoming. He said:

"I can't lend you the money. I'll guarantee an overdraft to your agents. For two hundred and fifty."

Well, then, he remained the sort of man who automatically lent money. He was glad.

The Colonel's face fell. His martially erect shoulders indeed collapsed. He exclaimed ruefully:

"Oh, I say, I thought you were the sort one could go to."

Tietjens said:

"It's the same thing. You can draw a cheque on your bank exactly as if I paid the money in."

The Colonel said:

"I *can*? It's the same thing? You're *sure*?" His questions were like the pleas of a young woman asking you not to murder her.

. . . He obviously was not a sponger. He was a financial virgin. There could not be a subaltern of eighteen in the whole army who did not know what it meant to have an overdraft guaranteed after a fortnight's leave. . . . Tietjens only wished they didn't. He said:

"You've practically got the money in your hand as you sit there. I've only to write the letter. It's impossible your agents should refuse my guarantee. If they do, I'll raise the money and send it you."

He wondered why he didn't do that last in any case. A year or so ago he would have had no hesitation about overdrawing his account to any extent. Now he had an insupportable objection. Like a hatred!

He said:

"You'd better let me have your address." He added, for his mind was really wandering a little. There was too much talk! "I suppose you'll go to No. IX Red Cross at Rouen for a bit."

The Colonel sprang to his feet:

"My God, what's that?" he cried out. "Me . . . to No. IX."

Tietjens exclaimed:

"I don't know the procedure. You said you had . . ."

The other cried out:

"I've got cancer. A big swelling under the armpit." He passed his hand over his bare flesh through the opening of his shirt, the long arm disappearing to the elbow. "Good God . . . I suppose when I said my pals had gone back on me you thought I'd asked them for help and been refused. I haven't. . . . They're all killed. That's the worst way you can go back on a pal, isn't it! Don't you understand men's language?"

He sat heavily down on his bed again.

He said:

"By jove, if you hadn't promised to let me have the money there would have been nothing for me but to make a hole in the water."

Tietjens said:

"Well, don't contemplate it now. Get yourself well looked after. What does Derry say?"

The Colonel again started violently:

"Derry! The M.O. . . . Do you think I'd tell him! Or little squits of subalterns? Or any man! You understand now why I wouldn't take Derry's beastly pill. How do I know what it mightn't do to . . ."

Again he passed his hand under his armpit, his eyes taking on a yearning and calculating expression. He added:

"I thought it a duty to tell you as I was asking you for a loan. You might not get repaid. I suppose your offer still holds good?"

Drops of moisture had hitherto made beads on his forehead; it now shone, uniformly wet.

"If you haven't consulted anybody," Tietjens said, "you mayn't have got it. I should have myself seen to right away. My offer still holds good!"

"Oh, I've got it, all right," the Colonel answered with an air of infinite sapience. "My old man — my governor — had it. Just like that. And he never told a soul till three days before his death. Neither shall I."

"I should get it seen to," Tietjens maintained. "It's a duty to your children. And the King. You're too damn good a soldier for the Army to lose."

"Nice of you to say so," the Colonel said. "But I've stood too much. I couldn't face waiting for the verdict."

. . . It was no good saying he had faced worse things. He very likely hadn't, being the man he was.

The Colonel said:

"Now if I could be any good!"

Tietjens said:

"I suppose I may go along the trenches now. There's a wet place . . ."

He was determined to go along the trenches. He had to . . . what was it . . . "find a place to be alone with Heaven." He maintained also his conviction that he must show the men his mealsack of a body, mooning along; but attentive.

A problem worried him. He did not like putting it since it might seem to question the Colonel's military efficiency. He wrapped it up: Had the Colonel any special advice as to keeping in touch with units on the right and left? And as to passing messages?

That was a mania with Tietjens. If he had had his way he would keep the battalion day and night at communication drill. He had not been able to discover that any precautions of that sort were taken in that unit at all. Or in the others alongside. . . .

He had hit on the Colonel's heel of Achilles.

In the open it became evident: more and more and more and always more evident! The news that General Campion was taking over that command had changed Tietjens' whole view of the world.

The trenches were much as he had expected. They conformed indeed exactly to the image he had had in the cellar. They resembled heaps of reddish gravel laid out ready to distribute over the roads of parks. Getting out of the dug-out had been like climbing into a trolley that had just been inverted for the purpose of discharging its load. It was a nasty job for the men, cleaving a passage and keeping under cover. Naturally the German sharp-shooters were on the lookout. Our problem was to get as much of the trench as you could set up by daylight. The German problem was to get as many of our men as possible. Tietjens would see that our men stayed under cover until nightfall; the commander of the unit opposite would attend to the sniping of as many men as he could. Tietjens himself had three first-class snipers left; they would attempt to get as many of the German snipers as they could. That was self-defence.

In addition a great many Enemy attentions would direct themselves to Tietjens' stretch of the line. The artillery would continue to plunk in a shell or so from time to time. They would not do this very often because it would invite the attention of our artillery and that might prove too costly. More or less heavy masses of high explosives would be thrown on to the line; what the Germans called *Minenwerfer* might project what our people called sausages. These being visible coming through the air, you posted lookouts who gave you warning in time to get under cover. So the Germans had rather abandoned the use of these, probably as being costly in explosives and not so very effective. They made, that is to say, good holes, but accounted for few men.

Airplanes with their beastly bullet-distributing hoppers — that is what they seemed like — would now and then duck along the trench, but not very often. The proceeding was, again, too costly: they would limit themselves as a rule to circling leisurely overhead and dropping things whilst the shrapnel burst round them — and spattered bullets over the trench. Flying pigs, aerial torpedoes, and other floating missiles, pretty, shining, silvery things with fins, would come through the air and would explode on striking the ground or after burying themselves. There was practically no end to their devices and the Huns had a new one every other week or so. They perhaps wasted themselves on new devices. A good many of them turned out to be duds. And a good many of their usually successful missiles turned out to be duds. They were undoubtedly beginning to feel the strain — mental and in their materials. So that if you had to be in these beastly places it was probably better to be in our trenches than theirs. Our war material was pretty good!

This was the war of attrition. . . . A mug's game! A mug's game as far as killing men was concerned, but not an uninteresting occupation if you considered it as a struggle of various minds spread all over the broad landscape in the sunlight. They did not kill many men and they expended an infinite number of missiles and a vast amount of thought. If you took six million men armed with loaded canes and stockings containing bricks or knives and set them against another six million men similarly armed, at the end of three hours four million on the one side and the entire six million on the other would be dead. So, as far as killing went, it really was a mug's game. That was what happened if you let yourself get into the hands of the applied scientist. For all these things were the products not of the soldier but of hirsute, bespectacled creatures who peered through magnifying glasses. Or of course, on our side, they would be shaven-cheeked and less abstracted. They were efficient as slaughterers in that they enabled the millions of men to be moved. When you had only knives you could not move very fast. On the other hand, your knife killed at every stroke: you would set a million men firing at each other with rifles from eighteen hundred yards. But few rifles ever registered a hit. So the invention was relatively inefficient. And it dragged things out!

And suddenly it had become boring.

They were probably going to spend a whole day during which the Germans would strain themselves, their intelligences flickering across the world, to kill a couple of Tietjens' men, and Tietjens would exercise all his care in the effort not to have even one casualty. And at the end of the day they would all be very tired and the poor b——y men would have to set to work to repair the trenches in earnest. That was the ordinary day's work.

He was going about it. . . . He had got "A" Company Commander to come up and talk to him about his fatigues. To the right of Headquarters the trenches appeared to have suffered less than to the left and it was possible to move quite a number of men without risk. "A" Company Commander was an astonishingly thin, bald man of fifty. He was so bald that his tin hat slid about all over his skull. He had been a small shipowner and must have married very late in life, for he spoke of having two children, one of five, one of seven. A pigeon pair. His business was now making fifty thousand a year for him. It pleased Tietjens to think that his children would be well provided for if he were killed. A nice, silent, capable man who usually looked into the distance rather abstractedly when he talked. He was killed two months' later, cleanly, by a bullet.

He was impatient that things had not got a move on. What had become of the big Hun *strafe?*

Tietjens said:

"You remember the Hun company-sergeant-major that surrendered to your crowd the night before last? The fellow who said he was going to open a little sweet-stuff shop in the Tottenham Court Road with the company money he had stolen? . . . Or perhaps you did not hear?"

The remembrance of that shifty looking N.C.O. in blue-grey that was rather smart for a man coming in during a big fight stirred up intensely disagreeable feelings from the bottom of Tietjens' mind. It was detestable to him to be in control of the person of another human being — as detestable as it would have been to be himself a prisoner . . . that thing that he dreaded most in the world. It was indeed almost more detestable, since to be taken prisoner was at least a thing outside your own volition, whereas to control a prisoner, even under the compulsion of discipline on yourself, implies a certain free-will of your own. And this had been an especially loathsome affair. Even normally, though it was irrational enough, prisoners affected him with the sense that they were unclean. As if they were maggots. It was not sensible, but he knew that if he had had to touch a prisoner he would have felt nausea. It was no doubt the product of his passionate Tory sense of freedom. What distinguished man from the brutes was his freedom. When, then, a man was deprived of freedom he became like a brute. To exist in his society was to live with brutes, like Gulliver amongst the Houyhnhnms!

And this unclean fellow had been a deserter in addition!

He had been brought in the H.Q. dug-out at three in the morning after the *strafe* had completely died out. It appeared that he had come over, ostensibly in the ordinary course of the attack. But he had lain all night in a shell hole, creeping in to our lines only when things were quiet. Previously to starting he had crammed his pockets with all the company money and even the papers that he could lay his hands on. He had been brought to H.Q. at that disagreeable hour because of the money and the papers, "A" Company judging that such things ought to be put in the hands at least of the Adjutant as quickly as possible.

The C.O., McKechnie, the Intelligence Officer, and the doctor had all, in addition to Tietjens himself, just settled in there, and the air of the smallish place was already fetid and reeking with service rum and whisky. The appearance of the German had caused Tietjens almost to vomit, and he was already in a state of enervation from having had to bring the battalion in. His temples were racked with a sort of neuralgia that he believed to be caused by eyestrain.

Normally, the questioning of prisoners before they reached Division was strongly discountenanced, but a deserter excites more interest than an ordinary prisoner, and the C.O. who was by then in a state of hilarious mutiny absolutely ordered Tietjens to get all he could out of the prisoner. Tietjens knew a little German: the Intelligence Officer who knew that language well had been killed. Dunne, replacing him, had no German.

The shifty, thin, dark fellow with even, unusually uneasy eyes, had answered questions readily enough: Yes, the Huns were fed up with the war; discipline had become so difficult to maintain that one of his reasons for deserting had been sheer weariness over the effort to keep the men under him in order. They had no food. It was impossible to get the men, in an advance, past any kind of food dumps. He was continually being unjustly reprimanded for his want of success, and standing there he cursed his late officers! Nevertheless, when the C.O. made Tietjens ask him some questions about an

Austrian gun that the Germans had lately introduced to that front and that threw a self-burying shell containing an incredible quantity of H.E., the fellow had clicked his heels together and had answered: *"Nein, Herr Offizier, das waere Landesverratung!"* . . . to answer that would be to betray one's country. His psychology had been difficult to grasp. He had explained as well as he could, using a few words of English, the papers that he had brought over. They were mostly exhortations to the German soldiers, circulars containing news of disasters to and the demoralisation of the Allied troops; there were also a few returns of no great interest — mostly statistics of influenza cases. But when Tietjens had held before the fellow's eyes a type-written page with a heading that he had now forgotten, the Sergeant had exclaimed: *"Ach, nicht das!"* . . . and had made as if to snatch the paper from Tietjens' fingers. Then he had desisted, realising that he was risking his life, no doubt. But he had become as pale as death, and had refused to translate the phrases that Tietjens did not understand; and indeed Tietjens understood practically none of the words, which were all technical.

He knew the paper contained some sort of movement orders; but he was by that time heartily sick of the affair and he knew that that was just the sort of paper that the staff did not wish men in the line to meddle with. So he dropped the matter, and the Colonel and the Pals being by that time tired of listening and not grasping what was happening, Tietjens had sent the fellow at the double back to Brigade under the charge of the Intelligence Officer and a heavier escort than was usual.

What remained to Tietjens of the affair was the expression that the fellow had used when asked what he was going to do with the Company money he had stolen. He was going to open a little sweet shop in the Tottenham Court Road. He had, of course, been a waiter, in old Compton Street. Tietjens wondered vaguely what would become of him. What did they do with deserters? Perhaps they interned them: perhaps they made them N.C.O.'s in prisoners' units. He could never go back to Germany. . . . That remained to him — and the horror and loathing he had felt at the episode, as if it had caused him personal deterioration. He had put the matter out of his mind.

It occurred to him now that, very likely, the urgent announcements from Staff of all sorts had been inspired by that very paper! The paper that loathsome fellow had tried to grab at. He remembered that he had been feeling so sick that he hadn't bothered to have the man handcuffed. . . . It raised a number of questions: Does a man desert and at the same time refuse to betray his country? Well, he might. There was no end to the contradictions in men's characters. Look at the C.O. An efficient officer and a muddled ass in one, even in soldiering matters!

On the other hand, the whole thing might be a plant of the Huns. The paper — the movement order — might have been meant to reach our Army Headquarters. On the face of it, important movement orders do not lie about in Company offices. Not usually. The Huns might be trying to call our attention to this part of the line whilst their real attack might be coming somewhere else. That again was unlikely because that particular part of the line was so weak owing to poor General Puffles' unpopularity with the great ones at home that the Huns would be mad if they attacked anywhere else. And the French were hurrying up straight to that spot in terrific force. He might, then, be a hero! . . . But he didn't look like a hero!

This sort of complication was wearisome nowadays, though once it would have delighted him to dwell on it and work it out with nice figures and calculations of stresses. Now his only emotion about the matter was that, thank God, it was none of his job. The Huns didn't appear to be coming.

He found himself regretting that the *strafe* was not coming after all. That was incredible. How could he regret not being put into immediate danger of death?

Long, thin, scrawny and mournful, with his tin hat now tilted forwards over his nose, the O.C. "A" Company gazed into futurity and remarked:

"I'm sorry the Huns aren't coming!"

He was sorry the Huns were not coming. Because if they came they might as well come according to the information supplied by that prisoner. He had captured that fellow. He might as well therefore get the credit. It might get him remembered if he put in for leave. He wanted leave. He wanted to see his children. He had not seen them for two years now. Children of five and seven change a good deal in two years. He grumbled on. Without any shame at the revelation of his intimate motives. The quite ordinary man! But he was perfectly to be respected. He had a rather grating chest voice. It occurred to Tietjens that that man would never see his children.

He wished these intimations would not come to him. He found

himself at times looking at the faces of several men and thinking that this or that man would shortly be killed. He wished he could get rid of the habit. It seemed indecent. As a rule he was right. But then, almost every man you looked at there was certain to get killed. . . . Himself excepted. He himself was going to be wounded in the soft place behind the right collar-bone.

He regretted that the *strafe* was not that morning coming! Because if they came they might as well come according to the information supplied by the prisoner he had examined in the stinking dug-out. His unit had captured the fellow. He would now be signing its H.Q. chits as Acting O.C. Ninth Glamorganshires. So he, Tietjens, had captured that fellow. And his perspicacity in having him sent immediately back to Brigade with his precious paper might get him, Tietjens, remembered favourably at Brigade H.Q. Then they would leave him in temporary command of his battalion. And if they did that he might do well enough to get a battalion of his own!

He astounded himself. . . . His mentality was that of O.C. "A" Company!

He said:

"It was damn smart of you to see that fellow was of importance and have him sent at the double to me." O.C. "A" Coy. grew red over all his grim face. So, one day, he, Tietjens, might flush with pleasure at the words of some squit with a red band round his hat!

He said:

"Even if the Germans don't come it might have been helpful. It might have been even more helpful. It might have been the means of keeping them back." Because of course if the Germans knew that we had got hold of their Movement Order they might change their plans. That would inconvenience them. It was not likely. There was perhaps not time for the news that we knew to have got through to their Important Ones. But it was possible. Such things had happened.

Aranjuez and the lance-corporal stood still and so silent in the sunlight that they resembled fragments of the reddish trench. The red gravel of the trenches began here, however, to be smirched with more agricultural marl. Later the trenches became pure alluvial soil and then ran down more smartly into stuff so wet that it was like a quicksand. A bog. It was there he had tried revetting with a siphon-drain. The thought of that extreme of his line reminded him. He said:

"You know all about keeping in communication with immediately neighbouring units?"

The grim fellow said:

"Only what they taught in the training camps at the beginning of the war, sir. When I joined up. It was fairly thorough, but it's all forgotten now."

Tietjens said to Aranjuez:

"You're Signalling officer. What do you know about keeping in communication with units on your right and left?"

Aranjuez, blushing and stammering, knew all about buzzers and signals. Tietjens said:

"That's only for trenches, all that. But, in motion. At your O.T.C. Didn't they practice you in keeping communication between troops in motion?"

They hadn't at the O.T.C. . . . At first it had been in the programme. But it had always been crowded out by some stunt. Rifle-grenade drill. Bomb-throwing. Stokes-gun drill. Any sort of machine drill as long as it was not moving bodies of men over difficult country — sand-hills, say — and hammering into them that they must keep in touch unit with unit or drop connecting files if a unit itself divided up.

It was perhaps the dominant idea of Tietjens, perhaps the main idea that he got out of warfare — that at all costs you must keep in touch with your neighbouring troops. When, later, he had to command the escorts over immense bodies of German prisoners on the march it several times occurred to him to drop so many connecting files for the benefit of the men or N.C.O.s — or even the officers, of his escort who had fallen out through sheer fatigue or disease, that he would arrive in a new camp at the day's end with hardly any escort left at all — say thirty for three thousand prisoners. The business of an escort being to prevent the escape of prisoners it might have been thought better to retain the connecting files for that purpose. But, on the other hand, he never lost a prisoner except by German bombs, and he never lost any of his stragglers at all.

He said to O.C. "A" Company:

"Please look after this matter in your Company. I shall arrange as soon as I can to transfer you to the outside right of the unit. If the men are doing nothing lecture them, please, yourself on this subject and talk very seriously to all lance-corporals, section leaders and oldest privates of platoons. And be good enough to get into communication at once with the Company Commander of the Wiltshires immediately on our right. In one of two ways the war is over. The war of trenches. Either the Germans will immediately drive us into the North Sea or we shall drive them back. They will then be in a state of demoralisation and we shall need to move fast. Lieutenant Aranjuez, you will arrange to be present when Captain Gibbs talks to his Company and you will repeat what he says in the other Companies."

He was talking quickly and distinctly, as he did when he was well, and he was talking stiltedly on purpose. He could not obviously call an officers' conference with a German attack possibly impending; but he was pretty certain that something of what he said would penetrate to nearly every ear of the Battalion if he said it before a Company Commander, a Signalling lieutenant and an Orderly Room lance-corporal. It would go through that the Old Man was dotty on this joke, and sergeants would see that some attention was paid to the matter. So would the officers. It was all that could be done at the moment.

He walked behind Gibbs along the trench which at this point was perfectly intact and satisfactory, the red gravel gradually giving place to marl. He remarked to the good fellow that in that way they would do something to checkmate the blasted civilians whose meddling with the processes of war had put them where they were. Gibbs agreed gloomily that civilian interference had lost the war. They so hated the regular army that whenever a civilian saw a trace of regular training remaining in this mud-fighting that they liked us to indulge in, he wrote a hundred letters under different names to the papers, and the War Secretary at once took steps to retain that hundred votes; Gibbs had been reading a home-newspaper that morning.

Tietjens surprised himself by saying:

"Oh, we'll beat them yet!" It was an expression of impracticable optimism. He sought to justify his words by saying that their Army Commander's having put up such a damn good fight in spite of the most criminal form of civilian interference had begun to put a stopper on their games. Campion's coming was a proof that soldiers were going to be allowed to have some say in the conduct of the war. It meant the single command. . . . Gibbs expressed a muted satisfaction. If the French took over those lines as they certainly would if they had the Single Command he would no doubt be able to go home and see his children. All their divisions would have to be taken out of the lines to be reorganised and brought up to strength.

Tietjens said:

"As to what we were talking about. . . . Supposing you detailed outside section leaders and another file to keep in touch with the Wiltshires and they did the same. Supposing that for purposes of recognition they wore handkerchiefs round their right and left arms respectively. . . . It has been done. . . ."

"The Huns," Captain Gibbs said grimly, "would probably pick them off specially. They'd probably pick off specially any one who had any sort of badge. So you would be worse off."

They were going at his request to look at a section of his trench. Orderly Room had ordered him to make arrangements for machine-gun performances there. He couldn't. It didn't exist. Nothing existed. He supposed that to have been the new Austrian gun. New probably, but why Austrian? The Austrians did not usually interest themselves much in high explosives. This one, whatever it was, threw something that buried itself and then blew up half the universe with astonishingly little noise and commotion; just lifted up, like a hippopotamus. He, Gibbs, had hardly noticed anything as you would have if it had been, say, a mine. When they came and told him that a mine had gone off there he would not believe them. . . . But you could see for yourself that it looked exactly as if a mine had been chucking things about. A small mine. But still a mine. . . .

In the shelter of the broken end of the trench a fatigue of six men worked with pick and shovel, patiently, two at a time. They threw up mud and stones and patted them and, stepping down into the thus created vacancy, threw up more mud and stones. Water oozed about, uncertain where to go. There must be a spring there. That hillside was honeycombed with springs. . . .

You would certainly have said there had been a mine there. If we had been advancing it would have been a small mine left by the Huns to cheer us up. But we had retreated on to ground we had always held. So it couldn't have been a mine.

Also it kicked the ground forward and backward and relatively little laterally, so that the deep hole it had created more resembled the entry into a rudimentary shaft than the usually circular shell-hole. A mound existed between Tietjens and "B" Company trench, considerably higher than you could see over. A vast mound; a miniature Primrose Hill. But much bigger than anything they had seen created by flying pigs or other aerial missiles as yet. Anyhow the mound was high enough to give Tietjens a chance to get round it in cover and shuffle down into "B" Company's line. He said to Gibbs:

"We shall have to see about that machine gun place. Don't come any further with me. Make those fellows keep their heads down and send them back if the Huns seem like sending over any more dirt."

VI

TIETJENS reclined on the reverse slope of the considerable mound in the sunlight. He had to be alone, to reflect on his sentimental situation and his machine guns. He had been kept so out of the affairs of the unit that he had suddenly remembered that he knew nothing whatever about his machine guns, or even about the fellow who had to look after him. A new fellow called Cobbe, who looked rather vacant, with an immense sunburnt nose and an open mouth. Not, on the face of him, alert enough for his job. But you never knew.

He was hungry. He had eaten practically nothing since seven the night before, and had been on his feet the greater part of the time.

He sent Lance-Corporal Duckett to "A" Company dug-out, to ask if they could favour him with a sandwich and some coffee with rum in it. He sent Second-Lieutenant Aranjuez to "B" Company to tell them that he was coming to take a look round on their men and quarters. "B" Company Commander for the moment was a very young boy just out from an O.T.C. It was annoying that he had an outside Company. But Constantine, the former Commander, had been killed the night before last. He was, in fact, said to be the gentleman whose remains hung in the barbed wire which was what made Tietjens doubtful whether it could be he. He should not have been so far to the left if he had been bringing his Company in. Anyhow, there had been no one to replace him but this boy — Bennett. A good boy. So shy that he could hardly give a word of command on parade, but yet with all his wits about him. And blessed with an uncommonly experienced Company sergeant-major. One of the original old Glamorganshires. Well, beggars could not be choosers. The Company had reported that morning five cases of the influenza that was said to be ravaging the outside world. Here then was another thing for which they had to thank the outside world — this band of rag-time solitaries! They let the outside world severely alone; they were, truly, hermits. Then the outside world did this to them. Why not leave them to their monastic engrossedness?

Even the rotten and detestable Huns had it! They were said by the Divisional news-sheets to have it so badly that whole Divisions were incapable of effective action. That might be a lie, invented for the purpose of heartening us; but it was probably true. The German men were apparently beastly underfed, and, at that, only on substitute-foods of relatively small percentage of nutritive value. The papers brought over by that N.C.O. had certainly spoken urgently of the necessity of taking every precaution against the spread of this flail. Another circular violently and lachrymosely assured the troops that they were as well fed as the civilian populations and the Corps of Officers. Apparently there had been some sort of scandal. A circular of which he had not had time to read the whole ended up with an assertion something like: "Thus the honour of the Corps of Officers has been triumphantly vindicated."

It was a ghastly thought, that of that whole vast territory that confronted them, filled with millions of half-empty stomachs that bred disorders in the miserable brains. Those fellows must be the most miserable human beings that had ever existed. God knows, the life of our own Tommies must be Hell. But those fellows . . . It would not bear thinking of.

And it was curious to consider how the hatred that one felt for the inhabitants of those regions seemed to skip in a wide trajectory over the embattled ground. It was the civilian populations and their rulers that one hated with real hatred. Now the swine were starving the poor devils in the trenches.

They were detestable. The German fighters and their Intelligence and staffs were merely boring and grotesque. Unending nuisances. For he was confoundedly irritated to think of the mess they had made of his nice clean trenches. It was like when you go out for an hour and leave your dog in the drawing-room. You come back and find that it has torn to pieces all your sofa-cushions. You would like to knock its head off. . . . So you would like to knock the German soldiers' heads off. But you did not wish them much real harm. Nothing like having to live in that hell on perpetually half-empty, windy stomachs with the nightmares they set up! Naturally influenza was decimating them.

Anyhow, Germans were the sort of people that influenza *would* bowl over. They were bores because they came for ever true to type. You read their confounded circulars and they made you grin whilst a little puking. They were like continual caricatures of themselves and they were continually hysterical. . . . Hypochondriacal. . . . Corps of Officers. . . . Proud German Army. . . . His Glorious Majesty. . . . Mighty Deeds. . . . Not much of the Rag-time Army about that, and that was welling out continuously all the time . . . Hypochondria!

A rag-time army was not likely to have influenza so badly. It felt neither its moral nor its physical pulse. . . . Still, here was influenza in "B" Company. They must have got it from the Huns the night before last. "B" Company had had them jump in on top of them; then and there had been hand-to-hand fighting. It was a nuisance. "B" Company was a nuisance. It had naturally been stuck into the dampest and lowest part of their line. Their company dug-out was reported to be like a well with a dripping roof. It would take "B" Company to be afflicted with such quarters. . . . It was difficult to see what to do — not to drain their quarters, but to exorcise their ill-luck. Still, it would have to be done. He was going into their quarters to make a *strafe*, but he sent Aranjuez to announce his coming so as to give the decent young Company Commander a chance to redd up his house. . . .

The beastly Huns! They stood between him and Valentine Wannop. If they would go home he could be sitting talking to her for whole afternoons. That was what a young woman was for. You seduced a young woman in order to be able to finish your talks with her. You could not do that without living with her. You could not live with her without seducing her; but that was the by-product. The point is that you can't otherwise talk. You can't finish talks at street corners; in museums; even in drawing-rooms. You mayn't be in the mood when she is in the mood — for the intimate conversation that means the final communion of your souls. You have to wait together — for a week, for a year, for a lifetime, before the final intimate conversation may be attained . . . and exhausted. So that . . .

That in effect was love. It struck him as astonishing. The word was so little in his vocabulary. . . . Love, ambition, the desire for wealth. They were things he had never known of as existing — as capable of existing within him. He had been the Younger Son, loafing, con-

temptuous, capable, idly contemplating life, but ready to take up
the position of the Head of the Family if Death so arranged matters.
He had been a sort of eternal Second-in-Command.

Now what the Hell was he? A sort of Hamlet of the Trenches! No,
by God he was not. . . . He was perfectly ready for action. Ready
to command a battalion. He was presumably a lover. They did things
like commanding battalions. And worse!

He ought to write her a letter. What in the world would she think
of this gentleman who had once made improper proposals to her;
balked; said "So long!" or perhaps not even "So long!" And then
walked off. With never a letter! Not even a picture postcard! For
two years! A sort of a Hamlet all right! Or a swine!

Well, then, he ought to write her a letter. He ought to say: "This
is to tell you that I propose to live with you as soon as this show is
over. You will be prepared immediately on cessation of active hostilities to put yourself at my disposal; please. Signed, "Xtopher
Tietjens, Acting O.C. 9th Glams." A proper military communication. She would be pleased to see that he was commanding a battalion. Or perhaps she would not be pleased. She was a Pro-German.
She loved these tiresome fellows who tore his, Tietjens', sofa-cushions
to pieces.

That was not fair. She was a Pacifist. She thought these proceedings pestilential and purposeless. Well, there were times when they
appeared purposeless enough. Look at what had happened to his
neat gravel walks. And to the marl too. Though that served the
purpose of letting him sit sheltered. In the sunlight! With any number of larks. Someone once wrote:

A myriad larks in unison sang o'er her, soaring out of sight!

That was imbecile really. Larks cannot sing in unison. They make
a heartless noise like that produced by the rubbing of two corks one
on the other. . . . There came into his mind an image. Years ago;
years and years ago, probably after having watched that gunner torment the fat Hun, because it had been below Max Redoubt. . . .
The sun was now for certain shining on Bemerton! Well, he could
never be a country parson. He was going to live with Valentine
Wannop! . . . he had been coming down the reverse side of the
range, feeling good. Probably because he had got out of that O.P.
which the German guns had been trying to find. He went down
with long strides, the tops of thistles brushing his hips. Obviously

the thistles contained things that attracted flies. They are apt to after a famous victory. So myriads of swallows pursued him, swirling round and round him, their wings touching; for a matter of twenty yards all round and their wings brushing him and the tops of the thistles. And as the blue sky was reflected in the blue of their backs — for their backs were below his eyes — he had felt like a Greek God striding through the sea. . . .

The larks were less inspiring. Really, they were abusing the German guns. Imbecilely and continuously, they were screaming imprecations and threats. They had been relatively sparse until just now. Now that the shells were coming back from a mile or so off, the sky was thick with larks. A myriad — two myriad — corks at once. Not in unison. Sang o'er him, soaring out of sight! . . . You might almost say that it was a sign that the Germans were going to shell you again. Wonderful "hinstinct" set by the Almighty in their little bosoms! It was perhaps also accurate. No doubt the shells as they approached more and more shook the earth and disturbed the little bosoms on their nests. So they got up and shouted; perhaps warning each other; perhaps mere defiance of the artillery.

He was going to write to Valentine Wannop. It was a clumsy swine's trick not to have written to her before. He had proposed to seduce her; hadn't done it, and had gone off without a word. . . . Considering himself rather a swell, too!

He said:

"Did you get a bit to eat, Corporal?"

The Corporal balanced himself before Tietjens on the slope of the mound. He blushed, rubbing his right sole on his left instep, holding in his right hand a small tin can and a cup, in his left an immaculate towel containing a small cube.

Tietjens debated whether he should first drink of the coffee and army rum to increase his zest for the sandwiches, or whether he should first eat the sandwiches and so acquire more thirst for the coffee. . . . It would be reprehensible to write to Valentine Wannop. The act of the cold-blooded seducer. Reprehensible! . . . It depended on what was in the sandwiches. It would be agreeable to fill the void below and inwards from his breast-bone. But whether do it first with a solid or warm moisture?

The lance-corporal was deft. . . . He set the coffee tin, cup, and towel on a flat stone that stuck out of that heap; the towel unfolded, served as a table-cloth; there appeared three heaps of ethereal sandwiches. He said he had eaten half a tin of warm mutton and haricot beans, whilst he was cutting the sandwiches. The meat in the sandwiches consisted of *foie gras*, that pile: bully beef reduced to a paste with butter that was margarine, anchovy paste out of a tin and minced onion out of pickles; the third pile was bully beef *nature*-seasoned with Worcester sauce. . . . All the materials he had at disposal!

Tietjens smiled on the boy at his work. He said this must be a regular *chef*. The boy said:

"Not a *chef*, yet, sir!" He had a camp stool hung on his trenching tool behind his hip. He had been chief assistant to one of the chief cooks in the Savoy. He had been going to go to Paris. "What you call a *marmiton*, sir!" he said. With his trenching tool he was scooping out a level place in front of the flat rock. He set the camp stool on the flattened platform.

Tietjens said:

"You used to wear a white cap and white overalls?"

He liked to think of the blond boy resembling Valentine Wannop dressed all in slim white. The lance-corporal said:

"It's different now, sir!" He stood at Tietjens' side, always caressing his instep. He regarded cooking as an Art. He would have preferred to be a painter, but Mother hadn't enough money. The source of supply dried up during the War. . . . If the C.O. would say a word for him after the War . . . He understood it was going to be difficult to get jobs after the War. All the blighters who had got out of serving, all the R.A.S.C., all the Lines of Communication men would get first chance. As the saying was, the further from the Line the better the pay. And the chance, too!

Tietjens said:

"Certainly I shall recommend you. You'll get a job all right. I shall never forget your sandwiches." He would never forget the keen, clean flavour of the sandwiches or the warm generosity of the sweet, be-rummed coffee! In the blue air of that April hillside. All the objects on that white towel were defined, with iridescent edges. The boy's face, too! Perhaps not physically iridescent. His breath, too, was very easy. Pure air! He was going to write to Valentine Wannop: "Hold yourself at my disposal. Please. Signed . . ." Reprehensible! Worse than reprehensible! You do not seduce the child of your father's oldest friend. He said.

"I shall find it difficult enough to get a job after the War!"

Not only to seduce the young woman, but to invite her to live a remarkably precarious life with him. It isn't done!

The lance-corporal said:

"Oh, sir; no, sir! . . . You're Mr. Tietjens, of Groby!"

He had often been to Groby of a Sunday afternoon. His mother was a Middlesbrough woman. Southbank, rather. He had been to the Grammar School and was going to Durham University when . . . Supplies stopped. On the eight nine fourteen. . . .

They oughtn't to put North Riding, Yorkshire, boys in Welsh-traditioned units. It was wrong. But for that he would not have to run against this boy of disagreeable reminiscences.

"They say," the boy said, "that the well at Groby is three hundred and twenty feet deep, and the cedar at the corner of the house a hundred and sixty. The depth of the well twice the height of the tree!" He had often dropped stones down the well and listened: they made an astonishingly loud noise. Long: like echoes gone mad! His mother knew the cook at Groby. Mrs. Harmsworth. He had often seen . . . he rubbed his ankles more furiously, in a paroxysm . . . Mr. Tietjens, the father, and him, and Mr. Mark and Mr. John and Miss Eleanor. He once handed Miss Eleanor her riding crop when she dropped it. . . .

Tietjens was never going to live at Groby. No more feudal atmosphere! He was going to live, he figured, in a four-room attic flat, on the top of one of the Inns of Court. With Valentine Wannop. *Because* of Valentine Wannop!

He said to the boy:

"Those German shells seem to be coming back. Go and request Captain Gibbs as soon as they get near to take his fatigues under cover until they have passed."

He wanted to be alone with Heaven. . . . He drank his last cup of warm, sweetened coffee, laced with rum. . . . He drew a deep breath. Fancy drawing a deep breath of satisfaction after a deep draft of warm coffee, sweetened with condensed milk and laced with rum! . . . Reprehensible! Gastronomically reprehensible! . . . What would they say at the Club? . . . Well, he was never going to be at the Club! The Club claret was to be regretted! Admirable claret. And the cold side-board!

But, for the matter of that, fancy drawing deep breaths of satisfaction over the mere fact of lying in command of a battalion! — on a slope, in the clear air, with twenty thousand — two myriad! — corks making noises overhead and the German guns directing their projectiles so that they were slowly approaching! Fancy!

They were, presumably, trying out their new Austrian gun. Methodically, with an infinite thoroughness. If, that is to say, there really was a new Austrian gun. Perhaps there wasn't. Division had been in a great state of excitement over such a weapon. It stood in Orders that everyone was to try to obtain every kind of information about it, and it was said to throw a projectile of a remarkable, high explosive efficiency. So Gibbs had jumped to the conclusion that the thing that had knocked to pieces his projected machine-gun emplacement had been the new gun. In that case they were trying it out very thoroughly.

The actual report of the gun or guns — they fired every three minutes, so that might mean that there was only one and that it took about three minutes to re-load — was very loud and rather high in tone. He had not yet heard the actual noise made by the projectile, but the reports from a distance had been singularly dulled. When, presumably, the projectile had effected its landing, it bored extraordinarily into the ground and then exploded with a time-fuse. Very likely it would not be very dangerous to life, but, if they had enough of the guns and the H.E. to plaster the things all along the Line, and if the projectiles worked as efficiently as they had done on poor Gibbs' trench, there would be an end of trench-warfare on the Allied side. But, of course, they probably had not either enough guns or enough high explosive and the thing would very likely act less efficiently in other sorts of soils. They were very likely trying that out. Or, if they were firing with only one gun they might be trying how many rounds could be fired before the gun became ineffective. Or they might be trying only the attrition game: smashing up the trenches, which was always useful, and then sniping the men who tried to repair them. You could bag a few men in that way, now and then. Or, naturally, with planes. . . . There was no end to these tiresome alternatives! Presumably, again, our planes might stop that gun or battery. Then it would stop!

Reprehensible! . . . He snorted! If you don't obey the rules of your club you get hoofed out, and that's that! If you retire from the post or Second-in-Command of Groby, you don't have to . . . oh, attend battalion parades! He had refused to take any money from Brother Mark on the ground of a fantastic quarrel. But he had not any quarrel with Brother Mark. The sardonic pair of them were just matching obstinacies. On the other hand you had to set to the tenantry an example of chastity, sobriety, probity, or you could not take their beastly money. You provided them with the best Canadian seed corn; with agricultural experiments suited to their soils; you sat on the head of your agent; you kept their buildings in repair; you apprenticed their sons; you looked after their daughters, when they got into trouble and after their bastards, your own or another man's. But you must reside on the estate. *You must reside on the estate.* The money that comes out of those poor devils' pockets must go back into the land so that the estate and all on it, down to the licensed beggars, may grow richer and richer and richer. So he had invented his fantastic quarrel with Brother Mark; because he was going to take Valentine to live with him. You could not have a Valentine Wannop having with you in a Groby the infinite and necessary communings. You could have a painted doxy from the servants' hall, quarrelling with the other maids, who would want her job, and scandalising the parsons for miles round. In their sardonic way the tenants appreciated that: it was in the tradition and all over the Riding they did it themselves. But not a lady, the daughter of your father's best friend! They wanted Quality women to *be* Quality and they themselves would go to ruin, spend their dung "and seed" money on whores and wreck the fortunes of the Estate, sooner than that you should indulge in infinite conversation. . . . So he hadn't taken a penny of their money from his brother, and he wouldn't take a penny when he in turn became Groby. Fortunately, there was the heir. . . . Otherwise he could not have gone with that girl!

Two pangs went through him. His son had never written to him; the girl might have married a War Office clerk! On the re-bound! That was what it would be: a civilian War Office clerk would be the most exact contrast to himself! . . . But the son's letters would have been stopped by the mother. That was what they did to people who were where *he* was. As the C.O. had said! And Valentine Wannop, who had listened to his conversation, would never want to mingle intimately in another's! Their communion was immutable and not to be shaken!

So he was going to write to her: freckled, downright, standing square on feet rather widely planted apart, just ready to say: "Oh, *chuck* it, Edith Ethel!" She made the sunlight!

Or no, by Heavens, he could not write to her! If he stopped one or went dotty. . . . Wouldn't it make it infinitely worse for her to know that his love for her had been profound and immutable? It would make it far worse, for by now the edges of passion had probably worn less painful. Or there was the chance of it! . . . But impenitently he would go on willing her to submit to his will; through mounds thrown up by Austrian projectiles and across the seas. They would do what they wanted and take what they got for it!

He reclined, on his right shoulder, feeling like some immense and absurd statue: a collection of meal-sacks done in mud, with grotesque shorts revealing his muddy knees. . . . The figure on one of Michael Angelo's Medici tombs. Or perhaps his *Adam* . . . He felt the earth move a little beneath him. The last projectile must have been pretty near. He would not have noticed the sound, it had become such a regular sequence. But he noticed the quiver in the earth. . . .

Reprehensible! He said. For God's sake *let* us be reprensible! And have done with it! We aren't Hun strategists for ever balancing pros and cons of militant morality!

He took, with his left hand, the cup from the rock. Little Aranjuez came round the mound. Tietjens threw the cup downhill at a large bit of rock. He said to Aranjuez's wistful, enquiring eyes:

"So that no toast more ignoble may ever be drunk out of it!"

The boy gasped and flushed:

"Then you've got someone that you love, sir!" he said in his tone of hero-worship. "Is she like Nancy, in Bailleul?"

Tietjens said:

"No, not like Nancy. . . . Or, perhaps, yes, a little like Nancy!" He did not want to hurt the boy's feelings by the suggestion that anyone unlike Nancy could be loved. He felt a premonition that that child was going to be hurt. Or, perhaps, it was only that he was already so suffering.

The boy said:

"Then you'll get her, sir. You'll certainly get her!"

"Yes, I shall probably get her!" Tietjens said.

The lance-corporal came, too, round the mound. He said that "A" Company were all under cover. They went all together round the heap in the direction of "B" Company's trench down into which they slid. It descended sharply. It was certainly wet. It ended practically in a little swamp. The next battalion had even some yards of sand-bag parapet before entering the slope again with its trench. This was Flanders. Duck country. The bit of swamp would make personal keeping in communication difficult. Where Tietjens had put in his

tile-siphons a great deal of water had exuded. The young O.C.
Company said that they had had to bale the trench out, until they
had made a little drain down into the bog. They baled out with
shovels. Two of the shovels still stood against the brushwood revetments of the parapet.

"Well, you should not leave your shovels about!" Tietjens shouted.
He was feeling considerable satisfaction at the working of his siphon.
In the meantime we had begun a considerable artillery demonstration. It became overwhelming. There was some sort of Bloody Mary
somewhere a few yards off, or so it seemed. She pooped off. The
planes had perhaps reported the position of the Austrian gun. Or we
might be *strafing* their trenches to make them shut up that weapon.
It was like being a dwarf at a conversation, a conflict — of mastodons.
There was so much noise it seemed to grow dark. It was a mental
darkness. You could not think. A Dark Age! The earth moved.

He was looking at Aranjuez from a considerable height. He was
enjoying a considerable view. Aranjuez's face had a rapt expression
— like that of a man composing poetry. Long dollops of liquid mud
surrounded them in the air. Like black pancakes being tossed. He
thought: "Thank God I did not write to her. We are being blown
up!" The earth turned like a weary hippopotamus. It settled down
slowly over the face of Lance-Corporal Duckett who lay on his side,
and went on in a slow wave.

It was slow, slow, slow . . . like a slowed-down movie. The earth
manœuvred for an infinite time. He remained suspended in space.
As if he were suspended as he had wanted to be in front of that
cockscomb in whitewash. Coincidence!

The earth sucked slowly and composedly at his feet.

It assimilated his calves, his thighs. It imprisoned him above the
waist. His arms being free, he resembled a man in a life-buoy. The
earth moved him slowly. It was solidish.

Below him, down a mound, the face of little Aranjuez, brown,
with immense black eyes in bluish whites, looked at him. Out of
viscous mud. A head on a charger! He could see the imploring lips
form the words: "Save me, Captain!" He said: "I've got to save
myself first!" He could not hear his own words. The noise was incredible.

A man stood over him. He appeared immensely tall because Tietjens' face was on a level with his belt. But he was a small Cockney
Tommy really. Name of Cockshott. He pulled at Tietjens' two arms.

Tietjens tried to kick with his feet. Then he realised it was better not to kick with his feet. He was pulled out. Satisfactorily. There had been two men at it. A second, a corporal had come. They were all three of them grinning. He slid down with the sliding earth towards Aranjuez. He smiled at the pallid face. He slipped a lot. He felt a frightful burning on his neck, below and behind the ear. His hand came down from feeling the place. The finger tips had no end of mud and a little pinkishness on them. A pimple had perhaps burst. He had at least two men not killed. He signed agitatedly to the Tommies. He made gestures of digging. They were to get shovels.

He stood over Aranjuez, on the edge of liquid mud. Perhaps he would sink in. He did not sink in. Not above his boot tops. He felt his feet to be enormous and sustaining. He knew what had happened. Aranjuez was sunk in the issuing hole of the spring that made that bog. It was like being on Exmoor. He bent down over an ineffable, small face. He bent down lower and his hands entered the slime. He had to get on his hands and knees.

Fury entered his mind. He had been sniped at. Before he had had that pain he had heard, he realised, an intimate drone under the hellish tumult. There was reason for furious haste. Or, no. . . . They were low. In a wide hole. There was no reason for furious haste. Especially on your hands and knees.

His hands were under the slime, and his forearms. He battled his hands down greasy cloth; under greasy cloth. *Slimy*, not greasy! He pushed outwards. The boy's hands and arms appeared. It was going to be easier. His face was now quite close to the boy's, but it was impossible to hear what he said. Possibly he was unconscious. Tietjens said: "Thank God for my enormous physical strength!" It was the first time that he had ever had to be thankful for great physical strength. He lifted the boy's arms over his own shoulders so that his hands might clasp themselves behind his neck. They were slimy and disagreeable. He was short in the wind. He heaved back. The boy came up a little. He was certainly fainting. He gave no assistance. The slime was filthy. It was a condemnation of a civilisation that he, Tietjens, possessed of enormous physical strength, should never have needed to use it before. He looked like a collection of mealsacks; but at least he could tear a pack of cards in half. If only his lungs weren't . . .

Cockshott, the Tommie, and the corporal were beside him, grinning. With the two shovels that ought not to have stood against the parapet of their trench. He was intensely irritated. He had tried to indicate with his signs that it was Lance-Corporal Duckett that they were to dig out. It was probably no longer Lance-Corporal Duckett. It was probably by now "it." The body! He had probably lost a man, after all!

Cockshott and the corporal pulled Aranjuez out of the slime. He came out reluctantly, like a lugworm out of sand. He could not stand. His legs gave way. He drooped like a flower done in slime. His lips moved, but you could not hear him. Tietjens took him from the two men who supported him between the arms and laid him a little way up the mound. He shouted in the ear of the Corporal:

"Duckett! Go and dig out Duckett! At the double!"

He knelt and felt the boy's back. His spine might have been damaged. The boy did not wince. His spine might be damaged all the same. He could not be left there. Bearers could be sent with a stretcher if one was to be found. But they might be sniped coming. Probably, he, Tietjens, could carry that boy, if his lungs held out. If not, he could drag him. He felt tender, like a mother, and enormous. It might be better to leave the boy there. There was no knowing. He said: "Are you wounded?" The guns had mostly stopped. Tietjens could not see any blood flowing. The boy whispered: "No, sir!" He was, then, probably just faint. Shell shock, very likely. There was no knowing what shell shock was or what it did to you. Or the mere vapour of the projectile.

He could not stop there.

He took the boy under his arm as you might do a roll of blankets. If he took him on his shoulders he might get high enough to be sniped. He did not go very fast, his legs were so heavy. He bundled down several steps in the direction of the spring in which the boy had been. There was more water. The spring was filling up that hollow. He could not have left the boy there. You could only imagine that his body had corked up the springhole before. This had been like being at home where they had springs like that. On the moors, digging out badgers. Digging earth drains, rather. Badgers have dry lairs. On the moors above Groby. April sunlight. Lots of sunlight and skylarks.

He was mounting the mound. For some feet there was no other way. They had been in the shaft made by that projectile. He inclined to the left. To the right would take them quicker to the trench, but he wanted to get the mound between them and the sniper. His breathing was tremendous. There was more light falling on them.

Exactly! . . . Snap! Snap! Snap! . . . Clear sounds from a quarter of a mile away. . . . Bullets whined overhead. Long sounds, going away. Not snipers. The men of a battalion. A chance! Snap! Snap! Snap! Bullets whined overhead. Men of a battalion get excited when shooting at anything running. They fire high. Trigger pressure. *He* was now a fat, running object. Did they fire with a sense of hatred or fun! Hatred probably. Huns have not much sense of fun.

His breathing was unbearable. Both his legs were like painful bolsters. He would be on the relatively level in two steps if he made them. . . . Well, make them! . . . He was on the level. He had been climbing, up clods. He *had* to take an immense breath. The ground under his left foot gave way. He had been holding Aranjuez in front of his own body as much as he could, under his right arm. As his left foot sank in, the boy's body came right on top of him. Naturally this stiffish earth in huge clods had fissures in it. Apertures. It was not like regular digging.

The boy kicked, screamed, tore himself loose. . . . Well, if he wanted to go! The scream was like a horse's in a stable on fire. Bullets had gone overhead. The boy rushed off, his hands to his face. He disappeared round the mound. It was a conical mound. He, Tietjens, could now crawl on his belly. It was satisfactory.

He crawled. Shuffling himself along with his hips and elbows. There was probably a text-book way of crawling. He did not know it. The clods of earth appeared friendly. For bottom soil thrown to the top they did not feel or smell so very sour. Still, it would take a long time to get them into cultivation or under grass. Probably, agriculturally speaking, that country would be in pretty poor condition for a long time. . . .

He felt pleased with his body. It had had no exercise to speak of for two months — as second-in-command. He could not have expected to be in even the condition he was in. But the mind had probably had a good deal to do with that! He had, no doubt, been in a devil of a funk. It was only reasonable. It was disagreeable to think of those Hun devils hunting down the unfortunate. A disagreeable business. Still, we did the same. . . . That boy must have been in a devil of a funk. Suddenly. He had held his hands in front of his face. Afraid to see. Well, you couldn't blame him. They ought not to send out schoolgirls. He was like a girl. Still, he ought to have stayed to see that he, Tietjens, was not pipped. He might have thought he was hit from the way his left leg had gone down. He would have to be *strafed*. Gently.

Cockshott and the corporal were on their hands and knees digging with the short-handled shovels that are known as trenching-tools. They were on the rear side of the mound.

"We've found im, sir," the corporal said. "Regular buried. Just seed is foot. Dursen't use a shovel. Might cut im in arf!"

Tietjens said:

"You're probably right. Give me the shovel!" Cockshott was a draper's assistant, the corporal a milkman. Very likely they were not good with shovels.

He had had the advantage of a boyhood crowded with digging of all sorts. Duckett was buried horizontally, running into the side of the conical mound. His feet at least stuck out like that, but you could not tell how the body was disposed. It might turn to either side or upwards. He said:

"Go on with your tools above! But give me room."

The toes being to the sky, the trunk could hardly bend downwards. He stood below the feet and aimed terrific blows with the shovel eighteen inches below. He liked digging. This earth was luckily dryish. It ran down the hill conveniently. This man had been buried probably ten minutes. It seemed longer, but was probably less. He ought to have a chance. Probably earth was less suffocating than water. He said to the corporal:

"Do you know how to apply artificial respiration? To the drowned?"

Cockshott said:

"I do, sir. I was swimming champion of Islington baths!" A rather remarkable man, Cockshott. His father had knocked up the arm of a man who tried to shoot Mr. Gladstone in 1866 or thereabouts.

A lot of earth falling away, obligingly, after one withdrawal of the shovel Lance-Corporal Duckett's thin legs appeared to the fork, the knees drooping.

Cockshott said:

" 'E aint rubbin' 'is ankles this journey!"

The corporal said:

"Company C'mander is killed, sir. Bullet clean thru the ed!"

It annoyed Tietjens that here was another head wound. He could not apparently get away from them. It was silly to be annoyed, because in trenches a majority of wounds had to be head wounds. But Providence might just as well be a little more imaginative. To oblige one. It annoyed him, too, to think that he had *strafed* that boy just before he was killed. For leaving his shovels about. A *strafe* leaves a disagreeable impression on young boys for quite half an hour. It was probably the last incident in his life. So he died depressed. . . . Might God be making it up to him!

He said to the corporal:

"Let me come." Duckett's left hand and wrist had appeared, the hand drooping and improbably clean, level with the thigh. It gave the line of the body; you could clear away beside him.

" 'E wasn't on'y twenty-two," the corporal said. Cockshott said: "Same age as me. Very particular 'e was about your rifle pull-throughs."

A minute later they pulled Duckett out, by the legs. A stone might have been resting on his face, in that case his face would have been damaged. It wasn't, though you had had to chance it. It was black, but asleep. . . . As if Valentine Wannop had been reposing in an ash-bin. Tietjens left Cockshott applying artificial respiration very methodically and efficiently to the prostrate form.

It was to him a certain satisfaction that, at any rate, in that minute affair he hadn't lost one of the men but only an officer. As satisfaction it was not military correct, though as it harmed no one there was no harm in it. But for his men he always felt a certain greater responsibility; they seemed to him to be there infinitely less of their own volition. It was akin to the feeling that made him regard cruelty to an animal as a more loathsome crime than cruelty to a human being, other than a child. It was no doubt irrational.

Leaning, in the communication trench, against the corrugated iron that boasted a great whitewashed A, in a very clean thin Burberry boasting half a bushel of badges of rank — worsted crowns and things! — and in a small tin hat that looked elegant, was a slight figure. How the *devil* can you make a tin hat look elegant! It carried a hunting switch and wore spurs. An Inspecting General. The General said benevolently:

"Who are you?" and then with irritation: "Where the devil is the officer commanding this Battalion? Why can't he be found?" He added: "You're disgustingly dirty. Like a blackamoor. I suppose you've an explanation."

Tietjens was being spoken to by General Campion. In a hell of a temper. He stood to attention like a scarecrow.

He said:

"I am in command of this Battalion, sir. I am Tietjens, second-in-command. Now in command temporarily. I could not be found because I was buried. Temporarily."

The General said:

"You . . . Good God!" and fell back a step, his jaw dropping. He said: "I've just come from London!" And then: "By God, you don't stop in command of a Battalion of mine a second after I take over!" He said: "They said this was the smartest battalion in my unit!" and snorted with passion. He added: "Neither my galloper nor Levin can find you or get you found. And there you come strolling along with your hands in your pockets!"

In the complete stillness, for, the guns having stopped, the skylarks, too, were taking a spell, Tietjens could hear his heart beat out of little dry scraping sounds from his lungs. The heavy beats were very accelerated. It gave an effect of terror. He said to himself:

"What the devil has his having been in London to do with it?" And then: "He wants to marry Sylvia! I'll bet he went to marry Sylvia!" That was what his having been to London had to do with it. It was an obsession with him: the first thing he said when surprised and passionate.

They always arranged these periods of complete silence for the visits of Inspecting Generals. Perhaps the Great General Staffs of both sides arrange that for each other. More probably our guns had split themselves in the successful attempt to let the Huns know that we wanted them to shut up — that we were firing with what Papists call a special intention. That would be as effective as a telephone message. The Huns would know there was something up. Never put the other side in a temper when you can help it.

He said:

"I've just had a scratch, sir. I was feeling in my pockets for my field-dressing."

The General said:

"A fellow like you has no right to be where he can be wounded. Your place is the lines of communication. I was mad when I sent you here. I shall send you back."

He added:

"You can fall out. I want neither your assistance nor your information. They said there was a damn smart officer in command here. I wanted to see him. . . . Of the name of . . . Of the name of . . . It does not matter. Fall out. . . ."

Tietjens went heavily along the trench. It came into his head to say to himself:

"It *is* a land of Hope and Glory!" Then he exclaimed: "By God! I'll take the thing before the Commander-in-Chief. I'll take the thing before the King in Council if necessary. By God I will!" The old fellow had no business to speak to him like that. It was importing personal enmity into service matters. He stood still reflecting on the terms of his letter to Brigade. The Adjutant Notting came along the trench. He said:

"General Campion wants to see you, sir. He takes over this Army on Monday." He added: "You've been in a nasty place, sir. Not hurt, I trust!" It was a most unusual piece of loquacity for Notting.

Tietjens said to himself:

"Then I've got five days in command of this unit. He can't kick me out before he's in command." The Huns would be through them before then. Five days' fighting! Thank God!

He said:

"Thanks. I've seen him. No, I'm all right. Beastly dirty!"

Notting's beady eyes had a tinge of agony in them. He said:

"When they said you had stopped one, sir, I thought I should go mad. We *can't* get through the work!"

Tietjens was wondering whether he should write his letter to Brigade before or after the old fellow took over. Notting was saying:

"The doctor says Aranjuez will get through all right."

It would be better, if he were going to base his appeal on the grounds of personal prejudice. Notting was saying:

"Of course he will lose his eye. In fact it . . . it is not practically there. But he'll get through."

Part Three

COMING INTO THE SQUARE was like being suddenly dead, it was
so silent and so still to one so lately jostled by the innumerable crowd and deafened by unceasing shouts. The
shouting had continued for so long that it had assumed the appearance of being a solid and unvarying thing, like life. So the silence
appeared like Death; and now she had death in her heart. She was
going to confront a madman in a stripped house. And the empty
house stood in an empty square all of whose houses were so eighteenth-century and silver grey and rigid and serene that they ought
all to be empty too and contain dead, mad men. And was this
the errand? For to-day when all the world was mad with joy? To
become bear-ward to a man who had got rid of all his furniture and
did not know the porter — mad without joy!

It turned out to be worse than she expected. She had expected
to turn the handle of a door of a tall, empty room; in a space made
dim with shutters she would see him, looking suspiciously round over
his shoulder, a grey badger or a bear taken at its dim occupations.
And in uniform. But she was not given time even to be ready. In
the last moment she was to steel herself incredibly. She was to become the cold nurse of a shell-shock case.

But there was not any last moment. He charged upon her. There
in the open. More like a lion. He came, grey all over, his grey hair —
or the grey patches of his hair — shining, charging down the steps,
having slammed the hall door. And lopsided. He was carrying under
his arm a diminutive piece of furniture. A cabinet.

It was so quick. It was like having a fit. The houses tottered. He regarded her. He had presumably checked violently in his clumsy stride. She hadn't seen because of the tottering of the houses. His stone-blue eyes came fishily into place in his wooden countenance — pink and white. Too pink where it was pink and too white where it was white. Too much so for health. He was in grey homespuns. He should not wear homespuns or grey. It increased his bulk. He could be made to look . . . Oh, a fine figure of a man, let us say!

What was he doing? Fumbling in the pocket of his clumsy trousers. He exclaimed — she shook at the sound of his slightly grating, slightly gasping voice — :

"I'm going to sell this thing. . . . Stay here." He had produced a latchkey. He was panting fiercely beside her. Up the steps. He was beside her. Beside her. Beside her. It was infinitely sad to be beside this madman. It was infinitely glad. Because if he had been sane she would not have been beside him. She could be beside him for long spaces of time if he were mad. Perhaps he did not recognise her! She might be beside him for long spaces of time with him not recognising her. Like tending your baby!

He was stabbing furiously at the latchhole with his little key. He *would*: that was normal. He was a stab-the-keyhole sort of clumsy man. She would not want that altered. But she would see about his clothes. She said: "I am deliberately preparing to live with him for a long time!" Think of that! She said to him:

"Did you send for me?"

He had the door open; he said, panting — his *poor* lungs!

"No." Then: "Go in!" and then: "I was just going . . ."

She was in his house. Like a child. . . . He had not sent for her. . . . Like a child faltering on the sill of a vast black cave.

It *was* black. Stone flags. Pompeian-red walls scarred pale-pink where fixed hall-furniture had been removed. Was it *here* she was going to live?

He said, panting, from behind her back:

"Wait here!" A little more light fell into the hall. That was because he was gone from the doorway.

He was charging down the steps. His boots were immense. He lolloped all over on one side because of the piece of furniture he had under his arm. He was grotesque, really. But joy radiated from his homespuns when you walked beside him. It welled out; it enveloped you. . . . Like the warmth from an electric heater, only that did not make you want to cry and say your prayers — the haughty oaf.

No, but he was not haughty. Gauche, then! No, but he was not gauche. . . . She could not run after him. He was a bright patch, with his pink ears and silver hair. Gallumphing along the rails in front of the eighteenth-century houses. *He* was eighteenth-century all right. . . . But then the eighteenth century never went mad. The only century that never went mad. Until the French Revolution; and that was either not mad or not eighteenth-century.

She stepped irresolutely into the shadows; she returned irresolutely to the light. . . . A long hollow sound existed: the sea saying: Ow, Ow, Ow along miles and miles. It was the armistice. It was Armistice Day. She had forgotten it. She was to be cloistered on Armistice Day! Ah, not cloistered! Not cloistered there. My beloved is mine and I am his! But she might as well close the door!

She closed the door as delicately as if she were kissing him on the lips. It was a symbol. It was Armistice Day. She ought to go away; instead she had shut the door on . . . Not on Armistice Day! What was it like to be . . . changed!

No! She ought not to go away! She ought not to go away! She ought *not*! He had told her to wait. She was not cloistered. This was the most exciting spot on the earth. It was not her fate to live nun-like. She was going to pass her day beside a madman; her night, too. . . . Armistice Night! That night would be remembered down unnumbered generations. Whilst one lived that had seen it the question would be asked: What did you do on Armistice Night? My beloved is mine and I am his!

The great stone stairs were carpetless: to mount them would be like taking part in a procession. The hall came in straight from the front door. You had to turn a corner to the right before you came to the entrance of a room. A queer arrangement. Perhaps the eighteenth century was afraid of draughts and did not like the dining-room door near the front entrance. . . . My beloved is . . . Why does one go repeating that ridiculous thing. Besides it's from the *Song of Solomon*, isn't it? *The Canticle of Canticles!* Then to quote it is blasphemy when one is . . . No, the essence of prayer is volition, so the essence of blasphemy is volition. She did not want to quote the thing. It was jumped out of her by sheer nerves. She was afraid. She was waiting for a madman in an empty house. Noises whispered up the empty stairway!

She was like Fatima. Pushing open the door of the empty room. He might come back to murder her. A madness caused by sex ob-

sessions is not infrequently homicidal. . . . What did you do on
Armistice Night? "I was murdered in an empty house!" For, no doubt
he would let her live till midnight.

But perhaps he had not got sex obsessions. She had not the shadow
of a proof that he had; rather that he hadn't! Certainly, rather that
he hadn't. Always the gentleman.

They had left the telephone! The windows were duly shuttered,
but in the dim light from between cracks the nickel gleamed on
white marble. The mantel-shelf. Pure Parian marble, the shelf supported by rams' heads. Singularly chaste. The ceilings and rectilinear
mouldings in an intricate symmetry. Chaste, too. Eighteenth-century.
But the eighteenth century was not chaste. . . . *He* was eighteenth-
century.

She ought to telephone to her mother to inform that Eminence
in untidy black with violet tabs here and there of the grave step that
her daughter was . . .

What was her daughter going to do?

She ought to rush out of the empty house. She ought to be trembling with fear at the thought that he was coming home very likely
to murder her. But she wasn't. What was she? Trembling with
ecstasy? Probably. At the thought that he was coming. If he murdered her. . . . Can't be helped! She was trembling with ecstasy
all the same. She must telephone to her mother. Her mother might
want to know where she was. But her mother never *did* want to know
where she was. She had her head too screwed on to get into mischief! . . . Think of *that*!

Still, on such a day her mother might like to. They ought to exchange gladnesses that her brother was safe for good, now. And
others, too. Normally her mother was irritated when she rang up.
She would be at her work. It was amazing to see her at work. Perhaps she never would again. Such untidiness of papers. In a little
room. Quite a little room. She never would work in a big room because a big room tempted her to walk about and she could not
afford the time to walk about.

She was writing at two books at once now. A novel. . . . Valentine
did not know what it was about. Her mother never let them know
what her novels were about till they were finished. And a woman's
history of the War. A history by a woman for women. And there
she would be sitting at a large table that hardly left room for more
than getting round it. Grey, large, generous-featured and tired, she

would be poking over one set of papers on one side of the table or just getting up from over the novel, her loose pince-nez falling off; pushing round the table between its edge and the wall to peer at the sheets of the woman's history that were spread all over that region. She would work for ten minutes or twenty-five or an hour at the one and then for an hour and a half or half an hour or three-quarters at the other. What a muddle her dear old head must be in!

With a little trepidation she took the telephone. It had got to be done. She could not live with Christopher Tietjens without first telling her mother. Her mother ought to be given the chance of dissuading. They say you ought to give a lover a chance of a final scene before leaving him or her for good. Still more your mother. That was jannock.

It broke the word of promise to the ear, the telephone! . . . Was it blasphemy to quote Shakespeare when one was going to. . . . Perhaps bad taste. Shakespeare, however, was not spotless. So they said. . . . Waiting! Waiting! How much of one's life wasn't spent waiting, with one's weight boring one's heels into the ground. . . . But *this* thing was dead. No roar came from its mouth and when you jabbed the little gadget at the side up and down no bell tinked. . . . It had probably been disconnected. They had perhaps cut him off for not paying. Or he had cut it off so that she might not scream for the police through it whilst he was strangling her. Anyhow they were cut off. They would be cut off from the world on Armistice Night. . . . Well, they would probably be cut off for good!

What nonsense. He had not known that she was coming. He had not asked her to come.

So, slowly, slowly she went up the great stone staircase, the noises all a-whispering up before her . . . "So, slowly, slowly she went up and slowly looked about her. Henceforth take warning by the fall. . . ." Well, she did not need to take warning: she was not going to fall in the way Barbara Allen did. Contrariwise!

He had not sent for her. He had not asked Edith Ethel to ring her up. Then presumably she felt humiliated. But she did not feel humiliated! It was in effect fairly natural. He *was* quite noticeably mad, rushing out, lopsided, with bits of furniture under his arm and no hat on his noticeable hair. Noticeable! That was what he was. He would never pass in a crowd! . . . He *had* got rid of all his furniture as Edith Ethel had alleged. Very likely he had not recognised the porter, too. She, Valentine Wannop, had seen him going to sell his furniture. Madly! Running to do it. You do not run when you are selling furniture if you are sane. Perhaps Edith Ethel had seen him running along with a table on his head. And she was by no means certain that he had recognised her, Valentine Wannop!

So Edith Ethel might have been almost justified in ringing her up. Normally it would have been an offence, considering the terms on which they had parted. Considering that Edith Ethel had accused her of having a child by this very man! It was pretty strong, even if she had seen him running about the Square with furniture, and even if there had been no one else who could help. . . . But she ought to have sent her miserable rat of a husband. There was no excuse!

Still, there had been nothing else for her, Valentine, to do. So there was no call for her to feel humiliated. Even if she had not felt for this man as she did she would have come, and, if he had been very bad, would have stayed.

He had not sent for her! this man who had once proposed love to her and then had gone away without a word and who had never so much as sent her a picture-postcard! Gauche! Haughty! Was there any other word for him? There could not be. Then she ought to feel humiliated. But she did not.

She felt frightened, creeping up the great staircase, and entering a great room. A very great room. All white, again with stains on the walls from which things had been removed. From over the way the houses confronted her, eighteen-centuryishly. But with a touch of gaiety from their red chimney-pots . . . And now she was spying, with her heart in her mouth. She was terribly frightened. This room was inhabited. As if set down in a field, the room being so large, there camped. . . . A camp-bed for the use of officers, G.S. one, as the saying is. And implements of green canvas, supported on crossed white wood staves: a chair, a bucket with a rope handle, a washing-basin, a table. The bed was covered over with a flea-bag of brown wool. She was terribly frightened. The further she penetrated the house the more she was at his mercy. She ought to have stayed downstairs. She was spying on him.

These things looked terribly sordid and forlorn. Why did he place them in the centre of the room? Why not against a wall? It is usual to stand the head of a bed against a wall when there is no support for the pillows. Then the pillows do not slip off. She would change

. . . No, she would not. He had put the bed in the centre of the room because he did not want it to touch walls that had been brushed by the dress of. . . . You must not think bad things about that woman!

They did not look sordid and forlorn. They looked frugal. And glorious! She bent down and drawing down the flea bag at the top, kissed the pillows. She would get him linen pillows. You would be able to get linen now. The war was over. All along that immense line men could stand up!

At the head of the room was a dais. A box of square boarding, like the model-throne artists have in studios. Surely she did not receive her guests on a dais; like Royalty. She was capable . . . *You must not*. . . . It was perhaps for a piano. Perhaps she gave concerts. It was used as a library now. A row of calf-bound books stood against the wall on the back edge of the platform. She approached them to see what books he had selected. They must be the books he had read in France. If she could know what books he had read in France she would know what some of his thoughts there had been. She knew he slept between very cheap cotton sheets.

Frugal and glorious. That was he! And he had designed this room to love her in. It was the room she would have asked. . . . The furnishing . . . Alcestis never had. . . . For she, Valentine Wannop, was of frugal mind, too. And his worshipper. Having reflected glory. . . . Damn it, she was getting soppy. But it was curious how their tastes marched together. He had been neither haughty nor gauche. He had paid her the real compliment. He had said: "Her mind so marches with mine that she will understand."

The books were indeed a job lot. Their tops ran along against the wall like an ill-arranged range of hills; one was a great folio in calf, the title indented deep and very dim. The others were French novels and little red military text-books. She leaned over the dais to read the title of the tall book. She expected it to be Herbert's Poems or his *Country Parson*. . . *He* ought to be a Country Parson. He never would be now. She was depriving the church of. . . . Of a Higher Mathematician, really. The title of the book was *Vir. Obscur.*

Why did she take it that they were going to live together? She had no official knowledge that he wanted to. But *they* wanted to TALK. You can't talk unless you live together. Her eye, travelling downwards along the dais caught words on paper. They threw themselves up at her from among a disorder of half a dozen typed pages;

they were in big, firm, pencilled letters. They stood out because they were pencilled; they were:

A man could stand up on a bleedin' 'ill!

Her heart stopped. She must be out of condition. She could not stand very well, but there was nothing to lean on to. She had — she didn't know she had — read also the typed words:

"Mrs. Tietjens is leaving the model cabinet by Barker of Bath which she believes you claim. . . ."

She looked desperately away from the letter. She did not want to read the letter. She could not move away. She believed she was dying. Joy never kills. . . . But it . . . *"fait peur."* "Makes afraid." Afraid! Afraid! Afraid! There was nothing now between them. It was as if they were already in each other's arms. For surely the rest of the letter must say that Mrs. Tietjens had removed the furniture. And his comment — amazingly echoing the words she had just thought — was that he could stand up. But it wasn't in the least amazing. My beloved is mine. . . . Their thoughts marched together; not in the least amazing. They could now stand on a hill together. Or get into a little hole. For good. And talk. For ever. She must not read the rest of the letter. She must not be certain. If she were certain she would have no hope of preserving her . . . Of remaining . . . Afraid and unable to move. She would be forced to read the letter because she was unable to move. Then she would be lost. She looked beseechingly out of the window at the house-fronts over the way. They were friendly. They would help her. Eighteenth-century. Cynical, but not malignant. She sprang right off her feet. She could move then. She hadn't had a fit.

Idiot. It was only the telephone. It went on and on. Drrinn; drinnnn; drRinn. It came from just under her feet. No, from under the dais. The receiver was on the dais. She hadn't consciously noticed it because she had believed the telephone was dead. Who notices a dead telephone?

She said — it was as if she was talking into his ear, he so pervaded her — she said:

"Who are you?"

One ought not to answer all telephone calls, but one does so mechanically. She ought not to have answered this. She was in a compromising position. Her voice might be recognised. Let it be recognised. She desired to be known to be in a compromising position! What did you do on Armistice Day!

A voice, heavy and old, said:

"You *are* there, Valentine. . . ."

She cried out:

"Oh, poor *mother*. . . . But he's not here." She added: "He's not been here with me. I'm still only waiting." She added again: "The house is empty!" She seemed to be stealthy, the house whispering round her. She seemed to be whispering to her mother to save her and not wanting the house to hear her. The house was eighteenth-century. Cynical. But not malignant. It wanted her undoing, but knew that women liked being . . . ruined.

Her mother said, after a long time:

"Have you *got* to do this thing? . . . My little Valentine . . . My little Valentine!" She wasn't sobbing.

Valentine said:

"Yes, I've got to do it!" She sobbed. Suddenly she stopped sobbing.

She said quickly:

"Listen mother. I've had no conversation with him. I don't know even whether he's sane. He appears to be mad." She wanted to give her mother hope. Quickly. She had been speaking quickly to get hope to her mother as quickly as possible. But she added: "I believe that I shall die if I cannot live with him."

She said that slowly. She wanted to be like a little child trying to get truth home to its mother.

She said:

"I have waited too long. All these years." She did not know that she had such desolate tones in her voice. She could see her mother looking into the distance with every statement that came to her, thinking. Old and grey. And majestic and kind. . . . Her mother's voice came:

"I have sometimes suspected. . . . My poor child. . . . It has been for a long time?" They were both silent. Thinking. Her mother said:

"There isn't any practical way out?" She pondered for a long time. "I take it you have thought it all out. I know you have a good head and you are good." A rustling sound. "But I am not level with these times. I should be glad if there were a way out. I should be glad if you could wait for each other. Or perhaps find a legal . . ."

Valentine said:

"Oh, mother, don't cry!" . . . "Oh, mother, I can't. . . ." . . .

"Oh, I will come. . . . Mother, I will come back to you if you order it." With each phrase her body was thrown about as if by a wave. She thought they only did that on the stage. Her eyes said to her:
. . . *"Dear sir,*
"Our Client, Mrs. Christopher Tietjens of Groby-in-Cleve-land . . ."
They said:
"After the occurrence at the Base-Camp at . . ."
They said:
"Thinks it useless . . ."
. She was agonised for her mother's voice. The telephone hummed in E-flat. It tried B. Then it went back to E-flat. Her eyes said:
"Proposes when occasion offers to remove to Groby . . ." in fat, blue typescript. She cried agonisedly:
"Mother. Order me to come back or it will be too late. . . ."
She had looked down, unthinkingly . . . as one does when standing at the telephone. If she looked down again and read to the end of the sentence that contained the words "It is useless," it would be too late! She would know that his wife had given him up!
Her mother's voice came, turned by the means of its conveyance into the voice of a machine of Destiny.
"No I can't. I am thinking."
Valentine placed her foot on the dais at which she stood. When she looked down it covered the letter. She thanked God. Her mother's voice said:
"I cannot order you to come back if it would kill you not to be with him." Valentine could feel her late-Victorian advanced mind, desperately seeking for the right plea — for any plea that would let her do without seeming to employ maternal authority. She began to talk like a book, an august Victorian book; Morley's *Life of Glad-stone*. That was reasonable: she wrote books like that.
She said they were both good creatures of good stock. If their consciences let them commit themselves to a certain course of action they were probably in the right. But she begged them, in God's name to assure themselves that their consciences *did* urge that course. She *had* to talk like a book!
Valentine said:
"It is nothing to do with conscience." That seemed harsh. Her mind was troubled with a quotation. She could not find it. Quotations ease strain; she said: "One is urged by blind destiny!" A Greek

quotation, then! "Like a victim upon an altar. I am afraid; but I consent!" . . . Probably Euripides; the *Alcestis* very likely! If it had been a Latin author the phrases would have occurred to her in Latin. Being with her mother made her talk like a book. Her mother talked like a book: then *she* did. They *must*; if they did not they would scream. . . . But they were English ladies. Of scholarly habits of mind. It was horrible. Her mother said:

"That is probably the same as conscience — race conscience!" She could not urge on them the folly and disastrousness of the course they appeared to propose. She had, she said, known too many irregular unions that had been worthy of emulation and too many regular ones that were miserable and a cause of demoralisation by their examples. . . . She was a gallant soul. She could not in conscience go back on the teachings of her whole life. She wanted to. Desperately! Valentine could feel the almost physical strainings of her poor, tired brain. But she could not recant. She was not Cranmer! She was not even Joan of Arc. So she went on repeating:

"I can only beg and pray you to assure yourself that not to live with that man will cause you to die or to be seriously mentally injured. If you think you can live without him or wait for him, if you think there is any hope of later union without serious mental injury I beg and pray . . ."

She could not finish the sentence . . . It was fine to behave with dignity at the crucial moment of your life! It was fitting, it was proper. It justified your former philosophic life. And it was cunning. Cunning!

For now she said:

"My child! my little child! You have sacrificed all your life to me and my teaching. How can I ask you now to deprive yourself of the benefit of them?"

She said:

"I *can't* persuade you to a course that might mean your eternal unhappiness!" . . . The *can't* was like a flame of agony!

Valentine shivered. That was cruel pressure. Her mother was no doubt doing her duty; but it was cruel pressure. It was very cold. November is a cold month. There were footsteps on the stairs. She shook.

"Oh, he is coming. He is coming!" she cried out. She wanted to say: "Save me!" She said: "Don't go away! Don't . . . Don't go away!" What do men do to you, men you love? Mad men. He was carrying a sack. The sack was the first she saw as he opened the door. Pushed it open; it was already half-open. A sack was a dreadful thing for a madman to carry. In an empty house. He dumped the sack down on the hearthstone. He had coal-dust on his right forehead. It was a heavy sack. Bluebeard would have had in it the corpse of his first wife. Borrow says that the gipsies say: "Never trust a young man with grey hair!" He had only half-grey hair and he was only half young. He was panting. He must be stopped carrying heavy sacks. Panting like a fish. A great motionless carp, hung in a tank.

He said:

"I suppose you would want to go out. If you don't we will have a fire. You can't stop here without a fire."

At the same moment her mother said:

"If that is Christopher I will speak to him."

She said away from the mouthpiece:

"Yes, let's go out. Oh, oh, oh. Let's go out. . . . Armistice . . . My mother wants to speak to you." She felt herself to be suddenly a little Cockney shop-girl. A midinette in an imitation Girl Guide's uniform. "Afride of the gentleman, my dear." Surely one could protect oneself against a great carp! She could throw him over her shoulder. She had enough Ju Jitsu for that. Of course a little person trained to Ju Jitsu can't overcome an untrained giant if he expects it. But if he doesn't expect it she can.

His right hand closed over her left wrist. He had swum towards her and had taken the telephone in his left. One of the window-panes was so old it was bulging and purplish. There was another. There were several. But the first one was the purplishest. He said:

"Christopher Tietjens speaking!" He could not think of anything more recherché to say than that — the great inarticulate fellow! His hand was cool on her wrist. She was calm, but streaming with bliss. There was no other word for it. As if you had come out of a bath of warm nectar and bliss streamed off you. His touch had calmed her and covered her with bliss.

He let her wrist go very slowly. To show that the grasp was meant for a caress! It was their first caress!

Before she had surrendered the telephone she had said to her mother:

"He doesn't know. . . . Oh, realise that he doesn't know!"

She went to the other end of the room and stood watching him.

He heard the telephone from its black depths say:

"How are you, my dear boy? My dear, dear boy; you're safe for good." It gave him a disagreeable feeling. This was the mother of the young girl he intended to seduce. He intended to. He said:

"I'm pretty well. Weakish. I've just come out of hospital. Four days ago." He was never going back to that bloody show. He had his application for demobilisation in his pocket. The voice said:

"Valentine thinks you are very ill. Very ill, indeed. She came to you because she thinks that." She hadn't come, then, because . . . But, of course, she would not have. But she might have wanted them to spend Armistice Day together! She might have! A sense of disappointment went over him. Discouragement. He was very raw. That old devil, Campion! Still, one ought not to be as raw as that. He was saying, deferentially:

"Oh, it was mental rather than physical. Though I had pneumonia all right." He went on saying that General Campion had put him in command over the escorts of German prisoners all through the lines of several armies. That really nearly had driven him mad. He couldn't bear being a beastly gaoler.

Still — Still! — he saw those grey spectral shapes that had surrounded and interpenetrated all his later days. The image came over him with the mood of repulsion at odd moments — at the very oddest; without suggestion there floated before his eyes the image, the landscape of greyish forms. In thousands, seated on upturned buckets, with tins of fat from which they ate at their sides on the ground, holding up newspapers that were not really newspapers; on grey days. They were all round him. And he was their gaoler. He said: "A filthy job!"

Mrs. Wannop's voice said:

"Still, it's kept you alive for us!"

He said:

"I sometimes wish it hadn't!" He was astonished that he had said it; he was astonished at the bitterness of his voice. He added: "I don't mean that in cold blood of course," and he was again astonished at the deference in his voice. He was leaning down, positively, as if over a very distinguished, elderly, seated lady. He straightened himself. It struck him as distasteful hypocrisy to bow before an elderly lady when you entertained designs upon her daughter. Her voice said:

"My dear boy . . . my dear, almost son . . ."

Panic overcame him. There was no mistaking those tones. He

looked round at Valentine. She had her hands together as if she were wringing them. She said, exploring his face painfully with her eyes:

"Oh, be kind to her. Be kind to her. . . ."

Then there had been revelation of their . . . you couldn't call it intimacy!

He never liked her Girl Guides' uniform. He liked her best in a white sweater and a fawn-coloured short skirt. She had taken off her hat — her cowboyish hat. She had had her hair cut. Her fair hair.

Mrs. Wannop said:

"I've got to think that you have saved us. To-day I have to think that you have saved us. . . . And of all you have suffered." Her voice was melancholy, slow, and lofty.

Intense, hollow reverberations filled the house. He said:

"That's nothing. That's over. You don't have to think of it."

The reverberations apparently reached her ear. She said:

"I can't hear you. There seems to be thunder."

External silence came back. He said:

"I was telling you not to think of my sufferings."

She said:

"Can't you wait? You and she? Is there *no* . . ." The reverberations began again. When he could again hear she was saying:

". . . Has had to contemplate such contingencies arising for one's child. It is useless to contend with the tendency of one's age. But I had hoped . . ."

The knocker below gave three isolated raps, but the echoes prolonged them. He said to Valentine:

"That's the knocking of a drunken man. But then half the population might well be drunk. If they knock again, go down and send them away."

She said:

"I'll go in any case before they can knock again."

She heard him say as she left the room — she could not help waiting for the end of the sentence; she *must* gather all that she could as to that agonising interview between her mother and her lover. Equally, she must go or she would go mad. It was no good saying that her head was screwed on straight. It wasn't. It was as if it contained two balls of string with two ends. On the one her mother pulled, on the other, he. . . . She heard him say:

"I don't know. One has desperate need. Of talk. I have not really spoken to a soul for two years!" Oh, blessed, adorable man! She heard him going on, getting into a stride of talk:

"It's that that's desperate. I'll tell you. I'll give you an instance. I was carrying a boy. Under rifle-fire. His eye got knocked out. If I had left him where he was his eye would not have been knocked out. I thought at the time that he might have been drowned, but I ascertained afterwards that the water never rose high enough. So I am responsible for the loss of his eye. It's a sort of monomania. You see, I am talking of it now. It recurs. Continuously. And to have to bear it in complete solitude . . ."

She was not frightened going now down the great stairs. They whispered, but she was like a calm Fatima. *He* was Sister Anne, and a brother, too. The enemy was fear. She must not fear. He rescued her from fear. It is to a woman that you must come for refuge from regrets about a boy's eyes.

Her physical interior turned within her. He had been under fire! He might never have been there, a grey badger, a tender, tender grey badger leaning down and holding a telephone. Explaining things with tender care. It was lovely how he spoke to her mother; it was lovely that they were all three together. But her mother would keep them apart. She was taking the only way to keep them apart if she was talking to him as she had talked to her.

There was no knowing. She had heard him say:

He was pretty well. . . . "Thank God!" . . . Weakish. . . . "Ah, give *me* the chance to cherish him!" He had just come out of hospital. Four days ago. He had had pneumonia all right, but it had been mental rather than physical. . . .

Ah, the dreadful thing about the whole war was that it had been — the suffering had been — mental rather than physical. And they had not thought of it. . . . He had been under fire. She had pictured him always as being in a Base, thinking. If he had been killed it would not have been so dreadful for him. But now he had come back with his obsessions and mental troubles. . . . And he needed his woman. And her mother was forcing him to abstain from his woman! That was what was terrible. He had suffered mental torture and now his pity was being worked on to make him abstain from the woman that could atone.

Hitherto, she had thought of the War as physical suffering only; now she saw it only as mental torture. Immense miles and miles of

anguish in darkened minds. That remained. Men might stand up
on hills, but the mental torture could not be expelled.

She ran suddenly down the steps that remained to her and was
fumbling at the bolts of the front door. She was not skilful at that.
She was thinking about the conversation that dreadfully she felt to
be continuing. She must stop the knocking. The knocker had stayed
for just long enough for the abstention of an impatient man knocking on a great door. Her mother was too cunning for them. With
the cunning that makes the mother wild-duck tumble apparently
broken-winged just under your feet to decoy you away from her
little things. STORGE, Gilbert White calls it! For, of course, she
could never have his lips upon hers when she thought of that crafty,
beloved, grey Eminence sitting at home and shuddering. . . . But
she *would*!

She found the gadget that opened the door — the third she had
tried amongst incomprehensible, painted century-old fixings. The
door came open exactly upon a frustrated sound. A man was being
propelled towards her by the knocker to which he held. . . . She
had saved *his* thoughts. Without the interruption of the knocker he
might be able to see that mother's device was just cunning. They
were cunning, the great Victorians. . . . Oh, poor mother!

A horrible man in uniform looked at her hatefully, with piercing,
hollow, black eyes in a fallen-away face. He said:

"I must see that fellow Tietjens; you're not Tietjens!" As if she
were defrauding him. "It's urgent," he said. "About a sonnet. I was
dismissed the Army yesterday. *His* doing. And Campion's. His wife's
lover!"

She said fiercely:

"He's engaged. You can't see him. If you want to see him you must
wait!" She felt horror that Tietjens should ever have had to do with
such a brute beast. He was unshaven; black. And filled with hatred.
He raised his voice to say:

"I'm McKechnie. Captain McKechnie of the Ninth. Vice-Chancellor's Latin Prizeman! One of the Old Pals!" He added: "Tietjens
forced himself in on the Old Pals!"

She felt the contempt of the scholar's daughter for the Prizeman;
she felt that Apollo with Admetus was as nothing for sheer disgust
compared with Tietjens buried in a band of such beings.

She said:

"It is not necessary to shout. You can come in and wait."

At all costs Tietjens must finish his conversation with her mother undisturbed. She led this fellow round the corner of the hall. A sort of wireless emanation seemed to connect her with the upper conversation. She was aware of it going on, through the wall above, diagonally; then through the ceiling in perpendicular waves. It seemed to work inside her head, her end of it, like waves, churning her mind.

She opened the shutters of the empty room round the corner, on the right. She did not wish to be alone in the dark with this hating man. She did not dare to go up and warn Tietjens. At all costs he must not be disturbed. It was not fair to call what her mother was doing, cunning. It was instinct, set in her breast by the Almighty, as the saying is. . . . Still, it was early-Victorian instinct! Tremendously cunning in itself.

The hateful man was grumbling:

"He's been sold up, I see. That's what comes of selling your wife to Generals. To get promotion. They're a cunning lot. But he overreached himself. Campion went back on him. But Campion, too, overreached *him*self. . . ."

She was looking out of the window, across the green square. Light was an agreeable thing. You could breathe more deeply when it was light. . . . Early Victorian instinct! . . . The Mid-Victorians had had to loosen the bonds. Her mother, to be in the van of Mid-Victorian thought, had had to allow virtue to "irregular unions." As long as they were high-minded. But the high-minded do not consummate irregular unions. So all her books had showed you high-minded creatures contracting irregular unions of the mind or of sympathy; but never carrying them to the necessary conclusion. They would have been ethically at liberty to, but they didn't. They ran with the ethical hare, but hunted with the ecclesiastical hounds. . . . Still, of course, she could not go back on her premises just because it was her own daughter!

She said:

"I beg your pardon!" to that fellow. He had been saying:

"They're too damn cunning. They overreach themselves!" Her mind spun. She did not know what he had been talking about. Her mind retained his words, but she did not understand what they meant. She had been sunk in the contemplation of Early-Victorian Thought. She remembered the long — call it "liaison" of Edith Ethel Duchemin and little Vincent Macmaster. Edith Ethel, swathed in opaque crêpe, creeping widow-like along the very palings she could see across the square, to her high-minded adulteries, amidst the whispered applause of Mid-Victorian England. So circumspect and right! . . . She had her thoughts to keep, all right. Well under control! . . . Well, she had been patient.

The man said agonisedly:

"My filthy, bloody, swinish uncle, Vincent Macmaster. *Sir* Vincent Macmaster! And this fellow Tietjens. All in a league against me. . . . Campion too. . . . But he overreached himself. . . . A man got into Tietjens' wife's bedroom. At the Base. And Campion sent him to the front. To get him killed. Her other lover, you see?"

She listened. She listened with all her attention straining. She wanted to be able to . . . She did not know what she wanted to be able to do! The man said:

"Major-General Lord Edward Campion, V.C., K.C.M.G., tantivy tum, tum, etcetera. Too cunning. Too b——y cunning by half. Sent Tietjens to the front too to get him killed. Me too. We all three went up to Division in a box-car — Tietjens, his wife's lover, and me. Tietjens confessed that bleedin' swab. Like a beastly monk. Told him that when you die — *in articulo mortis,* but you won't understand what that means! — your faculties are so numbed that you feel neither pain nor fear. He said death was no more than an anæsthetic. And that trembling, whining pup drank it in. . . . I can see them now. In a box-car. In a cutting."

She said:

"You've had shell-shock? You've got shell-shock now!"

He said, like a badger snapping:

"I haven't. I've got a bad wife. Like Tietjens. At least she isn't a bad wife. She's a woman with appetites. She satisfies her appetites. That's why they're hoofing me out of the Army. But at least, I don't sell her to Generals. To Major-General Lord Edward Campion, VC., K.C.M.G., etc. I got divorce leave and didn't divorce her. Then I got second divorce leave. And didn't divorce her. It's against my principles. She lives with a British Museum Palæontologist and he'd lose his job. I owe that fellow Tietjens a hundred and seventy quid. Over my second divorce leave. I can't pay him. I didn't divorce, but I've spent the money. Going about with my wife and her friend. On principle!"

He spoke so inexhaustibly and fast, and his topics changed so quickly that she could do no more than let the words go into her

ears. She listened to the words and stored them up. One main line
of topic held her; otherwise she could not think. She only let her
eyes run over the friezes of the opposite houses. She gathered that
Tietjens had been unjustly dismissed by Campion, whilst saving two
lives under fire. McKechnie grudgingly admitted heroism to Tietjens.
in order to blacken the General. The General wanted Sylvia Tietjens.
So as to get her he had sent Tietjens into the hottest part of the line.
But Tietjens had refused to get killed. He had a charmed life. That
was Provvy spiting the General. All the same, Providence could not
like Tietjens, a cully who comforted his wife's lover. A dirty thing to
do. When Tietjens would not be killed the General came down into
the Line and *strafed* him to Hell. Didn't she, Valentine, understand
why? He wanted Tietjens cashiered so that he, Campion, might be
less disgustingly disgraced for taking up with the wife. But he had
overreached himself. You can't be cashiered for not being on the
spot to lick a General's boots when you are saving life under rifle-
fire. So the General had to withdraw his words and find Tietjens
a dirty scavenger's job. Made a bleedin' gaoler of him!

She was standing in the doorway so that this fellow should not
run upstairs to where the conversation was going on. The windows
consoled her. She only gathered that Tietjens had had great mental
trouble. He must have. She knew nothing of either Sylvia Tietjens or
the General except for their beautiful looks. But Tietjens must have
had great mental trouble. Dreadful!

It was hateful. How could she stand it! But she must, to keep this
fellow from Tietjens, who was talking to her mother.

And . . . if his wife was a bad wife, didn't it . . .

The windows were consoling. A little dark boy of an officer passed
the railings of the house, looking up at the windows.

McKechnie had talked himself hoarse. He was coughing. He began
to complain that his uncle, Sir Vincent Macmaster, had refused him
an introduction to the Foreign Office. He had made a scene at the
Macmasters' already that morning. Lady Macmaster — a haggard
wanton, if there ever was one — had refused him access to his uncle,
who was suffering from nervous collapse. He said suddenly:

"Now about this sonnet: I'm at least going to show this fellow. . . ." Two more officers, one short, the other tall, passed the
window. They were laughing and calling out. ". . . that I'm a better
Latinist than he. . . ."

She sprang into the hall. Thunder again had come from the door.

In the light outside a little officer with his half profile towards her seemed to be listening. Beside him was a thin lady, very tall. At the bottom of the steps were the two laughing officers. The boy, his eye turned towards her, with a shrinking timidity you would have said, exclaimed in a soft voice:

"We've come for Major Tietjens. . . . This is Nancy. Of Bailleul, you know!" He had turned his face still more towards the lady. She was unreasonably thin and tall, the face of her skin drawn. She was much the older. Much. And hostile. She must have put on a good deal of colour. Purplish. Dressed in black. She ducked a little.

Valentine said:

"I'm afraid . . . He's engaged. . . ."

The boy said:

"Oh, but he'll see us. This is Nancy, you know!"

One of the officers said:

"We said we'd look old Tietjens up. . . ." He had only one arm. She was losing her head. The boy had a blue band round his hat. She said:

"But he's dreadfully urgently engaged. . . ."

The boy turned his face full on her with a gesture of entreaty.

"Oh, but . . ." he said. She nearly fell, stepping back. His eye-socket contained nothing; a disorderly reddish scar. It made him appear to be peering blindly; the absence of the one eye blotted out the existence of the other. He said in Oriental pleading tones:

"The Major saved my life; I must see him!" The sleeveless officer called out:

"We said we'd look old Tietjens up. . . . IT's armi . . . hick. . . . At Rouen in the pub . . ." The boy continued:

"I'm Aranjuez, you know! Aranjuez. . . ." They had only been married last week. He was going to the Indian Army to-morrow. They *must* spend Armistice Day with the Major. Nothing would be anything without the Major. They had a table at the Holborn.

The third officer — he was a very dark, silky-voiced, young Major — crept slowly up the steps, leaning on a stick, his dark eyes on her face.

"It *is* an engagement, you know!" he said. He had a voice like silk and bold eyes. "We really did make an engagement to come to Tietjens' house to-day. . . . Whenever it happened . . . a lot of us. In Rouen. Those who were in Number Two."

Aranjuez said:

"The C.O.'s to be there. He's dying, you know. And it would be nothing without the Major. . . ."

She turned her back on him. She was crying because of the pleading tones of his voice and his small hands. Tietjens was coming down the stairs, mooning slowly.

II

STANDING at the telephone, Tietjens had recognised at once that this was a mother, pleading with infinite statesmanship for her daughter. There was no doubt about that. How could he continue to . . . to entertain designs on the daughter of this voice? . . . But he *did*. He couldn't. He did. He *couldn't*. He did. . . . You may expel Nature by pleading . . . *tamen usque recur.* . . . She must recline in his arms before midnight. Having cut her hair had made her face look longer. Infinitely attracting. Less downright: with a refinement. Melancholy! Longing! One must comfort.

There was nothing to answer to the mother on sentimental lines. He wanted Valentine Wannop enough to take her away. That was the overwhelming answer to Mrs. Wannop's sophistications of the advanced writer of a past generation. It answered her then; still more it answered her now, to-day, when a man could stand up. Still, he could not overwhelm an elderly, distinguished, and inaccurate lady! It is not done.

He took refuge in the recital of facts. Mrs. Wannop, weakening her ground, asked:

"*Isn't* there any legal way out? Miss Wanostrocht tells me your wife . . ."

Tietjens answered:

"I can't divorce my wife. She's the mother of my child. I can't live with her, but I can't divorce her."

Mrs. Wannop took it lying down again, resuming her proper line. She said that he knew the circumstances and that if his conscience . . . And so on and so on. She believed, however, in arranging things quietly if it could be done. He was looking down mechanically, listening. He read that our client Mrs. Tietjens of Groby-in-Cleveland requests us to inform you that after the late occurrences at a Base Camp in France she thinks it useless that you and she

should contemplate a common life for the future. . . . He had contemplated that set of facts enough already. Campion during his
leave had taken up his quarters at Groby. He did not suppose that
Sylvia had become his mistress. It was improbable in the extreme.
Unthinkable! He had gone to Groby with Tietjens' sanction in order
to sound his prospects as candidate for the Division. That is to say
that, ten months ago, Tietjens had told the General that he might
make Groby his headquarters as it had been for years. But, in that
communication trench he had not told Tietjens that he had been at
Groby. He had said "London," specifically.

That *might* be an adulterer's guilty conscience but it was more
likely that he did not want Tietjens to know that he had been under
Sylvia's influence. He had gone for Tietjens bald-headed, beyond all
reason for a Commander-in-Chief speaking to a Battalion Commander. Of course he might have the wind up at being in the
trenches and being kept waiting so near the area of a real *strafe* as
he might well have taken that artillery lark to be. He might have
let fly just to relieve his nerves. But it was more likely that Sylvia
had bewildered his old brains into thinking that he, Tietjens, was
such a villain that he ought not to be allowed to defile the face of
the earth. Still less a trench under General Campion's control.

Campion had afterwards taken back his words very handsomely —
with a sort of distant and lofty deprecation. He had even said that
Tietjens had deserved a decoration, but that there were only a certain number of decorations now to be given and that he imagined
that Tietjens would prefer it to be given to a man to whom it would
be of more advantage. And he did not like to recommend for decoration an officer so closely connected with himself. He said this before
members of his staff . . . Levin and some others. And he went on,
rather pompously, that he was going to employ Tietjens on a very
responsible and delicate duty. He had been asked by H.M. Government to put the charge over all enemy prisoners between Army H.Q.
and the sea in charge of an officer of an exceptionally trustworthy
nature, of high social position and weight; in view of the enemy's
complaints to The Hague of ill-treatment of prisoners.

So Tietjens had lost all chance of distinction, command pay,
cheerfulness, or even equanimity. And all tangible proof that he had
saved life under fire — if the clumsy mud-bath of his incompetence
could be called saving life under fire. He could go on being discredited by Sylvia till kingdom come, with nothing to show on the

other side but the uncreditable fact that he had been a gaoler. Clever old General! Admirable old godfather-in-law!

Tietjens astonished himself by saying to himself that if he had had any proof that Campion had committed adultery with Sylvia he would kill him! Call him out and kill him. . . . That of course was absurd. You do not kill a General Officer commanding in chief an Army. And a good General, too. His reorganisation of that Army had been everything that was shipshape and soldierly; his handling it in the subsequent fighting had been impeccably admirable. It was in fact the apotheosis of the Regular Soldier. That alone was a benefit to have conferred on the country. He had also contributed by his political action to forcing the single command on the Government. When he had gone to Groby he had let it be quite widely known that he was prepared to fight that Division of Cleveland on the political issue of single command or no single command — and to fight it in his absence in France. Sylvia no doubt would have run the campaign for him!

Well, that, and the arrival of the American troops in large quantities, had no doubt forced the hand of Downing Street. There could no longer have been any question of evacuating the Western Front. Those swine in their corridors were scotched. Campion was a good man. He was good — impeccable! — in his profession; he had deserved well of his country. Yet, if Tietjens had had proof that he had committed adultery with his, Tietjens', wife he would call him out. Quite properly. In the eighteenth-century traditions for soldiers. The old fellow could not refuse. He was of eighteenth-century traditions, too.

Mrs. Wannop was informing him that she had had the news of Valentine's having gone to him from a Miss Wanostrocht. She had, she said, at first agreed that it was proper that Valentine should look after him if he were mad and destitute. But this Miss Wanostrocht had gone on to say that she had heard from Lady Macmaster that Tietjens and her daughter had had a liaison lasting for years. And . . . Mrs. Wannop's voice hesitated . . . Valentine seemed to have announced to Miss Wanostrocht that she intended to live with Tietjens. "Maritally," Miss Wanostrocht had expressed it.

It was the last word alone of Mrs. Wannop's talk that came home to him. People would talk. About him. It was his fate. And hers. Their identities interested Mrs. Wannop, as novelist. Novelists live on gossip. But it was all one to him.

The word "Maritally!" burst out of the telephone like a blue light! That girl with the refined face, the hair cut longish, but revealing its thinner refinement. . . . That girl longed for him as he for her! The longing had refined her face. He must comfort . . .

He was aware that for a long time, from below his feet a voice had been murmuring on and on. Always one voice. Who could Valentine find to talk to or to listen to for so long? Old Macmaster was almost the only name that came to his mind. Macmaster would not harm her. He felt her being united to his by a current. He had always felt that her being was united to his by a current. This then was the day!

The war had made a man of him! It had coarsened him and hardened him. There was no other way to look at it. It had made him reach a point at which he would no longer stand unbearable things. At any rate from his equals! He counted Campion as his equal; few other people, of course. And what he wanted he was prepared to take. . . . What he had been before, God alone knew. A Younger Son? A Perpetual Second-in-Command? Who knew. But to-day the world changed. Feudalism was finished; its last vestiges were gone. It held no place for him. He was going — he was damn well going! — to make a place in it for . . . A man could now stand up on a hill, so he and she could surely get into some hole together!

He said:

"Oh, I'm not destitute, but I was penniless this morning. So I ran out and sold a cabinet to Sir John Robertson. The old fellow had offered me a hundred and forty pounds for it before the war. He would only pay forty to-day — because of the immorality of my character." Sylvia had completely got hold of the old collector. He went on: "The Armistice came too suddenly. I was determined to spend it with Valentine. I expected a cheque to-morrow. For some books I've sold. And Sir John was going down to the country. I had got into an old suit of *mufti* and I hadn't a civilian hat." Reverberations came from the front door. He said earnestly:

"Mrs. Wannop. . . . If Valentine and I can, we will. . . . But to-day's to-day! . . . If we can't we can find a hole to get into. . . . I've heard of an antiquity shop near Bath. No special regularity of life is demanded of old furniture dealers. We should be quite happy! I have also been recommended to apply for a vice-consulate. In Toulon, I believe. I'm quite capable of taking a practical hold of life!"

All the Government Departments, staffed of course by non-combatants, were aching to transfer those who had served to any other old Department. The Department of Statistics would transfer him. . . .

A great many voices came from below stairs. He could not leave Valentine to battle with a great number of voices. He said:

"I've got to go!" Mrs. Wannop's voice answered:

"Yes; do. I'm very tired."

He came mooning slowly down the stairs. He smiled. He exclaimed:

"Come up, you fellows. There's some hooch for you!" He had a royal aspect. An all-powerfulness. They pushed past her and then past him on the stairs. They all ran up the stairs, even the man with the stick. The armless man shook hands with his left hand as he ran. They exclaimed enthusiasms. . . . On all celebrations it is proper for His Majesty's officers to exclaim and to run upstairs when whiskey is mentioned. How much the more so to-day!

They were alone now in the hall, he on a level with her. He looked into her eyes. He smiled. He had never smiled at her before. They had always been such serious people. He said:

"We shall have to celebrate! But I'm not mad. I'm not destitute!" He had run out to get money to celebrate with her. He had meant to go and fetch her. To celebrate that day together.

She wanted to say: "I am falling at your feet. My arms are embracing your knees!"

Actually she said:

"I suppose it is proper to celebrate together to-day!"

Her mother had made their union. For they looked at each other for a long time. What had happened to their eyes? It was as if they had been bathed in soothing fluid: they could look the one at the other. It was no longer the one looking and the other averting the eyes, in alternation. Her mother had spoken between them. They might never have spoken of themselves! In one heart-beat a-piece whilst she had been speaking they had been made certain that their union had already lasted many years. . . . It was warm; their hearts beat quietly. They had already lived side by side for many years. They were quiet in a cavern. The Pompeian red bowed over them; the stairways whispered up and up. They would be alone together now. For ever!

She knew that he desired to say "I hold you in my arms. My lips are on your forehead. Your breasts are being hurt by my chest!"

He said:

"Who have you got in the dining-room? It used to be the dining-room!"

Dreadful fear went through her. She said:

"A man called McKechnie. Don't go in!"

He went toward danger, mooning along. She would have caught at his sleeve, but Cæsar's wife must be as brave as Cæsar. Nevertheless she slipped in first. She had slipped past him before at a hangingstile. A Kentish kissing gate. She said:

"Captain Tietjens is here!" She did not know whether he was a Captain or a Major. Some called him one, some another.

McKechnie looked merely grumbling: not homicidal. He grumbled:

"Look here, my bloody swine of an uncle, your pal, has had me dismissed from the army!"

Tietjens said:

"Chuck it. You know you've been demobilised to go to Asia Minor for the Government. Come and celebrate." McKechnie had a dirty envelope. Tietjens said: "Oh, yes. The sonnet. You can translate it under Valentine's inspection. She's the best Latinist in England!" He said: "Captain McKechnie: Miss Wannop!" ·

McKechnie took her hand:

"It isn't fair. If you're such a damn good Latinist as that . . ." he grumbled.

"You'll have to have a shave before you come with us!" Tietjens said.

They three went up the stairs together, but they two were alone. They were going on their honeymoon journey. . . . The bride's going away! . . . She ought not to think such things. It was perhaps blasphemy. You go away in a neatly shining coupé with cockaded footmen!

He had re-arranged the room. He had positively re-arranged the room. He had removed the toilet-furnishings in green canvas: the camp-bed — three officers on it — was against the wall. That was his thoughtfulness. He did not want these people to have it suggested that she slept with him there. . . . Why not? Aranjuez and the hostile thin lady sat on green canvas pillows on the dais. Bottles leaned against each other on the green canvas table. They all held glasses. They were in all five of H.M. Officers. Where had they come from? There were also three mahogany chairs with green rep, sprung seats. Fat seats. Glasses were on the mantelshelf. The thin, hostile lady held a glass of dark red in an unaccustomed manner.

They all stood up and shouted:

"McKechnie! Good old McKechnie!" "Hurray McKechnie!" "Mc-Kechnie!" opening their mouths to the full extent and shouting with all their lungs. You could see that!

A swift pang of jealousy went through her.

McKechnie turned his face away. He said:

"The Pals! The old pals!" He had tears in his eyes.

A shouting officer sprang from the camp-bed — her nuptial couch! Did she *like* to see three officers bouncing about on her nuptial couch? What an Alcestis! She sipped sweet port! It had been put into her hand by the soft, dark, armless major! — The shouting officer slapped Tietjens violently on the back. The officer shouted:

"I've picked up a skirt. . . . A proper little bit of fluff, sir!"

Her jealousy was assuaged. Her lids felt cold. They had been wet for an instant or so: the moisture had cooled! It's salt of course! . . . She belonged to this unit! She was attached to him . . . for rations and discipline. So she was attached to it. Oh, happy day! Happy, happy day! . . . There was a song with words like that. She had never expected to see it. She had never expected . . .

Little Aranjuez came up to her. His eyes were soft, like a deer's, his voice and little hands caressing. . . . No he had only one eye! Oh dreadful! He said:

"You are the Major's dear friend . . . He made a sonnet in two and a half minutes!" He meant to say that Tietjens had saved his life.

She said:

"Isn't he wonderful!" Why?

He said:

"He can do anything! Anything! . . . He ought to have been . . ."

A gentlemanly officer with an eye-glass wandered in. . . . Of course they had left the front door open. He said with an exquisite's voice:

"Hullo, Major! Hullo, Monty! . . . Hullo, the Pals!" and strolled to the mantelpiece to take a glass. They all yelled, "Hullo, Duck-foot. . . . Hullo, Brassface!" He took his glass delicately and said: "Here's to hoping! . . . The mess!"

Aranjuez said:

"Our only V.C. . . ." Swift jealousy went through her.

Aranjuez said:

"*I* say . . . that *he* . . ." Good boy! Dear boy! Dear little brother!
. . . Where was her own brother? Perhaps they were not going to
be on terms any more! All around them the world was roaring. They
were doing their best to make a little roaring unit there, the tide
creeping into silent places!

The thin woman in black on the dais was looking at them. She
drew her skirts together. Aranjuez had his little hands up as if he were
going to lay them pleadingly on her breast. Why pleadingly? . . .
Begging her to forget his hideous eye-socket. He said:

"Wasn't it splendid . . . wasn't it ripping of Nancy to marry me
like this? . . . We shall all be such friends."

The thin woman caught her eye. She seemed more than ever to
draw her skirts away though she never moved. . . . That was because she, Valentine, was Tietjens' mistress. . . . There's a picture
in the National Gallery called *Titian's Mistress*. . . . She passed
perhaps with them all for having . . . The woman smiled at her, a
painfully forced smile. For Armistice. . . . She, Valentine, was outside the pale. Except for holidays and days of National rejoicing. . . .

She felt . . . nakedish, at her left side. Sure enough Tietjens was
gone. He had taken McKechnie to shave. The man with the eyeglass looked critically round the shouting room. He fixed her and
bore towards her. He stood over, his legs wide apart. He said:

"Hey! Hullo! Who'd have thought of seeing *you* here? Met you
at the Prinseps'. Friend of friend Hun's, aren't you?" He said:

"Hullo, Aranjuez! Better?"

It was like a whale speaking to a shrimp: but still more like an
uncle speaking to a favourite nephew! Aranjuez blushed with sheer
pleasure. He faded away as if in awe before tremendous eminences.
For him she too was an eminence. His life-hero's . . . woman!

The V.C. was in the mood to argue about politics. He always was.
She had met him twice during evenings at friends' called Prinsep.
She had not known him because of his eye-glasses; he must have put
that up along with his ribbon. It took your breath away: like a drop
of blood illuminated by a light that never was.

He said:

"They say you're receiving for Tietjens! Who'd have thought it? You're a pro-German — he's such a sound Tory. Squire of Groby and all, eh what?"

He said:

"Know Groby?" He squinted through his glasses round the room. "Looks like a mess this . . . Only needs the *Vie Parisienne* and the *Pink Un* . . . Suppose he has moved his stuff to Groby. He'll be going to live at Groby, now. The war's over!"

He said:

"But you and old Tory Tietjens in the same room . . . By Jove the war's over. . . . The lion lying down with the lamb's nothing . . ." He exclaimed "Oh damn! Oh, damn, damn, damn. . . . I say . . . I didn't mean it. . . . Don't cry. My dear little girl. My dear Miss Wannop. One of the best I always thought you. You don't suppose . . ."

She said:

"I'm crying because of Groby really. . . . It's a day to cry on anyhow. . . . You're quite a good sort, really!"

He said:

"Thank you! Thank you! Drink some more port! He's a good fat old beggar, old Tietjens. A good officer!" He added: "Drink a *lot* more port!"

He had been the most asinine, creaking, "what about your king and country," shocked, outraged and speechless creature of all the many who for years had objected to her objecting to men being unable to stand up. . . . Now he was a rather kind brother!

They were all yelling.

"Good old Tietjens! Good old Fat Man! Pre-war hooch! He'd be the one to get it!" No one like Fat Man Tietjens. He lounged at the door; easy; benevolent. In uniform now. That was better. An officer, yelling like an enraged Redskin, dealt him an immense blow behind the shoulder blades. He staggered, smiling into the centre of the room. An officer gently pushed her into the centre of the room. She was against him. Khaki encircled them. They began to yell and to prance, most joining hands. Others waved the bottles and smashed underfoot the glasses. Gipsies break glasses at their weddings. The bed was against the wall. She did not like the bed to be against the wall. It had been brushed by . . .

They were going round them: yelling in unison:

"Over here! Pom Pom Over here! Pom Pom!
That's the word, that's the word; Over here. . . ."

At least they weren't over there! They were prancing. The whole
world round them was yelling and prancing round. They were the
centre of unending roaring circles. The man with the eye-glass had
stuck a half-crown in his other eye. He was well-meaning. A brother.
She had a brother with the V.C. All in the family.

Tietjens was stretching out his two hands from the waist. It was
incomprehensible. His right hand was behind her back, his left in
her right hand. She was frightened. She was amazed. Did you ever!
He was swaying slowly. The elephant! They were dancing! Aranjuez
was hanging on to the tall woman like a kid on a telegraph pole. The
officer who had said he had picked up a little bit of fluff . . . well,
he had! He had run out and fetched it. It wore white cotton gloves
and a flowered hat. It said: "Ow! Now!" . . . There was a fellow
with a most beautiful voice. He led: better than a gramophone. Better. . . .

Les petites marionettes, font! font! font. . . .

On an elephant. A dear, meal-sack elephant. She was setting out
on . . .

The Last Post

Oh Rokehope is a pleasant place
If the fause thieves would let it be

Part One

HE LAY STARING at the withy binders of his thatch shelter; the grass was infinitely green; his view embraced four counties; the roof was supported by six small oak sapling-trunks, roughly trimmed and brushed from above by apple boughs. French crab-apple! The hut had no sides.

The Italian proverb says: He who allows the boughs of trees to spread above his roof invites the doctor daily. Words to that effect! He would have grinned, but that might have been seen.

For a man who never moved, his face was singularly walnut-coloured; his head, indenting the skim-milk white of the pillows should have been a gipsy's, the dark, silvered hair cut extremely close, the whole face very carefully shaven and completely immobile. The eyes moved, however, with unusual vivacity, all the life of the man being concentrated in them and their lids.

Down the path that had been cut in swathes from the knee-high grass and led from the stable to the hut, a heavy elderly peasant rolled in his gait. His over-long, hairy arms swung as if he needed an axe or a log or a full sack to make him a complete man. He was broad-beamed, in cord breeches very tight in the buttocks; he wore black leggings, an unbuttoned blue waistcoat, a striped flannel shirt, open at the perspiring neck and a square, high hat of black felt.

He said:

"Want to be shifted?"

The man in the bed closed his eyelids slowly.

"'Ave a droper cider?"

The other again similarly closed his eyes. The standing man sup-

ported himself with an immense hand, gorilla-like, by one of the
oaken posts.

"Best droper cider ever I tasted," he said, "'Is Lordship give me.
'Is Lordship sester me: 'Gunning,' 'e ses. . . . The day the vixen
got into keeper's coop enclosure . . ."

He began and slowly completed a very long story going to prove
that English noble landlords preferred foxes to pheasants. Or should!
English landowners of the right kidney.

'Is Lordship would no more 'ave that vixen killed or so much as
flurried, she being gravid like than . . . Dreadful work a gravid
vixen can do among 'encoops with pheasant poults. . . . Have to
eat fer six or seven, she have! All a-growing. . . . So 'is Lordship
sester Gunning. . . .

And then the description of the cider. . . . 'Ard! Thet cider was
'arder than a miser's 'art or 'n ole maid's tongue. Body it 'ad. Strength
it 'ad. Stans to reason. Ten-year cider. Not a drop was drunk in
Lordship's 'ouse under ten years in cask. Killed three sheep a week
fer his indoor and outdoor servants. An' three hundred pigeons. The
pigeon-cotes is a hundred feet high an' the pigeons nesteses in 'oles
in the inside walls. Clap-nests a 'ole wall at a go an' takes the squabs.
Times is not what they was but 'is Lordship keeps on. An always
will!

The man in the bed — Mark Tietjens — continued his own
thoughts:

Old Gunning lumbered slowly up the path towards the stable, his
hands swinging. The stable was a tile-healed, thatched affair, no real
stable in the North Country sense — a place where the old mare
sheltered among chickens and ducks. There was no tidiness amongst
South Country folk. They hadn't it in them, though Gunning could
bind a tidy thatch and trim a hedge properly. All-round man. Really
an all-round man; he could do a great many things. He knew all
about fox-hunting, pheasant-rearing, wood-craft, hedging, dyking, pig-
rearing and the habits of King Edward when shooting. Smoking
endless great cigars! One finished, light another, throw away the
stub . . .

Fox-hunting, the sport of kings with only twenty per cent of the
danger of war! He, Mark Tietjens, had never cared for hunting; now
he would never do any more; he had never cared for pheasant-
shooting. He would never do any more. Not couldn't; wouldn't from
henceforth. . . . It annoyed him that he had not taken the trouble

to ascertain what it was Iago said, before he had taken Iago's resolution. . . . *From henceforth he never would speak word.* . . . Something to that effect: but you could not get that into a blank verse line.

Perhaps Iago had not been speaking blank verse when he had taken his, Mark Tietjens' resolution . . . *Took by the throat the circumciséd dog and smote him.* . . . Good man, Shakespeare! All-round man in a way, too. Probably very like Gunning. Knew Queen Elizabeth's habits when hunting; also very likely how to hedge, thatch, break up a deer or a hare or a hog, and how to serve a writ and write bad French. Lodged with a French family somewhere in a Crutched Friars or the Minories. Somewhere.

The ducks were making a great noise on the pond up the hill. Old Gunning in the sunlight lumbered between the stable-wall and the raspberry canes, uphill. The garden was all uphill. Mark looked across the grass up at the hedge. When they turned his bed round he looked down on the house. Rough, grey stone.

Half round, he looked across the famous four counties; half round, the other way on, he could see up a steep grass-bank to the hedge on the main roadside. Now he was looking uphill across the tops of the hay-grass, over the raspberry canes at the hedge that Gunning was going to trim. . . . Full of consideration for him, they were, all the lot of them. For ever thinking of finding possible interests for him. He did not need it. He had interests enough.

Up the pathway that was above, beyond the hedge, on a grass slope, went the Elliot children — a lanky girl of ten with very long, corn-coloured hair; a fat boy of five in a sailor's suit — unspeakably dirty. The girl too long in the legs and ankles, her hair limp . . . War-starvation in early years! Well, that was not his, Mark Tietjens', fault. He had given the nation the Transport it needed: the nation should have found the food. They had not, so the children had long thin legs and wristbones that protruded on pipe-stems. All that generation! . . . No fault of his! He had managed the Transport as it should be managed. His department had. His own department, built up by himself from junior temporary clerk to senior permanent official; he had built it up, from the day of his entrance thirty years ago, to the day of his resolution never more to speak word.

Nor yet stir a finger! He had to be in this world, in this nation. Let them care for him, for he was done with them. . . . He knew the sire and dam of every horse from Eclipse to Perlmutter. That was

enough for him. They helped him to read all that could be read
about racing. He had interests enough!

The ducks on the pond continued to make a great noise, churning
the water, up the hill, boisterously with their wings, and squawking.
If they had been hens there would have been something the matter —
a dog chasing them. Ducks did not signify. They went mad, con-
tagiously. Like nations or all the cattle of a county.

Gunning, lumbering past the raspberry canes, took a bud or so
and squeezed the pale things between finger and thumb. Looking
for traces of maggots. Pale green leaves the raspberry had: a fragile
plant among the robuster rosaceæ. That was not starvation, but race.
Their commissariat was efficient enough, but presumably they were
not gross feeders. Gunning began to trim the hedge with sharp,
brushing blows of his bagging hook. There was still far too much
bramble among the quickset: in a week the hedge would be un-
sightly again.

They kept the hedge low so that he should be amused by passen-
gers on the path, though they would really have preferred to let it
grow high so that passers-by should not see into the orchard. . . .
Well, he had seen passers-by. More than they thought for! . . .
What in hell was Sylvia's game? And that old ass Edward Campion's? . . . Well, he, Mark, was not going to interfere. There was
undoubtedly something up. . . . Marie Léonie — formerly Charlotte — knew neither of that precious couple by sight: she had certainly seen them peer down over the hedge. . . .

They — it was more of their considerateness — had contrived a
broad shelf on the left corner post of his shelter. So that birds should
amuse him. He had always sought after larger quarry! . . . A hedge-
sparrow, noiseless and quaker-grey, was ghost-like on his shelf. It
flitted hiding itself deep in hedgerows. He thought of it as an American bird — or perhaps that was because there were so many Americans about there, though he never saw them. . . . A voiceless nightingale, slim, long, thin-billed, almost without markings as becomes
a bird that seldom sees the sun, but lives in the deep twilight of
deep hedges. . . . American because it ought to wear a scarlet letter.
Nearly all he knew of Americans came from a book he had once read
— about a woman like a hedge-sparrow, creeping furtive in hedgerows
and getting into trouble with a priest. . . . But no doubt there were
other types.

This desultory, slim, obviously Puritan bird, inserted its thin bill into the dripping that Gunning had put on the shelf for the tomtits. The riotous tomtit, the great tit, the bottle-tit . . . all that family love dripping. The hedge-sparrow obviously did not; the dripping on that warmish June day had become oleaginous. The hedge-sparrow, its bill all greased, mumbled its upper mandible with its lower but took no more dripping. It looked at Mark's eyes. Because these regarded it motionlessly it uttered a long warning note and flitted, noiseless, into invisibility. All hedge things ignore you whilst you move on and do not regard them. The moment you stay still and fix your eyes on them they warn the rest of the hedge and flit off. This hedge-sparrow no doubt had its young within ear-shot. Or the warning might have been just co-operative.

Marie Léonie née Riotor, was coming up the steps and then the path. He knew that by the sound of her breathing. She stood beside him, shapeless in her long pinafore of printed cotton, holding a plate of soup and saying:

"Mon pauvre homme! Mon pauvre homme! Ce qu'ils ont fait de toi!"

She began a breathless discourse in French. She was of the large, blond, Norman type; in the middle forties, her extremely fair hair very voluminous and noticeable. She had lived with Mark Tietjens for twenty years now, but she had always refused to speak a word of English, having an invincible scorn for both language and people of her adopted country.

Her discourse poured on. She had set the little tray with the plate of reddish-yellowish soup on a flat shelf of wood that turned out on a screw from underneath the bed; in the soup was a shining clinical thermometer that she moved and regarded from time to time, beside the plate a glass syringe, graduated. She said that *Ils* — They — had combined to render her soup of vegetables uneatable. They would not give her *navets de Paris* but round ones, like buttons; they contrived that the carrots should be *pourris* at their bottom ends; the leeks were of the consistency of wood. They were determined that he should not have vegetable soup because they wanted him to have meat juice. They were anthropophagi. Nothing but meat, meat, meat! That girl! . . .

She had always in the Grey's Inn Road had Paris turnips from Jacopo's in Old Compton Street. There was no reason why you should not grow *navets de Paris* in this soil. The Paris turnip was barrel-shaped, round, round, round like an adorable little pig till it turned into its funny little tail. That was a turnip to amuse you; to change and employ your thoughts. *Ils* — he and she — were incapable of having their thoughts changed by a turnip.

Between sentences she ejaculated from time to time:

"My poor man! What they have made of you?"

Her volubility flowed over Mark like a rush of water over a grating, only a phrase or so now and then coming to his attention. It was not unpleasant; he liked his woman. She had a cat that she made abstain from meat on a Friday. In the Gray's Inn Road that had been easier, in a large room decorated with innumerable miniatures and silhouettes representing members of the Riotor family and its branches. Mme Riotor *mère* and Mme Riotor *grand'mère* too had been miniature painters and Marie Léonie possessed some astonishingly white statuary by the distinguished sculptor Casimir-Bar, a life-long friend of her family who had only never been decorated because of a conspiracy. So he had a great contempt for decorations and the decorated. Marie Léonie had been accustomed to repeat the voluminous opinions of Monsieur Casimir-Bar on the subject of decorations at great length on occasion. Since he, Mark, had been honoured by his sovereign she had less frequently recited them. She admitted that the democracy of to-day had not the sterling value that had distinguished democrats of the day of her parents, so it might be better to *caser* oneself — to find a niche amongst those whom the State distinguished.

The noise of her voice, which was deep-chested and not unpleasing, went on. Mark regarded her with the ironic indulgence that you accord to a child, but indeed, when he had been still in harness it had rested him always to come home as he had done every Thursday and Monday and not infrequently on a Wednesday when there had been no racing. It had rested him to come home from a world of incompetent imbeciles and to hear this brain comment on that world. She had views on virtue, pride, downfalls, human careers, the habits of cats, fish, the clergy, diplomats, soldiers, women of easy virtue, Saint Eustachius, President Grévy, the purveyors of comestibles, custom-house officers, pharmacists, Lyons silk weavers, the keepers of boarding-houses, garotters, chocolate-manufacturers, sculptors other than M. Casimir-Bar, the lovers of married women, housemaids. . . . Her mind in fact was like a cupboard, stuffed, packed with the most incongruous materials, tools, vessels, and débris. Once the door was opened you never knew what would tumble out or be followed by what. That was restful to Mark as foreign travel might have been — only he had never been abroad except when his father, before his accession to Groby, had lived in Dijon for his children's education. That was how he knew French.

Her conversation had another quality that continually amused him: she always ended it with the topic with which she had chosen to begin. Thus, to-day having chosen to begin with *navets de Paris*, with Paris turnips she would end, and it amused him to observe how on each occasion she would bring the topic back. She might be concluding a long comment on ironclads and have to get back suddenly to custards because the door-bell rang while her maid was out, but accomplish the transition she would before she answered the bell. Otherwise she was frugal, shrewd, astonishingly clean and healthy.

Whilst she was giving him his soup, inserting the glass syringe in his lips at half minute intervals which she timed by her wrist-watch, she was talking about furniture. . . . *Ils* would not let her apply to the species of rabbit-hutches in the salon a varnish that she imported from Paris; Monsieur her brother-in-law had really exhibited when she had actually varnished a truly discreditable chair — had exhibited a distraction that had really filled her with amusement. It was possible that the fashion of the day was for furniture of decrepitude or gross forms. That *they* would not let her place in the salon the newly gilt arm-chair of her late mother or the sculptural group representing Niobe and some of her offspring by the late Monsieur Casimir-Bar or the over-mantel clock that was an exact reproduction in bronze of the Fountain of the Medicis in the gardens of the Luxembourg at Paris — that was a matter of taste. *Elle* might very well feel umbrage that she, Marie Léonie, should possess articles of such acknowledged prestige. For what could be more unapproachable than a Second Empire fauteuil newly gilt and maintained, she could assure the world, at such a pitch of glitter as dazzled the eyes? *Elle* might very well feel umbrage when you considered that the skirt that she wore when gardening was . . . Well, in short was what it was! Nevertheless in that skirt she allowed herself to be seen by the clergyman. But why did *Il* who was admittedly a man of honour and sensibility and reputed to know all the things of this world and perhaps of the next — why did He join in the infinitely stupid conspiracy against the work of the great genius Casimir-Bar? She, Marie Léonie, could understand that He, in his

difficult situation would not wish to give permission to instal in the
Salon works at which *Elle* took umbrage because her possessions
did not include objects of art which all the world acknowledged to
be of classic rank, not to mention the string of pearls which she,
Marie Léonie, Riotor by birth, owed to the generosity of him, Mark,
and her own economies. And other objects of value and taste. That
was reasonable. If your woman is poorly *dot*-ed . . . let us call it
dot-ed . . . because, certainly she, Marie Léonie, was not one to
animadvert upon those in situations of difficulty. . . . It would ill
become her so to do! Nevertheless a great period of years of honesty,
frugality, regularity of life and cleanliness . . . And she asked Mark
if he had ever seen in *her* parlour traces of mud such as on wet days
she had certainly observed in the salon of a certain person. . . .
And certain revelations she could make as to what had used to be
the condition of a cupboard under the stairs and the state to be
observed behind certain presses in the kitchen! But if you have not
had experience in the control of domestics, what would you? . . .
Nevertheless a stretch of years passed in the state of housewifeliness
such as she had already adumbrated upon gave one the right to
comment — of course — with delicacy, upon the *ménage* of a young
person even though her delicate situation might avert from her
comment of an un-Christian nature as to certain other facts. It
did however seem to her, Marie Léonie, that to appear before a
clergyman in a skirt decorated with no less than three visible *tâches*
of petrol, wearing gloves encrusted with mud as you encrust a truffle
with paste before baking it under the cinders — and holding, of all
implements, a common gardening-trowel. . . . And to laugh and
joke with him! . . . Surely the situation called for a certain — let
them call it, retirement of demeanour. She was far from according
to the Priest the extravagant privileges to which priests laid claim.
The late Monsieur Casimir-Bar was accustomed to say that if we
accorded to our *soi-disant* spiritual advisers all that they would take
we should lie upon a bed that had neither sheets, *eidredons*, pillows,
bolsters, nor settle. And she, Marie-Léonie, was inclined to agree
with Monsieur Casimir-Bar, though, as one of the heroes of the
barricades in 1848, he was apt to be a little extreme in his tenets.
Still a vicar is in England a functionary of the State and as such
should be received with a certain modesty and reserve. On the
other hand — she, Marie Léonie — formerly Riotor, her mother having been born Lavigne-Bourdreau and having in consequence a sus-

picion of Huguenot blood so that she, Marie Léonie, might be expected to know how the Protestant clergy should be received — she, then, Marie Léonie, from the little window on the side of the stairs, had distinctly seen *Elle* lay one hand on the shoulder of that clergyman and point — point, mind you, with the *trowel* — to the open front door and say — she had distinctly heard the words: "Poor man, if you have hunger you will find Mr. Tietjens in the dining-room. He is just eating a sandwich. It's hungry weather!" . . . That was six months ago, but Marie Léonie's ears still tingled at the words and the gesture. A trowel! To point with a *trowel; pensez y!* If a trowel why not a *main de fer*, a dustpan? Or a vessel even more homely! . . . And Marie Léonie chuckled.

Her grandmother Bourdreau remembered a crockery-merchant of the ambulating sort who had once filled one of those implements — a *vase de nuit* — but of course new, with milk and had offered the whole gratuitously to any passer-by who would drink the milk. A young woman called Laborde accepted his challenge there in the market-place of Noisy-Lebrun. She has lost her fiancé who found the gesture exaggerated. But he was a farceur, that crockery-dealer!

She drew from the pocket of her pinafore several folded pages of a newspaper and from under the bed a double picture-frame — two frames hinged together so that they would close. She inserted a sheet of the paper between the two frames and then hung the whole on a piece of picture wire that depended from the roof-tree beneath the thatch. Two braccs of picture-wire too came from the supporting posts, to right and left. They held the picture-frames motionless and a little inclined towards Mark's face. She was agreeable to look at, stretching up her arms. She lifted his torso with great strength and infinite solicitude, propped it a little with the pillows and looked to see that his eyes fell on the printed sheet. She said:

"You can see well, like that?"

His eyes took in the fact that he was to read of the Newbury Summer Meeting and the one at Newcastle. He closed them twice to signify Yes! The tears came into hers. She murmured:

"Mon pauvre homme! Mon pauvre homme! What they have done to you!" She drew from another pocket in her pinafore a flask of eau de cologne and a wad of cotton-wool. With that, moistened, she wiped even more solicitously his face and then his thin, mahogany hands which she uncovered. She had the air of women in

France when they change the white satin clothes and wash the faces
of favourite Virgins at the church doors in August.

Then she stood back and apostrophised him. He took in that the
King's filly had won the Berkshire Foal plate and the horse of a
friend the Seaton Delaval Handicap, at Newcastle. Both might have
been expected. He had meant to go to the Newcastle meeting this
year and give Newbury a by. During the last year when he had gone
racing he had done rather well at Newbury so he had then thought
he would try Newcastle for a change and, whilst he was there, take
a look at Groby and see what that bitch Sylvia was doing with the
house. Well, that was done with. They would presumably bury him
at Groby.

She said, in deep, rehearsed, tones:

"My Man!" She might almost have well said: "My Deity!" "What
sort of life is this we lead here? Was there ever anything so singular
and unreasonable? If we sit to drink a cup of tea, the cup may at
any moment be snatched from our mouths; if we recline upon a
divan — at any moment the divan may go. I do not comment on
this that you lie by night as by day for ever here in the open air,
for I understand that it is by your desire and consent that you lie
here and I will never exhibit aversion from that which you desire
and that to which you consent. But cannot you bring it about that
we should inhabit a house of some reason, one more suited to human beings of this age, and one that is less of a procession of goods
and chattels? You can bring that about. You are all-powerful here.
I do not know what are your resources. It was never your habit to
tell me. You kept me in comfort. Never did I express a desire that
you did not satisfy, though it is true that my desires were always
reasonable. So I know nothing though I read once in a paper that
you were a man of extravagant riches and that can hardly all have
vanished for there can have been fewer men of as great a frugality
and you were always fortunate and moderate in your wagers. So I
know nothing and I would scorn to ask of these others, for that
would imply doubt of your trust in me. I do not doubt that you
have made arrangements for my future comfort and I am in no uncertainty of the continuance of those arrangements. It is not material
fears that I have. But all this appears to be a madness. Why are
we here? What is the meaning of all this? Why do you inhabit this
singular erection? It may be that the open air is of necessity for your
malady. I do not believe that you lived in perpetual currents of air

in your chambers, though I never saw them. But on the days you gave to me you had everything of the most comfortable and you seemed contented with my arrangements. And your brother and his woman appear so mad in all the other affairs of life that they may well be mad in this also. Why then will you not end it? You have the power. You are all-powerful here. Your brother will spring from one corner to the other of this lugubrious place in order to anticipate your slightest wish. *Elle*, too!"

Stretching out her hands she had the air of a Greek woman who invoked a deity, she was so large and fair and her hair was so luxuriantly blond. And indeed, to her, in his mystery and silence he had the air of a deity who could discharge unthinkable darts and vouchsafe unimaginable favours. Though all their circumstances had changed, that had not changed, so that even his immobility enhanced his mystery. In all their life together, not merely here, he had been silent whilst she had talked. On the two regular days of the week on which he had been used to visit her, from the moment when she would open her door exactly at seven in the evening and see him in his bowler hat with his carefully rolled umbrella, his racing glasses slung diagonally across him, to the moment when, next morning at half-past ten she would brush his bowler and hand him that and his umbrella, he would hardly speak a word — he would speak such few words as to give the idea of an absolute taciturnity whilst she entertained him with an unceasing flow of talk and of comments on the news of the Quartier — of the French colonists of that part of London, or on the news in the French papers. He would remain seated on a hard chair, bending slightly forward, with, round the corners of his mouth little creases that suggested an endless, indulgent smile. Occasionally he would suggest that she should put half a sovereign upon a horse; occasionally he would bring her an opulent present, heavy gold bangles floridly chased and set with large emeralds, sumptuous furs, expensive travelling trunks for when she had visited Paris or went to the seaside in the autumn. That sort of thing. Once he had bought her a complete set of the works of Victor Hugo bound in purple morocco and all the works that had been illustrated by Gustave Doré, in green calf, once a hoof of a racehorse, trained in France, set in silver in the form of an inkstand. On her forty-first birthday — though she had no idea how he had ascertained that it was her forty-first birthday — he had given her a string of pearls and had taken her to a hotel at Brighton kept by an ex-prize-fighter. He had told her to wear the pearls at dinner, but to be careful of them because they had cost five hundred pounds. He asked her once about her investment of her savings and when she had told him that she was investing in French *rentes viagères* he had told her that he could do better than that for her and afterwards, from time to time he had told her of odd but very profitable ways of investing small sums.

In this way, because his gifts filled her with rapture on account of their opulence and weightiness, he had assumed for her the aspect by degrees of a godhead who could bless — and possibly blast — inscrutably. For many years after he had first picked her up in the Edgeware Road outside the old Apollo she had regarded him with suspicion since he was a man and it is the nature of men to treat women with treachery, lust, and meanness. Now she regarded herself as the companion of a godhead, secure and immune from the evil workings of Fortune — as if she had been seated on the shoulder of one of Jove's eagles, beside his throne. The Immortals had been known to choose human companions; when they had so done, fortunate indeed had been the lot of the chosen. Of them she felt herself to be one.

Even his seizure had not deprived her of her sense of his widespreading and inscrutable powers and she could not rid herself of the conviction that if he would, he could talk, walk, and perform the feats of strength of a Hercules. It was impossible not to think so; the vigour of his glance was undiminished and it was the dark glance of a man, proud, alert, and commanding. And the mysterious nature and occurrence of the seizure itself only confirmed her subconscious conviction. The fit had come so undramatically that although the several pompous and, for her nearly imbecile, English physicians who had been called in to attend on him, agreed that some sort of fit must have visited him as he lay in his bed, that had done nothing to change her mind. Indeed, even when her own Doctor, Drouant-Rouault, asserted with certitude and knowledge that this was a case of fulminant hemiplegia of a characteristic sort, though her reason accepted his conclusion, her subconscious intuition remained the same. Doctor Drouant-Rouault was a sensible man; that he had proved by pointing out the anatomical excellence of the works of sculpture by Monsieur Casimir-Bar and agreeing that only a conspiracy of rivals could have prevented his arriving at the post of President of the Ecole des Beaux Arts. He was then, a man of sense and his reputation amongst the French tradesmen of the Quarter stood very high. She had never herself needed the attentions of a doctor. But if you needed a doctor, obviously you went to a Frenchman and acquiesced in what he said.

But although she acquiesced in words to others, and indeed to herself, she could not convince herself in her *for intérieur*, nor indeed had she arrived at that amount of exterior conviction without some argument at least. She had pointed out, not only to Doctor Drouant-Rouault, but she had even conceived it to be her duty to point out to the English practitioners to whom she would not otherwise have spoken, that the man lying there in her bed was a North-Countryman, from Yorkshire where men were of an inconceivable obstinacy. She had asked them to consider that it was not unusual for Yorkshire brothers and sisters or other relatives to live for decades together in the same house and never address a word to each other and she had pointed out that she knew Mark Tietjens to be of an unspeakable determination. She knew it from their lifelong intimacy. She had never, for instance, been able to make him change his diet by an ounce in weight or the shaking of a pepperpot as to flavour — not once in twenty years during which she had cooked for him. She pleaded with these gentlemen to consider as a possibility that the terms of the armistice were of such a nature as to make a person of Mark's determination and idiosyncrasies resolve to withdraw himself for ever from all human contacts and, that if he did so determine, nothing would cause him to change his determination. The last word he had spoken had been whilst one of his colleagues at the Ministry had been telephoning to tell her, for Mark's information, what the terms of the Armistice were. At the news, which she had had to give him over her shoulder, he had made from the bed some remark. He had been recovering from double pneumonia at the time. What the remark had been she could not exactly repeat; she was almost certain that it had been to the effect — in English — that he would never speak again. But she was aware that her own predilection was sufficient to bias her hearing. She had felt herself at the news that the Allies did not intend to pursue the Germans into their own country — she had felt herself as if she could say to the High Official at the other end of the telephone that she would never speak word to him and his race again. It was the first thing that had come into her mind and no doubt it had been the first thing to come into Mark's.

So she had pleaded with the doctors. They had paid practically no attention to her and she was aware that that was very likely due to her ambiguous position as the companion, until lately without any legal security, of a man whom they considered as in no position to continue his protection of her. That she in no way resented; it was in the nature of English male humanity. The Frenchman had naturally listened with deference, bowing even a little. But he had remarked with a sort of deaf obstinacy: Madame must consider that the occasion of the stroke only made more certain that it *was* a stroke. And that argument to her, as Frenchwoman, must seem almost controvertible. For the betrayal of France by her Allies at the supreme moment of triumph had been a crime the news of which might well cause the end of the world to seem desirable.

II

SHE continued to stand beside him and to apostrophise him until it should be time to turn round the framed newspaper so that he could read the other side of the sheet. What he read first contained the remarks of various writers on racing. That he took in rapidly, as if it were a mere *hors d'œuvre*. She knew that he regarded with contempt the opinions of all writers on racing, but the two who wrote in this particular sheet with less contempt than the others. But the serious reading began when she turned the page. Here were endless, serried columns of the names of race-horses, their jockeys, and entrants at various race-meetings, their ages, ancestries, former achievements. That he would peruse with minuteness and attention. It would cost him just under an hour. She would have liked to stay with him whilst he read it, for the intensive study of matters connected with race-horses had always been their single topic of communion. She had spent almost sentimental hours leaning over the back of his arm-chair reading news of the turf simultaneously with himself, and the compliments he had been used to pay her over her predictions of Form, if they were the only compliments he ever paid her, had filled her with the warm pleasure and confusion that she might have felt had he addressed the same compliments to her on the subject of her person. She did not indeed need compliments from him as to her person; his complete contentment with her sufficed—but she had rejoiced in, and now missed, these long, quiet times of communing. She remarked to him indeed that Seattle had won her race as she had several days ago predicted because there had been no other competitors in any way of the same class as the filly, but there had been no answering, half contemptuous grunt of acquiescence such as in the old days had been hers.

An aeroplane had droned overhead and she had stepped out to look up at the bright toy that, shone upon by the sun, progressed slowly across the pellucid sky. When she went in, in answer to the double closing of his lids that meant that he acquiesced in the turning of his news-sheet, she unhitched one brace from the oaken post to his right and, walking round his bed attached the brace on the post to his left, doing the reverse with the brace that had gone to the left. In that way the picture-frames turned completely round and exhibited the other side of the newspaper.

It was a contrivance that daily excited her annoyance and, as usual, she expressed herself. This was another instance of the madness of They — of her brother-in-law and his woman. Why had they not obtained one of those ingenious machines, like an arm of bright brass supporting a reading-shelf of agreeably varnished mahogany, that you clamped to a bedstead and could adjust at any angle? Why indeed had They not procured one of those huts for the tuberculous that she had seen depicted in a catalogue? Such huts could be painted in agreeable stripes of green and vermilion, thus presenting a gay appearance, and they could be turned upon a pivot so as to meet the rays of the sun or avoid the currents of air caused by the wind? What could be the explanation of this mad and gross structure? A thatched roof supported on posts without walls! Did they desire him to be blown out of his bed by the draughts? Did they merely desire to enrage her? Or could it be that their resources were of such exiguity that they could not afford the conveniences of modern civilisation?

She might well have thought that to be the case. But how could it be, in face of the singular behaviour of Monsieur her *beau-frère* in the matter of the statuary of Casimir-Bar the great sculptor? She had offered to contribute to the expenses of the establishment even at the cost of the sacrifice of what she held most dear and how singular had been Monsieur Christophère's behaviour. During their absence on the occasion of the great sale at Wingham Priory she had ordered the amiable if gross Gunning and the semi-imbecile carpenter to descend from her room to the salon that admirable *Niobe* and the admittedly incomparable *Thetis informing Neptune of the death of a Son-in-law,* not to mention her newly re-gilt Second-Empire fauteuil. And in that gloomy wilderness how had they not shone in their respective whiteness and auriference! The pose of the *Niobe* how passionate, the action of the *Thetis* how spirited and how at the same time pathetic! And she had seized the opportunity to varnish with a special preparation imported from the City of the Arts the only chair in the salon that was not too rough to be susceptible of varnish even though it came from Paris herself. A clumsy affair at that — of the epoch of Louis the Thirteenth of France, though heaven knew whose epoch that was here. Without doubt that of Cromwell the regicide!

And Monsieur must needs seize the moment of his entry on this thus enlivened scene to exhibit the only display of emotion that she had ever known him vouchsafe. For otherwise Monsieur had the pose of being at least as self-contained if not as absolutely taciturn as Mark himself. She asked Mark: was that the moment for what was after all, if you analysed it, a manifestation of attachment for his young woman? What else could it be? *Il* — Monsieur their relative, passed for a man of unbounded knowledge. He knew all knowledge. He could not but be aware of the supreme value of the work of Casimir-Bar who, but for the machinations of his rival Monsieur Rodin and his confrères, must have attained to the highest honours in France. But not only had Monsieur with hisses and tut-tuts of anger ordered Gunning and the carpenter at once to remove the statuary and the fauteuil from the salon where she had exhibited them — with heaven knew how much reluctance — with a view to their attracting the attention of a chance customer — for chance customers did come in Their absence without rendezvous. . . . Not only that, but Monsieur to gratify the perhaps not unnatural envy of *Elle* had cast meretricious doubts on the pecuniary value of the works of Casamir-Bar themselves. Everyone knew how the Americans to-day were stripping the unfortunate land of France of her choicest art treasures; the enormous prices they paid; the avidity they showed. Yet that man had tried to persuade her that her statues were worth no more than a few shillings a-piece. It was incomprehensible. He was in want of money to the extent of turning their house into a mere depot for dilapidated objects in rough wood and battered brass.

He had contrived to obtain singular prices for these forlorn objects from insane Yankees who came great distances to purchase these débris from him. Yet when he was offered pieces of the utmost beauty in the most perfect condition he just simply turned the objects down with scoffing.

For herself, she respected passion — though she could have imagined an object of passion more calculated to excite that feeling than *Elle*, whom for convenience she would call her *belle-sœur*. She at least was broad-minded and moreover she understood the workings of the human heart. It was creditable for a man to ruin himself for the object of his affections. But this at least she found exaggerated.

And what, then, was this determination to ignore the developments of modern genius? Why would they not purchase for Mark a reading-desk with a brass arm that should indicate to the neighbours and dependants that at least he was a person of condition? Why no revolving hut? There were certain symptoms of that age that were disquieting. She would be the first to acknowledge that. They had only to read in the papers of the deeds of assassins, highway robbers, of the subversive and the ignorant who everywhere seized the reins of power. But what was to be said against such innocent things as the reading-desk, the revolving hut, and the aeroplane? Yes, the aeroplane!

Why did they ignore the aeroplane? They had told her that the reason why they had been unable to provide her with *navets de Paris* was that the season was becoming too advanced for the sowing of the seeds of those admirable and amusing vegetables which, seen advancing through the pale electric lights of the early hours of the morning, piled symmetrically as high as the first floors of the hotels, on the marketcarts, provided one of the gayest spectacles of the night-life of la Ville Lumière. They had said that to procure the seeds from Paris would demand at least a month. But supposing they had sent a letter by aeroplane, requesting the despatch of the seeds equally by aeroplane, to procure them, as all the world knew, would be a matter merely of a few hours. And, having thus brought the matter back to turnips again she concluded:

"Yes, mon pauvre homme, they have singular natures, our relatives — for I will include the young woman in that category. I at least am broad-minded enough for that. But they have singular natures. It is a strange affair!"

She departed up the path towards the stable, speculating on the nature of her man's relatives. They were the relatives of a godhead — but godheads had relatives of a singular nature. Let Mark figure as Jupiter; well, Jupiter had a son called Apollo who could not be regarded as exactly *fils de famille*. His adventures had been of the most irregular. Was it not known that he had spent a long space of time with the shepherds of King Admetus, singing and carousing? Well, Monsieur Tietjens might for convenience be regarded as a sort of Apollo, now amongst the shepherds of Admetus and complete with female companion. If he did not often sing he also concealed the tendencies that had brought about his downfall. He was quiet enough about the house, extraordinary as the house might be. *Elle* also. If their relationship was irregular it presented no aspects of reprehensible festivity. It was a sufficiently serious *collage*. That at least ran in the family.

She came round the rough balks of the side of the stable upon Gunning, seated on the stone-sill of the door, cutting with a broad-bladed clasp-knife considerable chunks out of a large meat pasty. She surveyed his extended leggings, his immense be-mired boots and his unshaven countenance and remarked in French that the shepherds of Admetus were probably differently dressed. They certainly were in all the performances of the *Alceste* that she had seen. But perhaps he served his turn.

Gunning said that he supposed he had to go on duty again. She, he supposed, was going to bottle off the cider or she would not have had him bring down that 'ere cask. She was to be careful to tie the carks tight; it would get itself a 'ed, proper.

She said that if she, a Norman of a hundred generations did not know how to handle cider it would be a strange thing and he said that it would be a pity if that cider went wrong after all the trouble they 'ad 'ad.

He brushed the crumbs of his demolished pipe off the cords of his breeches, carefully picking up the larger fragments of crust and inserting them into his mouth between his broad, red lips. He asked if 'er Ladyship knew whether the Cahptn wanted the mare that afternoon. If not 'e might's well turn 'er on the Common. She said that she did not know; the Captain had said nothing to her about it. He said he supposed 'e might's well. Cramp said 'e would not have the settee ready to go to the station 'fore mornin'. If she would wait there he would go git some tepid water and they would moisten the eggs. She did not ask better.

He scrambled to his feet and lumbered down the stone path towards the house. She stood in the bright day regarding the long grass of the orchard, the gnarled, whitened trunks of the fruit trees, the little lettuces like aligned rosettes in the beds, and the slope of the land towards the old stones of the house that the boughs of the apple trees mostly hid. And she acknowledged that, in effect, she did not ask better. A Norman, if Mark had died in the ordinary course, she would no doubt have gone back to the neighbourhood either of Falaise or Bayeux from which place came the families of her grandmother and grandfather respectively. She would probably have married a rich farmer or a rich grazier and, by choice, she would have pursued a life of bottling off cider and moistening the eggs of sitting hens. She had had her training as a *coryphée* at the Paris Opera and no doubt if she had not made her visit to London with the Paris Opera troupe and if Mark had not picked her up in the Edgeware road where her lodgings had been, she would have lived with some man in Clichy or Auteuil until with her economies she would have been able, equally, to retire to one or other of the *pays* of her families, and marry a farmer, a butcher, or a grazier. She acknowledged, for the matter of that, that she would probably not have raised more succulent *poulets au grain* or more full-bodied cider than came from the nest-boxes and the presses here and that she was leading no other life than that which she had always contemplated. Nor indeed would she have wanted any other henchman than Gunning who if you had given him a blue-blouse with stitchery and a *casquette* with a black leather peak would have passed for any peasant in Caen market.

He swung up the path, carrying gingerly a large blue bowl, just as if his blouse bellied out round him; he had the same expression of the mouth, the same intonation. It was nothing that she obstinately spoke French to him. On his subjects he could tell by intuition what her answers to his questions were and by now she understood him well enough.

He said that he had better take the 'ens off the nesteses fer fear they peck 'er 'ands and giving her the bowl, brought out from the shadows a protesting, ruffled and crooning hen before which he dropped a handful of bran paste and a lettuce leaf. He came out with another and another. Many more! Then he said she could go in and sprinkle the eggs. He said that it always bothered him to turn the eggs; his clumsy ol' 'ands bruk 'em 's often as not. He said:

"Wait whilst I brings out ol' mare. Bit o' grass wunt do'er much mischief."

The hens swollen to an enormous size paraded hostilely against one another about her feet; they clucked, crooned, pecked at lumps of paste, drank water eagerly from an iron dog-trough. With an exaggerated clatter of hoofs old mare emerged from the stable. She was aged nineteen, obstinate, bitter, very dark bay, extremely raw-boned. You might fill her with oats and mash five times a day, but she would not put on flesh. She emerged into the light from the door with the trot of a prima donna, for she knew she had once been a famous creature. The hens fled; she bit into the air showing immense teeth. Gunning opened the orchard gate, just at hand; she went out at a canter, checked, crumpled her knees together, fell on her side and rolled and rolled; her immense lean legs were incongruous, up in the air.

"Yes," Marie Léonie said, "pour moi-même je ne demanderais pas mieux!"

Gunning remarked:

"Don't show 'er age, do she? Gambolling like a five-day lamb!" His voice was full of pride, his grey face joyful. 'Is Lordship once sed thet ol' mare had orter be put in the 'Orse Show up to Lunnon. Some yeers ago that was!

She went into the dark, warm, odorous depths of the hen-house-stable shed; the horse-box being divided off from the hen half by wire netting, nest-boxes, blankets extended on use-poles. She had to bend down to get into the hen-half. The cracks of light between the uprights of the walls blinked at her. She carried the bowl of tepid water gingerly, and thrust her hand into the warm hay hollows. The eggs were fever-heat or thereabouts; she turned them and sprinkled in the tepid water; thirteen, fourteen, fourteen, eleven — that hen was a breaker! — and fifteen. She emptied out the tepid water and from other nests took out egg after egg. The acquisition gratified her.

In an upper box a hen brooded low. It crooned menacingly, then screamed with the voice of poultry disaster as her hand approached it. The sympathetic voices of other hens outside came to her,

screaming with poultry disaster — and other hens on the Common.
A rooster crowed.

She repeated to herself that she did not demand a better life than
this. But was it not the self-indulgence to be so contented? Ought she
not to be, still, taking steps for her future — near Falaise or Bayeux?
Did one not owe that to oneself? How long would this life last
here? And, still more, when it broke up, *how* would it break up?
What would *Ils* — the strange people — do to her, her savings, her
furs, trunks, pearls, turquoises, statuary, and newly gilt Second Empire chairs and clocks? When the Sovereign died what did the Heir,
his concubines, courtiers, and sycophants do to the Maintenon of
the day? What precautions ought she not to be taking against that
wrath to come? There must be French lawyers in London. . . .

Was it to be thought that *Il* — Christopher Tietjens, clumsy, apparently slow-witted, but actually gifted with the insight of the
supernatural . . . Gunning would say: The Captain, he never says
anything, but who knows what he thinks? He perceives everything.
. . . Was it to be thought then that, once Mark was dead and he
actual owner of the place called Groby and the vast stretch of coal-
bearing land that the newspaper had spoken of, Christopher Tietjens would maintain his benevolent and frugal dispositions of to-
day? It was truly thinkable. But, just as he appeared slow-witted and
was actually gifted with the insight of the supernatural, so he might
well now maintain this aspect of despising wealth and yet develop
into a true Harpagon as soon as he held the reins of power. The rich
are noted for hardness of heart, and brother will prey upon brother's
widow sooner than on another.

So that, certainly, she ought to put herself under the protection
of the Authorities. But then, what Authorities? The long arm of
France would no doubt protect one of her nationals even in this remote and uncivilised land. But would it be possible to put that machinery in motion without the knowledge of Mark — and what dreadful steps might Mark not take in his wrath if he thought that she had
set machinery in motion?

There appeared nothing for it but to wait, and that side of her
nature being indolent, perhaps being alone indolent, she was aware
that she was contented to wait. But was such a course right? Was
it doing justice to herself or to France? For it is the duty of the
French citizen, by industry, frugality, and vigilance to accumulate
goods; and it was above all the duty of the French citizen to carry

back accumulated hoards to that distressed country, stripped bare as she was by the perfidious Allies. She might herself rejoice in these circumstances, these grasses, orchards, poultry, cider-presses, vegetable-gardens — even if the turnips were not of the Paris *navet* variety! She might not ask for better. But there might be a little *pays*, near Falaise, or in the alternative, near Bayeux, a little spot that she might enrich with these spoils from the barbarians. If every inhabitant of a *pays* in France did the same would not France again be prosperous, with all its *clochers* tolling out contentment across smiling acres? Well, then!

Standing gazing at the poultry whilst Gunning with a hone smoothed out some notches from his bagging hook, previous to going on duty again, she began to reflect on the nature of Christopher Tietjens, for she desired to estimate what were her chances of retaining her furs, pearls and gilt articles of vertu. . . . By the orders of the doctor who attended daily on Mark — a dry, sandy, no doubt perfectly ignorant person — Mark was never to be left out of sight. He was of opinion, this doctor, that one day Mark might move — physically. And there might be great danger if ever he did move. The lesions, if there were in his brain, might then be re-started with fatal effects — some such talk. So they must never let him out of their sight. For the night they had an alarm that was connected by a wire from his bed to hers. Hers was in a room that gave onto the orchard. If he so much as stirred in his bed the bell would ring in her ear. But indeed she rose every night, over and over again to look from her window into his hut; a dim lantern illuminated his sheets. These arrangements appeared to her to be barbarous, but they met the views of Mark and she was thus in no position to question them. . . . So she had to wait whilst Gunning honed out his sickle-shaped, short-handled blade.

It had all then begun — all the calamities of the world began amidst the clamours and intoxications of that dreadful day. Of Christopher Tietjens till then she had known little or nothing. For the matter of that, of Mark himself she had known little or nothing until a very few years ago. She had known neither his name, nor how he occupied himself, nor yet where he lived. It had not been her business to enquire so she had never made enquiries. Then one day — after thirteen years — he had awakened one morning with an attack of bronchitis after a very wet Newmarket Craven Meeting.

He had told her to go to his office with a note addressed to his chief clerk, to ask for his letters and to tell them to send a messenger to his chambers to get some clothes and necessaries.

When she had told him that she did not know what his office was nor where were his chambers nor even his surname he had grunted. He had expressed neither surprise nor gratification, but she knew that he had been gratified — probably with himself for having chosen a woman companion who displayed no curiosity rather than with her for having displayed none. After that he had had a telephone installed in her rooms and not infrequently he would stay later of a morning than had been his habit, letting a messenger from the office bring letters or fetch documents that he had signed. When his father had died he had put her into mourning.

By that date, gradually, she had learned that he was Mark Tietjens of Groby, an immense estate somewhere in the North. He employed himself at an office of the Government in Whitehall — apparently with questions of railways. She gathered, chiefly from ejaculations of the messenger, that he treated his Ministry with contempt, but was regarded as so indispensable that he never lost his post. Occasionally the office would ring up and ask her if she knew where he was. She would gather from the papers afterwards that that was because there had been a great railway accident. On those occasions he would have been absent at a race-meeting. He gave the office, in fact, just as much of his time as he chose, no more and no less. She gathered that, with his overpowering wealth, it was of no account to him except as an occupation of leisure time between meetings and she gathered that he was regarded as an occult power amongst the rulers of the nation. Once, during the war when he had hurt his hand, he dictated to her a note of a confidential nature to one of the Cabinet Ministers. It had concerned itself with Transport and its tone had been that of singular polite contempt.

For her he was in no way astonishing. He was the English Milor with *le Spleen*. She had read of him in the novels of Alexander Dumas, Paul de Kock, Eugene Sue and Ponson du Terrail ·He represented the England that the Continent applauded — the only England that the Continent applauded. Silent, obstinate, inscrutable, insolent, but immensely wealthy and uncontrollably generous. For herself, *elle ne demandait pas mieux*. For there was about him nothing of the unexpected. He was as regular as the Westminster Chimes; he never exacted the unexpected of her and he was all-powerful and never in the wrong. He was, in short, what her countrywomen called *sérieux*. No Frenchwoman asks better than that of lover or husband. It was the *collage sérieux* par excellence: they were as a *ménage* sober, honest, frugal, industrious, very wealthy, and seriously saving. For his dinner twice a week she cooked him herself two mutton chops with all but an eighth of an inch of the fat pared off, two mealy potatoes, as light and as white as flour, an apple pie with a very flaky crust which he ate with a wedge of Stilton and some pulled bread and butter. This dinner had never varied once in twenty years except during the season of game when on alternate weeks a pheasant, a brace of grouse or of partridges would come from Groby. Nor in the twenty years had they once been separated for a whole week except that every late summer he spent a month at Harrogate. She always had his dress-shirts washed for him by her own laundress in the Quartier. He spent almost every week-end in one country house or another using at most two dress-shirts and that only if he stayed till Tuesday. English people of good class do not dress for dinner on Sundays. That is a politeness to God because theoretically you attend evening service and you do not go to church in the country in evening dress. As a matter of fact you never go to evening service — but it is complimentary to suggest by your dress that you might be visited by the impulse. So, at least Marie Léonie Tietjens understood the affair.

She was looking out on the Common that sloped up to beech trees, at the poultry — bright chestnut birds extremely busy on the intense green of the browsed grass. The great rooster reminded her of the late Monsieur Rodin, the sculptor who had conspired against Casimir-Bar. She had once seen Rodin in his studio, conducting some American ladies round his work and he had precisely resembled a rooster kicking its leg back and drooping its wings in the dust round a new hen. Only round a new one. Naturally! . . . This rooster was a tremendous Frenchman. *Un vrai de la vraie!* You could imagine nothing more unlike Christopher Tietjens! . . . The backward-raking legs on the dancing toes; the gait of a true master of deportment at an academy of young ladies! The vigilant clear eye cocking up every minute. . . . Hark! A swift shadow ran over the ground: the sparrow hawk! The loud, piercing croon of that Father of his Country! How the hens all re-echoed it; how the chickens ran to their mothers and all together to the shadow of the hedge! Monsieur the hawk would have no chance amidst that outcry. The hawk flits silent and detests noise. It will bring the poultry-keeper with his gun! . . . All is dis-

covered because of the vigilance of Milord Chantecler
are those who reprove him because his eyes are always
because he has a proud head. But that is his function — tha
lantry. Perceive him with a grain of corn; how he flies upon it
invites with cries! His favourite — the newest — hens run c
joyously to him! How he bows, droops and prances, holding the
of corn in his powerful bill, depositing it, pecking to bruise it
then depositing it before his sultana of the moment. Nor will he co
plain if a little ball of fluff runs quickly and pecks the grain from h
bill before Madame Partlet can take it from him. His gallantry has
been wasted, but he is a good father! . . . Perhaps there is not even
a grain of corn when he issues his invitations: perhaps he merely calls
his favourites to him that he may receive their praise or perform the
act of Love. . . .

He is then the man that a woman desires to have vouchsafed her.
When he smites his wing feathers behind his back and utters his
clarion cry of victory over the hawk that now glides far away down
the hill, his hens come out again from the shadows, the chickens
from beneath their mothers' wings. He has given security to his country and in confidence they can return to their avocations. Different
indeed from that Monsieur Christopher who even when he was still
a soldier more than anything resembled a full, grey, coarse meal-sack
short in the wind and with rolling, hard-blue eyes. Not hard eyes,
but of a hard blue! And yet, curiously, he too had some of the spirit
of Chantecler beneath his rolling shoulders of a farmyard boar. Obviously you could not be your brother's brother and not have some
traces of the Milor. . . . The spleen too. But no one could say that
her Mark was not a proper man. *Chic* in an eccentric manner, but,
oh yes, *chic*! And that was his brother.

Naturally he might try to despoil her. That is what brother does
to brother's widow and children. . . . But, on occasion, he treated
her with a pompous courtesy — a parade. On the first time he had
seen her — not so long ago that; only during that period of the war
that had been without measurable time — he had treated her to
heavy but expressive gestures of respect and words of courtesy in an
old-fashioned language that he must have learned at the Théatre
Français whilst they still played *Ruy Blas*. French was a different
thing now, that she must acknowledge. When she went to Paris —
which she did every late summer whilst her man went to Harrogate —
the language her nephews spoke was a different affair — without grace,

y. Certainly without respect! Oh, la, la! When
up her inheritance that would be a sharper kind
man ever Christopher Tietjens'! Whilst she lay on
ith those young fellows and their wives would be all
presses and armoires like a pack of wolves. . . . *La*
ell, that was very proper. It showed the appropriate spirit
ition. What was a good mother for if not to despoil her hus-
relatives in the interests of their joint children!

Christopher had been as courteous as a well-trained meal-sack
the *dix-huitième*. Eighteenth-century! Older still, *période Molière!*
When he had come into her room that had been dimly lit with a
veilleuse — a night-light; they are so much more economical than
shaded electric lights! — he had precisely suggested to her a lumbering character from Molière as presented at the Comédie Française;
elaborate of phrase and character, but protuberant in odd places.
She might in that case have supposed that he entertained designs on
her person; but with his eyes sticking out in elaborate considerateness
he had only come to break to her the news that his brother was about
to make an honest woman of her. That had been Mark's phrase. It is
of course only God that can do that. . . . But the enterprise had had
the full concurrence of Monsieur the Heir-Apparent.

He had indeed been active whilst she slumbered in a hooded-chair
after four days and three nights on her feet. She would have surrendered the body of Mark to no human being but his brother. Now
the brother had come to tell her not to be alarmed — panting with
nervousness and shortness of breath. . . . Bad lungs both the brothers had! Panting he had come to tell her not to be alarmed at finding
in her man's room two priests, an official, a lawyer and a lawyer's
clerk. . . . These black-robed people attend on death, bringing will-
forms and the holy oils. The doctor and a man with oxygen cylinders
had been there when she had gone to repose herself. It was a pretty
congregation of the vultures that attend on us during life.

She had started at once to cry out. That undoubtedly was what
had made him nervous — the anticipation that she would cry out
sharply in the black, silent London that brooded between air-raids. In
that silence, before sleep had visited her peignoir-enveloped, and
therefore clumsyish, form, she had been aware of Christopher's activities on the telephone in the passage. It had struck her that he might
have been warning the Pompes Funèbres! . . . So she had begun to
scream: the sound that irresistibly you make when death is about to

descend. But he had agitated himself to soothe her — for all the world like Monsieur Sylvain on the boards of Molière's establishment! He spoke that sort of French, in a hoarse whisper, in the shadows of the night-light . . . assuring her that the priest was for marriage, with license of the Archevêque de Cantorbéri such as in London you got in those days from Lambeth Palace for thirty pounds sterling. That enabled you to make any woman honest at any hour of the day or night. The lawyer was there to have a will re-signed. Marriage in this singular country invalidates any previous will. So, Tietjens (Christophère) assured her.

But then, if there was that haste there was danger of death! She had often speculated as to whether he would or would not marry her as an act of death-bed contrition. Rather contemptuously as great lords with *le Spleen* make their peace with God. She screamed; in silent, black London. The night-light wavered in its saucer.

He crepitated out that his brother was doubling, in this new will, his posthumous provision for her. With provision for the purchase of a house in France if she would not inhabit the Dower House at Groby. A Louis Treize dower-house. It was his idea of consolation. He affected to be business-like. . . . These English. But then, perhaps they do not go through your presses and wardrobes whilst your corpse is still warm!

She screamed out that they might take away their marriage papers and will-forms, but to give her her man again. If they had let her give him her *tisanes* instead of . . .

With her breast heaving she had cried into that man's face:

"I swear that my first act when I am Madame Tietjens and have the legal power will be to turn out all these men and give him infusions of poppy-heads and lime-flowers." She expected to see him recoil, but he had said:

"In heaven's name do, my dear sister. It might save him and the nation!"

It was silly of him to talk like that. These fellows had too much pride of family. Mark did no more than attend to Transport. Well, perhaps transport in those days had its importance. Still, probably Tietjens, Christopher, over-rated the indispensableness of Tietjens, Mark. . . . That would have been three weeks or a month before the Armistice. They were black days. . . . A good brother, though. . . .

In the other room, whilst papers were signing, after the *curé* in his *calotte* and all, had done reading from his book, Mark had signed to her to bend her head down to him and had kissed her. He whispered:

"Thank God there is one woman-Tietjens who is not a whore and a bitch!" He winced a little; her tears had fallen on his face. For the first time, she had said:

"Mon pauvre homme, ce qu'ils ont fait de toi!" She had been hurrying from the room when Christopher had stopped her. Mark had said:

"I regret to put you to further inconvenience . . ." in French. He had never spoken to her in French before. Marriage makes a difference. They speak to you with ceremony out of respect for themselves and their station in life. You also are at liberty to address them as your *pauvre homme*.

There had to be another ceremony. A man looking like a newly dressed gaol-bird stepped out with his book like an office register. With a blue-black jowl. He married them over again. A civil marriage, this time.

It was then that, for the first time, she had become aware of the existence of another woman-Tietjens, Christopher's wife. . . . She had not known that Christopher had a wife. Why was not she there? But Mark with his labouring politeness and chest had told her that he exaggerated the formality of the marriage because if both he and Christopher died she, Marie Léonie Tietjens, might have trouble with a certain Sylvia. The Bitch! . . . Well, she, Marie Léonie, was prepared to face her legitimate sister-in-law.

III

THE LITTLE maid, Beatrice, as well as Gunning, regarded Marie Léonie with paralysed but bewildered obedience. She was 'Er Ladyship, a good mark, a foreign Frenchy. That was bad. She was extraordinarily efficient about the house and garden and poultry-yard, a matter for mixed feelings. She was fair, not black-avised, a good mark; she was buxom, not skinny, like the real Quality. A bad mark because she was, then, not real Quality; but a qualifiedly good mark because if you 'as to 'ave Quality all about you in the 'ouse tis better not to 'ave real Quality. . . . But on the whole the general feeling was favourable because like themselves she was floridly blond. It made 'er 'uman like. Never you trust a dark woman and if you marries a dark man 'e will treat you bad. In the English countryside it is like that.

Cabinet-maker Cramp who was a remnant of the little dark persistent race that once had peopled Sussex regarded her with distrust that mingled with admiration for the quality of the varnish that she imported from Paris. Proper French polish that were. He lived in the cottage just across the path on the Common. 'E couldn' say as 'ow 'e liked the job the Governor give 'im. He had to patch up and polish with beeswax — not varnish — rough stuff such 's 'is granf'er 'ad 'ad. An 'ad got rid of. Rough ol' truck. Moren n 'undred yeers old. N' more!

He had to take bits of old wood out of one sort of old truck and fit it into missing bits of other old truck. Bought old Moley's pig-pound boards that had been Little Kingsworth church stalls, the Cahptn 'ad; n 'ad 'im, Cramp, use'm for all manner of patchin's up. The Captain had bought too ol' Miss' Cooper's rabbit 'utch. Beautifully bevelled the panels was too which cleaned up n beeswaxed. Cramp would acknowledge that. Made him match the bevelling in the timber from Kingsworth Church stalls for one of the missing doors, an' more of the timber fer the patching. Proper job, he, Cramp, had made of it too; he would say that. 'N it looked proper when it was finished — a long, low press, with six bevelled doors; beautiful purfling on the edges. Like some of the stuff 'Is Lordship 'ad in the Tujer Room at Fittleworth House. Moren n 'undred yeers old. Three undred. Four . . . There's no knowin.

'N no accountin' fer tastes. 'E would say 'e 'ad n eye — the Cahptn 'ad. Look at a bit of ol' rough truck the Cahptn would n see it was older than the Monument to Sir Richard Atchinson on Tadworth 'Ill that was set up in the year 1842 to celebrate the glorious victory of Free Trade. So the Monument said. Lug a bit of rough ol' truck out of the back of a cow-house where it had been throwed — the Cahptn would. And his, Cramp's, heart would sink to see the ol' mare come back, some days, the cart full of 'en-coops, n leaden pig-truffs, n pewter plates that 'ad been used to stop up 'oles in cow-byres.

'N off it would all go to Murrikay. Queer place Murrikay must be — full of the leavins of ol' England. Pig-troughs, hen-coops, rabbit-hutches, wash-house coppers that no one now had any use for. He loaded 'em when he'd scrubbed, and silver-sanded and beeswaxed-n-turpentined 'em, onto the ol' cart, n put to ol' mare, n down to station, n on to Southampton n off to New York. Must be a queer place yon! Hadn't they no cabinet-makers or ol' rough truck of ther own?

Well, it took all sorts to make a world n thank God fer that. He, Cramp, had a good job, likely to last 'im 'is lifetime because some folks wus queer in the 'ed. The ol' lumber went out yon and his, Cramp's missus, was gettin' together a proper set of goods. A tidy treat their sittin' room looked with aspidistras in mahogany tripods, 'n a Wilton carpet 'n bamboo cheers 'n mahogany whatnots. A proper woman Missus Cramp was, if sharp in the tongue.

Miss's Cramp she didn't give so much fer 'Er Ladyship. She was agin Foreigners. All German spies they wus. Have no truck with them she wouldn't. 'Oo noo if they wus 's much 's married. Some says they wus, some says they wasn'. But you couldn' take in Miss' Cramp . . . 'N Quality! What was to show that they were real Quality. Livin how they did wasn' Quality manners. Quality was stuck up 'n wore shiny clothes 'n had motor-cars 'n statues 'n palms 'n ball-rooms 'n conservatories. 'N didn' bottle off the cider 'n take the eggs 'n speak queer lingo to th' handy-man. 'N didn' sell the cheers they sat on. The four younger children also didn' like 'Er Ladyship. Never called 'em pretty dears she did nor give 'em sweeties nor rag-dolls nor apples. Smacked 'em if she found 'em in the orchard. Never so much s give 'em red flannel capes in the winter.

But Bill the eldest liked 'Er Ladyship. Called 'er a proper right 'un. Never stopped tarkin' of 'er. 'N *she* 'ad statues in 'er bedroom, 'n fine gilt cheers, 'n clocks, 'n flowerin plants. Bill e'd made fer 'Er Ladyship what she called 'n eightyjare. In three stories, to stand in a corner 'n hold knick-knacks. Out of fretwork to a pettern she'd give 'im. Varnished proper, too. A good piece of work if he shouldn't say so. . . . But Miss's Cramp she'd never been allowed in 'er Ladyship's bedroom. A proper place it was. Fit fer a Countess! If Miss's Cramp could be allowed to see it she'd maybe change her opinions. . . . But Miss's Cramp she said: "Never you trust a fair woman," bein' dark.

The matter of the cider however, did give him to think. Proper cider it was, when they was given a bottle or two. But it wasn't Sussex cider. A little like Devonshire cider, more like Herefordshire. But not the same as any. More head it had 'n was sweeter, 'n browner. 'N not to be drunk s' freely! Fair scoured you it did if you drunk's much's a quart!

The little settlement was advancing furtively to the hedge. Cramp put his bald poll out of his work-shed and then crept out. Mrs. Cramp, an untidy, dark, very thin woman emerged over her door-sill, wiping her hands on her apron. The four Cramp children at different stages of growth crept out of the empty pig-pound. Cramp was not going to buy his winter pigs till next fortnightly fair at Little Kingsworth. The Elliott children with the milk-can came at a snail's pace down the green path from the farm; Mrs. Elliott, an enormous woman with untidy hair, peered over her own hedge which formed a little enclosure on the Common; Young Hogben, the farmer's son, a man of forty, very thick-set, appeared on the path in the beech-wood, ostensibly driving a great black sow. Even Gunning left his brushing and lumbered to the edge of the stable. From there he could still see Mark in his bed, but also, looking downwards between the apple-trunks he could see Marie Léonie bottle the cider, large, florid and intent, in the open dairying-shed where water ran in a v-shaped wooden trough.

"Runnin' t' cider out of cask with a chube!" Mrs. Cramp screamed up the hill to Mrs. Elliott. "'Ooever 'eered!" Mrs. Elliott rumbled huskily back at Mrs. Cramp. All these figures closed in furtively; the children peering through tiny interstices in the hedge and muttering one to the other: "'Ooever 'eered. . . . Foreign ways I call it. . . . A glass chube . . . 'Ooever 'eered." Even Cramp, though, wiping his bald head with his carpenter's apron, he admonished Mrs. Cramp to remember that he had a good job — even Cramp descended from the path to the hedge-side and stood so close — peering over — that the thorns pricked his perspiring chest through his thin shirt. They said to the baker who wearily followed his weary horse up the steep path, coming from the deep woods below: It had ought to be stopped. The police had ought to know. Bottling cider by means of a glass tube. And standing the cider in running water. Where was the excise? Rotting honest folks guts! Poisoning them. No doubt the governor could tell them a tale about that if he could speak or move. The police had ought to know. . . . Showing off, with cider in running water — to cool it when first bottled! 'Ooever 'eered! Just because they 'ad a Ladyship to their tail. 'N more money than better folks. Not so much money either. Reckon they'd come to smash 'n be sold up like 'Igginson at Fittleworth. Set 'isself up fer Quality, 'e did too! . . . 'N not so much of a Ladyship, neither. Not so much more of a Ladyship as us if the truth was known. Not an Earl or a Lord, only a baronite-ess at that, supposin' we all 'ad our rights. . . . The police had ought to be brought into this affair!

A number of members of the Quality, on shining horses, their leathers creaking beautifully, rode at a walk up the path. They were the real Quality. A fine old gentleman, thin as a lath, clean face, hooky nose, white moustache, lovely cane, lovely leggings. On 'Is Lordship's favourite hack. A bay mare. A fine lady, slim as a boy, riding astride as they do to-day though they did not use to. But times change. On the Countess's own chestnut with white forehead. A bad-tempered horse. She must ride well, that lady. Another lady, grey-haired, but slim too, riding side-saddle in a funny sort of get-up. Long skirt with panniers and three-cornered hat like the ones you see in pictures of highwaymen in the new pub in Queens Norton. Sort of old-fashioned she looked. But no doubt it was the newest pattern. Things is so mixed up nowadays. 'Is Lordship's friends could afford to do as they pleased. A boy, eighteen, maybe. Shiny leggings too: all their clothes is shiny. Rides well, too, the boy. Look how his legs nip into Orlando — the chief whip's horse. Out for an airing. 'Is Lordship's groom of the stud only too glad if the horses can get exercise in hay-cutting time. The real Quality.

They reined in their horses a little further up the road, and sat staring down into the orchard. They had ought to be told what was going on down there. Puts white powder into the cider along o' the sugar. The Quality ought to be told. . . . But you do not speak to the Quality. Better if they do not notice you. You never know. They sticks together. Might be friends of Tietjenses for all you know. You don't *know* Tietjenses ain't Quality. Better git a move on or something might 'appen to you. You hear!

The boy in the shiny leggings and clothes — bareheaded he was, with shiny fair hair and shiny cheeks — exclaimed in a high voice:

"I say, mother, I don't like this spying!" And the horses started and jostled.

You see. They don't like this spying. Get a move on. And all that peasantry got a move on whilst the horses went slowly up hill. Queer things the Gentry can do to you still if they notice you. It is all very well to say this is a land fit for whatever the word is that stands for simple folk. But they have the police and the keepers in their hands, and your cottages and livings.

Gunning went out at the garden gate beside the stable and shouted objurgations at Young Hogben.

"Hey, don't you drive that sow. She's as much right on Common as you."

The great sow was obstinately preceding the squat figure of Young Hogben who hissed and squeaked behind her. She flapped her great ears and sniffed from side to side, a monument of black imperturbability.

"You keep your 'ogs out of our swedes!" Young Hogben shouted amidst objurgations. "In our forty acre she is all day 'n all night too!"

"You keep your swedes outen our 'ogs," Gunning shouted back swinging his gorilla arms like a semaphore. He advanced onto the Common. Young Hogben descended the slope.

"You fence your 'ogs in same's other folks 'as to do," Young Hogben menaced.

"Folks as abuts on Commons 'as to fence out, not fence in," Gunning menaced. They stood foot to foot on the soft sward menacing each other with their chins.

"'S Lordship sold Tietjens's to the Cahptn without Common rights," the farmer said. "Ask Mr. Fuller."

"'S Lordship could no more sell Tietjens's 'thout Common rights 'n you could sell milk without drinking rights. Ast Lawyer Sturgis!" Gunning maintained. Put arsenic in among 'is roots, Young Hogben maintained that he would. Spend seven years up to Lewes Jail if 'e did, Gunning maintained. They continued for long in the endless quarrel that obtains between tenant-farmer who is not Quality but used to brutalising his hinds, and gentleman's henchman who is used to popularity amongst his class and the peasantry. The only thing upon which they agreed was that you wouldn't think there 'adnt been no war. The war ought to have given tenant farmers the complete powers of local tyrants; it should have done the same for gentlemen's bailiffs. The sow grunted round Gunning's boots, looking up for grains of maize that Gunning usually dropped. In that way sows come to heel when you call them however far away they may be on the Common.

Down through the garden by the zig-zag path that dropped right away from the hard road up the hill — Tietjens's went up the slope to the hedge there — descended the elderly lady who was singularly attired in the eyes of the country people. She considered that she was descended, not by blood, but by moral affinity from Madame de Maintenon, therefore she wore a long grey riding skirt with panniers, and a three-cornered, grey felt hat and carried a riding switch of green shagreen. Her thin grey face was tired but authoritative, her hair which she wore in a knot beneath her hat was luminously grey, her pince-nez rimless.

Owing to the steepness of the bank on which the garden rose the path of sea-pebbles zigzagged across most of its width, orange-coloured because it had been lately sanded. She went furtively between quince-trunks, much like the hedge-sparrow, flitting a stretch and then stopping for the boy with the shining leggings stolidly to overtake her.

She said that it was dreadful to think that the sins of one's youth could so find one out. It ought to make her young companion think. To come at the end of one's life to inhabiting so remote a spot! You could not get there with automobiles. Her own Delarue-Schneider had broken down on the hill-road in the attempt to get there yesterday.

The boy, slim in the body, but heavy in the bright red cheeks, with brown hair, truly shiny leggings and a tie of green, scarlet and white stripes, had a temporarily glum expression. He said nevertheless with grumbling determination that he did not think this was playing the game. Moreover hundreds of motors got up that hill; how else would people come to buy the old furniture? He had already told Mrs. de Bray Pape that the carburettors of Delarue-Schneiders were a wash-out.

It was just that, Mrs. Pape maintained, that was so dreadful a thought. She went swiftly down another zigzag of the path and then faltered.

It was that that was dreadful in these old countries, she said. Why could they never learn? Take example! Here were the descendants of a great family, the Tietjenses of Groby, a haunt of ancient peace, the one reduced to a no doubt dreadful state by the sins of his youth, the other to making a living by selling old furniture.

The youth said she was mistaken. She must not believe all that his mother hinted to her. His mother was all right, but her hints went further than facts warranted. If he wanted to let Groby to Mrs. de Bray Pape it was because he hated swank. His uncle also hated swank. . . . He mumbled a little and added: "And . . . my father!" Moreover it was not playing the game. He had soft brown eyes that were now clouded and he was blushing.

He mumbled that mother was splendid but he did not think she ought to have sent him there. Naturally she had her wrongs. For himself he was a Marxist-Communist. All Cambridge was. He therefore, of course, approved of his father's living with whom he wished. But there were ways of doing things. Because you were advanced you did not have to treat women with discourtesy. The reverse, rather. He was painfully agitated by the time he overtook the tired lady at the corner of the next zigzag.

She wanted him not to misunderstand her. No discredit attached in her eyes to the pursuit of selling old furniture. Far from it. Mr. Lemuel of Madison Avenue might be called a dealer in old furniture. It was of course Oriental which made a difference. But Mr. Lemuel was a most cultivated man. His country house at Crugers in the State of New York was kept up in a style that would have done credit to the *grands seigneurs* of pre-Revolutionary France. But from that to this . . . what a downfall!

The house — the cottage — was by now nearly below her feet, the roof extremely high, the windows sunk very deep in grey stone and very small. There was a paved semi-circular court before the door, the space having been cut out of the orchard bank and walled with stones. It was extravagantly green, sunk in greenery and the grass that came nearly to Mrs. Pape's middle was filled with hiding profusions of flowers that were turning to seed. The four counties swept away from under her, hedges like string going away, enclosing fields, to the hills on the very distant horizon; the country near at hand wooded. The boy beside her took a deep breath as he always did when he saw a great view. On the moors above Groby, for instance. Purple they were.

"It *isn't* fit for human habitation!" the lady exclaimed with the triumphant intonation of one who sees · great truth confirmed. "The houses of the poor in these old countries beggar even pity. Do you suppose they so much as have a bath?"

"I should think my father and uncle were personally *clean!*" the boy said. He mumbled that this was supposed to be rather a show-place. He could trust his father indeed to find rather a show-place to live in. Look at the rock plants in the sunk garden! He exclaimed: "Look here! Let's go back!"

Mrs. Pape's perturbation gave way to obstinacy. She exclaimed.

"Never!" She had a mission from the poor boy's injured mother. She would never look Sylvia Tietjens in the face if she flinched. Sanitation went before anything. She hoped to leave the world a better place before she passed over. She had Authority conferred on

her. Metempsychosistically. She believed that the soul of Madame de
Maintenon, the companion of Louis the Fourteenth had passed into
her. How many convents had not the Maintenon set up and how
rigidly had she not looked after the virtue and the sanitation of the
inhabitants? That was what she, Mrs. Millicent de Bray Pape, looked
to. She had in the South of France — the Riviera — a palace, erected
by Mr. Behrens the celebrated architect — after the palace of the
Maintenon at Sans Souci. But sanitated! She asked the young man
to believe her. The boudoir appeared to be only a panelled boudoir:
very large because of the useless vanity of le Raw Solale. Madame
de Maintenon would have been content without such vanity. . . .
But only touch a spring in the panels and every sort of bathing
arrrangement presented itself to you hidden in the wall. Sunken
baths; baths above ground; douches with sea-water extra-iodised; lateral douches with and without bath-salts dissolved in the water.
That was what she called making the world a little better.

The boy mumbled that he was not in principle against the old
tree's coming down. He was indeed in principle against his uncle's
and his father's adoption of the peasant life. This was an industrial
age. The peasant had always spoilt every advance in the ideas of the
world. All the men at Cambridge were agreed as to that. He exclaimed:

"Hi! You can't do that. . . . Not go through standing *hay!*"

Every fibre of his country-boy landowner's soul was outraged as
he saw the long trail of satiny grey that followed Mrs. de Bray
Pape's long skirts. How were his father's men to cut hay that had
been trampled like that? But, unable to bear any longer the suspense of the spectacular advance towards Mark Tietjens along
those orange zigzags, Mrs. de Bray Pape was running straight down
the bank towards the unwalled, thatched hut. She could see it
through the tops of the apple tree.

The boy, desperately nervous, continued to descend the zigzag
paths that would take him into the very purlieus of his father's
house — onto the paved court where there were rock plants between
the interstices. His mother *ought* not to have forced him to accompany Mrs. de Bray Pape. His mother was splendid. Divinely beautiful; athletic as Atalanta or Betty Nuthall, in spite of her sufferings.
But she ought not to have sent Mrs. de Bray Pape. It was *meant* as a
sort of revenge. General Campion had not approved. He could see
that, though he had said: "My boy, you ought always to obey your

dear mother! She has suffered so much. It is your duty to make it up to her by fulfilling her slightest whim. An Englishman always does his duty to his mother!"

Of course it was the presence of Mrs. de Bray Pape that forced the General to say that. Patriotism. General Campion was deadly afraid of mother. Who wasn't? But he would hardly have enjoined upon a son to go and spy upon his father and his father's . . . companion if he had not wanted to show Mrs. de Bray Pape how superior English family ties were to those of her country. They ragged each other about that all day long.

And yet he did not know. The dominion of women over those of the opposite sex was a terrible thing. He had seen the old General whimper like a whipped dog and mumble in his poor white moustache. . . . Mother was splendid. But wasn't sex a terrible thing. . . . His breath came short.

He covered two foot of pebbles with the orange sand rolled into them. A tidy job it must be rolling on that slope! Still the actual gradient was not so steep on the zigzags. One in sixteen perhaps. He covered another two feet of pebbles with orange sand rolled in. How could he? How could he cover another two? His heels were trembling!

Four counties ran out below his feet. To the horizon! *He showed him the kingdoms of the earth.* As great a view as above Groby, but not purple and with no sea. Trust Father to settle where you could see a great view by going up hill. Vox *adhaesit.* . . . "His feet were rooted to the earth." . . . No, *vox adhaesit faucibus* meant that his voice stuck to his jaws. Palate rather. His palate was as dry as sawdust! How *could* he do it! . . . A terrible thing! They called it Sex! . . . His mother had coerced him into this dry palate and trembling heels by the force of her sex fever. Dreadful good-nights they had had in her boudoir, she forcing and forcing him with arguments to go. To come here. Beautiful Mother! . . . Cruel! Cruel!

The boudoir all lit up. Warm! Scented! Mother's shoulders! A portrait of Nell Gwynn by Sir Peter Lely. Mrs. de Bray Pape wanted to buy it. Thought she could buy the earth, but Lord Fittleworth only laughed. . . . How had they all got forced down there? By Mother. . . . To spy on Father. Mother had never taken much stock of Fittleworth — good fellow Fittleworth, good landlord! — till last winter when she had got to know that Father had bought this place. Then it was Fittleworth, Fittleworth, Fittleworth! Lunches, dinner, dances at the Ambassador's. Fittleworth wasn't saying no. Who could say no to Mother, with her figure in the saddle, and her hair?

If he had known when they came down to Fittleworth's last winter what he knew now! He knew now that his mother, come down for the hunting, though she had never taken much stock in hunting . . . Still, she could ride. Jove, she could ride. He had gone queer all over again and again at first in taking those leaps that she took laughing. Diana, that's what she was. . . . Well, no, Diana was . . . His mother, come down for the hunting was there to torment Father and his . . . companion. She had told him. Laughing in that way she had. . . . It must be sex cruelty! . . . Laughing like those Leonardi-do-da . . . Well, Vinci women. A queer laugh, ending with a crooked smile. . . . In corresponding with Father's servants. . . . Dressing up as a housemaid and looking over the hedge.

How *could* she do it? *How?* How could she force him to be here? What would Monty, the Prime Minister's son, Dobles, Porter — fat ass because his father was too beastly rich! — what would his set think at Cambridge. They were all Marxist-Communists to a man. But still . . .

What would Mrs. Lowther think if she *really* knew. . . . If she could have been in the corridor one night when he came out from his mother's boudoir! He would have had the courage to ask her then. Her hair was like floss silk, her lips like cut pomegranates. When she laughed she threw up her head. . . . He was now warm all over, his eyes wet and warm.

When he had asked if he ought to — if *she* wanted him to — do whatever his mother wanted whether or no he approved. . . . If his mother asked him to do what he thought was a mean action. . . . But that had been on the Peacock Terrace with the famous Fittleworth Seven Sister Roses. . . . How she went against the roses! . . . In a yellow . . . No, moth-coloured . . . Not yellow, not yellow. Green's forsaken, but yellow's forsworn. Great pity filled him at the thought that Mrs. Lowther might be forsaken. But she must not be forsworn . . . moth-coloured silk. Shimmering. Against pink roses. Her fine, fine hair, a halo. She had looked up and sideways. She had been going to laugh with her lips like cut pomegranates. . . . She had told him that as a rule it was a good thing to do what one's mother wanted when she was like Mrs. Christopher Tietjens. Her soft voice . . . Soft Southern voice . . . Oh, when she laughed at Mrs. de Bray Pape. . . . How could she be a friend of Mrs. de Bray Pape's? . . .

If it hadn't been sunlight. . . . If he had come on Mrs. Lowther as he came out of his mother's boudoir. He would have had courage. At night. Late. He would have said: "If you are really interested in my fate tell me if I ought to spy upon my father and his . . . companion!" She would not have laughed, late at night. She would have given him her hand. The loveliest hands and the lightest feet. And her eyes would have dimmed. . . . Lovely, lovely pansies! Pansies are heartsease. . . .

Why did he have these thoughts: these wafts of intolerable . . . oh, desire! He was his mother's son. . . . His mother was . . . He would kill anyone who said it. . . .

Thank God! Oh thank God! He was down on the crazy paving level with the house. AND *there was another path went up to Uncle's Mark's shed.* The Blessed Virgin — who was like Helen Lowther! — had watched over him. He had not to walk under those little deep, small-paned windows.

His father's . . . companion might have been looking out. He would have fainted. . . .

His father was a good sort of man. But he too must be . . . like Mother. If what they said was true. Ruined by dissolute living. But a good, grey man. The sort of man to be tormented by Mother. Great spatulate fingers. But no one had ever tied flies like Father. Some he had tied years ago were the best he, Mark Tietjens junior of Groby, had yet. And Father loved the wine-coloured moor. *How* could he stifle under these boughs! A house overhung by trees is unsanitary. They all say that . . .

But what a lovely glimpse under the trees. Sweet-williams along the path. Light filtered by boughs. Shadow. Gleams in the little window-panes. Wallstones all lichen. That's England. If he could spend a while here with Father . . .

Father had been matchless with horses. Women too. . . . What an inheritance was his, Mark Tietjens, junior's! If he could spend a while here. . . . But his Father slept with . . . If she came out of the door . . . She must be beautiful. . . . No they said she was not a patch on Mother. He had overheard that at Fittleworth's. Or Helen Lowther. . . . But his father had had his pick! . . . If he chose then to sleep with . . .

If she came out of the door he would faint. . . . Like the Venus

of Botti. . . . A crooked smile . . . No, Helen Lowther would protect. . . . He might fall in love with his father's . . . What do you
know of what will happen to you when you come in contact with the
Bad Woman . . . of advanced views . . . They said she was of
Advanced Views. And a Latinist. . . . He was a Latinist. Loved it!

Or his father might with Hel . . . Hot jealousy filled. His father
was the sort of man . . . She might . . . Why did over- . . . people like Mother and Father beget children?

He kept his eyes fascinatedly fixed on the stone porch of the cottage whilst he stumbled up the great stone slabs to the path. The
path led to Uncle Mark's wall-less thatched hut. . . . No form
filled the porch. What was to become of him? He had great wealth;
terrific temptation would be his. His mother was no guide. His
father might have been better. . . . Well, there was Marxian-Com-
munism. They all looked to that now, in his set at Cambridge.
Monty, the Prime Minister's son with black eyes; Dobles, Campion's
nephew, lean as a rat; Porter, with a pig's snout, but witty as hell.
Fat ass!

IV

MARK TIETJENS thought that a cow or a hog must have got into
the orchard there was such a rushing in the grass. He said to himself
that that damn Gunning was always boasting about his prowess as a
hedger; he might see that his confounded hedges kept out the beasts
from the Common. An unusual voice — unusual in its intonation —
remarked:

"Oh, Sir Mark Tietjens, this is dreadful!"

It appeared to be dreadful. A lady in a long skirt — an apparently
elderly Di Vernon out of *Waverley* which was one of the few novels
Mark had read — was making dreadful havoc with the standing grass.
The beautiful, proud heads swayed and went down as she rushed,
knee-deep amongst it; stopped, rushed again across his view and
then stopped apparently to wring her hands and once more explain
that it was dreadful. A tiny rabbit, scared out by her approach, scut-
tered out under his bed and presumably down into the vegetables.
Marie Léonie's Mistigris would probably get it and, since it was
Friday, Marie Léonie would be perturbed.

The lady pushed through the remaining tall grass that stood be-

tween them, and had the air of rising up at his bed-foot. She was
rather a faint figure — like the hedge-sparrow. In grey, with a grey
short coat and a waistcoat with small round buttons and a three-
cornered hat. A tired, thin face. . . . Well, she must be tired, pushing through that long grass with a long skirt. She had a switch of
green shagreen. The hen tomtit that lived in the old shoe they had
tucked on purpose under his thatch uttered long warning cries. The
hen tomtit did not like the aspect of this apparition.

She was devouring his face with her not disagreeable eyes and
muttering:

"Dreadful! Dreadful!" An aeroplane was passing close overhead.

She looked up and remarked almost tearfully:

"Hasn't it struck you that but for the sins of your youth you might
be doing stunts round these good-looking hills? Now!"

Mark considered the matter, fixedly returning her glance. For an
Englishman the phrase "the sins of your youth" as applied to a
gentleman's physical immobility implies only one thing. It never had
occurred to him that that implication might be tacked on to him.
But of course it might. It was an implication of a disagreeable, or
at least a discrediting, kind because, in his class they had been accustomed to consider that the disease was incurred by consorting
with public women of a cheap kind. He had never consorted with
any woman in his life but Marie Léonie who was health exaggerated.
But if he had had to do with women he would have gone in for
the most expensive sort. And taken precautions! A gentleman owes
that to his fellows!

The lady was continuing:

"I may as well tell you at once that I am Mrs. Millicent de Bray
Pape. And hasn't it struck you that but for *his* depravity — un-
bridled depravity — your brother might to-day be operating in Capel
Court instead of peddling old furniture at the end of the world?"

She added disconcertingly:

"It's nervousness that makes me talk like this. I have always been
shy in the presence of notorious libertines. That is my education."

Her name conveyed to him that this lady was going to occupy
Groby. He saw no objection to it. She had indeed written to ask
him if he saw any objection to it. It had been a queerly written
letter, in hieroglyphs of a straggling and convoluted kind. . . . "I
am the lady who is going to rent your mansion Groby from my friend
Mrs. Sylvia."

It had struck him then — whilst Valentine had been holding the letter up for him to read . . . pretty piece, Valentine, nowadays; the country air suited her — that this woman must be an intimate friend of his brother's wife Sylvia. Otherwise she would have said "Mrs. Sylvia Tietjens" at least.

Now he was not so certain. This was not the sort of person to be an intimate friend of that bitch's. Then she was a catspaw. Sylvia's intimates — amongst women — were all Bibbies and Jimmies and Marjies. If she spoke to any other woman it was to make use of her — as a lady's-maid or a tool.

The lady said:

"It must be agony to you to be reduced to letting your ancestral home. But that does not seem to be a reason for not speaking to me. I meant to ask the Earl's housekeeper for some eggs for you, but I forgot. I am always forgetting. I am so active. Mr. de Bray Pape says I am the most active woman from here to Santa Fé."

Mark wondered: why Santa Fé? That was probably because Mr. Pape had olive-tree plantations in that part of the United States. Valentine had told him over the letter that Mr. Pape was the largest olive-oil merchant in the world. He cornered all the olive-oil and all the straw-covered flasks in Provence, Lombardy, California, and informed his country that you were not really refined if you used in your salads oil that did not come out of a Pape Quality flask. He showed ladies and gentlemen in evening dress starting back from expensively laid dinner tables, holding their noses and exclaiming "Have you no *Pape's*!" Mark wondered where Christopher got his knowledge, for naturally Valentine had the information from him. Probably Christopher had looked at American papers. But why should one look at American papers? Mark himself never had. Wasn't there the *Field*? . . . He was a queer chap, Christopher.

The lady said:

"It *isn't* a reason for not speaking to me! It isn't!"

Her greyish face flushed slowly. Her eyes glittered behind her rimless pince-nez. She exclaimed:

"You are probably too haughtily aristocratic to speak to me, Sir Mark Tietjens. But I have in me the soul of the Maintenon; you are only the fleshly descendant of a line of chartered libertines. That is what Time and the New World have done to redress the balance of the old. It is we who are keeping up the status of the *grands seigneurs* of old in your so-called ancestral homes."

He thought she was probably right. Not a bad sort of woman: she would naturally be irritated at his not answering her. It was proper enough.

He never remembered to have spoken to an American or to have thought about America. Except of course during the war. Then he had spoken to Americans in uniform about Transport. He hadn't liked their collars, but they had known their jobs as far as their jobs went — which had been asking to be provided with a disproportionate amount of transport for too few troops. He had had to wring that transport out of the country.

If he had had his way he wouldn't have. But he hadn't had his way because the Governing Classes were no good. Transport is the soul of a war: the spirit of an army had used to be in its feet, Napoleon had said. Something like that. But those fellows had starved the army of transport; then flooded it with so much it couldn't move; then starved it again. Then they had insisted on his finding enormously too much transport for those other fellows who used it for disposing of smuggled typewriters and sewing machines that came over on transports. . . . It had broken his back, that and solitude. There had not been a fellow he could talk to in the Government towards the end. Not one who knew the difference between the ancestry of Persimmon and the stud form of Sceptre or Isinglass. Now they were paying for it.

The lady was saying to him that her spiritual affinity was probably a surprise to Sir Mark. There was none the less no mistake about it. In every one of the Maintenon's houses she felt instantly at home; the sight in any Museum of any knick-knack or jewel that had belonged to the respectable companion of Louis Quatorze startled her as if with an electric shock. Mr. Quarternine, the celebrated upholder of the metempsychosistic school had told her that those phenomena proved beyond doubt that the soul of the Maintenon had returned to earth in her body. What, as against that, were the mere fleshly claims of Old Family?

Mark considered that she was probably right. The old families of his country were a pretty inefficient lot that he was thankful to have done with. Racing was mostly carried on by English nobles from Frankfort-on-the-Main. If this lady could be regarded as speaking allegorically she was probably right. And she had had to get a soul from somewhere.

But she talked too much about it. People ought not to be so tre-

mendously fluent. It was tiring; it failed to hold the attention. She
was going on.

He lost himself in speculations as to her reason for being there,
trampling on his brother's grass. It would give Gunning and the
extra hands no end of an unnecessary job to cut. The lady was talking about Marie Antoinette. Marie Antoinette had gone sledging on
salt in summer. Trampling down haygrass was really worse. Or no
better. If everyone in the country trampled on grass like that it would
put up the price of fodder for transport animals to something pro-
hibitive.

Why had she come there? She wanted to take Groby furnished.
She might for him. He had never cared about Groby. His father had
never had a stud worth talking about. A selling plater or two. He
himself had never cared for hunting or shooting. He remembered
standing on Groby lawn watching the shooting parties take to the
hills on the Twelfth and feeling rather a fool. Christopher, of course,
loved Groby. He was younger and hadn't expected to own it.

A pretty muck Sylvia might have made of the place by now — if
her mother had let her. Well, they would know pretty soon. Christopher would be back, if the machine did not break his obstinate
neck. . . . What, then, was this woman doing here? She probably
represented a new turn of the screw that that unspeakable woman
was administering to Christopher.

His sister-in-law Sylvia represented for him unceasing, unsleeping
activities of a fantastic kind. She wanted, he presumed, his brother
to go back and sleep with her. So much hatred could have no other
motive. . . . There could be no other motive for sending this American lady here.

The American lady was telling him that she intended to keep up at
Groby a semi-regal state — of course with due domestic modesty.
Apparently she saw her way to squaring that circle! . . . Probably
there are ways. There must be quite a lot of deucedly rich fellows
in that country! How did they reconcile doing themselves well with
democracy? Did their valets sit down to meals with them, for instance? That would be bad for discipline. But perhaps they did not
care about discipline. There was no knowing.

Mrs. de Bray Pape apparently approved of having footmen in
powder and the children of the tenants kneeling down when she
drove out in his father's coach and six. Because she intended to use

his father's coach and six when she drove over the moors to Red-car or Scarboro'. That, Mrs. de Bray Pape had been told by Sylvia, was what his father had done. And it was true enough. That queer old josser, his father, had always had out that monstrosity when he went justicing or to the Assizes. That was to keep up his state. He didn't see why Mrs. de Bray Pape shouldn't keep up hers if she wanted to. But he did not see the tenant's children kneeling to the lady! Imagine old Scot's children at it or Long Tom o' th' Clough's; . . . Their grandchildren of course. They had called his father "Tietjens" — some of them even "Auld Mark!" to his face. He him-self had always been "Young Mark" to them. Very likely he was still. These things do not change any more than the heather on the moors. He wondered what the tenants would call her. She would have a tough time of it. They weren't her tenants; they were his and they jolly well knew it. These fellows who took houses and castles furnished thought they jolly well hired descent from the family. There had been before the war a fellow from Frankfort-on-the-Main took Lindisfarne or Holy Island or some such place and hired a bagpiper to play round the table while they ate. And closed his eyes whilst the fellow played reels. As if it had been a holy occasion. . . . Friend of Sylvia's friends in the Government. To do her credit she would not stop with Jews. The only credit she had to her tail!

Mrs. de Bray Pape was telling him that it was not undemocratic to have your tenants' children kneel down when you passed.

A boy's voice said:

"Uncle Mark!" Who the devil could that be? Probably the son of the people he had week-ended with. Bowlby's maybe; or Teddy Hope's. He had always liked children and they liked him.

Mrs. de Bray Pape was saying that, yes, it was good for the tenants' children. The Rev. Dr. Slocombe, the distinguished educationalist, said that these touching old rites should be preserved in the in-terests of the young. He said that to see the Prince of Wales at the Coronation kneeling before his father and swearing fealty had been most touching. And she had seen pictures of the Maintenon having it done when she walked out. *She* was now the Maintenon, there-fore it must be right. But for Marie Antoinette . . .

The boy's voice said:

"I hope you will excuse . . . I *know* it isn't the thing . . ."

He couldn't see the boy without turning his head on the pillow

and he was not going to turn his head. He had a sense of someone
a yard or so away at his off-shoulder. The boy at least had not come
through the standing hay.

He did not imagine that the son of anyone he had ever week-
ended with would ever walk through standing hay. The young generation were a pretty useless lot, but he could hardly believe they
would have come to that yet. Their sons might. . . . He saw visions
of tall dining-rooms lit up, with tall pictures, and dresses, and the
sunset through high windows over tall grasses in the parks. He was
done with that. If any tenants' children ever knelt to him it would
be when he took his ride in his wooden coat to the little church
over the moors. . . . Where his father had shot himself.

That had been a queer go. He remembered getting the news. He
had been dining, at Marie Léonie's. . . .

The boy's voice was, precisely, apologising for the fact that that
lady had walked through the grass. At the same time Mrs. de Bray
Pape was saying things to the discredit of Marie Antoinette whom
apparently she disliked. He could not imagine why anyone should
dislike Marie Antoinette. Yet very likely she was dislikable. The
French who were sensible people had cut her head off, so *they* presumably disliked her. . . .

He had been dining at Marie Léonie's, she standing, her hands
folded before her, hanging down, watching him eat his mutton chops
and boiled potatoes when the porter from his Club had phoned
through that there was a wire for him. Marie Léonie had answered
the telephone. He had told her to tell the porter to open the telegram and read it to her. That was a not unusual proceeding. Tele-
grams that came to him at the Club usually announced the results
of races that he had not attended. He hated to get up from the
dinner-table. She had come back slowly and said still more slowly
that she had bad news for him; there had been an accident; his father
had been found shot dead.

He had sat still for quite a time; Marie Léonie also had said nothing. He remembered that he had finished his chops, but had not
eaten his apple-pie. He had finished his claret.

By that time he had come to the conclusion that his father had
probably committed suicide and that he — he, Mark Tietjens — was
probably responsible for his father's having done that. He had got
up, then, told Marie Léonie to get herself some mourning and had
taken the night train to Groby. There had been no doubt about it

when he got there. His father had committed suicide. His father was not the man, unadvisedly, to crawl through a quicken-hedge with his gun at full-cock behind him, after rabbits. . . . It had been proposed.

There was, then, something soft about the Tietjens' stock — for there had been no real and sufficient cause for the suicide. Obviously his father had had griefs. He had never got over the death of his second wife: that was soft for a Yorkshireman. He had lost two sons and an only daughter in the war: other men had done that and got over it. He had heard through him, Mark, that his youngest son — Christopher — was a bad hat. But plenty of men had sons who were bad hats. . . . Something soft then about the stock! Christopher certainly was soft. But that came from the mother. Mark's step-mother had been from the south of Yorkshire. Soft people down there; a soft woman. Christopher had been her ewe lamb and she had died of grief when Sylvia had run away from him! . . .

The boy with a voice had got himself into view towards the bottom of the bed, near Mrs. de Bray Pape. . . . A tallish slip of a boy, with slightly chawbacony cheeks, high-coloured, lightish hair, brown eyes. Upstanding, but softish. Mark seemed to know him, but could not place him. He asked to be forgiven for the intrusion, saying that he knew it was not the thing.

Mrs. de Bray Pape was talking improbably about Marie Antoinette, whom she very decidedly disliked. She said that Marie Antoinette had behaved with great ingratitude to Madame de Maintenon — which must have been difficult. Apparently, according to Mrs. de Bray Pape, when Marie Antoinette had been a neglected little girl about the Court of France Madame de Maintenon had befriended her, lending her frocks, jewels, and perfumes. Later Marie Antoinette had persecuted her benefactor. From that had arisen all the woes of France and the Old World in general.

That appeared to Mark to be to mix history. Surely the Maintenon was a hundred years before the other. But he was not very certain. Mrs. de Bray Pape said, however, that she had those little-known facts from Mr. Regibald Weiler, the celebrated professor of social economy at one of the Western universities.

Mark returned to the consideration of the softness of the Tietjens stock whilst the boy gazed at him with eyes that might have been imploring or that might have been merely moonstruck. Mark could not see what the boy could have to be imploring about, so it was

probably just stupidity. His breeches, however, were very nicely cut.
Very nicely indeed. Mark recognised the tailor — a man in Conduit
Street. If that fellow had the sense to get his riding breeches from
that man he could not be quite an ass. . . .

That Christopher was soft because his mother did not come from
the north of Yorkshire or Durham might be true enough — but that
was not enough to account for the race dying out. His, Mark's, father
had no descendants by his sons. The two brothers who had been
killed had been childless. He himself had none. Christopher. . . .
Well, that was debatable!

That he, Mark, had practically killed his own father he was ready
to acknowledge. One made mistakes: that was one. If one made
mistakes one should try to repair them, otherwise one must, as it
were, cut one's losses. He could not bring his father back to life; he
hadn't, equally, been able to do anything for Christopher. . . . Not
much, certainly. The fellow had refused his brass. . . . He couldn't
really blame him.

The boy was asking him if he would not speak to them. He said
he was Mark's nephew, Mark Tietjens, junior.

Mark took credit to himself because he did not stir a hair. He
had so made up his mind, he found, that Christopher's son was
not his son that he had almost forgotten the cub's existence. But
he ought not to have made up his mind so quickly: he was astonished to find from the automatic working of his brain that he so
had. There were too many factors to be considered that he had
never bothered really to consider. Christopher had determined that
this boy should have Groby: that had been enough for him, Mark.
He did not much care who had Groby.

But the actual sight of this lad whom he had never seen before,
presented the problem to him as something that needed solution.
It came as a challenge. When he came to think of it, it was a challenge to him to make up his mind finally as to the nature of Woman.
He imagined that he had never bothered his head about that branch
of the animal kingdom. But he found that, lying there, he must
have spent quite a disproportionate amount of his time in thinking
about the motives of Sylvia.

He had never spoken much with any but men — and then mostly
with men of his own class and type. Naturally you addressed a few
polite words to your week-end hostess. If you found yourself in the
rose-garden of a Sunday before church with a young or old woman

who knew anything about horses, you talked about horses or Goodwood or Ascot to her for long enough to show politeness to your hostess's guests. If she knew nothing about horses you talked about the roses or the irises or the weather last week. But that pretty well exhausted it.

Nevertheless he knew all about women; of that he was confident. That is to say that, when in the course of conversation or gossip he had heard the actions of women narrated or commented on, he had always been able to supply a motive for those actions sufficient to account for them to his satisfaction or to let him predict with accuracy what course the future would take. No doubt twenty years of listening to the almost ceaseless but never disagreeable conversation of Marie Léonie had been a liberal education.

He regarded his association with her with complete satisfaction — as the only subject for complete satisfaction to be found in the contemplation of the Tietjens family. Christopher's Valentine was a pretty piece enough and had her head screwed confoundedly well on. But Christopher's association with her had brought such a peck of troubles down on his head that, except for the girl as an individual, it was a pretty poor choice. It was a man's job to pick a woman who would neither worry him nor be the cause of worries. Well, Christopher had picked two — and look at the results!

He, himself, had been completely unmistaken — from the beginning. He had first seen Marie Léonie on the stage of Covent Garden. He had gone to Covent Garden in attendance on his step-mother, his father's second wife — the soft woman. A florid, gentle, really saintly person. She had passed around Groby for a saint. An Anglican saint, of course. That was what was the matter with Christopher. It was the soft streak. A Tietjens had no business with saintliness in his composition! It was bound to get him looked on as a blackguard!

But he had attended Covent Garden as a politeness to his step-mother who very seldom found herself in Town. And there, in the second row of the ballet he had seen Marie Léonie — slimmer of course in those days. He had at once made up his mind to take up with her and, an obliging commissionaire having obtained her address for him from the stage-door he had, towards twelve-thirty, walked along the Edgeware Road towards her lodgings. He had intended to call on her; he met her, however, in the street. Seeing her there he had liked her walk, her figure, her neat dress.

He had planted himself, his umbrella, his billycock hat and all, squarely in front of her — she had neither flinched nor attempted to bolt round him! — and had said that, if at the end of her engagement in London, she cared to be placed "*dans ses draps*," with two hundred and fifty pounds a year and pin money to be deliberated on, she might hang up her cream-jug at an apartment that he would take for her in St. John's Wood Park which was the place in which in those days most of his friends had establishments. She had preferred the neighbourhood of the Gray's Inn road as reminding her more of France.

But Sylvia was quite another pair of shoes. . . .

That young man was flushing all over his face. The young of the tomtit in the old shoe were getting impatient; they were chirruping in spite of the alarm-cries of the mother on the boughs above the thatch. It was certainly insanitary to have boughs above your thatch, but what did it matter in days so degenerate that even the young of tomtits could not restrain their chirpings in face of their appetites.

That young man — Sylvia's by-blow — was addressing embarrassed remarks to Mrs. de Bray Pape. He suggested that perhaps his uncle resented the lady's lectures on history and sociology. He said they had come to talk about the tree. Perhaps that was why his uncle would not speak to them.

The lady said that it was precisely giving lessons in history to the dissolute aristocracy of the Old World that was her mission in life. It was for their good, resent it how they might. As for talking about the tree, the young man had better do it for himself. She now intended to walk around the garden to see how the poor lived.

The boy said that in that case he did not see why Mrs. de Bray Pape had come at all. The lady answered that she had come at the sacred behest of his injured mother. That ought to be answer enough for him. She flitted, disturbedly, from Mark's view.

The boy, swallowing visibly in his throat, fixed his slightly protruding eyes on his uncle's face. He was about to speak, but he remained for a long time, silent and goggling. That was a Christopher Tietjens trick — not a Tietjens family trick. To gaze at you a long time before speaking. Christopher had it, no doubt, from his mother — exaggeratedly. She would gaze at you for a long time. Not unpleasantly of course. But Christopher had always irritated him, even as a small boy. . . . It is possible that he, Mark, himself, might not be as he was if Christopher hadn't gazed at him for a long time, like a, stuck pig. On the morning of that beastly day. Armistice Day. . . . Beastly.

Cramp's eldest son, a bugler in the second Hampshires, went down the path, his bugle shining behind his khaki figure. Now they would make a beastly row with that instrument. On Armistice Day they had played the Last Post on the steps of the church under Marie Léonie's windows. . . . The Last Post! . . . The Last of England! He remembered thinking that. He had not by then had the full terms of that surrender, but he had had a dose enough of Christopher's stuck-piggedness! . . . A full dose! He didn't say he didn't deserve it. If you make mistakes you must take what you get for it. You shouldn't make mistakes.

The boy at the foot of the bed was making agonised motions with his throat: swallowing at his Adam's apple.

He said:

"I can understand, uncle, that you hate to see us. All the same it seems a little severe to refuse to speak to us!"

Mark wondered a little at the breakdown in communications that there must have been. Sylvia had been spying round that property and round and round and round again. She had had renewed interviews with Mrs. Cramp. It had struck him as curious taste to like to reveal to dependents — to reveal and to dwell upon, the fact that you were distasteful to your husband. If his woman had left him he would have preferred to hold his tongue about it. He certainly would not have gone caterwauling about it to the carpenter of the man she had taken up with. Still, there was no accounting for tastes. Sylvia had, no doubt, been so full of her own griefs that she, very likely had not listened to what Mrs. Cramp had said about his, Mark's, condition. During the one or two interviews he had had years ago with that bitch she had been like that. She had sailed in with her grievances against Christopher with such vigour that she had gone away with no ideas at all as to the conditions on which she was to be allowed to inhabit Groby. Obviously it taxed her mind to invent what she invented. You could not invent that sort of sex-cruelty stuff without having your mind a little affected. She could not, for instance, have invented the tale that he, Mark, was suffering for the sins of his youth without its taking it out of her. That is the ultimate retribution of Providence on those who invent gossip frequently. They go a little dotty. . . . The fellow — he could not call his name to mind, half Scotch, half Jew — who had told him the worst tales against Christopher, had gone a little dotty. He had grown a beard and wore a top-hat at inappropriate functions. Well, in effect, Christopher was a saint and Provvy invents retributions of an ingenious kind against those who libel saints.

At any rate that bitch must have become so engrossed in her tale that it had not come through to her that he, Mark, could not speak. Of course the results of venereal disease are not pleasant to contemplate and no doubt Sylvia having invented the disease for him had not liked to contemplate the resultant symptoms. At any rate that boy did not know — and neither did Mrs. de Bray Pape — that he did not speak; not to them, not to anybody. He was finished with the world. He perceived the trend of its actions, listened to its aspirations and even to its prayers, but he would never again stir lip or finger. It was like being dead — or being a God. This boy was apparently asking for absolution. He was of opinion that it was not a very sporting thing of himself and Mrs. Bray to come there. . . . It was however sporting enough. He could see that they were both as afraid of him, Mark, as of the very devil. Its taste might, however, be questioned. Still, the situation was unusual — as all situations are.

Obviously it was not in good taste for a boy to come to the house in which his father lived with a mistress, nor for the wife's intimate friend either. Still they apparently wanted, the one to let, the other to take, Groby. They could not do either if he, Mark, did not give permission, or at any rate if he opposed them. It was business, and business may be presumed to cover quite a lot of bad taste.

And in effect the boy was saying that his mother was, of course, a splendid person but that he, Mark junior, found her proceedings in many respects questionable. One could not however expect a woman — and an injured woman . . . The boy with his shining eyes and bright cheeks seemed to beg Mark to concede that his mother was at least an injured woman. . . . One could not expect, then, a wronged woman to see things eye to eye with . . . with young Cambridge! For, he hastened to assure Mark, his Set — the son of the Prime Minister, young Doble, and Porter, as well as himself, were unanimously of opinion that a man ought to be allowed to live with whom he liked. He was not therefore questioning his father's actions and, for himself, if the occasion arose, he would be very glad to shake his father's . . . companion . . . by the hand.

His bright eyes became a little humid. He said that he was not in effect questioning anything, but he thought that he, himself, would have been the better for a little more of his father's influence. He considered that he had been too much under his mother's influence. They noticed it, even at Cambridge! That, in effect, was the real snag when it came to be a question of dissolving unions once contracted. Scientifically considered. Questions of . . . of sex-attraction, in spite of all the efforts of scientists, remained fairly mysterious. The best way to look at it . . . the safest way, was that sex attraction occurred as a rule between temperamental and physical opposites because Nature desired to correct extremes. No one in fact could be more different than his father and mother — the one so graceful, athletic and . . . oh, charming. And the other so . . . oh, let us say perfectly honourable but lawless. Because, of course, you can break certain laws and remain the soul of honour.

Mark wondered if this boy was aware that his mother habitually informed everyone whom she met that his father lived on women. On the immoral earnings of women, she would infer when she thought it safe. . . .

The soul of honour, then, and masculinely clumsy and damn fine in his way. . . . Well, he, Mark Tietjens junior, was not there to judge his father. His Uncle Mark could see that he regarded his father with affection and admiration. But if Nature — he must be pardoned for using anthropomorphic expressions since they were the shortest way — if Nature then, meant unions of opposite characters to redress extremes in the children, the process did not complete itself with . . . in short with the act of physical union. For just as there were obviously inherited physical characteristics and no doubt inherited memory, there yet remained the question of the influence of temperament on temperament by means of personal association. So that for one opposite to leave the fruits of a union exclusively under the personal influence of the other opposite was very possibly to defeat the purposes of Nature. . . .

That boy, Mark thought, was a very curious problem. He seemed to be a good, straight boy. A little loquacious: still that was to be excused since he had to do all the talking himself. From time to time he had paused in his speech as if, deferentially, he wished to have Mark's opinion. That was proper. He, Mark, could not stand hobbledehoys — particularly the hobbledehoys of that age who appeared to be opinionative and emotional beyond the normal in hobbledehoys. Anyhow, he could not stand the Young once they were beyond the age of childhood. But he was aware that, if you want to conduct a scientific investigation, if you want to arrive, for yourself, at the truth of an individual's parentage — you must set aside your likes and dislikes.

Heaven knew, he had found Christopher, when he had been only one of the younger ones in his father's — he had found him irritating enough . . . a rather moony, fair brat, interested mostly in mathematics, with a trick of standing with those goggle eyes gazing bluely at you — years ago in and around, at first the nursery, then the stables at Groby. Then, if this lad irritated him it was rather an argument in favour of his being Christopher's son than Sylvia's by-blow by another man. . . . What was the fellow's name? A rank bad hat, anyhow.

The probability was that he *was* the other fellow's son. That woman would not have trepanned Christopher into the marriage if she hadn't at least thought that she was with child. There was nothing to be said against any wench's tricking any man into marrying her if she were in that condition. But once having got a man to give a name to your bastard you ought to treat him with some loyalty: it is a biggish service he has done you. That Sylvia had never done. . . . They had got this young springald into their — the Tietjenses' — family. There he was, with his fingers on Groby already. . . . That was all right. As great families as Tietjens' had had that happen to them.

But what made Sylvia pestilential was that she should afterwards have developed this sex-madness for his unfortunate brother.

There was no other way to look at it. She had undoubtedly lured Christopher on to marry her because she thought rightly or wrongly that she was with child by another man. They would never know — she herself probably did not know! — whether this boy was Christopher's son or the other's. English women are so untidy — shame-faced — about these things. That was excusable. But every other action of hers from that date had been inexcusable — except regarded as actions perpetrated under the impulsion of sex-viciousness.

It is perfectly proper — it is a mother's duty to give an unborn child a name and a father. But afterwards to blast the name of that father is more discreditable than to leave the child nameless. This boy was now Tietjens of Groby — but he was also the legal son of a father who had behaved unspeakably according to the mother. . . . And the son of a mother who had been unable to attract her man! . . . Who advertised the fact to the estate carpenter! If we say that the good of the breed is the supreme law, what sort of virtue was this?

It was all very well to say that every one of Sylvia's eccentricities had in view the sole aim of getting her boy's father to return to her. No doubt they might be. He, Mark, was perfectly ready to concede that even her infidelities, notorious as they had been, might have been merely ways of calling his unfortunate brother's attention back to her — of keeping herself in his mind. After the marriage Christopher, finding out that he had been a mere catspaw, probably treated her pretty coldly or ignored her — maritally. . . . And he was a pretty attractive fellow, Christopher. He, Mark, was bound nowadays to acknowledge that. A regular saint and Christian martyr and all that. . . . Enough to drive a woman wild if she had to live beside him and be ignored.

It is obvious that women must be allowed what means they can make use of to maintain — to arouse — their sex attraction for their men. That is what the bitches are for in the scale of things. They have to perpetuate the breed. To do that they have to call attention to themselves and to use what devices they see fit to use, each one according to her own temperament. That cruelty was an excitant he was quite ready, too, to concede. He was ready to concede anything to the woman. To be cruel is to draw attention to yourself; you cannot expect to be courted by a man whom you allow to forget you. But there probably ought to be a limit to things. You probably ought in this, as in all other things, to know what you can do and what you can't — and the proof of this particular pudding, as of all others, was in the eating. Sylvia had left no stone unturned in the determination to keep herself in her man's mind and she had certainly irretrievably lost her man: to another girl. Then she was just a nuisance.

A woman intent on getting a man back ought to have some system, some sort of scheme at the very least. But Sylvia — he knew it from the interminable talk that he had had with Christopher on Armistice night — Sylvia delighted most in doing what she called pulling the strings of shower-baths. She did extravagant things, mostly of a cruel kind, for the fun of seeing what would happen. Well, you cannot allow yourself fun when you are on a campaign. Not as to the subject matter of the campaign itself! If then you do what you want rather than what is expedient you damn well have to take what you get for it. *Damn* well!

What would have justified Sylvia, no matter what she did, would have been if she had succeeded in having another child by his brother. She hadn't. The breed of Tietjens was not enriched. Then she was just a nuisance. . . .

An infernal nuisance . . . For what was she up to now? It was perfectly obvious that both Mrs. de Bray Pape and this boy were here because she had had another outbreak of . . . practically Sadism. They were here so that Christopher might be hurt some more and she not forgotten. What then was the reason for this visit? What the deuce was it?

The boy had been silent for some time. He was gazing at Mark with the goggle-eyed gasping that had been so irritating in his father — particularly on Armistice Day. . . . Well, he, Mark, was apparently now conceding that this boy was probably his brother's son. A real Tietjens after all was to reign over the enormously long, grey house behind the fantastic cedar. The tallest cedar in Yorkshire; in England; in the Empire. . . . He didn't care. He who lets a tree overhang his roof calls the doctor in daily. . . . The boy's lips began to move. No sound came out. He was presumably in a great state!

He was undoubtedly like his father. Darker. . . . Brown hair, brown eyes, high-coloured cheeks all flushed now; straight nose, marked brown eyebrows. A sort of . . . scared, puzzled . . . what was it? . . . expression. Well, Sylvia was fair; Christopher was dark-haired with silver streaks, but fair-complexioned. . . . Damn it; this boy was more attractive than Christopher had been at his age and earlier. . . . Christopher hanging round the schoolroom door in Groby, puzzled over the mathematical theory of waves. He, Mark, hadn't been able to stand him or indeed any of the other children. There was sister Effie — *born* to be a curate's wife. . . . Puzzled! That was it! . . . That bothering woman, his father's second wife — the Saint! — had introduced the puzzlement strain into the Tietjenses. . . . This was Christopher's boy, saintly strain and all. Christopher was probably born to be a rural dean in a fat living, writing treatises on the integral calculus all the time except on Saturday afternoons. With a great reputation for saintliness. Well he wasn't the one and hadn't the other. He was an old-furniture dealer who made a stink in virtuous nostrils. . . . Provvy works in a mysterious way. The boy was saying now:

"The tree . . . the great tree . . . It darkens the windows. . . ."

Mark said: "Aha!" to himself. Groby Great Tree was the symbol of Tietjens. For thirty miles round Groby they made their marriage vows by Groby Great Tree. In the other Ridings they said that Groby Tree and Groby Well were equal in height and depth one to the other. When they were really imaginatively drunk Cleveland villagers would declare — would knock you down if you denied — that Groby Great Tree was 365 foot high and Groby Well 365 feet deep. A foot for every day of the year. . . . On special occasions — he could not himself be bothered to remember what — they would ask permission to hang rags and things from the boughs. Christopher said that one of the chief indictments against Joan of Arc had been that she and the other village girls of Domrèmy had hung rags and trinkets from the boughs of a cedar. Or maybe a thorn? Offering to fairies. . . . Christopher set great store by the tree. He was a romantic ass. Probably he set more store by the tree than by anything else at Groby. He would pull the house down if he thought it incommoded the tree.

Young Mark was bleating, positively bleating:

"The Italians have a proverb. . . . He who lets a tree overhang his house invites a daily call from the doctor . . . I agree myself. . . . In principle of course. . . ."

Well, that was that! Sylvia, then, was proposing to threaten to ask to have Groby Great Tree cut down. Only to threaten to ask. But that would be enough to agonise the miserable Christopher. You couldn't cut down Groby Great Tree. But the thought that the tree was under the guardianship of unsympathetic people would be enough to drive Christopher almost dotty — for years and years.

"Mrs. de Bray Pape," the boy was stammering, "is extremely keen on the tree's being . . . I agree in principle. . . . My mother wished you to see that — oh, in modern days — a house is practically unlettable if . . . So she got Mrs. de Bray Pape. . . . She hasn't had the courage though she swore she had. . . ."

He continued to stammer. Then he started and stopped, crimson. A woman's voice had called:

"Mr. Tietjens. . . . Mr. Mark . . . Hi . . . hup!"

A small woman, all in white, white breeches, white coat, white wide-awake, was slipping down from a tall bay with a white star on the forehead — a bay with large nostrils and an intelligent head. She waved her hand obviously at the boy and then caressed the horse's nostrils. Obviously at the boy. . . for it was impossible that Mark,

Senior, would know a woman who could make a sound like "Hi, hup!" to attract his attention.

Lord Fittleworth, in a square, hard hat, sat on an immense, coffin-headed dapple-grey. He had bristling, close-cropped moustaches and sat like a limpet. He waved his crop in the direction of Mark — they were such old friends — and went on talking to Gunning, who was at his stirrup. The coffin-headed beast started forward and reared a foot or so; a wild, brazen, yelping sound had disturbed it. The boy was more and more scarlet and as emotion grew on him, more and more like Christopher on that beastly day. . . . Christopher with a piece of furniture under his arm, in Marie Léonie's room, his eyes goggling out at the foot of the bed.

Mark swore painfully to himself. He hated to be reminded of that day. Now this lad and that infernal bugle that the younger children of Cramp had got hold of from their bugler-brother, had put it back damnably in his mind. It went on. At intervals. One child had another try, then another. Obviously then Cramp, the eldest, took it. It blared out. . . . Ta. . . . Ta. . . . Ta. . . . Ta, ti . . . ta-ta-ti. . . . Ta. . . . The Last Post. The B——y infernal Last Post. . . . Well, Christopher, as that day Mark had predicted, had got himself, with his raw sensibilities, into a pretty bloody infernal mess while some drunken ass had played the Last Post under the window. . . . Mark meant that whilst that farewell was being played he had had that foresight. And he hated the bugle for reminding him of it. He hated it more than he had imagined. He could not have imagined himself using profanity even to himself. He must have been profoundly moved. Deucedly and profoundly moved at that beastly noise. It had come over the day like a disaster. He saw every detail of Marie Léonie's room as it was on that day. There was, on the marble mantel-shelf under an immense engraving of the Sistine Madonna a feeding-cup over a night-light in which Marie Léonie had been keeping some sort of pap warm for him. Probably the last food to which he had ever helped himself. . . .

V

BUT no . . . that must have been about twelve or earlier or later on that infernal day. In any case he could not remember any subsequent meal he had had then; but he remembered an almost infinitely long period of intense vexation. Of mortification insofar as he could accuse himself of ever having felt mortified. He could still remember the fierce intaking of his breath through his nostrils that had come when Christopher had announced what had seemed to him then his ruinous intentions. . . . It had not been till probably four in the morning that Lord Wolstonemark had rung him up to ask him to countermand the transport that was to have gone out from Harwich. . . . At four in the morning, the idiotic brutes. His substitute had disappeared in the rejoicings in the sy—— and Lord Wolstonemark had wanted to know what code they used for Harwich because transport must at all costs be stopped. There was going to be no advance into Germany. . . . He had never spoken after that!

His brother was done for; the country finished; he was as good as down and out, as the phrase was, himself. Already in his deep mortification — yes — mortification! — he had said to Christopher that morning — the 11th November, 1918 — that he would never speak to him again. He hadn't at that moment meant to say that he would never speak to Christopher at all again — merely that he was never going to speak to him about the affairs of Groby! Christopher might take that immense, far-spreading, grey, bothersome house and the tree and the well and the moors and all the John Peel outfit. Or he might leave them. He, Mark, was never going to speak about the matter any more.

He remembered thinking that Christopher might have taken him to mean that he intended to withdraw, for what it was worth, the light of his countenance from the Christopher Tietjens *ménage*. Nothing had been further from his thoughts. He had a soft corner in his heart for Valentine Wannop. He had had it ever since sitting, feeling like a fool, in the ante-room of the War Office, beside her — gnawing at the handle of his umbrella. But, then, he had recommended her to become Christopher's mistress; he had at any rate begged her to look after his mutton chops and his buttons. So that it wasn't likely that when, a year or so later, Christopher announced that he really was at last going to take up with the young woman and to chance what came of it — it wasn't likely that he intended to dissociate himself from the two of them.

The idea had worried him so much that he had written a rough note — the last time that his hand had ever held a pen — to Christopher. He had said that a brother's backing was not of great use to a woman, but in the special circumstances of the case, he being Tietjens of Groby for what it was worth, and Lady Tietjens — Marie Léonie — being perfectly willing to be seen on all occasions with Valentine and her man it might be worth something, at any rate with tenantry and such like.

Well, he hadn't gone back on that!

But once the idea had come into his head it had grown and grown, on top of his mortification and his weariness. Because he could not conceal from himself that he was weary to death — of the office, of the nation, of the world and people. . . . People . . . he was tired of them! And of the streets, and the grass, and the sky and the moors! He had done his job. That was before Wolstonemark had telephoned and he still thought that he had done his job of getting things here and there about the world to some purpose.

A man is in the world to do his duty by his nation and his family. . . . By his own people first. Well, he had to acknowledge that he had let his own people down pretty badly — beginning with Christopher. Chiefly Christopher; but that reacted on the tenantry.

He had always been tired of the tenantry and Groby. He had been born tired of them. That happens. It happens particularly in old and prominent families. It was odd that Groby and the whole Groby business should so tire him; he supposed he had been born with some kink. All the Tietjenses were born with some sort of kink. It came from the solitude maybe, on the moors, the hard climate, the rough neighbours — possibly even from the fact that Groby Great Tree overshadowed the house. You could not look out of the schoolroom windows at all for its great, ragged trunk and all the children's wing was darkened by its branches. Black . . . funeral plumes. The Hapsburgs were said to hate their palaces — that was no doubt why so many of them, beginning with Juan Ort, had come muckers. At any rate they had chucked the royalty business.

And at a very early age he had decided that he would chuck the country-gentleman business. He didn't see that he was the one to bother with those confounded, hardheaded beggars or with those confounded wind-swept moors and valley bottoms. One owed the blighters a duty, but one did not have to live among them or see that they aired their bedrooms. It had been mostly swank that, always; and since the Corn Laws it had been almost entirely swank. Still, it is obvious that a landlord owes something to the estate from which he and his fathers have drawn their income for generations and generations.

Well, he had never intended to do it because he had been born tired of it. He liked racing and talking about racing to fellows who liked racing. He had intended to do that to the end.

He hadn't been able to.

He had intended to go on living between the office, his chambers, Marie Léonie's and week-ends with race-horse owners of good family until his eyes closed. . . . Of course God disposes in the end, even of the Tietjenses of Groby! He had intended to give over Groby, on the death of his father, to whichever of his brothers had heirs and seemed likely to run the estate well. That for a long time had seemed quite satisfactory. Ted, his next brother, had had his head screwed on all right. If he had had children he would have filled the bill. So would the next brother. . . . But neither of them had had children and both had managed to get killed in Gallipoli. Even sister Mary who was actually, next to him, a *maîtresse femme* if ever there was one, had managed to get killed as a Red Cross matron. *She* would have run Groby well enough — the great, blowsy, grey woman with a bit of a moustache.

Thus God had let him down with a bump on Christopher. . . . Well, Christopher would have run Groby well enough. But he wouldn't. Wouldn't own a yard of Groby land; wouldn't touch a penny of Groby money. He was suffering for it now.

They were both, in effect, suffering, for Mark could not see what was to become of either Christopher or the estate.

Until his father's death Mark had bothered precious little about the fellow. He was by fourteen years the younger: there had been ten children altogether, three of his own mother's children having died young and one having been soft. So Christopher had been still a baby when Mark had left Groby for good — for good except for visits when he had brought his umbrella and seen Christopher mooning at the schoolroom door or in his own mother's sitting-room. So he had hardly known the boy.

And at Christopher's wedding he had definitely decided that he would not see him again — a mug who had got trepanned into marrying a whore. He wished his brother no ill, but the thought of him made Mark sickish. And then, for years, he had heard the worst possible rumours about Christopher. In a way they had rather consoled Mark. God knows, he cared little enough about the Tietjens family — particularly for the children by that soft saint. But he would rather have any brother of his be a wrong 'un than a mug.

Then gradually from the gossip that went abroad he had come to think that Christopher was a very bad wrong 'un indeed. He could account for it easily enough. Christopher had a soft streak and what a woman can do to deteriorate a fellow with a soft streak is beyond belief. And the woman Christopher had got hold of — who had got hold of him — passed belief too. Mark did not hold any great opinion of women at all; if they were a little plump, healthy, a little loyal and not noticeable in their dress that was enough for him. . . . But Sylvia was as thin as an eel, as full of vice as a mare that's a wrong 'un, completely disloyal, and dressed like any Paris cocotte. Christopher, as he saw it, had had to keep that harlot to the tune of six or seven thousand a year, in a society of Jewish or Liberal cabinet minister's wives, all wrong 'uns too — and on an income of at most two. . . . Plenty for a younger son. But naturally he had had to go wrong to get the money.

So it had seemed to him . . . and it had seemed to matter precious little. He gave a thought to his brother perhaps twice a year. But then one day — just after the two brothers had been killed — their father had come up from Groby to say to Mark at the Club:

"Has it occurred to you that, since those two boys are killed that fellow Christopher is practically heir to Groby? You have no legitimate children have you?" Mark replied that he hadn't any bastards either and that he was certainly not going to marry.

At that date it had seemed to him certain that he was not going to marry Marie Léonie Riotor and certainly he was no going to marry anyone else. So Christopher — or at any rate Christopher's heir — must surely come in to Groby. It had not really, hitherto, occurred to him. But when it was thus put forcibly into his mind he saw instantly that it upset the whole scheme of his life. As he saw Christopher then, the fellow was the last person in the world to have charge of Groby — for you had to regard that as to some extent a cure of souls. And he himself would not be much better. He was hopelessly out of touch with the estate and, even though his father's land-steward was a quite efficient fellow, he himself at that date was so hopelessly immersed in the affairs of the then war that he would hardly have a moment of time to learn anything about the property.

There was therefore a breakdown in his scheme of life. That was already a pretty shaking sort of affair. Mark was accustomed to regard himself as master of his fate — as being so limited in his ambitions and so entrenched behind his habits and his wealth that, if circumstances need not of necessity bend to his will, fate could hardly touch him.

And it was one thing for a Tietjens younger son to be a bold sort of law-breaker — or at any rate that he should be contemptuous of restraint. It was quite another that the heir to Groby should be a soft sort bad hat whose distasteful bunglings led his reputation to stink in the nostrils of all his own class. If a younger son can be said to have a class! . . . At any rate in the class to which his father and eldest brother belonged. Tietjens was said to have sold his wife to her cousin the Duke at so contemptible a price that he was obviously penniless even after that transaction. He had sold her to other rich men — to bank managers, for instance. Yet even after that he was reduced to giving worthless cheques. If a man sold his soul to the devil he should at least insist on a good price. Similar transactions were said to distinguish the social set in which that bitch moved — but most of the men who, according to Ruggles, sold their wives to members of the government, obtained millions by governmental financial tips — or peerages. Not infrequently they obtained both peerages and millions. But Christopher was such a confounded ass that he had got neither the one nor the other. His cheques were turned down for twopences. And he was such a bungler that he must needs seduce the daughter of their father's oldest friend, must needs get her with child and let the fact be known to the whole world. . . .

This information he had from Ruggles — and it killed their father. Well, he, Mark was absolutely to blame: that was that. But — infinitely worse — it had made Christopher fiercely determined not to accept a single penny of the money that had become Mark's and that had been his father's. And Christopher was as obstinate as a hog. For that Mark did not blame him. It was a Tietjens job to be obstinate as a hog.

He couldn't, however, disabuse his mind of the idea that Christopher's refusal of Groby and all that came from Groby was as much a manifestation of the confounded saintliness that he got from his soft mother as of a spirit of resentment. Christopher *wanted* to rid himself of his great possessions. The fact that his father and brother had believed him to be what Marie Léonie would have called *maquereau* and had thus insulted him he had merely grasped at with eagerness as an excuse. He wanted to be out of the world. That was it. He wanted to be out of a disgustingly inefficient and venial world just as he, Mark, also wanted to be out of a world that he found almost more fusionless and dishonest than Christopher found it.

At any rate, at the first word that they had had about the heirship to Groby after their father's death, Christopher had declared that he, Mark, might take his money to the devil and the ownership of Groby with it. He proposed never to forgive either his father or Mark. He had only consented to take Mark by the hand at the urgent solicitation of Valentine Wannop. . . .

That had been the most dreadful moment of Mark's life. The country was, even then, going to the devil; his brother proposed to starve himself; Groby, by his brother's wish was to fall into the hands of that bitch. . . . And the country went further and further towards the devil and his brother starved worse and worse . . . and as for Groby . . .

The boy who practically owned Groby had, at the first sound of the voice of the woman who wore white riding-kit and called "Hi-hup!" — at the very first sound of her voice the boy had scampered off through the raspberry canes and was now against the hedge whilst she leaned down over him, laughing, and her horse leaned over behind her. Fittleworth was smiling at them benevolently and at the same time continuing his conversation with Gunning. . . .

The woman was too old for the boy who had gone scarlet at the sound of her voice. Sylvia had been too old for Christopher: she had got him on the hop when he had been only a kid. . . . The world went on.

He was nevertheless thankful for the respite. He had to acknowledge to himself that he was not as young as he had been. He had a great deal to think of if he was to get the hang of — he was certainly not going to interfere with — the world and having to listen to conversations that were mostly moral apophthegms had tired him. He got too many at too short intervals. If he had spoken he would not have, but, because he did not speak both the lady who was descended from the Maintenon and that boy had peppered him with moral points of view that all required to be considered, without leaving him enough time to get his breath mentally.

The lady had called them a corrupt and effete aristocracy. They were probably not corrupt but certainly, regarded as landowners, they were effete — both he and Christopher. They were simply bored at the contemplation of that terrific nuisance — and refusing to perform the duties of their post they refused the emoluments too. He could not remember that, after childhood, he had ever had a penny out of Groby. They would not accept that post: they had taken others. . . . Well, this was his, Mark's, last post. . . . He could have smiled at his grim joke.

Of Christopher he was not so sure. That ass was a terrific sentimentalist. Probably he would have liked to be a great landowner, keeping up the gates on the estate — like Fittleworth who was a perfect lunatic about gates. He was probably even now jaw-jawing Gunning about them, smacking his boot-top with his crop-handle. Yes — keeping up the gates and seeing that the tenants' land gave so many bushels of wheat to the acre or supported so many sheep the year round. . . . How many sheep would an acre keep all the year round and how many bushels of wheat should it give? He, Mark, had not the least idea. Christopher would know — with the difference to be expected of every acre of all the thousand acres of Groby. . . . Yes, Christopher had pored over Groby with the intentness of a mother looking at her baby's face!

So that his refusal to take on that stewardship might very well arise from a sort of craving for mortification of the spirit. Old Campion had once said that he believed — he positively believed, with shudders — that Christopher desired to live in the spirit of Christ. That had seemed horrible to the general, but Mark did not see that it was horrible, *per se*. . . . He doubted, however, whether Christ would have refused to manage Groby had it been his job. Christ was a sort of an Englishman and Englishmen did not as a rule refuse to do their jobs. . . . They had not used to; now no doubt they did. It was a Russian sort of trick. He had heard that even before the revolution great Russian nobles would disperse their estates, give their serfs their liberty, put on a hair shirt and sit by the roadside begging. . . . Something like that. Perhaps Christopher was a symptom that the English were changing. He himself was not. He was just lazy and determined — and done with it!

He had not at first been able to believe that Christopher was resolved — with a Yorkshire resolution — to have nothing to do with Groby or his, Mark's, money. He had nevertheless felt a warm admiration for his brother the moment the words had been said. Christopher would take none of his father's money; he would never forgive either his father or his brother. A proper Yorkshire sentiment, uttered coldly and as it were good-humouredly. His eyes, naturally, had goggled, but he had displayed no other emotion.

Nevertheless Mark had imagined that he might be up to some game. He might be merely meaning to bring Mark to his knees. . . . But how could Mark be more brought to his knees than by offering to give over Groby to his brother? It is true he had kept that up his sleeve whilst his brother had been out in France. After all there was no sense in offering a fellow who might be going to become food for powder the management of great possessions. He had felt a certain satisfaction in the fact that Christopher *was* going out, though he was confoundedly sorry too. He really admired Christopher for doing it — and he imagined that it might clear some of the smirchiness that must attach to Christopher's reputation in spite of what he now knew to be his brother's complete guiltlessness of the crime that had been attributed to him. He had of course been wrong — he had reckoned without the determined discredit that, after the war was over, the civilian population would contrive to attach to every man who had been to the front as a fighting soldier. After all that was natural enough. The majority of the male population was civilian and once the war was over and there was no more risk they would bitterly regret that they had not gone. They would take it out of the ex-soldiers all right!

So that Christopher had rather been additionally discredited than much helped by his services to the country. Sylvia had been able to put it, very reasonably, that Christopher was by nature that idle and dissolute thing, a soldier. That, in times of peace, had helped her a great deal.

Still, Mark had been pleased with his brother, and, once Christopher had been invalided back and had returned to his old-tin saving depot near Ealing, Mark had at once set wheels in motion to get his brother demobilised so that he might look after Groby. By that time Groby was inhabited by Sylvia, the boy, and Sylvia's mother. The estate just had to be managed by the land-steward who had served his father, neither Sylvia nor her family having any finger in that; though her mother was able to assure him, Mark, that the estate was doing as well as the Agricultural Committee of grocers and stock-jobbers would let it. They insisted on wheat being sown on exposed moors where nothing but heather had a chance, and active moorland sheep being fattened in water-bottoms full of liver fluke. But the land-steward fought them as well as one man could be expected to fight the chosen of a nation of small shop-keepers. . . .

And at that date — the date of Christopher's return to Ealing — Mark had still imagined that Christopher had really only been holding out for the possession of Groby. He was therefore disillusioned rather nastily. He had managed to get Christopher demobilised — without telling him anything about it — by just about the time when the Armistice came along. . . . And then he found that he really had put the fat in the fire!

He had practically beggared the wretched fellow who, counting on living on his pay for at least a year longer, had mortgaged his blood-money in order to go into a sort of partnership in an old-furniture business with a confounded American. And of course the blood-money was considerably diminished, being an allowance made to demobilised officers computed on the number of their days of service. So he had docked Christopher of two or three hundred pounds. That was the sort of mucky situation into which Christopher might be expected to be got in by his well-wishers. . . . There he had been, just before Armistice Day, upon the point of demobilisation and without an available penny! It appeared that he had to sell even the few books that Sylvia had left him when she had stripped his house.

That agreeable truth had forced itself on Mark at just the moment when he had been so rotten bad with pneumonia that he might be expected to cash in at any moment. Marie Léonie had indeed, of her own initiative, telephoned to Christopher that he had better come to see his brother if he wanted to meet him on this side of the grave.

They had at once started arguing — or rather each had started exposing his views. Christopher had stated what he was going to do and Mark had voiced his horror at what Christopher proposed. Mark's horror came from the fact that Christopher proposed to eschew comfort. An Englishman's duty is to secure for himself for ever, reasonable clothing, a clean shirt a day, a couple of mutton chops grilled without condiments, two floury potatoes, an apple pie with a piece of Stilton and pulled bread, a pint of Club médoc, a clean room, in the winter a good fire in the grate, a comfortable armchair, a comfortable woman to see that all these were prepared for you, and to keep you warm in bed and to brush your bowler and fold your umbrella in the morning. When you had that secure for life you could do what you liked provided that what you did never endangered that security. What was to be said against that?

Christopher had nothing to advance except that he was not going to live in that way. He was not going to live in that way unless he could secure that or something like it, by his own talents. His only available and at the same time marketable talent was his gift for knowing genuine old furniture. So he was going to make a living out of old furniture. He had had his scheme perfectly matured; he had even secured an American partner, a fellow who had as great a gift for the cajolement of American purchasers of old stuff as he, Christopher, had for its discovery. It was still the war then, but Christopher and his partner between them had predicted the American mopping up of the world's gold supply and the consequent stripping of European houses of old stuff. . . . At that you could make a living.

Other careers, he said, were barred to him. The Department of Statistics in which he had formerly had a post had absolutely cold-shouldered him. They were not only adamant, they were also vindictive against civil servants who had become serving soldiers. They took the view that those members of their staffs who had preferred serving were idle and dissolute fellows who had merely taken up arms in order to satisfy their lusts for women. Women had naturally preferred soldiers to civilians; the civilians were now getting back on them. That was natural.

Mark agreed indeed that it was natural. Before he had been interested in his brother as a serving soldier he had been inclined to consider most soldiers as incompetent about Transport and, in general, nuisances. He agreed too that Christopher could not go back to the Department. There he was certainly a marked man. He could possibly have insisted on his rights to be taken back even though his lungs, being by now pretty damaged by exposure, might afford them a pretext for legally refusing him. H.M. Civil Service and Departments have the right to refuse employment to persons likely to become unfit for good. A man who has lost an eye may be refused by any Department because he may lose the other and so become liable for a pension. But even if Christopher forced himself on the Department they would have their bad mark against him. He had been too rude to them during the war when they had tried to force him to employ himself in the faking of statistics that the Ministry had coerced the Department into supplying in order to dish the French who demanded more troops.

With that point of view Mark found himself entirely in sympathy. His long association with Marie Léonie, his respect for the way in which she had her head screwed on, the constant intimacy with the life and point of view of French individuals of the *petite bourgeoisie* which her gossip had given him — all these things together with his despair for the future of his own country had given him a very considerable belief in the destinies and indeed in the virtues of the country across the Channel. It would therefore have been very distasteful to him that his brother should take pay from an organisation that had been employed to deal treacherously with our Allies. It had indeed become extremely distasteful to him to take pay himself from a Government that had forced such a course upon the nation and he would thankfully have resigned from his office if he had not considered that his services were indispensable to the successful prosecution of the war which was then still proceeding. He wanted to be done with it, but at the moment he saw no chance. The war was by then obviously proceeding towards a successful issue. Owing to the military genius of the French who by then had the supreme command, the enemy nations were daily being forced to abandon great stretches of territory. But that only made the calls on Transport the greater whilst, if we were successfully and unwastefully to occupy the enemy capital as at that date he imagined that we obviously must, the demand for the provision of Transport must become almost unmeasurable.

Still, that was no argument for the re-entry of his brother into the service of the country. As he saw things, public life had become — and must remain for a long period — so demoralized by the members of the then Government with their devious foreign policies and their intimacies with a class of shady financiers such as had never hitherto had any finger in the English political pie — public life had become so discreditable an affair that the only remedy was for the real governing classes to retire altogether from public pursuits. Things in short must become worse before they could grow better. With the dreadful condition of ruin at home and foreign discredit to which the country must almost immediately emerge under the conduct of the Scotch grocers, Frankfort financiers, Welsh pettifoggers, Midland armament manufacturers and South Country incompetents who during the later years of the war had intrigued themselves into office — with that dreadful condition staring it in the face, the country must return to something like its old standards of North Country common sense and English probity. The old governing class to which he and his belonged might never return to power but, whatever revolutions took place — and he did not care! — the country must return to ex-acting of whoever might be its governing class some semblance of personal probity and public honouring of pledges. He obviously was out of it or he would be out of it with the end of the war, for even from his bed he had taken no small part in the directing of affairs at his office. . . . A state of war obviously favouring the coming to the top of all kinds of devious storm petrels; that was inevitable and could not be helped. But in normal times a country — every country — was true to itself.

Nevertheless he was very content that his brother should in the interim have no share in affairs. Let him secure his mutton chop, his pint of claret, his woman, and his umbrella and it mattered not into what obscurity he retired. But how was that to be secured? There were several ways.

He was aware, for instance, that Christopher was both a mathe-matician of no mean order and a churchman. He might perfectly well take orders, assume the charge of one of the three family livings that Mark had in his gift and, whilst competently discharging the duties of his cure, pursue whatever are the occupations of a well-cared-for mathematician.

Christopher, however, whilst avowing his predilection for such a life — which as Mark saw it was exactly fitted to his asceticism, his softness in general, and his private tastes — Christopher admitted that there was an obstacle to his assuming such a cure of souls — an ob-stacle of an insuperable nature. Mark at once asked him if he were in fact living with Miss Wannop. But Christopher answered that he had not seen Miss Wannop since the day of his second proceeding to the front. They had then agreed that they were not the sort of persons to begin a hidden intrigue and the affair had proceeded no further.

Mark was, however, aware that a person of Christopher's way of thinking might well feel inhibited from taking on a cure of souls if, in spite of the fact that he had abstained from seducing a young woman, he nevertheless privately desired to enter into illicit relations with her, and that that was sufficient to justify him in saying that an insuperable obstacle existed. He did not know that he himself agreed, but it was not his business to interfere between any man and his conscience in a matter of the Church. He was himself no very good Christian, at any rate as regards the relationships of men and women. Nevertheless the Church of England was the Church of England. No doubt had Christopher been a Papist he could have had the young woman for his housekeeper and no one would have bothered.

But what the devil, then, was his brother to do? He had been offered, as a sop in the pan, and to keep him quiet, no doubt, over the affair of the Department of Statistics, a vice-consulate in some Mediterranean port — Toulon or Leghorn or something of the sort. That might have done well enough. It was absurd to think of a Tietjens, heir to Groby, being under the necessity of making a living. It was fantastic, but if Christopher was in a fantastic mood there was nothing to be done about it. A vice-consulate is a potty sort of job. You attend to ships' manifests, get members of crews out of gaol, give old lady tourists the addresses of boarding houses kept by English or half-castes, or provide the vice-admirals of visiting British squadrons with the names of local residents who should be invited to entertainments given on the flagship. It was a potty job, but innocuous if it could be regarded as a sort of marking time. . . . And at that moment Mark still thought that Christopher was still holding out for some sort of concession on Mark's part before definitely assuming the charge of Groby, its tenants, and its mineral rights. . . . But there were insuperable objections to even the vice-consulate. In the first place the job would have been in the public service, a fact to which as has been said Mark strongly objected. Then the job was offered as a sort of a bribe. And, in addition, the consular service exacts from everyone who occupies a consular or vice-consular post the deposit of a sum of four hundred pounds sterling, and Christopher did not possess even so much as four hundred shillings. . . . And, in addition, as Mark was well aware, Miss Wannop might again afford an obstacle. A British vice-consul might possibly keep a Maltese or Levantine in a back street and no harm done, but he probably could not live with an English young woman of family and position without causing so much scandal as to make him lose his job. . . .

It was at this point that Mark again, but for the last time, asked his brother why he did not divorce Sylvia.

By that time Marie Léonie had retired to get some rest. She was pretty worn out. Mark's illness had been long and serious; she had nursed him with such care that during the whole time she had not been out into the streets except once or twice to go across the road

to the Catholic church where she would offer a candle or so to his
recovery and once or twice to remonstrate with the butcher as to the
quality of the meat he supplied for Mark's broths. In addition, on
many days, she had worked late, under Mark's directions on papers
that the office had sent him. She either could not or would not put
her man into the charge of any kind of night nurse. She alleged that
the war had mopped up every kind of available attendant on the sick,
but Mark shrewdly suspected that she had made no kind of effort
to secure an assistant. There was her national dread of draughts to
account for that. She accepted with discipline, if with despair, the
English doctor's dictum that fresh air must be admitted to the sick
room, but she sat up night after night in a hooded-chair, watching
for any change in the wind and moving in accordance a complicated
arrangement of screens that she maintained between her patient
and the open window. She had, however, surrendered Mark to his
brother without a murmur and had quietly gone to her own room to
sleep, and Mark, though he carried on almost every kind of conversation with his brother and though he would not have asked her to
leave them in order that he might engage on topics that his brother
might like to regard as private — Mark seized the opportunity to lay
before Christopher what he thought of Sylvia and the relationships
of that singular couple.

It amounted in the end to the fact that Mark wanted Christopher
to divorce his wife and to the fact that Christopher had not altered
in his views that a man cannot divorce a woman. Mark put it that if
Christopher intended to take up with Valentine it mattered practically
very little whether he married her after a divorce or not. What a man
has to do if he means to take up with a woman and as far as possible
to honour her is to make some sort of fight of it — as a symbol. Marriage, if you do not regard it as a sacrament — as no doubt it ought
to be regarded — was nothing more than a token that a couple intended to stick to each other. Nowadays people — the right people
— bothered precious little about anything but that. A constant
change of partners was a social nuisance; you could not tell whether
you could or couldn't invite a couple together to a tea-fight. And
society existed for social functions. That was why promiscuity was no
good. For social functions you had to have an equal number of men
and women or someone got left out of conversations and so you had
to know who, officially in the social sense, went with whom. Everyone knew that all the children of Lupus at the War Office were really

the children of a late Prime Minister so that presumably the Countess and the Prime Minister slept together most of the time but that did not mean that you invited the Prime Minister and the woman to social-official functions because they hadn't any ostensible token of union. On the contrary, you invited Lord and Lady Lupus together to all functions that would get into the papers, but you took care to have the Lady at any private, week-endish parties or intimate dinners to which the Chief was coming.

And Christopher had to consider that, if it came to marriage, ninety per cent of the inhabitants of the world regarded the marriage of almost everybody else as invalid. A Papist obviously could not regard a marriage before a registrar or a French *maire* as having any spiritual validity. At best it was no more than a demonstration of aspirations after constancy. You went before a functionary publicly to assert that you and a woman intended to stick to each other. Equally for extreme Protestants a marriage by a Papist priest, or a minister of any other sect, or a Buddhist Lama, had not the blessing of their own brand of Deity. So that really, to all practical intents, it was sufficient if a couple really assured their friends that they intended to stick together, if possible, for ever. If not, at least for years enough to show that they had made a good shot at it. Mark invited Christopher to consult whom he liked in his, Mark's, particular set and he would find that they agreed with his views.

So he was anxious that if Christopher intended to take up with the Wannop young woman he should take at least a shot at a divorce. He might not succeed in getting one. He obviously had grounds enough, but Sylvia might make counter-allegations, he, Mark, couldn't say with what chance of success. He was prepared himself to accept his brother's assertions of complete innocence, but Sylvia was a clever devil and there was no knowing what view a judge might take. Where there had been such a hell of a lot of smoke he might consider that there must be enough flame to justify refusing a divorce. There would no doubt be, thus — a beastly stink. But a beastly stink would be better than the sort of veiled ill-fame that Sylvia had contrived to get attached to Christopher. And the fact that Christopher had faced the stink and made the attempt would be at least that amount of tribute to Miss Wannop. Society was at least good-natured and was inclined to take the view that if a fellow had faced his punishment and taken it he was pretty well absolved. There might be people who would hold out against them, but Mark supposed that what Christopher wanted for himself and his girl was reasonable material comfort with a society of sufficient people of the right sort to give them a dinner or so a week and a week-end or so a month in the week-ending season.

Christopher had listened to his views with so much amiability that Mark began to hope that he would get his way in the larger matter of Groby. He was prepared to go further and to stake as much as his assurance that if Christopher would settle down at Groby, accept a decent income and look after the estate, he, Mark, would assure his brother and Valentine of bearable social circumstances.

Christopher, however, had made no answer at all beyond saying that if he tried to divorce Sylvia it would apparently ruin his old-furniture business. For his American partner assured him that in the United States if a man divorced his wife instead of letting her divorce him no one would do any business with him. He had mentioned the case of a man called Blum, a pretty warm stock-exchange man, who insisted on divorcing his wife against the advice of his friends; he found when he returned to the stockmarket that all his clients cold-shouldered him, so that he was ruined. And as these fellows were shortly going to mop up everything in the world, including the old-furniture trade, Christopher supposed that he would have to study their prejudices. He had come across his partner rather curiously. The fellow, whose father had been a German Jew but a naturalized American citizen, had been in Berlin mopping up German old furniture for sale in the American interior where he had a flourishing business. So, when America had come in on the side that was not German, the Germans had just simply dropped on Mr. Schatzweiler in their pleasant way, incorporated him in their forces and had sent him to the front as a miserable little Tommy before the Americans had been a month in the show. And there, amongst the prisoners he had had to look after, Christopher had found the little, large-eyed, sensitive creature, unable to speak a word of German, but just crazy about the furniture and tapestries in the French châteaux that the prisoners passed on their marches. Christopher had befriended him; kept him as far as possible separated from the other prisoners, who naturally did not like him, and had a good many conversations with him.

It had appeared that Mr. Schatzweiler had had a good deal to do, in the way of buying, with Sir John Robertson the old old-furniture buying millionaire who was a close friend of Sylvia's and had been so considerable an admirer of Christopher's furniture-buying gifts that he had, years ago, proposed to take Christopher into partnership with himself. At that time Christopher had regarded Sir John's proposals as outside the range of his future; he had then been employed in the Department of Statistics. But the proposal had always amused and rather impressed him. If, that is to say, that hardheaded old Scotsman who had made a vast fortune at his trade made to Christopher a quite serious business proposition on the strength of Christopher's *flair* in the matter of old woods and curves, Christopher himself might take his own gifts with a certain seriousness.

And by the time he came to be in command of the escort over those miserable creatures he had pretty well realised that, after the necessity for escorts was over he would jolly well have to consider how he was going to make a living for himself. That was certain. He was not going to re-insert himself amongst the miserable collection of squits who occupied themselves in his old Department; he was too old to continue in the Army; he was certainly not going to accept a penny from Groby sources. He did not care what became of him — but his not caring did not take any tragico-romantic form. He would be quite prepared to live in a hut on a hillside and cook his meals over three bricks outside the door — but that was not a method of life that was very practicable, and even that needed money. Everyone who served in the Army at the front knew how little it took to keep life going — and satisfactory. But he did not see the world, when it settled down again turning itself into a place fit for old soldiers who had learned to appreciate frugality. On the contrary, the old soldier would be chivvied to hell by a civilian population who abhorred him. So that merely to keep clean and out of debt was going to be a tough job.

In his long vigils in tents, beneath the moon with the sentries walking, challenging from time to time round the barbed wire stockades, the idea of Sir John's proposition had occurred to him with some force. It had gathered strength from his meeting with Mr. Schatzweiler. The little fellow was a shivering artist and Christopher had enough of superstition in him to be impressed by the coincidence of their having come together in such unlikely circumstances. After all Providence must let up on him after a time so why should not this unfortunate and impressively Oriental member of the Chosen people be a sign of a covenant? In a way he reminded Christopher of his former protégé, Macmaster — he had the same dark eyes, the same shape, the same shivering eagerness.

That he was a Jew and an American did not worry Christopher; he had not objected to the fact that Macmaster had been the son of a Scotch grocer. If he had to go into partnership and be thrown into close contact with anyone at all he did not care much who it was as long as it was not either a bounder or a man of his own class and race. To be in close mental communion with either an English bounder or an Englishman of good family would, he was aware, be intolerable to him. But, for a little, shivering artistic Jew, as of old for Macmaster he was quite capable of feeling a real fondness — as you might for an animal. Their manners were not your manners and could not be expected to be and whatever their intelligence they would have a certain little alertness, a certain exactness of thought. . . . Besides, if they did you in, as every business partner or protégé must be expected to do, you did not feel the same humiliation as you did if you were swindled by a man of your own race and station. In the one case it was only what was to be expected, in the other you were faced with the fact that your own tradition had broken down. And under the long strain of the war he had outgrown alike the mentality and the traditions of his own family and his own race. The one and the other were not fitted to endure long strains.

So he welcomed the imploring glances and the eventual Oriental gratitude of that little man in his unhappy tent. For, naturally, by communicating in his weighty manner with the United States Headquarters when he happened to find himself in its vicinity, he secured the release of the little fellow who was by now safely back somewhere in the interior of the North American Continent.

But before that happened he had exchanged a certain amount of Correspondence with Sir John and had discovered from him and from one or two chance members of the American Expeditionary Force that the little man was quite a good old-furniture dealer. Sir John had by that time gone out of business and his letters were not particularly cordial to Tietjens — which was only what was to be expected if Sylvia had been shedding her charms over him. But it had appeared that Mr. Schatzweiler had had a great deal of business with Sir John who had indeed supplied him with a great part of his material and so, if Sir John had gone out of business, Mr. Schatzweiler would need to find in England someone to take Sir John's place. And that was not going to be extraordinarily easy for what with the amount of his money that the Germans had mopped up — they had sold him immense quantities of old furniture and got paid for it and had then enlisted him in the ranks of their Brandenburgers where naturally he could do nothing with carved oak chests that had elaborate steel hinges and locks. . . . What, then, with that and his prolonged absence from the neighbourhood of Detroit where he had mostly found his buyers, Mr. Schatzweiler found himself extremely hampered in his activities. It therefore fell to Christopher, if he was to go into partnership with the now sanguine and charming Oriental, to supply an immediate sum of money. That had not been easy, but by means of mortgaging his pay and his blood-money and selling the books that Sylvia had left him he had at least been able to provide Mr. Schatzweiler with enough to make at least a start somewhere across the water. . . . And Mr. Schatzweiler and Christopher had between them evolved an ingenious scheme along lines that the American had long contemplated, taking into account the tastes of his countrymen and the nature of the times.

Mark had listened to his brother during all this with indulgence and even with pleasure. If a Tietjens contemplated going into trade he might at least contemplate an amusing trade carried on in a spirited manner. And what Christopher humorously projected was at least more dignified than stock-broking or bill-discounting. And he was pretty well convinced by this time that his brother was completely reconciled to him and to Groby.

It was about then and when he had again begun to introduce the topic of Groby that Christopher got up from the chair at the bedside and having taken his brother's wrist in his cool fingers remarked: "Your temperature's pretty well down. Don't you think it is about time that you set about marrying Charlotte? I suppose you mean to marry her before this bout is finished and you might have a relapse."

Mark remembered that speech perfectly well with the addition that if he, Christopher, hurried about it they might get the job done that night. It must therefore then have been about one o'clock of a day about three weeks before the 11th November, 1918.

Mark replied that he would be much obliged to Christopher, and Christopher, having aroused Marie Léonie and told her that he would be back in time to let her have a good night's rest, disappeared saying that he was going straight to Lambeth. In those days, supposing you could command thirty pounds or so there was no difficulty in getting married at the shortest possible notice and Christopher had promoted too many last minute marriages amongst his men not to know the ropes.

Mark viewed the transaction with a good deal of contentment. It had needed no arguing: if the proceeding had the approval of the heir-presumptive to Groby there was nothing more to be said against it. And Mark took the view that if he agreed to a proceeding that Christopher could only have counselled as heir-presumptive that was an additional reason for Mark's expecting that Christopher would eventually consent to administer Groby himself.

VI

THAT would have been three weeks before the 11th of November. His head boggled a little at computing what the actual date in October must have been. With his then pneumonia his mind had not much registered dates; days had gone by in fever and boredom. Still, a man ought to remember the date of his wedding. Say it had been the 20th of October, 1918. The 20th of October had been his father's birthday. When he came to think of it he could remember hazily that it was queer that he should be going out of life on the date his father had entered it. It made a sort of full stop. And it made a full stop that, practically on that day Papists entered into their own in Groby. He had, that is to say, made up his mind to the fact that Christopher's son would have Groby as a home even if Christopher didn't. And the boy was by now a full-fledged Papist, pickled and oiled and wafered and all. Sylvia had rubbed the fact in about a week ago by sending him a card for his nephew's provisional baptism and first communion about a week before. It had astonished him that he had not felt more bitter.

He had not any doubt that the fact had reconciled him to his marriage with Marie Léonie. He had told his brother a year or so ago that he would never marry her because she was a Papist, but he was aware that then he was only chipping at Spelden, the fellow that wrote *Spelden on Sacrilege*, a book that predicted all sorts of disaster for families who owned former Papist Church lands or who had displaced Papists. When he had told Christopher that he would never marry Charlotte — he had called her Charlotte for reasons of camouflage before the marriage — he had been quite aware that he was chipping at Spelden's ghost — for Spelden must have been dead a hundred years or so. As it were, he had been saying grimly if pleasantly to that bogey:

"Eh, old 'un. You see. You may prophesy disaster to Groby because a Tietjens was given it over the head of one of your fellows in Dutch William's time. But you can't frighten me into making an honest woman — let alone a Lady of Groby — out of a Papist."

And he hadn't. He would swear that no idea of disaster to Groby had entered his head at the date of the marriage. Now, he would not say; but of what he felt then he was certain. He remembered thinking whilst the ceremony was going on of the words of Fraser of Lovat before they executed him in the 'Forty Five. They had told him on the scaffold that if he would make some sort of submission to George II they would spare his body from being exhibited in quarters on the spikes of the buildings in Edinburgh. And Fraser had answered: "An the King will have my heid I care not what he may do with my ——" naming a part of a gentleman that is not now mentioned in drawing-rooms. So, if a Papist was to inhabit Groby House it mattered precious little if the first Lady Tietjens of Groby were Papist or Heathen.

A man as a rule does not marry his mistress whilst he has any kick in him. If he still aims at a career it might hinder him supposing she were known to have been his mistress, or of course a fellow who wants to make a career might want to help himself on by making a good marriage. Even if a man does not want to make a career he may think that a woman who has been his mistress as like as not may cuckold him after marriage, for, if she has gone wrong with him she would be more apt to go wrong elsewhere as well. But if a fellow is practically finished, those considerations disappear and he remembers that you go to hell if you seduce virgins. It is as well at one time or another to make your peace with your Creator. For ever is a long word and God is said to disapprove of unconsecrated unions.

Besides it would very likely please Marie Léonie, though she had never said a word about it and it would certainly dish Sylvia who was no doubt counting on being the first Lady Tietjens of Groby. And then, too, it would undoubtedly make Marie Léonie safer. In one way and another he had given his mistress quite a number of things that might well be desirable to that bitch, and neither his nor Christopher's lives were worth much, whilst Chancery can be a very expensive affair if you get into it.

And he was aware that he had always had a soft spot in his heart for Marie Léonie, otherwise he would not have provided her with the name of Charlotte for public consumption. A man gives his mistress another name if there is any chance of his marrying her so that it may look as if he were marrying someone else when he does it. *Marie Léonie Riotor* looks different from a casual Charlotte. It gives her a better chance in the world outside.

So it had been well enough. The world was changing and there was no particular reason why he should not change with it. . . . And he had not been able to conceal from himself that he was getting on the way. Time lengthened out. When he had come in drenched from one of the potty local meetings that they had to fall back on during the war he had known that something was coming to him because after Marie Léonie had tucked him up in bed he could not remember the strain of the winner of some handicap of no importance. Marie Léonie had given him a goodish tot of rum with butter in it and that might have made him hazy — but all the same that had never happened to him in his life before, rum or no rum. And by now he had forgotten even the name of the winner and the meeting. . . .

He could not conceal from himself that his memory was failing though otherwise he considered himself to be as sound a man as he had ever been. But when it came to memory, ever since that day his brain had checked at times as a tired horse will at a fence. . . . A tired horse!

He could not bring himself to the computation of what three weeks back from the 11th of November came to; his brain would not go at it. For the matter of that he could remember precious little of the events of that three weeks in their due order. Christopher had certainly been about, relieving Marie Léonie at night and attending to him with a soft, goggle-eyed attentiveness that only a man with a saint for a mother could have put up. For hours and hours he would read aloud in Boswell's *Life of Johnson* for which Mark had had a fancy.

And Mark could remember drowsing off with satisfaction to the sound of the voice and drowsing with satisfaction awake again, still to the sound of the voice. For Christopher had the idea that if his voice went droning on it would make Mark's slumbers more satisfactory.

Satisfaction. . . . Perhaps the last satisfaction that Mark was ever to know. For at that time — during those three weeks — he had not

been able to believe that Christopher really meant to
about the matter of Groby. How could you believe that a
who waited on you with the softness of a girl built of mealsacl
determined to . . . call it, break your heart. That was what it c
to . . . A fellow too who agreed in the most astounding mani,
with your views of things in general; a fellow for the matter of tha\
who knew ten times as much as you did. A damned learned fellow. . . .

Mark had no contempt for learning — particularly for younger
sons. The country was going to the dogs because of the want of education of the younger sons whose business it was to do the work of
the nation. It was a very old North Country rhyme that, that when
land is gone and money spent then learning is most excellent. No,
he had no contempt for learning. He had never acquired any because he was too lazy: a little Sallust, a little Cornelius Nepos, a
touch of Horace, enough French to read a novel and follow what
Marie Léonie said. . . . Even to himself he called her Marie Léonie
once he was married to her. It had made her jump at first!

But Christopher was a damned learned fellow. Their father, a
younger son at the beginning, had been damned learned too. They
said that even at his death he had been one of the best Latinists
in England — the intimate friend of that fellow Wannop, the Professor. . . . A great age at which to die by his own hand, his father's!
Why, if that marriage had been on the 29th October, 1918, his
father, then dead, must have been born on the 29th October what
. . . 1834. . . . No, that was not possible . . . No, '44. *His* father,
Mark knew, had been born in 1812 — before Waterloo!

Great stretches of time. Great changes! Yet Father had not been
an incult sort of a man. On the contrary, if he was burly and determined, he was quiet. And sensitive. He had certainly loved Christopher very dearly — and Christopher's mother.

Father was very tall; stooping like a toppling poplar towards the
end. His head seemed very distant, as if he hardly heard you. Iron-
grey; short-whiskered. Absent-minded towards the end. Forgetting
where he had put his handkerchief and where his spectacles were
when he had pushed them up onto his forehead. . . . He had been
a younger son who had never spoken to his father for forty years.
Grand-father had never forgiven him for marrying Miss Selby of
Biggen . . . not because it was marrying below him but because
Grand-father had wanted their mother for his eldest son. . . . And

ᵗʰ ᵃd been poor in their early childhood, wandering over the
ᵪ ment to settle at last in Dijon where they had kept some sort
ȼtate . . . a large house in the middle of the town with several
rvants. He never could imagine how their mother had done it on
our hundred a year. But she had. A hard woman. But Father had
kept in with French people and corresponded with Professor Wannop and Learned Societies. He had always regarded him, Mark, as
a dunce. . . . Father would sit reading in elegantly bound books, by
the hour. His study had been one of the show rooms of the house
in Dijon.

Did he commit suicide? If so then Valentine Wannop was his
daughter. There could not be much getting away from that, not that
it mattered much. In that case Christopher would be living with his
half-sister. . . . Not that it mattered much. It did not matter much,
to him, Mark . . . but his father was the sort of man that it might
drive to suicide.

A luckless sort of beggar, Christopher! . . . If you took the whole
conglobulation at its worst — the father suiciding, the son living with
his sister in open sin, the son's son not his son and Groby going over
to Papist hands. . . . That was the sort of thing that would happen
to a Tietjens of the Christopher variety: to any Tietjens who would
not get out or get under as he, Mark, had done. Tietjenses took what
they damn well got for doing what they damn well wanted to. Well,
it landed them in that sort of post. . . . A last post, for, if that boy
was not Christopher's, Groby went out of Tietjens' hands. There
would be no more Tietjenses. Spelden might well be justified.

The grand-father of Father scalped by Indians in Canada in the
war of 1810; the father dying in a place where he should not have
been — taking what he got for it and causing quite a scandal for the
Court of Victoria; the elder brother of Father killed drunk whilst
fox-hunting; Father suicided; Christopher a pauper by his own act
with a by-blow in his shoes. If then there were to be any more Tietjenses by both name and blood. . . . Poor little devils! They would
be their own cousins. Something like that. . . .

And possibly none the worse off for that. . . . Either Spelden or
Groby Great Tree had perhaps done for the others. Groby Great
Tree had been planted to commemorate the birth of Great-grand-
father who had died in a whoreshop — and it had always been whis-
pered in Groby, amongst the children and servants that Groby
Great Tree did not like the house. Its roots tore chunks out of the

foundations and two or three times the trunk had had to be bricke\
into the front wall of the house. They always quoted too the Italian\
saying about trees over the house. Obviously Christopher had told
it to his son and the young man had told it to Mrs. de Bray Pape.
That was why the saying had been referred to three times that day.
. . . Anyway it was an Italian tree! It had been brought as a sap-
ling from Sardinia at a time when gentlemen still thought about
landscape gardening. A gentleman in those days consulted his heirs
about tree planting. Should you plant a group of copper beeches
against a group of white maples over against the haha a quarter of
a mile from the house so that the contrast seen from the ball-room
windows should be agreeable — in thirty years' time. In those days
thought, in families, went in periods of thirty years, owner gravely
consulting the heirs who should see that development of light and
shade that the owner never would.

Nowadays the heir apparently consulted the owner as to whether
the tenant who was taking the ancestral home furnished might not
cut down trees in order to suit the sanitary ideas of the day. . . . An
American day! Well, why not. Those people could not be expected
to know how picturesque a contrast the tree would make against the
roofs of Groby Great House when seen from Peel's Moorside. They
would never hear of Peel's Moorside, or John Peel, or the coat so
grey. . . .

Apparently that was the meaning of the visit of that young colt
and Mrs. de Bray Pape. They had come to ask his, Mark's sanction as owner, to cut down Groby Great Tree. And then they had
funked it and bolted. At any rate the boy was still talking earnestly
to the woman in white over the hedge. As to where Mrs. de Bray
Pape had got to he had no means of knowing; she might be among
the potato rows studying the potatoes of the poor for all he knew.
He hoped she would not come upon Marie Léonie because Marie
Léonie would make short work of Mrs. de Bray Pape and be annoyed
on top of it.

But they were wrong to funk talking to *him* about cutting down
Groby Great Tree. He cared nothing about it. Mrs. de Bray Pape
might just as well have come and said cheerfully: "Hullo old cock,
we're going to cut down your bally old tree and let some light into
the house . . ." if that was the way Americans talked when they
were cheerful; he had no means of knowing. He never remembered
to have talked to an American. . . . Oh, yes, to Cammie Fittle-

worth. She had certainly been a dreadfully slangy young woman before her husband came into the title. But then Fittleworth was
confoundedly slangy too. They said he had to give up in the middle
of a speech he tried to make in the House of Lords because he
could not do without the word "toppin" which upset the Lord
Chancellor. . . . So there was no knowing what Mrs. de Bray Pape
might not have said if she had not thought she was addressing a
syphilitic member of an effete aristocracy mad about an old cedar
tree. But she might just as well have cheerfully announced it. He
did not care. Groby Great Tree had never seemed to like him. It
never seemed to like anybody. They say it never forgave the Tietjenses for transplanting it from nice warm Sardinia to that lugubrious
climate. . . . That was what the servants said to the children and
the children whispered to each other in the dark corridors.

But poor old Christopher! He was going to go mad if the suggestion were made to him. The barest hint! Poor old Christopher
who was now probably at that very minute in one of those beastly
machines overhead, coming back from Groby. . . . If Christopher
had to buy a beastly South Country show-cottage Mark wished he
would not have bought it so near a confounded air-station. However, he had expected probably, that beastly Americans would come
flying in the beastly machines to buy the beastly old junk. They did
indeed do so — sent by Mr. Schatzweiler who was certainly efficient
enough in the sending of cheques.

Christopher had nearly jumped out of his skin — that is to say
he had sat as still as a lump of white marble — when he had gathered
that Sylvia and, still more his own heir, wanted to let Groby furnished. He had said to Mark, over Sylvia's first letter: "You won't let
'em?" and Mark knew the agony that was behind his tallowy mask
and goggle eyes. . . . Perfectly white around the nostrils he went —
that was the sign!

And it had been as near an appeal as he had ever come — unless
the request for a loan on Armistice Day could be regarded as an
appeal. But Mark did not think that that could be regarded as a
score. In their game neither of them had yet made a real score.
Probably neither of them ever would: they were a stout pair of North
Countrymen whatever else could be said against them.

No, it hadn't been a score when Christopher had said: "You won't
let 'em let Groby," the day before yesterday: Christopher had been
in an agony, but he was not *asking* Mark not to let Groby be let; he

was only seeking information as to how far Mark would let the degradation of the old place go. Mark had let him pretty well know that Groby might be pulled down and replaced by a terra-cotta hotel before he would stir a finger. On the other hand Christopher had only to stir a finger and not a blade of grass between the cobbles in the Stillroom Yard could be grubbed up. . . . But by the rules of the game neither of them could give an order. Neither. Mark said to Christopher: "Groby's yours!" Christopher said to Mark: "Groby's yours!" With perfect goodhumour and coldness. So probably the place would fall to pieces or Sylvia would turn it into a bawdy house. . . . It was a good joke! A good, grim Yorkshire joke!

It was impossible to know which of them suffered more. Christopher, it is true, was having his heart broken because the house suffered — but, damn it, wasn't Mark himself pretty well heart-broken because Christopher refused to accept the house from him? . . . It was impossible to know which!

Yes, his confounded heart had been broken on Armistice Day in the morning — between the morning and the morning after. . . . Yes: after Christopher had been reading Boswell aloud, night after night for three weeks. . . . Was that playing the game? Was it playing the game to get no sleep if you had not forgiven your brother? . . . Oh, no doubt it was playing the game. You don't forgive your brother if he lets you down in a damn beastly way. . . . And of course it *is* letting a fellow down in a beastly — a beastly! — way to let him know that you believe he lives on the immoral earnings of his wife. . . . Mark had done that to Christopher. It was unforgivable all right. And equally, of course, you do not hurt your brother back except on the lines circumscribed by the nature of the offence: you are the best friend he has — except on the lines circumscribed by the offence; and you will nurse him like a blasted soft worm — except in so far as the lines circumscribed by the offence do not preclude your ministrations.

For, obviously the best thing Christopher could have done for his brother's health would have been to have accepted the stewardship of Groby — but his brother could die and he himself could die before he would do that. It was nevertheless a pretty cruel affair. . . . Over Boswell the two brothers had got as thick as thieves with an astonishing intimacy — and with an astonishing similarity. If one of them made a comment on Bennet Langton it would be precisely the comment that the other had on his lips. It was what asses call telep-

athy, nowadays . . . a warm, comfortable feeling, late at night
with the light shaded from your eyes, the voice going on through
the deep silence of London that awaited the crash of falling bombs.
. . . Well, Mark accepted Christopher's dictum that he himself was
an eighteenth-century bloke and was only forestalled when he had
wanted to tell Christopher that he was more old-fashioned still — a
sort of seventeenth-century Anglican who ought to be strolling in a
grove with Greek Testament beneath the arm and all. . . .

And, hang it all, there was room for him! The land had not
changed. . . . There were still the deep beech-woods making groves
beside the ploughlands and the rooks rising lazily as the plough
came towards them. The land had not changed. . . . Well, the
breed had not changed. . . . There was Christopher. . . . Only,
the times . . . they had changed. The rooks and the ploughlands
and the beeches and Christopher were there still. . . . But not the
frame of mind in the day. . . . The sun might rise and go above
the plough till it set behind the hedge and the ploughman went off
to the inn settle; and the moon could do the same. But they would
— neither sun nor moon — look on the spit of Christopher in all
their journeys. Never. They might as well expect to see a mastodon.
. . . And he, Mark, himself was an old-fashioned buffer. That was
all right. Judas Iscariot himself was an old-fashioned ass, once upon
a time!

But it was almost on the edge of not playing the game for Christopher to let that intimacy establish itself and all the time to cherish
that unforgivingness. . . . Not quite not playing the game, but almost. For hadn't Mark held out feelers? Hadn't he made conces-
sions? Hadn't his very marrying of Marie Léonie been by way of a
concession to Christopher? Didn't Christopher, if the truth was to
be known, want Mark to marry Marie Léonie because he, Christopher, wanted to marry Valentine Wannop and hadn't a hope? If
the truth were known . . . Well, he had made that concession to
Christopher, who was a sort of a person anyhow. But ought Christopher to have exacted — to have telepathically willed — that concession if he wasn't himself going to concede something? Ought he
to have forced him, Mark, to accept his mooning, womanly services
when the poor devil was already worn out with his military duties
of seeing old tins cleaned out day after day, and when he meant to
become a beastly old-furniture dealer and refuse Groby? For, upon
his soul, till the morning of Armistice Day Mark had accepted

Christopher's story of Mr. Schatzweiler as merely a good-humoured, grim threat . . . A sort of a feint at a threat. . . .

Well, probably it was playing the game all right: if Christopher thought it was jonnock, jonnock it was!

But . . . a damn beastly shock. . . . Why he had been practically convalescent, he had been out of bed in a dressing gown and had told Lord Wolstonemark that he could pile in as many papers as he liked from the office. . . . And then Christopher, without a hat and in a beastly civilian suit of light mulberry coloured Harris tweed, had burst into the room with a beastly piece of old furniture under his arm. . . . A sort of inlaid toy writing-desk. A model. For cabinet-makers! A fine thing to bring into a convalescent bedroom, to a man quietly reading Form T. O. LOUWR 1962. E 17 of the 10/11/18 in front of a clean fire. . . . And chalk-white about the gills the fellow was — with an awful lot of silver in his hair. . . . What age was he? Forty? Forty-three? God knew!

Forty . . . He wanted to borrow forty quid on that beastly piece of furniture. To have an Armistice Day Beanfeast and set up house with his gal! Forty quid! My God! Mark felt his bowels turning over within him with disgust. . . . The gal — that fellow's half-sister as like as not — was waiting in an empty house for him to go and seduce her. In order to celebrate the salvation of the world by seven million deaths!

If you seduce a girl you don't do it on forty pounds: you accept Groby and three, seven, ten thousand a year. So he had told Christopher.

And then he had got it. Full in the face. Christopher was not going to accept a penny from him. Never. Not ever! . . . No doubt about that, either. That fact had gone into Mark as a knife goes into a stag's throat. It had hurt as much, but it hadn't killed! Damn it, it might as well have! It might as well have. . . . Does a fellow do that to his own brother just because his own brother has called him . . . what is the word? *Maquereau!* . . . Probably a maquereau is worse than a pimp. . . . The difference between a flea and a louse, as Dr. Johnson said.

Eh, but Christopher was bitter! . . . Apparently he had gone round first to Sir John Robertson's with that jigamaree. Sir John had promised to buy it for a hundred pounds. It was a special sort of model signed by some duke of a Bath cabinet-maker in 1762. . . . Wasn't that the year of the American Rebellion? Well, Christopher had bought it in a junk-shop of sorts for a fiver and Sir John had promised him a hundred quid. He collected cabinet-maker's models; extraordinarily valuable they were. Christopher had spat out that this was worth a thousand dollars. . . . Thinking of his old-furniture customers!

When Christopher had used that word — with the blue pebbles sticking out of his white lard head — Mark had felt the sweat break out all over him. He had known it was all up. . . . Christopher had gone on: you expected him to spit electric sparks, but his voice was wooden. Sir John had said to him:

"Eh, no mon. You're a fine soldier now, raping half the girls in Flanders an Ealing and asking us to regard you as heroes. Fine heroes. And now you're safe. . . . A hundred pounds is a price to a Christian that is faithful to his lovely wife. Five pounds is as much as I'll give you for the model and be thankful it is five, not one, for old sake's sake!"

That was what Sir John Robertson had said to Christopher; that was what the world was like to serving soldiers in that day. You don't have to wonder that Christopher was bitter — even to his own brother with the sweat making his underlinen icy. He had said:

"My good chap. I won't lend you a penny on that idiotic jigamaree. But I'll write you a cheque for a thousand pounds this minute. Give me my cheque book from the table. . . ."

Marie Léonie had come into the room on hearing Christopher's voice. She liked to hear the news from Christopher. And she liked Christopher and Mark to have heated discussions. She had observed that they did Mark good: on the day when Christopher had first come there, three weeks before, when they certainly had heatedly discussed, she had observed that Mark's temperature had fallen from ninety-nine point six to ninety-eight point two. In two hours. . . . After all, if a Yorkshire man can quarrel he can live. They were like that, those others, she said.

Christopher had turned on her and said:

"Ma belle amie m'attend à ma maison; nous voulons célébrer avec mes camarades de régiment. Je n'ai pas le soue. Prêtez moi quarante livres, je vous en prie, madame!" He had added that he would leave his cabinet as a pledge. He was as stiff as a sentry outside Buckingham Palace. She had looked at Mark with some astonishment. After all, she might well be astonished. He himself had made no sign and suddenly Christopher had exclaimed:

"Prêtez les moi, prêtez les moi, pour l'amour de Dieu!"

Marie Léonie had gone a little white, but she had turned up her skirt and turned down her stocking and took out the notes.

"Pour le dieu d'amour, monsieur, je veux bien," she had said. . . . You never knew what a Frenchwoman would not say. That was out of an old song.

But the sweat burst out all over his face at the recollection: great drops of sweat.

VII

MARIE LÉONIE, a strong taste of apples in her mouth, strong odours of apples on the air, wasps around her and as if a snow-drift of down descending about her feet, was frowning seriously over Burgundy bottles into which ran cider from a glass tube that she held to their necks. She frowned because the task was serious and engrossing, because the wasps annoyed her and because she was resisting an impulse inside herself. It told her that something ailed Mark and urged her to go and look at him.

It annoyed her because as a rule she felt presages of something ailing Mark only at night. Only at night. During the day usually she felt in her *for intérieur* that Mark was like what he was only because he wanted so to be. His glance was too virile and dominant to let you think otherwise — the dark, liquid, direct glance! But at nightfall — or at any rate shortly after supper when she had retired to her room terrible premonitions of disaster to Mark visited her. He was dying where he lay; he was beset by the spectral being of the countryside; robbers, even, had crept upon him, though that was unreasonable. For all the countryside knew that Mark was paralysed and unable to store wealth in his mattress. . . . Still, nefarious strangers might see him and imagine that he kept his gold repeater watch beneath his pillow. . . . So she would rise a hundred times in a night and, going to the low, diamond-casement window, would lean out and listen. But there would be no sound: the wind in the leaves; the cry of water-birds overhead. The dim light would be in the hut, seen unmoving through the apple boughs.

Now, however, in broad daylight, towards the hour of tea, with the little maid on a stool beside her plucking the boiling-hens that were to go to market next day, with the boxes of eggs on their shelves, each egg wired to the bottom of its box wait'ng till she had time to date-stamp it — in the open potting-shed in the quiet, broad light of a summer day she was visited by a presage of something ailing Mark. She resented it, but she was not the woman to resist it.

There was, however, nothing to warrant it. From the corners of the house, to which she proceeded, she could see quite well the greater part of Mark's solitary figure. Gunning, being talked to by the English lord, held a spare horse by the bridle and was looking at Mark over the hedge, too. He exhibited no emotions. A young man was walking along the inside of the hedge between it and the raspberries. That was no affair of hers: Gunning was not protesting. The head and shoulders of a young woman — or it might be another young man — were proceeding along the outside of the hedge nearly level with the first one. That was equally no affair of hers. Probably they were looking at the bird's nest. There was some sort of bird's nest she had heard, in that thick hedge. There was no end to the folly of the English in the country as in the town: they would waste time over everything. This bird was a bottle . . . bottle something and Christopher and Valentine and the parson and the doctor and the artist who lived down the hill were crazy about it. They walked on tip-toe when they were within twenty yards. Gunning was allowed to trim the hedge, but apparently the birds knew Gunning. . . . For Marie Léonie all birds were *moineaux*, as who should say "sparrers" as in London they called them — just as all flowers were *giroflées* — as you might say wall-flowers. . . . No wonder this nation was going to rack and ruin when it wasted its time over preserving the nests of sparrers and naming innumerable wall-flowers! The country was well enough — a sort of suburb of Caen: but the people! . . . No wonder William, of Falaise, in Normandy subjugated them with such ease.

Now she had wasted five minutes, for the glass tubes, hinged on rubber, that formed her siphon from barrel to bottle had had per-force, to be taken out of the spile-hole, the air had entered into it, and she would have to put it back and suck once more at the tube until the first trickle of cider entered her mouth. She disliked having to do that; it wasted the cider and she disliked the flavour in the afternoon when one had lunched. The little maid also would say: "A — oh, meladyship, Ah *du* call thet queer!" . . . Nothing would cure that child of saying that though she was otherwise *sage et docile*. Even Gunning scratched his head at the sight of those tubes.

Could these savages never understand that if you want to have *cidre mousseux* — foaming — you must have as little sediment as possible? And that in the bottom of casks, even if they had not been moved for a long time there will always be sediment — particularly if you set up a flow in the liquids by running it from a tap near the bottom. So you siphon off the top of the great casks for bottling *mousseux* and bottle the rest of the cask and run the thickest into little thin-wood kegs with many hopes for freezing in the winter. . . . To make *calvados*, where you cannot have alembics because of the excise . . . In this unhappy country you may not have alembics for the distilling of apple-jack, plum-brandy or other *fines* — because of the excise! *Quel pays! Quels gens!*

They lacked industry, frugality — and above all, spirit! Look at that poor Valentine, hiding in her room upstairs because there were people about whom she suspected of being people from the English lord's house. . . . By rights that poor Valentine should be helping her with the bottling and ready to sell that lugubrious old furniture to visitors whilst her lord was away buying more old rubbish. . . . And she was distracted because she could not find some prints. They represented — Marie Léonie was well aware because she had heard the facts several times — street criers of ambulant wares in London years ago. There were only eight of these to be found. Where were the other four? The customer, a lady of title, was anxious for them. For presents for an immediate wedding! Monsieur my brother-in-law had come upon the four that were to make up the set at a sale two days before. He had recounted with satisfaction how he had found them on the grass. . . . It was supposed that he had brought them home; but they were not in the warehouse at Cramp the carpenter's, they were not to be found, left in the cart. They were in no drawer or press. . . . What was to prove that *mon beau-frère* had brought them home from the sale. He was not there: he was gone for a day and a half. Naturally he would be gone for a day and a half when he was most needed. . . . And where was he gone, leaving his young wife in that nervous condition? For a day and a half! He had never before been gone for a day and a half. . . . There was then something brewing; it was in the air; it was in her bones. . . . It was like that dreadful day of the Armistice when this miserable land betrayed the beautiful *pays de France*! . . . When monsieur had borrowed forty pounds of her. . . . In the name of heaven why did not he borrow another forty — or eighty — or a

hundred, rather than be distracted and distract Mark and his unhappy girl? . . .

She was not unsympathetic, that girl. She had civilisation. She
could talk of Philémon and Baucis. She had made her *bachot*, she
was what you would call *fille de famille*. . . . But without *chic* . . .
Without . . . Without . . . Well, she neither displayed enough
erudition to be a *bas bleu* — though she had enough erudition! —
not enouch *chic* to be a *femme légère* — a *poule* who would *faire la
noce* with her gallant. Monsieur the brother-in-law was no gay spark.
But you never know with a man. . . . The cut of a skirt; a twist of
the hair . . . Though to-day there was no hair to twist; but there is
the equivalent.

And it was a fact that you never knew a man. Look at the case of
Eleanor Dupont who lived for ten years with Duchamp of the Sor-
bonne. . . . Eleanor would never attend scrupulously to her attire
because her man wore blue spectacles and was a *savant*. . . . But
what happened. . . . There came along a little piece with a hat as
large as a cartwheel covered with greenstuff and sleeves up above her
ears — as the mode was then. . . .

That had been a lesson to her, Marie Léonie, who had been a girl
at the time. She had determined that if she achieved a *collage sérieux*
with a monsieur of eighty and as blind as a bat she would study the
modes of the day right down to the latest perfume. These messieurs
did not know it, but they moved among *femmes du monde* and the
fashionable cocottes and however much she at home might be the
little brown bird of the domestic hearth, the lines of her dresses,
her hair, her personal odour, must conform. Mark did not imagine;
she did not suppose he had ever seen a fashionable journal in her
apartments that were open to him or had ever suspected that she
walked in the Row on a Sunday when he was away. . . . But she
had studied these things like another. And more. For it is difficult
to keep with the fashion and at the same time appear as if you were
a serious *petite bourgeoise*. But she had done it: and observe the
results. . . .

But that poor Valentine. . . . Her man was attached enough,
and well he should be considering the affair in which he had landed
her. But always there comes the *pic des tempêtes*, the Cape Horn,
round which you must go. It is the day when your man looks at you
and says: "H'm, h'm," and considers if the candle is not more valuable than the game! Ah then . . . There are wise folk who put that

at the seventh year; other wise ones, at the second; others again at
the eleventh. . . . But in fact you may put it at any day on any
year — to the hundredth. . . . And that poor Valentine with four
spots of oil on her only skirt but two. And that so badly hung, though
the stuff no doubt was once good. One must concede that! They
make admirable tweeds in this country: better certainly than in
Roubaix. But is that enough to save a country — or a woman depend-
ant on a man who has introduced her into a bad affair?

A voice behind her said:

"I see you have plenty of eggs!" — an unusual voice of a sort of
breathless nervousness. Marie Léonie continued to hold the mouth
of her tube into the neck of a burgundy bottle; into this she had
already introduced a small screw of sifted sugar and an extremely
minute portion of a powder that she got from a pharmacist of
Rouen. This, she understood, made the cider of a rich brownness.
She did not see why cider should be brown but it was considered to
be less fortifying if it were light golden. She continued also to think
about Valentine who would be twittering with nerves at the window
whose iron-leaded casement was open above their heads. She would
have put down her Latin book and have crept to the window to
listen.

The little girl beside Marie Léonie had risen from the three-legged
stool and held a dead, white fowl with a nearly naked breast by its
neck. She said hoarsely:

"These 'ere be 'er Ladyship's settins of prize Reds." She was
blonde, red-faced and wore on her dull fair hair a rather large cap,
on her thin body a check blue cotton gown. " 'Arf a crownd a piece
the heggs be or twenty-four shillings a dozen if you take a gross."

Marie Léonie heard the hoarse voice with some satisfaction. This
girl whom they had only had for a fortnight seemed to be satisfactory
mentally; it was not her business to sell the eggs but Gunning's;
nevertheless she knew the details. Marie Léonie did not turn round:
it was not *her* business to talk to anyone who wanted to buy eggs
and she had no curiosity as to customers. She had too much else to
think about. The voice said:

"Half a crown seems a great deal for an egg. What is that in
dollars? This must be that tyranny over edibles by the producer of
which one has heard so much."

"Tiddn nothin' in dollars," the girl said. " 'Arf a dollar is two bob.
'Arf a crown is two 'n six."

The conversation continued, but it grew dim in Marie Léonie's thoughts. The child and the voice disputed as to what a dollar was — or so it appeared, for Marie Léonie was not familiar with either of the accents of the disputants. The child was a combative child. She drove both Gunning and the cabinet-maker Camp with an organ of brass. Of tin perhaps, like a penny whistle. When she was not grubbily working, she read books with avidity — books about Blood if she could get them. She had an exaggerated respect for the Family but none for any other soul in the world. . . .

Marie Léonie considered that, by now, she might have got down to the depth of the cask where you find sediment. She ran some cider into a clear glass, stopping the tube with her thumb. The cider was clear enough to let her bottle another dozen, she judged; then she would send for Gunning to take the spile-bung out of the next cask. Four sixty-gallon casks she had to attend to; two of them were done. She began to tire: she was not unfatigable if she was indefatigable. She began at any rate to feel drowsy. She wished Valentine could have helped her. But that girl had not much backbone and she, Marie Léonie, acknowledged that for the sake of the future it was good that she should rest and read books in Latin or Greek. And avoid nervous encounters.

She had tucked her up under an eiderdown on their four-post bed because They would have all the windows open and currents of air must above all be avoided by women. . . . *Elle* had smiled and said that it had once been her dream to read the works of Æschylus beside the blue Mediterranean. They had kissed each other. . . .

The maid beside her was saying that orfen 'n orfen she'd 'eared 'er farver 'oo was a dealer wen a lot of ol' 'ens, say, 'ad gone to three an nine say: "Make it two arf dollars!" They didn' 'ave dollars in thet country but they did 'ave 'arf dollars. N Capt'n Kidd th' pirate: 'e 'ad dollars, n' pieces of eight 'n' moi-dors too!

A wasp annoyed Marie Léonie; it buzzed almost on her nose, retired, returned, made a wide circuit. There were already several wasps struggling in the glass of cider she had just drawn; there were others in circles round spots of cider on the slats of wood on which the barrels were arranged. They drew in their tails and then expanded, ecstatically. Yet only two nights before she and Valentine had gone with Gunning all over the orchard with a lantern, a trowel and a bottle of prussic acid, stopping up holes along the paths and in banks. She had liked the experience; the darkness, the ring of light from the lantern on the rough grass; the feeling that she was out, near Mark and that yet Gunning and his lantern kept spiritual visitors away. . . . What she suffered between the desire to visit her man in the deep nights and the possibility of coming up against *revenants* . . . Was it reasonable? . . . What women had to suffer for their men! Even if they were faithful. . . .

What the unfortunate *Elle* had not suffered! . . .

Even on what you might call her *nuit de noces*. . . . At the time it had seemed incomprehensible. She had had no details. It had merely seemed fantastic: possibly even tragic because Mark had taken it so hardly. Truly she believed he had become insane. At two in the morning, beside Mark's bed. They had — the two brothers — exchanged words of considerable violence whilst the girl shivered; and was determined. That girl had been determined. She would not go back to her mother. At two in the morning. . . . Well, if you refuse to go back to your mother at two in the morning you kick indeed your slipper over the mill!

The details of that night came back to her, amongst wasps and beneath the conversation of the unseen woman, in the shed where the water ran in the trough. She had set the bottles in the trough because it is a good thing to cool cider before the process of fermentation in the bottles begins. The bottles with their shining necks of green glass were an agreeable spectacle. The lady behind her back was talking of Oklahoma. . . . The cowboy with the large nose that she had seen on the film at the Piccadilly Cinema had come from Oklahoma. It was no doubt somewhere in America. She had been used to go to the Piccadilly Cinema on a Friday. You do not go to the theatre on a Friday if you are *bien pensant*, but you may regard the cinema as being to the theatre what a *repas maigre* is as against a meal with meat. . . . The lady speaking behind her came apparently from Oklahoma: she had eaten prairie chickens in her time. On a farm. Now, however, she was very rich. Or so she told the little maid. Her husband could buy half Lord Fittleworth's estate and not miss the money. She said that if only people here would take example . . .

On that evening they had come thumping on her door. The bell had failed to wake her after all the noise in the street that day. . . . She had sprung into the middle of the floor and flown to save Mark . . . from an air-raid. She had forgotten that it was the Armistice. . . . But the knocking had gone on on the door.

Before it had stood monsieur the brother-in-law and that girl in a dark blue girl-guides' sort of uniform. Both chalk-white and weary to death. As if they leaned one against another. . . . She had been for bidding them go away, but Mark had come out of the bedroom; in his nightshirt with his legs bare. And hairy! He had bidden them come in, roughly, and had got back into bed. . . . That had been the last time he had been on his legs! Now, he having been in bed so long, his legs were no longer hairy, but polished. Like thin glazed bones!

She had recalled his last gesture. He had positively used a gesture, like a man raving. . . . And indeed he was raving. At Christopher. And dripping with sweat. Twice she had wiped his face whilst they shouted at each other.

It had been difficult to understand what they said because they had spoken a sort of *patois*. Naturally they returned to the language they spoke in their childhoods — when they were excited, these unexcitable people! It resembled the *patois* of the Bretons. Harsh . . .

And, for herself she had been all concerned for the girl. Naturally she had been concerned for the girl. One is a woman. . . . At first she had taken her for a little piece from the streets. . . . But even for a little piece from the streets . . . Then she had noticed that there had been no rouge; no imitation pearl necklace. . . .

Of course when she had gathered that Mark was pressing money on them she had felt different. Different in two ways. It could not be a little piece. And then her heart contracted at the idea of money being given away. They might be ruined. It might be these people instead of her Paris nephews who would pillage her corpse. But the brother-in-law pushed the thought of money away from him with both hands. If she — *Elle* — wanted to go with him she must share his fortune. . . . What a country! What people!

There had seemed to be no understanding them then. . . . It had appeared that Mark insisted that the girl should stop there with her lover; the lover on the contrary insisted that she should go home to her mother. The girl kept saying that on no account would she leave Christopher. He could not be left. He would die if he was left. . . . And indeed that brother-in-law had seemed sick enough. He panted worse than Mark.

She had eventually taken the girl to her own room. A little, agonised, fair creature. She had felt inclined to enfold her in her arms but she had not done so. Because of the money. . . . She might as well have. It was impossible to get these people to touch money. She would now give no little to lend that girl twenty pounds for a frock and some undergarments.

The girl had sat there without speaking. It had seemed for hours. Then some drunken man on the church steps opposite had begun to play the bugle. Long calls. . . . Tee . . . Teee . . . TEEEE . . . Ta-heee . . . To-hee . . . Continuing for ever. . . .

The girl had begun to cry. She had said that it was dreadful. But you could not object. It was the Last Post they were playing. For the Dead. You could not object to their playing the Last Post for the Dead that night. Even if it was a drunken man who played and even if it drove you mad. The Dead ought to have all they could get.

If she had not made the necessary allowance that would have seemed to Marie Léonie an exaggerated sentiment. The English bugle notes could do no good to the French dead and the English losses were so negligible in quantity that it hardly seemed worth while to become *emotionnée* when their funeral call was played by a drunken man. The French papers estimated the English losses at a few hundreds; what was that as against the millions of her own people? . . . But she gathered that this girl had gone through something terrible that night with the wife, and being too proud to show emotion over her personal vicissitudes she pretended to find an outlet because of the sounds of that bugle. . . . Well, it was mournful enough. She had understood it when Christopher, putting his face in at the crack of the door had whispered to her that he was going to stop the bugle because its sound was intolerable to Mark.

The girl apparently had been in a reverie for she had not heard him. She, Marie Léonie, had gone to look at Mark and the girl sat there, on the bed. Mark was by then quite quiescent. The bugle had stopped. To cheer him she had made a few remarks about the inappropriateness of playing, for a negligible number of dead, a funeral call at three in the morning. If it had been for the French dead — or if her country had not been betrayed. It was betraying her country to have given those assassins an armistice when they were far from their borders. Merely that was treachery on the part of these sham Allies. They should have gone right through those monsters slaying them by the million, defenceless, and then they should have laid waste their country with fire and sword. Let them too know what it was to suffer as France had suffered. It was treachery enough not to have done that and the child unborn would suffer for it.

But there they waited, then, even after that treachery had been done, to know what were the terms of even that treachery. They might even now not intend to be going to Berlin. . . . What then was Life for?

Mark had groaned. In effect he was a good Frenchman. She had seen to that. The girl had come into the room. She could not bear to be alone. . . . What a night of movement and cross movement. She had begun to argue with Mark. Hadn't there, she had asked, been enough of suffering? He agreed that there had been enough of suffering. But there must be more. . . . Even out of justice to the poor bloody Germans. . . . He had called them the poor bloody Germans. He had said that it was the worst dis-service you could do to your foes not to let them know that remorseless consequences follow determined actions. To interfere in order to show fellows that if they did what they wanted they need not of necessity take what they got for it was in effect to commit a sin against God. If the Germans did not experience that in the sight of the world there was an end of Europe and the world. What was to hinder endless recurrences of what had happened near a place called Gemmenich on the 4th of August, 1914, at six o'clock in the morning? There was nothing to hinder it. Any other state from the smallest to the largest might . . .

The girl had interrupted to say that the world had changed and Mark, lying back exhausted on his pillows had said with a sort of grim sharpness:

"It is you who say it. . . . Then you must run the world. . . . I know nothing about it. . . ." He appeared exhausted.

It was singular the way those two discussed — discussed "the situation" at three-thirty in the morning. Well, nobody wanted to be asleep that night, it seemed. Even in that obscene street mobs went by, shouting and playing concertinas. She had never heard Mark discuss before — and she was never to hear him discuss again. He appeared to regard that girl with a sort of aloof indulgence; as if he were fond of her but regarded her as over-learned, too young, and devoid of all experience. Marie Léonie had watched them and listened with intentness. In twenty years, these three weeks had for the first time showed her her man in contact with his people. The contemplation had engrossed her.

She could nevertheless see that her man was exhausted in his inner being and obviously that girl was tried beyond endurance. Whilst she talked she appeared to listen for distant sounds. . . . She kept on recurring to the idea that punishment was abhorrent to the modern mind. Mark stuck to his point that to occupy Berlin was not punishment, but that not to occupy Berlin was to commit an intellectual sin. The consequences of invasion is counter-invasion and symbolical occupation, as the consequence of over-pride, is humiliation. For the rest of the world, he knew nothing of it; for his own country that was logic — the logic by which she had lived. To abandon that logic was to abandon clearness of mind: it was mental cowardice. To show the world Berlin occupied, with stands of arms and colours on her public places was to show that England respected logic. Not to show the world that was to show that England was mentally cowardly. We dare not put the enemy nations to pain because we shrank from the contemplation.

Valentine had said: "There has been too much suffering!"

He had said:

"Yes, you are afraid of suffering. . . . But England is necessary to the world. . . . To my world. . . . Well, make it your world and it may go to rack and ruin how it will. I am done with it. But then . . . do you accept the responsibility!"

A world with England presenting the spectacles of moral cowardice will be a world on a lower plane. . . . If you lower the record for the mile you lower the standard of blood-stock. Try to think of that. If Persimmon had not achieved what it did the French Grand Prix would be less of an event and the trainers at Maisons Laffite would be less efficient; and the jockeys, and the stable lads, and the sporting writers. . . . A world profits by the example of a steadfast nation. . . .

Suddenly Valentine said:

"Where is Christopher?" with such intentness that it was like a blow.

Christopher had gone out. She exclaimed:

"But you must not let him go out. . . . He is not fit to go out alone. . . . He has gone out to go back. . . ."

Mark said:

"Don't go. . . ." For she had got to the door. "He went out to stop the Last Post. But you may play the Last Post, for me. Perhaps he has gone back to the Square. He had presumably better see what has happened to his wife. I should not myself."

Valentine had said with extraordinary bitterness:

"He shall not. He shall not." She had gone.

It had come through to Marie Léonie partly then and partly subsequently that Christopher's wife had turned up at Christopher's empty house that was in the Square only a few yards away. They had gone back late at night probably for purposes of love and had found her there. She had come for the purpose of telling them that she was going to be operated on for cancer so that with their sensitive natures they could hardly contemplate going to bed together at that moment.

It had been a good lie. That Mrs. Tietjens was a *maîtresse femme*. There was no denying that. She herself was engaged for those others both by her own inclinations and the strong injunctions of her husband, but Mme Tietjens was certainly ingenious. She had managed to incommode and discredit that pair almost as much as any pair could be incommoded and discredited, although they were the most harmless couple in the world.

They had certainly not had an agreeable festival on that Armistice Day. Apparently one of the officers present at their dinner of celebration had gone raving mad; the wife of another of Christopher's comrades of the regiment had been rude to Valentine; the colonel of the regiment had taken the opportunity to die with every circumstance of melodrama. Naturally all the other officers had run away and had left Christopher and Valentine with the madman and the dying colonel on their hands.

An agreeable *voyage de noces*. . . . It appeared that they had secured a four-wheel cab in which with the madman and the other they had driven to Balham — an obscure suburb, with sixteen celebrants hanging all over the outside of the cab and two on the horse's back — at any rate for a couple of miles from Trafalgar Square; they were not of course interested in the interior of the cab; they were merely gay because there was to be no more suffering. Valentine and Christopher had got rid of the madman somewhere in Chelsea at an asylum for shell-shock cases. There he had remained ever since. But the authorities would not take the colonel so they had driven on to Balham, the colonel making dying speeches about the late war, his achievements, the money he owed Christopher. . . . Valentine had appeared to find that extremely trying. The man died in the cab.

They had had to walk back into Town because the driver of the four-wheeler was so upset by the death in his cab that he could not drive. Moreover the horse was foundered. It had been twelve, midnight, before they reached Trafalgar Square. They had had to struggle through packed crowds nearly all the way. Apparently they were happy at the accomplishment of their duty — or their benevolence.

They stood on the top step of St. Martin's Church, dominating the square that was all illuminated and packed and roaring, with bonfires made of the paving wood and omnibuses and the Nelson Column going up and the fountain-basins full of drunkards, and orators and bands. . . . They stood on the top step, drew deep breaths and fell into each other's arms. . . . For the first time — though apparently they had loved each other for a lustrum or more. . . . What people!

Then, at the top of the stairs in the house in the Inn they had perceived Sylvia, all in white! . . .

Apparently she had been informed that Christopher and that girl were in communication — by a lady who did not like Christopher because she owed him money. A Lady Macmaster. Apparently there was no one in the world who did not dislike Christopher because they owed him money. The colonel and the lunatic and the husband of the lady who had been rude to Valentine . . . all, all! Right down to Mr. Schatzweiler who had only paid Christopher one cheque for a few dollars out of a great sum and had then contracted a nervous break-down on account of the sufferings he had gone through as a prisoner of war.

But what sort of a man was that Christopher to have in his hands the fortunes of a woman. . . . Any woman!

Those were practically the last words her Mark had ever spoken to her, Marie Léonie. She had been supporting him whilst he drank a *tisane* she had made in order that he might sleep, and he had said gravely:

"It is not necessary that I should ask you to be kind to Mademoiselle Wannop. Christopher is incapable of looking after her. . . ." His last words, for immediately afterwards the telephone bell had rung. He had just before seemed to have a good deal of temperature and it had been whilst his eyes were goggling at her, the thermometer that she had stuck in his mouth gleaming on his dark lips, and whilst she was regretting letting him be tormented by his family that the sharp drilling of the telephone had sounded from the hall. Immediately the strong German accent of Lord Wolstonemark had, with its accustomed disagreeableness, burred in her ear. He had said that the Cabinet was still sitting and they desired to know at once the code that Mark used in his communications with various ports. His second-in-command appeared to be lost amongst the celebrations of that night. Mark had said with a sort of grim irony from the bedroom that if they wanted to stop his transport going out they might just as well

not use cypher. If they wanted to use a twopenny halfpenny economy as window dressing for the elections they'd have to have, they
might as well give it as much publicity as they could. Besides, he did
not believe they would get into Germany with the transport they had.
A good deal had been smashed lately.

The Minister had said with a sort of heavy joy that they were not
going into Germany, and that had been the most dreadful moment
of Marie Léonie's life; but with her discipline she had just simply
repeated the words to Mark. He had then said something she did not
quite catch, and he would not repeat what he had said. She said as
much to Lord Wolstonemark and the chuckling accent said that he
supposed that that was the sort of news that would rattle the old boy.
But one must adapt oneself to one's day; the times were changed.

She had gone from the instrument to look at Mark. She spoke to
him; she spoke to him again. And again — rapid words of panic. His
face was dark purple and congested; he gazed straight before him.
She raised him; he sank back inertly.

She remembered going to the telephone and speaking in French
to the man at the other end. She had said that the man at the other
end was a German and a traitor; her husband should never speak to
him or his fellows again. The man had said: "Eh, what's that? Eh?
. . . Who are you?"

With appalling shadows chasing up and down in her mind she had
said:

"I am Lady Mark Tietjens. You have murdered my husband. Clear
yourself from off my line, murderer!"

It had been the first time she had ever given herself that name; it
was indeed the first time she had ever spoken in French to that Ministry. But Mark had finished with the Ministry, with the Government, with the nation. . . . With the world.

As soon as she could get that man off the wire she had rung up
Christopher. He had come round with Valentine in tow. It had certainly not been much of a *nuit de noces* for that young couple.

Part Two

SYLVIA TIETJENS, using merely the persuasion of her left knee edged her chestnut bay nearer to the bay mare of the shining General. She said:

"If I divorce Christopher, will you marry me?"

He exclaimed with the vehemence of a shocked hen:

"Good God, no!"

He shone everywhere except in such parts of his grey tweed suit as would have shown by shining that they had been put on more than once. But his little white moustache, his cheeks, the bridge but not the tip of his nose, his reins, his Guards' tie, his boots, martingale, snaffle, curb, fingers, fingernails — all these gave evidence of interminable rubbings. . . . By himself, by his man, by Lord Fittleworth's stable-hands, grooms. . . . Interminable rubbings and supervisions at the end of extended arms. Merely to look at him you would know that he was something like Lord Edward Campion, Lieutenant General retired, K.C.M.G. (military) M.P.V.C., M.C., D.S.O. . . . So he exclaimed: "Good God, no!" and using a little-finger touch on his snaffle-rein made his mare recoil from Sylvia Tietjens' chestnut. Annoyed at its mate's motion, the bad-tempered chestnut with the white forehead showed its teeth at the mare, danced a little and threw out some flakes of foam. Sylvia swayed a little backwards and forwards in her saddle, and smiled downwards into her husband's garden.

"You can't, you know," she said, "expect to put an idea out of my head just by flurrying the horses. . . ."

"A man," the General said between "Comeups" to his mare, "does not marry his . . ."

His mare went backwards a pace or two into the bank and then a pace forwards.

"His what?" Sylvia asked with amiability. "You can't be going to call me your cast mistress. No doubt most men would have a shot at it. But I never have been even your mistress. . . . I have to think of Michael!"

"I wish," the General said vindictively, "that you would settle what that boy is to be called. . . . Michael or Mark!" He added: "I was going to say: 'his godson's wife.' . . . A man may not marry his godson's wife."

Sylvia bent over to stroke the neck of the chestnut.

"A man," she said, "cannot marry any man's wife. . . . But if you think that I am going to be the second Lady Tietjens after that . . . French hairdresser's widow . . ."

"You would prefer," the General said, "to go to India. . . ."

Visions of India went through their hostile minds. They looked down from their horses over Tietjens's in West Sussex, over a house with a high-pitched, tiled roof with deep windows in the grey local stone. He nevertheless saw names like Akhbar Khan, Alexander of Macedon, the son of Philip, Delhi, the Massacre at Cawnpore. . . . His mind, given over from boyhood to the contemplation of the largest jewel in the British Crown, spewed up those romances. He was member for the West Cleveland Division and a thorn in the side of the Government. They *must* give him India. They knew that if they did not he could publish revelations as to the closing days of the late war. . . . He would naturally never do that. One does not blackmail even a Government.

Still, to all intents he *was* India.

Sylvia also was aware that he was to all intents and purposes India. She saw receptions in Government Houses in which, habited with a tiara, she too would be INDIA. . . . As someone said in Shakespeare:

> I am dying, Egypt, dying! Only
> I will importune Death a while until
> Of many thousand kisses this poor last
> Is laid upon thy lips. . . .

She imagined it would be agreeable, supposing her to betray this old Pantaloon India to have a lover, gasping at her feet, exclaiming: "I am dying, India, dying. . . ." And she with her tiara, very tall. In white, probably. Probably satin!

The General said:

"You know you cannot possibly divorce my godson. You are a Roman Catholic."

She said, always with her smile:

"Oh, *can't* I? . . . Besides it would be of the greatest advantage to Michael to have for a step-father the Field Marshal. . . ."

He said with impotent irritation:

"I wish you would settle whether that boy's name is Michael or Mark!"

She said:

"He calls himself Mark. . . . I call him Michael because I hate the name of Mark. . . ."

She regarded Campion with real hatred. She said that upon occasion she would be exemplarily revenged upon him. "Michael" was a Satterthwaite name, "Mark," the name for a Tietjens eldest son. The boy had originally been baptised and registered as Michael Tietjens. At his reception into the Roman Church he had been baptised "Michael Mark." Then had followed the only real deep humiliation of her life. After his Papist baptism the boy had asked to be called Mark. She had asked him if he really meant that. After a long pause — the dreadful long pauses of children before they render a verdict! — he had said that he intended to call himself Mark from then on. . . . By the name of his father's brother, of his father's father, grandfather, great-grandfather. . . . By the name of the irascible apostle of the lion and the sword. . . . The Satterthwaites, his mother's family, might go by the board.

For herself, she hated the name of Mark. If there was one man in the world whom she hated because he was insensible of her attraction it was Mark Tietjens who lay beneath the thatched roof beneath her eyes. . . . Her boy, however, intended, with a child's cruelty to call himself Mark Tietjens. . . .

The General grumbled:

"There is no keeping track with you. . . . You say now you would be humiliated to be Lady Tietjens after that Frenchwoman. . . . But you have always said that that Frenchwoman is only the concubine of Sir Mark. . . . You say one thing, then you say another. . . . What is one to believe?"

She regarded him with sunny condescension. He grumbled on:

"One thing, then another. . . . You say you cannot divorce my godson because you are a Roman Catholic. Nevertheless you begin divorce proceedings and throw all the mud you can over the miserable fellow. Then you remember your creed and don't go on. . . . What sort of game is this?" She regarded him still ironically but with good humour across the neck of her horse.

He said:

"There's *really* no fathoming you. . . . A little time ago — for months on end — you were dying of . . . of internal cancer in short . . ."

She commented with the utmost good temper:

"I didn't want that girl to be Christopher's mistress. . . . You would think that no man with any imagination at all *could* . . . I mean with his wife in that condition. . . . But of course when she insisted . . . Well, I wasn't going to stop in bed, in retreat, all my life. . . ."

She laughed good-humouredly at her companion.

"I don't believe you know anything about women," she said. "Why should you? Naturally Mark Tietjens married his concubine. Men always do as a sort of deathbed offering. You will eventually marry Mrs. Partridge if I do not choose to go to India. You think you will not, but you will. . . . As for me I think it would be better for Michael if his mother were Lady Edward Campion — of India! — than if she were merely Lady Tietjens the second of Groby with a dowager who was once a cross-Channel fly-by-night. . . ." She laughed and added: "Anyhow, the sisters at the Blessed Child said that they never saw so many lilies — symbols of purity — as there were at my tea-parties when I was dying. . . . You'll admit yourself you never saw anything so ravishing as me amongst the lilies and the tea-cups with the great crucifix above my head. . . . You were singularly moved! You swore you would cut Christopher's throat yourself on the day the detective told us that he was really living here with that girl. . . ."

The General exclaimed:

"About the Dower House at Groby. . . . It's really damned awkward. . . . You swore to me that when you let Groby to that damned American madwoman I could have the Dower House and keep my horses in Groby stables. But now it appears I can't. . . . It appears . . ."

"It appears," Sylvia said, "that Mark Tietjens means to leave the Dower House at the disposal of his French concubine. . . . Anyhow you can afford a house of your own. You're rich enough!"

The General groaned:

"Rich enough! My God!"

She said:

"You have still — trust *you*! — your younger son's settlement. You have still your Field Marshal's pay. You have the interest on the grant the nation made you at the end of the war. You have four hundred a year as a member of Parliament. You have cadged on me for your keep and your man's keep and your horses' and grooms' at Groby for years and years. . . ."

Immense dejection covered the face of her companion. He said:

"Sylvia. . . . Consider the expenses of my constituency. . . . One would almost say you hated me!"

Her eyes continued to devour the orchard and garden that were spread out below her. A furrow of raw, newly turned earth ran from almost beneath their horses' hoofs nearly vertically to the house below. She said:

"I suppose that is where they get their water supply. From the spring above here. Cramp the carpenter says they are always having trouble with the pipes!"

The General exclaimed:

"Oh, Sylvia. And you told Mrs. de Bray Pape that they had no water-supply so they could not take a bath!"

Sylvia said:

"If I hadn't she would never have dared to cut down Groby Great Tree. . . . Don't you see that for Mrs. de Bray Pape people who do not take baths are outside the law? So, though she's not really courageous, she will risk cutting down their old trees. . . ." She added: "Yes, I almost believe I do hate misers, and you are more next door to a miser than anyone else I ever honoured with my acquaintance. . . ." She added further: "But I should advise you to calm yourself. If I let you marry me you will have Satterthwaite pickings. Not to mention the Groby pickings till Michael comes of age and the — what is it — ten thousand a year you will get from India. If out of all that you cannot skimp enough to make up for house-room at my expense at Groby you are not half the miser I took you for!"

A number of horses with Lord Fittleworth and Gunning came up from the soft track outside the side of the garden and onto the hard road that bordered the garden's top. Gunning sat one horse without his feet in the stirrups and had the bridles of two others over his elbows. They were the horses of Mrs. de Bray Pape, Mrs. Lowther and Mark Tietjens. The garden with its quince trees, the old house with its immensely high-pitched roof such as is seen in countries where wood was plentiful, the thatch of Mark Tietjens' shelter and the famous four counties ran from the other side of the hedge out to infinity. An aeroplane droned down towards them, miles away. Up from the road ran a slope covered with bracken to many great beech trees, along a wire hedge. That was the summit of Cooper's Common. In the stillness the hoofs of all those horses made a noise like that of desultorily approaching cavalry. Gunning halted his horses at a little distance; the beast Sylvia rode was too ill-tempered to be approached.

Lord Fittleworth rode up to the General and said:

"God damn it, Campion, Helen Lowther ought not to be down there. Her ladyship will give me no rest for a fortnight!" He shouted at Gunning: "Here you, blast you, you old scoundrel, where's the gate Speeding complains you have been interfering with." He added to the general: "This old scoundrel was in my service for thirty years yet he's always counterswinging the gates in your godson's beastly fields. Of course a man has to look after his master's interests, but we shall have to come to some arrangement. We can't go on like this." He added to Sylvia:

" It isn't the sort of place Helen ought to go to, is it? All sorts of people living with all sorts. If what you say is true . . ."

The Earl of Fittleworth gave in all places the impression that he wore a scarlet tail coat, a white stock with a fox-hunting pin, white buckskin breeches, a rather painful eyeglass and a silk tophat attached to his person by a silken cord. Actually he was wearing a square, black felt hat, pepper and salt tweeds and no eyeglass. Still he screwed up one eye to look at you and his lucid dark pupils, his contracted swarthy face with grey whiskers and bristling black-grey moustache gave him, perched on his immense horse, the air of a querulous but very masterful monkey.

He considered that he was out of earshot of Gunning and so continued to the other two: "Oughtn't to give away masters before their servants. . . . But it *isn't* any place for the niece of the President of a Show that Cammie has most of her money in. Anyhow she will comb my whiskers!" Before marrying the Earl Lady Fittleworth had been Miss Camden Grimm. "Regular Aga . . . Agapemone if what you say is true. A queer go for old Mark at his age."

The General said to Fittleworth:

"Here, I say, she says I am a regular miser. . . . You don't have any complaints, say, from your keepers that I don't tip enough? That's the real sign of a miser!"

Fittleworth said to Sylvia:

"You don't mind my talking like that of your husband's establishment, do you?" He added that in the old days they would not have talked like that before a lady about her husband. Or perhaps, by Jove, they would have! His grandfather had kept a . . .

Sylvia was of opinion that Helen Lowther could look after herself. Her husband was said not to pay her the attentions that a lady has a right to expect of a husband. So if Christopher . . .

She took an appraising sideways glance at Fittleworth. That peer was going slightly purple under his brown skin. He gazed out over the landscape and swallowed in his throat. She felt that her time for making a decision had come. Times changed, the world changed; she felt heavier in the mornings than she had ever used to. She had had a long, ingenious talk with Fittleworth the night before, on a long terrace. She had been ingenious even for her, but she was aware that afterwards Fittleworth had had a longer bedroom talk with his Cammie. Over even the greatest houses a certain sense of suspense broods when the Master is talking to the Mistress. The Master and the Mistress — upon a word, usually from the Master — take themselves off and the house-guests, at any rate in a small party, straggle, are uncertain as to who gives the signal to retire, suppress yawns even. Finally the butler approaches the most intimate guest and says that the Countess will not be coming down again.

That night Sylvia had shot her bolt. On the terrace she had drawn for the Earl a picture of the *ménage* whose garden she now looked down on. It stretched out below her, that little domain as if she were a goddess dominating its destinies. But she was not so certain of that. The dusky purple under Fittleworth's skin showed no diminution. He continued to gaze away over his territory, reading it as if it were a book — a clump of trees gone here, the red roof of a new villa grown up there in among the trees, a hop-oast with its characteristic cowl gone from a knoll. He was getting ready to say something. She had asked him the night before to root that family out of that slope.

Naturally not in so many words. But she had drawn such a picture of Christopher and Mark as made it, if the peer believed her, almost a necessity for a conscientious nobleman to do his best to rid his countryside of a plague-spot. . . . The point was whether Fittleworth would choose to believe her because she was a beautiful woman with a thrilling voice. He was terribly domestic and attached to his Trans-Atlantic female as only very wicked dark men late in life can contrive to be when they come of very wicked, haughty, and influential houses. They have as it were attended on the caprices of so many opera singers and famous professionals that they get the knack when, later in life they take capricious or influential wives, of very stiffly but minutely showing every sort of elaborate deferences to their life-partners. That is born with them.

So that the fate of that garden and that high-pitched roof was in fact in the hands of Cammie Fittleworth — in so far as great peers to-day have influence over the fates of their neighbours. And it is to be presumed that they have some.

And men are curious creatures. Fittleworth stiffened at queer places. He had done so last night. He had nevertheless stood a good deal in the way of allegations from her. It had to be remembered that Mark Tietjens was an old acquaintance of his — not as intimate as he would have been if the Earl had had children, for Mark preferred houses of married people who had children. But the Earl knew Mark very well. . . . Now a man listening to gossip about another man whom he knows very well will go pretty far in the way of believing what a beautiful woman will tell him about that other man. Beauty and truth have a way of appearing to be akin; and it is true that no man knows what another man is doing when he is out of sight.

So that in inventing or hinting at a ruinous, concealed harem, with consequent disease to account for Mark's physical condition and apparent ruin she thought she was not going altogether too far. She had at any rate been ready to chance it. It is the sort of thing a man will believe about his best friend even. He will say: "Only think . . . all the while old X . . . was appearing such a quiet codger he was really . . ." And the words rivet conviction.

So that appeared to get through.

Her revelations as to Christopher's financial habits had not appeared to do so well. The Earl had listened with his head on one side whilst she had let him gather that Christopher lived on women — on the former Mrs. Duchemin, now Lady Macmaster, for instance. Yes, to that the Earl had listened with deference, and it had seemed a fairly safe allegation to make. Old Duchemin was known to have left a pot of money to his widow. She had a very nice little place not six or seven miles away from where they stood.

And it had come rather naturally to bring in Edith Ethel, for not so long ago Lady Macmaster had actually paid Sylvia a visit. It was about the late Macmaster's debt to Christopher. That was a point about which Lady Macmaster was and always had seemed to be a little cracky. She had actually visited Sylvia in order to see if Sylvia would not use her influence with Christopher. To get him to remit the debt!

Apparently Christopher had not carried his idiocy as far as might be expected. He had dragged that wretched girl down to those penurious surroundings, but he was not going to let her and the child she appeared to be going to have suffer actual starvation or even to suffer from too great worry. And apparently, to satisfy a rather uneasy vanity, years before Macmaster had given Christopher a charge on his life insurance. Macmaster, as she well knew, had sponged unmercifully on her husband and Christopher had certainly formerly regarded the money he had advanced as a gift. She herself had many times upbraided him about it: it had appeared to her one of Christopher's worst unbearablenesses.

But apparently the charge on the life insurance still existed and was now a charge on that miserable fellow's rather extensive estate. At any rate the insurance company refused to pay over any money to the widow until the charge was satisfied. . . . And the thought that Christopher was doing for that girl what, she was convinced, he never would have done for herself had added a new impulse to Sylvia's bitterness. Indeed her bitterness had by now given way almost entirely to a mere spirit of tormentingness — she wanted to torture that girl out of her mind. That was why she was there now. She imagined Valentine under the high roof suffering tortures because she, Sylvia, was looking down over the hedge.

But the visit of Lady Macmaster had certainly revived her bitterness as it had suggested to her new schemes of making herself a nuisance to the household below her. Lady Macmaster in widow's weeds of the most fantastic crape that gave to her at once the elegance and the portentousness of a funeral horse had really seemed more than a little out of her mind. She had asked Sylvia's opinion of all sorts of expedients for making Christopher loosen his grip and she had continued her supplications even in correspondence. At last she had

hit on a singular expedient. . . . Some years before, apparently,
Edith Ethel had had an affair of the heart with a distinguished
Scottish Litterateur, now deceased. Edith Ethel, as was well known,
had acted as Egeria to quite a number of Scottish men of letters.
That was natural; the Macmasters' establishment was Scottish, Macmaster had been a Critic and had had government funds for the relief of indigent men of letters and Edith Ethel was passionately
cultured. You could see that even in the forms her crape took and in
how she arranged it around her when she sat or agitatedly rose to
wring her hands.

But the letters of this particular Scot had outpassed the language
of ordinary Egerianishness. They spoke of Lady Macmaster's eyes,
arms, shoulders, feminine aura. . . . These letters Lady Macmaster
had proposed to entrust to Christopher for sale to Trans-Atlantic
collectors. She said they ought to fetch $30,000 at least and with
the 10% commission that Christopher might take he might consider himself as amply repaid for the four thousand odd that Macmaster's estate owed him.

And this had appeared to Sylvia to be so eccentric an expedient
that she had felt the utmost pleasure in suggesting that Edith Ethel
should drive up to Tietjens's with her letters and have an interview —
if possible with Valentine Wannop in the absence of Tietjens. This
she calculated would worry her rival quite a bit — and even if it did
not do that she, Sylvia, would trust herself to obtain subsequently
from Edith Ethel a great many grotesque details as to the Wannop's
exhausted appearance, shabby clothing, worn hands.

For it is to be remembered that one of the chief torments of the
woman who has been abandoned by a man is the sheer thirst of
curiosity for material details as to how that man subsequently lives.
Sylvia Tietjens for a great number of years had tormented her husband. She would have said herself that she had been a thorn in his
flesh, largely because he had seemed to her never inclined to take
his own part. If you live with a person who suffers from being put
upon a good deal and if that person will not assert his own rights
you are apt to believe that your standards as gentleman and Christian are below his, and the experience is lastingly disagreeable. But
in any case Sylvia Tietjens had had reason to believe that for many
years, for better or for worse — and mostly for worse — she had been
the dominating influence over Christopher Tietjens. Now, except for
extraneous annoyances, she was aware that she could no longer influ-

ence him either for evil or for good. He was a solid, four-square lump of meal-sacks too heavy for her hauling about.

So that the only real pleasure she had was when, at night in a circle of cosy friends she could assert that she was not even yet out of his confidence. Normally she would not — the members of her circle would not have — made confidantes of her ex-husband's domestics. But she had had to chance whether the details of Christopher's *ménage* as revealed by the wife of his carpenter would prove to her friends sufficiently amusing to make them forget the social trespass she committed in consorting with her husband's dependants and she had to chance whether the carpenter's wife would not see that, by proclaiming her wrongs over the fact that her husband had left her, she was proclaiming her own unattractiveness.

She had hitherto chanced both, but the time, she was aware, was at hand when she would have to ask herself whether she would not be better off if she were what the French call *rangée* as was the wife of the Commander in Chief in India than as a free-lance woman owing her popularity entirely to her own exertions. It would be slightly ignominious to owe part of her prestige to a pantaloon like General Lord Edward Campion K.C.B., but how restful might it not be! To keep your place in a society of Marjies and Beatties — and even of Cammies, like the Countess of Fittleworth — meant constant exertion and watchfulness, even if you were comfortably wealthy and well-born — and it meant still more exertion when your staple capital for entertainment was the domestic misfortune of a husband that did not like you.

She might well point out to Marjie, Lady Stern, that her husband's clothes lacked buttons and his companion all imaginable chic; she might well point out to Beattie, Lady Elsbacher, that according to her husband's carpenter's wife, the interior of her husband's home resembled a cave encumbered with packing cases in dark-coloured wood, whereas in her day . . . Or she might even point out to Cammie, Lady Fittleworth, to Mrs. de Bray Pape and Mrs. Luther that, having a defective water supply, her husband's woman probably provided him only with difficulty with baths. . . . But every now and then someone — as had been the case once or twice with the three American ladies — would point out, a little tentatively, that her husband was by now Tietjens of Groby to all intents and purposes. And people — and in particular American ladies — would attach particular importance before her to English county gentlemen who had turned down titles and the like. Her husband had not turned down a title; he had not been able to, for much as Mark had desired to refuse a baronetcy at the last moment he had been given to understand that he couldn't. But her husband had practically turned down a whole great estate and the romantic aspect of that feat was beginning to filter through to her friends. For all her assertions that his seeming poverty was due to dissolute living and consequent bankruptcy, her friends would occasionally ask her whether in fact his poverty was not simply a voluntary affair, the result either of a wager or a strain of mysticism. They would point out that she and her son at least had all the symptoms of considerable wealth as a sign rather that Christopher did not desire wealth or was generous, than that he had no longer money to throw away. . . .

There were symptoms of that sort of questioning of the mind rising up in the American ladies whom Cammie Fittleworth liked to have staying with her. Hitherto Sylvia had managed to squash them. After all, the Tietjens household below her feet was a singular affair for those who had not the clue to its mystery. She had the clue herself; she knew both about the silent feud between the two brothers and about their attitude to life. And if it enraged her that Christopher should despise things that she so valued it none the less gratified her to know that, in the end, she was to be regarded as responsible for that silent feud and the renunciation that it had caused. It was her tongue that had set going the discreditable stories that Mark once had believed against his brother.

But if she was to retain her power to blast that household with her tongue she felt she ought to have details. She must have corroborative details. Otherwise she could not so very convincingly put over her picture of abandoned corruption. You might have thought that her coercing Mrs. de Bray Pape and her son into making that rather outrageous visit and in awakening Mrs. Lowther's innocent curiosity as to the contents of the cottage she had been inspired solely by the desire to torment Valentine Wannop. But she was aware that there was more than that to it. She might get details of all sorts of queernesses that, triumphantly, to other groups of listeners she could retail as proof of her intimacy with that household.

If her listeners showed any signs of saying that it was queer that a man like Christopher who appeared to be a kindly group of sacks should actually be a triply crossed being compounded of a Lovelace, Pandarus, and a Satyr she could always answer: "Ah, but what can you expect of people who have hams drying in their drawing room!" Or if others alleged that it was queer, if Valentine Wannop had Christopher as much under her thumb as she was said to have, even by Sylvia, that she should still allow Christopher to run an Agapemone in what was after all her own house, Sylvia would have liked to be able to reply: "Ah, but what can you expect of a woman upon whose stairs you will find, side by side, a hairbrush, a frying pan, and a copy of Sappho!"

That was the sort of detail that Sylvia needed. The one item she had: The Tietjenses, she knew from Mrs. Carpenter Cramp, had an immense fireplace in their living-room and, after the time-honoured custom they smoked their hams in that chimney. But to people who did not know that smoking hams in great chimneys was a time-honoured custom the assertion that Christopher was the sort of person who dried hams in his drawing room would bring up images of your finding yourself in a sort of place where hams reclined on the sofa-cushions. Even that to the reflective would not necessarily be proof that the perpetrator was a Sadic lunatic — but few people are reflective and at any rate it was queer, and one queerness might be taken as implying another.

But as to Valentine she could not get details enough. You had to prove that she was a bad housekeeper and a blue stocking in order that it should be apparent that Christopher was miserable — and you had to prove that Christopher was miserable in order to make it apparent that the hold that Valentine Wannop certainly had over him was something unholy. For that, it was necessary to have details of misplaced hairbrushes, frying pans, and copies of Sappho.

It had, however, been difficult to get those details. Mrs. Cramp when appealed to had made it rather plain that, far from being a bad housekeeper Valentine Wannop did no housekeeping at all whereas Marie Léonie — Lady Mark — was a perfect devil of a ménagère. Apparently Mrs. Cramp was allowed no further into the dwelling than the wash house — because of half-pounds of sugar and dusters that Mrs. Cramp in the character of charwoman had believed to be her perquisites. Marie Léonie hadn't.

The local doctor and the parson, both of whom visited the house, had contributed only palely coloured portraits of the young woman. Sylvia had gone to call on them and making use of the Fittleworth ægis — hinting that Lady Cammie wanted details of her humbler neighbours for her own instruction — Sylvia had tried to get behind the professional secrecy that distinguished parsons and doctors. But she had not got much behind. The parson gave her the idea that he thought Valentine rather a jolly girl, very hospitable and with a fine tap of cider at disposal and fond of reading under trees — the classics mostly. Very much interested also in rock-plants as you could see by the bank under Tietjens's windows. . . . Their house was always called Tietjens's. Sylvia had never been under those windows and that enraged her.

From the doctor, Sylvia, for a faint flash, gained the impression that Valentine enjoyed rather poor health. But it had only been an impression arising from the fact that the doctor saw her every day — and it was rather discounted by the other fact that the doctor said that his daily visits were for Mark who might be expected to pop off at any moment. So he needed careful watching. A little excitement and he was done for. . . . Otherwise Valentine seemed to have a sharp eye for old furniture as the doctor knew to his cost, for in a small way he collected himself. And he said that at minor cottage-sales and for small objects Valentine could drive a bargain that Tietjens himself never achieved.

Otherwise, from both the doctor and the parson, she had an impression of Tietjens's as a queer household — queer because it was so humdrum and united. She really herself had expected something more exciting! Really. It did not seem possible that Christopher should settle down into tranquil devotion to brother and mistress after the years of emotion she had given him. It was as if a man should have jumped out of a frying pan into — a duckpond.

So, as she looked at the red flush on Fittleworth's face an almost mad moment of impatience had overcome her. This fellow was about the only man who had ever had the guts to stand up to her. . . . A fox-hunting squire: an extinct animal!

The trouble was, you could not tell quite how extinct he was. He might be able to bite as hard as a fox. Otherwise she would be running down, right now, running down that zigzag orange path to that forbidden land.

That she had hitherto never dared. From a social point of view it would have been outrageous, but she was prepared to chance that. She was sure enough of her place in Society and if people will excuse a man's leaving his wife they will excuse the wife's making at least one or two demonstrations that are a bit thick. But she had simply not dared to meet Christopher; he might cut her.

Perhaps he would not. He was a gentleman and gentlemen do not usually cut women with whom they have slept. . . . But he might. . . . She might go down there and in a dark low-ceilinged room be making some sort of stipulation — God knew what, the first that came into her head — to Valentine. You can always make up some sort of reason for approaching the woman who has supplanted you. But he might come mooning in, and suddenly stiffen into a great, clumsy — oh adorable! — face of stone.

That was what you would not dare to face. That would be death. She could imagine him going out of the room, rolling his shoulders. Leaving the whole establishment to her, closing only himself in invisible bonds — closed to her by the angel with the flaming sword. . . . That was what he would do. And that before the other woman. He had come once very near it and she had hardly recovered from it. That pretended illness had not been so much pretended as all that! She had smiled angelically, under the great crucifix, in the convent that had been her nursing-home — angelically, amongst lilies, upon the General, the sisters, the many callers that gradually came to her teas. But she had had to think that Christopher was probably in the arms of his girl, and he had let her go when she had, certainly physically, needed his help.

But that had not been a calm occasion, in that dark empty house. . . . And he had not, at that date, enjoyed the favours, the domesticity, of that young woman. He hadn't had a chance of comparison, so that the turning-down need not count. He had treated her barbarously — as social counters go it had been helpful to her — but only at the strong urge of a young woman driven to fury. That could be palliated. It hardly indeed affected her now as a reverse. Looked at reasonably, if a man comes home intending to go to bed with a young woman who has bewitched him for a number of years and finds another woman who tells him that she has cancer and does a very creditable faint from the top of the stairs and then — in spite of practice and being as hard as nails — puts her ankle out of joint, he has got to choose between the one and the other. And the other in this case had been vigorous, determined on her man, even vituperative. Obviously Christopher was not the sort of man who would *like* seducing a young woman whilst his wife was dying of internal cancer, let alone a sprained ankle. But the young woman

had arrived at a stage when she did not care for any delicacies or
their dictates.

No; that Sylvia had been able to bear. But if now the same
thing happened, in dim, quiet daylight, in a tranquil old room . . .
that she would not be able to face! It is one thing to acknowledge
that your man has gone — there is no irrevocability about going.
He may come back when the other woman is insignificant, a blue
stocking, entirely unnoticeable. . . . But if he took the step — the responsibility! — of cutting you, that would be to put between you a
barrier that no amount of weariness with your rival could overstep.

Impatience grew upon her. The fellow was away in an aeroplane.
Gone North. It was the only time she had ever *known* of him as
having gone away. It was her only chance of running down those
orange zigzags. And now — it was all Lombard Street to a China
apple that Fittleworth intended to disapprove of her running down.
And you could not ignore Fittleworth.

II

No, you could not ignore Fittleworth. As a fox-hunting squire he
might be an extinct monster — though then again he might not:
there was no knowing. But as a wicked, dark, adept with bad women,
and come of a race that had been adepts with women good and bad
for generations, he was about as dangerous a person as you could
find. That gross, slow, earthy, obstinate fellow, Gunning, could
stand grouchily up to Fittleworth, answer him back and chance what
Fittleworth could do to him. So could any cottager. But then they
were his people. She wasn't . . . she, Sylvia Tietjens, and she did
not believe she could afford to outface him. Nor could half England.

Old Campion wanted India — probably she herself wanted Campion to have India. Groby Great Tree was cut down and if you
have not the distinction — if you rid yourself of the distinction, of
Groby Great Tree just to wound a man to the heart — you may as
well take India. Times were changing but there was no knowing
how the circumstances of a man like Fittleworth changed. He sat
his horse like a monkey and gazed out over his land as his people
had done for generations, bastard or legitimate. And it was all very
well to regard him as merely a country squire married to a Trans-

Atlantic nobody and so out of it. He hopped up to London — he and his Cammie too — and he passed unnoticeably about the best places and could drop a word or so here and there; and for all the countess' foreign and unknown origin she had access to ears that could well be dangerous for aspirants to India. Campion might have his war-services and his constituency. But Cammie Fittleworth was popular in high places and Fittleworth had his hounds and, when it came even to constituencies, the tradesmen of a couple of counties. And he was wicked.

It had been obvious to her for a long time that God would one day step in and intervene for the protection of Christopher. After all Christopher was a good man — a rather sickeningly good man. It is, in the end, she reluctantly admitted, the function of God and the invisible Powers to see that a good man shall eventually be permitted to settle down to a stuffy domestic life . . . even to chaffering over old furniture. It was a comic affair — but it was the sort of affair that you had to admit. God is probably — and very rightly — on the side of the stuffy domesticities. Otherwise the world could not continue — the children would not be healthy. And certainly God desired the production of large crops of healthy children. Mind doctors of to-day said that all cases of nervous breakdown occurred in persons whose parents had not led harmonious lives.

So Fittleworth might well have been selected as the lightning conductor over the house of Tietjens. And the selection was quite a good one on the part of the Unseen Powers. And no doubt predestined! There was no accident about Mark's being under the ægis — if that was what you called it — of the Earl. Mark had for long been one of the powers of the land, so had Fittleworth. They had moved in the same spheres — the rather mysterious spheres of Good People — who ruled the destinies of the nation in so far as the more decorative and more splendid jobs were concerned. They must have met about, here and there, constantly for years. And Mark had indicated that it was in that neighbourhood that he wanted to end his days simply because he wanted to be near the Fittleworths who could be calculated on to look after his Marie Léonie and the rest of them.

For the matter of that, Fittleworth himself, like God, was on the side of the stuffy domesticities and on the side of women who were in the act of producing healthy children. Early in life he had had a woman to whom he was said to have been hopelessly attached and whom he had acquired in romantic circumstances — a famous dancer whom he had snapped up under the nose of a very Great Person indeed. And the woman had died in childbirth — or had given birth to an infant child and gone mad and committed suicide after that achievement. At any rate for months and months, Fittleworth's friends had had to sit up night after night with him so that he might not kill himself.

Later — after he had married Cammie in the search for a domesticity that, except for his hounds he had made really almost stuffy — he had interested himself — and of course his countess — in the cause of providing tranquil conditions for women before childbirth. They had put up a perfectly lovely lying-in almshouse right under their own windows, down there.

So there it was — and, as she took her sideways glance at Fittleworth high up there in the air beside her, she was perfectly aware that she might be in for such a duel with him as had seldom yet fallen to her lot.

He had begun it by saying: "God damn it, Campion, ought Helen Lowther to be down there?" Then he had put it, as upon her, Sylvia's information, that the cottage was in effect a disorderly house. But he had added: "If what you say is true?"

That of course was distinctly dangerous, for Fittleworth probably knew quite well that it had been at her, Sylvia's instigation that Helen Lowther *was* down there. And he was letting her know that if it *was* at her instigation and if the house was really in her belief a brothel, his countess would be frightfully displeased. Frightfully!

Helen Lowther was of no particular importance, except to the Countess — and, of course, to Michael. She was one of those not unattractive Americans that drift over here and enjoy themselves with frightfully simple things. She liked visiting ruins and chattering about nothing in particular and galloping on the downs and talking to old servants and she liked the adoration of Michael. Probably she would have turned down the adoration of anyone older.

And the Countess liked to preserve the innocence of young American women. The Countess was fiftyish now and of a generation that preserved a certain stiffness along with a certain old-fashioned broadness of mind and outspokenness. She was of a class of American that had once seemed outrageously wealthy and who, if in the present stage of things they did not seem overwhelming, yet retained an aspect of impressive comfort and social authority and she moved in a set most of whose individuals, American, English, or even French, were of much the same class, at least by marriage, as herself. She tolerated — she even liked — Sylvia, but she might well get mad if from under her roof Helen Lowther, who was in her charge, should come into social contact with an irregular couple. You never knew when that point of view might not crop up in women of that date and class.

Sylvia, however, had chanced it. She had to — and in the end it could only be pulling the string of one more showerbath. It was a showerbath formidably charged — but that was her vocation in life and, if Campion had to lose India, she could always pursue her vocation in other countrysides. She was tired, but not as tired as all that!

So Sylvia had chanced saying that she supposed Helen Lowther could look after herself and had added a salacious quip to keep the speech in character. She knew nothing really of Helen Lowther's husband, who was probably a lean man with some avocation in a rather dim West. But he could not be very *impressionné* or he would not let his attractive young wife roam for ever over Europe, alone.

His Lordship gave no further sign beyond repeating that if that fellow was the sort of fellow Mrs. Tietjens said he was, her Ladyship would properly curl his whiskers. And in face of that Sylvia simply had to make a concession to the extent of saying that she did not see why Helen Lowther could not visit a show cottage that was known, apparently, over half America. And perhaps buy some old sticks.

His Lordship removed his gaze from the distant hills and turned a long, cool, rather impertinent glance on her. He said:

"Ah, if it's only that . . ." and nothing more. And, at that, she chanced it again:

"If," she said slowly too, "you think Helen Lowther is in need of protection I don't mind if I go down and look after her myself!"

The General, who had tried several interjections, now exclaimed:

"Surely you wouldn't meet that fellow!" . . . And that rather spoilt it.

For Fittleworth could take the opportunity to leave her to do what he was at liberty to regard as the directions of her natural protector. Otherwise he must have said something to give away his attitude. So she had to give away more of her own with the words:

"Christopher is not down here. He has taken an aeroplane to York

— to save Groby Great Tree. Your man Speeding saw him when he went to get your saddle. Getting into a plane." She added: "But he's too late. Mrs. de Bray Pape had a letter yesterday to say the tree had been cut down. At her orders!"

Fittleworth said: "Good God!" Nothing more!

The General regarded him as one fearing to be struck by lightning. Campion had already told her over and over again that Fittleworth would rage like a town bull at the bare idea that the tenant of a furnished house should interfere with its owner's timber. . . . But Fittleworth merely continued to look away, communing with the handle of his crop. That called, Sylvia knew for another concession and she said:

"Now, Mrs. de Bray Pape has got cold feet. Horribly cold feet. That's why she's down there. She's got the idea that Mark may have her put in prison!" She added further:

"She wanted to take my boy, Michael, with her to intercede. As the heir he has some right to a view!"

And from those speeches of hers Sylvia had the measure of her dread of that silent man. She was more tired than she thought and the idea of India more attractive.

At that point Fittleworth exclaimed:

"Damn it all, I've got to settle the hash of that fellow Gunning!"

He turned his horse's head along the road and beckoned the General towards him with his crop-handle. The General gazed back at her appealingly, but Sylvia knew that she had to stop there and await Fittleworth's verdict from the General's lips. She wasn't even to have any duel of sous-entendus with Fittleworth.

She clenched her fingers on her crop and looked towards Gunning. . . . If she was going to be asked by the Countess through old Campion to pack up, bag and baggage, and leave the house she would at least get what she could out of that fellow whom she had never yet managed to approach.

The horses of the General and Fittleworth, relieved to be out of the neighbourhood of Sylvia's chestnut, minced friendlily along the road, the mare liking her companion.

"This fellow Gunning," his Lordship began . . . He continued with great animation:

"About these gates . . . You are aware that my estate carpenter repairs. . . ."

Those were the last words she heard and she imagined Fittleworth continuing for a long time about his bothering gates in order to put the General quite off his guard — and no doubt for the sake of manners. Then he would drop in some shot that would be terrible to the old General. He might even cross-question him as to facts, with sly, side questions, looking away over the country.

For that she cared very little. She did not pretend to be a historian: she entertained rather than instructed. And she had conceded enough to Fittleworth. Or perhaps it was to Cammie. Cammie was a great, fat, good-natured dark thing with pockets under her liquid eyes. But she had a will. And by telling Fittleworth that she had not incited Helen Lowther and the two others to make an incursion into the Tietjens' household Sylvia was aware that she had made an important concession.

She hadn't intended to weaken. It had happened. She had intended to chance conveying the idea that she wanted to worry Christopher and his companion into leaving that country.

The heavy man with the three horses approached slowly, with the air of a small army in the narrow road. He was grubby and unbuttoned, but he regarded her intently with eyes a little bloodshot. He said from a distance something that she did not altogether understand. It was about her chestnut. He was asking her to back that 'ere chestnut's tail into the hedge. She was not used to being spoken to by the lower classes. She kept her horse along the road. In that way the fellow could not pass. She knew what was the matter. Her chestnut would lash out at Gunning's charges if they got near its stern. In the hunting season it wore a large "K" on its tail.

Nevertheless the fellow must be a good man with horses; otherwise he would not be perched on one with the stirrups crossed over the saddle in front of him and lead two others. She did not know that she would care to do that herself nowadays; there had been a time when she would have. She had intended to slip down from the chestnut and hand it over to Gunning. Once she was down on the road he could not very well refuse. But she felt disinclined to cock her leg over the saddle. He looked like a fellow who could refuse.

He refused. She had asked him to hold her horse whilst she went down and spoke to his master. He had made no motion towards doing so; he had continued to stare fixedly at her. She had said:

"You're Captain Tietjens' servant, aren't you? I'm his wife. Staying with Lord Fittleworth!"

He had made no answer and no movement except to draw the back of his right hand across his left nostril — for lack of a handkerchief. He said something incomprehensible — but not conciliatory. Then he began a longer speech. That she understood. It was to the effect that he had been thirty years, boy and man with his Lordship and the rest of his time with the Cahptn. He also pointed out that there was a hitching post and chain by the gate there. But he did not advise her to hitch to it. The chestnut would kick to flinders any cart that came along the road. And the mere idea of the chestnut lashing out and injuring itself caused her to shudder; she was a good horsewoman.

The conversation went with long pauses. She was in no hurry; she would have to wait till Campion or Fittleworth came back — with the verdict, probably. The fellow, when he used short sentences, was incomprehensible because of his dialect. When he spoke longer she got a word or two out of it.

It troubled her a little, now, that Edith Ethel might be coming along the road. Practically she had promised to meet her at that spot and at about that moment, Edith Ethel proposing to sell her love-letters to Christopher — or through him. . . . The night before she had told Fittleworth that Christopher had bought the place below her with money he had from Lady Macmaster because Lady Macmaster had been his mistress. Fittleworth had boggled at that . . . it had been at that moment that he had gone rather stiff to her.

As a matter of fact Christopher had bought that place out of a windfall. Years before — even before she had married him — he had had a legacy from an aunt and in his visionary way had invested it in some Colonial — very likely Canadian — property or invention or tramway concession because he considered that some remote place, owing to its geographical position on some road — was going to grow. Apparently during the war it had grown and the completely forgotten investment had paid nine and sixpence in the pound. Out of the blue. It could not be helped. With a monetary record of visionariness and generosity such as Christopher had behind him, some chickens must now and then come home — some visionary investment turn out sound, some debtor turn honest. She understood even that some colonel who had died on Armistice night and to whom Christopher had lent a good sum in hundreds had turned honest. At any rate his executors had written to ask her for Christopher's address with a view to making payments. She hadn't at the time known Christopher's address, but no doubt they had got it from the War Office or somewhere.

No doubt with windfalls like those he had kept afloat, for she did not believe the old-furniture business as much as paid its way. She had heard through Mrs. Cramp that the American partner had embezzled most of the money that should have gone to Christopher. You should not do business with Americans. Christopher, it is true, had years ago — during the war — predicted an American invasion — as he always predicted everything. He had indeed said that if you wanted to have money you must get it from where money was going to; in other words, if you wanted to sell, you must prepare to sell what was wanted. And they wanted old furniture more than anything else. She didn't mind. She was already beginning a little campaign with Mrs. de Bray Pape to make her re-furnish Groby — to make her export all the clumsy eighteen-forty mahogany that the great house contained, to Sante Fé or wherever it was that Mr. Pape lived alone, and to re-furnish with Louis Quatorze as befitted the spiritual descendant of the Maintenon. The worst of it was that Mr. Pape was stingy.

She was, indeed, in a fine taking that morning — Mrs. de Bray Pape. In hauling out the stump of Groby Great Tree the woodcutters had apparently brought down two-thirds of the ball-room exterior wall and that vast, gloomy room, with its immense lustres was wrecked along with the old school-rooms above it. As far as she could make out from the steward's letter Christopher's boyhood's bedroom had practically disappeared. . . . Well, if Groby Great Tree did not like Groby House it had finely taken its dying revenge. . . . A nice shock Christopher would get! Anyhow Mrs. de Bray Pape had pretty well mangled the great dovecote in erecting in it a new power station.

But apparently it was going to mangle the Papes to the tune of a pretty penny and apparently Mr. Pape might be expected to give his wife no end of a time. . . . Well, you can't expect to be God's Vicegerent of England without barking your shins on old, hard things.

No doubt Mark knew all about it by now. Perhaps it had killed him. She hoped it hadn't because she still hoped to play him some tidy little tricks before she had done with him. . . . If he were dead or dying beneath that parallelogram of thatch down among the apple boughs all sorts of things might be going to happen. Quite inconvenient things.

There would be the title. She quite definitely did not want the title and it would become more difficult to decry Christopher. People with titles and great possessions are vastly more difficult to decry than impoverished commoners, because the scale of morality changes. Titles and great possessions expose you to great temptations — you may be excused if you succumb. It is scandalous, on the other hand, that the indigent should have any fun!

So that sitting rather restfully in the sunlight on her horse, Sylvia felt like a general who is losing the fruits of victory. She did not much care. She had got down Groby Great Tree: that was as nasty a blow as the Tietjenses had had in ten generations.

But then a queer, disagreeable thought went through her mind, just as Gunning at last made again a semi-comprehensible remark. Perhaps in letting Groby Great Tree be cut down God was lifting the ban off the Tietjenses. He might well.

Gunning, however, had said something like:

"Shuddn' gaw dahn theer. Ride Boldro up to farm n' put he in loose box." She gathered that if she would ride her horse to some farm he could be put in a loose box and she could rest in the farmer's parlour. Gunning was looking at her with a queer, intent look. She could not just think what it meant.

Suddenly it reminded her of her childhood. Her father had had a head gardener just as gnarled and just as apparently autocratic. That was it. She had not been much in the country for thirty years. Apparently country people had not changed much. Times change; probably people do not, much.

For it came back to her with sudden extraordinary clearness. The side of a greenhouse, down there in the west where she had been "Miss Sylvia, oh, Miss *Sylvia*," for a whole army of protesting retainers, and that old, brown, gnarled fellow, who was equally "Mr. Carter" for them all, except her father. Mr. Carter had been potting geranium shoots and she had been teasing a little white kitten. She was thirteen with immense plaits of blond hair. The kitten had escaped from her and was rubbing itself, its back arched against the leggings of Mr. Carter, who had a special affection for it. She had proposed — merely to torment Mr. Carter — to do something to the kitten, to force its paws into walnut shells perhaps. She had so little meant to hurt the kitten that she had forgotten what it was she had proposed to do. And suddenly the heavy man, his bloodshot eyes fairly blazing, had threatened if she so much as blew on that kitten's fur, to thrash her on a part of her anatomy on which public school-boys rather than young ladies are usually chastised . . . so that she would not be able to sit down for a week, he had said.

Oddly enough it had given a queer pleasure, that returned always with the recollection. She had never otherwise in her life been threatened with physical violence, but she knew that within herself the emotion had often and often existed: If only Christopher had thrashed her within an inch of her life . . . Or yes — there had been Drake. . . . He had half killed her on the night before her wedding to Christopher. She had feared for the child within her! That emotion had been unbearable!

She said to Gunning — and she felt for all the world as if she were trying a torment on Mr. Carter of years ago:

"I don't see why I need go to the farm. I can perfectly well ride Boldero down this path. I must certainly speak to your master."

She had really no immediate notion of doing anything of the sort, but she turned her horse towards the wicket gate that was a little beyond Gunning.

He scrambled off his horse with singular velocity and under the necks of those he led. It was like the running of an elephant and, with all the reins bunched before him, he almost fell with his back on the little wicket back towards whose latch she had been extending the handle of her crop. . . . She had not meant to raise it. She swore she had not meant to raise it. The veins stood out in his hairy, open neck and shoulders. He said: No, she didn't!

Her chestnut was reaching its teeth out towards the led horses. She was not certain that he heard her when she asked if he did not know that she was the wife of the Captain, his master; and guest of Lord Fittleworth, his ex-master. Mr. Carter certainly had not heard her years ago when she had reminded him that she was his master's daughter. He had gone on fulminating. Gunning was doing that, too — but more slowly and heavily. He said first that the Cahptn would tan her hide if she so much as disturbed his brother by a look; he would hide her within an inch of her life. As he had done already.

Sylvia said that by God he never had; if he said he had, he lied. Her immediate reaction was to resent the implication that she was not as good a man as Christopher. He seemed to have been boasting that he had physically corrected her.

Gunning continued drily:

"You put it in th' papers yourself. My ol' missus read it me. Powerful set on Sir Mark's comfort, the Cahptn is. Throw you down stairs, the Cahptn did n' give you cancer. It doesn' show!"

That was the worst of attracting chivalrous attentions from professional people. She had begun divorce proceedings against Christopher, in the way of a petition for restitution of conjugal rights, compounding with the shade of Father Consett and her conscience as a Roman Catholic by arguing that a petition for the restoration of your husband from a Strange Woman is not the same as divorce proceedings. In England at that date it was a preliminary measure and caused as much publicity as the real thing to which she had no intention of proceeding. It caused quite a terrific lot of publicity because her counsel, in his enthusiasm for the beauty and wit of his client — in his chambers the dark, Gaelic, youthful K. C. had been impressively sentimental in his enthusiasm — learned counsel had overstepped the rather sober bounds of the preliminary stage of these cases. He knew that Sylvia's aim was not divorce, but the casting of all possible obloquy on Christopher, and in his fervid Erse oratory he had cast as much mud as an enthusiastic terrier with its hind legs out of a fox's hole. It had embarrassed Sylvia herself, sitting brilliantly in Court. And it had roused the judge, who knew something of the case, having, like half London of his class, taken tea with the dying Sylvia beneath the crucifix and amongst the lilies of the nursing-home that was also a convent. The judge had protested against the oratory of Mr. Sylvian Hatt but Mr. Hatt had got in already a lurid picture of Christopher and Valentine in a dark, empty house on Armistice Night, throwing Sylvia downstairs and so occasioning her a fell disease from which, under the Court's eyes, she was now fading. This had distressed Sylvia herself, for, rather with the idea of showing the court and the world in general what a fool Christopher was to have left her for a little brown sparrow, she had chosen to appear in all radiance and health. She had hoped for the appearance of Valentine in Court. It had not occurred.

The judge had asked Mr. Hatt if he really proposed to bring in evidence that Captain Tietjens and Miss Wannop had enticed Mrs. Tietjens into a dark house — and on a shake of the head that Sylvia had not been able to refrain from giving Mr. Hatt, the judge had made some extremely rude remarks to her counsel. Mr. Hatt was at that time standing as parliamentary candidate for a Midland borough and was anxious to attract as much publicity as that or any other case would give him. He had, therefore, gone bald-headed for the judge, even accusing him of being indifferent to the sufferings he was causing to Mr. Hatt's fainting client. Rightly handled impertinence to a judge will gain quite a number of votes on the Radical side of Midland constituencies, judges being supposed to be all Tories.

Anyhow the case had been a fiasco and for the first time in her life Sylvia had felt mortification; in addition she had felt a great deal of religious fear. It had come into her mind in court — and it came with additional vividness there above that house, that, years ago in her mother's sitting-room in a place called Lobscheid, Father Consett had predicted that if Christopher fell in love with another woman, she, Sylvia, would perpetrate acts of vulgarity. And there she had been, not only toying with the temporal courts in a matter of marriage, which is a sacrament, but led undoubtedly into a position that she had to acknowledge was vulgar. She had precipitately left the court when Mr. Hatt had for the second time appealed for pity for her — but she had not been able to stop him. . . . Pity! She appeal for pity! She had regarded herself as — she had certainly desired to be regarded as — the sword of the Lord smiting the craven and the traitor to Beauty! And was it to be supported that she was to be regarded as such a fool as to be decoyed into an empty house! Or as to let herself be thrown downstairs! . . . But *qui facit per alium* is herself responsible and there she had been in a position as mortifying as would have been that of any city clerk's wife. The florid periods of Mr. Hatt had made her shiver all over and she had never spoken to him again.

And her position had been broadcasted all over England — and now, here in the mouth of this gross henchman it had recurred. At the most inconvenient moment. For the thought suddenly recurred, sweeping over with immense force: God had changed sides at the cutting down of Groby Great Tree.

The first intimation she had had that God might change sides had occurred in that hateful court and had, as it were, been prophesied by Father Consett. That dark saint and martyr was in Heaven, having died for the Faith, and undoubtedly he had the ear of God. He had prophesied that she would toy with the temporal courts. Immediately she had felt herself degraded, as if strength had gone out from her.

Strength had undoubtedly gone out from her. Never before in her life had her mind not sprung to an emergency. It was all very well to say that she could not move physically either backwards or forwards for fear of causing a stampede amongst all those horses and that, therefore, her mental uncertainty might be excused. But it was the finger of God — or of Father Consett, who as saint and martyr, was the agent of God. . . . Or, perhaps, God, Himself, was here really taking a hand for the protection of His Christopher, who was undoubtedly an Anglican saint. . . . The Almighty might well be dissatisfied with the relatively amiable Catholic saint's conduct of the case in which the saint of the other persuasion was involved. For surely Father Consett might be expected to have a soft spot for her whereas you could not expect the Almighty to be unfair even to Anglicans. . . . At any rate, up over the landscape, the hills, the sky, she felt the shadow of Father Consett, the arms extended as if in a gigantic cruciform — and then above and behind that an . . . an August Will!

Gunning, his bloodshot eyes fixed on her, moved his lips vindictively. She had, in face of those ghostly manifestations across hills and sky, a moment of real panic. Such as she had felt when they had been shelling near the hotel in France when she had sat amidst palms with Christopher under a glass roof. . . . A mad desire to run — or as if your soul ran about inside you like a parcel of rats in a pit awaiting an unseen terrier.

What was she to do? What the devil was she to do? . . . She felt an itch. . . . She felt the very devil of a desire to confront at least Mark Tietjens . . . even if it should kill the fellow. Surely God could not be unfair! What was she given beauty — the dangerous remains of beauty! — for if not to impress it on the unimpressible! She ought to be given the chance at least once more to try her irresistible ram against that immovable post. . . . She was aware. . . .

Gunning was saying something to the effect that if she caused Mrs. Valentine to have a miscarriage or an idiot child 'Is Lordship would flay all the flesh off 'er bones with 'is own ridin' crop. 'Is Lordship 'ad fair done it to 'im. Gunning 'isself, when 'e lef' 'is missis then eight and a 'arf munce gone to live with old Mother Cressy! The child was bore dead.

The words conveyed little to her. . . . She was aware. . . . She was aware. . . . What was she aware of? She was aware that God — or perhaps it was Father Consett that so arranged it, more diplomatically, the dear! — desired that she should apply to Rome for the dissolution of her marriage with Christopher and that she should then apply to the civil courts. She thought that probably God desired that Christopher should be freed as early as possible, Father Consett suggesting to Him the less stringent course.

A fantastic object was descending at a fly-crawl the hill road that went almost vertically up to the farm amongst the beeches. She did not care!

Gunning was saying that that wer why 'Is Lordship giv 'im th' sack. Took away the cottage an ten bob a week that 'Is Lordship allowed to all as had been in his service thritty yeer.

She said: "What! What's that?" Then it came back to her that Gunning had suggested that she might give Valentine a miscarriage. . . .

Her breath made in her throat a little clittering sound like the trituration of barley ears; her gloved hands, reins and all were over her eyes, smelling of morocco leather; she felt as if within her a shelf dropped away — as the platform drops away from beneath the feet of a convict they are hanging. She said: "Could . . ." Then her mind stopped, the clittering sound in her throat continuing. Louder. Louder.

Descending the hill at the fly's pace was the impossible. A black basket-work pony phaeton, the pony — you always look at the horse first — four hands too big; as round as a barrel, as shining as a mahogany dining-table, pacing for all the world like a *haute école* circus steed and in a panic bumping its behind into that black vehicle. It eased her to see . . . But, . . . fantastically horrible, behind that grotesque coward of a horse, holding the reins, was a black thing, like a funeral charger; beside it a top hat, a white face, a buff waistcoat, black coat, a thin, Jewish beard. In front of that a bare, blond head, the hair rather long — on the front seat, back to the view. Trust Edith Ethel to be accompanied by a boy-poet cicisbeo! Training Mr. Ruggles for his future condition as consort!

She exclaimed to Gunning:

"By God, if you do not let me pass I will cut your face in half . . ."

It was justified! This in effect was too much — on the part of

Gunning and God and Father Consett. All of a heap they had
given her perplexity, immobility and a dreadful thought that was
gripping her vitals. . . . Dreadful! Dreadful!

She must get down to the cottage. She must get down to the
cottage.

She said to Gunning:

"You damn fool. . . . You *damn* fool. . . . I want to save . . ."

He moved up — interminably — sweating and hairy from the gate
on which he had been leaning, so that he no longer barred her way.
She trotted smartly past him and cantered beautifully down the
slope. It came to her from the bloodshot glance that his eyes gave her
that he would like to outrage her with ferocity. She felt pleasure.

She came off her horse like a circus performer to the sound of
"Mrs. Tietjens! Mrs. Tietjens," in several voices from above. She let
the chestnut go to hell.

It seemed queer that it did not seem queer. A shed of log-parings
set upright, the gate banging behind her. Apple branches spreading
down; grass up to the middle of her grey breeches. It was Tom
Tiddler's Grounds; it was near a place called Gemmenich on the
Fourth of August 1914 . . . But just quietude: quietude.

Mark regarded her boy's outline with beady, inquisitive eyes. She
bent her switch into a half loop before her. She heard herself say:

"Where are all these fools? I want to get them out of here!"

He continued to regard her, beadily, his head like mahogany
against the pillows. An apple bough caught in her hair.

She said:

"Damn it all, *I* had Groby Great Tree torn down: not that tin
Maintenon. But, as God is my Saviour I would not tear another
woman's child in the womb!"

He said:

"You poor bitch! You poor bitch! The riding has done it!"

She swore to herself afterwards that she had heard him say that,
for at the time she had had too many emotions to regard his speaking
as unusual. She took indeed a prolonged turn in the woods before
she felt equal to facing the others. Tietjens's had its woods onto
which the garden gave directly.

Her main bitterness was that they had this peace. She was cutting
the painter, but they were going on in this peace; her world was
waning. It was the fact that her friend Bobbie's husband, Sir Ga-

briel Blantyre — formerly Bosenheim — was cutting down expenses like a lunatic. In her world there was the writing on the wall. Here they could afford to call her a poor bitch — and be in the right of it, as like as not!

III

VALENTINE was awakened by the shrill overtones of the voice of the little maid coming in through the open window. She had fallen asleep over the words "*Saepe te in somnis vidi!*" to a vision of white limbs in the purple Adriatic. Eventually the child's voice said:

"We only sez 'mem' to friends of the family!" shrilly and self-assertively.

She was at the casement, dizzy and sickish with the change of position and the haste — and violently impatient of her condition. Of humanity she perceived only the top of a three-cornered grey hat and a grey panniered skirt in downward perspective. The sloping tiles of the potting-shed hid the little maid; aligned small lettuce plants like rosettes on the dark earth ran from under the window, closed by a wall of sticked peas, behind them the woods, slender grey ash trunks going to a great height. They were needed for shelter. They would have to change their bedroom; they could not have a night nursery that faced the north. The spring onions needed pricking out; she had meant to put the garden pellitory into the rocks in the half-circle, but the operation had daunted her. Pushing the little roots into crevices with her fingers; removing stones, trowelling in artificial manure, stooping, dirtying her fingers would make her retch. . . .

She was suddenly intensely distressed at the thought of those coloured prints. She had searched the whole house — all imaginable drawers, cupboards, presses. It was like their fate that when they had at last got a good — an English — client their first commission from her should go wrong. She thought again of every imaginable, unsearched parallelogram in the house, standing erect, her head up, neglecting to look down on the intruder.

She considered all their customers to be intruders. It was true that Christopher's gifts lay in the way of old-furniture dealing — and farming. But farming was ruinous. Obviously if you sold old furniture straight out of use in your own house it fetched better prices than from a shop. She did not deny Christopher's ingenuity — or that he was right to rely on her hardihood. He had at least the right so to rely. Nor did she mean to let him down. Only . . .

She passionately desired little Chrissie to be born in that bed with the thin fine posts, his blond head with the thin, fine hair on those pillows. She passionately desired that he should lie with blue eyes gazing at those curtains on the low windows. . . . Those! With those peacocks and globes. Surely a child should lie gazing at what his mother had seen whilst she was awaiting him! .

And, where were those lost prints? . . . Four parallelograms of faint, silly colour. Promised for to-morrow morning. The margins needed breadcrumbing. . . . She imagined her chin brushing gently, gently back and forward on the floss of his head; she imagined holding him in the air as, in that bed, she lay, her arms extended upwards, her hair spread on those pillows! Flowers perhaps spread on that quilt. Lavender!

But if Christopher reported that one of those dreadful people with querulous voices wanted a bedroom complete. . . .

If she begged him to retain it for her! Well, he would. He prized her above money. She thought — ah, she knew — that he prized the child within her above the world.

Nevertheless she imagined that she would go all on to the end with her longings unvoiced. . . . Because there was the game. . . . His game . . . oh, hang it, *their* game! And you have to think whether it is worse for the unborn child to have a mother with unsatisfied longings or a father beaten at his . . . No, you must not call it a game. Still, roosters beaten by other roosters lose their masculinity. . . . Like roosters, men. . . . Then, for a child to have a father lacking masculinity . . . for the sake of some peacock and globe curtains, spindly bed-posts, old, old glass tumblers with thumb-mark indentations . . .

On the other hand, for the mother, the soft feeling that those things give! . . . The room had a barrel-shaped ceiling, following the lines of the roof almost up to the roof tree; dark oak beams, bees-waxed — ah, that beeswaxing! Tiny, low windows almost down to the oaken floor. . . . You would say, too much of the show-place, but you lived into it. You lived yourself into it in spite of the Americans who took, sometimes embarrassed, peeps from the doorway.

Would they have to peek into the nursery? Oh, God, who knew? What would he decree? It was an extraordinary thing to live with

⁊ . . . . What was the name of the place . . . a pretty
Buy a living where George Herbert had been par-

᾿e the bye, remember to tell Marie Léonie that it was
rpington labelled 42, not the Red 16 that she had put
of Indian Runners under. She had found that Red 16
ally broody, though she had come on afterwards. It was
t Marie Léonie had not the courage to put eggs under
hens because they pecked her whereas she, Valentine, had
urage to take the chickens when the settings hatched, because
ιe shells and gumminesses that might be in the nests. . . . Yet
ther of them wanted courage. . . . Hang it all, neither of them
anted courage or they would not be living with Tietjens's. It was like
ᴐeing tied to buffaloes!

And yet. . . . How you wanted them to change!

'Bremersyde. . . . No that was the home of the Haigs. . . . Tide
what will and tide what tide, there shall be Haigs at Bremersyde.
. . . . Perhaps it was Bemersyde! . . . Bemerton, then. George Herbert, rector of Bemerton, near Wilton, Salisbury. . . . That was what
Chrissie was to be like. . . . She was to imagine herself sitting with
her cheek on Chrissie's floss-silk head, looking into the fire and
seeing in the coals, Chrissie, walking under elms beside plough-
lands. *Elle ne demandait*, really, *pas mieux*!

If the country would stand it! . . .

Christopher presumably believed in England as he believed in
Provvy — because the land was pleasant and green and comely. It
would breed true. In spite of showers of Americans descended from
Tiglath Pileser and Queen Elizabeth and the end of the industrial
system and the statistics of the shipping trade, England with its
pleasant, green comeliness would go on breeding George Herberts
with Gunnings to look after them. . . . Of course with Gunnings!

The Gunnings of the land were the rocks on which the lighthouse
was built — as Christopher saw it. And Christopher was always right.
Sometimes a little previous. But always right. Always right. The rocks
had been there a million years before the lighthouse was built, the
lighthouse made a deuce of a movable flashing — but it was a mere
butterfly. The rocks would be there a million years after the light
went for the last time out.

Gunnings had been in the course of years, painted blue, a Druid-
worshipper, later, a Duke Robert of Normandy, illiterately burning

towns and begetting bastards — and eventually — actually at the moment — a man of all works, half-full of fidelity, half blatant, hairy. A retainer you would retain as long as you were prosperous and dispensed hard cider and overlooked his blear-eyed peccadilloes with women. He would go on. . . .

The point was whether the time had come for another Herbert of Bemerton. Christopher thought it had; he was always right, always right. But previous. He had predicted the swarms of Americans buying up old things. Offering fabulous prices. He was right. The trouble was they did not pay when they offered the fabulous prices: when they did pay they were as mean as . . . she was going to say Job. But she did not know that Job was particularly mean. That lady down below the window would probably want to buy the signed cabinet of Barker of 1762 for half the price of one bought in a New York department store and manufactured yesterday. . . . And she would tell Valentine she was a bloodsucker — even if — to suppose the ridiculous! — Valentine let her have it at her own price. On the other hand Mr. Schatzweiler talked of fantastic prices. . . .

Oh, Mr. Schatzweiler, Mr. Schatzweiler, if you would only pay us ten per cent. of what you owe us I could have all the pink fluffies, and three new gowns and keep the little old lace for Chrissie — and have a proper dairy, and not milk goats. And cut the losses over the confounded pigs and put up a range of glass in the sunk garden where it would not be an eye-sore. . . . As it was, the age of fairy-tales was not, of course, past. They had had windfalls, lovely windfalls when infinite ease had seemed to stretch out before them. . . . A great windfall when they had bought this place; little ones for the pigs and old mare. . . . Christopher was that sort of fellow; he had sowed so many golden grains that he could not be always reaping whirlwinds. There must be some halcyon days. . . .

Only it was deucedly awkward now — with Chrissie coming and Marie Léonie hinting all day that, as she was losing her figure, if she could not get the grease stains out of her skirt she would lose the affections of Christopher. And they had not got a stiver. . . . Christopher had cabled Schatzweiler. But what was the use of that? . . . Schatzweiler would be finely dished if she lost the affections of Christopher — because poor old Chris could not run any old junk shop without her! . . . She imagined cabling Schatzweiler — about the four stains on the skirt and the necessity for elegant lying-in gowns. Or else he would lose Christopher's assistance. . . .

The conversation down below raised its tones. She heard the tweeny maid ask why, if the American lady was a friend of the family, she did not know 'Er Ladyship theere? . . . Of course it was easy to understand: these people came, all of them, with letters of introduction from Schatzweiler. Then they insisted that they were friends of the family. It was perhaps nice of them — because most English people would not want to know old-furniture dealers.

The lady below exclaimed in a high voice:

"That Lady Mark Tietjens! That! Mercy me, I thought it was the cook!"

She, Valentine, ought to go down and help Marie Léonie. But she was not going to. She had the sense that hostile presences were creeping up the paths and Marie Léonie had given her the afternoon off . . . For the sake of the future, Marie Léonie had said. And *she* had said that she had once expected her own future to offer the reading of Æschylus beside the Ægean sea. Then Marie Léonie had kissed her and said she knew that she, Valentine would never rob her of her belongings after Mark died!

An unsolicited testimonial, that; but of course Marie Léonie would desire her not to lose the affections of Christopher: Marie Léonie would say to herself that in that case Christopher might take up with a woman who *would* want to rob Marie Léonie of her possessions after Mark died.

The woman down below announced herself as Mrs. de Bray Pape, descendant of the Maintenon, and wanted to know if Marie Léonie did not think it reasonable to cut down a tree that overhung your house. Valentine desired to spring to the window: she sprang to the old panelled door and furiously turned the key in the lock. She ought not to have turned the key so carelessly; it had a knack of needing five or ten minutes' manipulation before you could unlock the door again. . . . She ought to have sprung to the window and cried out to Mrs. de Bray Pape:

"If you so much as touch a leaf of Groby Great Tree we will serve you with injunctions that it will take half your life and money to deal with!"

She ought to have done that to save Christopher's reason. But she could not, she could not! It was one thing living with all the tranquillity of conscience in the world in open sin. It was another, confronting elderly Americans who knew the fact. She was determined to remain shut in there. An Englishman's house may no longer be his castle — but an Englishwoman's castle is certainly her own bedroom. When once, four months or so ago, the existence of little Chrissie being manifest, she had expressed to Christopher the idea that they ought no longer to go stodging along in penury, the case being so grave; they ought to take some of the Groby money — for the sake of future generations. . . .

Well, she had been run down. . . . At that stage of parturition, call it, a woman is run down and hysterical. . . . It had seemed to her overwhelmingly the fact that a breeding woman ought to have pink fluffy things next her quivering skin and sprayings of, say, Houbigant all over her shoulders and hair. For the sake of the child's health.

So she had let out violently at poor wretched old Chris who was faced with the necessity for denying his gods and she had slammed to and furiously locked that door. Her castle had been her bedroom with a vengeance then — for Christopher had been unable to get in or she to get out. He had had to whisper through the keyhole that he gave in; he was dreadfully concerned for her. He had said that he hoped she would try to stick it a little longer, but, if she would not, he would take Mark's money.

Naturally she had not let him — but she *had* arranged with Marie Léonie for Mark to pay a couple of pounds more a week for their board and lodging and as Marie Léonie had perforce taken over the housekeeping they had found things easing off a little. Marie Léonie had run the house for thirty shillings a week less than she, Valentine, had ever been able to do — and run it streets better. Streets and streets! So they had had money at least nearly to complete their equipments of table linen and the layette. . . . The long and complicated annals!

It was queer that her heart was nearly as much in Christopher's game as was his own. As house-mother she ought to have grabbed after the last penny — and goodness knew the life was strain enough. Why do women back their men in unreasonable romanticisms? You might say that it was because if their men had their masculinities abated — like defeated roosters! — the women would suffer in intimacies. . . . Ah, but it wasn't that! Nor was it merely that they wanted the buffaloes to which they were attached to charge.

It was really that she had followed the convolutions of her man's mind. And ardently approved. She disapproved with him of riches, of the rich, of the frame of mind that riches confers. If the war had done nothing else for them — for those two of them — it had induced them at least to instal Frugality as a deity. They desired to live hard even if it deprived them of the leisure in which to think high! She agreed with him that if a ruling class loses the capacity to rule — or the desire! — it should abdicate from its privileges and get underground.

And having accepted that as a principle, she could follow the rest of his cloudy obsessions and obstinacies.

Perhaps she would not have backed him up in his long struggle with dear Mark if she had not considered that their main necessity was to live high. . . . And she was aware that why, really, she had sprung to the door rather than to the window, had been that she had not desired to make an unfair move in that long chess game; on behalf of Christopher. If she had had to see Mrs. de Bray Pape or to speak to her it would have been disagreeable to have that descendant of a king's companion look at her with the accusing eyes of one who thinks: "You live with a man without being married to him!" Mrs. de Bray Pape's ancestress had been able to force the king to marry her. . . . But that she would have chanced: they had paid penalty enough for having broken the rules of the Club. She could carry her head high: not obtrusively high, but sufficiently! For, in effect they had surrendered Groby in order to live together and she had endured sprays of obloquy that seemed never to cease to splash over the garden hedges . . . in order to keep Christopher alive and sane!

No, she would have faced Mrs. de Bray Pape. But she would hardly, given Christopher's half-crazed condition, have kept herself from threatening Mrs. Pape with dreadful legal consequences if she touched Groby Great Tree. That would not have been jonnock. That would have been to interfere in the silent Northern struggle between the brothers. That she would never do, even to save Christopher's reason — unless she were jumped into it! . . . That Mark did not intend to interfere between Mrs. Pape and the tree she knew — for when she had read Mrs. Pape's letter to him he had signified as much to her by means of his eyes. . . . Mark she loved and respected because he was a dear — and because he had backed her through thick and thin. Without him . . . There had been a moment on that dreadful night. . . . She prayed God that she would not have to think again of that dreadful night. . . . If she had to see Sylvia again she would go mad, and the child within her. . . .

Deep, deep within her the blight would fall on the little thread of brain!

Mrs. de Bray Pape, God be thanked, provided diversion for her mind. She was speaking French with an eccentricity that could not be ignored.

Valentine could see, without looking out of the window, Marie Léonie's blank face and the equal blankness with which she must have indicated that she did not intend to understand. She imagined her standing, motionless, pinafored and unmerciful before the other lady who beneath the three-cornered hat was stuttering out:

"Lady Tietjens, mwaw Madam de Bray Pape desire coo-pay la arbre. . . ."

Valentine could hear Marie Léonie's steely tones saying:

"On dit 'l'arbre,' Madame!"

And then the high voice of the little maid:

"Called us 'the pore' she did, your ladyship. . . . Ast us why we could not take example!"

Then a voice, soft for these people, and with modulations:

"Sir Mark seems to be perspiring a great deal. I was so free as to wipe . . ."

Whilst, above, Valentine said: "Oh Heaven!" Marie Léonie cried out: "Mon Dieu!" and there was a rush of skirts and pinafore.

Marie Léonie was rushing past a white, breeched figure, saying:

"Vous, une étrangère, avez osé. . . ."

A shining, red-cheeked boy was stumbling slightly from before her. He said, after her back:

"Mrs. Lowther's handkerchief is the smallest, softest . . ." He added to the young woman in white: "We'd better go away. . . . Please let's go away. . . . It's not sporting. . . ." A singularly familiar face; a singularly moving voice.

"For God's sake let us go away. . . ."

Who said "For God's sake!" like that — with staring blue eyes?

She was at the door frantically trying to twist the great iron key; the lock was of very old hammered iron work. The doctor ought to be telephoned to. He had said that if Mark had fever or profuse sweats he should be telephoned to at once. Marie Léonie would be with him; it was her, Valentine's, duty to telephone. The key would not turn; she hurt her hand in the effort. But part of her emotion was due to that bright-cheeked boy. Why should he have said that it was not sporting of them to be there? Why had he exclaimed for

God's sake to go away? The key would not turn. It stayed solid, like
a piece of the old lock. . . . Who was the boy like? She rammed her
shoulder against the unyielding door. She must not do that. She cried
out.

From the window — she had gone to the window intending to tell
the girl to set up a ladder for her, but it would be more sensible to
tell her to telephone! — she could see Mrs. de Bray Pape. That lady
was still haranguing the girl. And then on the path, beyond the lettuces and the newly sticked peas, arose a very tall figure. A very tall,
thin, figure. Portentous. By some trick. of the slope, figures there always appeared very tall. . . . The figure appeared leisurely: almost
hesitant. Like the apparition of the statue of the Commander in Don
Juan, somehow. It appeared to be preoccupied with its glove: undoing its glove. . . .

Very tall, but with too much slightness of the legs. . . . A woman
in hunting-breeches! Grey against the tall ash-stems of the spinney.
You could not see her face because you were above her, in the window, and her head was bent down! In the name of God! . . .

There wafted over her a sense of the dreadful darkness in the old
house at Grays Inn on that dreadful night. . . . She must not think
of that dreadful night because of little Chrissie deep within her. She
felt as if she held the child covered in her arms, as if she were looking upwards, bending down over the child. Actually she was looking
downwards. . . . Then she had been looking upwards — up the dark
stairs. At a marble statue, the white figure of a woman, the Nike . . .
the Winged Victory. It is like that on the stairs of the Louvre. She
must think of the Louvre, not Grays Inn. They were, in a Pompeian
ante-room, Etruscan tombs, with guardians in uniform, their hands
behind their backs. Strolling about as if they expected you to steal a
tomb. . . .

She had — they had — been staring up the stairs. The house had
seemed unnaturally silent when they had entered. Unnaturally. . . .
How can you seem more silent than silent. But you *can*! They had
seemed to tiptoe. She had, at least. Then light had shone above —
coming from an opened door, above. In the light had been the white
figure that had said it had cancer!

She must not think about these things!

Such rage and despair had swept over her as she had never before
known. She cried to Christopher, dark, beside her, that the woman
lied. She had not got cancer. . . .

She must not think about these things.

The woman on the path — in grey riding-clothes — approached slowly. The head still bent down. Undoubtedly she had silk under-things beneath all that grey cloth . . . Well, *they* — Christopher and Valentine — gave her them.

It was queer how calm she was. That of course was Sylvia Tietjens. Let it be. She had fought for her man before and so she could again; the Russians should not have . . . The old jingle ran in her calm head. . . .

But she was also desperately perturbed: trembling at the thought of that dreadful night! Christopher had wanted to go with Sylvia after she had fallen downstairs. A good theatre fall, but not good enough. But she, Valentine, had shouted: No! He was never going with Sylvia again. *Finis Sylviae et magna.* . . . In the black night. . . . Maroons had gone on firing. They could hear!

Well, she was calm. The sight of that figure was not going to hurt the tiny brain that worked deep within her womb. Nor the tiny limbs! She was going to slub the warm, soap-transfused flannel onto those little legs in the warm of the great hearth. . . . Nine hams up that chimney! Chrissie looking up and laughing. . . . That woman would never again do that! Not to a child of Christopher's. Not to any man's child, belike!

That had been Sylvia Tietjens' son! With a girl in white breeches! . . . Well, who was she to prevent a son's seeing his father? She felt on her arm the weight of her own son. With that there she could confront the world!

It was queer! That woman's face was all blurred. . . . Blubber-ingly! The features swollen, the eyes red! . . . Ah, she had been thinking, looking at the garden and the stillness: "If I had given Christopher that I should have kept him!" But she would never have kept him. Had she been the one woman in all the world he would never have looked at her. Not after he had seen her. Valentine Wannop!

Sylvia had looked up, contemplatively — as if into the very win-dow. But she could not see into the window. She must have seen Mrs. de Bray Pape and the girl for it became apparent why she had taken off her glove. She now had a gold vanity box in her hand: looking in at the mirror and moving her right hand swiftly before her face . . . Remember: it was *we* who gave her that gold thing. Remember! Remember it hard!

Sudden anger came over her. That woman must never come into their house-place before whose hearth she was to bathe the little Chrissie! Never! Never! The place would be polluted. She knew, only by that, now she loathed and recoiled from that woman.

She was at the lock. The key turned. . . . See what emotion at the thought of harm to your unborn child can do for you! Subconsciously her right hand had remembered how you pressed the key upwards when you made it turn. . . . She must not run down the narrow stairs. The telephone was in a niche on the inner side of the great ingle. The room was dim: very long, very low. The Barker cabinet looked very rich with its green, yellow, and scarlet inlays. She was leaning sideways in the nook between the immense fireplace and the room wall, the telephone receiver at her ear. She looked down her long room — it opened into the dining-room, a great beam between. It was dark, gleaming, rich with old bees-waxed woods. . . . Elle ne demandait pas mieux . . . the phrase of Marie Léonie occurred constantly to her mind. . . . She did not ask better — if only the things were to be regarded as theirs! She looked into the distant future when things would spread out tranquilly before them. They would have a little money, a little peace. Things would spread out . . . like a plain seen from a hill. In the meantime they had to keep all on going. . . . She did not in effect grumble at that . . . as long as strength and health held out.

The doctor — she pictured him, long, sandy and very pleasant, suffering too from an incurable disease and debts, life being like that! — the doctor asked cheerfully on the telephone how Mark was. She said she did not know. He was said to have been profusely sweating. . . . Yes, it was possible that he might have been having a disagreeable interview. The doctor said:

"Tut! Tut! And yourself?" He had a Scotch accent, the sandy man. . . . She suggested that he might bring along a bromide. He said: "They've been bothering you. Don't let them!" She said she had been asleep — but they probably would. She added: "Perhaps you would come quickly!" . . . Sister Anne! Sister Anne! For God's sake Sister Anne! If she could get a bromide into her it would pass like a dream.

It was passing like a dream. Perhaps the Virgin Mary exists. . . . If she does not, we must invent her to look after mothers who can not . . . But she could! She, Valentine Wannop!

The light from the doorway that was open onto the garden was ob-

scured. A highwayman in skirts with panniers stood in the room
against the light. It said:

"You're the saleswoman, I guess. This is a most insanitary place
and I hear you have no bath. Show me some things. In the Louie
Kaators style." It guessed that it was going to re-furnish Groby in
Louie Kaators style. Did she, Valentine, as saleswoman suppose that
They — her employers — would meet her in the expense. Mr. Pape
had had serious losses in Miami. They must not suppose that the
Papes could be bled white. This place ought to be pulled down as
unfit for human habitation and a model workman's cottage built
in its place. People who sold things to rich Americans in this country were sharks. She herself was descended spiritually from Madame
de Maintenon. It would be all different if Marie Antoinette had
treated the Maintenon better, She, Mrs. de Bray Pape, would have
the authority in the country that she ought to have. She had been
told that she would be made to pay an immense sum for having
cut down Groby Great Tree. Of course the side wall of the house
had fallen in. These old houses could not stand up to modern inventions. She, Mrs. de Bray Pape, had employed the latest Australian
form of tree-stump extractor — the Wee Whizz Bang. . . . But did
she, as saleswoman, doubtless more intimate with her employers than
was necessary, considering the reputation of that establishment . . .
did she consider . . .

Valentine's heart started. The light from the doorway was again
obscured. Marie Léonie ran panting in. Sister Anne, in effect! She
said: "Le telephone! Vite!"

Valentine said:

"J'ai déjà telephoné. . . . Le docteur sera ici dans quelques minutes. . . . Je te prie de rester à côté de moi!" . . . "I beg you to remain beside me!" Selfish! Selfish! But there was a child to be born.
. . . Anyhow Marie Léonie could not have got out of that door. It
was blocked. . . . Ah! . . .

Sylvia was looking down on Valentine. You could hardly see her
face against the light. . . . Well, it did not amount to more than
that. . . . She was looking down because she was so tall; you could
not see her face against the light. Mrs. de Bray Pape was explaining
what spiritual descent from *grands seigneurs* did for you. . . .

Sylvia was bending her eyes on Valentine. That was the phrase.
She said to Mrs. de Bray Pape:

"For God's sake hold your *damned* tongue. Get out of here!"

Mrs. de Bray Pape had not understood. For the matter of that neither did Valentine take it in. A thin voice from a distance thrilled:

"Mother! . . . Mo . . . ther!"

She — IT — for it was more like a statue than a human being. . . . Marvellous how she had made her face up. . . . Three minutes before it had been all . . . be-blubbered! It was flawless now — Dark-shadowed under the eyes. And sorrowful. And tremendously dignified. And *kind*! Damn! Damn! Damn!

It occurred to Valentine that this was only the second time that she had seen that face.

Its stillness now was terrible!

What was she waiting for before she began upon the Billingsgate they would both have to use before they parted? For she, Valentine, had her back against the wall. She heard herself begin to say:

"You have spoilt . . ."

She could not continue. You cannot very well tell a person that their loathsomeness is so infectious as to spoil your baby's bathing place. It is not done!

Marie Léonie said in French to Mrs. de Bray Pape that Madame Tietjens did not require her presence. Mrs. de Bray Pape did not understand. It is difficult for a Maintenon to understand that her presence is not required.

The first time that she, Valentine, had seen that face — in Edith Ethel's drawing room, she had thought how kind — how blindingly kind it was. Those lips had approached her mother's cheeks and the tears had been in Valentine's eyes. It had said — that face of a statue — that it must kiss Mrs. Wannop for her kindness to Christopher. Damn it all, she might as well kiss her, Valentine now. But for her there would have been no Christopher.

You must not say Damn it all. The war is over . . . Ah, but its backwashes, when would *they* be over?

It said — that woman's voice was so perfectly expressionless that you could continue appropriately to call it "it" — it said coldly to Mrs. de Bray Pape:

"You hear! The lady of the house does not require your presence. Please go away."

Mrs. de Bray Pape had been explaining that she intended refurnishing Groby in the Louis Quatorze style.

It occurred to Valentine that this position had its comicalities.

Mrs. de Bray Pape did not know her, Valentine. Marie Léonie did not know who that figure was.

They could miss a good deal of the jam. . . . Jam to-morrow, jam yesterday. . . . Where was the jam? . . . That figure had said "The lady of the house." Delicately. *Quelle delicatesse!*

But she did not appear denunciatory. She dropped sideways: pensive. Puzzled. As if at the ways of God. As if stricken by God and puzzled at his ways. . . . Well, she might be.

She caught at the telephone shelf. The child had moved within her. It wanted her to be called Mrs. Tietjens in its own house. This woman stood in the way. She could not give a father's name to the little thing. So he protested within her. Dark it was growing. Hold up there.

Someone was calling: "Valentine!"

A boy's voice called:

"Mother! Mother!"

A soft voice said:

"Mrs. Tietjens!"

What things to say in her child's hearing! . . . Mother! Mother! . . . Her mother was in Pontresina, complete with secretary in black alpaca. . . . The Italian Alps!

Dark! . . . Marie Léonie said in her ear: "Tiens toi debout, ma chérie!"

Dark, dark night; cold, cold snow — Harsh, Harsh, wind and lo! — Where shall we shepherds go, God's son to find?

Edith Ethel was reading from a letter to Mrs. de Bray Pape. She said: "As an American of culture you will be interested. . . . From the great poet!" . . . A gentleman held a top-hat in front of his face, as if he were in church. Thin, with dull eyes and a Jewish beard! Jews keep their hats on in church. . . .

Apparently she, Valentine Wannop, was going to be denounced before the congregation! Did they bring a scarlet letter? . . . They were Puritans enough, she and Christopher. The voice of the man with the Jewish beard — Sylvia Tietjens had removed the letter from the fingers of Edith Ethel. . . . Not much changed Edith Ethel! Face a *little* lined. And pale. And suddenly reduced to silence — the voice of the man with the beard said:

"After all! It does make a difference. He is virtually Tietjens of . . ." He began to push his way backwards, outwards. A man trying to leave through the crowd at the church door. He said to Valentine oddly interrogative:

"Mrs. . . . eh Tietjens!" And then: "Par*don*!" Attempting a French accent!

Edith Ethel remarked:

" wanted to say to Valentine: if I effect the sale personally I do not see that any commissions should be payable."

Sylvia Tietjens said they could discuss that outside. Valentine was aware that, some time before a boy's voice had said: "Mother, is this sporting?" It occurred to Valentine to wonder if it was sporting of people to call her "Mrs. Tietjens" under Sylvia Tietjens' nose. Of course she had to be Mrs. Tietjens before the servants. She heard herself say:

"I am sorry Mr. Ruggles called me Mrs. Tietjens before you!"

The eyes of the statue were if possible doubly bent on her!

The bitter answer came to her as if from stiff lips:

"An the King will have my head I carena what he may do with my . . ."

It affected Valentine disagreeably — with a pang of jealousy. What it amounted to was that Sylvia said: "You have my man, so you may as well have his name." But by using a saying that Christopher used habitually — and that Mark had used habitually when he could speak — by using then a Tietjens-family saying she asserted that she too had belonged to the Tietjens family, and, before Valentine, had been intimate with their sayings to the point of saturation.

That statue went on speaking.

It said:

"I wanted to get those people out. . . . And to see . . ." It spoke very slowly. Marmoreally. The flowers in the jug on the fald-stool needed more water. Marigolds. Orange. . . . A woman is upset when her child moves within her. Sometimes more, sometimes less. She must have been very upset: there had been a lot of people in the room; she knew neither how they had come nor how they had gone. She said to Marie Léonie:

"Dr. Span is bringing some bromide. . . . I can't find those . . ."

Marie Léonie was looking at that figure; her eyes stuck out of her head like Christopher's. She said, as still as a cat watching a mouse:

"Qui este elle? C'est bien la femme?"

It looked queerly like a pilgrim in a ballet, now, that figure against the light — the long legs slightly bent gave that effect. Actually this was the third time she had seen it — but in the dark house she had not really seen the face. . . . The features had been contorted and thus not the real features: these were the real features. There was about that figure something timid. And noble. It said:

"Sporting! Michael said: 'Be sporting, mother!' . . . But sporting. . . ." It raised its hand as if to shake a fist at heaven. The hand struck the beam across the ceiling; that roof was so low. And dear! It said:

"It was Father Consett really . . . They can all, soon, call you Mrs. Tietjens. Before God, I came to drive those people out. . . . But I wanted to see how it was you kept him. . . ."

Sylvia Tietjens was keeping her head turned aside, drooping. Hiding a tendency to tears, no doubt. She said to the floor:

"I say again, as God hears me, I never thought to harm your child. His child. . . . But any woman's. . . . Not harm a child . . . I have a fine one, but I wanted another . . . with its littleness. . . . It's the riding has done it. . . ." Someone sobbed!

She looked loweringly then at Valentine:

"It's Father Consett in heaven that has done this. Saint and martyr, desiring soft things! I can almost see his shadow across these walls now it's growing dark. You hung him: you did not even shoot him though I say you shot him to save my feelings. . . . And it's you who will be going on through all the years. . . ."

She bit into a small handkerchief that she had in her hand, concealed. She said:

"Damn it, I'm playing pimp to Tietjens of Groby — leaving my husband to you! . . ."

Someone again sobbed.

It occurred to Valentine that Christopher had left those prints at old Hunt's sale in a jar on the field. They had not wanted the jar. Then Christopher had told a dealer called Hudnut that he could have that jar and some others against a little carting service. . . . He would be tired, when he got back, Christopher. But he would have to go to Hudnut's, Gunning could not be trusted. They must not disappoint Lady Robinson. . . .

Marie Léonie said:

"C'est lamentable qu'un seul homme puisse inspirer deux passions pareilles dans deux femmes. . . . C'est le martyre de notre vie!"

Yes, it was lamentable that a man could inspire two such passions in two women. Marie Léonie went to look after Mark. Sylvia Tiet-

jens was gone. They say joy never kills. She fell straight down
onto the floor Lumpishly. . . . It was lucky they had the Bussorah
rug otherwise Chrissie . . . They had no money. . . . Poor . . .
poor . . .

IV

MARK TIETJENS had lain considering the satisfaction of a great night
he had lately passed. Or perhaps not lately; at some time.

Lying out there in the black nights the sky seemed enormous.
You could understand how somewhere heaven could be concealed
in it. And tranquil at times. Then you felt the earth wheeling through
infinity.

Night birds cried overhead: herons, ducks, swans even; the owls
kept closer to the ground, beating along the hedgerows. Beasts became busy in the long grass. They rustled busily, then paused for
long. No doubt a rabbit ran till it found an attractive plantain. Then
it nibbled for a long time without audible movement. Now and then
cattle lowed, or many lambs — frightened by a fox maybe. . . .

But there would nevertheless be long silences. . . . A stoat would
get onto the track of the rabbit. They would run, run, run brushing
through the long grass, then out into the short meadow and round
and round, the rabbit squealing. Loudly at first.

In the dim illumination of his night-light dormice would climb
up the posts of his shelter. They would remain regarding him with
beads of eyes. When the rabbits squealed they would hunch themselves together and shiver. They knew it meant S . . t . . o . . at —
stoat! Their turn soon!

He despised himself a little for attending to these minutiae — as if
one were talking down to a child. . . . On his great night the whole
cattle of the county had been struck with panic; you heard them
crashing down through the hedges and miles down into the silent
valleys.

No! He had never been one to waste his time and mind on small
mammals and small birds. . . . The Flora and Fauna of Blankshire!
. . . Not for him. It was big movements interested him: "wherein
manifesteth itself the voice of God!" . . . Very likely that was true.
Transport! Panic in cattle over whole counties. In people, over whole
continents!

Once years — oh, years and years ago, when he had been aged twelve and on a visit to Grandfather he had taken a gun to Redcar Sands from Groby, over the moors, and with one shot he had brought down two terns, a sandpiper, and a herring gull. Grandfather had been so delighted with his prowess — though naturally the shot had been a fluke — that he had the things stuffed and there they were in Groby Nursery to this day. The herring gull stiff on a mossy rock; the sandpiper doing obeisance before it, the terns flying, one on each side. Probably that was the only memorial to him, Mark Tietjens, at Groby. The younger children had been wont to refer with awe to "Mark's bag," for long years afterwards. The painted background had been Bamborough Castle with lashings of foam and blue sky. It was a far cry from Redcar to Bamborough — but that was the only background the bird-stuffing chap in Middlesboro could paint for sea-birds. For larks and the like he had a cornfield in the Vale of York; for nightingales, poplar trees. . . . Never heard that nightingales were particularly partial to poplars!

. . . Nightingales disturbed the majesty of great nights; for two months out of the year, more or less, according to the nature of the season. He wasn't decrying the beauty of their voices. Hearing them you felt like seeing a good horse win the St. Leger. No other things in the world could do it — just as there was no place in the world like Newmarket Heath on a breezy day. . . . But they limited the night. It was true that nightingales deep down in the spinney near where Gunning's hut must be — say a quarter of a mile away — could make you think of great distance, echoing up through the deep woods. Woods dripping with dew beneath the moon. . . . And air-raids not so long ago! The moon brought air-raids and its shining was discouraged. . . . Yes, nightingales made you think of distance just as the night-jar for ever crepitating from twilight to dawn seemed to measure a fragment of eternity. . . . But only fragments! The great night was itself eternity and the Infinite. . . . The spirit of God walking on the firmament.

Cruel beggars, nightingales: they abused one another with dis-tended throats all through the nights. Between the gusts of gales you could hear them shouting on — telling their sitting-hens that they — each one — were the devils of fellows, the other chap, down the hill by Gunning's hut, being a bedraggled, louse-eaten, braggart. . . . Sex ferocity!

Gunning lived in a bottom, in a squatter's cottage, they said. With

a thatch like Robinson Crusoe's bonnet. A wise-woman's cottage.
He lived with the wise-woman, a chalk-white-faced slattern. . . .
And a grand-daughter of the wise-woman whom, because she had a
cleft palate and only half a brain the parish, half out of commiseration, half for economy, had nominated mistress in the school up
the hill. No one knew whether Gunning slept with the wise-woman
or the grand-daughter; for one or the other he had left his missus
and Fittleworth had tanned his hide and taken his cottage from
him. He thrashed them both impartially with a hunting thong every
Saturday night — to teach them, and to remind them that for them
he had lost his cottage and the ten bob a week Fittleworth allowed
such hinds as had been in his service thirty years. . . . Sex ferocity
again!

> And how shall I thy true love know from another one?
> Oh, by his cockled hat and staff and by his sandalled shoon!

An undoubted pilgrim had suggested irresistibly the lines to him!
. . . It was, naturally, that bitch Sylvia. Wet eyes she had! . . .
Then some psychological crisis was going on inside her. Good for her.
  Good for Val and Chris, possibly. There was no real knowing.
. . . Oh, but there was. Hear to that: the bitch-pack giving tongue!
Heard ye ever the like to that, sirs. She had had Groby Great Tree
torn down. . . . But as God was her maker she would not tear an-
other woman's child . . .
  He felt himself begin to perspire. . . . Well, if Sylvia had come
to that his, Mark's, occupation was gone. He would no longer have
to go on willing against her; she would drop into the sea in the wake
of their family vessel and be lost to view. . . . But damn it, she
must have suffered to be brought to that extreme. . . . Poor bitch!
Poor bitch! The riding had done it. . . . She ran away, a handkerchief to her eyes.
  He felt satisfaction and impatience. There was some place to
which he desired to get back. But there were also things to be done:
to be thought out. . . . If God was beginning to temper the wind
to these flayed lambs . . . Then . . . He could not remember what
he wanted to think about. . . . It was — no, not exasperating.
Numb! He felt himself responsible for their happiness. He wanted
them to go rubbing along, smooth with the rough, for many long,
unmarked years. . . . He wanted Marie Léonie to stay with Valentine until after her deliverance and then go to the Dower House at

Groby. She was Lady Tietjens. She knew she was Lady Tietjens and she would like it. Besides she would be a thorn in the flesh of Mrs. . . . He could not remember the name. . . .

He wished that Christopher would get rid of his Jewish partner so as to addle a little brass. It was their failing as Tietjenses that they liked toadies. He himself had bitched all their lives by having that fellow Ruggles years ago sharing his rooms. Because he could not have borne to share with an equal and Ruggles was half Jew, half Scotchman. Christopher had had for toadies firstly Macmaster, a Scot, and then this American Jew. Otherwise he, Mark, was reconciled with things. Christopher no doubt was wise in his choice. He had achieved a position in which he might — with just a little more to it — anticipate jogging away to the end of time, leaving descendants to carry on the country without swank.

Ah. . . . It came to his mind to remember, almost with pain. He had accepted nephew Mark as nephew Mark: a strong slip. A good boy. . . . But there was the point . . . the point! The boy had the right sort of breeches. . . . But if there were incest. . . .

Crawling through a hedge after a rabbit was thinkable. Father had been in the churchyard to shoot rabbits to oblige the vicar. There was no doubt of that. He did not want rabbits. . . . But supposing he had mis-hit a bunny and the little beast had been throwing gymnastics on the other side of the quickset? Father would have crawled through then rather than go all the way to the lych-gate and round. Decent men put their mis-hits out of their agony as soon as possible. Then there was motive. And as for not putting his gun out of action before crawling through the quickset. . . . Many good, plucked men had died like that. . . . *And father had grown absent-minded!* . . . There had been farmer Lowther had so died; and Pease of Lobhall; and Pease of Cullercoats. All good plucked farmers. . . . Crawling through hedges rather than go round, and with their guns at full cock! And not absent-minded men. . . . But he had remembered . . . just now, he had remembered that father had grown absent-minded. He would put a paper in one of his waistcoat pockets and fumble for it in all his other pockets a moment after; he would push his spectacles up onto his forehead and search all the room for them; he would place his knife and fork in his plate and whilst talking take another knife and fork from beside it and begin again to eat. . . . Mark remembered that his father had done that twice during the last meal they had eaten together — whilst he, Mark, had been presenting the fellow Ruggles's account of Christopher's misdeeds. . . .

Then it need not be incumbent on him, Mark, to go up to his father in heaven and say: "Hullo, sir. I understand you had a daughter by the wife of your best friend, she being now with child by your son." Rather ghostly to introduce yourself to the awful ghost of your father. . . . Of course you would be a ghost yourself. Still, not, with your billycock hat, umbrella, and racing-glasses, an awful ghost! . . . And to say to your father: "I understand that you committed suicide!"

Against the rules of the Club. . . . For I consider it no grief to be going there where so many great men have preceded me. Sophocles that, wasn't it? So, on his authority it was a damn good club. . . .

But he did not have to anticipate that *mauvais quart d'heure*! Dad quite obviously did not commit suicide. He wasn't the man to do so. So Valentine was not his daughter and there was no incest. It is all very well to say that you care little about incest. The Greeks made a hell of a tragic row about it. . . . Certainly it was a weight off the chest. He had always been able to look Christopher in the eyes — but he would be able to do it better than ever now. Comfortably! It is uncomfortable to look a man in the eyes and think: You sleep between incestuous sheets.

That then was over. The worst of it rolled up together. No suicide. No incest. No by-blow at Groby. . . . A Papist there. . . . Though how you could be a Papist and a Marxian-Communist passed his, Mark's comprehension. . . . A Papist at Groby and Groby Great Tree down. . . . The curse was perhaps off the family!

That was a superstitious way to look at it — but you must have a pattern to interpret things by. You can't really get your mind to work without it. The blacksmith said: By hammer and hand all art doth stand! . . . He, Mark Tietjens, for many years interpreted all life in terms of Transport. . . . Transport be thou my God. . . . A damn good God. . . . And in the end, after a hell of a lot of thought and of work the epitaph of him, Mark Tietjens, ought by rights to be: "*Here lies one whose name was writ in sea-birds!*" As good an epitaph as another.

He must get it through to Christopher that Marie Léonie should have that case of stuffed birds with Bamborough and all, in her bedroom at Groby Dower House. It was the last permanent record of her man. . . . But Christopher would know that. . . .

It was coming back. A lot of things were coming back. . . . He could see Redcar Sands running up towards Sunderland, grey, grey. Not so many factory chimnies then, working for him, Mark Tietjens! Not so many! And the sandpipers running in the thin of the tide, bowing as they ran; and the shovellers turning over stones and the terns floating above the viscous sea. . . .

But it was great nights to which he would not turn his attention; great black nights above the purple moors. . . . Great black nights above the Edgeware Road where Marie Léonie lived . . . because, above the blaze of lights of the old Apollo's front, you had a sense of immense black spaces. . . .

Who said he was perspiring a great deal? Well, he *was* perspiring!

Marie Léonie, young, was bending over him. . . . Young, young, as he had first seen her on the stage of Covent Garden. . . . In white! . . . Doing agreeable things to his face with a perfume like that of Heaven itself! . . . And laughing sideways as Marie Léonie had laughed when first he presented himself before her in his billy-cock hat and umbrella! . . . The fine, fair hair! The soft voice!

But this was silly. . . . That was nephew Mark with his cherry-red face and staring eyes. . . . And this was his light of love! . . . Naturally. Like uncle, like nephew. He would pick up with the same type of woman as his uncle. That made it certain that this was no by-blow! Pretty piece against the apple boughs!

He wanted great nights, then! — Young Mark, though, should not pick up with a woman older than himself. Christopher had done that and look!

Still, things were takking oop! . . . Do you remember the York-shireman who stood with his chin just out of the water on Ararat Top as Noah approached. And: "It's boon to tak oop!" said the Yorkshireman. . . . It's bound to clear up!

A great night, with room enough for Heaven to be hidden there from our not too perspicacious eyes. . . . It was said that an earth-quake shock imperceptible to our senses set those cattle and sheep and horses and pigs crashing through all the hedges of the county. And it was queer: before they had so started lowing and moving Mark was now ready to swear that he had heard a rushing sound. He probably had not! One could so easily self-deceive oneself! The cattle had been panicked because they had been sensible of the presence of the Almighty walking upon the firmament. . . .

Damn it all: there were a lot of things coming back. He could have sworn he heard the voice of Ruggles say: "After all he is virtually Tietjens of Groby!" . . . By no fault of yours, old cock! But now you will be cadging up to him. . . . Now there speaks Edith Ethel Macmaster! A lot of voices passing behind his head. Damn it all, could they all be ghosts drifting before the wind! . . . Or damn it all, was he himself dead! . . . No, you were probably not profane when you were dead.

He would have given the world to sit up and turn his head round and see. Of course he could, but that would give the show away! He credited himself with being too cunning an old fox for that! To have thrown dust in their eyes for all these years! He could have chuckled!

Fittleworth seemed to have come down into the orchard. What the devil could Fittleworth want? It was like a pantomime. Fittleworth in effect was looking at him. He said:

"Hello, old bean. . . ." Marie Léonie was looking from beside his elbow. He said: "I've driven all these goats out of your hen-roost. . . ." Good-looking fellow, Fittleworth. His Lola Vivaria had been a garden-peach. Died in child-birth. No doubt that' was why he had troubled to come. Fittleworth said: Cammie said to give Mark her love for old time's sake. Her dear love! And as soon as he was well to bring her ladyship down.

Damn this sweat. With its beastly tickling he would grimace and give the show away. But he would like Marie Léonie to go to the Fittleworths'. Marie Léonie said something to Fittleworth.

"Yes, yes, me lady!" says Fittleworth. Damn it, he did look like a monkey as some people said. . . . But if the monkeys we were descended from were as good-looking . . . Probably he had good-looking legs. . . . How beautiful upon the mountains are the feet of them that bring good tidings to Zion! . . .

Fittleworth added earnestly and distinctly that his sister-in-law, Sylvia, *begged* Mark to understand that she had not sent that flock of idiots down here. Sylvia also said that she was going to divorce his, Mark's, brother and dissolve her marriage with the sanction of Rome. . . . So they would all be a happy family down there, soon. . . . Anything Cammie could do . . . And because of Mark's unforgettable services to the country . . .

Name was written in. . . . Lettest thou thy servant. . . divorce in peace!

Marie Léonie begged Fittleworth to go away now. Fittleworth said he would, but joy never kills! So long, old . . . old friend! The clubs they had been in together! . . .

But one went to a far better Club than . . . His breathing was a little troublesome. . . . It was darkish, then light again.

Christopher was at the foot of his bed. Holding a bicycle and a lump of wood. Aromatic wood, a chunk sawn from a tree. His face was white; his eyes stuck out. Blue pebbles. He gazed at his brother and said:

"Half Groby wall is down. Your bedroom's wrecked. I found your case of sea-birds thrown on a rubble heap."

It was as well that one's services were unforgettable!

Valentine was there, panting as if she had been running. She exclaimed to Christopher:

"You left the prints for Lady Robinson in a jar you gave to Hudnut the dealer. How could you? Oh, how could you? How are we going to feed and clothe a child if you do such things?"

He lifted his bicycle wearily round. You could see he was dreadfully weary, the poor devil. Mark almost said:

"Let him off, the poor devil's worn out!"

Heavily, like a dejected bulldog, Christopher made for the gate. As he went up the green path beyond the hedge, Valentine began to sob.

"How are we to live? How are we ever to live?"

"Now I must speak," Mark said to himself.

He said:

"Did ye ever hear tell o' t' Yorkshireman. . . . On Mount Ara . . . Ara . . ."

He had not spoken for so long. His tongue appeared to fill his mouth; his mouth to be twisted to one side. It was growing dark. He said:

"Put your ear close to my mouth . . ." She cried out!

He whispered:

> " 'Twas the mid o' the night and the barnies grat
> And the mither beneath the mauld heard that."

. . "An old song. My nurse sang it. . . . Never thou let thy barnie weep for thy sharp tongue to thy goodman. . . . A good man! . . . Groby Great Tree is down. . . ."

He said: "Hold my hand!"

She inserted her hand beneath the sheet and his hot hand closed on hers. Then it relaxed.

She nearly cried out for Marie Léonie.

The tall, sandy, much-liked doctor came through the gate.

She said:

"He spoke just now. . . . It has been a torturing afternoon. . . . Now I'm afraid . . . I'm afraid he's . . ."

The doctor reached his hand beneath the sheet, leaning down. He said:

"Go get you to bed. . . . I will come and examine you. . . ."

She said:

"Perhaps it would be best not to tell Lady Tietjens that he spoke. . . . She would have liked to have his last words. . . . But she did not need them as much as I."

ABOUT THE AUTHOR

FORD MADOX FORD was born Ford Madox Hueffer in 1873, and died in 1939. Dante Gabriel and William Michael Rosetti were his uncles. His first book, a fairy story, was published when he was nineteen; he became the author of thirty-nine books, four of which were in collaboration with Joseph Conrad, and hundreds of articles. Mr. Ford was the editor of *The English Review* and later of *The Transatlantic Review*. After the First World War, he lived most of his life in France and the United States, teaching during his last few years at Olivet College in Michigan. Besides *Parade's End*, some of the best known of his books are *The Good Soldier* and *It Was a Nightingale*.